READER'S DIGEST CONDENSED BOOKS

READER'S DIGEST ASSOCIATION (CANADA) LTD.
215 Redfern Ave., Montreal, Que. H3Z 2V9

Editor: Deirdre Gilbert
Assistant Editor: Anita Winterberg
Design: Andrée Payette
Production Manager: Holger Lorenzen

FIRST EDITION
PRINTED IN THE U.S.A.

READER'S DIGEST CONDENSED BOOKS

In this volume

LET ME CALL YOU SWEETHEART
by Mary Higgins Clark

Kerry McGrath is a dedicated prosecutor and a devoted mother. When her daughter's face is cut in a car accident, Kerry is relieved that the plastic surgeon who treats her is the eminent Dr. Charles Smith. Then Kerry notices something bizarre. Two of Smith's patients bear an uncanny resemblance to Suzanne Reardon, a young woman killed eleven years earlier. Why would Dr. Smith create look-alikes of a murder victim? A chilling tale of obsession by the reigning queen of suspense. / Page 7

CHILDREN OF THE DUST
by Clancy Carlile

They are children of the Oklahoma Territory: he, the son of a Cheyenne chief; she, the daughter of the white superintendent of an Indian school. Growing up, Corby White and Rachel Maxwell are the best of friends. But when they grow beyond childhood friendship, they find their world divided by forces larger than themselves. Their one ally is Gypsy Smith, a renegade lawman who is as determined as they are to live free. Land and love, betrayal and revenge are at the heart of this thrilling saga of the Old West. / Page 151

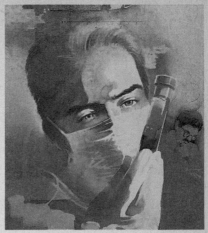

MRS. POLLIFAX AND THE LION KILLER
by Dorothy Gilman

Emily Pollifax, folksy grandmother and fearless CIA agent, has battled everything from terrorists to drug lords. But when she travels to the African nation of Ubangiba, she confronts a new opponent— lions! No one has seen the beasts, but their razor-sharp claws have left a telltale trail and brought fear to the entire country. As the number of victims rises, Mrs. Pollifax must summon all her lionhearted courage to defeat the unseen threat. A charming tale of derring-do as only the intrepid Mrs. P. can do it. / Page 343

THE MAGIC BULLET
by Harry Stein

A cure for cancer: The odds against finding one are monumental. But this is just the kind of challenge researcher Dan Logan lives for. Accepted by the world-famous American Cancer Foundation, Dan is thrilled to be battling the killer alongside scientists he thought were the best in the business. What he finds instead are vicious turf wars, faked data—even sabotage. And when Dan actually hits upon a promising drug compound, he learns that he has human enemies as lethal as the disease he came to fight. / Page 429

Let Me Call You Sweetheart

Mary Higgins Clark

She'd seen that face before. It was remarkably beautiful, yet somehow disturbing. Especially when it began to appear in her nightmares. . . .

As often as humanly possible he tried to put Suzanne out of his mind. Sometimes he achieved peace for a few hours or even managed to sleep through the night. It was the only way he could function, go about the daily business of living.

Did he still love her or only hate her? He could never be sure. She had been so beautiful, with those luminous mocking eyes, that cloud of dark hair, those lips that could smile so invitingly or pout so easily, like a child being refused a sweet.

And now, nearly eleven years later, Kerry McGrath would not let Suzanne rest. Questions and more questions! It could not be tolerated. She had to be stopped. And she would be stopped, he thought. No matter what.

1

Wednesday
October 11th

KERRY smoothed the skirt of her dark green suit, straightened the narrow gold chain on her neck and ran her fingers through her collar-length, dusky blond hair. Her entire afternoon had been a mad rush, leaving the courthouse at two thirty, picking up Robin at school, driving from Ho-Ho-Kus through the heavy traffic of Routes 17 and 4, then over the George Washington Bridge to Manhattan, finally parking the car and arriving at the doctor's office just in time for Robin's four-o'clock appointment.

Now, after all the rush, Kerry could only sit and wait. She had

9

wanted to be with Robin while the stitches were removed, but the nurse had been adamant. "During a procedure Dr. Smith will not permit anyone except a nurse in the room with a patient."

"But she's only ten!" Kerry had protested. Then she reminded herself that she should be grateful that Dr. Smith had been the one called in after the accident. The nurses at St. Luke's-Roosevelt Hospital had assured her he was a wonderful plastic surgeon. The emergency-room doctor had even called him a miracle worker.

Reflecting back on that day, a week ago, Kerry realized she still hadn't recovered from the shock of that phone call. She'd been working late at the courthouse in Hackensack, preparing for the murder case she would be prosecuting, taking advantage of the fact that Robin's father, Kerry's ex-husband, Bob Kinellen, had unexpectedly invited Robin to see New York City's Big Apple Circus.

At six thirty her phone had rung. It was Bob. There had been an accident. A van had rammed into his Jaguar while he was pulling out of the parking garage. Robin's face had been cut by flying glass. She'd been rushed to St. Luke's-Roosevelt, and a plastic surgeon had been called. Otherwise she seemed fine, although she was being examined for internal injuries.

Remembering that terrible evening, Kerry shook her head. She tried to push out of her mind the agony of the hurried drive from New Jersey into New York, dry sobs shaking her body, her lips forming a prayer: Please, God, don't let her die. She's all I have. Please, she's just a baby. Don't take her from me.

Robin was in surgery when Kerry had arrived at the hospital, so she had sat in the waiting room, Bob next to her—with him but not with him. He had a wife and two other children now. Kerry could still feel the overwhelming relief she had experienced when Dr. Smith had finally appeared and in a formal and oddly condescending manner had said, "Fortunately, the lacerations did not deeply penetrate the dermis. Robin will not be scarred. I want to see her in my office in one week."

The cuts proved to be her only injuries, and Robin had bounced back from the accident, missing only two days of school. It was just today, on their way into New York for the appointment, that she'd sounded frightened when she asked, "I will be okay, won't I, Mom? I mean, my face won't be all messed up?"

With her wide blue eyes, oval face, high forehead and sculptured features, Robin was a beautiful child and the image of her father. Kerry had reassured her with a heartiness she hoped was truthful. Now, to distract herself, Kerry looked around the waiting room, tastefully furnished with several couches and chairs covered in a small floral print. A woman who appeared to be in her early forties, wearing a bandage across her nose, was among those waiting to be called inside. Another, who looked somewhat anxious, was confiding to her attractive companion, "Now that I'm here, I'm glad you made me come. You look fabulous."

She does, Kerry thought as she self-consciously reached into her bag for her compact. Snapping it open, she examined herself in the mirror, deciding that today she looked every minute of her thirty-six years. She brushed the powder puff over her nose, trying to cover the spray of detested freckles; studied her eyes; and decided that whenever she was tired, as she was today, their hazel color changed from green to muddy brown. With a sigh she closed the compact and smoothed back the half bang that needed trimming. Anxiously she fastened her gaze on the door that led to the examining rooms. Why was it taking so long to remove Robin's stitches?

A moment later the door opened. Kerry looked up expectantly. Instead of Robin, however, there emerged a young woman who seemed to be in her mid-twenties, a cloud of dark hair framing the petulant beauty of her face. Kerry studied the high cheekbones, exquisitely shaped pouty lips, luminous eyes, arched brows.

Kerry's throat tightened. I know you, she thought. But from where? She swallowed, her mouth suddenly dry.

Once the woman had left, Kerry went over to the receptionist and explained that she thought she might know the lady who just came out of the doctor's office. Who was she?

The name Barbara Tompkins, however, meant nothing to her. She must have been mistaken. Still, when she sat down again, an overwhelming sense of déjà vu filled her mind. The effect was so chilling, she actually shivered.

11

KATE CARPENTER HAD BEEN with Dr. Charles Smith as a surgical nurse for four years, working with him on the operations he performed in the office. She considered him a genius. Still, she sometimes wondered why she stayed with him. He was so brusque with everyone, patients as well as staff, that he often seemed rude. Lately, he was getting increasingly bad-tempered. Potential new clients were offended by his manner and more and more frequently were canceling scheduled procedures. The only ones he treated with flattering care were the recipients of the special "look," and that was another thing that bothered Mrs. Carpenter.

She glanced at her watch. As she had expected, after Dr. Smith had finished examining Barbara Tompkins, the latest recipient of the look, he had gone into his office and closed the door. What did he do in there? she wondered. He had to realize he was running late. That little girl, Robin, had been sitting in examining room 3 for half an hour. After the doctor saw one of the special patients, he always seemed to need time to himself.

"Mrs. Carpenter. . . ."

Startled, the nurse looked up from her desk. Dr. Smith was staring down at her. "I think we've kept Robin Kinellen waiting long enough," he said accusingly. Behind rimless glasses his eyes were frosty.

"I DON'T like Dr. Smith," Robin said matter-of-factly as Kerry maneuvered the car out of the parking garage on Ninth Street off Fifth Avenue.

Kerry looked at her quickly. "Why not?"

"He's scary. At home when I go to Dr. Wilson, he always makes jokes. But Dr. Smith didn't even smile. He acted like he was mad at me. He said something about how some people are given beauty, while others attain it, but in neither case must it ever be wasted."

Robin was indeed quite beautiful, but why would a doctor say such an odd thing to a child? Kerry wondered.

"I'm sorry I told him I hadn't finished fastening my seat belt when the van hit Daddy's car," Robin added. "That's when Dr. Smith started lecturing me."

12

Kerry glanced at her daughter again. Robin always fastened her seat belt. Kerry tried to keep anger out of her voice as she said, "Daddy probably took off out of the garage in a hurry."

"He just didn't notice I hadn't had time to buckle it," Robin said defensively, picking up on the edge in her mother's voice.

Kerry felt heartsick for her daughter. Bob Kinellen had walked out on them both when Robin was a baby. Now he was married to his senior partner's daughter and was the father of a five-year-old girl and a three-year-old boy. Robin was crazy about her father, and when he was with her, he made a big fuss over her. But he disappointed her so often, calling at the last minute to break a scheduled date. Because his second wife did not like to be reminded that he had another child, Robin was never invited to his home. As a result, she hardly even knew her half brother and sister.

On the rare occasion when he does come through and finally takes her out, look what happens, Kerry thought. She decided not to pursue the subject. Instead she said, "Why don't you try to snooze till we get to Uncle Jonathan and Aunt Grace's?"

"Okay. I bet they have a present for me."

WHILE they waited for Kerry and Robin to arrive for dinner, Jonathan and Grace Hoover were sharing their customary late afternoon martini in the living room of their home in Old Tappan, New Jersey, overlooking Lake Tappan.

A handsome couple in their early sixties, they had been married nearly forty years, tied by bonds and needs that went beyond affection and habit. Over that time they seemed almost to have grown to resemble each other: Both had patrician features framed by luxuriant heads of hair—his pure white with natural waves, hers short and curly, still peppered with traces of brown. There was, however, a distinctive difference in their bodies. Jonathan sat tall and erect in a high-backed wing chair, while Grace reclined on a sofa opposite him, an afghan over her useless legs, a wheelchair nearby. For years she had been a victim of rheumatoid arthritis.

Jonathan remained devoted to her. The senior partner of a major New Jersey law firm, he had also been a state senator for some twenty years but had several times turned down the opportunity to run for governor. Anyone who knew him well knew Grace was the reason, and secretly wondered if he didn't harbor some vague resentment that her condition had held him back. If he did, however, he certainly never showed it.

Now, as Grace sipped her martini, she glanced anxiously at the clock on the mantel. "Aren't they running late?"

"Kerry's a good driver," Jonathan reassured her. "Don't worry."

"I know. It's just . . ." The sentence did not have to be completed; Jonathan understood fully. Ever since twenty-one-year-old Kerry, about to start law school, had answered their ad for a house sitter, they'd come to think of her as a surrogate daughter. That had been fifteen years ago, and during that time Jonathan had been of frequent help to Kerry in guiding and shaping her career, most recently using his influence to get her name on the governor's shortlist of candidates for a judgeship.

Ten minutes later the welcome sound of door chimes heralded Kerry and Robin's arrival. As Robin had predicted, there was a gift waiting for her: a book and a quiz game for her computer. After dinner she took the book into the library and curled up in a chair, while the adults lingered over coffee.

With Robin out of earshot, Grace quietly asked, "Kerry, those marks on Robin's face will fade, won't they?"

"I asked Dr. Smith the same thing. He not only practically guaranteed their disappearance, he made me feel as though I'd insulted him by expressing any concern."

As she sipped the last of her coffee, Kerry thought about the woman she had seen earlier in Dr. Smith's office. She looked across the table at Jonathan and Grace. "An odd thing happened while I was waiting for Robin," she said. "There was someone in Dr. Smith's office who looked so familiar, I even asked the receptionist what her name was. I'm sure I don't know her, but I just couldn't shake the sensation that we had met before. She gave me a creepy feeling. Isn't that odd?"

"What did she look like?" Grace asked.

"A knockout in a kind of come-hither, sensually provocative

way," Kerry reflected. "Maybe she was one of Bob's old girl-friends." She shrugged. "Oh, well. It's going to bug me till I figure it out."

YOU'VE *changed my life, Dr. Smith.* That was what Barbara Tompkins had said to him as she left his office earlier today. And he knew it was true. From a plain, almost mousy woman he'd transformed her into a beauty. More than a beauty, actually. Now she had spirit. She wasn't the same insecure young woman who had come to him a year ago. "I saw what you did for one of our clients," she had said. "I just inherited some money from my aunt. Can you make me pretty?"

At the time, she had been working in a small public relations firm in Albany. Now she was working in Manhattan at a large, prestigious PR firm. She had always had brains, but combining those brains with that special kind of beauty had truly changed her life.

Dr. Smith saw his last patient for the day at six thirty. Then he walked the three blocks down Fifth Avenue to his converted carriage house in Washington Mews. It was his habit to go home, relax over a bourbon and soda and then decide where he wanted to dine. He lived alone and almost never ate in.

Tonight an unaccustomed restlessness overcame him. Of all the women, Barbara Tompkins was most like *her.* Just seeing Barbara was an emotional, almost cathartic experience. He had overheard her telling Mrs. Carpenter that she was dining that night with a client in the Oak Room at The Plaza Hotel.

Almost reluctantly he got up. What would happen next was inevitable. He would go to the Oak Room, see if there was a small table from which he could observe Barbara while he dined. With any luck she wouldn't see him. But even if she did, he would merely wave. She had no reason to think that he was following her.

AFTER they got home from dinner with Jonathan and Grace, and long after Robin was asleep, Kerry continued to work. Her office was in the study of the house she had moved to after the divorce. She had been able to get it at a good price, when the real estate

15

market was low, and she loved it. Fifty years old, it was a Cape Cod with double dormers, set on a heavily treed two-acre lot.

Tomorrow she would be cross-examining the defendant in a murder case. He was a good actor. On the stand his version of events seemed entirely plausible. He claimed his superior had constantly belittled him, so much so that one day he had snapped and killed her. His attorney was going for manslaughter. It was Kerry's job to show that this was a carefully planned vendetta against a boss who for good reasons had passed him over for promotion. It had cost her her life. Now he has to pay, Kerry thought.

It was one o'clock before she was satisfied that she had laid out all the points she wanted to make. Wearily she climbed the stairs to the second floor, glanced in on a peacefully sleeping Robin, then went across the hallway to her own room.

Five minutes later, clad in her favorite nightshirt, she snuggled down into the queen-size brass bed she had bought in a tag sale. She closed her eyes, wondering why she felt so uneasy.

She woke at five, then managed to doze off until six. It was in that hour that the dream came to her for the first time. She was in the waiting room of a doctor's office. There was a woman lying on the floor who, through large, unfocused eyes, was staring into nothingness. A cloud of dark hair framed the petulant beauty of her face. A knotted cord was twisted around her neck. As Kerry watched, the woman got up, removed the cord from her neck and went over to the receptionist to make an appointment.

DURING the evening it crossed Bob Kinellen's mind to call and see how Robin had made out at the doctor's, but the thought had come and gone without being acted on. His father-in-law and the law firm's senior partner, Anthony Bartlett, had appeared at the Kinellens' house after dinner to discuss strategy in the upcoming income tax evasion trial of James Forrest Weeks, the firm's most important—and controversial—client.

Weeks, a multimillion-dollar real estate developer and entrepreneur, was a heavy contributor to political campaigns and a donor to numerous charities. He was also rumored to have connections with the Mob, and the U.S. Attorney General's office had been trying to pin something on him for years. It had been the financially rewarding job of Bartlett and Kinellen to represent him during those past investigations. Until now the feds had always fallen short of enough evidence for a solid indictment.

"This time Jimmy is in serious trouble," Anthony Bartlett said as he sat across from his son-in-law in the study of the Kinellen home in Englewood Cliffs, New Jersey. He sipped a brandy. "Which, of course, means we're in serious trouble with him."

In the ten years since Bob had joined the firm, he had seen it become almost an extension of Weeks Enterprises, so closely were they entwined. In fact, if Jimmy were to be found guilty, Bartlett and Kinellen as a viable law firm would be finished.

"Barney's the one I worry about," Bob said quietly. Barney Haskell was Jimmy Weeks's chief accountant and codefendant in the current case. Intense pressure was being put on him to turn government witness in exchange for a plea bargain.

Anthony Bartlett nodded. "Agreed."

"And for more than one reason," Bob continued. "I told you about the accident and that Robin was being treated by a plastic surgeon, but I didn't tell you his name. It's Charles Smith."

Anthony Bartlett sat bolt upright. "Not the one who . . . ?"

"Exactly. Knowing my ex-wife, the assistant prosecutor, it's only a matter of time before she makes the connection."

"Oh, that's just great," Bartlett said miserably.

2

Thursday
October 12th

THE Bergen County prosecutor's office was located on the second floor of the courthouse. It housed thirty-five assistant prosecutors, seventy investigators and twenty-five secretaries, as well as Franklin Green, the prosecutor. Despite the heavy workload and the serious, often macabre, nature of the business, an air of camaraderie existed within the office. Kerry loved working there.

She regularly received enticing offers from law firms, but despite the financial temptations, she had elected to stay put and now had worked her way up to the position of trial chief. In the process she had earned a reputation as a smart, tough and scrupulous lawyer.

Two judges had just retired from the bench, and in his capacity as a state senator, Jonathan Hoover had submitted Kerry's name to replace one of them. She did not admit even to herself how much she wanted it. The big law firms offered much more money, but a judgeship represented the kind of achievement that no money could compete with.

By the standards of the windowless cubbyholes assigned to new assistants, Kerry's office was reasonably sized, and she had personalized it with plants that edged the windowsills and with framed pictures that Robin had taken.

She stared at the stacks of files that completely covered her battered wooden desk, then sat down and picked up one of them. The business at hand was the trial session starting in an hour.

The murdered supervisor had two teenage sons, whom she had been raising alone. Who was going to take care of them now? Suppose something happened to me, Kerry thought. Where would Robin go? Surely not to her father; she would not be happy, nor welcome, in his new household. But Kerry also couldn't picture her own mother and stepfather, both over seventy and living in Colorado, raising a ten-year-old. Pray God I stay around, she thought as she turned her attention to the file in front of her.

At ten of nine her phone rang. It was Frank Green, the prosecutor. "Kerry, I know you're on your way to court, but stop by for just a minute."

"Of course."

She found Green seated behind his desk. Craggy-faced, with shrewd eyes, at fifty-two he'd kept the hard physique that had made him a college football star. His smile seemed odd, she thought. Did he just have his teeth bonded? If so, he's smart. They'll photograph well when he's nominated in June.

There was no question that Green was preparing for the gubernatorial campaign. The attention he was paying to his wardrobe was obvious. An editorial had said that since the present governor had served so well for two terms and Green was his handpicked successor, it seemed likely he would be chosen to lead the state. After that, Green became known to his staff as Our Leader.

Kerry admired Green's legal skills. Her reservation about him was that several times he had let an assistant who had made an honest mistake hang out to dry. Green's first loyalty was to himself.

Now he said, "Come in, Kerry. I just wanted to hear how Robin is doing."

She briefly told him about the checkup.

"Robin was with her father at the time of the accident, wasn't she?" he asked.

"Yes. Bob was driving."

"By the way, your ex may be running out of luck. I don't think he's going to get Jimmy Weeks off this time. Word is they're going to nail him, and I hope they do. He's a crook and maybe worse." He made a gesture of dismissal. "You're cross-examining the defendant today, aren't you?"

"Yes."

"Knowing you, I'm almost sorry for him. Good luck."

3

Monday
October 23rd

ALMOST two weeks later Kerry was still basking in the satisfaction of the now concluded trial. She had gotten her murder conviction. At least the sons of the murdered woman would not have to grow up knowing that their mother's killer would be walking the streets in five or six years. That would have happened if the jury had fallen for the manslaughter defense. Murder carried a mandatory thirty-year sentence, without parole.

Now, once again seated in the reception area of Dr. Smith's office, Kerry opened her briefcase and pulled out a newspaper. This was Robin's second checkup and should be routine, so she could relax. Besides, she was anxious to read the latest about the

Jimmy Weeks trial. As Frank Green had predicted, the consensus was that it would not go well for the defendant. Previous investigations for bribery, insider trading and money laundering had been dropped for lack of sufficient evidence. This time the prosecutor was said to have an airtight case.

Bob had introduced Kerry to Jimmy Weeks once, when she had bumped into them in a restaurant. Now she studied his picture as he sat with her ex-husband at the defense table. Take away that thousand-dollar suit and phony air of sophistication, and you've got a thug, she thought. In the picture Bob's arm was draped protectively around the back of Weeks's chair, their heads close together. Kerry remembered how Bob used to practice that gesture.

She scanned the article, then dropped the newspaper back into her briefcase, remembering how appalled she had been when, shortly after Robin was born, Bob had told her he had accepted a job with Bartlett and Associates. "All their clients have one foot in jail," she had protested. "And the other foot should be there."

"And they pay their bills on time," Bob had replied. "Kerry, you stay in the prosecutor's office if you want. I have other plans."

A year later he had announced that those plans included marrying Alice Bartlett.

Ancient history, Kerry told herself now as she glanced toward the examining rooms, the door to which was just opening.

Immediately Kerry froze, and her glance became a stare. The young woman who emerged had a face framed by a cloud of dark hair, pouty lips, wide-set eyes, arched brows. It wasn't the same woman she had seen last time—but it looked like her. Could the two be related? If they were patients, surely Dr. Smith couldn't be trying to make them look alike, she thought. And why did that face remind her so much of someone else that it had brought on a nightmare?

"Ms. McGrath."

Kerry turned to see Mrs. Carpenter, the nurse, beckoning to her to come to the doctor's office. As Kerry followed her, she said, "That woman who just left—what's her name?"

"Pamela Worth," Mrs. Carpenter said. "Here we are."

20

Robin was seated across the desk from the doctor, her hands folded in her lap, her posture unusually straight. Kerry saw the look of relief on her daughter's face when their eyes met. The doctor indicated that Kerry should take the chair next to Robin. His expression was intense. "I've explained to Robin that many people come to me seeking the kind of beauty that was freely given to her. It is her duty to safeguard it. Robin told me her father was driving the car at the time of the accident. I urge you to warn him to take better care of his daughter. She is irreplaceable."

ON THE way home, at Robin's request, they stopped for dinner at Valentino's in Park Ridge. "I like the shrimp there," Robin explained. But when they were settled at a table, she said, "Daddy brought me here once." Her voice was wistful.

So that's why this is the restaurant of choice, Kerry thought. Since the accident Bob had phoned Robin only once, and that had been during school hours. The message on the answering machine was that he guessed she was in school and that must mean she was doing great. There was no suggestion she return his call.

When the waiter had taken their orders, Robin said, "Mom, I don't want to go back to Dr. Smith anymore. He's creepy."

Kerry's heart sank. It was exactly what she had been thinking. Her next thought was that she only had his word that the angry red lines on Robin's face would disappear. I've got to have someone else check her out, she thought. Trying to sound matter-of-fact, she said, "Oh, I guess he's all right, even if he does have the personality of a wet noodle." She was rewarded by Robin's grin.

"Even so," she continued, "he doesn't want to see you for another month, and after that, maybe not at all, so don't worry about him. It's not his fault he was born without charm."

Robin laughed. "Forget the charm. He's a major creep."

When the food arrived, they sampled each other's choices and gossiped. Robin had a passion for photography and was taking a basic course in technique. Her present assignment was to capture the autumn leaves in transition. "I know the ones I took this week with the colors at their peak will be terrific. Now I can't wait till

21

a good storm starts scattering everything. Won't that be great?"

"Nothing like a good storm scattering everything," Kerry agreed.

They decided to skip dessert. The waiter had just returned Kerry's credit card when she heard Robin gasp.

"What is it, Rob?" Kerry asked.

"Daddy's here. He sees us." Robin jumped up.

"Wait, Rob. Let him come over to you," Kerry said quietly. She turned, and her eyes widened. Following the maître d', Bob was accompanied by another man—Jimmy Weeks.

As usual, her ex-husband looked stunning. Even a long day in court did not leave a sign of fatigue on his handsome face. Never a wrinkle or a rumple about you, Kerry thought, aware that in Bob's presence she always had the impulse to check her makeup, smooth her hair, straighten her jacket.

On the other hand, Robin looked ecstatic as her father approached. Happily she returned Bob's hug. "I'm sorry I missed your call, Daddy."

Oh, Robin, Kerry thought. Then she realized that Jimmy Weeks was looking down at her. "I met you here last year," he said. "Glad to see you again, Mrs. Kinellen."

"I dropped that name long ago. It's back to McGrath. But you have a good memory, Mr. Weeks." Kerry's tone was impersonal.

"You bet I have a good memory." Weeks's smile made the remark seem like a joke. "It helps when you're remembering a very attractive woman."

Spare me, Kerry thought, smiling tightly. She turned from him as Bob released Robin. Now he stretched out his hand to her. "Kerry, what a nice surprise."

"It's usually a surprise when we see you, Bob." Kerry bit her lip. She hated herself when she jabbed at Bob in front of their daughter. She forced a smile. "We're just leaving."

When they were settled at their table, Jimmy Weeks observed, "Your ex-wife sure doesn't like you much, Bobby."

Kinellen shrugged. "Kerry should lighten up. She takes everything too seriously. I wish she'd meet someone."

"What happened to your kid's face?"

"Flying glass in a fender bender. She'll be fine."

"Did you make sure she had a good plastic surgeon?"

"Yes. What do you feel like eating, Jimmy?"

"What's the doctor's name? Maybe he's the same one my wife went to."

Bob Kinellen cursed the lousy luck of meeting Kerry and Robin and having Jimmy ask about the accident. "Charles Smith," he said finally.

"Charles Smith? You've got to be kidding."

"I wish I were."

"Well, I hear he's retiring soon. He's got health problems."

Kinellen looked startled. "How do you know that?"

Jimmy looked at him coldly. "I keep tabs on him. You figure out why. It shouldn't take too long."

THAT night the dream returned. Again Kerry was standing in a doctor's office. A young woman was lying on the floor, a cord knotted around her neck, her dark hair framing a face with wide, unfocused eyes, a mouth open as though gasping for breath, the tip of a pink tongue protruding. In her dream Kerry tried to scream, but only a moaning protest came from her lips. A moment later Robin was shaking her. "Mom. Mom, wake up. What's wrong?"

Kerry opened her eyes, "Oh, Rob, what a rotten nightmare. Thanks."

When Robin had returned to her room, Kerry lay awake, pondering the dream. This time there had been flowers scattered over the woman's body. Roses. Sweetheart roses.

She sat up suddenly. That was it! The women in Dr. Smith's office. She knew now who they looked like.

Suzanne Reardon, the victim in the Sweetheart Murder Case. It had been nearly eleven years since she had been murdered by her husband, Skip Reardon. It had gotten a lot of press attention—crime of passion and roses scattered over the beautiful victim.

The day I started in the prosecutor's office was the day the jury found the husband guilty, Kerry thought. The papers had been

23

plastered with pictures of Suzanne. I'm sure I'm right, she told herself. But why would two of Dr. Smith's patients be look-alikes for a murder victim?

PAMELA Worth had been a mistake. That thought kept Dr. Charles Smith sleepless virtually all Monday night. Even the beauty of her newly sculptured face could not compensate for her graceless posture, her harsh, loud voice.

I should have known, he thought. And, in fact, he had known. But he hadn't been able to help himself. Her bone structure made her a ridiculously easy candidate for such a transformation. And feeling that transformation take place under his fingers had made it possible for him to relive something of the excitement of the first time. What would he do when it wasn't possible to operate anymore? he wondered. That time was approaching. The slight tremor in his right hand would become more pronounced.

He switched on the light that illuminated the picture on the wall opposite his bed. He looked at it each night before he fell asleep. She was so beautiful. But now, without his glasses, the woman in the picture became distorted, as she had looked in death.

"Suzanne," he murmured. Then, as the pain of memory engulfed him, he threw an arm over his eyes, blocking out the image. He could not bear to remember how she had looked then, robbed of her beauty, her eyes bulging, the tip of her tongue protruding over her slack lower lip and drooping jaw.

4

Tuesday
October 24th

ON TUESDAY morning the first thing Kerry did when she got to her office was phone her mentor and friend, Jonathan Hoover.

As always, it was comforting to hear his voice. Kerry got right to the point. "Jonathan, Robin had her checkup with Dr. Smith yesterday, and everything seems to be fine, but I'd be more comfortable with a second opinion. Do you know a good plastic surgeon?"

"No, but let me make some inquiries. Did something happen to make you decide on this?"

"Yes and no. I'll tell you about it when I see you."

"I'll get back to you with a name this afternoon."

"Thanks, Jonathan."

"You're welcome, Your Honor."

"Jonathan, don't say that. You'll jinx me."

As the phone clicked, she heard him chuckle.

Next Kerry dialed Joe Palumbo, one of the best investigators in the prosecutor's office. When he answered with his usual "Yup," she asked, "Joe, have you got lunch plans?"

"Not a one, Kerry. Want to take me to Solari's?"

Kerry laughed. "I'd love to, but I have something else in mind. Were you involved with the Reardon homicide about ten or eleven years ago? The one the media called the Sweetheart Murder."

"That was a biggie. No, I wasn't, but as I remember, it was pretty open and shut. Our Leader made his name on that one."

Kerry knew that Palumbo was not enamored of Frank Green. "Something has come up that has me curious about that case. I want you to dig out everything the *Record* printed on it," she said. Kerry could picture Joe good-naturedly rolling his eyes.

"For you, Kerry, sure. But why? That case is long gone."

"Ask me later."

Kerry's lunch was a sandwich at her desk. At one thirty Palumbo came in carrying a bulging envelope. "As requested."

Kerry looked at him affectionately. Short, graying, twenty pounds overweight and with a ready smile, Joe had a disarmingly benevolent appearance that did not reflect his ability to home in on seemingly unimportant details. She had worked with him on some of her most important cases. "I owe you one," she said.

"Forget it. See you later."

Kerry was planning to take the file home and read it after dinner. But she could not resist pulling out the top clipping. It was a recent item noting that Skip Reardon's fifth appeal for a new trial had been turned down by the New Jersey Supreme Court and that his attorney, Geoffrey Dorso, had vowed to find grounds for another appeal. Dorso's quote was, "I'll keep trying until Skip Reardon walks out of that prison exonerated. He's an innocent man."

Of course, she thought, all lawyers say that.

FOR the second night in a row Bob Kinellen dined with his client Jimmy Weeks. Both men were somber. It was almost certain Barney Haskell, Weeks's codefendant, was going to cop a plea.

"Even if Haskell does plead, I think I can destroy him on the stand," Kinellen assured Jimmy.

"You *think* you can destroy him. That's not good enough, Bob. I'm beginning to worry about you. It's about time you got yourself a backup plan."

Bob Kinellen let the remark pass. He opened the menu. "I'm meeting Alice at Jason Arnott's later. Were you planning to go?"

"Hell, no. I don't need any more of his introductions. You should know that. They've done me enough harm already."

KERRY and Robin sat in companionable silence in the family room. Because of the chilly evening, they had decided to have a fire, which in their case meant turning on the gas jet and then pressing the button that sent flames shooting through the artificial logs. Kerry was allergic to smoke, as she explained to visitors.

Robin laid out her change-of-season pictures on the coffee table. "What a terrific night," she said with satisfaction. "Cold and windy. I should get the rest of the pictures soon. Bare trees, lots of leaves on the ground."

Kerry sat in her favorite armchair, her feet on a hassock. She looked up. "Don't remind me of the leaves. I get tired."

"Why don't you get a leaf blower?"

"I'll give you one for Christmas."

"Funny. What are you reading, Mom?"

"Come here, Rob." Kerry held up a newspaper clipping with a picture of Suzanne Reardon. "Do you recognize that lady?"

"She was in Dr. Smith's office yesterday."

"You've got a good eye, but it's not the same person." Kerry had just begun reading the account of Suzanne Reardon's murder. Her husband, millionaire contractor Skip Reardon, claimed he had found her at midnight on the floor in the foyer of their luxurious home in Alpine. She had been strangled. Sweetheart roses were scattered over her body.

It was twenty minutes later when Kerry read the clipping that made her gasp. Skip Reardon had been charged with the murder after his father-in-law, *Dr. Charles Smith*, had told the police that his daughter lived in fear of her husband's insane jealousy. *Dr. Smith was Suzanne Reardon's father!* Incredible, Kerry thought. Is that why he's giving her face to other women? How bizarre.

"What's the matter, Mom? You look funny," Robin said.

"Nothing. Just interested in a case." Kerry looked at the clock on the mantel. "Nine o'clock, Rob. You'd better pack it in. I'll come up to say good night."

As Robin gathered her pictures, Kerry let the clipping fall into her lap. She had heard of parents who could not recover from the death of a child, who left the child's room unchanged, just as the child had left it. But to "re-create" her, and do it over and over? That went beyond grief, surely.

Slowly she stood up and followed Robin upstairs. After she kissed her daughter good night, she went back downstairs, made a cup of cocoa and continued to read.

The case against Skip Reardon did seem open and shut. He admitted that he and Suzanne had quarreled at breakfast the morning of her death. He admitted that he had come home at six o'clock that evening and found her arranging roses in a vase. When he asked her where they had come from, she told him it was none of his business. He said he told her that whoever sent them was welcome to her, that he was getting out. Then he claimed he had gone back to his office, had a couple of drinks, fallen asleep on the couch and returned home at midnight, to find her body.

There had been no one, however, to corroborate what he said. The file contained part of the trial transcript, including Skip's testimony. The prosecutor had hammered at him until he became confused and seemed to contradict himself.

27

What a terrible job his lawyer had done in preparing him to testify, Kerry thought. She didn't doubt that with the prosecutor's strong circumstantial case, it had been imperative that Reardon take the stand to deny he had killed Suzanne. But it was obvious that Frank Green's scathing cross-examination had completely unnerved him. There's no question, she thought, that Reardon had helped to dig his own grave.

Kerry had actually gone in to witness the sentencing. Now she thought back to that day. When the judge asked him if he wanted to say anything before sentence was passed, he had once again protested his innocence.

Geoff Dorso had been with Reardon that day, serving as assistant counsel to Reardon's defense lawyer. Although Kerry didn't know him firsthand and had never argued against him in court, Geoff had built a solid reputation as a criminal defense lawyer in the ten years since then.

She came to the clipping about the sentencing. It included a quote from Skip Reardon: "I am innocent of the death of my wife. I never hurt her. I never threatened her. Her father, Dr. Charles Smith, is a liar. Before God and this court, I *swear* he is a liar."

Despite the warmth from the fire, she shivered.

EVERYONE knew, or thought they knew, that Jason Arnott had family money. He had lived in Alpine for fifteen years, ever since he had bought the old Halliday house, a twenty-room mansion with a splendid view of Palisades Interstate Park.

Jason was in his early fifties, of average height, with scant brown hair, weathered eyes and a trim figure. He traveled extensively, talked vaguely of investments in the Orient and loved beautiful things. His home, with its exquisite antique furniture, fine paintings and delicate *objets d'art,* was a feast for the eyes. A superb host, Jason entertained lavishly and was in return besieged with invitations from the great, the near great and the merely rich. His friends found him colorful, a little mysterious and totally engaging.

What they didn't know was that Jason was a thief. No one ever seemed to piece together that after a decent interval virtually all the homes he visited were burglarized. No one guessed that Jason had several identities and a secret dwelling in a remote area of New York's Catskill Mountains, where he was known to his widely scattered neighbors as a recluse. If his house in Alpine was exquisite, the one in the Catskills was breathtaking, for it was there that Jason kept the pieces from his looting escapades that he could not bear to part with.

Everything in Alpine had been bought with money received for stolen property Jason had sold. There was nothing there that would ever catch the attention of someone with a photographic memory for a stolen possession. Jason could say with confidence, "Yes, that's quite nice, isn't it? I got it at Sotheby's in an auction last year."

Nevertheless, he had had a few narrow escapes. One of the worst happened eleven years ago when his cleaning woman in Alpine had spilled the contents of her pocketbook. When she retrieved them, she missed her sheet of paper containing the security pass codes for four homes in Alpine. Jason had jotted them down, replaced the paper before the woman knew it was gone and then, tempted beyond control, had burglarized the four homes: the Ellots, the Ashtons, the Donnatellis. And the Reardons. Jason still shuddered with the memory of that horrific night.

But that was years ago, and Skip Reardon was securely in prison. Tonight the party was in full swing. Jason smilingly acknowledged the gushing compliments of Alice Bartlett Kinellen.

"I hope Bob will be able to make it," Jason told her.

"Oh, he'll be along. He knows better than to disappoint me."

Alice was a beautiful Grace Kelly–type blonde, with none of that late princess's charm or warmth. Alice was cold as ice. Also boring and possessive, Jason thought. How does Kinellen stand her?

"He's having dinner with Jimmy Weeks," Alice confided as she sipped champagne.

"Well, I hope Jimmy comes too," Jason said sincerely. "I like him." But he knew Jimmy wouldn't come. Weeks hadn't been to one of his parties in years. In fact, he had given a wide berth to Alpine after Suzanne Reardon's murder. Eleven years ago Jimmy Weeks had met Suzanne at a party in Jason Arnott's house.

5

*I*T WAS clear that Frank Green was irritated. The smile that he flashed so readily to show off his newly whitened teeth was nowhere in evidence as he looked across his desk at Kerry. I should have known, she thought, that of all people, Frank wouldn't want to hear anyone questioning the case that made him, and especially not now, with talk of his candidacy for governor so prevalent.

After reading the newspaper file on the Sweetheart Murder Case last night, Kerry had gone to bed trying to decide what she should do regarding Dr. Smith. Should she confront him, ask him point-blank why he was re-creating his daughter in the faces of other women? Odds were he would throw her out of the office and deny everything. Finally she had decided that the best place to start was with Frank Green, since he had tried the case. Now that she had filled him in on the reason she was inquiring about the case, it was obvious that her question "Do you think there is any possibility Dr. Smith was lying when he testified against Skip Reardon?" was not going to result in a friendly response.

"Kerry," Green said, "Skip Reardon killed his wife. He knew she was playing around. The very day he killed her, he had called his accountant to find out how much a divorce would cost him, and he went bananas when he was told he would have to pay through the nose. He was a wealthy man, and Suzanne had given up a lucrative modeling career to become a full-time wife. So questioning Dr. Smith's veracity at this point is a waste of time."

"But there's something wrong with Dr. Smith," Kerry said slowly. "Frank, I'm not trying to make trouble, but I swear to you that Smith is more than a grief-stricken father."

Green looked at his watch. "Kerry, you just finished a big case. You're about to take on another one. You've got a judgeship pending. It's too bad Robin was treated by Suzanne Reardon's father. If anything, he wasn't an ideal witness. There wasn't a drop of emotion in him when he talked about his daughter. I was thankful the jury even believed his testimony. Do yourself a favor and forget it."

It was clear the meeting was over.

Back in her office, Kerry sat gazing into space. She could understand Frank Green's alarm at her raising questions about his star witness in the Sweetheart Murder Case. Dr. Smith is probably an obsessively grieving father, she told herself, and Skip Reardon is probably one of the countless murderers who say "I didn't do it."

Even so, she knew she couldn't let it rest at that. On Saturday, when she took Robin to the plastic surgeon Jonathan had recommended, she would ask the doctor if he would even consider giving a number of women the same face.

At six thirty that evening Geoff Dorso glanced at the stack of messages that had come in while he was in court.

Thirty-eight years old, Geoff was tall and lean. His jet-black hair and olive skin were evidence of his Italian ancestry. His intensely blue eyes came from his Irish-English grandmother. Still a bachelor, he looked the part. His selection of ties was hit and miss, and his clothes usually had a slightly rumpled look. But the stack of messages was an indication of his excellent reputation as an attorney.

As he leafed through them, he suddenly raised his eyebrows. There was a request to call Assistant Prosecutor Kerry McGrath. She had left both her office and home numbers. What's that about? he wondered. Over the years he had met Kerry at bar association dinners, and he knew she was up for a judgeship, but he didn't really know her. The call intrigued him. It was too late to get her at the office. He decided he would try her now, at home.

"I'll get it," Robin called as the phone rang.

It's probably for you anyhow, Kerry thought as she tested the spaghetti. I thought telephonitis didn't set in until the teen years, she mused. Then Robin yelled for her to pick up. She hurried across the kitchen to the phone. An unfamiliar voice said, "Kerry."

"Yes."

"Geoff Dorso here."

31

It had been an impulse to leave the message for him. Afterward, she was uneasy about having done it. If Frank Green heard that she was contacting Skip Reardon's attorney, he would not be happy. "Geoff, this is probably not relevant, but my daughter had an accident recently and was treated by Dr. Charles Smith."

"Charles Smith?" Dorso interrupted. "Suzanne Reardon's father!"

"Yes. That's the point. There is something bizarre going on with him." She told him about the two women who resembled Suzanne.

"You mean Smith is actually giving them his daughter's face?" Dorso exclaimed. "What the hell is that about?"

"That's what troubles me. It occurred to me that if I could read the entire trial transcript, I'd have a better handle on Dr. Smith. I can get one through the office, but that would take time, and I don't want it getting around that I'm looking for it."

"I'll have a copy in your office tomorrow," Dorso promised.

"No. Better to send it to me here. I'll give you the address."

As he jotted it down, he said, "I'd like to bring it up myself and talk to you. Would tomorrow night be all right? About six thirty?"

"I guess that would be okay."

"See you then. And thanks, Kerry." The phone clicked.

Kerry looked at the receiver. She hadn't missed the excitement in Dorso's voice. I shouldn't have used the word bizarre, she thought. I've started something I may not be able to finish.

TODAY Dr. Charles Smith had cleared his calendar completely. As he drove down East Sixty-eighth Street toward the brownstone where the public relations firm Barbara Tompkins worked for was located, his eyes widened at his good luck. There was a parking spot across from the entrance of her building; he could sit there and watch for her to leave.

When she finally did appear in the doorway, he smiled involuntarily. She looked lovely. As he had suggested, she wore her hair full and loose around her face—the best style to frame her new features. As she hailed a cab, he turned on the ignition of his black Mercedes and began to follow. They drove south, the cab finally stopping at The Four Seasons on East Fifty-second. Barbara must be meeting someone for a drink there, he thought. The bar would be crowded now. It would be easy for him to slip in undetected.

Shaking his head, he decided to drive home instead. The glimpse of her had been enough. Almost too much. For a moment he had really believed that she was Suzanne. Now he just wanted to be alone. A sob rose in his throat. As the traffic inched downtown, he repeated over and over, "I'm sorry, Suzanne. I'm sorry."

6

Thursday
October 26th

*I*F JONATHAN Hoover happened to be in Hackensack, he usually tried to persuade Kerry to join him for a quick lunch.

Today, over a hamburger at Solari's, the restaurant around the corner from the courthouse, Kerry filled him in on the Suzanne Reardon look-alikes and her boss's less-than-favorable reaction to her suggestion that she might look into the old murder case.

Jonathan was deeply concerned. "Kerry, I don't remember much about that case, but I think you should stay out of it, especially considering Frank Green's involvement—very public, as I recall—in securing the conviction. Look at the realities here. Governor Marshall has served two terms and can't run for a consecutive third, but he loves his job. He wants Frank to take his place. Between us, they've got a deal. Green is to be governor for four years; then he runs for the U.S. Senate with Marshall's support."

"And Marshall moves back into the governor's mansion."

"Exactly. As of now it's a foregone conclusion that Green will get the nomination. But if you reopen the Reardon case, do you know what the media would do if it were suggested that Green sent an innocent man to prison for life?"

"Jonathan, you're getting way ahead of me. I'm not going in with that supposition. I just feel that Dr. Smith has a big problem, and it may have affected his testimony. If he lied, it really casts doubt in my mind as to whether Reardon is guilty."

Jonathan's expression became serious. "Kerry, if you embarrass

33

Frank Green and put his nomination in jeopardy, chances are you can kiss your judgeship good-bye." He paused, then took Kerry's hand. "Give this lots of thought before you do anything. I know you'll make the right decision."

PROMPTLY at six thirty that evening the chiming of the doorbell sent Robin racing to greet Geoff Dorso. Kerry had told her he was coming and that they would be going over a case. Robin had promised to finish her homework in her room while Kerry was busy.

She inspected Dorso with benevolence and ushered him into the family room. "My mother will be right down," she said. "I'm Robin."

"I'm Geoff Dorso. How does the other guy look?" Geoff asked. With a smile he indicated the still vivid marks on her face.

Robin grinned. "I flattened him. Actually, it was a fender bender, with some flying glass."

"It looks as though it's healing fine."

"Dr. Smith, the plastic surgeon, says it is. Mom says you know him. I think he's creepy."

"Robin!" Kerry had just come downstairs.

"From the mouths of babes," Dorso said, smiling. "Kerry, it's good to see you."

"Good to see you, Geoff." I hope I mean it, Kerry thought as her gaze fell on the bulging briefcase under Dorso's arm. "Robin. . . ."

"I know. Homework." With a wave of her hand Robin headed for the staircase.

Geoff Dorso smiled after her. "Nice kid, Kerry, and she's a knockout. In another five years you'll have to barricade the door."

"A scary prospect. Geoff, coffee, a drink, a glass of wine?"

"No, thanks. I don't want to take too much of your time." He laid his briefcase on the coffee table. "Shall we go over this in here?"

"Sure." She sat next to him on the couch as he took out two thick volumes of bound paper. "The trial transcript," he said. "One thousand pages of it. Frankly, I'm ashamed of the defense we mounted. Skip wasn't properly prepared to take the stand. The state's witnesses weren't vigorously questioned. And we only called two character witnesses for Skip, when we should have called twenty."

"Why was it handled that way?" Kerry asked.

"Tim Farrell had been a good defense lawyer once, but when Skip Reardon hired him, he was past his prime and burned out. He just wasn't interested in another murder case."

"Couldn't you have filled the gap?"

"No, not really. I was just out of law school and didn't have much to say about anything. I had very little participation in the trial at all. I was basically a gofer for Farrell. As inexperienced as I was, though, it was obvious to me that the trial was handled badly."

"And Frank Green tore him apart on cross-examination."

"As you read, he got Skip to admit that he and Suzanne had quarreled that morning, that he'd spoken to his accountant to find out what a divorce would cost, that he'd gone home again at six and quarreled with Suzanne. The coroner estimated time of death to be between six and eight o'clock, so Skip could, by his own testimony, be placed at the scene at the time of the murder."

"From the account I read, Reardon claimed he went back to his office, had a couple of drinks and fell asleep. That's pretty thin."

"It's thin but it's true. Skip had established a very successful business building quality homes. Recently he had expanded into shopping malls. He often put on work clothes and spent the day with a crew. That's what he'd done that day before coming back to work at the office. The guy was tired.

"Skip is convinced," he continued, "that Suzanne was involved with another man, perhaps even more than one. What precipitated the second quarrel, when he went home at six o'clock, was that he found her arranging a bunch of red roses—sweetheart roses, I think the press called them—that he had not sent her. The prosecution maintained that he went into a rage, strangled her, then threw the roses over her body. He swears that he didn't, that when he left, Suzanne was still blithely puttering with the flowers."

"Did anyone check the local florists to see if an order for the roses had been placed with one of them?"

"Farrell did at least do that. Nothing turned up."

Geoff stood up. "I know it's a lot to ask, Kerry, but after you read this transcript, I want you to come with me to Trenton State Prison.

Talk to Skip yourself. I swear you'll hear the ring of truth when he tells you his story."

She walked with Geoff to the door. "I'll call you in the next few days," she promised.

IN TRENTON State Prison, Skip Reardon lay on the bunk of his cell, watching the six-thirty news. After ten years in this place he had managed for the most part to set himself on a middle course. In the beginning he had fluctuated between wild hope when an appeal was pending, and crashing despair when it was rejected. Now his usual state of mind was weary resignation.

In his most despondent moments Skip allowed himself to think back over the years before the murder and to realize just how crazy he had been. He and Beth Taylor had practically been engaged. Then at Beth's urging he had gone alone to a party her sister and her surgeon husband were giving. Beth had come down with a bug, but she hadn't wanted him to miss the fun.

Yeah, *fun*, Skip thought ironically, remembering that night. Suzanne and her father had been there. Even now he could not forget how she looked the first time he saw her. He had known immediately she meant trouble, but he fell for her anyway.

Now the daydream he allowed himself was that by some miracle he was free to go back to building houses. He had loose-leaf books filled with designs. Whenever Beth came to see him, he would show her the latest ones and they would talk about them as though he really would one day be able to go back to the job he had loved—building homes.

Only now he had to wonder, What would people be living in when he finally got out of this terrible place?

KERRY started reading the transcript after Robin went to bed. By the time she laid it down, she had pages of notes and questions.

The roses: If Skip Reardon didn't send them, who *did?*

Dolly Bowles, the baby-sitter in the house across the street from the Reardon home the night of the murder: She claimed she saw a car in front of the Reardons' house at nine o'clock that night. But neighbors were having a party at the time, and a number of their guests had parked in the street. Dolly had made a particularly poor witness in court. Frank Green had brought out the fact that she had reported "suspicious-looking" people in the neighborhood on six separate occasions that year. In each instance the suspect turned out to be a legitimate deliveryman.

There had been a series of burglaries in Alpine around the time of Suzanne Reardon's death. Skip Reardon claimed that some of Suzanne's jewelry was missing. But a tray full of valuable jewelry was found on the dresser.

As she undressed for bed that night, Kerry decided there were two things she had to do: talk with Dr. Smith and visit Skip Reardon at the state prison in Trenton.

7

Saturday
October 28th

AT TEN o'clock Saturday morning Kerry and an impatient Robin were in Livingston, New Jersey, in the office of Dr. Ben Roth, a noted plastic surgeon.

"I'm going to miss the soccer game," Robin fretted.

"You'll be a little late, that's all," Kerry soothed. "Don't worry."

"Very late," Robin protested. "Why couldn't he see me this afternoon after the game?"

"Perhaps if you'd sent the doctor your schedule, he could have worked around it," Kerry teased.

"Oh, Mom."

"You can bring Robin in now, Ms. McGrath," the receptionist announced.

Dr. Roth, in his mid-thirties, warm and affable, was a welcome change from Dr. Smith. He examined Robin's face carefully. "The lacerations probably looked pretty bad right after the accident, but they were what we call superficial. They didn't deeply penetrate the dermis. You haven't got any problems."

Robin looked relieved. "Great. Thanks, Doctor. Let's go, Mom."

"Wait in the reception area, Robin. I'll be out in a moment. I want to talk to the doctor." Kerry's voice carried what Robin called the tone. It meant "no arguments."

"Okay," Robin said with an exaggerated sigh as she departed.

"I know you have patients waiting, so I won't be long, Doctor, but there is something I must ask you," Kerry said.

A few minutes later Kerry rejoined Robin, and they rushed to the soccer field. Unlike Kerry, Robin was not a natural athlete, and Kerry had spent long hours working with her, because Robin's heart was set on being a good player. Now, as she watched Robin confidently kick the ball past the goalie, she reflected on Dr. Roth's flat answer to her question: "It's a fact that some surgeons give everyone the same nose or chin or eyes, but I find it extremely unusual that any surgeon would in essence clone the faces of his patients."

At eleven thirty she caught Robin's eye and waved good-bye. Robin would go home from the game with her best friend, Cassie, and would spend the afternoon at her house.

Then Kerry got on the road to the state prison in Trenton. She had arranged to meet Geoff Dorso there at one forty-five.

KERRY found Geoff waiting for her in the area where visitors were registered. They talked little while they waited for their three-o'clock meeting with Skip Reardon. Promptly at three, a guard approached them and told them to follow him.

Kerry did not know what she expected Skip Reardon to look like now. It had been ten years since she had sat in at his sentencing. The impression she had retained of him was of a tall, good-looking young man with red hair. But more than his appearance, it was his statement that had been burned into her mind: *Dr. Charles Smith is a liar. Before God and this court, I swear he is a liar!*

Reardon appeared, dressed in prison denims and an open-necked prison-issue shirt. The red hair was streaked with gray, but except for the lines around his eyes, he still looked much as Kerry recalled him. A smile brightened his face as Geoff introduced him. A hopeful smile, Kerry realized with a sinking heart.

Geoff got right to the point. "Skip, as I told you, Ms. McGrath wants to ask you some questions."

Kerry smiled, then went straight to the question that was to her the crux of this meeting. "In his testimony Dr. Smith swore that his daughter—your wife—was afraid of you and that you had threatened her. You maintain he was lying, but what purpose would he have in lying about that?"

Reardon's hands were folded on the table in front of him. "Ms. McGrath, if I had any explanation for Dr. Smith's actions, maybe I wouldn't be here now. Suzanne and I were married four years, and during that time I never saw that much of Smith. She'd go into New York and have dinner with him occasionally, or he'd come out to the house, but usually when I was away on a business trip. At the time, my construction business was booming. I was building all over the state. I'd be gone a couple of days at a time on a fairly regular basis. Whenever I was with Dr. Smith, he never acted as though he didn't like me. And he certainly didn't act as though he thought his daughter's life was in danger."

"What was his attitude toward her?"

"When I was in parochial school, the nuns got mad at us for talking in church and told us we should have reverence for a holy place. Well, that's the way Smith treated her. With reverence."

An odd word to use about a father's attitude toward his daughter, Kerry thought.

"He was also protective of her," Reardon added. "One night the three of us were driving somewhere for dinner and he noticed Suzanne hadn't put on her seat belt. So he launched into a lecture about taking care of herself. He actually got angry about it."

The same way he lectured Robin and me, Kerry thought.

"How did she act toward him?"

"Respectful, mostly. Although toward the end—before she was killed—she seemed to be kind of irritated at him."

Kerry then ventured into other aspects of the case, asking Skip about his testimony that just prior to the murder he had noticed Suzanne wearing expensive jewelry he had not given her.

"Ms. McGrath, I wish you'd talk to my mother. She could tell

39

you. She has a picture of Suzanne from one of the papers, taken at a charity affair. It shows her with an old-fashioned diamond pin on the lapel of her suit. The picture was taken only a couple of weeks before she was murdered. I swear to you that that pin and a couple of other pieces of jewelry, none of which I gave her, were in her jewelry box that morning. I remember because it was one of the things we argued about. Those pieces weren't there the next day."

"You mean someone took them?"

"I don't know if someone took them or if she gave them back to someone, but I tell you there was jewelry missing the next morning. I told this to the cops, but it was obvious from the beginning that they didn't believe me. They thought that I was trying to make it look like she had been robbed and killed by an intruder.

"Something else," Reardon continued. "My dad was in World War Two and was in Germany for two years after the war. He brought back a miniature picture frame that he gave to my mother when they became engaged. My mother gave that frame to Suzanne and me when we were married. Suzanne put my favorite picture of her in it and kept it on the night table in our room. When my mother and I sorted Suzanne's things before I was arrested, Mom noticed it was missing. I know it was there that last morning."

"Are you saying that the night Suzanne died, someone came in and stole some jewelry and a picture frame?" Kerry asked.

"I'm telling you what I know was missing."

Kerry looked up from her notes and peered into the eyes of the man facing her. "Skip, what was your relationship with your wife?"

Reardon sighed. "When I met her, I fell like a ton of bricks. She was gorgeous, the kind of woman who makes a guy feel ten feet tall. After we were married . . ." He paused. "It was all heat and no warmth. I was raised to think you're supposed to make a go of marriage, that divorce was a last resort. And of course, there were some good times. But was I happy? No. But I was so busy building up my company that I was able to avoid dealing with it.

"As for Suzanne, she seemed to have everything she wanted. The money was rolling in. She was at the club every day playing golf. I built her her dream house, and she spent two years furnishing it.

There's a guy who lives in Alpine—Jason Arnott—who really knows antiques. He took Suzanne to auctions and told her what to buy. She was like a kid who wanted every day to be Christmas. She loved to be at affairs that got press coverage so her picture would be in the paper. I thought she was happy, but as I look back, I'm sure she stayed with me because she hadn't found any better setup."

"Until . . ." Geoff prompted.

"Until someone she met became important," Reardon continued. "That was when I noticed jewelry I hadn't seen before. Some pieces were antiques, others very modern. She claimed her father gave them to her, but I could tell she was lying. Her father has all her jewelry now, including everything I gave her."

When the guard indicated time was up, Reardon stood and looked squarely at Kerry. "Ms. McGrath, I shouldn't be here. Somewhere out there the guy who killed Suzanne is walking around. And somewhere, there has to be something that will prove it."

Geoff and Kerry walked to the parking lot together. "Why don't we grab something fast for lunch?" he said.

"I've got to get back. Geoff, I have to tell you that from what I heard today, I can't see a single reason for Dr. Smith to lie about Skip Reardon. Reardon says that they had a reasonably cordial relationship. You heard him say that he didn't believe Suzanne when she told him that her father had given her some pieces of jewelry. If he started getting jealous about those pieces, well . . ." She did not finish the sentence.

8

Sunday
October 29th

O N SUNDAY morning Robin served at the ten-o'clock Mass. As Kerry watched the processional move down the aisle, she was reminded of how, as a child, she had wanted to be a server and was told that only boys were allowed. Things change, she mused. I never thought I'd see my daughter on the altar; I never thought I'd be divorced; I never thought that someday I'd be a judge. *Might* be

41

a judge, she corrected herself. She knew Jonathan was right. Embarrassing Frank Green could be a fatal blow to her appointment. Yesterday's visit to Skip Reardon might have been a serious mistake. Why mess up her life again? She had done it once.

She knew she had worked her way through the emotional gamut with Bob Kinellen—first loving him, then being heartbroken when he left her, then angry at him and contemptuous of herself that she had not seen him for the opportunist that he was. If only Bob had been the person I believed he was, she thought. If only he were the person *he* thinks he *is.* By now they would have been married eleven years. By now surely she would have had other children. She'd always wanted three.

As she watched Robin carry the ewer of water and the lavabo bowl to the altar in preparation for the consecration, her daughter looked up and met Kerry's gaze. Her brief smile caught at Kerry's heart. What am I complaining about? she asked herself. I have her. As unions go, Bob's and mine may have been far from perfect, but at least something good came of it. No one else except us could have had exactly this wonderful child, she reasoned.

As she watched, her mind jumped to another parent and child, to Dr. Smith and Suzanne. She had been the unique result of his and his former wife's genes. In his testimony Dr. Smith had stated that after their divorce his wife moved to California and remarried, and he had permitted Suzanne to be adopted by the second husband, thinking that was in her best interests. "But after her mother died, she came to me," he had said. "She needed me."

Skip Reardon had said that Dr. Smith's attitude toward his daughter bordered on reverence. When Kerry heard that, a question that took her breath away had raced through her mind. Dr. Smith had transformed other women to look like his daughter. But no one had ever asked whether he had operated on Suzanne.

Kerry and Robin had just finished lunch when Bob called, suggesting he take Robin out to dinner that night. He explained that Alice had taken the children to Florida for a week and he was driving to the Catskills to look at a ski lodge they might buy. Would Robin want to accompany him? he asked.

Robin's enthusiastic response resulted in Bob's picking her up an hour later. The unexpected free afternoon gave Kerry a chance to spend more time going over the Reardon trial transcript.

GEOFF Dorso loved football and was an ardent Giants fan. Nevertheless, on Sunday afternoon, sitting in Giants Stadium, his mind was less on the close game with the Dallas Cowboys than on Kerry McGrath's reaction to Skip Reardon and the trial transcript. Had she read it yet? he wondered. He had hoped she would bring it up while they were waiting to see Skip, but she hadn't. He tried to tell himself that it was her training to be skeptical, that her seemingly negative attitude after the visit to Skip didn't have to mean that she was washing her hands of the case.

When the Giants squeaked through with a last-second field goal as the game ended, Geoff shared in the cheering but declined to join his friends for a couple of beers. Instead he went home and called Kerry.

He was elated when she admitted she had read the transcript and had a number of questions. "I'd like to get together again," he said. Then a thought struck him. She can only say no, he reasoned as he asked, "By any chance, would you be free for dinner tonight?"

DOLLY Bowles had been sixty when she moved in with her daughter in Alpine. That had been twelve years ago, when she was first widowed. She had not wanted to impose, but the truth was, she was nervous about being alone. And, in fact, there was a basis for her nervousness. When she was a child, she had opened the door for a deliveryman who turned out to be a burglar. She still had nightmares about the way he had tied up both her and her mother and ransacked the house. As a result, she tended to be suspicious of all strangers, and several times had irritated her son-in-law by pushing the panic button on the alarm system when she had been alone in the house and had heard strange noises.

Her daughter, Dorothy, and her son-in-law, Lou, traveled frequently. Their children had still been at home when Dolly moved in with them, and she had been a help in taking care of them.

43

Once the children had gone off on their own, Dolly had become the neighborhood baby-sitter, which worked out wonderfully. She genuinely enjoyed children. The only time people got annoyed was when she made one of her calls to report suspicious-looking persons to the police. But she hadn't done that in ten years, not since she was a witness at the Reardon murder trial. She shuddered every time she thought of that. The prosecutor had made such a fool of her. Dorothy and Lou had been mortified. "Mother, I begged you not to talk to the police," Dorothy had snapped at the time.

But Dolly had known Skip Reardon and liked him and felt she had to try to help him. Besides, she really had seen that car, as had Michael, the five-year-old boy with all the learning problems she had been minding that night. She was sure she had made out a 3 and an L on the license plate. But the prosecutor had held up a license plate at the back of the courtroom, and she hadn't been able to read it. And he had gotten her to admit that she was very fond of Skip because he had dug her car out of a snowdrift one night.

Dolly knew that just because Skip had been nice to her didn't mean that he couldn't be a murderer, but in her heart she felt he was innocent. Sometimes even now, when she was baby-sitting across the street from the Reardon house, she would think about the night Suzanne was murdered. And she would think about little Michael—his family had moved away several years ago—and how he had pointed to the strange black car and said, "Poppa's car."

Dolly could not know that on this Sunday evening as she sat looking out the window at what used to be the Reardon house, some ten miles away, at Villa Cesare in Hillsdale, Geoff Dorso and Kerry McGrath were talking about her.

By TACIT agreement Kerry and Geoff refrained from any discussion of the Reardon case until coffee was served. During the meal Geoff talked about growing up in Manhattan with four sisters.

"I envy you," Kerry said. "I'm an only child, and I used to love to visit friends' houses where there was a big family. My father died when I was nineteen, and my mother remarried when I was twenty-one and moved to Colorado. I see her twice a year."

Geoff's eyes softened. "That doesn't give you much family support," he said.

"No, I guess not, but Jonathan and Grace Hoover have helped to fill the gap. They've been wonderful to me, almost like parents."

Over coffee they finally discussed the Reardon case. Kerry began by saying frankly, "I sat in on the sentencing ten years ago, and the look on Skip's face and what he said were imprinted in my memory. I've heard a lot of guilty people swear they were innocent, but there was something about his statement that got to me."

"Because he was telling the truth."

Kerry looked directly at him. "I warn you, Geoff, I intend to play devil's advocate, and while reading that transcript raises a lot of questions for me, it doesn't convince me Reardon is innocent. Neither did yesterday's visit. I still think it's damaging that the very day Suzanne died, Reardon discussed divorce and apparently flipped when he learned what it might cost him."

"Kerry, Suzanne had already cost Skip a fortune. She was a big-time shopaholic, buying whatever struck her fancy." He paused. "No. Being angry and being vocal about it is one thing. But there's a difference between blowing off steam and murder. If anything, even though a divorce was going to be expensive, he was relieved that his sham marriage was going to be over, so he could get on with his life."

They talked about the sweetheart roses. "I absolutely believe Skip neither brought nor sent them," Geoff said. "So if we accept that, we then have the factor of another person."

As Geoff was paying the bill, they both agreed that Dr. Smith's testimony was the linchpin that had convicted Skip Reardon. "Ask yourself this," Geoff urged. "Dr. Smith claimed that Suzanne was afraid of Skip's jealous rages. But if she were so afraid of him, how could she stand there and flaunt flowers another man had sent her? Besides, no one testified in corroboration of Smith's testimony. The Reardons were a popular couple. Surely if Skip were abusive to Suzanne, someone would have come forward to say so."

"Perhaps," Kerry conceded. "But based on the information the jury was given, they had no reason not to believe Dr. Smith."

They were quiet on the drive home. As Geoff walked Kerry to her door, he reached for her key. "My mother said you should always open the door for the lady. I hope that's not too sexist."

"No. Not for me at least. But maybe I'm just old-fashioned." The sky was blue-black and brilliant with stars. A sharp wind was blowing, and Kerry shivered from the chill.

Geoff noticed, and quickly turned the key, then pushed open the door, making no move to indicate that he expected her to invite him in. Instead he said, "Where do we go from here?"

"I'm going to see Dr. Smith as soon as possible."

"Then we'll talk in the next few days." Geoff smiled briefly and started down the porch steps. Kerry closed the door and walked into the living room, but did not immediately turn on the light. She realized she was still savoring the moment when Geoff had taken the key from her hand and opened the door for her. Then she went to the window and watched as his car disappeared down the street.

DADDY is such fun, Robin thought. She didn't get to see him much, but when they were together, he was great.

They had inspected the ski lodge Bob Kinellen was thinking about buying. She thought it was cool, but he said it was a disappointment. "I want one where we can ski to the door," he had said, and then he'd laughed. "We'll just keep looking."

Now they were talking over shrimp and scallops. He had just promised to take her skiing, just the two of them. "Sometime when Mom's on a date." He winked.

"Oh, Mom doesn't date much," Robin told him. "A lawyer came to the house the other night. He was nice. But I think it was just business."

Bob Kinellen had been only partially involved in the conversation. Now he became attentive. "What was his name?"

"Geoff Dorso. He brought over a big file for Mommy to read."

When her father suddenly became quiet, Robin had the guilty feeling that maybe she had said too much, that maybe he was mad at her. When he dropped her off, she was glad to be home.

IRST thing Monday morning Kerry called Dr. Smith's office. Mrs. Carpenter answered. "I'd like an appointment to speak with the doctor as soon as possible," Kerry said. "It's important."

"What is this in reference to, Ms. McGrath?"

Kerry decided to gamble. "Tell the doctor it's about Suzanne."

She waited nearly five minutes, then heard Dr. Smith's cold, precise voice. "What do you want, Ms. McGrath?" he asked.

"I want to talk to you about Skip Reardon, Doctor, and I'd appreciate doing it as soon as possible."

By the time she hung up, he had agreed to meet her in his office at seven thirty the next morning. It meant she would have to leave home by six thirty, so she would have to arrange for a neighbor to phone Robin to make sure she didn't fall back asleep. Otherwise Robin would be fine. She always walked to school with two girl-friends, and she was old enough to get herself a bowl of cereal.

Just before lunch Kerry asked Joe Palumbo to stop by her office. "I have a little extracurricular situation I need your help with," she told him when the investigator slumped in a chair in front of her desk. "The Reardon case." She told him about the Suzanne look-alikes and Dr. Charles Smith. Hesitantly she admitted that she had also visited Reardon in prison and that she was beginning to have her doubts about the way the case had been handled.

Palumbo whistled.

"Keep this just between us, Joe. Frank Green is not happy about my interest in the case."

"I wonder why," Palumbo murmured.

"The point is that Green himself told me that Dr. Smith was an unemotional witness. Strange for a father of a murder victim, wouldn't you say? On the stand Dr. Smith testified that he and his wife had separated when Suzanne was a baby and that a few years later he allowed her to be adopted by her stepfather, a man named Wayne Stevens, and that she grew up in Oakland, California. I'd be interested in learning what kind of girl Suzanne was, growing up, and I want to see a picture of her when she was a teenager."

She had pulled out several pages of the Reardon trial transcript. Now she shoved them across the desk to Palumbo. "Here's the testimony of a baby-sitter who claims she saw a strange car in front of the Reardon house the night of the murder. She lives—or lived—with her daughter in Alpine. Check her out for me, okay?"

Palumbo's eyes reflected keen interest. "It will be a pleasure, Kerry. I'd love to see Our Leader on the hot seat for a change."

"Look, Joe, Frank Green's a good guy," Kerry protested. "I'm not interested in upsetting things for him. But if there's a chance the wrong man is in jail, I feel it's my duty to explore it."

"Don't get me wrong," Palumbo said. "Green's an okay guy. It's just that I would prefer someone who doesn't run for cover every time someone in this office is taking heat."

LATE that afternoon Geoff Dorso's secretary buzzed him on the intercom. "Miss Taylor is here. She says it's important."

For Beth Taylor to show up without calling first, it had to be important. "Send her in," Geoff said.

When his secretary escorted Beth into his office, Geoff came around his desk and kissed her affectionately. Whenever he saw her, the same thought always flashed into his mind: What a different life Skip would have had if he had married Beth Taylor.

Beth was Skip's age, almost forty now, about five feet six, a comfortable size 12, with brown hair, lively brown eyes and a face that radiated intelligence and warmth. She had been a teacher when she and Skip were dating fifteen years ago. Since then she had earned her master's degree and now worked as a guidance counselor in a nearby school.

By her expression today it was obvious she was deeply troubled. She came directly to the point. "Geoff, I talked to Skip on the phone last night. He sounds terribly depressed. I'm worried. There's so much talk about cutting off repeated appeals from convicted murderers. Skip has practically been kept alive on the hope that someday one of the appeals will be upheld. If he gives up that hope, he'll want to die. He told me about that assistant prosecutor visiting him. He's sure she doesn't believe him."

"Do you think he's becoming suicidal?" Geoff asked quickly. "If so, I should warn the warden."

"No, no! Don't even think about reporting that! I don't mean he'd do anything to himself now. He knows he'd be killing his mother too." Mrs. Reardon had had a heart attack shortly after Skip's conviction and another one five years ago. Beth threw out her hands in a helpless gesture. "Geoff," she burst out, "is there any hope I can give him?"

If this were a week ago, Geoff thought, I'd have had to tell her no. Kerry McGrath's call, however, had made a difference. Careful not to sound overly encouraging, he told Beth about the two women Kerry had seen in Dr. Smith's office and of Kerry's growing interest in the case.

Beth's eyes were filling with tears. "Then Kerry McGrath still is looking into the case?"

"Very definitely. She's quite something, Beth." As Geoff heard himself saying those words, he was visualizing Kerry—the way she tucked a lock of blond hair behind her ear as she was concentrating, the joyful pride that emanated from her when she talked about her daughter. He was hearing her slightly husky voice and seeing the almost shy smile she gave him when he had taken the key and opened the door for her.

"Geoff, if there are grounds for another appeal, do you think we made a mistake by not telling about me?"

Beth's question yanked him back to the present. She was referring to an aspect of the case that had never come out. Just prior to Suzanne's death, Skip and Beth had bumped into each other, and Skip had insisted on taking her to lunch. He had confessed to her how unhappy he was and how much he regretted their breakup.

Skip and Beth started to see each other again. On the night Suzanne died, they were scheduled to have dinner together. She had had to cancel at the last minute, however, and it was then that Skip had gone home to find Suzanne arranging the roses.

At the time of the trial Geoff had agreed with Skip's chief counsel, Tim Farrell, that to put Beth on the stand was a double-edged sword. The prosecution no doubt would try to make it seem that in addition to avoiding the expense of a divorce, Skip Reardon had another compelling reason for killing his wife. On the other hand, Beth's testimony might have been effective in dispelling Dr. Smith's contention that Skip was insanely jealous of Suzanne.

Until Kerry had told him about Dr. Smith and the look-alikes, Geoff had been sure they had made the right decision. Now he was less sure. He looked squarely at Beth. "I want Kerry to meet you and to hear your story. If we have any chance at all for a new and successful appeal, all the cards have to be on the table."

10

Tuesday
October 31st

*W*HEN she was ready to leave the house for her early morning appointment with Dr. Smith, Kerry shook awake a protesting Robin. "Come on, Rob," she urged. "You're always telling me I treat you like a baby."

"You do," Robin mumbled.

"All right. I'm giving you a chance to prove your independence. Get up now. Mrs. Weiser will phone at seven to be sure you didn't fall back asleep. I left cereal and juice out."

Robin yawned and closed her eyes.

"Rob, please."

"Okay." With a sigh Robin swung her legs over the side of the bed. Her hair fell forward over her face as she rubbed her eyes.

Kerry smoothed it back and kissed the top of her head. "Now remember, don't open the door for anyone. I'll set the alarm. You deactivate it when you're ready to leave, then reset it."

"I know. I know." Robin sighed dramatically.

Kerry grinned. "I know I've given you the same spiel a thousand times. See you tonight. Alison will be here at three."

Alison was the high school student who stayed with Robin after school until Kerry came home.

"See you, Mom."

Robin listened to Kerry's steps going down the stairs. Just for a minute, Robin thought as she slipped back into bed. I'll just lie here for a minute more.

At seven o'clock, after the phone had rung six times, she sat up and answered it. "Oh, thanks, Mrs. Weiser. Yes, I'm sure I'm up."

I am now, she thought as she hurried out of bed.

DR. SMITH let Kerry in himself. Even the minimal courtesy he had shown on Robin's visits was lacking this morning. He did not greet her except to say, "I can give you twenty minutes, Ms. McGrath, and not a second more." He led her to his private office.

If that's the way we're going to play it, Kerry thought, fine. When she was seated across his desk from him, she said, "Dr. Smith, after seeing two women emerge from this office who startlingly resemble your murdered daughter, Suzanne, I became curious enough about the circumstances of her death to take time this last week to read the transcript of Skip Reardon's trial."

She did not miss the look of hatred that came over Dr. Smith's face at the mention of Reardon's name. She leaned forward. "Dr. Smith, your testimony is the reason Skip Reardon is in prison. You said he was insanely jealous, that your daughter was afraid of him. He swears that he never threatened her."

"He's lying." The voice was flat, unemotional.

"But if Suzanne was in fear for her life, why did she stay with him?" she asked.

The morning sun flooded the room and shone on Smith's rimless glasses, so that Kerry could not see his eyes. Could they possibly be as flat as his voice? she wondered. "Because unlike her mother— my former wife—Suzanne had a commitment to her marriage," he responded after a pause. "The grave mistake of her life was to fall in love with Reardon. An even graver mistake was not to take his threats seriously."

Kerry realized she was getting nowhere. It was time to ask the question that had occurred to her earlier. "Dr. Smith, did you ever perform surgery on your daughter?"

51

It was immediately clear that her question outraged him. "Ms. McGrath, I belong to the school of physicians who would never, except in dire emergency, treat a family member. Beyond that, the question is insulting. Suzanne was a natural beauty."

"You've made at least two women resemble her. Why?"

Dr. Smith looked at his watch. "I'll answer this final question, and then you will have to excuse me." He took off his glasses and rubbed his forehead. "I operate on women who look in the mirror and see sagging skin or baggy eyes. I raise and clamp the forehead under the hairline. I tighten the skin and pull it up behind the ears. I take twenty years off their appearance, but more than that, I transform their self-deprecation into self-worth."

His voice rose. "I could show you before and after pictures of accident victims whom I have helped. You ask me why several of my patients resemble my daughter. I'll tell you why. Because in these ten years a few plain and unhappy young women came into this office and I was able to give them her kind of beauty." Dr. Smith stood up. "And now, this discussion is over."

There was nothing Kerry could do except follow him from the room. As she walked behind him, she noticed that he was holding his right hand rigidly against his side. Was that a tremor? Yes, it was.

At the door he said, "Ms. McGrath, you must understand that the sound of Skip Reardon's name sickens me. Please call Mrs. Carpenter and give her the name of another physician to whom she can forward Robin's file. I do not want to hear from you or see you or your daughter again."

He was so close to her that Kerry stepped back involuntarily. There was something genuinely frightening about the man. His eyes, filled with hatred, seemed to burn through her. If he had a gun in his hand right now, I swear he'd use it, she thought.

AFTER she locked the door and started down the steps, Robin noticed the small dark car parked across the street. Strange cars weren't common on this street, especially at this hour, but she didn't know why this one gave her an especially funny feeling. It was cold. She shifted her books to her left arm and zipped her

jacket the rest of the way to her neck, then quickened her steps. She was meeting Cassie and her other friend at the corner a block away, and she was a couple of minutes late.

The street was quiet. Now that the leaves were almost gone, the trees had a bare, unfriendly look. Robin wished she had remembered to wear gloves.

When she reached the sidewalk, she glanced across the street. The driver's window in the strange car was opening slowly. She stared at it, hoping to see a familiar face inside. Then she saw a hand reach out, pointing something at her. Suddenly panicked, Robin began to run. With a roar the car came rushing across the road toward her. Just as she thought it was going to come up the curb and hit her, it swerved into a U-turn and raced down the block. Sobbing, Robin ran across the lawn of their neighbor's house and frantically rang the doorbell.

WHEN Joe Palumbo called Dolly Bowles and explained that he was an investigator with the Bergen County prosecutor's office, she sounded a little guarded. But after he told her that one of the assistant prosecutors, Kerry McGrath, wanted to hear about the car Dolly had seen in front of the Reardon house the night of the murder, she announced that she had followed the trial Kerry McGrath recently had prosecuted and was so glad that the man who shot his supervisor had been convicted. She told Palumbo that if Kerry McGrath wanted to talk to her, it would be fine.

"Well, actually," Joe told her somewhat lamely, "I'd like to come over and talk to you right now. Maybe Kerry will come later."

There was a pause. Palumbo could not know that Dolly was remembering the derisive expression on the face of Prosecutor Green when he cross-examined her at the trial.

Finally she spoke. "I think," she said with dignity, "that I would be more comfortable discussing that night with Kerry McGrath."

IT WAS nine forty-five before Kerry got to the courthouse, much later than she normally arrived. Anticipating the possibility of receiving a bit of flak about it, she had phoned to say she had an

54

errand and was going to be late. She knew Frank Green would have a fit if he learned that her errand was to see Dr. Smith.

When she punched in the code that admitted her to the prosecutor's office, the switchboard operator looked up and said, "Kerry, go right into Mr. Green's office. He's expecting you."

Oh, boy, Kerry thought. But as soon as she walked into Green's office, she could see he was not angry. As usual, he came directly to the point. "Kerry, Robin is with your neighbor Mrs. Weiser. She is all right."

Kerry felt her throat tighten. "Then what's wrong?"

"We're not sure. According to Robin, you left the house at six thirty." There was a glint of curiosity in Green's eyes.

"Yes, I did."

"When Robin left later, she said she noticed a strange car across the street. When she reached the sidewalk, the window on the driver's door opened, and she saw a hand holding some kind of object. She couldn't tell what it was, and she wasn't able to see the driver's face. Then the car veered across the street so suddenly she thought it would come up on the sidewalk and hit her, but it went into a U-turn and took off. Robin ran to your neighbor's."

Kerry sank into a chair. "She's there now?"

"Yes. You can call her, or go home if that would reassure you. Does Robin have an overactive imagination, Kerry, or is it possible someone was trying to frighten her and, ultimately, you?"

"Why would anyone want to frighten Robin or me?"

"It's happened before in this office. You've just completed a case that got a lot of media attention. The guy you got convicted of murder was an out-and-out sleaze and still has friends."

"Yes, but those I met seemed to be pretty decent people," Kerry said. "And to answer your first question, Robin is a levelheaded kid. She wouldn't imagine something like this."

"Call her," Green directed.

Robin answered Mrs. Weiser's telephone on the first ring. "I knew you'd call, Mom. I'm okay now. I want to go to school. Mrs. Weiser said she'd drive me. And Mom, I've still got to go out this afternoon. It's Halloween."

Kerry thought quickly. Robin was better off in school than sitting at home thinking about the incident. "All right, but I'll pick you up at school at quarter of three. I don't want you walking home." And I'll be right with you when you trick-or-treat, she thought. When she hung up, she said, "Frank, is it all right if I leave early today?"

His smile was genuine. "Of course it is. Kerry, I don't have to tell you to question Robin carefully. We have to know if there's any chance someone really was watching for her."

Later Joe Palumbo stopped by Kerry's office and told her about his call to Dolly Bowles. "She'll only talk to you, Kerry."

"Let me phone her now."

Her six-word greeting, "Hello, Mrs. Bowles, I'm Kerry McGrath," led to being on the receiving end of a ten-minute monologue. Palumbo leaned back in the chair as with some amusement he watched Kerry try to interject a word. Finally she hung up. "Dolly Bowles is not a happy camper about the way she was treated by this office ten years ago," Kerry said. "That was the gist of the conversation. The rest is that her daughter and son-in-law don't want her talking about the murder or what she saw anymore, and they're coming back from a trip tomorrow. If I want to see her, it's got to be about five o'clock today. That's going to take some juggling." She told Palumbo about Robin and the incident that morning.

The investigator rose to his feet. "I'll meet you at your place at five," he suggested. "While you're with Mrs. Bowles, let me take Robin for a hamburger. I'd like to talk to her about this morning." When he saw the look of disapproval on Kerry's face, he added, "Kerry, you're smart, but you're not going to be objective about this. Don't do my job for me."

Kerry studied Joe thoughtfully. He was always a little disheveled, but he was just about the best there was at his job. It would be very helpful to have his spin on this. "Okay," she agreed.

On Tuesday afternoon, Halloween, Jason Arnott drove from Alpine to the remote area in the Catskills where his sprawling country home, hidden by the surrounding mountain range, concealed his priceless stolen treasures. He was glad to get away. He was tired.

Over the weekend he had gone to Maryland and burglarized a Chevy Chase home at which he had attended a party a few months earlier. At that gathering the hostess, Myra Hamilton, had rattled on about her son's wedding on October 28 in Chicago, effectively announcing that the house would be empty on that date.

The house was not large, but it was exquisite, filled with precious items. Jason had salivated over a sapphire-blue Fabergé desk seal with a gold egg-shaped handle. That and a delicate three- by five-foot Aubusson with a central rosace that they used as a wall hanging were now in the trunk of his car on their way to his retreat. Unconsciously, Jason frowned. He was not experiencing his usual sensation of triumph at having achieved his goal. A vague worry was nagging at him. Mentally he reviewed the Hamilton operation.

After leaving the Hamilton home, as he had inched his way into traffic on Route 240, two police cars, sirens screaming and lights flashing, had raced past him and turned left onto the street he had just exited. It was obvious that they were on their way to the Hamilton house. It meant that he had somehow triggered a silent alarm that operated independently of the master system, which he had disengaged upon entering.

What other kind of security did the Hamiltons have? he wondered. It was so easy to conceal cameras now. He had been wearing the stocking mask he always put on during a burglary, but at one point he had pulled it up to examine a bronze figurine, a foolish thing to do—it had proved to be of no real value.

One chance in a million that a camera caught my face, Jason reassured himself now as he pulled into his driveway. Maddie, the cleaning woman—stolid and unquestioning woman that she was— would have left everything shining. He knew she didn't recognize the difference between an Aubusson and a ten-dollar-a-yard carpet remnant, but she took pride in her work. In ten years she had never so much as chipped a cup.

He parked the car at the side door, and with the rush of anticipation that always surged over him when he came here, he entered the house and reached for the light switch. Once again, the sight of so many beautiful things made his lips and hands moist with pleasure. A few minutes later, after his new treasures were safely inside, he locked the door and drew the bolt. His evening had begun.

His first task was to carry the Fabergé seal upstairs and place it on the antique dressing table in the master bedroom. Once it was in place, he leaned over to compare it with the miniature frame that had been on his night table for the past eleven years.

The frame represented one of the few times he had been fooled. It was a decent Fabergé copy, but certainly not the real thing. That seemed so obvious now. The blue enamel looked muddy when compared to the deep color of the desk seal. The gold border encrusted with pearls was nothing like authentic Fabergé workmanship. But from inside that frame Suzanne's face gazed back at him.

He didn't like to think about that night, almost eleven years ago. He had gone in through the open window of the sitting room of the master-bedroom suite. He knew the house was supposed to be empty. That very day, Suzanne had told him about her dinner engagement for the evening and the fact that Skip would not be home. He had the security code, but when he got there, he saw that the window was wide open. When he entered the bedroom, he spotted the miniature frame on top of the night table. From across the room it looked authentic. He was examining it closely when he heard a raised voice. Suzanne! Panicking, he had dropped the frame in his pocket and hidden in a closet.

Looking down at the frame now, Jason wondered what perverse reason had kept him from removing Suzanne's picture from it. But as he stared at it, he understood that the picture made it easier for him to blot out the memory of how gruesome and distorted Suzanne's features had been when he made his escape.

GEOFF Dorso phoned Kerry just as she was about to leave the office. "I saw Dr. Smith this morning," she told him hurriedly, "and I'm seeing Dolly Bowles around five. I can't talk now. I've got to meet Robin at school."

"Kerry, I'm anxious to know what happened with Dr. Smith and what you learn from Dolly Bowles. Can we have dinner?"

"I don't want to go out tonight, but if you don't mind pasta . . ."

"I'm Italian, remember?"

"About seven thirty?"

"I'll be there."

WHEN she picked up Robin at school, it was clear to Kerry that her daughter's mind was much more on Halloween than on the early morning incident. Taking her cue from Robin, Kerry dropped the subject, for now at least. When they reached home, she gave Robin's sitter the afternoon off. This is the way other mothers live, she thought as, with several of them, she trailed a cluster of trick-or-treating children. She and Robin arrived home just in time to let Joe Palumbo in.

He was carrying a bulging briefcase, which he tapped with a satisfied smile. "The office investigation of the Reardon case," he said. "It'll have Dolly Bowles's original statement. Let's see how it compares with what she has to say now." He looked at Robin, who was wearing a witch's costume. "That's some outfit, Rob."

"It was between this and being a corpse," Robin told him.

Kerry did not realize she had winced until she caught the look of understanding in Palumbo's eyes. "I'd better be on my way," she said hurriedly.

During the twenty-minute drive to Alpine, Kerry realized her nerves were on edge. She had finally gotten Robin to talk briefly about the incident that morning. By then Robin was trying to play the whole thing down. Kerry wanted to believe that someone had simply stopped to check an address and then realized he was on the wrong block. But Kerry knew her daughter would not have exaggerated the incident.

As SOON as Kerry parked in the driveway of the massive Tudor house, the door was yanked open. Dolly Bowles was a small woman with gray hair and a narrow, inquisitive face. She was already talking when Kerry reached her: ". . . just like your picture in the *Record*. I was so sorry I couldn't make it to the trial of that awful man who killed his supervisor."

59

Still talking, she led Kerry into a cavernous foyer and indicated a small sitting room to the left. "Let's go in here. That living room is too big for my taste."

She's a sweet woman, Kerry thought, but I'm just not in the mood for this. "Mrs. Bowles, let's talk about the night Suzanne Reardon died."

Fifteen minutes later, after hearing all about how Michael, the little boy Dolly was minding that night, had serious developmental problems, Kerry had isolated one nugget of information.

"You say the car you saw parked in front of the Reardons' did not belong to one of the neighbors' guests. Why are you so sure?"

"Because I talked to those people myself. They were entertaining three other couples, all from Alpine, and after Mr. Green made me feel like such a fool on the stand, I called each of them. And you know what? None of those guests was driving Poppa's car."

"Poppa's car!" Kerry exclaimed incredulously.

"That's what Michael called it. You see, he had a real problem with colors. You'd point to a car and ask him what color it was, and he wouldn't know. But he could pick out one that was familiar or one that looked just like a familiar car. When he said 'Poppa's car' that night, he had to have been pointing at the black Mercedes four-door sedan. You see, he called his grandfather Poppa and loved to ride with him in his car—his black Mercedes four-door sedan. It was dark, but the torchlight at the end of the Reardons' driveway was on, so he could see it clearly."

"Mrs. Bowles, you testified that *you* had seen the car."

"Yes, although it wasn't there at seven thirty, when I got to Michael's house, and when he pointed it out, it was pulling away, so I didn't get a good look at it. Still, I had an impression of a 3 and an L on the license plate. I tried to tell Skip Reardon's attorney about this. His name was Farrer—no, Farrell. He told me that hearsay evidence from a developmentally disabled child would only dilute my testimony that I'd seen the car. But I don't see why I couldn't have told the jury that Michael became all excited when he thought he had seen his grandfather's car. I think that would have helped."

JONATHAN HOOVER WAS NOT enjoying his predinner martini this evening. Usually he savored this time of day, sipping his drink and sitting in his wing chair by the fire, conversing with Grace.

He looked at his wife. Nowadays she always wore long flowing hostess gowns that concealed the steadily progressing deformity of her legs and feet. Propped up as she was, in a half-lying position on the couch, the curvature in her spine was not apparent, and her luminous gray eyes were beautiful against the alabaster white of her complexion. Only her hands, the fingers gnarled and twisted, were visible indicators of her devastating illness. She gave him a wry smile. "You're upset about something, Jon."

Jonathan raised his eyebrows. "It's Kerry, Grace. I'm afraid she has no intention of letting go of the Reardon case. Last night I persuaded the governor to delay submitting to the senate the names of candidates for appointment to the bench."

"Jonathan!"

"It was the only thing I could do short of asking him to withhold Kerry's appointment for the present. I had no choice. Grace, Prescott Marshall has been an outstanding governor. Working with him, I've been able to lead the senate in getting necessary reforms into law. I want Marshall back in four years. I'm no great fan of Frank Green, but as governor, he'll be a good benchwarmer and won't undo what Marshall and I have accomplished. On the other hand, if Green fails and the other party gets in, everything we've accomplished will be taken apart."

Suddenly he looked very tired to Grace, and every minute of his sixty-two years.

"Let's invite Kerry and Robin to dinner Sunday," Grace said. "That will give you a chance to talk sense to her. I don't think anyone's future should be sacrificed for that Reardon man."

"Yes. I'll call her tonight," Jonathan said.

GEOFF Dorso rang the doorbell at exactly seven thirty and once again was greeted by Robin. She was still wearing her witch's costume and makeup. Her eyebrows were thick with charcoal. Pasty white powder covered her skin except where the lacerations streaked her chin and cheek. A wig of tangled black hair flapped around her shoulders.

Geoff jumped back. "You scared me."

"Great," Robin said enthusiastically. "I'm due at a party, and there's a prize for the scariest costume."

"You'll win in a landslide," Geoff told her as he stepped into the foyer. Then he sniffed. "Something smells good."

"Mom's making garlic bread," Robin explained, then called, "Mom, Mr. Dorso's here."

The kitchen was at the back of the house. Geoff smiled as the door swung open and Kerry emerged, drying her hands on a towel. She was dressed in green slacks and a green cowlneck sweater. Geoff could not help but notice how the overhead light accentuated the gold streaks in her hair and the spray of freckles across her nose. She looks about twenty-three, Geoff thought, then realized that her warm smile did not disguise the concern in her eyes.

"Geoff, good to see you. Go inside and be comfortable. I have to walk Robin down the block to a party."

"Why not let me do that?" Geoff suggested. "I've still got my coat on."

"I guess that would be okay," Kerry said slowly, "but be sure to see her inside the door. Don't just leave her at the driveway."

"Mom," Robin protested, "I'm not scared anymore. Honest."

"Well, I am."

What's that about? Geoff wondered. He said, "Kerry, I was forever dropping my sisters off and picking them up, and heaven help me if I didn't see them safely inside. Get your broom, Robin."

As they walked along the quiet street, Robin told him about the car that had frightened her. "Mom acts cool about everything, but I can tell she's freaking out," she confided. "She worries about me too much. I'm sort of sorry I told her about it."

Geoff stopped short and looked down at her. "Robin, listen to me. It's a lot worse *not* to tell your mother when something like that happens. Promise me you won't make that mistake."

"I won't, Mr. Dorso. I already promised Mom." The painted witch's lips separated in a mischievous smile. "I'm real good at keeping promises, except when it comes to getting up on time. I hate getting up."

"So do I," Geoff agreed fervently. "And call me Geoff."

FIVE minutes later, when he was sitting on a counter stool in the kitchen watching Kerry make a salad, Geoff decided to try a direct approach. "Robin told me about this morning," he said. "Is there a reason to worry?"

Kerry was tearing freshly washed lettuce into the salad bowl. "One of our investigators, Joe Palumbo, talked to Robin this afternoon. He's concerned. Robin was so specific about the window opening and a hand appearing with something pointing at her. Joe suggested that somebody might have taken her picture."

Geoff heard the tremor in Kerry's voice. "But why?"

"I don't know. Frank Green thinks it might be connected to that case I just prosecuted. I don't agree. Maybe some nut saw Robin and developed a fixation." She began to tear the lettuce with savage force. "The point is, how do I protect her?"

"It's pretty tough to carry that worry alone," Geoff said quietly.

"You mean because I'm divorced? Because there is no man here to take care of her? You've seen her face. That happened when she was with her father. Robin and I are better off alone." She ripped at a piece of lettuce, then said apologetically, "I'm sorry, Geoff. I'm not much company right now. But then, that doesn't matter. What is important are my meetings with Dr. Smith and Dolly Bowles."

Over salad and garlic bread Kerry told him about her encounter with Dr. Smith. "He hates Skip Reardon," she said. "It's a different kind of hatred. What I mean is that typically, relatives of victims despise the murderer and want him to be punished, but their anger is so entwined with grief that both emotions are flying out of them. Parents will show you baby pictures of the murdered daughter, tell you she won a spelling bee in the eighth grade. Then they break down and cry. And one of them, usually the father, will tell you he'd like to pull the switch on the killer himself. But I didn't get any of that from Smith. From him I got only hatred."

"What does that say to you?" Geoff asked.

"It says we need to know more about Smith's relationship with Suzanne. Don't forget, by his own testimony he hadn't laid eyes on her from the time she was an infant till she was nearly twenty. From her pictures you can see she was a remarkably attractive woman."

Kerry stood up. "Think about that while I put together the pasta. Then I want to tell you about Dolly Bowles and Poppa's car."

Geoff was almost unaware of how delicious the linguine with clam sauce tasted as he listened to Kerry's report of her visit to Dolly Bowles. "The thing is," she concluded, "from what Dolly tells me, little Michael might have been a very reliable witness."

"Tim Farrell interviewed Dolly Bowles himself," Geoff recalled. "I kind of remember a reference to a learning-disabled five-year-old seeing a car, but I passed over it."

"It's a long shot," Kerry said, "but Joe Palumbo, the investigator who spoke to Robin, brought the Reardon file with him this afternoon. I want to go through it to see what names might have come up—of men Suzanne was getting cozy with. It shouldn't be too hard to check with the motor vehicle division to see if any of them owned a black Mercedes sedan eleven years ago." She looked at the clock over the kitchen stove. "Plenty of time," she said.

Geoff knew she was talking about getting Robin. "What time is the party over?"

"Nine. How about some coffee?"

"Fine. And while we're having it, I'll give you the background of Skip Reardon's relationship with Beth Taylor."

When he finished telling her about Beth and Skip, Kerry said, "I can see why Farrell was afraid to use Beth as a witness. But if Skip was in love with her at the time of the murder, it takes some of the credibility away from Dr. Smith's testimony."

"Exactly. Skip's whole attitude about seeing Suzanne arranging flowers given to her by another man can be summed up in two words—good riddance."

The phone rang, and Geoff looked at his watch. "I'll get Robin while you're on the phone."

"Thanks." Kerry reached for the receiver. "Hello." She listened, then said warmly, "Oh, Jonathan, I was going to call you."

Geoff got up with a "see you" motion of his hand and went to get his coat.

As they walked back home, Robin said she'd had a good time at the party even though she hadn't won a prize for her costume.

"You win some, you lose some, Robin."

The moment Kerry opened the door for them, Geoff could see that something was terribly wrong. It was an obvious effort for Kerry to keep a smile on her face as she listened to Robin's enthusiastic description of the party. Finally Kerry said, "Okay, Robin. It's after nine, and you promised. . . ."

"I know. Off to bed." Robin kissed Kerry quickly. "Love you, Mom. Good night, Geoff." She bounced up the stairs.

Geoff watched as Kerry's mouth began to quiver. He took her arm and led her into the kitchen. "What's the matter?"

She tried to keep her voice steady. "The governor was supposed to submit three names to the senate tomorrow for approval of judicial appointments. Mine was to be one of them. Jonathan has asked the governor to postpone the action for now."

"Senator Hoover did that to you!" Geoff exclaimed. "I thought he was your big buddy." Then he stared at her. "Wait. Does this have something to do with the Reardon case and Frank Green?"

He didn't need her nod to know he was right. "Kerry, that's lousy. But you said postponed, not withdrawn."

"I know. But I can't expect Jonathan to go out on a limb for me. I told him about seeing Dr. Smith and Dolly Bowles, and he wasn't impressed. He feels that by reopening this case, I am questioning Frank's capability and wasting taxpayers' money on a case that was decided ten years ago. He pointed out that five appeals courts have confirmed Reardon's guilt." She shook her head as though trying to clear her mind. "I'm sorry to have wasted your time this way, Geoff, but I guess I've decided that Jonathan's right. A murderer is in prison, put there by a jury of his peers, and the courts have been consistent in upholding his conviction. Why do I think I know something they don't? I'm just going to have to let this drop."

Geoff's face tightened in suppressed anger. "Very well, then. Good-bye, Your Honor," he said. "Thanks for the pasta."

11

*I*N THE laboratory of FBI headquarters in Washington, D.C., four agents watched the computer screen freeze on the profile of the thief who had broken into the Hamilton home in Chevy Chase over the weekend. At first the image taken by the hidden camera had seemed impossibly blurry, but after some electronic enhancement a few details of the face were visible. It's still pretty difficult to see much more than his nose and the outline of his mouth, thought Si Morgan, the senior agent. Nonetheless, it might jog someone's memory.

"Get a couple of hundred of these run off and see that they're circulated to the families in every break-in that matches the Hamilton case profile. It's not much, but at least we now have a chance of getting that bastard." Morgan's face turned grim. "And I hope when we get him, we can match his thumbprint to the one we found the night Congressman Peale's mother lost her life because she'd canceled her plans to go away for the weekend."

IT WAS still early morning as Wayne Stevens sat reading the newspaper in the family room of his comfortable Spanish-style house in Oakland, California. Retired two years from his modestly successful insurance business, he was a contented man. He had been married to his third wife, Catherine, for eight years now and in that time had come to realize that his first two marriages had left much to be desired. That was why when the phone rang, he had no premonition that the caller would evoke unpleasant memories.

The voice had a distinct East Coast accent. "Mr. Stevens, I'm Joe Palumbo, an investigator for the Bergen County, New Jersey, prosecutor's office. Was your stepdaughter Suzanne Reardon?"

"Suzanne Reardon? I don't know anyone by that name. Wait a minute," he said. "You're not talking about Susie, are you?"

"Is that what you called Suzanne?"

"I had a stepdaughter we called Susie, but her name was Sue Ellen, not Suzanne." Then he realized the inspector was using the past tense. "Has something happened to her?"

Joe Palumbo gripped the phone. "You don't know that Suzanne, or Susie, as you call her, was murdered eleven years ago?"

"Dear God." Wayne Stevens's voice fell to a whisper. "No, I didn't know. I send her a note every Christmas in care of her father, Dr. Charles Smith, but I've heard nothing from her in years."

"When did you last see her?"

"Eighteen years ago, shortly after my second wife, Jean, her mother, died. Susie was a troubled, unhappy and, frankly, *difficult* girl. I was a widower when her mother and I married. I had two young daughters, and I adopted Susie. Jean and I raised the three together. After Jean died, Susie received the proceeds of an insurance policy and announced that she was moving to New York. She was nineteen. A few months later I received a note from her saying she wanted nothing more to do with any of us. She said that she was going to live with her real father. Well, I phoned Dr. Smith, but he was extremely rude. He told me that it had been a grave mistake to allow me to adopt his daughter. What happened to her?"

"Ten years ago her husband was convicted of killing her in a jealous rage."

Images ran through Wayne Stevens's head: Susie as a whiny toddler, a plump, scowling teenager. Susie glowering at her stepsisters when their dates came to pick them up. "Jealous because she was involved with another man?" he asked slowly.

"Yes." Joe heard the bewilderment in the other man's voice and knew that Kerry's instinct was right when she had asked him to delve into Suzanne's background. "Mr. Stevens, would you describe your stepdaughter's physical appearance?"

"Sue was . . ." Stevens hesitated. "She was not a pretty girl."

"Do you have pictures of her?" Palumbo asked.

"Of course. But if this happened over ten years ago, why are you bringing it up now?"

"Because one of our assistant prosecutors thinks there's more to the case than came out at the trial."

And boy, was Kerry's hunch right! Joe thought as he hung up the phone after having secured Wayne Stevens's promise to send pictures of Susie by overnight mail.

KERRY was barely settled in her office Wednesday morning when her secretary told her that Frank Green wanted to see her.

He did not waste words. "What happened, Kerry? I understand that the governor has postponed presenting the nominations for judgeship. The indication was that he was having a problem with your inclusion. Is something wrong? Is there anything I can do?"

Well yes, as a matter of fact there is, Frank, Kerry thought. You can tell the governor that you welcome any inquiry that might reveal a gross miscarriage of justice, even if you're left with egg on your face. You could be a stand-up guy, Frank.

Instead she said, "Oh, I'm sure it will all go through soon."

"You're not on the outs with Senator Hoover, are you?"

"He's one of my closest friends."

As she turned to go, the prosecutor said, "Kerry, it stinks waiting for these appointments. Hey, I get nightmares hoping my own nomination doesn't get screwed up somewhere."

Back in her office, she tried desperately to keep her mind on the trial schedule. The grand jury had just indicted a suspect in a bungled gas station holdup. The attendant had been shot and was in intensive care. If he didn't make it, the charge would be murder.

They had planned that Robin would hold the Bible when she was sworn in. Jonathan and Grace had insisted that they would buy her judicial robes. "I, Kerry McGrath, do solemnly swear . . ."

Tears stung her eyes as she heard Jonathan's impatient voice again: *Kerry, five appeals courts have found Reardon guilty. What's the matter with you?* Well, he was right. Later this morning she would call him and tell him that she had dropped the whole matter.

DEIDRE Reardon had heard the discouragement in her son's voice when they spoke on Tuesday, which was why she decided on Wednesday to make the long trip to the Trenton prison to see him.

A small woman who had passed on to her son her red hair and

warm blue eyes, Deidre Reardon now looked every day of her age, which would soon be seventy. Her step had lost much of its bounce. Her health had forced her to give up her sales job at A&S, and now she supplemented her Social Security check by doing some clerical work at the parish office. The money she had saved during the years when Skip was doing so well and was so generous to her was gone, most of it spent on the unsuccessful appeals.

She arrived at the prison in midafternoon. Because it was a weekday, they could only communicate by telephone, with a window between them. The minute she saw the look on Skip's face, Deidre knew that the one thing she feared had happened. Skip had given up hope. "Skip, what's the matter?" she asked.

"Mom, Geoff called last night. That prosecutor who came down to see me—she's not going to follow up. She's pretty much washed her hands of me. I made Geoff be honest." Skip told her that he had refused Beth's call today. "Beth has to get on with her life. She never will if all her life is tied up with worrying about me."

"Skip, Beth loves you."

"Let her love someone else. I did, didn't I?"

"Oh, Skip." Deidre Reardon felt the shortness of breath that always preceded the stabbing pain in her chest. The doctor had warned that she was going to need a bypass operation if the angioplasty next week didn't work. She hadn't told Skip about that. She wouldn't now either.

Deidre bit back tears as she saw the hurt in her son's eyes. Involuntarily she reached out her hand and touched the glass. "Skip, don't you dare let me down by talking like this."

Their time was up too quickly. Deidre managed not to cry until after the guard had led Skip away. Then she dabbed her eyes fiercely and waited for the chest pain to pass before walking briskly out.

It feels like November, Barbara Tompkins thought as she walked the ten blocks from her office to her apartment. She should have worn a heavier coat. But what did a few blocks of discomfort matter when she felt so good? It had been a dizzying year since she moved to Manhattan from Albany. Dizzying but exciting. Barbara

69

was having a wonderful time. There wasn't a day that she didn't rejoice in the miracle that Dr. Smith had performed for her.

But as she walked the last block to her apartment, she glanced nervously over her shoulder. Last night she had had dinner with some clients in The Mark Hotel. When they were leaving, she had noticed Dr. Smith seated alone at a small table off to the side. Last month she had caught a glimpse of him in the Oak Room at The Plaza. And last week, when she met clients at The Four Seasons, she had had the impression that someone was watching her from a car across the street when she hailed a taxi.

Barbara felt a surge of relief as the doorman greeted her. Then once again she looked over her shoulder. A black Mercedes was stopped in traffic directly in front of the apartment building. There was no mistaking the driver: Dr. Smith.

Barbara walked quickly into the foyer of her building. As she waited for the elevator, she thought, He *is* following me. But what can I do about it?

AT NINE o'clock Kerry looked in on Robin, who was in bed reading. "Lights out," she said as she went over to tuck her in.

As Robin snuggled down under the covers, she said, "Mom, I like Geoff. He's neat."

Geoff. Kerry didn't want to think about his derisive, dismissive comment when he left last night. *Good-bye, Your Honor.*

"When is he coming back?" Robin asked.

Kerry was evasive. "Oh, I don't know. He really just came because of a case he's been working on."

Robin looked troubled. "I guess I shouldn't have told Daddy about that."

"What do you mean?"

"I didn't mean to talk about you to him, but I said a lawyer had come to the house on business, and Daddy asked who it was."

"And you said Geoff Dorso. There's nothing wrong with that."

"I don't know. Daddy seemed to get upset with me. We'd been having fun; then he got quiet and said it was time to get home."

"Rob, Daddy's involved in a very tough case right now. Maybe you had kept his mind off it for a while, and then he started thinking about it again."

"Do you really think so?" Robin's eyes brightened.

"I really think so," Kerry said firmly as she turned out the light.

She went downstairs, planning to balance her checkbook. But when she got to her desk, she gazed for a long minute at the Reardon file Joe Palumbo had given her. Then she shook her head. Forget it, she told herself. Stay out of it.

But it wouldn't hurt just to take a look, she reasoned. She picked it up, carried it to her favorite chair, laid the file on the hassock at her feet and reached for the first batch of papers.

The record showed that the call had come in at twelve twenty a.m. Skip Reardon had dialed the operator and shouted at her to connect him to the Alpine police. "My wife is dead. My wife is dead," he had repeated over and over. The police reported they had found him kneeling beside her, crying. The vase the roses had been in was overturned, the roses scattered over the body.

Kerry's eyes narrowed when she saw that a Jason Arnott had been questioned in the course of the investigation. Skip Reardon had mentioned him to her. In his statement Arnott described himself as an antiques expert who for a commission would accompany women to auctions and advise them in their bidding. He said he enjoyed entertaining, and Suzanne often came to his parties, sometimes with Skip, but usually alone. The investigator had checked with mutual friends of both Suzanne's and Arnott's and found no suggestion of any romantic interest between them.

Nothing new here, Kerry decided when she had completed half the file. Sorry, Geoff. Her eyes were burning. She would skim through the rest of the file tomorrow. But as she went to close it, she glanced at the next report—an interview with a caddie at the Palisades Country Club, where Suzanne and Skip Reardon were members. A name caught her eye, and she picked up the next batch of papers, all thought of sleep suddenly gone.

The caddie, Michael Vitti, was a fountain of information about Suzanne. "Everybody loved to caddie for her. She gave big tips. She played with lots of the men. She was good, and I mean *good.*

71

A lot of the wives got sore at her because the men all liked her."

Vitti had been asked if he thought Suzanne was involved with any of the men. "Oh, I don't know about that," he said. "I never saw her alone with anyone." But when pressed, he said that just maybe there was something going on between Suzanne and Jimmy Weeks.

It was Jimmy Weeks's name that had jumped out at Kerry. According to the investigator's notes, Weeks, on being questioned about Suzanne, absolutely denied that he had ever seen her outside the club. He said he had been having a serious relationship with another woman at that time, and besides, he had an ironclad alibi for the entire night of the murder.

Then Kerry read the last of the caddie's interview. He admitted that Mr. Weeks treated all the women pretty much alike and called most of them things like honey, darlin' and lovey.

The caddie was asked if Weeks had a special name for Suzanne. The answer was, "Well, a couple of times I heard him call her sweetheart."

Kerry let the papers drop in her lap. Jimmy Weeks. Bob's client. Was that why Bob's attitude changed so suddenly when Robin told him that Geoff Dorso had come to see her on business? It was fairly widely known that Geoff represented Skip Reardon and had been trying for ten years to get him a new trial. Was Bob, as Weeks's counsel, afraid of what a new trial might entail for his client?

A couple of times I heard him call her sweetheart. The words haunted Kerry.

12

Thursday
November 2nd

O N THURSDAY morning Kate Carpenter arrived at the office at quarter of nine. The first patient wasn't arriving until ten o'clock, so Dr. Smith had not come in yet. The receptionist was at her desk, a worried look on her face. "Kate, Barbara Tompkins wants you to phone her, and she specifically asked that Dr. Smith not be told about her call. She says it's very important. I told her you'd be along very soon. She's waiting at home to hear from you."

Kate went into the closet-size private office the accountant used, closed the door and dialed Tompkins's number. With increasing dismay she listened as Barbara related her conviction that Dr. Smith was following her. "I don't know what to do," she said. "I'm so grateful to him. But I'm frightened."

"He's never approached you?"

"No."

"Then let me think about it and talk to a few people. I beg you not to discuss this with anyone else. Dr. Smith has a wonderful reputation. It would be terrible to have it destroyed."

"I'll never be able to repay Dr. Smith for what he did for me," Barbara said quietly. "But please get back to me quickly."

AT FOUR o'clock Thursday afternoon Joe Palumbo received delivery of an Express Mail package from Wayne Stevens in Oakland, California. He immediately slit it open and reached inside for the two stacks of snapshots held together with rubber bands. A note was clipped to one of them. It read:

Dear Mr. Palumbo,

The full impact of Susie's death hit me only after I began putting these photos together for you. Susie was not an easy child to raise. I think these pictures tell the story. My daughters were very attractive. Susie was not. That led to intense jealousy and unhappiness on Susie's part. Susie's mother, my wife, had great difficulty watching her stepdaughters enjoy their teen years, while her own child was basically friendless. I'm afraid the situation caused a great deal of friction in our home. I always hoped that a mature Susie would show up at the door one day and have a wonderful reunion with us.

But for now, I hope these pictures will help.

Sincerely,
Wayne Stevens

Twenty minutes later Joe went into Kerry's office and dropped the snapshots on her desk. "Just in case you think Susie became a beauty because of a new hairdo," he commented.

AT FIVE O'CLOCK KERRY PHONED Dr. Smith's office. He had left for the day. Anticipating that, she next asked, "Is Mrs. Carpenter available?" When Kate Carpenter came to the phone, Kerry said, "Mrs. Carpenter, how long have you been with Dr. Smith?"

"Four years, Ms. McGrath. Why are you asking?"

"Because I wondered if you were there when Dr. Smith operated on his daughter, Suzanne, or had a colleague operate on her. I can tell you what she looked like. Both Barbara Tompkins and Pamela Worth are dead ringers for Dr. Smith's daughter."

The woman gasped. "I didn't know Dr. Smith had a daughter."

"She died nearly eleven years ago—murdered, as the jury decided, by her husband. Dr. Smith was the principal witness against him. Mrs. Carpenter, I must talk to Dr. Smith, and I doubt very much that he will agree to see me. Is he going to be in on Monday?"

"Yes, but he has a very full schedule. He won't be done until sometime after four o'clock."

"I'll be there then, but don't tell him I'm coming." A question occurred to Kerry. "What kind of car does Dr. Smith drive?"

"The same one he's always driven. A black four-door Mercedes sedan."

Kerry gripped the phone. "You say 'always driven.' You mean he *always* selects a black Mercedes sedan?"

"I mean he drives the same one he's driven for at least twelve years. I know because I've heard him talking about it to one of his patients who happens to be a Mercedes executive."

"Thank you, Mrs. Carpenter."

WHEN Geoff Dorso got home on Thursday night, he stood at the window of his condominium in the Meadowlands and stared at the New York skyline. All day the memory of how he had sarcastically called Kerry "Your Honor" had been plaguing him.

What a hell of a nerve I had, he thought. Kerry was decent enough to call me and ask to read the transcript. She was decent enough to talk to Dr. Smith and Dolly Bowles. She made the trek to Trenton to meet Skip. Why shouldn't she worry about losing her judgeship, especially if she honestly doesn't believe that Skip is innocent? I owe her an apology, he thought, although I wouldn't blame her if she hung up on me. It was a cheap shot to insinuate that she was being self-serving.

One thing, however, had come out of all this, he reminded himself. Kerry might not believe in Skip's innocence, but she had opened two lines of inquiry that he would follow up on: Dolly Bowles's story of Poppa's car, and Dr. Smith's bizarre need to duplicate Suzanne's face in other women.

Geoff reached for the phone, took a deep breath and dialed Kerry's number.

WHEN Kerry got home and the sitter had left, Robin looked at her critically. "You look bushed, Mom. Tough day?"

"You could call it that. How was your day?"

"Fine. I think Andrew likes me."

"Really!" Kerry knew that Andrew was considered the coolest boy in the fifth grade. "How do you know that?"

"He told Tommy that even with my face banged up, I'm better-looking than most of the dorks in our class."

Kerry grinned. "Now that's what I call a compliment."

"That's what I thought. What are we having for dinner?"

"How does a cheeseburger sound?"

"Perfect."

The phone rang and Robin grabbed it. It was for her. She tossed the receiver to Kerry. "I'll take it upstairs, okay? It's Cassie."

When she heard Robin's exuberant "I'm on," Kerry replaced the receiver, carried the mail into the kitchen and began to sort through it. A plain white envelope with her name and address in block printing caught her eye. She slit it open, pulled out a snapshot and went cold. It was a color Polaroid of Robin coming down the walk outside their house. She was dressed in the dark blue slacks she had worn the day she had been frightened by the car.

Kerry's lips felt rubbery. Her breath came in short, fast gasps. Who did this? Who would take Robin's picture, drive a car at her, then mail the picture to me? Hearing Robin clattering down the stairs, she shoved the picture into her pocket.

75

"Mom, Cassie reminded me that I'm supposed to be watching the Discovery Channel now. The program is about what we're studying in science. That doesn't count as entertainment, does it?"

"No, of course not. Go ahead."

The phone rang again as Kerry sank into a chair. It was Geoff Dorso. She cut off his apologies. "Geoff, I just opened the mail." And she told him about the picture. "Robin was right," she half whispered. "There *was* someone watching her from that car. Suppose he had pulled her into it."

Geoff heard the fear and despair in her voice. "Kerry, don't say anything else. I'm on my way. I'll be there in half an hour."

Dr. Smith sat in his library that evening in his usual chair, sipping his usual after-office cocktail. It had been a terrible mistake to follow Barbara Tompkins last night. When his car was caught in traffic in front of her apartment building, he thought she might have seen him. On the other hand, midtown Manhattan was a place where people did frequently catch a glimpse of people they knew. So his being there really wasn't so unusual.

But a quick, casual glimpse wasn't enough. He wanted to see Barbara again. Really see her. Talk to her. She wasn't Suzanne. No one could be. But like Suzanne, the more Barbara became accustomed to her beauty, the more her personality enhanced it. He recalled the sullen, plain creature who had first appeared in his office; within a year of the operation Suzanne had capped the transformation with her total change of personality.

Smith smiled faintly, remembering Suzanne's provocative body language, the subtle moves that made every man turn to look at her. She had even lowered the tone of her voice until it had a husky, intimate quality. When he had commented on her personality transformation, she had said, "I had two good teachers—my stepsisters. We reversed the fairy tale. They were the beauties, and I was ugly Cinderella. Only instead of a fairy godmother, I have you."

Toward the end, however, his Pygmalion fantasy turned into a nightmare. The respect and affection Suzanne seemed to have for him began to fade. She no longer listened to his counsel. Toward the end she had gone beyond simple flirting. How many times had he warned her that she was playing with fire, that Skip Reardon would be capable of murder if he found out the way she was carrying on? Any husband of a woman that desirable would be capable of murder, Dr. Smith thought.

With a jolt he looked down angrily at his empty glass. Now there wouldn't be another chance to reach the perfection he had achieved in Suzanne. He would have to give up surgery before a disaster occurred. It was too late. He knew he was in the beginning stages of Parkinson's.

If Barbara wasn't Suzanne, she was of all his living patients the most striking example of his genius. He reached for the phone.

Surely that wasn't stress in her voice, he thought when Barbara Tompkins picked up the receiver and said hello. "Barbara, my dear, is anything wrong? This is Dr. Smith."

Her gasp was audible, but then she said quickly, "Oh, no, of course not. How are you, Doctor?"

"I'm fine. I'm stopping in at Lenox Hill Hospital to see an old friend who is terminal, and I know I'll be feeling a bit down. Would you have mercy on me and join me for dinner? I could stop by for you about seven thirty."

"I—I don't know. . . ."

"Please, Barbara." He tried to sound playful. "You did say that you owed me your new life. Why not spare me two hours of it?"

"Of course."

"Wonderful. Seven thirty, then."

"All right, Doctor."

She almost sounded as though he had forced her into meeting him, he thought as he hung up. If so, it was one more way in which she was beginning to resemble Suzanne.

JASON Arnott could not shake the feeling that something was wrong. He had spent the day in New York with fifty-two-year-old Vera Shelby Todd, on an endless hunt for Persian carpets.

A Rhode Island Shelby, Vera lived in one of the handsome manor houses in Tuxedo Park, New York, and was used to getting her way.

After her first husband died, she had married Stuart Todd but decided to keep the Tuxedo Park place. Now, using Todd's seemingly unlimited checkbook, Vera frequently availed herself of Jason's infallible eye for rare finds and bargains.

Jason had first met Vera at a gala the Shelbys gave in Newport. When she realized how relatively close he lived to her Tuxedo Park home, she had begun inviting him to her parties. It had amused Jason when she had told him every detail of the police investigation into the Newport robbery he had committed years before.

"My cousin Judith was so upset," Vera had confided. "She couldn't understand why someone would take the Picasso and pass up the van Eyck. So she brought in some art expert, and he said that she had a discriminating criminal: The van Eyck is a fake. Judith was furious, but for the rest of us who had had to listen to her bragging about her peerless knowledge of the great masters, it's become a family joke."

Today, after having exhaustively examined ludicrously expensive rugs, with Vera finding none of them to be exactly what she had in mind, Jason was wild to get away from her. But at her insistence they had lunch at The Four Seasons. The pleasant interlude perked Jason up, until, as she finished her espresso, Vera had said, "Oh, did I forget to tell you? You remember how five years ago my cousin Judith's place in Rhode Island was burglarized?"

Jason had pursed his lips. "Of course. Terrible experience."

Vera nodded. "I should say. But yesterday Judith got a photograph from the FBI. There was a recent burglary in Chevy Chase, and a hidden camera caught the robber. The FBI thinks it may be the same person who broke into Judith's house."

Jason had felt every nerve in his body tingle. He had only met Judith Shelby a few times and hadn't seen her in almost five years. Obviously, she hadn't recognized him. Yet. "Was it a clear picture?" he asked casually.

Vera laughed. "No, not at all. Judith says she could just about make out something of the nose and mouth. She threw it out."

Jason stifled a sigh of relief.

"According to the information with the photograph, that man is dangerous," Vera continued. "He's wanted for questioning in the murder of Congressman Peale's mother. She apparently stumbled in on him during a robbery at her house. Judith almost went home early the night her place was burglarized. Just think what might have happened if she'd found him there."

Nervously Jason pursed his lips. They had tied him to the Peale death!

ON HIS way home to Alpine, Jason thought about that awful night in Congressman Peale's house. He had been in the hallway carrying the painting when he heard footsteps coming up the stairs. He had barely had time to hold the painting in front of his face when light flooded the hallway. Then he had heard the quavering gasp, "Oh, dear God," and knew it was the Congressman's mother. He hadn't intended to hurt her. He had rushed toward her, holding the painting as a shield, intending only to knock her down and grab her glasses. He had spent a long time talking with her at Peale's inaugural party, and he knew she was blind as a bat without them.

But the heavy picture frame caught the side of her head harder than he had intended, and she toppled down the stairs. He knew from the final gurgle she made before she went still that she was dead. For months afterward he had looked over his shoulder, expecting someone to come toward him with handcuffs.

Should he cut and run? he asked himself now as he crossed the George Washington Bridge. Under other identities he had plenty of money in negotiable securities. Maybe he should leave the country immediately. On the other hand, if the photograph was as indistinguishable as Judith Shelby found it . . .

By the time he exited onto the road into Alpine, he had made up his mind. With the exception of this photograph he was almost sure he had left no tracks. No, he would not panic. But no more jobs for a long time. This was a warning.

He got home at quarter of four and went through the mail. One envelope caught his eye, and he slit it open, pulled out the contents and burst out laughing. Surely no one would link him to that vaguely comical figure with the stocking mask pushed up and the grainy caricature of a profile literally inches away from the copy of the Rodin figurine.

"Vive le junk!" Jason exclaimed. He settled in the den for a nap. Vera's constant stream of talk had exhausted him. When he awoke, it was time for the six-o'clock news. The lead story was that Jimmy Weeks's codefendant, Barney Haskell, was rumored to be cutting a deal with the attorney general. He was hinting he could tie Jimmy to a murder that someone else was serving time for.

Nothing like the deal I could cut, Jason thought. It was a comforting reminder. But of course it would never happen.

ROBIN turned off the science program just as the doorbell rang. She was delighted to hear Geoff Dorso's voice in the foyer and came running out to greet him. She could see that both his face and her mother's were serious. Maybe they had a fight, she thought, and want to make up.

Throughout the meal Robin noticed that her mother was unusually quiet, while Geoff was funny, telling stories about his sisters. Geoff is so nice, Robin thought. He reminded her of Jimmy Stewart in that movie she watched with her mother every Christmas, *It's a Wonderful Life*. He had the same sort of shy, warm smile and hesitant voice, and the kind of hair that looked as though it wouldn't ever really stay in place.

But Robin noticed that her mother seemed to be only half listening to Geoff's stories. It was obvious something was up between them and that they needed to talk—without her in the room. So she decided to make the big sacrifice and work on her science project in her room. After she had helped clear the table, she announced her plans and caught the look of relief in her mother's eyes.

Geoff listened for the click of Robin's bedroom door, then said to Kerry, "Let's see the picture."

Kerry reached into her pocket, drew it out and handed it to him.

Geoff studied it carefully. "It looks to me as though Robin had it straight when she told what had happened," he said. "Someone caught her coming head-on from the house."

"Then she was right about the car racing toward her. But Geoff, why?"

"I don't know, Kerry. But I do know that this has to be treated seriously. Did you let Bob know?"

"Good Lord, it never occurred to me. Of course Bob has to know about this."

"I'd want to know if it were my child," Geoff agreed. "Look, why don't you give him a call and let me pour us another coffee?"

Bob was not at home. Alice was coldly civil to Kerry. "He's still at the office," his wife said. "Is there a message I can give him?"

Only that his oldest child is in danger, Kerry thought. "I'll call Bob at the office. Good-bye, Alice."

Bob Kinellen paled as he listened to Kerry's recounting of what had happened to Robin. He had no doubt who had taken the picture. It had Jimmy Weeks's signature all over it. That was the way he worked. Start a war of nerves, then step it up. Next week there would be another picture. Never a threat. No notes. Just a picture. A get-the-message-or-else situation.

When Bob hung up, he slammed his fist on the desk. Jimmy was spinning out of control. They both knew that it was all over if Haskell completed his deal with the U.S. Attorney. Especially if Haskell got wind of Kinellen's ex-wife's looking into the Reardon murder case. It might occur to him that he had another way to sweeten any deal he was trying to make with the prosecution.

Weeks figured that Kerry would probably call me about the picture, Bob thought. It's his way of telling me to warn her away from the Reardon case. But what Weeks doesn't know is that Kerry doesn't get scared off. In fact, if she perceived that picture as a warning to her, it would be like waving a red flag in front of a bull.

Dr. Smith took Barbara Tompkins to Le Cirque, a very chic, very expensive restaurant in midtown Manhattan. He had picked her up at her apartment and did not miss the fact that she had been ready to leave immediately. Her coat was on a chair in the foyer, her purse on the table beside it. She did not offer him an apéritif.

She doesn't want to be alone with me, he had thought.

But at the restaurant, with so many people around them and the attentive maître d' hovering nearby, Barbara visibly relaxed. "It's a lot different from Albany," she said. "I'm still like a kid having a daily birthday."

He was stunned for a moment by her words. Suzanne had compared herself to a kid with an ever present Christmas tree and gifts always waiting to be opened. But from being an enchanted child, Suzanne had changed into an ungrateful adult. I asked so little of her, he thought. Shouldn't an artist be allowed to take pleasure in his creation?

Warmth filled him now as he noticed that in this room crowded with attractive, elegant women, sidelong glances rested on Barbara. He pointed that out to her. She shook her head slightly, as though dismissing the suggestion. His eyes became cold. "Don't take it for granted, Suzanne. That would be insulting to me."

It was only later, after he had seen her back to her apartment, that he asked himself if he had called her Suzanne. And if so, how many times had he slipped?

He sighed and leaned back, closing his eyes. As the cab jostled downtown, Charles Smith reflected how easy it had been to drive past Suzanne's house when he was starved for a glimpse of her. She invariably sat in front of the television and never bothered to draw the drapes. He would see her curled up in her favorite chair, or sometimes he would be forced to witness her sitting on the couch with Skip Reardon, shoulders touching in the casual intimacy he could not share.

Barbara wasn't married. From what he could tell, there wasn't anyone special in her life. Tonight he had asked her to call him Charles. He thought about the bracelet Suzanne had been wearing when she died. Should he give it to Barbara? Would it endear him to her?

He had given Suzanne several pieces of jewelry. Fine jewelry. But then she had started accepting other pieces from other men and demanding that he lie for her.

Smith felt the glow from being with Barbara ooze away.

GEOFF STUDIED KERRY'S GRAVE face after she called Bob, aware of the hint of sadness in her hazel eyes, the vulnerability in her overall posture. He wanted to put his arms around her, to tell her to lean on him. But he knew she didn't want that. Kerry McGrath did not expect or want to lean on anyone. He tried again to apologize for his remark to her the other night. "I had a hell of a nerve," he said. "I know that if you believed in your heart that Skip Reardon was innocent, you of all people would not hesitate to help him. You're a stand-up guy, McGrath."

Am I? Kerry wondered. It was not the moment to share with Geoff the information she had found in the prosecutor's file about Jimmy Weeks. She wanted to see Dr. Smith again first. He had angrily denied that he had touched Suzanne surgically, but he had never said that he hadn't sent her to someone else.

As Geoff was leaving a few minutes later, they stood for a moment in the foyer. "I like being with you," he told her, "and that has nothing to do with the Reardon case." He leaned down and brushed her cheek with his lips.

13

Friday
November 3rd

THE plea bargaining was not going well for Barney Haskell. At seven a.m. on Friday he met attorney Mark Young in his law office in Summit. The head of Barney's defense team, Young was about the same age he was, fifty-five, but there the resemblance ended, Barney thought sourly. Young was smoothly elegant even at this early hour, dressed in his thousand-dollar suit that seemed to fit like a second skin. Barney bought his suits off the rack. Jimmy Weeks never paid him enough to allow him to do otherwise. Now he was facing years in prison if he stuck with Jimmy.

Barney knew he had the innocent look of a dumb bank clerk, an aspect that had always been helpful. People tended not to notice or remember him. Even the guys closest to Weeks never paid much attention to him. None of them had realized he was the one who converted the under-the-table cash into investments and took care of bank accounts all over the world.

"We can get you into the Witness Protection Program," Young was saying. "But only after you've served a minimum of five years."

"Too much," Barney grunted.

"Look, you've been hinting you can tie Jimmy to a murder," Young said. "Barney, you've got to put up or shut up. The feds would love to hang a murder on Weeks. If he's in for life, his organization probably would collapse. That's what they're gunning for."

"I can tie him to one. Then they'll have to prove he did it. Isn't there talk that Brandon Royce, the U.S. Attorney on this case, is thinking about running for governor against Frank Green?"

"If each gets his party's nomination," Young commented. "Barney, you'll have to stop talking in circles. You'd better trust me with whatever it is you're hinting about. Otherwise I won't be able to help you."

A frown momentarily crossed Barney's cherubic face. Then his forehead cleared and he said, "All right. I'll tell you. Remember the Sweetheart Murder Case, the one involving that sexy young wife who was found dead with roses scattered all over her, the case that Frank Green made his name on?"

Young nodded. "I remember. He got a conviction on the husband." His eyes narrowed. "You're not saying Weeks was connected to that case?"

"You remember how the husband claimed he didn't give his wife those roses?" At Young's nod, Haskell continued. "Jimmy Weeks sent those roses to Suzanne Reardon. I should know. I delivered them to her house the night she died. There was a card with them that Jimmy wrote himself. I'll show you what was on it."

Barney reached for his pen and the telephone message pad. A moment later he handed over the pad. "Jimmy called Suzanne 'sweetheart,' " he explained. "He had a date with her that night."

Young examined the paper. It held six notes of music with five words written underneath: "I'm in love with you." It was signed "J." He hummed the notes, then looked at Barney. "The opening notes of the song 'Let Me Call You Sweetheart,' " he said.

"Uh-huh. Followed by the rest of the first line of the song, *'I'm in love with you.'*"

"Where is this card?"

"That's the point. Nobody mentioned it being in the house when the body was found. But Jimmy was crazy about that woman, and it drove him nuts that she played up to other guys. When he sent her those flowers, he had already given her an ultimatum that she had to get a divorce—and stay away from other men."

"What was her reaction?"

"Oh, she liked to make him jealous. One of our guys tried to warn her that Jimmy could be dangerous, but she just laughed. My guess is that that night she went too far. Throwing those roses over her body is just the kind of thing Jimmy would do."

"And the card was missing?"

Barney shrugged. "You didn't hear nothing about it at the trial. I was ordered to keep my mouth shut about her. I do know that she kept Jimmy waiting or stood him up that night. A couple of the guys told me he exploded and said he'd kill her. You know Jimmy's temper. And there was one other thing. Jimmy had bought her some expensive jewelry. I know because I paid for it and kept a copy of the receipts. There was a lot of talk about jewelry at the trial, stuff the husband claimed he hadn't given her. But anything they found, the father swore he gave her."

Mark Young tore the sheet of paper off the pad, folded it and put it into his breast pocket. "Barney, I think you're going to be able to enjoy a wonderful new life in Ohio. You've delivered the U.S. Attorney a chance not only to nail Jimmy for murder but also to annihilate Frank Green for prosecuting an innocent man."

They smiled across the desk at each other. "Tell them I don't want to live in Ohio," Barney joked.

They left the office together and walked down the corridor to the bank of elevators. When one arrived and the doors started to part, Barney sensed immediately that something was wrong. There was no light on inside. Gut instinct made him turn to run.

He was too late. He died immediately, moments before Mark Young felt the first bullet shred the lapel of his thousand-dollar suit.

KERRY HEARD ABOUT THE DOUBLE homicide on WCBS Radio as she was driving to work. The bodies were discovered by Mark Young's private secretary. Mike Murkowski, the prosecutor of Essex County, said it appeared both men had been robbed. They might have been followed into the building by potential muggers and then lost their lives when they tried to resist. Barney Haskell had been shot in the back of his head and neck.

The CBS reporter asked if the fact that Barney Haskell was rumored to be about to connect Jimmy Weeks to a murder was being considered as a possible motive for the double slaying. The prosecutor's sharp answer was, "No comment."

It sounds like a Mob hit, Kerry thought as she snapped off the radio. And Bob represents Jimmy Weeks. Wow, what a mess!

BOB Kinellen did not hear the news about Barney Haskell and Mark Young until he entered the courthouse at ten of nine and the media pounced on him. As soon as he heard what had happened, he realized he had been expecting it. How could Haskell have been so stupid as to think Jimmy would let him live to testify against him?

Kinellen managed to appear appropriately shocked, and escaped to the courtroom.

Jimmy was already there. "Heard about Haskell?" he asked.

"Yes, I did, Jimmy."

"Nobody's safe. These muggers are everywhere."

"I guess they are, Jimmy."

"It kind of levels the playing field though, doesn't it, Bobby?"

"Yes, I would say so."

"But I don't like a level playing field."

"I know that, Jimmy."

"Just so you know."

Bob spoke carefully. "Jimmy, someone sent my ex-wife a picture of our little girl, Robin. It was taken as she was leaving for school on Tuesday by the same person who was in a car that made a U-turn right in front of her. Robin thought he was going to run her over."

"They always joke about New Jersey drivers, Bobby."

"Jimmy, nothing had better happen to my daughter."

"I don't know what you're talking about. When are they going to make your ex-wife a judge and get her out of the prosecutor's office? She shouldn't be poking around in other people's business."

Bob knew that his question had been asked and answered. One of Jimmy's people had taken the picture of Robin. He, Bob, would have to get Kerry to back off investigating the Reardon case. And he had better see to it that Jimmy was acquitted in this one.

"Good morning, Jimmy. Morning, Bob."

Bob looked up to see his father-in-law, Anthony Bartlett, slip into the chair next to Jimmy.

"Very sad about Haskell and Young," Bartlett murmured.

"Tragic," Jimmy said.

At that moment the sheriff's officer motioned to the prosecutor and Bob and Bartlett to step inside the judge's chambers. A somber Judge Benton looked up from his desk. "I assume you have all been made aware of the tragedy involving Mr. Haskell and Mr. Young." The attorneys nodded quietly.

"As difficult as it will be, I believe that given the time already invested in this trial, it should proceed. Fortunately, the jury is sequestered and won't be exposed to this news, including the speculation that Mr. Weeks may be involved. I will simply tell them that Mr. Haskell's case is no longer before them. I will instruct them not to speculate on what happened and not to let it affect their consideration of Mr. Weeks's case. Okay, let's continue."

They returned to the courtroom, and the jury filed in. Bob could see the quizzical looks on their faces as they looked over to Haskell's and Young's empty chairs. As the judge instructed them not to speculate on what had happened, Bob knew damn well that that was exactly what they were doing. They think Haskell pleaded guilty, Bob thought. That's not going to help us.

KERRY was just leaving the office at five o'clock when Bob phoned. She caught the tension in his voice. "Kerry, I need to stop by for a few minutes. Will you be home in an hour or so?"

"Yes."

"I'll see you then," he said, and hung up.

What was bringing Bob to the house? she wondered. Concern about the picture of Robin she'd received? She reached for her coat, remembering wryly how for the year and a half of her marriage, she had joyfully rushed home from work to spend the evening with Bob Kinellen.

When she arrived home, Robin looked at her accusingly. "Mom, why did Alison pick me up at school and drive me home? She wouldn't give me a reason, and I felt like a jerk."

Kerry looked at the sitter. "I won't hold you up, Alison. Thanks."

When Robin and Kerry were alone, she looked into Robin's indignant face. "That car that frightened you . . ." she began.

When she was finished, Robin sat very still. "It's kind of scary, isn't it, Mom?"

"Yes, it is."

"I wish you'd told me last night."

"I didn't know how to, Rob. I was too uptight myself."

"So what do we do now?"

"Take a lot of precautions until we find out who was across the street last Tuesday and why he was there."

"Do you think if he comes back, he'll run me over next time?"

Kerry wanted to shout, "No, I don't." Instead she moved over to the couch where Robin was sitting and put an arm around her.

Robin dropped her head onto her mother's shoulder. "In other words, if the car comes at me again, duck."

"That's why the car isn't going to get the chance, Rob."

"Does Daddy know about this?"

"I called him last night. He's coming up in a little while."

Robin sat upright. "Because he's worried about me?"

She's pleased, Kerry thought, as though Bob has done her a favor. "Of course he's worried about you."

"Cool. Mom, can I tell Cassie about this?"

"No. Not until we know who's pulling this—"

"And have cuffed him," Robin interjected.

"Exactly. Once that's done, then you can talk about it."

"Okay. What are we going to do tonight?"

"We'll send out for pizza. I rented a couple of movies."

The mischievous look Kerry loved came into Robin's face. "R-rated, I hope."

She's trying to make me feel better, Kerry thought. She's not going to let me know how scared she is.

At ten of six Bob arrived. With a whoop of joy Robin ran into his arms. "What do you think about me being in danger?" she asked.

"You two visit while I get changed," Kerry said.

Bob released Robin. "Don't be long, Kerry," he said hurriedly. "I can only stay a few minutes."

Kerry saw the instant pain on Robin's face and wanted to throttle Bob. Struggling to keep her tone of voice even, she responded, "Down in a minute."

She changed quickly into slacks and a sweater, but deliberately waited upstairs for ten minutes. Then, as she was about to come down, there was a knock at her door and Robin called, "Mom."

"Come in." Kerry started to say "I'm ready," when she saw the look on Robin's face. "What's wrong?"

"Nothing. Dad asked me to wait up here while he talks to you."

"I see."

Bob was standing in the middle of the study, obviously uncomfortable. What did he do to upset Robin? Kerry wondered. Probably spent the whole time telling her how rushed he was.

He turned when he heard her footsteps. "Kerry, I've got to get back to the office. But there's something very important I have to tell you." He pulled a small sheet of paper out of his pocket. "You heard what happened to Barney Haskell and Mark Young?"

"Obviously."

"Kerry, Jimmy Weeks has a way of getting information. For example, he knows that you went to see Reardon in prison."

"Does he?" Kerry stared at her ex-husband. "What difference would that make to him?"

"Kerry, don't play games. I'm worried. Jimmy is desperate." He handed her a sheet of paper. On it were six musical notes and the words "I'm in love with you." It was signed "J."

"What's this supposed to be?" Kerry asked as she mentally hummed the notes. Then, before Bob had a chance to answer, she understood, and her blood ran cold. They were the opening notes to the song "Let Me Call You Sweetheart."

"Where did you get this, and what does it mean?" she snapped.

"It's a copy of a note they found in Mark Young's breast pocket at the morgue. It's Haskell's writing. I'm certain it's connected to the plea bargain Haskell was trying to make."

"The plea bargain? You mean the homicide he was hinting he could connect Jimmy Weeks to was the Sweetheart Murder?" Kerry could not believe what she was hearing. "Jimmy *was* involved with Suzanne Reardon, wasn't he? Bob, are you telling me that whoever took Robin's picture and came within an inch of running her over works for Jimmy Weeks, and this is his way of scaring me off?"

"Kerry, I'm not saying anything except leave it alone. For Robin's sake, *leave it alone.*"

"Does Weeks know you're here?"

"He knows that for Robin's sake, I'd warn you."

"Wait a minute." Kerry looked at her former husband with disbelief. "Let me get this straight. You're here to warn me off because your client—the thug and murderer you represent—has given you a threat to convey to me. Oh, Bob, how low you have gone."

"Kerry, I'm trying to save my child's life."

"Your child? All of a sudden she's so important to you? Do you know how many times you've devastated her when you didn't show up to see her? It's insulting. Now get out." As he turned, she snatched the paper from his hand. "But I'll take this."

"Give that to me." Kinellen grabbed her hand, forcing her fingers open and pulling the paper from her.

"Dad, let go of Mom!"

They both whirled to see Robin standing in the doorway, the fading scars bright once more against the ashen pallor of her face.

Dr. Smith had left the office at four twenty, only a minute or so after his last patient—a post–tummy-tuck checkup—had departed.

Kate Carpenter was glad to see him go. She found it disturbing just to be around him lately. She had noticed that the tremor in his hand had become more pronounced, but her concern went beyond the physical. The phone calls from Barbara Tompkins and Kerry McGrath had convinced her that mentally there was something radically wrong with the doctor as well. The most frustrating thing for Kate, though, was that she didn't know where to turn. Charles Smith was—or at least had been—a brilliant surgeon. She didn't want to see him drummed out of the profession.

At four thirty Barbara Tompkins phoned. "Mrs. Carpenter, I've had it. Last night Dr. Smith called and practically demanded that I have dinner with him. But then he kept calling me Suzanne. I'm sorry, I know I owe him a lot, but this is getting to me. I find that even at work I'm looking over my shoulder, expecting to see him lurking somewhere. I can't stand it."

Kate Carpenter knew she couldn't stall any longer. The one possible person in whom she might confide was Robin Kinellen's mother, Kerry McGrath. Kate knew she was a lawyer, an assistant prosecutor in New Jersey, but also a mother who was very grateful that Dr. Smith had treated her daughter in an emergency. Kate also realized that Kerry McGrath knew more about Dr. Smith's personal background than did she or anyone else on his staff. She wasn't sure why Kerry had been checking on the doctor, but Kate didn't feel that it was for any harmful purpose.

Feeling like Judas, Kate gave Barbara Tompkins the home number of Bergen County assistant prosecutor Kerry McGrath.

FOR a long time after Bob left, Kerry and Robin sat on the sofa, not talking, shoulders touching, legs up on the coffee table. Then, choosing her words carefully, Kerry said, "Whatever the scene you just witnessed might have implied, Dad loves you very much, Robin. His worry is for you. I don't admire the fixes he gets himself into, but I respect his feeling for you."

"You got mad at him when he said he was worried about me."

"Oh, come on, those were just words. He makes me so angry sometimes. Anyhow, I know that you're not going to grow up to be the kind of person who lets herself drift into problems that are obvious to everyone else, then pleads situational ethics—meaning 'this may be wrong, but it's necessary.' "

"That's what Dad's doing?"

"*I* think so."

"Does he know who took my picture?"

"He *suspects* he knows. It has to do with a case Geoff has been working on and that he's tried to get me to help him with. He's trying to get a man out of prison that he's convinced is innocent."

"Are you helping him with it?"

"Actually, I'd pretty well decided that by getting involved, I was stirring up a hornet's nest for no reason. Now I'm beginning to think I may have been wrong, that Geoff's client indeed may have been unfairly convicted. But I'm certainly not going to put you in any danger to prove it. I promise you that."

Robin stared ahead for a moment and then turned to her mother. "Mom, that's totally unfair. You're putting Dad down for something, and then you're doing the same thing. Isn't *not* helping Geoff 'situational ethics' if you think his client shouldn't be in prison?"

"Robin!"

"I mean it. Now can we order the pizza? I'm hungry."

Shocked, Kerry watched as her daughter stood up and reached for the bag with the video movies they were planning to watch. Robin examined the titles, chose one and put it into the VCR. Just before she turned it on, she said, "Mom, I really think that guy in the car was just trying to scare me. I don't mind if you drop me off at school and Alison picks me up. What's the dif?"

Kerry stared at her daughter, then shook her head. "The dif is that I'm proud of you and ashamed of myself." She gave Robin a hug and went into the kitchen to order the pizza.

A few minutes later, as she was getting out plates for the pizza, the phone rang and a hesitant voice said, "Ms. McGrath, I'm Barbara Tompkins. I apologize for bothering you, but Mrs. Carpenter in Dr. Smith's office suggested that I call you."

As she listened, Kerry grabbed a pen and began jotting notes on the message pad: "Dr. Smith was consulted by Barbara. . . . He showed her a picture. . . . Asked her if she wanted to look like this woman. . . . Operated on her. . . . Now is calling her Suzanne and stalking her."

Finally Tompkins said, "Ms. McGrath, I'm so grateful to Dr. Smith. He's turned my life around. I don't want to report him to the police or hurt him in any way. But I can't let this go on."

"Have you ever felt you were in physical danger from him?" Kerry asked.

There was a brief hesitation before Tompkins answered slowly, "No, not really. I mean, he's never forced himself on me physically. But I do get a sense occasionally of terrible, restrained anger in him, and that it could easily be unleashed, maybe on me."

"Barbara, I'm going to see Dr. Smith on Monday. He doesn't know it, but I am. From what you tell me, I think he's suffering from some sort of breakdown, and I hope he might be persuaded to seek help. But I can't advise you not to speak to the police if you're frightened. In fact, I think you should."

"Not yet. There's a business trip I was going to make next month, but I can rearrange my schedule and take it next week. I'd like to talk to you when I come back; then I'll decide what to do."

WHEN she hung up, Kerry sank into a kitchen chair. The situation was getting much more complicated. Dr. Smith had been stalking Barbara Tompkins. Had he also been stalking his own daughter? If so, it was likely that it was *his* Mercedes Dolly Bowles and little Michael had seen in front of the Reardon house the night of the murder. Had Joe Palumbo checked the partial plate number Bowles claimed to have seen against Smith's car?

But if Dr. Smith had turned on Suzanne the way Barbara Tompkins feared he might turn on her, if he was the one responsible for her death, then why was Jimmy Weeks so afraid of being connected to Suzanne Reardon's murder?

I need to know more about Dr. Smith's relationship with Suzanne before I see him, Kerry thought. That antiques dealer, Jason Arnott—he might be the one to speak to. According to the notes in the file, he went into New York frequently with Suzanne to auctions. Perhaps Dr. Smith met them sometimes.

She placed a call to Arnott, leaving a message to call her back. Kerry then debated about making one more call.

It would be to Geoff, asking him to set up a second meeting at the prison with Skip Reardon. Only this time she would want to have both his mother and his girlfriend, Beth Taylor, there as well.

JASON Arnott had planned to stay quietly at home on Friday night, but when Amanda Coble phoned to invite him to dinner at the Ridgewood Country Club, he had accepted gladly. The Cobles were his kind of people—superrich but marvelously unpretentious. Richard was an international banker and Amanda an interior designer. Jason knew she appreciated his expertise in antiques. They would be a welcome diversion after the disquieting time he had spent in New York yesterday with Vera Todd.

He drove up to the front door of the club just as the Cobles surrendered their car to the parking valet. He was a moment behind them going through the front entrance, then waited as they greeted a distinguished-looking couple who were just leaving. He recognized the man immediately: Senator Jonathan Hoover. He'd been at a couple of political dinners where Hoover put in an appearance, but they'd never met face to face.

The woman was in a wheelchair but still managed to look regal in a deep blue dinner suit with a skirt that came to the tips of high-laced shoes. He had heard that Mrs. Hoover was disabled but had never seen her before. With an eye that instantly absorbed the smallest detail, he noted the position of her hands, clasped together, partially concealing the swollen joints of her fingers.

She must have been a knockout when she was young and before her illness, he thought as he studied the still stunning features dominated by sapphire-blue eyes.

Amanda Coble glanced up and saw him. "Jason, you're here." She waved him over and made the introductions. "We're talking about those terrible murders in Summit this morning. Both Senator Hoover and Richard knew the lawyer, Mark Young."

"It's pretty clear it was a Mob hit," Richard Coble said angrily.

"I agree," Jonathan Hoover said. "And so does the governor. We all know how he's cracked down on crime these eight years, and now we need Frank Green to keep up the good work."

"Jonathan," Grace Hoover murmured reprovingly. "You can tell it's an election year, can't you, Amanda?" As they all smiled, she added, "Now we mustn't keep you any longer."

"My wife has been keeping me in line since we met," Jonathan Hoover explained to Jason. "Nice meeting you, Mr. Arnott."

"Mr. Arnott, haven't we met before?" Grace Hoover asked suddenly. "I feel as though I know you."

Jason felt his internal alarm system kick in, sending out a strong warning. "I don't think so," he answered slowly. I'm sure I'd have remembered, he thought. So what makes her think we've met?

"Well, I'm sure I'm wrong. Good-bye."

Even though the Cobles were their usual interesting selves, Jason spent the evening heartily wishing he had stayed home.

When he got back to his house at ten thirty, his day was further ruined by listening to the one message on his answering machine. It was from Kerry McGrath, who introduced herself as a Bergen County assistant prosecutor, gave her phone number and asked him to call her at home till eleven or first thing in the morning. She explained that she wanted to talk to him unofficially about his late neighbor and friend, the murder victim, Suzanne Reardon.

ON FRIDAY evening Geoff Dorso went to dinner at his parents' home in Essex Fells. His sister Marian, her husband, Don, and their two-year-old twins had come in from Boston for the weekend, and his mother had planned a family gathering.

Geoff parked in front of the rambling Tudor house his parents had bought twenty-seven years ago for one tenth of its present value. He went up the walk and let himself into the noisy warmth, so typical when three generations of the Dorso clan gathered.

After effusive greetings to the Boston branch and a casual hello to the siblings he saw regularly, Geoff managed to escape into the book-lined study with his father. Edward Dorso poured a Scotch for his son. A retired attorney who had specialized in corporate law, he had known and liked Mark Young and was anxious to hear any behind-the-scenes information about his murder that Geoff might have picked up in court.

"I can't tell you much, Dad," Geoff said. "It's hard to believe that muggers just happened to botch a robbery and kill Young just when his fellow victim, Haskell, was about to plea-bargain in return for testifying against Jimmy Weeks."

Before his father could comment, a chorus of voices from outside the study shouted, "Grandpa, Uncle Geoff, dinner's ready."

"Go ahead, Dad. I'll be right behind you. I want to check my messages." When Geoff heard Kerry's husky, low voice on the answering machine tape, he pressed the receiver to his ear. Was Kerry actually saying that she wanted to go to the prison and see Skip again? That she wanted to have his mother and Beth Taylor there?

"Hallelujah!" Geoff said aloud, and headed to the dining room.

After his father concluded the blessing, his mother added, "And we're so grateful to have Marian and Don and the twins with us."

"Mother, it's not as though we live at the North Pole," Marian protested, winking at Geoff. "Boston is three and a half hours away."

"You can all laugh at me," his mother said, "but I love seeing my family together. It's wonderful to have three of you girls settled, and Vickey with a steady boyfriend as nice as Kevin."

Geoff watched as she beamed at that couple.

"Now if I could just get our only son to find the right girl. . . ." Her voice trailed off as everyone turned to smile indulgently at Geoff, who grimaced, then smiled back, reminding himself that when his mother wasn't riding this horse, she was a very interesting woman who had taught medieval literature at Drew University for twenty years. In fact, he had been named Geoffrey because of her great admiration for Chaucer.

Between courses Geoff slipped back into the den and phoned Kerry. He was thrilled that she sounded glad to hear from him. "Kerry, can you go down and see Skip tomorrow? I know his mother and Beth will drop everything to be there when you come."

"I want to, Geoff, but I don't know if I can. I'd be a wreck leaving Robin, even at Cassie's house."

"Then I've got a better idea. I'll pick you both up, and we can leave Robin here with my folks. My sister and her husband and their kids are here, and the other grandchildren will be dropping by. Robin will have plenty of company, and if that isn't enough, my brother-in-law is a captain in the Massachusetts State Police. Believe me, she'll be safe."

14

*J*ASON Arnott lay sleepless most of the night, trying to decide how to treat the call from Assistant Prosecutor Kerry McGrath. By seven a.m. he'd made up his mind. He would return her call and inform her that he would be delighted to meet with her, provided it would not take too long. His excuse would be that he was about to leave on a business trip. To the Catskills, Jason promised himself. I'll hide out at the house. In the meantime this will all blow over. The decision made, he finally fell into a sound sleep.

He called Kerry McGrath first thing when he woke up at nine thirty. He was relieved to hear what seemed to be genuine gratitude in her tone.

"Mr. Arnott, I appreciate your calling, and I assure you this is unofficial," she said. "Your name came up as having been a friend and antiques expert for Suzanne Reardon. Something has developed about that case, and I'd very much appreciate an opportunity to talk to you about Suzanne and her father, Dr. Charles Smith. I promise I'll only take a few minutes of your time."

She meant it. Jason could spot a phony—had made a career of it—and she wasn't a phony. It wouldn't be hard to talk about Suzanne, he told himself. He frequently had shopped with her the way he had shopped with Vera Shelby Todd the other day. Suzanne had been at many of his parties, but so had dozens of other people. No one could make anything of that.

Jason was totally amenable to Kerry's suggestion that she visit him within the hour.

KERRY DECIDED TO BRING ROBIN with her when she drove to Jason Arnott's house. She knew that it had upset Robin to see her struggling with Bob over the note the night before, and the drive to Alpine would give them a half hour each way to chat. She blamed herself for the scene with Bob. She should have realized he wouldn't let her have the note. Anyhow, she knew what it said. She had jotted it down just as she had seen it so she could show it to Geoff.

It was a sunny, crisp day, the kind that renews the spirit. Now that she had decided to see the Reardon case through, she was determined to do it quickly. She told Robin about the plan for her to visit Geoff's family while she went to Trenton on business.

"Because you're worried about me," Robin said matter-of-factly.

"Yes," Kerry admitted. "I want you where I know you'll be okay." She glanced down at her directions. "We're not far. Now Rob, when we get to Mr. Arnott's, you come in with me, but you do know I have to talk privately to him. You brought a book?"

"Uh-huh. I wonder how many of Geoff's nieces and nephews will be there today. Let's see, he has four sisters. The youngest isn't married. The one next to Geoff has three kids, a boy who's nine— he's the one closest to my age—and a girl who's seven and a boy who's four. Geoff's second sister has four kids, and then there's the one with the two-year-old twins."

"Rob, for heaven sake, when did you learn all this?" Kerry asked.

"The other night at dinner. Geoff was talking about them. You were kind of out of it. I mean, I could tell you weren't listening. Anyhow, I think it will be cool to go down there."

Five minutes later they drove up a winding road to Jason Arnott's European-style mansion, a breathtaking combination of stone, stucco, brick and wood, with towering leaded-pane windows.

"Wow!" Robin said as Kerry parked in the driveway.

Jason's greeting was cordial. "Ms. McGrath—and is this your assistant?"

"I said it would be an unofficial visit, Mr. Arnott." Kerry introduced Robin. "Perhaps she could wait somewhere while we talk?"

"She'll be comfortable in the study." Arnott indicated a room to the left of the entrance hall. "You and I can go into the library."

This place is like a museum, Kerry thought as she followed Arnott. She would have loved to stop and study the exquisite paintings. Keep your mind on what you're doing, she warned herself.

When she and Arnott were seated opposite each other on handsome morocco armchairs, she said, "Mr. Arnott, Robin suffered some facial injuries in a car accident several weeks ago and was treated by Dr. Charles Smith."

Arnott raised his eyebrows. "Suzanne Reardon's father?"

"Exactly. On each of two follow-up visits, I saw a patient in his office who bore a startling resemblance to Suzanne Reardon."

Arnott stared at her. "By coincidence, I hope. Surely you're not saying that he is deliberately re-creating Suzanne?"

"An interesting choice of words, Mr. Arnott. I'm here because I need to know Suzanne better. I need to know about her relationship with her father and with her husband."

Arnott leaned back, looked up at the ceiling and clasped his hands under his chin. "Let me start with meeting Suzanne. It would be about twelve years ago now. One day she simply rang the bell. I must tell you she was an extraordinarily beautiful girl. She introduced herself and explained that she and her husband were building a house in the neighborhood, that she wanted to furnish it with antiques and that she'd heard that I went with friends to assist them in their bidding at auctions."

"And you became Suzanne's adviser?"

"Yes. Eventually she and I became good friends; in fact, I still miss her very much. She added a great deal to my parties."

"Did Skip come with her?"

"Seldom. He was bored, and frankly, my guests did not find him simpatico. Now don't misunderstand me. He was a well-mannered and intelligent young man, but he was different from most of the people I know. He was the kind of man who got up early, worked hard and had no interest in idle chatter."

"How would you judge the relationship between Suzanne and Skip?"

"Unraveling. At first they seemed to be fond of each other, but eventually it became clear that she was bored with him. Toward the end they did very little together."

"Dr. Smith said Skip was jealous of Suzanne and that he had threatened her."

"If he did, Suzanne did not confide that to me."

"How well did you know Dr. Smith?" Kerry asked.

"As well as any of her friends did, I suppose. If I went into New York with Suzanne on days when his office was closed, he often joined us. Finally, though, his attention seemed to annoy her. She made no effort to hide her impatience with him."

"You knew that she had been raised by her mother and a stepfather?"

"Yes. She told me her growing-up years were miserable. Her stepsisters were jealous of her looks. She once said, 'Talk about Cinderella—in some ways I lived her life.' "

That answers my next question, Kerry thought. Obviously, Suzanne had not confided to Arnott that she had grown up as the plain sister named Susie.

"Do you know if Suzanne was involved with another man? Specifically, was she seeing Jimmy Weeks?"

Arnott seemed to consider before answering. "I introduced her to Jimmy Weeks in this very room. They were quite taken with each other. As you may know, there is a feeling of power about Weeks, and that attracted Suzanne. After they met, he started appearing frequently at the Palisades Country Club, where she spent a lot of her time. Jimmy was a member as well."

"Was she happy about that?"

"Oh, very. Although I don't think she let Jimmy know it. She enjoyed making him jealous. Do you remember the scene in *Gone With the Wind* where Scarlett collects everyone else's beaux? Well, that was Suzanne. It didn't make her very popular with women."

"And Dr. Smith's reaction to her flirting?"

"Outraged, I would say. I think that if it had been possible, Smith would have built a guardrail around her to keep others away."

"If your theory is correct, Mr. Arnott, wouldn't that be a reason for Dr. Smith to resent Skip Reardon?"

"I think it went deeper than that. I think he hated him."

"Mr. Arnott, did you have any reason to think that Suzanne was given jewelry by any man other than her husband and father?"

"If she was, I wasn't privy to it. I do know Suzanne had some very fine pieces. Skip bought her a number of things, and she also had several older pieces that I believe her father gave her."

Or so he said, Kerry thought. She got up. "Mr. Arnott, do you think Skip Reardon killed Suzanne?"

He rose to his feet. "Ms. McGrath, I consider myself very knowledgeable about antiques. I'm less good at judging people. But isn't it true that love and money are the two greatest reasons to kill? I'm sorry, but in this case both seem to apply to Skip."

FROM a window Jason watched Kerry's car disappear down the driveway. Thinking over their brief exchange, he felt he had been sufficiently detailed to seem helpful, sufficiently vague so that she, like both the prosecution and defense ten years ago, would decide there was no purpose in questioning him further.

Do I think Skip Reardon killed Suzanne? No, I don't, Ms. McGrath, he thought. I think that, like far too many men, Skip might have been *capable* of murdering his wife. Only that night someone else beat him to it.

SKIP Reardon had endured what was arguably one of the worst weeks of his life. Ever since Geoff had told him that Assistant Prosecutor Kerry McGrath was no longer interested in his case, it was as though a Greek chorus were chanting endlessly inside his head, "Twenty more years. Twenty more years." All week, instead of reading or watching television at night, Skip had stared at the framed pictures on the walls of his cell.

Beth was in most of them. He had made up his mind. He would not let Beth visit him anymore. She had to get on with her life, he reasoned. She'd be forty her next birthday. She should meet someone else, get married, have kids. She loved children. There was something else that Skip decided: He wasn't going to waste any more time designing houses with the dream that someday he would get to build

101

them. By the time he got out of prison—if he ever did get out—he would be in his sixties. It would be too late to start again.

That was why on Saturday morning, when Geoff called and told him that Kerry McGrath was coming down to see him as well as his mother and Beth, the news angered him. "What does McGrath want to do, Geoff?" he asked. "Show Mom and Beth exactly why they're wasting their time trying to get me out of here?"

"Shut up, Skip," Geoff snapped. "Kerry's interest in you and this murder case is causing her a hell of a lot of trouble, including a threat to her ten-year-old daughter if she doesn't pull out."

"A threat? Who?" Skip looked at the receiver he was holding as though it had suddenly become an alien object. It was impossible to comprehend that Kerry McGrath's daughter had been threatened because of him.

"We're sure Jimmy Weeks is the 'who.' For some reason he's afraid to have the investigation reopened. Now listen, Kerry wants to go over every inch of this case with you and with your mother and Beth. This is the best chance we have had of getting you out. It may also be the last."

Skip heard the click in his ear. In spite of himself, the flicker of hope he thought he had extinguished jumped back to life.

GEOFF picked up Kerry and Robin at one o'clock. When they reached Essex Fells, he brought them into the house and introduced them around. At the end of the family dinner the night before, he had explained to the adults the circumstances of his bringing Robin for a visit. Immediately his mother's instincts had zeroed in on the fact that the woman Geoff insisted on calling "Robin's mother" might have special significance for her son.

Now he detected the approval in his mother's eyes as she took in Kerry's appearance. Kerry was wearing a belted camel-hair coat over matching slacks. A hunter-green turtleneck sweater accentuated the green tones in her hazel eyes. Her hair was brushed loosely over her collar.

Robin was delighted to hear that all nine grandchildren were somewhere in the house. She watched as the two-year-old twins, chased by their four-year-old cousin, pell-melled past them. "Sort of like baby rush hour around here," she observed happily. "See you later, Mom."

In the car, Kerry leaned back against the seat and sighed deeply. "You're not worried, are you?" Geoff asked quickly.

"No, not at all. That was an expression of relief. And now let me fill you in on what I didn't tell you before."

"Like what?"

"Like Suzanne's years growing up. Like what Dr. Smith is up to with one of the patients he's given Suzanne's face to. And like what I learned from Jason Arnott this morning."

Deidre Reardon and Beth Taylor were already in the visitors reception room when Geoff and Kerry arrived at the prison. While they waited to be called, Kerry chatted with Beth, whom she liked immediately.

Promptly at three o'clock they were led to the area where family members and friends were allowed contact visits with the prisoners. It was more crowded today than it had been when Kerry last visited. When Skip was escorted in and his handcuffs removed, Beth held back while Deidre hugged her son. Then Kerry watched as Beth and Skip looked at each other. The expressions on their faces and the restraint of their kiss told more of what was between them than would have the most ardent embrace. Kerry vividly remembered that day in court when she had seen the agony on Skip's face as he was sentenced to a minimum of thirty years, and had listened to his heartrending protest that Dr. Smith was a liar. Thinking back on it, she realized that she had felt she heard the ring of truth in Skip Reardon's voice that day.

Kerry had brought a yellow pad on which she had written a series of questions. Briefly she told them everything that had impelled her to make this second visit: Dolly Bowles's story about the Mercedes the night Suzanne died; the fact that Suzanne had been extremely plain growing up; Dr. Smith's bizarre re-creation of her face when operating on current patients; Smith's attraction to Barbara Tompkins; the fact that Jimmy Weeks's name had come up in the investigation; and, finally, the threat to Robin.

Kerry felt that it was a credit to the three of them that after their initial shock over hearing the disclosures, they did not waste time reacting among themselves. Beth Taylor reached for Skip's hand as she asked Kerry, "What can we do now?"

"First, let's clear the air by saying I now have grave doubts whether Skip is guilty, and I'll do my best to help Geoff get the verdict reversed. A week ago, Skip, you surmised after we talked that I didn't believe you. That really isn't accurate. What I thought was that there was nothing I had heard for you or against you—nothing that would provide grounds for a new appeal. Dr. Smith's testimony is the main reason you were convicted, Skip. The one great hope is to discredit that testimony. And the only way I can see to do that is to back him into a corner by confronting him with some of his lies."

For the remainder of the visit Kerry fired questions at them. "Skip, did Suzanne ever mention Jimmy Weeks?"

"Only casually," he said. "I knew he was a member of the club and that she sometimes played golf with him."

"Isn't Weeks the man on trial for income tax evasion?" Deidre Reardon asked.

Kerry nodded, then turned to Skip. "I want you to describe the jewelry you believe Suzanne received from another man."

"One piece was a gold bracelet with zodiac figures. The Capricorn symbol, encrusted with diamonds, was the centerpiece. Suzanne was a Capricorn. It was obviously very expensive. She told me her father had given it to her, but when I thanked him for his generosity to her, he didn't know what I was talking about."

"That's the kind of item we might be able to trace. We can put out a flyer to jewelers in New Jersey for openers," Kerry said.

Skip told her about an emerald-and-diamond ring that looked like a wedding band.

"Another one she claimed her father gave her?"

"Yes. Her story was that he was making up for the years he hadn't given her anything. She said that some of the pieces were family

jewelry from his mother. That was easier to believe. She also had a flower-shaped diamond pin that was obviously very old."

"I remember that one," Deidre Reardon said. "It had a smaller bud-shaped pin attached to it by a silver chain. I still have a picture I cut out of one of the local papers showing Suzanne wearing it at some fund-raiser. Another heirloom-type piece was the diamond bracelet Suzanne was wearing when she died, Skip."

"Where was Suzanne's jewelry that night?" Kerry asked.

"Except for what she was wearing, in her jewelry case on top of her dressing table," Skip said.

"Skip, according to your testimony, several items were missing from your bedroom that night."

"Two that I'm positive of. One was the flower pin. And I can swear that a miniature frame that was on the night table was gone."

"Describe it to me," Kerry said.

"Let me, Skip," Deidre Reardon interrupted. "You see, Kerry, that little frame was exquisite, a blue enamel oval with a gold border that was encrusted with pearls. It was reputed to be a Fabergé. My husband bought it in Germany after the war. It was my wedding present to Skip and Suzanne."

"Suzanne put a picture of herself in it," Skip explained.

"When did you last see that frame, Skip?" Kerry asked.

"It was there that last morning when I got dressed. That night, when the detectives told me they were taking me in for questioning, one of them came up to the bedroom with me while I got a sweater. The frame was gone."

"If Suzanne was involved with someone else, is it possible she gave that picture of herself to someone that day?"

"No," Skip said. "It was one of her best pictures, and she liked looking at it. And I don't think even she would have had the guts to give my mother's wedding present away."

"And it never showed up?" Kerry asked.

"Never. But when I tried to say it might have been stolen, the prosecutor argued that if a thief had been there, all that jewelry would have been gone."

The bell signaled the end of visiting hours. When Skip got up, he put one arm around his mother, the other around Beth, and drew them to him. Over their heads he looked at Kerry and Geoff and smiled. "Kerry, you find a way to get me out of this place, and I'll build a house for you that you'll never want to leave for the rest of your life." Then he laughed. "In this place I can't believe I said that."

Across the room convict Will Toth was sitting with his girlfriend, but he gave most of his attention to the group with Skip Reardon. Last week he had recognized Kerry McGrath when she visited Skip. He would know her anywhere—McGrath was the reason he was in this hellhole. She had been the prosecutor at his trial.

As Will kissed his girlfriend good-bye, he whispered, "Call your brother as soon as you get home and tell him to pass the word that McGrath was down here again today and taking lots of notes."

Si Morgan, senior FBI agent in charge of investigating the Hamilton theft, was in his office on Saturday afternoon going over a computer printout. He had asked the Hamiltons, along with burglary victims in similar cases, to furnish names of all guests who attended any gathering at their homes during the several months before they were victimized. The computer had created an alphabetized list of about a dozen names that appeared frequently. The first one was Arnott, Jason.

Nothing there, Si thought. Arnott had been quietly investigated a couple of years ago and passed as clean. Maybe it wouldn't hurt to run a check on him again. But Morgan was more interested in another name, Sheldon Landi, who had his own public relations firm. Landi certainly rubs shoulders with the beautiful people, Si mused. He doesn't make much money, yet he lives high.

The FBI had sent out six hundred flyers with the security-camera photo to the names culled from the guest lists. So far they had received thirty tips, one of them from a woman who thought the culprit might be her ex-husband. "He robbed me blind the whole time we were married, and he has that kind of pointy chin I see in the picture," she'd explained.

Now, as he leaned back in his chair, Si thought about that call and smiled. The woman's ex-husband was a United States Senator.

15

*K*ERRY and Robin were on their way to Jonathan and Grace
Hoover's for Sunday dinner.

Sunday is such a family day, Kerry reflected as she drove. Robin
and I are darn lucky to have Jonathan and Grace.

Robin interrupted her thoughts. "Mom, Geoff's mother thinks
he likes you. So do I. We talked about it."

"You what?"

"We talked about it. Mrs. Dorso said that Geoff never, ever
brings a date home. She told me you're the first since his prom
days. She said that it was because his little sisters used to play tricks
on his dates and that now he's gun-shy."

"Probably," Kerry said offhandedly. She turned her mind from
the realization that coming back from the prison, she had been so
weary that she had closed her eyes for just a minute and awakened
later, resting against Geoff's shoulder. And that it had felt so natural, so right.

THE visit with Grace and Jonathan Hoover was, as expected,
thoroughly agreeable. Kerry knew that at some point they would
get around to discussing the Reardon case, but it wouldn't be
before coffee was served. That was when Robin was free to leave
the table to read or try one of the new computer games Jonathan
always had waiting for her.

As they ate, Jonathan entertained them with talk about the legis-
lative sessions and the budget the governor was trying to get
through. "You see, Robin," he explained, "politics is like a football
game. The governor is the coach, and the leaders of his party in the
senate and the assembly are the quarterbacks."

"That's you, isn't it?" Robin interrupted.

"Yes, I guess you could call me that," Jonathan agreed.

Kerry smiled. "Robin, I hope you realize how lucky you are to be learning the workings of government from someone like Uncle Jonathan."

"All very selfish," Jonathan assured them. "By the time Kerry is sworn in for the Supreme Court in Washington, we'll be getting Robin elected to the legislature and have her on her way too."

Here it comes, Kerry thought. "Rob, if you're finished, you can see what's up with the computer."

"There's something there you'll like, Robin," Jonathan told her.

The housekeeper was going around with the coffeepot. From here on, it's all going downhill, Kerry thought.

She did not wait for Jonathan to ask about the Reardon case. Instead she presented everything to him and Grace exactly as she knew it, and concluded by saying, "It's clear Dr. Smith was lying on the stand. It's also clear that Jimmy Weeks has some very important reason not to want that case reopened. Otherwise why would he or his people be involving Robin?"

"Bob Kinellen actually threatened that something could happen to Robin?" Grace's tone was icy with contempt.

"Warned is the better word, I think." Kerry turned, appealing to Jonathan. "Look, you must understand that I don't want to upset anything for Frank Green. And Jonathan, dammit, I want to be a judge. I know I can be a good one. But what kind of judge would I make if, as a prosecutor, I turned my back on something that more and more appears to be a flagrant miscarriage of justice?"

"I suppose we do what we must," Grace said quietly.

"I'm not trying to ride a horse down Main Street and wave to the crowd. If something is wrong, I'd like to find out what it is and then let Geoff Dorso carry the ball. I'm going to see Dr. Smith tomorrow. The key is to discredit his testimony. I frankly think he's on the verge of a breakdown. Stalking someone is a crime. If I can push him enough to get him to admit that he lied, that he didn't give Suzanne that jewelry, that someone else may well have been involved, then we've got a new ball game. Geoff Dorso can file a motion for a new trial. By then Frank could be governor."

"But you, my dear, may not be a member of the judiciary," Jonathan said. "You're very persuasive, Kerry, and I admire you even while I worry about what this may cost you. First and fore-most, though, is Robin. You must take the threat to her seriously."

"I do, Jonathan. She won't be left alone for a minute."

"Kerry, anytime you feel your house isn't safe, leave her here," Grace urged. "Our security is excellent."

Kerry put her hand over Grace's fingers and gave them a hint of a squeeze. "I love you two," she said simply. "Jonathan, please don't be disappointed that I have to do this."

"I'm proud of you, I guess," Jonathan said. "I'll do my best to keep your name in for the appointment, but . . ."

"But don't count on it. I know," Kerry said slowly. "Goodness, choices can be pretty tough, can't they?"

"I think we'd better change the subject," Jonathan said briskly. "But keep me posted, Kerry."

16

Monday
November 6th

THE sequestered jury in the Jimmy Weeks trial did not know about the assassination of Barney Haskell and Mark Young, but the media were making sure that everyone else did.

A frightened witness, whose identity was not revealed, had finally phoned the police. He had been on his way to withdraw cash from an ATM and had seen a dark blue Toyota pull into the parking lot of the small building that housed Mark Young's law office. That was at ten after seven. The front right tire of the witness's car had felt wobbly, and he had pulled over to the curb to examine it. He was crouched beside it when he saw the door of the office building open again and a man run back to the Toyota. His face was obscured, but he was carrying what appeared to be an oversized gun. The witness got part of the Toyota's out-of-state license number. Good police work tracked the car down and identified it as one that had been stolen Thursday night in Philadelphia. Late Friday its burned-out frame was found in Newark.

In light of that evidence, it was obviously a Mob hit, and no doubt ordered by Jimmy Weeks. But the police were unsure how to prove it. The witness could not identify the gunman. The car was gone. The gun was undoubtedly now at the bottom of a river.

ON MONDAY morning Grace Hoover stayed in bed longer than usual. Even though the house was comfortably warm, the winter cold somehow found its way into her bones and joints. Her hands and fingers and legs and knees and ankles ached fiercely.

Years ago, at the onset of her illness, Grace had decided she would never succumb to self-pity. Even so, on her darkest days she admitted to herself that besides the constantly increasing pain, it had been devastating to have to lessen her activities. She had been one of the few wives who actually enjoyed going to the many affairs that a politician such as Jonathan had to attend. She relished the adulation Jonathan received. She was so proud of him. He should have been governor. She knew that.

She had enjoyed going to the country club for dinner the other night. It was the first time in many weeks that she had been out. But that Jason Arnott—isn't it funny that I can't get him out of my mind? she thought. She had asked Jonathan about him again, but he could reason only that possibly she had been at some fund-raiser Arnott may have attended.

It had been a dozen years since Grace went to any of those big events. By then she had been on two canes and disliked jostling crowds. No, it was something else that triggered her memory of him. Oh, well, she said to herself, it will come in time.

The housekeeper, Carrie, came into the bedroom with a tray. "I thought you'd be ready for a second cup of tea around now," she said cheerfully.

"I am, Carrie. Thanks."

Carrie laid down the tray and propped up the pillows. "There. That's better." She reached into her pocket and pulled out a folded sheet of paper. "Oh, Mrs. Hoover, this was in the wastebasket in the senator's study. I know he was throwing it away, but I still want to ask if it's all right if I take it. All my grandson talks about is being an FBI agent. He'd get such a kick out of seeing a genuine flyer they sent out." She unfolded it and handed it to Grace.

Grace glanced at it and started to hand it back, then stopped. Jonathan had shown this to her on Friday afternoon, joking, "Anyone you know?" The covering letter explained that the flyer was being sent to anyone who had been a guest in homes that were burglarized shortly afterward. The grainy, almost indistinguishable picture was of a felon in the process of committing a robbery. He was believed to be responsible for many similar break-ins, almost all of them following a party or social function of some kind. One theory was that he might have been a guest.

"I know the Peales' Washington home was broken into a few years ago," Jonathan had said. "Terrible business. I had been there to Jock's victory party. Two weeks later his mother came home early and must have walked in on the thief. She was found at the bottom of the staircase with a broken neck, and the John White Alexander painting was missing."

Maybe it was because I know the Peales that I paid so much attention to this picture, Grace thought as she gripped the flyer. The camera must have been below him, the way his face is angled.

She studied the blurry image—the narrow neck, sharp-tipped nose, pursed lips. It wasn't what you'd notice when you look directly at someone's face, she thought. But when you're looking up at him from a wheelchair, you see him from this angle.

I would swear this looks like that man I met at the club the other night, Jason Arnott, Grace thought. Was it possible?

"Carrie, I'd like to keep this for a bit. Would you hand me the phone, please?" A moment later Grace was speaking to Amanda Coble, who had introduced her to Jason Arnott at the club. She confessed that she was still plagued by the impression that she had met him before. Where did he live? she asked. What did he do?

When she hung up, Grace sipped the now cooling tea and studied the picture again. According to Amanda, Arnott was an art and antiques expert, and he traveled in the best social circles from Washington to Newport.

Grace called Jonathan in his Trenton office. She told him she believed Jason Arnott was the burglar the FBI was looking for.

"That's quite an accusation, dear," Jonathan said cautiously.

"I've got good eyes, Jonathan. You know that."

"Yes, I do," he agreed quietly. "And frankly, if it were anyone other than you, I would hesitate to pass the name along to the FBI. I don't want to put anything in writing, but give me the confidential number on that flyer. I'll make a phone call."

"No," Grace said. "As long as you agree that it's all right to speak to the FBI, I'll make the call. If I'm dead wrong, you're not connected to it. If I'm right, I get to feel that I've done something useful again. I very much liked Jock Peale's mother when I met her years ago. I'd love to be the one who found her killer. No one should be allowed to get away with murder."

DR. CHARLES Smith was in a very bad mood. He had spent a solitary weekend, made more frustratingly lonely by the fact that he could not reach Barbara Tompkins. Saturday had been such a beautiful day, he thought she might enjoy a drive along the Hudson. He got her answering machine, however, and she did not return his call. Sunday was no better.

On Monday morning he tried Barbara at the office and was told she was on a two-week business trip to California. Now he really was upset. He knew that was a lie. At dinner on Thursday, Barbara had mentioned something about looking forward to a business lunch at La Grenouille this Wednesday.

For the rest of Monday, Smith found it difficult to concentrate on his patients. Not that his schedule was very busy. He seemed to have fewer and fewer patients, and those who came in for initial consultation seldom came back. Not that he really cared—so few of them had the potential for genuine beauty. When his three-thirty appointment canceled, he decided to go home early. He would get the car and drive up to Barbara's office. She usually left a few minutes after five, but he wanted to be there early just in case. The thought that she might be deliberately evading him was intolerable. If that was true . . .

He was just stepping from his office-building lobby onto Fifth Avenue when he saw Kerry McGrath approaching.

"Dr. Smith, I'm glad I caught you," Kerry said. "It's very important that I speak to you."

"Ms. McGrath, Mrs. Carpenter and the receptionist are still in the office. Any assistance you require can be handled by them." He tried to walk past her.

She fell into step beside him. "Dr. Smith, neither of them is responsible for putting an innocent man in prison."

Charles Smith reacted as though she had thrown hot tar on him. "How dare you!" He stopped and grabbed her arm.

Kerry realized suddenly that he was about to strike her. His face was contorted with fury. A man passing by looked at them curiously and stopped. "Are you all right, miss?" he asked.

"Am I all right, Doctor?" Kerry asked, her voice calm.

Smith released her arm. "Of course. Of course." He started to walk quickly down Fifth Avenue.

Kerry kept stride with him. "Dr. Smith, you will have to talk to me eventually. It would be much better to hear me out now, before some very unpleasant situation occurs."

He did not respond.

She stayed next to him. She realized his breathing was rapid. "Dr. Smith, I don't care how fast you walk. I can outrun you. Shall we go back to your office, or is there someplace we could get a cup of coffee? We have got to talk. Otherwise I'm afraid you're going to be arrested and charged with being a stalker."

"Charged . . . with . . . what?" Again Smith whirled to face her.

"You have frightened Barbara Tompkins with your attention. Did you frighten Suzanne as well, Doctor? You were there the night she died, weren't you? Two people saw a black Mercedes in front of the house. One remembered part of the license plate—a 3 and an L. Today I learned that your license plate has an 8 and an L. Close enough, I would say. Now, where shall we talk?"

He continued to stare at her for several moments, anger still flaring in his eyes. She watched as resignation gradually took its place. "I live down this street," he said, no longer looking at her. They were near the corner, and he pointed to the left.

Kerry took the words as an invitation. Am I making a mistake going inside with him? she wondered. But she decided she might not get this chance again.

At number 28 Washington Mews, Smith reached for his key and with a precise gesture inserted it in the lock, turned it and pushed the door open. "Come in if you insist, Ms. McGrath," he said.

THE tips continued to filter in to the FBI from people who had been guests at one or more of the various burglarized homes. They now had twelve potential leads, but Si Morgan thought he had struck gold when on Monday afternoon his chief suspect, Sheldon Landi, admitted that his public relations firm was a cover for his real activity.

Landi had been invited in for questioning, and for a brief moment Si thought he was about to hear a confession. Then Landi, his hands twisting together, whispered, "Have you ever read *Tell All?*"

"That's a supermarket tabloid, isn't it?" Si asked.

"Yes. One of the biggest." Landi's voice dropped as he said, "This must not go beyond this room, but I'm its chief writer. If it ever gets out, I'll be dropped by all my friends."

So much for that, Si thought, after Landi left. That little gossip-monger wouldn't have the guts to pull off any of those jobs.

At quarter of four one of the three investigators working on the Hamilton case came in. "Si, there's someone on the Hamilton case confidential line I think you should talk to. Her name is Grace Hoover. Her husband is New Jersey state senator Hoover, and she thinks she saw the guy we're looking for. It's one of the birds whose name has come up before—Jason Arnott."

"Arnott!" Si grabbed the phone. "Mrs. Hoover, I'm Si Morgan."

As he listened, he decided that Grace Hoover was the kind of witness lawmen pray to find. She was logical and articulate in explaining how, looking up from her wheelchair, her eyes were probably at the same angle as the lens of the surveillance camera in the Hamilton house.

"Looking straight at Mr. Arnott, you would think his face was fuller than it appears when you're looking up at him," she explained. "Also, when I asked him if we knew each other, his lips pursed together tightly. I think it may be a habit he has when he's concentrating. Notice how they're scrunched in your picture. My feeling is that when the camera caught him, he was concentrating on that statuette. Deciding whether or not it was genuine. My friend tells me he's quite an expert on antiques."

"Yes, he is." Si Morgan was excited. "Mrs. Hoover, I can't tell you how much I appreciate this call."

When Si hung up, he sent for his three investigators. He told them he wanted Arnott followed round the clock. Judging from the investigation they had made of him two years ago, if he was the thief, he had done an excellent job of concealing his tracks. It would be better to trail him for a while. He might just lead them to where he was keeping stolen property.

"If this isn't another red herring and we can get proof he's committed the burglaries," Si said, "our next job will be to nail the Peale murder on him. The boss wants that one solved big-time. The President's mother used to play bridge with Mrs. Peale."

DR. SMITH's study was clean but shabby, Kerry noticed. The ivory silk lampshades, the kind she remembered from her grandmother's house, were darkened with age. One of them had been scorched. To Kerry the room seemed frozen in time.

She slipped off her coat, but Dr. Smith did not attempt to take it from her. She draped it on the arm of a chair and sat down.

Smith sat rigidly erect in a high-backed chair opposite her. "What do you want, Ms. McGrath?" The rimless glasses enlarged eyes that chilled with their hostile probing.

"I want the truth," Kerry said evenly. "I want to know why you claimed you gave Suzanne jewelry that, in fact, was given to her by another man. I want to know why you lied about Skip Reardon. He never threatened Suzanne. What possible reason would you have for swearing that he did?"

"Skip Reardon killed my daughter. He strangled her so viciously that her eyes hemorrhaged, her tongue hung out of her mouth like a dumb animal's. . . ." His voice trailed off. What had started as an angry outburst ended almost as a sob.

116

"I realize how painful it must have been for you to examine those pictures, Dr. Smith." Kerry spoke softly. "But why have you always blamed Skip for the tragedy?"

"He was her husband. He was insanely jealous. It was clear to everyone."

"Doctor, you are wrong. Skip was not jealous of Suzanne. He did know she was seeing someone else." Kerry waited. "But so was he."

Smith's head jerked as though she had slapped him. "That's impossible. He was married to an exquisite woman, and he worshipped her."

"*You* worshipped her, Doctor." Kerry hadn't expected to say that, but when she did, she knew it was true. "You put yourself in his position, didn't you? If you had been Suzanne's husband and had found out she was involved with another man, you'd have been capable of murder, wouldn't you?" She stared at him.

He did not blink. "How dare you! Suzanne was my daughter!" he said coldly. "Now get out of here." He stood and moved toward Kerry as though he might grab her to throw her out.

Kerry jumped up, clutching her coat, and stepped back. With a glance she checked to see that, if necessary, she could get around him to the front door. "No, Doctor," she said, "*Susie Stevens* was your daughter. *Suzanne* was your creation. And you felt you owned her, just as you believe you own Barbara Tompkins. Doctor, you were in Alpine the night Suzanne died. Did you kill her?"

"Kill Suzanne? Are you crazy?"

"But you were there."

"I was not!"

"Oh, yes you were, and we're going to prove it. We're going to reopen the case and get the innocent man you condemned out of prison. You were jealous of him, Dr. Smith. You punished him because he had constant access to Suzanne and you didn't."

"That's not true." The words escaped through clenched teeth.

Kerry saw that Smith's hand was trembling violently. She lowered her voice, took a more conciliatory tone. "Dr. Smith, if you didn't kill your daughter, someone else surely did. But it wasn't Skip Reardon. I believe you loved Suzanne in your own way. I

117

believe you wanted her murderer to be punished. But do you know what you've done? You've given Suzanne's killer a free ride. He's out there singing your praises for covering up for him. If we had the jewelry Skip is sure you didn't give Suzanne, we could try to trace it, try to find out who did give it to her. Skip is certain that at least one piece is missing and may have been taken that night."

"He's lying."

"No, he isn't. And something else was stolen that night—a picture of Suzanne in a miniature frame. It had been on her night table. Did you take it?"

"I was not in that house the night Suzanne died!"

"Then who borrowed your Mercedes that night?"

Smith's "Get out!" was a guttural howl.

Kerry knew she had better not stay any longer. She circled around him but at the door turned to him again. "Dr. Smith, Barbara Tompkins spoke to me. She is alarmed. She moved up a business trip solely to get away from you. When she returns, I'm going to personally escort her to the police to lodge a complaint against you."

She opened the door to the old carriage house, and a blast of cold air swept into the foyer. "Unless," she added, "you come to terms with the fact that you need help. And unless you satisfy me that you have told the truth about what happened the night Suzanne died. And unless you give me the jewelry you suspect may have been given to her by a man other than you or her husband."

As KERRY thrust her hands into her pockets for the three-block walk to her car, she was aware neither of Smith's probing eyes studying her from behind the study window nor of the stranger parked on Fifth Avenue who picked up his cellular phone and called in a report of her visit in Washington Mews.

U.S. ATTORNEY Brandon Royce, in cooperation with the Middlesex and Ocean County prosecutor's offices, obtained a search warrant for both the permanent residence and the summer home of the late Barney Haskell. Living apart from his wife most of the

time, Barney resided in a pleasant split-level house in Edison. His neighbors there said Barney had never bothered with any of them but was always polite if they met face to face.

His other home, a modern two-story structure overlooking the ocean on Long Beach island, was where his wife resided year-round. Neighbors there told investigators that during the summer Barney was around a lot. He spent a good amount of time fishing on his twenty-three-foot Chris-Craft. His other hobby was carpentry. A couple of neighbors said his wife had invited them in to show off the massive white-oak hutch Barney had made to house their entertainment center last year. It seemed to be his pride and joy.

The investigators knew that Barney had to have had solid evidence against Jimmy Weeks to back up his attempted plea bargain. They also knew that if they didn't find it quickly, Jimmy's people would ferret it out and destroy it.

Despite the protests of Barney's widow, who cried that this was her home and that they had no right to destroy it, they took apart everything, including the oak hutch that was nailed to the wall of the television room. When they had ripped the wood from the plaster, they found a large safe.

As the media gathered outside, television cameras recorded the arrival of a retired safecracker now on the payroll of the U.S. government. Fifteen minutes later the safe was opened, and shortly afterward, at four fifteen that afternoon, U.S. Attorney Royce received a call from chief investigator Les Howard.

A second set of books for Weeks Enterprises had been found, as well as datebooks going back fifteen years, in which Barney had chronicled Jimmy's appointments along with his own notations. There were also shoe boxes with copies of receipts for high-tag items, including jewelry for Jimmy's various girlfriends, which Barney had flagged "No sales tax paid."

"It's a bonanza, a treasure trove," Howard assured Royce. "Barney must have been preparing since day one to barter his way out of prison by throwing Jimmy to us if they ever got indicted."

After Royce hung up the phone, he savored the splendid news. "Thanks, Barney," he said aloud. "I knew you'd come through."

JASON ARNOTT HAD AWAKENED late on Sunday morning with flulike symptoms and decided not to go to the Catskill house as planned. Instead he spent the day in bed, getting up only long enough to prepare some light food for himself. He brought books and newspapers to his room and spent the day reading, in between sipping orange juice and dozing. Every few hours, however, he compulsively pulled out the FBI flyer to reassure himself that no one could possibly tie him to that grainy caricature of a picture.

By Monday evening he was feeling much better and had completely convinced himself that the flyer was not a threat. There was no question. He was safe. He promised himself that tomorrow or Wednesday he would drive up to the Catskills and spend a few days enjoying his treasures.

Jason could not know that FBI agents had already obtained a court order allowing them to tap his phone and were now quietly surveilling his house. From now on he wouldn't make a single move without being observed and without being followed.

MONDAY night, when Kerry got home, she found Alison gone and Geoff and Robin in the kitchen. "I thought you might be game for a Dorso home-cooked meal," Geoff said. "Very simple menu: lamb chops, a salad and baked potato."

Kerry realized she was both tense and hungry. "Sounds wonderful," she sighed as she unbuttoned her coat.

Geoff quickly moved to take it from her. It seemed natural that as he put it over one arm, he slid the other arm around her and kissed her cheek. "Hard day at the factory?"

For a brief moment she let her face rest in the warm spot beneath his neck. "There have been easier ones."

Robin said, "Mom, I'm going upstairs to finish my homework, but I do think since I'm the one in danger, I should know exactly what's going on. What did Dr. Smith say when you saw him?"

"Finish your homework. I promise a full report later."

"Okay."

Geoff had turned on the gas fire in the family room. He had brought in sherry and had glasses ready alongside the bottle on the coffee table there. "I hope I'm not making myself too much at home," he apologized.

Kerry sank onto the couch and kicked off her shoes. She shook her head and smiled. "No, you're not."

"Tell me about Smith."

"I got to him, Geoff. I know I did. The guy is cracking up. If he doesn't start telling the truth, my next move is to get Barbara Tompkins to file a stalking complaint against him. The prospect of that shocked him, I could tell. I think rather than risk having that happen, he'll come through and we'll get some answers."

She stared into the fire, watching the flames lick at the artificial logs. Then she added slowly, "I told Smith that maybe the reason he was so anxious to see Skip convicted was because *he* was the one who killed Suzanne. Geoff, I think he was in love with her, not as a daughter, maybe not even as a woman, but as his *creation*."

She turned to him. "Think about this scenario. On the evening of the murder, Dr. Smith drives out to see Suzanne. Skip has come and gone, just as he claimed. Suzanne is in the foyer arranging flowers from another man. Don't forget, the card was never found. Smith is angry, hurt and jealous. It isn't just Skip he has to contend with; now it's Jimmy Weeks as well. In a fit of rage he strangles Suzanne, and because he's always hated Skip, he takes the card and makes up the story of Suzanne being afraid of Skip."

"It makes sense," Geoff said slowly. "But then why would Jimmy Weeks be so worried about your reopening the case?"

"I've thought about that. And, in fact, you could make the argument that he was involved with Suzanne. That they quarreled that night, and he murdered her."

"You've made a damn good case for either scenario," Geoff said. "Did you happen to listen to the news on the way home?"

"My brain needed a rest. I listened to the golden oldies."

"You made a better choice. But if you had listened to a news station, you'd know that the stuff Barney Haskell was planning to swap for a plea bargain is now in the U.S. Attorney's hands. Apparently Barney kept records like nobody else. Tomorrow, if Frank Green is smart, instead of resisting your investigation, he'll request access to any records they can find of jewelry Weeks bought in the months before Suzanne's murder. If we can tie him to stuff like the zodiac bracelet, we've got proof Smith was a liar." He stood up. "I would say, Kerry McGrath, that you have sung for your supper. Wait here. I'll let you know when it's ready."

GEOFF left at nine o'clock. When the door closed behind him, Robin said, "Mom, this guy Dad is defending? From what you tell me, Dad's not going to win the case. Will that be bad for him?"

"No one likes to lose a case, but no. I think the best thing that could ever happen to your father is to see Jimmy Weeks convicted."

"You're sure Weeks is the one who's trying to scare me?"

"Yes, I'm about as sure as I can get. That's why the sooner we can find out his connection to Suzanne Reardon, the sooner he won't have any reasons to try to scare us off."

"Geoff's a defense attorney, isn't he?"

"Yes, he is."

"Would Geoff ever defend a guy like Jimmy Weeks?"

"No, Robin. I'm pretty sure he wouldn't."

"I don't think he would either."

At nine thirty Kerry remembered that she'd promised to report to Jonathan and Grace about her meeting with Dr. Smith. "You think he may break down and admit he lied?" Jonathan asked when she reached him.

"I think so."

Grace was on the other extension. "Let's tell Kerry my news, Jonathan. Kerry, today I've either been a good detective or made an awful fool of myself."

Kerry had not thought it important to bring up Arnott's name on Sunday when she told Jonathan and Grace about Dr. Smith and Jimmy Weeks. When she heard what Grace had to say about Arnott, she was glad that neither one of them could see the expression on her face. Jason Arnott—Suzanne Reardon's friend. If he was a thief, and if, according to the FBI flyer Grace described, he was also a murder suspect, where did he fit in the conundrum surrounding the Sweetheart Murder Case?

123

DR. CHARLES SMITH SAT FOR long hours after he had forced Kerry to leave. *Stalker! Murderer! Liar!* The accusations she had thrown at him made him shudder with revulsion. It was the same revulsion he felt when he looked at a maimed or ugly face. He could feel his very being tremble with the need to change it, to redeem it.

Stalker! To call him a stalker because a brief glimpse of the near perfection he had created gave him pleasure! And did she really think he could have murdered Suzanne? Burning misery raced through him as he lived again the moment when he had found Suzanne in the foyer. Suzanne—but not Suzanne. That distorted creature with bulging, hemorrhaged eyes and protruding tongue—that was not the exquisite creature he had created. Even her body appeared awkward and unlovely, crumpled as it was, the left leg twisted under the right one, those fresh red roses scattered over her, a mocking tribute to death.

He remembered how he had cursed Suzanne because she had not heeded his warnings. She had married Reardon against his wishes. "Wait," he had urged her. "He's not good enough for you."

"In your eyes no one will ever be good enough for me," she had shouted back.

He had endured the way they looked at each other, the way their hands clasped across the table, the way they sat together, side by side, on the couch. To have to endure all that had been bad enough, but it was too much when Suzanne became restless and began seeing other men, none of them worthy of her, and then came to him, asking for favors, saying, "You must let Skip think you bought me this . . . and this . . . and this. . . ."

Or she would say, "Why are you so upset? You told me I should have all the good times I've missed. Well, I'm having them. Skip works too hard. He isn't fun."

Murderer? No, Skip was the murderer. As he stood over Suzanne's body, Smith had known exactly what had happened. Her loutish husband had come home to find her with flowers from another man, and he had exploded. Just as *I* would, Smith had thought, when his eye fell on the card half hidden by Suzanne's body.

And then, standing there over her, a whole scenario had played itself out in his mind. Skip, the jealous husband—a jury might be lenient with a man who killed his wife in a moment of passion. He might get off with a light sentence. Or maybe even no sentence at all. I won't let that happen, he had vowed. Smith remembered how he had closed his eyes, blotting out the distorted face in front of him and, instead, seeing Suzanne in all her beauty. Suzanne, I promise you that!

It had not been hard to keep the promise. All he had to do was take the card that had come with the flowers, then go home and wait for the inevitable call that would tell him that Suzanne, his daughter, was dead.

When the police had questioned him, he had told them that Skip was insanely jealous, that Suzanne feared for her life, and obeying the last request she made of him, he claimed he had given her all the pieces of jewelry that Skip had questioned.

No, let Ms. McGrath say all she might want. The murderer was in jail. And he would stay there.

It was almost ten o'clock when Charles Smith got up. It was all over. He couldn't operate anymore. He no longer wanted to see Barbara Tompkins. She disgusted him. He went into the bedroom, opened the small safe in the closet and took out a gun. It would be so easy. Where would he go? he wondered. He did believe that the spirit moves on. Reincarnation? Maybe. Maybe this time he would be born Suzanne's peer. Maybe they would fall in love. A smile played on his lips.

As he was about to close the safe, he looked at Suzanne's jewelry case. Suppose McGrath was right. Suppose it hadn't been Skip who had taken Suzanne's life. McGrath had said that person was laughing now, mockingly grateful for the testimony that had condemned Skip.

There was a way to rectify that. If Reardon was not the killer, then McGrath would have all that she needed to find the man who had murdered Suzanne.

Smith reached for the jewelry case, laid the gun on top of it and carried both to his desk in the study. Then with precise movements he took out a sheet of stationery and unscrewed the top from his pen. When he was finished writing, he wrapped the jewelry case and the note together and forced them into one of the Federal Express mailers he kept at home for convenience. He addressed the package to "Assistant Prosecutor Kerry McGrath, Bergen County Prosecutor's Office, Hackensack, New Jersey." Then he put on his coat and walked the eight blocks to the Federal Express drop.

It was just eleven o'clock when he returned home. He took off his coat, picked up the gun, went back into the bedroom and stretched out on the bed, still fully dressed. He turned off all the lights except the one that illuminated Suzanne's picture. He would end this day with her and begin the new life at the stroke of midnight. The decision made, he felt calm, even happy.

At eleven thirty the doorbell rang. Who? he wondered. Angrily he tried to ignore it, but a persistent finger was pressed against it. He was sure he knew what it was. Once there had been an accident on the corner, and a neighbor had run to him for help. After all, he was a doctor. If there had been an accident, just this one more time his skill might be put to use.

Dr. Charles Smith unlocked and opened his door, then slumped against it as a bullet found its mark between his eyes.

17

Tuesday
November 7th

O N TUESDAY morning Deidre Reardon and Beth Taylor were already in the reception room of Geoff Dorso's law office when he arrived at nine o'clock.

"Geoff, I'm so sorry to come without calling first," Beth said, "but Deidre has to go into the hospital for an angioplasty tomorrow morning. I know it will rest her mind if she has a chance to talk to you for a few minutes."

"Sure," Geoff said heartily. "Come back to my office. I'm sure the coffeepot's on."

"We will only stay five minutes," Beth promised as Geoff placed a coffee mug in front of her. "It's been a glimpse of heaven to think that finally there's real hope for Skip. And we are grateful for everything you are doing."

"Kerry saw Dr. Smith yesterday," Geoff said. "She thinks she got to him. But there are other developments as well." He told them about Barney Haskell's records. "We may at last have a chance to track the source of the jewelry we think Weeks gave Suzanne."

"That's one of the reasons we're here," Deidre Reardon told him. "Remember I said I had a picture that showed Suzanne wearing the missing antique diamond pin? With all the talk about the jewelry the other day, I felt it important for you to have it."

She handed him a manila envelope. From it he extracted a page from *Palisades Community Life,* a tabloid-size weekly paper. The group picture from the Palisades Country Club took up four columns. Geoff recognized Suzanne Reardon immediately. Her outstanding beauty leaped from the page. She was standing at a slight angle, and the camera had clearly caught the sparkling diamonds on the lapel of her jacket. "This is the double pin that disappeared," Deidre explained, pointing to it.

"I'm glad to have this," Geoff said. "When we get a copy of those records Haskell kept, we may be able to trace the pin."

It almost hurt to see the eager hope on both their faces. Don't let me fail them, he prayed as he walked them back to the reception room. At the door he hugged Deidre. "Now remember, you get this angioplasty over and start feeling better. We can't have you sick when they unlock the door for Skip."

"Geoff, I haven't walked barefoot through hell this long to check out now."

After having taken care of a number of client calls and queries, Geoff decided to call Kerry. Maybe she would want a fax of the picture Deidre had brought in. Or maybe I just want to talk to her, he admitted to himself.

When her secretary put her through, Kerry's frightened voice sent chills through Geoff. "I just opened a Federal Express package that Dr. Smith sent me. Inside was a note and Suzanne's jewelry case and the card that must have come with the sweetheart roses. He admits he lied about Skip and the jewelry. He said by the time I read this, he'll have committed suicide."

"My God, Kerry, did—"

"No. You see, he *didn't*. Geoff, Mrs. Carpenter from his office just called me. When Dr. Smith didn't come in for an early appointment and didn't answer the phone, she went to his house. She found his body lying in the foyer. He'd been shot and the house ransacked. Was someone looking for the jewelry? Geoff, who is doing this? Will Robin be next?"

JASON Arnott awoke at nine thirty Tuesday morning. Other than some residual achiness in his legs and back, he was over the bug that had laid him low over the weekend, and was looking forward to finally getting to his hideaway. He decided to call ahead. He enjoyed arriving there to find the heat on and the refrigerator stocked.

Inside what seemed to be a repair van of Public Service Electric and Gas, the signal came that Arnott was making a call. As the agents listened, they smiled triumphantly at each other. "I think we are about to trace the foxy Mr. Arnott to his lair," the senior agent on the job observed. They listened as Jason concluded the conversation by saying, "Thank you, Maddie. I should be there by one."

FRANK Green was trying a case, and it was noon before Kerry caught him in his office and was able to inform him of Smith's murder and the Federal Express packet she had received from him that morning. She was fully composed now, relieved by the knowledge that Joe Palumbo was parked outside Robin's school, waiting to escort her home.

Green went carefully through the contents of the jewelry box, comparing each piece with those Smith had mentioned in the letter he had included in the package to Kerry. "'Zodiac bracelet,'" he read. "That's right here. 'Emerald-and-diamond ring.' That's here. 'Antique diamond bracelet.'" He held it up. "That's a beauty."

"Yes. You may remember Suzanne was wearing it when she was murdered. There was one more piece, an antique diamond double pin that Skip Reardon had described. Dr. Smith doesn't mention it, and apparently he didn't have it, but Geoff just faxed me a picture from a local newspaper showing Suzanne wearing that pin. It never showed up in the items found at the house. You can see it's very much like the antique bracelet."

As Kerry looked closely at the blurred reproduction, it evoked a mother-and-child image. The pin was in two parts, Deidre had explained, the larger being a flower, the smaller a bud. They were attached by a chain. Kerry studied it for a moment, perplexed because it looked oddly familiar.

"We'll watch out for this pin to see if it is mentioned in Haskell's receipts," Green promised. "Now let's get this straight. Everything the doctor mentioned, excluding this particular pin, is the total of the jewelry Suzanne asked the doctor to tell Skip he gave her?"

"According to what Smith wrote in his letter, and it does coincide with what Skip Reardon told me."

Green put down Smith's letter. "Kerry, do you think you were followed when you went to see Smith yesterday?"

"I think now I probably was. That's why I'm so concerned about Robin's safety."

"We'll keep a squad car outside your house tonight, but I wouldn't be unhappy to have you and Robin in some more secure place with all this coming to a head. Jimmy Weeks is a cornered animal. They may be able to tie him to tax fraud, but with what you've uncovered, we may be able to tie him to a murder."

"You mean because of the card Jimmy sent with the roses?"

"Exactly. No clerk in a flower shop drew those musical notes. Imagine describing an inscription like that over the phone. From what I understand, Weeks is a pretty good amateur musician. With that card—and if the jewelry ties in to those receipts—the Reardon case is a whole new ball game."

"And if Skip is granted a new trial, he'll be entitled to release on bail pending that trial—or dismissal of the charges?"

"If the scenario plays out, I'll recommend that," Green agreed.

"But Frank," Kerry said, "there's a reason why the murder scenario may not play out, even if we can tie Jimmy Weeks to Suzanne." Kerry filled him in on Jason Arnott's connection to Suzanne and Grace Hoover's theory that he was a professional thief.

"Even if he is, are you tying him to Suzanne Reardon's murder?" Green asked.

"I'm not sure," Kerry said slowly. "It depends on whether or not he is involved in those thefts."

"Sit tight. We can get that flyer faxed in from the FBI right away." Green pressed the intercom. "We'll find out who's running the investigation."

Less than five minutes later his secretary brought in the flyer. Green pointed at the confidential number. "Tell them to put me through to the top guy on this."

Sixty seconds later Green was on the phone with Si Morgan. He turned on the speakerphone so Kerry could listen. "It's breaking now," Morgan said. "Arnott has another place, in the Catskills. We've decided to ring the doorbell and see if the housekeeper will talk to us. We'll keep you posted."

Kerry turned toward the detached voice coming out of the speakerphone. "Mr. Morgan, this is terribly important. If you can still contact your agent, ask him to inquire about a miniature oval picture frame. It's blue enamel surrounded with pearls. It may hold a picture of a beautiful dark-haired woman. If it's there, we'll be able to connect Jason Arnott to a murder case."

"I'll have my agent ask about it and get back to you."

"What was that about?" Green asked as he snapped off the speaker.

"Skip Reardon swears that a miniature frame disappeared from the master bedroom the day Suzanne died. That and the antique pin are the two things we can't account for." Kerry leaned over and picked up the picture of Suzanne wearing the antique pin. "Isn't it funny? I feel as though I've seen a pin like that before—I mean, the little one joined to the big one."

She put the picture down. "Jason Arnott spent a great deal of time with Suzanne, Frank. Let's say he fell for her too. He gave her the antique pin and the bracelet. It's exactly the kind of jewelry he would select. Then he realized that she was fooling around with Jimmy Weeks. Maybe he came in that night and saw the sweetheart roses and the card we believe Jimmy sent."

"You mean he killed her and took back the pin?"

"And her picture. From what Mrs. Reardon tells me, it's a beautiful frame."

"Why not the bracelet?"

"While I was waiting for you this morning, I looked at the pictures taken of the body before it was moved. Suzanne had a gold link bracelet on her left hand. You can see it in the picture. The diamond bracelet, which was on the other arm, doesn't show. I checked the records. It was pushed up on her arm under the sleeve of her blouse, so that it wasn't visible. She may have shoved it out of sight because she was aware her attacker had come to retrieve it. If so, it worked. He didn't find it."

While they waited for Morgan to call back, Green and Kerry worked together to prepare a flyer, with pictures of the jewelry in question, that would be distributed to New Jersey jewelers.

At one point Frank observed, "Kerry, do you realize that a tip from our state senator's wife may catch the murderer of Congressman Peale's mother? Then if Arnott is tied to the Reardon case . . ."

Frank Green, gubernatorial candidate, Kerry thought. He's already figuring how to sugarcoat having convicted an innocent man! Well, that's politics, I guess.

MADDIE Platt, Jason Arnott's housekeeper, was not aware of the car that followed her when she stopped at the market. Nor did she notice it following her to the rambling country house owned by the man she knew as Nigel Grey.

She let herself in and ten minutes later was startled when the doorbell rang. Nobody ever dropped in at this house. Furthermore, Mr. Grey had given her strict orders never to admit anyone. When she peeked out the side window, she saw a neatly dressed man standing on the top step. He saw her and held up a badge identifying him as an FBI agent. "FBI, ma'am. Would you please open the door so I can talk to you?"

Nervously Maddie opened the door. Now she stood inches from the badge showing the unmistakable FBI seal and identifying picture of the agent.

"Good afternoon, ma'am. I'm FBI agent Milton Rose. I don't mean to startle or upset you, but it's important that I speak with you about Mr. Jason Arnott. You're his housekeeper, aren't you?"

"Sir, I don't know any Mr. Arnott. This house is owned by Mr. Nigel Grey, and I've worked for him for many years. He's due here this afternoon; in fact, he should be here shortly. And I can tell you right now—I am under strict orders not to ever let anyone in this house without his permission."

"Ma'am, I'm not asking to come in. I don't have a search warrant. But I still need to talk to you. Your Mr. Grey is really Jason Arnott, who we suspect has been responsible for dozens of burglaries involving fine art and other valuable items. He might even be responsible for a murder."

"Oh, heavens," Maddie gasped. Certainly Mr. Grey had always been completely a loner here, but she had just assumed that this Catskill home was where he escaped to for privacy and relaxation. She now realized that he might well have been "escaping" here for very different reasons.

Agent Rose went on to describe to her many of the stolen pieces of art and other items that had disappeared from homes where Arnott had previously attended social functions. Sadly she confirmed that virtually all of these items were in this house. And yes, the miniature oval blue frame, with a woman's picture in it, was on his night table.

"Ma'am, I must ask you to come with us. I'm sure you didn't know what was happening, and you're not in any trouble. But we are going to make a telephone application for a search warrant so that we can search Mr. Arnott's home and arrest him."

Gently Agent Rose led the bewildered Maddie to the waiting car. "I can't believe this," she cried. "I just didn't know."

KERRY WENT BACK TO HER office after the call from Si Morgan came through. She was now convinced that Arnott was irrevocably tied in some way to Suzanne Reardon's death. Just how, though, would have to wait until he was in FBI custody and she and Frank Green had a chance to interrogate him.

There was a pile of messages on her desk. One, from Jonathan Hoover, was marked "Urgent." She called him immediately.

"Thanks for calling back, Kerry. I have to come over to Hackensack, and I want to talk to you. Buy you lunch?"

A few weeks ago he had started the conversation with "Buy you lunch, Judge?" Kerry knew the omission today was not accidental. Jonathan played it straight. If the political fallout from her investigation cost Frank Green the nomination, she would have to forget about a judgeship, no matter how justified she had been.

"Of course, Jonathan."

"Solari's at one thirty."

She was sure she knew why he was calling. He had heard about Dr. Smith and was worried about her and Robin.

She dialed Geoff's office. He was having a sandwich at his desk. "I'm glad I'm sitting down," he told her when she filled him in about Arnott.

"The FBI will be photographing and cataloguing everything they find in the Catskill house. When Green and I go up to talk to Arnott, we want Mrs. Reardon along to positively identify the picture frame. Have you called Skip about Dr. Smith's letter?"

"Right after I talked to you."

"What was his reaction?"

"He started to cry." Geoff's voice became husky. "I did too. He's going to get out, Kerry, and you're the reason."

"No, you and Robin are. I was ready to turn my back on him."

"We'll argue about that another time. Kerry, Deidre Reardon's on the other phone. She's going in for an angioplasty tomorrow, but I'll ask her to postpone it. I'll talk to you later. I don't want you and Robin alone in your place tonight."

Before Kerry left to meet Jonathan, she dialed Joe Palumbo's cellular phone. He answered on the first ring. "Palumbo."

"It's Kerry, Joe."

"Recess is over. Robin is back inside. I'm parked in front of the entrance. I'll drive her home and stay with her and the sitter. Don't worry, Momma. I'll take good care of your baby."

"I know you will. Thanks, Joe."

It was time to meet Jonathan. As she hurried out to the corridor and rushed through the just closing elevator door, Kerry kept thinking about the missing pin. Something about it seemed so familiar. The two parts. The flower and the bud, like a mother and child. A momma and a baby. Why did that ring a bell?

Jonathan was already seated at the table. He got up when he saw her coming. His brief, familiar hug was reassuring. "You look very tired, young lady," he said. "Or is it very stressed?"

Whenever he talked to her like that, Kerry felt a rush of gratitude that Jonathan in so many ways had been a surrogate father to her.

"It's been quite a day so far," she said as she sat down. "Did you hear about Dr. Smith?"

"Grace called me. She heard the news when she was having breakfast. Sounds like more of Weeks's handiwork. We're both heartsick with worry about Robin."

"So am I. But one of our investigators is with her."

The waiter was at the table. "Let's order," Kerry suggested, "and then I'll fill you in."

They both decided on onion soup, which arrived almost immediately. While they were eating, she told him about the package with all the jewelry and the letter from Dr. Smith.

"You make me ashamed that I tried to dissuade you from your investigation, Kerry," Jonathan said quietly. "I'll do my best, but if the governor decides Green's nomination is in jeopardy, it would be like him to take it out on you."

"Well, at least there's hope," Kerry said. "And we can thank Grace for the tip she gave the FBI." She told Jonathan what she had learned about Jason Arnott. "Frank Green is dying to announce that the cat burglar who murdered Congressman Peale's mother was captured because of a tip from the wife of Senator Hoover. You're going to come out of this as his best friend, and who can blame him? Heaven knows you're probably the most respected politician in New Jersey."

Jonathan smiled. "We can always stretch the truth and say that Grace consulted Green first and he urged her to make the call." Then the smile vanished. "Kerry, is there a possibility that Arnott is the one who took that picture of Robin?"

"No way. Robin's father passed along the warning and in essence admitted that Jimmy Weeks had that picture taken."

"What's the next step?"

"Frank Green and I will bring Deidre Reardon up to the Catskills first thing tomorrow morning to identify that miniature frame. Arnott should be being cuffed right about now. They'll keep him in the local jail for the present. Once they start connecting the stolen goods to specific burglaries, they'll arraign him in different locations. My guess is they're itching to try him first for the murder of Congressman Peale's mother. And of course, if he was responsible for Suzanne Reardon's death, we'll want to try him here."

"Suppose he won't talk?"

"We're sending flyers to all the jewelers in New Jersey. My guess is that one of them will recognize the more contemporary jewelry and tie it to Weeks, and that the antique bracelet will turn out to be from Arnott. When it was found on Suzanne's arm, it obviously had a new clasp, and the bracelet is so unusual some jeweler might remember it."

"Then you expect to leave early in the morning for the Catskills?"

"Yes. I'm certainly not going to leave Robin alone, though. If Frank wants to be on the road early, I'll have the sitter stay over."

"I have a better idea. Let Robin stay with us tonight. Our house has state-of-the-art security. You know that. I'll be there, of course, and I don't know whether you realize that even Grace has a gun in her night-table drawer. I taught her to use it years ago. Besides, I think it would be good for Grace to have Robin visit. She's been rather down lately, and Robin is such fun to have around."

Kerry smiled. "Yes, she is." She thought for a moment. "Jonathan, that really could work. I want to go through the Reardon file with a fine-tooth comb before we question Arnott. Robin's

135

crazy about you and Grace, and she loves the pink guest room."

"It used to be yours, remember?"

"Sure. How could I forget?"

JASON Arnott knew there was something terribly wrong the minute he walked in the door of his Catskill home and realized that Maddie was not there.

If Maddie's not here and she didn't leave a note, then something is happening. It's all over, he thought. How long before they would close in on him? Soon, he was sure.

Suddenly he was hungry. He rushed to the refrigerator and pulled out a bottle of Pouilly-Fuissé and the smoked salmon he had asked Maddie to pick up. He prepared a plate of salmon and poured a glass of wine. Then, carrying them with him, he began to walk through the house. A kind of final tour, he thought as he assessed the riches around him. The tapestry in the dining room—exquisite. The Aubusson in the living room—a privilege to walk by such beauty.

He would need a lawyer, of course. A good lawyer. But who? A smile made his lips twitch. He knew just the one: Geoffrey Dorso, who for ten years had so relentlessly worked for Skip Reardon. Dorso might be willing to take on a new client, especially one who could give him evidence that would help him spring poor Reardon.

The front doorbell rang. Arnott ignored it. It rang again, then continued persistently. Then the back doorbell started to chime. Surrounded, he thought. Ah, well. He had known it would happen someday. If he had only obeyed his instincts last week and left the country. He sipped the last of the wine, decided another glass would be welcome and went back to the kitchen. There were faces at all the windows now, self-satisfied faces.

Arnott nodded to them and held up the glass in a mocking toast. As he sipped, he walked to the back door, opened it, then stood aside as they rushed in. "FBI, Mr. Arnott," they shouted. "We have a warrant to search your home."

"Gentlemen, gentlemen," he murmured. "I beg you to be careful."

KERRY CALLED ROBIN AT THREE thirty. She and Alison were at the computer, Robin told her, playing one of the games Uncle Jonathan and Aunt Grace had given her. Kerry told her the plan: "I have to work late tonight and be on the way by seven tomorrow. Jonathan and Grace really would like to have you stay with them, and I'd feel good knowing you're there."

Robin was delighted. "I'm going to ask Aunt Grace if I can pull out her old photo albums again," she said. "I love looking at the old clothes and hairstyles, and I might get some ideas, since our next assignment in camera class is to create a family album so that it really tells a story."

"Yeah, there are some great pictures there. I used to love to go through those albums when I was house-sitting," Kerry reminisced. "I used to count how many different servants Aunt Grace and Uncle Jonathan grew up with. I still think about them sometimes when I'm pushing the vacuum."

Robin giggled. "Well, hang in there. You may win the lottery someday. Love you, Mom."

At five thirty Geoff phoned from his car. "Guess what?" He didn't wait for an answer. "Jason Arnott wants to see me immediately. He wants me to take his case."

"Would you represent him?"

"I couldn't, because he's connected to the Reardon case, and I wouldn't if I could. I told him that, but he still insists on seeing me."

"Geoff! Don't let him tell you anything that would have lawyer-client privilege."

Geoff chuckled. "Thank you, Kerry. I never would have thought of that."

Kerry laughed with him, then explained the arrangement she had made for Robin for the night. Geoff signed off, promising to call and report to her after he had seen Arnott.

IT WAS ten o'clock before Kerry had finished her work and left the now quiet office. So now, Kerry thought, the murderer is the man who visited that house between the time Skip left at around six thirty and when the doctor arrived at around nine o'clock. Which one had killed Suzanne? she wondered. Jason Arnott? Jimmy Weeks? It all came back to the jewelry. If she could prove that Arnott gave Suzanne those valuable antique pieces, there was no way he could get away with saying it was a gift of pure friendship.

Realizing suddenly that she was starving, she drove to the diner around the corner and had a hamburger, french fries and coffee. Substitute a cola for the coffee, and you have Robin's favorite meal, she thought, sighing inwardly. I have to say I miss my baby.

The momma and the baby. . . . The momma and the baby.

Why did that singsong phrase keep echoing in her head? Something about it seemed wrong, so terribly wrong. But what? She should have called and said good night to Robin before she left her office, she thought. Why hadn't she? Kerry ate quickly and got back into the car. It was twenty of eleven—much too late to call. She was just pulling out of the lot when the car phone rang. It was Jonathan.

"Kerry," he said, his voice low and taut, "Robin is in with Grace. She doesn't know I'm calling. She didn't want me to worry you. But after Robin fell asleep, she had a terrible nightmare. I think you should come over. So much has been going on. She needs you."

"I'll be right there." Kerry pressed her foot on the accelerator and rushed to get to her child.

IT WAS a long and miserable ride from New Jersey up the thruway to the Catskills. An icy rain began falling around Middletown, and traffic slowed to a crawl. It was a quarter of ten before a tired and hungry Geoff Dorso arrived at the Ellenville police headquarters, where Jason Arnott was being held.

Handcuffed, Arnott was escorted into the conference room. Geoff had not seen the man in the nearly eleven years since Suzanne's death. Now he studied him closely. Arnott was somewhat more full-faced than Geoff remembered, but he still had that same urbane, world-weary expression. The lines around his eyes suggested fatigue, but the cashmere turtleneck still looked fresh under his tweed jacket. Country gentleman, cultivated connoisseur, Geoff thought. Even in these circumstances he looks the part.

"It's good of you to come, Geoff," Arnott said amiably.

"I really don't know why I'm here," Geoff replied. "As I warned you on the phone, you are now connected to the Reardon case. My client is Skip Reardon. I can tell you that nothing you may say to me is a privileged communication. I am not your lawyer. I will repeat anything you say to the prosecutor, because I intend to try to place you in the Reardon house the night of Suzanne's death."

"Oh, I was there. That's why I sent for you. I intend to be a witness for Skip. But in exchange, once he is cleared, I want you to represent me. There won't be any conflict of interest then."

"Look," Geoff said, "I've spent ten years of my life representing an innocent man who got sent to prison. If you killed Suzanne, or know who did, and let Skip rot in that cell all this time, I'd burn in hell before I would raise a finger to help you."

"Now that's the kind of determination I want to hire." Arnott sighed. "Very well. Let's try it this way. You're a criminal defense attorney. You know who the good ones are. Promise to find me the best attorney money can buy, and I'll tell you what I know of Suzanne Reardon's death—which, incidentally, I am not responsible for."

Geoff stared at the man for a moment, considering his offer. "Okay, but I want a signed and witnessed statement that any information you give me will not be privileged and that I can use it in any way I see fit to assist Skip Reardon."

"Of course."

A stenotypist took down Arnott's brief statement. When he and a couple of witnesses had signed it, he said, "Have you been thinking about what lawyer I should have?"

"Yes," Geoff said. "George Symonds, from Trenton. He's an excellent trial lawyer and a superb negotiator."

"They're going to try to convict me of deliberate murder in the death of Mrs. Peale. I swear it was an accident."

"If there's a way to get it down to felony murder, he'll find it. At least you wouldn't face the death penalty."

"Call him now."

Geoff knew that Symonds lived in Princeton, having once been to dinner at his home. He also remembered that Symonds's phone was listed in his wife's name. Using his cellular phone, Geoff made the call in Arnott's presence. It was ten thirty.

Ten minutes later Geoff put the phone back. "All right. You've got a top-drawer lawyer. Now talk."

"I had the misfortune to be in the Reardon house at the time Suzanne died," Arnott said, his manner suddenly grave. "Suzanne was so wildly careless of her jewelry that the temptation proved too great. Suzanne had told me Skip was not going to be home that evening and that she had a date with Jimmy Weeks. Odd as it may seem, she had quite a crush on him."

"Was he in the house while you were there?"

Arnott shook his head. "No. As I understood it, she was meeting Jimmy early that night. Obviously, I was wrong. There were a few lights on downstairs when I got to Suzanne's house, but that was normal. They came on automatically. From the back I could see that the windows of the master bedroom were wide open. It was child's play to climb up, since the second-story roof of that very modern house slopes almost to the ground."

"What time was that?"

"Precisely eight o'clock. I was on my way to a dinner party in Cresskill. One of the reasons for my long and successful career is that almost invariably I could furnish an impeccable set of witnesses as to my whereabouts on particular nights."

"You went into the house," Geoff encouraged.

"Yes. There wasn't a sound, so I assumed everyone was away as planned. I had no idea that Suzanne was still downstairs. I went through the sitting room of the bedroom suite, then over to the night table. I'd only seen the picture frame in passing and had never been sure if it was a genuine Fabergé. I picked it up and was studying it when I heard Suzanne's voice. She was shouting at someone."

"What was she saying?"

"Something to the effect of 'You gave them to me, and they're mine. Now get out. You bore me.' "

You gave them to me, and they're mine. The jewelry, Geoff

thought. "So that must mean that Jimmy Weeks *was* there," he reasoned.

"Oh, no. I heard a man shout, 'I have to have them back,' but it was much too refined a voice to have been Jimmy Weeks, and it certainly wasn't poor Skip." Arnott sighed. "At that point I dropped the frame in my pocket, almost unconsciously. A dreadful copy as it turns out, but I have enjoyed having Suzanne's picture. She was so entertaining. I do miss her."

"You dropped the frame in your pocket," Geoff prodded.

"And realized suddenly that someone was coming upstairs. I jumped into Suzanne's closet and tried to hide behind her long gowns. I hadn't closed the door completely."

"Did you see who it was?"

"No, not the face."

"What did that person do?"

"Made straight for the jewelry case, picked among Suzanne's baubles and took something. Then, apparently not finding everything he wanted, he began frantically going through all the drawers. After only a few minutes he either found what he was looking for or gave up. Fortunately, he didn't go through the closet. I waited as long as I could, and then, knowing that something was terribly wrong, I slipped downstairs. That's when I saw her."

"What jewelry did Suzanne's killer take from that case?"

"Given what I learned during the trial, I'm sure it must have been the flower-and-bud pin. It really was a beautiful piece."

"Did whoever gave Suzanne that pin also give her the antique bracelet?"

"Oh, yes. I think he was trying to find the bracelet as well."

"Do you know who gave Suzanne the bracelet and the pin?"

"Of course I know. Suzanne kept few secrets from me. Now mind you, I can't swear he was the one in the house that night, but it does make sense. My testimony will help to deliver the real murderer. That's why I should have some consideration, don't you agree?"

"Mr. Arnott, who gave Suzanne the bracelet and pin?"

Arnott smiled. "You won't believe me when I tell you."

IT TOOK KERRY TWENTY-FIVE minutes to drive to the Hoovers' home, in Old Tappan. Every turn of the wheel seemed interminable. Robin, brave little Robin, who always tried to hide how scared she was—it had finally become too much for her. I never should have left her with anyone else, Kerry thought. Even Jonathan and Grace. From now on, *I'll* take care of my baby, Kerry vowed.

The momma and the baby. There was that phrase again.

She was entering Old Tappan. Only a few minutes more now.

Robin had seemed so pleased at the prospect of being with Grace and Jonathan and of going through the photo albums.

The photo albums.

Kerry turned into the Hoovers' driveway. Almost unconsciously she realized that the sensor lights did not go on.

The photo albums.

The flower-and-bud pin.

She had seen it before.

On Grace.

Years ago, when Kerry first started to work for Jonathan. Grace used to wear her jewelry then. Many pictures in the album showed her wearing it. Grace had joked when Kerry admired that pin. She'd called it the momma and the baby.

Suzanne Reardon was wearing Grace's pin in that newspaper picture! That must mean . . . Jonathan? Could he have given it to her?

She remembered now that Grace had told her that she had asked Jonathan to put all her jewelry in the safe-deposit box. "I can't put it on without help, and I can't get it off without help, and I would only worry about it if it were still in the house."

Last night, after I came home, I told Jonathan I thought Smith would crack, Kerry realized. Oh, my God! He must have shot Smith.

Kerry stopped in front of the handsome limestone residence. She pushed the car door open and rushed up the steps.

Robin was with a murderer.

Kerry did not hear the faint pealing of the car telephone as she pressed her finger on the doorbell.

GEOFF TRIED TO PHONE KERRY at home. When there was no answer, he tried her car phone. Where was she? he wondered frantically. He was dialing Frank Green's office when the guard led Arnott away.

"The prosecutor's office is closed. If this is an emergency, dial . . ."

Geoff swore as he dialed the emergency number. Robin was staying with the Hoovers. Where was Kerry? Finally someone answered the emergency line.

"This is Geoff Dorso. I absolutely must reach Frank Green. It concerns a breaking murder case. Give me his home number."

"I can tell you he's not there. He was called out because of a murder in Oradell, sir."

"Can you get through to him?"

"Yes. Hold on."

It was a full three minutes before Green got on the line. "Geoff, I'm in the middle of something. This had better be important."

"It is. Very important. It has to do with the Reardon case. Frank, Robin Kinellen is staying at Jonathan Hoover's home tonight. I've just learned that Jonathan Hoover gave that antique jewelry to Suzanne Reardon. He'd been having an affair with her. I think he's our killer, and Robin is with him."

There was a long pause. Then in an unemotional voice Frank Green said, "I'm in the home of an old man who specialized in repairing antique jewelry. He was murdered early this evening. There's no evidence of robbery, but his son tells me his Rolodex with the names of his customers is missing. I'll get the local cops over to Hoover's place fast."

JONATHAN opened the door for Kerry. The house was dimly lit and very quiet. "She's settled down," he said. "It's all right."

Kerry's fists were hidden in the pockets of her coat, clenched in fear and anger. Still, she managed to smile. "Oh, Jonathan, this is such an imposition for you and Grace. I should have known Robin would be frightened. Where is she?"

"Back in her room now. Fast asleep."

143

Am I crazy? Kerry wondered as she followed Jonathan upstairs. Did my imagination go hog-wild? He seems so normal.

They came to the door of the guest bedroom—the pink room, as Robin called it, because of the soft pink walls and draperies. Kerry pushed the door open. In the glow of a small night-light she could see Robin on her side, her long brown hair scattered on the pillow. In two strides Kerry was beside the bed.

Robin's cheek was cupped in her palm. She was breathing evenly. Kerry looked up at Jonathan. He was at the foot of the bed, staring at her. "She was so upset. After you got here, you decided to take her home," he said. "See—her bag with her school clothes and books is packed and ready. I'll carry it for you."

"Jonathan, there was no nightmare. She didn't wake up, did she?" Kerry said, her voice even.

"No," he said indifferently. "And it would be easier for her if she didn't wake up now." In the dim light Kerry saw that he was holding a gun.

"Jonathan, what are you doing? Where's Grace?"

"Grace is fast asleep, Kerry. It was better that way. Sometimes I can tell that one of her more powerful sedatives is necessary to ease the pain. I dissolve it in the hot cocoa I bring her every night."

"Jonathan, what do you want?"

"I want to keep on living just as we're living now. I want to be president of the senate and friend of the governor. I want to spend my remaining years with my wife, whom I really do love, still. Sometimes men stray, Kerry. They let young, beautiful women flatter them. Perhaps I was susceptible because of Grace's problem. I knew it was foolish of me; I knew it was a mistake. Then all I wanted to do was to take back the jewelry I had so stupidly given that vulgar Reardon girl, but she wouldn't part with it."

He waved the revolver at Robin. "Pick her up. There isn't any more time."

"Jonathan, what are you going to do?"

"Only what I have to do, and then only with great regret. Kerry, Kerry, why did you feel you had to tilt at windmills? What did it matter that Reardon was in prison? What did it matter that

Suzanne's father claimed as his gift the bracelet that could have so desperately harmed me? Those things were meant to be. I was supposed to continue to serve the state I love and to live with the wife I love. It was sufficient penance to know that Grace had so easily spotted my betrayal."

Jonathan smiled. "She is quite marvelous. She showed me that newspaper picture and said, 'Doesn't that remind you of my flower-and-bud pin? It makes me want to wear it again. Please get it out of the safe-deposit box, dear.' She knew, and I knew that she knew, Kerry. And suddenly . . . I felt soiled."

"And you killed Suzanne."

"She not only refused to return my wife's gems but had the gall to tell me she had a new boyfriend—Jimmy Weeks. My Lord, the man's a thug. A mobster."

"Mom." Robin was stirring. Her eyes opened. She sat up. "Mom." She smiled. "Why are you here?"

"Get out of bed, Rob. We're leaving now." He's going to kill us, she thought. She put her arm around Robin.

Sensing that something was wrong, Robin shrank against her. "Mom?"

"It's all right," Kerry assured her.

"Uncle Jonathan?" Robin had seen the gun.

"Don't say anything else, Robin," Kerry said quietly. What can I do? she thought. He's crazy. He's out of control. If only Geoff hadn't gone to see Jason Arnott. Geoff would have helped. Somehow Geoff would have helped.

As they were going down the stairs, Jonathan said quietly, "Give me your car keys, Kerry. I'll follow you out, and then you and Robin will get in the trunk."

Oh, God, Kerry thought. He'll kill us and drive us somewhere and leave the car, and it will look like a Mob killing. It will be blamed on Jimmy Weeks.

Jonathan spoke again as they crossed the foyer. "I am truly sorry, Robin. Now open the door slowly, Kerry."

Kerry bent down to kiss Robin. "Rob, when I spin around, you run," she whispered. "Run next door and keep screaming."

"The door, Kerry," Jonathan prodded.

Slowly she opened it. He had turned off the porch lights so that the only illumination was the faint glow thrown off by the torchère at the end of the driveway. "My key is in my pocket," she said. She turned, then screamed, "Run, Robin!"

At the same moment she threw herself across the foyer at Jonathan. She heard the gun go off as she hurtled toward him, then felt a burning pain in the side of her head, followed by waves of dizziness. The marble floor of the foyer rushed up to greet her. Around her she was aware of a cacophony of sound: Another gunshot. Robin screaming for help, her voice fading into the distance. Sirens approaching.

Then suddenly Grace's broken cry, "I'm sorry, Jonathan. I couldn't let you do this," she said. "Not to Kerry and Robin."

Kerry managed to pull herself up and press her hand against the side of her head. Blood was trickling down her face, but the dizziness was receding. As she looked up, she saw Grace slide from her wheelchair onto the floor, drop the pistol from her swollen fingers and gather her husband's body in her arms.

18

Tuesday
February 6th

THE courtroom was packed for the swearing-in ceremony of Assistant Prosecutor Kerry McGrath to the judiciary. The festive hum of voices subsided into silence when the door from the chambers opened and a stately procession of black-robed judges marched in to welcome a new colleague.

Kerry quietly walked from the side of the chamber and took her place to the right of the bench as the judges went to the chairs reserved for them in front of the guests.

She looked out at the assembly. Her mother and stepfather had flown in from Colorado for the ceremony. They were sitting with Robin, who was ramrod straight on the edge of her seat, her eyes wide with excitement. There was barely a trace of the lacerations that had brought them to that fateful meeting with Dr. Smith.

Geoff was in the next row with his mother and father. Kerry thought of how he had rushed down in the FBI helicopter to come to her in the hospital, how he had been the one to comfort a hysterical Robin and then bring her home to his family when the doctor insisted Kerry stay overnight. Now she blinked back tears at what she saw in his face as he smiled at her.

Kerry thought of Jonathan and Grace. They had planned to be present too. Grace had sent a note.

> I am going home to South Carolina and will live with my sister. I blame myself for what happened. I knew Jonathan was involved with that woman. I also knew it wouldn't last. If only I had ignored that picture in which she was wearing my pin, none of this would have happened. I didn't care about the jewelry. That was my way of warning Jonathan to give her up. Please forgive me and forgive Jonathan if you can.

Can I? Kerry wondered. Grace saved my life, but Jonathan would have killed Robin and me to save himself. Grace knew Jonathan had been involved with Suzanne and might even have been her murderer, yet she let Skip Reardon rot in prison all those years.

Skip, his mother and Beth were somewhere in the crowd. Skip and Beth were getting married next week; Geoff would be best man.

It was customary for a few close friends or associates to make brief remarks before the swearing-in. Frank Green went first. "Searching my memory, I cannot imagine any person—man or woman—who is more suited to assume this high position than Kerry McGrath. Her sense of justice led her to request me to reopen a murder case. Together we faced the appalling fact that a vengeful father had condemned his daughter's husband to prison, while the real killer was enjoying freedom. We . . ."

That's my boy, Kerry thought. Lemonade from lemons. But in the end, Frank had stood by her. He had personally met with the governor and urged that her name be placed before the senate for confirmation.

Frank had been the one to clear up the Jimmy Weeks connection to Suzanne Reardon. One of his sources, a small-time hood who had been a gofer for Jimmy, supplied the answer. Suzanne had indeed been involved with Jimmy, and he had given her jewelry. He had also sent the roses to her that night and was supposed to meet her for dinner. When she didn't show up, he had become furious and in drunken anger had even said he would kill her. Since Weeks was not given to idle threats, a couple of his people thought he really had been the murderer. He was always afraid that if his connection to her came out, her death would be pinned on him.

Now the assignment judge, Robert McDonough, was speaking, talking about how when Kerry came into the courtroom for the first time ten years ago as a brand-new assistant prosecutor, she looked so young that he thought she was a college kid on a summer job.

I was a brand-new bride too, Kerry thought wryly. Bob was an assistant prosecutor then. I only hope he has the brains to stay away from Jimmy Weeks and his ilk from now on, she mused. Weeks had been convicted on all counts. Now he was facing another trial for tampering with a juror. Bob had narrowly missed being indicted himself. Maybe all this would scare Bob before it was too late.

Judge McDonough was smiling at her. "Well, Kerry, I think it's time," he said.

Robin came forward, carrying the Bible. Kerry raised her right hand, placed her left hand on the Bible and began to repeat after Judge McDonough: " 'I, Kerry McGrath, do solemnly swear . . .' "

ABOUT THE AUTHOR

Mary Higgins Clark

I t's a brilliant spring afternoon, and Mary Higgins Clark has just returned from a grueling four hours of book signing. If she's exhausted, you'd never know it. She takes a moment to show a visitor the breathtaking view from the terrace of her sixteenth-floor Manhattan apartment. Then she settles down to chat about her latest novel.

Clark explains that she and her longtime editor at Simon & Schuster, Michael Korda—himself a topflight novelist—have a tradition. "Whenever I finish a book, Michael gives me about a week off; then he invites me to dinner to discuss the next one." In the case of *Let Me Call You Sweetheart*, it was Korda who suggested she write about a plastic surgeon. And right there in the restaurant she started spinning her tale. "The magic word in suspense writing is 'suppose,'" says Clark. "I asked myself, suppose this surgeon is giving a number of women the same face. Why is he doing it?"

Clark's supposings have led her to an unbroken string of fourteen best sellers, as well as to the presidency of the Mystery Writers of America, an honorary doctorate from Villanova University, and even the French Grand Prix de Littérature Policière. And through it all, a lot of book signings!

PHOTO: BERNARD VIDAL

CLANCY CARLILE

CHILDREN OF THE DUST

The Oklahoma
land rush. For some,
a time-honored way
of life was ending.
For others, the
dream of a
lifetime was
just beginning.

Chapter One

Superintendent John Maxwell stood at his office window. Gazing across the schoolyard and agency grounds toward the prairies beyond, he saw a wagon coming, pulled by two bone-gaunt horses. He recognized the driver as John Black Bear. Beside him was a boy.

The wagon stopped at the hitching rail in front of the school building. John Black Bear got down, but the boy was reluctant to follow. John Black Bear had to lift him from the wagon.

Superintendent Maxwell, slipping into his frock coat, went out to the schoolyard, where the first-grade Indian students were learning to play white children's games. As he approached the wagon, John Black Bear said, "Maxwell," friendly but unsmiling. Though nearly toothless and dressed in tattered remnants of white man's clothing, John Black Bear was a man of great solemnity, as became a leader of the Human Beings.

"Black Bear, *nimahaeaman*." Maxwell offered his hand.

Black Bear pumped it three times mechanically, as if it were the handle of a water pump, then said, "I bring this boy. His mother say him go white man's school, become white man."

Noting the boy's worn and dirty clothes and the look in his darting eyes of a hungry wolf whelp, Maxwell assumed that he had been brought to the agency boarding school not so much for an education as for some new clothes and something to eat.

Black Bear said, "This boy is the son of Chief Cloud Walker. Him father gone long time white man's prison. Boy's mother, Rainbow Woman, soon die of white man's coughing sickness. Rainbow Woman Christian now, want boy learn white man's medicine."

Speaking Cheyenne, Maxwell asked the boy his name.

"Hokoxc—Little Raven," Black Bear volunteered.

Maxwell offered to shake hands. The boy edged farther behind Black Bear's legs.

"Afraid white man. Hear stories how white man kill Human Beings." He used the old word for "Cheyennes"—Tsistsistas—meaning "the People," or "the Human Beings," as if there were no others.

"You will not be hurt here," Maxwell assured the boy in Cheyenne, then turned to a group of first-grade girls jumping rope nearby. He beckoned to one of the girls and said in Cheyenne, "This is Martha Washington. Martha is also of the Hehyo band. Martha has been here for a year and has never been hurt. Ask her."

But Little Raven only stared at her as if her schoolgirl's uniform—plain blue jacket and skirt, white blouse, high-button shoes, and black stockings—disgusted him.

"Martha, run fetch Miss Tibbens," Maxwell said in English. "Tell her we have a new student."

Miss Kate Tibbens was the school's matron. An elderly woman with heavy hips and a pouter-pigeon bosom, she dressed severely in ankle-length dark muslin. From her desk she took a piece of candy and went down to meet the new arrival.

"My-my-my," she clucked. "Isn't he a handsome little brave, though? Would you like some candy?"

The boy shrank away. Maxwell spoke to him again in Cheyenne, but it took Black Bear to persuade the boy to go into the school, and even then his moccasined steps were wary.

Grasping Little Raven's arm, Miss Tibbens said, "Come along now. You'll like it here," and pulled him up the steps.

Miss Clarksdale, the school's seamstress, was in the sewing room conducting a crocheting class.

"Sorry to interrupt," Miss Tibbens said, "but we have a new boy.

First we have a haircut," she informed him, raising her voice in an attempt to make him understand English, and mimed cutting off his shoulder-length hair. "I suspect there may be a few bugs in there."

A few of the girls tittered. The boy tried to jerk away and run.

"Now, now. It won't hurt. If you would do the honors, Miss Clarksdale?" Miss Tibbens said. "I think I'll have to hold him."

Miss Clarksdale took from her sewing kit a pair of scissors and, examining the boy's hair, said, "Oh, yes, some cooties in there."

The girls tittered again, and the boy, without so much as a sound, suddenly bit Miss Clarksdale's hand, then struck Miss Tibbens in the stomach. Miss Clarksdale screamed and fell backward, crashing into the students. Chairs were overturned. Girls shrieked. Miss Tibbens made a grab for the boy. Agile as a monkey, he scrambled to a tall cabinet, clambered up the face of it as easily as scaling a ladder, and crouched on top, facing the room, teeth bared, panting.

Maxwell dashed into the room. "What's going on?"

"We were just about to give him a haircut," Miss Tibbens said. "He's a wildcat."

Maxwell took a few steps toward the crouching boy. *"Henova, naha?"* he said. John Black Bear entered, and Maxwell spoke in English. "Tell him to come on down. Nobody's going to hurt him."

Black Bear frowned disapprovingly, though there was pride and amusement in his eyes. "Shame on you, Little Raven. It is your mother's wish that you become a student here. Is this how you honor her wish?"

The ferocity in the boy's face dissolved. His eyes brimmed with tears as he was coaxed down from the cabinet.

Maxwell sent Miss Tibbens and Miss Clarksdale to the doctor to have their injuries tended. The girls he excused from class, and after they were gone and the door had been shut, he again spoke to the boy in Cheyenne. "Little Raven, we are not your enemy. We want to help you. Will you give us your trust?"

The boy stared at Black Bear, and Black Bear nodded.

Aware that Cheyenne custom held hospitality and trust to be inseparable, Maxwell asked Little Raven to share the evening meal with him and his family. Although such an invitation to a student

155

was unique, Maxwell saw that this boy would need special handling, not only because he was wild and mistrustful but also because he was Chief Cloud Walker's son. If Maxwell could make a successful student out of this boy, the other children on the reservation would be less reluctant to attend the white man's school.

THE Maxwells' house had a front porch, unpainted clapboard walls, and a picket fence around the yard to keep the animals and Indians out. There was a small corral and barn in the back, where the Maxwells kept two horses, a cow, two pigs, and some chickens.

When Maxwell came home with the boy, his wife took him aside. "Is this the boy that attacked Miss Tibbens and Miss Clarksdale today?" she whispered. "What if he attacks one of us?"

"Nora, the boy was just frightened out of his wits. He's never been around white people before."

"Then wouldn't he feel better eating with his own kind?"

"Not when he can't speak a word of English and the others are forbidden to speak anything else. At least I can talk to him, and I seem to be the only one he feels safe around. He wouldn't let them cut his hair unless I was right there."

"Never mind," she said, "I ought to've known," and turned from him. "Rachel," she called, "set a plate for the boy."

Maxwell and Nora sat at opposite ends of an oilcloth-covered table. Dexter, Nora's son by her first marriage, sat opposite Little Raven, whose hair had been cut so short it stood up like the quills of an alarmed porcupine. He now wore a schoolboy's uniform.

Rachel, six years old, sat next to Little Raven. She had quick hazel eyes, a light sprinkling of freckles across her nose, and long, wavy auburn hair tied back with a pink ribbon. As her father was saying grace, Rachel turned her head to look at the boy. He didn't bow his head like everyone else; he was, after all, a heathen. She was surprised that he was ignoring all her efforts to catch his eye. As the food was being passed around, she tried a more direct approach.

"What's your name?"

"Hasn't got one yet," Maxwell said.

"Well then, what's his Indian name?"

156

"Little Raven."

"I know! Let's name him Corby," she cried.

She had recently raised an injured raven chick. She had named it Corby, and tended it until it had healed enough to fly away.

"Corby? Too unusual," Maxwell said. "The Bureau wants them to have simple, ordinary white names. George, for instance. Or Walter. How about Walter?"

"Oh, please, Daddy, let's do name him Corby." Rachel took a swallow of buttermilk, leaving a white mustache on her upper lip, which she slurped off with the tip of her tongue.

"Stop that," Nora admonished. "Mind your manners, young lady. You have to set a good example." She looked in disgust toward the boy, who had lowered his head over his plate and was picking the chicken out of the gravy with his fingers.

"Please, Daddy?" Rachel said.

"Well, what about a last name? Dexter? Got any ideas?"

Dexter pondered, then said, "Why not name him White? We could sure use more whites around here."

Quick to neutralize Dexter's sarcasm by taking him seriously, Maxwell said, "Why not? That's a good name."

After supper Rachel followed her father and Corby out onto the front porch. "Good night, Corby White," she said.

The boy stared blankly.

She pointed to his chest. "Corby. You Corby." She pointed to herself. "Rachel. I'm Rachel."

It was then the boy uttered his first word since arriving at the agency. "Ray-chil," he said in a whisper. "Ray-chil."

"Yes, yes!" she cried. "I'm Rachel. You're Corby."

The boy gestured in sign language. *"Nahavesheeton,"* he said.

Rachel looked at her father. "Means 'we are friends,' " he said.

Rachel smiled, pleased as though she had been given a new pet to replace the little raven that had flown away.

THE Cheyenne-Arapaho reservation was located in the western portion of Indian Territory. The agency on the reservation consisted of twenty-five buildings, most of them fronting on a large

157

treeless square. Among the buildings were the agent's office and dwelling, a post office, a boardinghouse, a missionary church, and two general stores. But the most impressive building was the school. Three stories high, with twenty-two rooms, a belfry, and four huge brick chimneys, it towered over the countryside.

In the days following Corby White's arrival, Maxwell often watched the students at play from his office windows. Rachel and a few other white children were among them, but it was Corby's small figure that Maxwell's eyes sought. Over the months he saw the boy slowly become integrated into the groups and games, and he was pleased to see that it was usually Rachel who served as his friend and sponsor.

At first Corby wasn't prized as a teammate in games, because he didn't know the rules, but he learned fast and eventually could hold a bat and wallop a ball as hard as any of the others. He also did well in the classroom. He had quickly picked up English, and even Miss Tibbens was willing to admit that the boy might have some promise. She began to admire in him the same qualities that Maxwell had been quick to admire: his spunk, his quickness of mind, his stoic composure, his almost manly dignity. Indeed, Corby was exactly the kind of boy Maxwell would have wanted for a son, the kind of son he had once hoped Nora would give him.

He had first met Nora Bingham when he was a teacher at the St. Louis Normal School. Nora had been the wife of the school's chaplain, Clyde Bingham. When Mr. Bingham died of a sudden illness, leaving Nora a widow with a five-year-old son, Maxwell found himself spending more and more time in her company. He always found her to be a good and respectable woman, a woman who believed in doing her duty toward her family and church. Moreover, even though she never wore cosmetics or fancy clothes and was five or six years older than Maxwell, he found her attractive. Frail, yes, and sometimes excessively self-righteous perhaps, but a good person, one who would make a man a good and faithful wife. Also, when Maxwell was offered a job by the Bureau of Indian Affairs, Nora hinted that she would welcome the opportunity to become the wife of a schoolteacher on an Indian reservation. It seemed to appeal to her sense of martyrdom.

So they were married and moved to the Cheyenne-Arapaho reservation in Indian Territory. Maxwell was soon promoted to superintendent of the agency school, and within a year Nora gave birth to Rachel. Although Maxwell couldn't have been more pleased with his daughter, he was very disappointed to learn from the doctor that Nora might not survive another pregnancy. He tried to reconcile himself to the idea that Dexter, Nora's son by Clyde Bingham, was the only son he would ever have. And that was too bad, because however hard he tried to be a good stepfather and to like Dexter, they just didn't get along. Among the things he disliked about the boy was his tendency to be a bully, and one of the things he most admired about Corby White was his refusal to be bullied.

At first Dexter only sneered at Corby, testing him. But because Corby ignored him, Dexter's provocations finally became physical. Once, in the dining hall, as he passed the table where Corby was sitting with Rachel, he swung his elbow out and hit the back of Corby's head just as he was lifting a glass of milk. Milk splashed down Corby's shirt and over the table, but he didn't even look around. Dexter smiled, wondering just how far he could push the little redskin before he would react.

It was months later, on a Saturday afternoon in late May, when Dexter found out. The students—boys mostly—were gathered on the square for the first baseball game of the '85 school year. Everything was going along fine until Corby came to bat. Dexter was the pitcher, and a good one. That was why it was hard to believe that his first pitch to Corby was so wild that Corby had to duck to keep from being hit in the head. Dexter shrugged apologetically.

"Here comes a good one," he yelled, and threw.

Corby ducked again, but this time the ball hit him on the shoulder and, glancing upward, smashed against his head just above his ear. He was knocked to the ground, blinded for a moment by pinpoints of bright lights. He shook his head to clear his vision, and then, without warning, he picked up a stone and hurled it at Dexter.

Dexter threw up his hands to protect his face. The stone hit him in the chest. Shock and disbelief twisted his face for a moment, and then he rushed at Corby. Instead of running, Corby brought the bat

159

up and held it poised to strike. As soon as Dexter came in range, Corby swung with all his strength. Dexter threw up his arms to protect his head, and the bat hit his left forearm. There was a loud crack, sounding as if the bat had splintered. But Dexter's bewildered wail signaled that it was not the bat that had broken.

With his left arm dangling uselessly, Dexter grabbed for Corby with his right arm, crying, "I'll kill you. I'll kill you!" Then he fell on Corby and pinned him to the ground, slamming his face into the dirt, shouting over and over, "You redskin bastard, I'll kill you!"

Rachel pushed through the crowd and sprang onto Dexter's back, pulling at him, punching him, crying, "Don't, Dexter! Let him be."

Dexter wrenched her off his shoulders and flung her sprawling into the dirt in a flurry of high-button shoes and petticoats. But she sprang to her feet and was instantly on him again, pulling his hair, crying, "Let him alone! Let him alone!"

Dexter flung her away again, but now, emboldened by Rachel's example, a few of the bigger Indian boys placed restraining hands on him, saying, "Enough, Dexter. You hurt him too much."

Dexter appeared to allow the boys to mollify him, though it was really the increasing pain throbbing through his broken arm that caused him to stop. With tears flooding his eyes, he got up. His forearm was swelling rapidly and turning purple.

Maxwell broke through the spectators. Corby was sitting up now, glaring at Dexter. Rachel was on her knees beside him, brushing away the pebbles and dirt that had been embedded in his face.

"Come on, let's get you to the doctor," Maxwell said to Dexter.

"I'm gonna kill him," Dexter said as Maxwell led him away.

Rachel sat on the ground by Corby. "I'm glad you hurt him good," she said. "Now maybe he'll leave you alone."

But Corby knew better. Now he knew he and Dexter would be enemies always, until death.

Chapter Two

THERE were twelve bands of Southern Cheyennes on the reservation. The Hehyo band—about three hundred and twenty in all—came to the agency in late June of that year, 1885, to collect its annuities and rations. Included in the rations was a beef disbursement, which was a special event because it was conducted as a mock hunt. The band of Indians was split into family groups, and each group was given a longhorn steer as its meat ration. The wild Texas steers would be released from the corral out onto the open prairie, and a small group of mounted Indian men would chase them in an attempt to recapture some of the excitement of the buffalo hunts of years gone by. The night before, the band would perform the buffalo dance, a ritual intended to assure a good kill.

The Hehyo band was named after its principal chief, an old man whose full name was Ehohotohehyo—He Follows His Father's

Ways—but that was too much for white people to pronounce, so they shortened it. As was his custom whenever he visited the agency, Chief Hehyo stopped at the agent's office, where the agent, Elijah Tanner, a one-eyed man with a snuff-stained beard, met him. The chief told Agent One-eye—as he was called by the Indians—that he had a message for Little Raven, the boy of the Hehyo band who had now been a student at the reservation school for almost a year, a message that must be given in person. So a clerk was sent to fetch both the boy and Superintendent Maxwell, and when they arrived, the chief shook hands with Maxwell.

"*Namahaovo, veho* Maxwell," he said in a gravelly voice.

"*Namahaovo,*" Maxwell responded. "How is my friend?"

"I grow old, my friend. Soon I will travel the Hanging Road to the Spirit Land. You must visit my lodge once more before I go."

"I will visit again soon, although I am confident you will be among us for many winters yet."

The chief turned to the boy, who, shy and respectful, dressed in his school uniform, waited to be noticed. "Is it really you, Little Raven? They have made you into a fine white boy. What is your white name?"

Corby glanced up at Maxwell for permission to speak his native tongue, and when Maxwell nodded, he said, "I am now called Corby White, Grandfather," using the honorary form of address of a young Cheyenne to a respected elder of the tribe.

"A strange name. What does it mean in the white man's tongue?"

The boy was embarrassed. "I do not know, Grandfather."

The chief grunted, eternally bemused by the white man's customs, and then said, "Corby White, I must tell you that your mother has gone to the Spirit Land."

Corby seemed unable to respond.

"Two sleeps ago. Her dying wish was that I tell her son that he must not mourn. She said to tell her son that she would be joyful in the Spirit Land with the white man's god called Jesus." Then, having performed his duty, Chief Hehyo nodded his dismissal.

Maxwell and Corby left the office. Putting an arm around the boy's small shoulders, Maxwell said, "I'm sorry about your mother."

As they were passing in front of Maxwell's house, on their way back to the school, Rachel darted out to meet them. Ignoring her mother's calls to come back, she slammed through the front gate. "What's wrong?" she asked.

"My mother is dead," Corby announced in a voice of mingled sorrow and excitement at the drama death had conferred upon him.

From her place behind the curtained windows, Nora watched, and when Maxwell and Rachel returned from the school, Nora sent Rachel out to the barn to help Dexter do the chores.

"Now there's no use telling me they're not friends," Nora said to Maxwell. "I saw her holding his hand."

"For heaven's sake, Nora, the boy's mother just died. She was only expressing sympathy. And anyway, so what if they are friends?"

"John, that little savage tried to kill Dexter, her own brother."

"I've told you, it was just a schoolyard fight between two kids."

"Attacking Dexter with a baseball bat! The least you could do is forbid her to be friends with that—that dirty little Indian."

"And that's it, isn't it? That's the real reason you hate him so much—because he's Indian. Well, I'll tell you again, hating people because of their race is dangerous foolishness, and I certainly am not going to allow a daughter of mine to—"

"Daughter of *yours*? She's *my* daughter, too!" But then a look of consternation crossed her face, and she added as if to herself, "Though, God help me, sometimes I wonder. . . ."

"What? You wonder what?"

Nora sat down on a straight-backed chair and crossed her arms. "Sometimes I don't think I know her at all. Like last Sunday. I got her all prettied up to go to church, and five minutes later I find her in the dirt playing marbles with some boys—Indian boys. And I found myself wondering if she was my child—*my* child."

"Nora," he gently admonished, "we've been over this."

"You always take her side against me," she said, getting up and turning back to the hot kitchen stove. "Never mind. Go on. Wash up. Let me finish getting supper."

Outside on the porch, he noted the many new tepees being erected close to the agency buildings. Three of the tepees had been set up near his barn, and he guessed that some of the Indians would no doubt end up sleeping in his hayloft after the buffalo dance.

He could see Rachel and Dexter in the cow pen. Dexter was milking the cow with his one good hand, and Rachel was feeding the cow oats from her cupped hands. As Maxwell watched her, his heart was flooded with love. He wondered once again at the puzzling antagonism between Nora and Rachel, an antagonism that had apparently begun before Rachel was even born, taken from her womb by cesarean section. Nora had hovered between life and death for days after the birth, unable to nurse the child. He had been forced to look for a wet nurse, and the only one available was a squaw named Black Kettle, who had a five-month-old daughter of her own. Black Kettle came to the house three times a day, sat on the back porch dangling her moccasined feet into the flower bed, and chewed tobacco while the two babies suckled greedily.

Rachel's only bad times came when she grew hungry at night. Maxwell tried to appease her with a formula of goat's milk and syrup, but she would regurgitate the liquid within minutes and begin crying. Finally Maxwell began to let Black Kettle take the child with her at night to the Indian camp. She would bring Rachel back every morning, fed and content.

Nora's recovery was slow and fitful. Bedridden for almost two months, she knew nothing of Rachel's nursing arrangement until the day she decided she was strong enough to get up. She stepped out onto the back porch and saw Rachel being nursed by Black Kettle. Horrified, she retrieved the baby and accused Maxwell of deceiving her. "I'll nurse her myself from now on." But she had ceased lactating, and two days later, after Rachel had begun to cry almost constantly, she held the child out to Maxwell. "Take her," she said. "I have nothing to give her. Take her back to that savage."

And from that day forward, until the time came when she could subsist on solid foods, Rachel spent not only her nights but most of her days, too, with Black Kettle in the Indian camp, where, happy and brash as a bear cub, she could crawl naked through the ashes and dirt in front of Black Kettle's tepee.

She was just over a year old when Nora reclaimed her and began the task of trying to make the child over into her own image. In time, Rachel submitted to being dressed up like a doll, and loved the attention that her well-scrubbed prettiness brought her, but it was never more than a game to her. When she'd had enough, she was likely to be found toddling off toward Black Kettle's camp or playing with some Indian kids behind the barn. By the time Rachel was five years old, it had begun to be clear that the gulf between mother and daughter would never be bridged. Nora believed that the milk from that savage's breasts had put Rachel forever beyond her reach.

Now as he stood on the back porch, Maxwell was jarred from his ruminations by the sound of Nora's dropping a pan in the kitchen. He turned to the washstand and washed his face and hands in the basin. When Rachel came up from the barn with a bucket of milk, he followed her into the kitchen.

Near the end of the meal that evening Nora saw something in the window that caused her to cry out in terror, startling everyone at the table. Maxwell turned to see three Indians with painted faces staring in at them, their noses against the panes.

"No need to panic," he said, and got up to go outside. He knew they meant no harm. It was just that to most Indians, windows in a white man's dwelling were put there for passersby to peer in.

The three Indians nodded and grunted when Maxwell came out, and one of them greeted him as a friend. It was Blue Horse, who asked, "Does Maxwell's lodge have coffee for his friends?"

"I regret that I do not," Maxwell said. "But I will bring tobacco to the dance, and we will share a pipe."

"*Pava,*" the Indian grunted. "Good." Then they went on their way.

When he went back into the house, Maxwell found Nora slumped forward in her chair, her face hidden in her hands. He touched her shoulder. "You all right?"

She slowly lifted her head. "I'm going to lie down," she murmured. Pushing herself up, she tottered toward the front bedroom. At such moments her only recourse was to lie down, put a cool wet cloth over her eyes, and pray for the blessed release of sleep.

But there would be no sleep for her that night. The buffalo dance had begun.

JOHN MAXWELL AND THE Tanner brothers—Elijah, the agent, and Brady P., the chief of the Indian police—stood on the gallery of the agency's headquarters building. With them were many other agency officials and employees. They were there to meet Chief Cloud Walker and three other high-ranking Cheyenne chiefs, all of whom had been held for four years as military prisoners and were now being returned to the reservation.

The prisoners had been the leaders in what became known as the breakout of '82, in which more than three hundred Cheyennes and Arapahos had left the reservation and made a desperate dash for their old homelands on the Great Plains. Having left in one of the coldest winters ever known in the region, they suffered terribly from cold and hunger, and when the army finally caught up with them—what was left of them—near Ogallala, Nebraska, a battle ensued in which thirteen soldiers were killed. The Indians suffered more than a hundred casualties, men and women, but refused to surrender until they were completely out of food and ammunition.

Chief Cloud Walker and the other leaders of the breakout had been brought back to the reservation, tried, and sentenced to life imprisonment. But in 1887, after they had served four years in the military stockade at Fort Marion, Florida, the Great White Father in Washington commuted their sentences as a peace gesture. Now they were being escorted back to the reservation by a squad of 5th Cavalry troopers from Fort Reno. The squad was under the command of a lieutenant but was actually led by Gypsy Smith, a mixed-blood Negro Cherokee, Fort Reno's chief of scouts.

In addition to the agency officials, many Indians had come to the agency to meet Cloud Walker and the other prisoners.

Corby watched his father's return from a window in the boys' third-floor dormitory. He had wanted to go out to welcome him, but the school's rules did not permit any meetings between the students and their parents. Bureau of Indian Affairs policy required that young Indian students be totally severed from their families for the duration of their education. Otherwise too many students would take the opportunity to escape and go back to the blanket.

At first Corby wasn't sure which of the prisoners was his father.

Since he had been only four years old when his father was taken away to prison, he had only a vague memory of what he looked like. He focused on the prisoner who seemed to be the center of attention. Corby guessed that this was his father, the legendary Chief Cloud Walker, though he didn't look very imposing at the moment, with his hair short and uneven and his dusty gray prison uniform hanging on him like rags on a scarecrow.

Bringing the troopers to a halt in front of the administration building, the lieutenant presented some papers to Agent Tanner. The prisoners climbed out of the wagon and into a swarm of welcoming Indians. In the forefront was Black Buffalo Woman, Cloud Walker's wife number one, who presented him with the reins to a gray stallion and then gave him a bundle she was cradling in her arms. Cloud Walker took from the bundle an elaborately decorated Ghost Dance shirt. He didn't bother to unbutton the prison shirt he wore, but simply ripped it off and flung it away, to the accompanying cheers and shouts of the Indians. Then he pulled on the Ghost Dance shirt, and a look of pride and defiance came over his face. He vaulted onto the back of the gray stallion without using the stirrup.

Agent Tanner borrowed his brother's .44 Colt and fired it into the air. When the Indians gave him their attention, he shouted, "Cloud Walker and the other prisoners have been released into my custody, and if they break the law in any way, if they try to stir up the Indians and make trouble for the government, they will be returned to prison for the rest of their lives. Is that understood?"

Cloud Walker's only acknowledgment was a sullen stare.

"And there's one more thing," Tanner said loudly. "The Great White Father in Washington knows that many of you have been practicing a new religion called the Ghost Dance, and he knows that Cloud Walker has become a leader of this cult. The Great White Father says there is to be no more Ghost Dancing."

A roar of outrage arose from the Indians. Cloud Walker restored order by holding up his hand for silence; then he spoke.

"I understand your words, and I am not surprised by them. This order was to be expected." Like the legendary Indian orators of the old days, he gave a songlike cadence to his words, as if they were

167

being spoken to the accelerating beat of a drum. "Everything that we have ever cherished has been taken from the Human Beings by the white man. First the white man killed all our buffalo."

There was a murmuring chorus of agreement from the Indians. "Then the white man took our land and our freedom."

A dramatic pause, another chorus of agreement, and then Cloud Walker pointed toward the school. "The white man has even taken our children and our language. And now"—a longer pause this time—"the white man would take away our religion, our dreams."

A few warriors close to Cloud Walker shook their rifles over their heads and began chanting the old war cry *"Hoka hey!"*

Alarmed, the young lieutenant ordered his men to fall into a phalanx in front of the gallery, to protect the whites, but Gypsy Smith, the mixed-blood chief of scouts, quickly assumed authority. "No guns!" he shouted. "They got women and children with 'em. They didn't come here to fight."

Then Cloud Walker spoke again. "Is it possible that the white man thinks there will be a day when he will see no more Ghost Dancers among the Human Beings? As long as I live, that day will never be, because from this day forward my name will be Ghost Dancer. And if the white man would put all the Ghost Dancers in jail, let him start with me. *Namatoan*—I have finished speaking," he added, and spun his horse around and rode out of the agency. The Indians closed in behind him and followed in his wake.

"Well," said Police Chief Brady P. Tanner, "that troublemaker didn't learn a thing in prison, did he?"

As MAXWELL crossed the square, he saw Gypsy Smith approaching. "Scuse me, Mr. Maxwell," the scout said as he drew near, "I was wondering if I could ask you something."

Maxwell stopped and looked up at him. Gypsy Smith was in his late thirties, a tall, gangling man wearing a worn and soiled army coat and fringed buckskin pants. On his right hip he wore a low-holstered .44 Colt, on his left side he carried a huge hunting knife in a fringed and beaded buckskin sheath, and in his left hand he carried a Winchester rifle. He wore a faded, brown, wide-brimmed hat from under which sprang a mass of hair that was neither kinky like a Negro's nor straight like an Indian's, but was instead a pile of woolly black curls. And his face was such an even blend of Indian and Negro features that people were often unsure if he was one or the other. During his early days in the Territory a buffalo skinner had mistaken him for a Gypsy and tagged him with the name. His real name was Wannicha Smith, but very few people knew that.

"Name's Gypsy Smith," he said.

"I know. Something I can do for you?"

Gypsy gestured that they resume walking. "Well, it's like this. You think a man old as me can still learn to read and write?"

Maxwell turned and stared at him. This man, who seemed so mild mannered, was a killer—not a murderer, but at least a man who, for presumably lawful reasons, was known to have killed many men. "You?" he said. "You want to learn to read and write?"

Gypsy said with a crooked grin, "I guess I'd be too old."

"No, no, it's not that. Sure, you could learn if you wanted to, but, well, it'd mean going to school, sitting in a classroom. . . ."

"Yeah, I reckon I'd look pretty silly, a grown man sitting in a schoolroom with them kids?"

"No, no, I didn't mean that. I mean, how could you? An army scout stationed a good four-hour ride from here?"

"Oh, I ain't gonna be a scout much longer. I been hearing 'bout how this Dawes Act's gonna do away with the reservations, and the Indians are gonna be forced to settle down on farms. So the army ain't gonna need no more scouts like me. I figure I can make a living catching some wild horses now and again. Well, that'd leave me some time to go to school. See what I mean?"

They stopped again at the steps leading to the school.

"Yes, I see." Maxwell was touched in his teacher's soul to find someone who really wanted to learn, especially since that someone was a bona fide killer. "Well, all right. Anytime you're ready to begin, just come to my office, and we'll get you enrolled."

"You don't think the kids'll laugh at me?"

"At *you?*" Maxwell chuckled. "No, Mr. Smith, I don't think anybody's going to laugh at *you.*"

Chapter Three

CORBY was surprised when he came to his homeroom reading class one morning to find that Gypsy Smith was his new bench mate. He remembered seeing Gypsy in the Hehyo village a few times. Known among the Human Beings as Moxthaveho—Black White Man—he was a highly respected warrior and tamer of horses.

They proved to be good bench mates, Corby and Gypsy, and a real friendship between them began one day when their teacher asked the students to take turns reading. Gypsy stood, awkward as any schoolboy, and began a stumbling reading from his textbook.

" 'Jack . . . went to . . . fe . . . fe . . .' " he read.

" 'Fetch,' " Corby whispered behind his hand.

" '. . . *fetch* Jane. They went to the . . . me . . . me . . .' "

" 'Meeting,' " Corby supplied.

" '. . . *meeting*,' " Gypsy said in triumph.

When Gypsy finished and sat down again, he whispered from the side of his mouth, "Thanks, *navestax*. That's one I owe you."

Corby blushed. *Navestax* was a word used to address a brother in a warrior band, and to be called that by Moxthaveho was enough to make him almost giddy with a sense of importance.

After that, they sometimes met in the school's dining hall to help each other with their homework, and one day Gypsy, to show his gratitude, offered to take Corby along on a wild-horse hunt.

The prospect excited Corby for a moment, and then, crestfallen, he said, "But I cannot leave the school. It is not permitted."

"I reckon that's best," Gypsy said. "You stay in school, learn all you can as long as you can."

Corby stammered, "My—my father . . ."

"I know. Your father don't put much store in white man's learning. I've known Ghost Dancer for a long time now, and always respected him, but he's wrong about this schooling business."

"They say the Ghost Dance will . . ." He ran his finger over the cover of a McGuffey reader on the table in front of him.

"I tell you, *navestax*, there ain't no dance that's gonna bring back the buffalo and the Indian dead. The Indian wars are over. The Indians lost, and the sooner we face that, the better off we're gonna be. What we got to do now is get educated. Learn to read and write. That's where the white man gets his power from—books."

Gypsy's being away from school three or four times a year to catch mustangs interfered with his lessons, but he took his McGuffey reader with him. On those stretches of prairie where the horses could walk for hours with hardly a break in rhythm, Gypsy would read as he rode along. It wasn't long before he could read popular pulp-paper fiction, and newspaper stories about the General Allotment Act of 1887, the so-called Dawes Act. He learned that a Senator Dawes from Massachusetts introduced the bill in Congress that cleared the way for much of Indian Territory to be settled by homesteaders. The bill would force the Indians to give up the tribal lands they held in common in exchange for individual ownership of one-hundred-and-sixty-acre allotments. So once more the politicians were going to move the Indians off the land promised to them "in perpetuity."

"The lying scoundrels," Gypsy said of the politicians.

But the politicians didn't plan for all the reservations to be thrown open at the same time; it would be done one reservation at a time. The first land to be opened for settlement would be the Oklahoma District, a tract on which no Indians had yet been sent to live. The Oklahoma District—more than two million acres of prime ranching and farming land smack in the middle of Indian Territory—was bordered on the north by the Cherokee Outlet, on the south by the Chickasaw Nation, on the west by the Cheyenne-Arapaho reservation, and on the east by a number of smaller reservations of the Shawnee and other tribes. This land had originally been set aside for future Indian reservations, but the politicians had changed their minds and decided to give it to homesteaders instead.

Gypsy learned all this by doggedly deciphering the newspapers, and by the time the opening of the Oklahoma District was drawing near, he was able to read the letter he received from a man in Topeka, Kansas. The letter asked him if he would go to Tennessee to bring back a wagon train of colored settlers to make the run into the Oklahoma District. He showed the letter to Maxwell.

Maxwell adjusted the glasses on the bridge of his nose and leaned forward. " 'Oklahoma Immigration Association.' " His eyes went to the signature at the bottom of the page. "Well, well, would you look at that! Jolson Mossburger."

"I read 'bout him in the newspapers once or twice. Some high muck-a-muck colored man up in Kansas, ain't he?"

"One of the best-known colored men in the country, in fact. Was once United States ambassador to Liberia, or something like that, and now he's some kind of elected official in Kansas. Read something a couple of weeks ago about his trying to get hundreds of thousands of Negroes in the South to make the run for homesteads. Seems he wants to make an all-colored territory, Negroes and Indians, with him as the first governor when it becomes a state." After a pause to appreciate the scope of such grand ambitions, he asked, "You going to take the job?"

Gypsy scratched the nape of his neck. "Don't rightly know. Tell the truth, I don't hold much with sodbusters—all fences and plowed fields. Fact is, I like this country the way it is."

"Well, they're coming, whether you help 'em or not."

"I 'spect so," Gypsy said, and figured that if they were coming anyway, where was the harm in giving them a hand? Still, he'd have to know how much the job paid and how long it would last before he could make up his mind, so he got Maxwell to help him write a letter to Mr. Mossburger, saying he needed more information.

A few days later a telegram was delivered to him. It was from Topeka, Kansas, requesting him to meet Mr. Jolson Mossburger five days hence at Guthrie Station in the Oklahoma District. Mossburger was scheduled to stop over for a day to meet with some prospective wagon-train guides, one of whom he hoped would be Gypsy. Could Gypsy come?

GUTHRIE Station, a small collection of buildings alongside the Santa Fe railroad tracks, had once been a stagecoach stop. Most of the buildings were weather-beaten clapboard and log structures.

Gypsy stopped to let his mare drink from the horse trough beneath the water tank alongside the tracks, then rode to the hotel, where four horses were tied to the hitching rail. The saloon was a smoke-darkened, low-ceilinged room with a crude plank bar on one side, plank tables with chairs on the other, and a big stone fireplace at the far end, in which roared a fire. Behind the bar was Roy Lipscomb, the owner, a paunchy man with tousled hair and unshaven jowls. His wife, a Tonkawa squaw, was at that moment in the kitchen cooking a dinner of rattlesnake stew for the hotel's guests.

There were three of them, all black. Gypsy knew one of them, Chickasaw Charlie, who lived with the Chickasaw Indians and had himself a Chickasaw wife. The other two were Joe Peek and Nat Sayers, and like Gypsy, they were men of the Plains who dressed in bits and pieces of agency-issue clothes and Indian geegaws.

"We all after the same job?" Gypsy asked after he had joined them at their table for a drink.

"Naw," said Chickasaw Charlie in his thick southern accent. "Way I hear it, they beating the bushes for every colored man they can find in the Territory. Say they wants us go down south and bring back as many of them po' ignorant dirt farmers as we can."

"You gonna do it?"

"I 'spect so. I got a squaw to feed and about umpteen in-laws." He pushed the bottle of whiskey across the table. "Have another."

"Not now, thanks. Gotta take care of my horse and grab a bunk."

He paid Lipscomb fifty cents, for a bunk for himself and a stable for his mare. "How the bedbugs these days?" he asked.

"Real hungry," Lipscomb said. "They been looking forward to seeing you again, Gypsy."

As Gypsy was leading his mare around to the crumbling adobe stables behind the hotel, he noticed a blurred movement on the southern horizon. Horses and riders, seven or eight of them; not Indians, cowboys maybe, though there would be little reason for cowboys to be in the Oklahoma District now that the government had moved the ranchers out to make way for the homesteaders.

Their presence made him a little edgy, but he went on to the stable and unsaddled his mare and gave her a rubdown while she

173

munched oats from a nose bag. Then he took his saddlebags and bedroll and started for the back door of the saloon but stopped when he saw two riders coming. He thought he recognized one of the horses—a piebald with unusual markings, easy to spot—as being one of the mounts in the gang of cowboys he had seen a little while ago. Why had they split off from the others? And where were the others? What were they up to?

Gypsy went back into the saloon, had some of the rattlesnake stew, and when the train carrying Mossburger arrived, he and the others went out to meet it. The only other persons on the platform were five bedraggled Indians, their ponies tied to the hitching rail beside the station house. Gypsy wondered what had happened to the two riders he had seen approaching town. They'd had plenty of time to arrive, yet there was no piebald among the horses.

The locomotive screeched to a steaming stop directly beneath the water tank, putting the two passenger cars directly abreast of the platform. A few Indians got off, followed by three Negroes, one of whom could only have been Jolson Mossburger: a light-skinned man in a brown derby hat, a high stiff collar, a black silk vest, spats, and pin-striped pants. He was followed by two other light-skinned Negroes, both dressed in suits and ties.

"Is this all of you?" Mossburger asked after introductions.

"Fur's I knows," Chickasaw Charlie said, glancing around the platform. "How many was you 'specting?"

"Ah, well," Mossburger said, and led them back to a table in the saloon and ordered a pot of hot black coffee.

"Gentlemen," he announced, "the Oklahoma Immigration Association needs you. Your colored brothers and sisters in the South need you. After twenty-five years of 'freedom,' the Negro race is as bad off as it ever was. They're no longer called slaves, but they're still working the white man's lands with the white man's mules. They're still being lynched—one hundred and sixty-two lynchings in the South during the last year—and a colored school or church or home is burned down almost every day by the Ku Klux Klan.

"Well, our people have to have a land of their own, and this is it—Oklahoma! Here," he said, taking from his satchel a sheaf of flyers. "This is what we're doing to make a Negro homeland a reality." He started to pass the flyers around, but suddenly stopped as if he had thought of something. "Can any of you read?"

Gypsy said with a grin, "Sure, I can."

The flyer from the Oklahoma Immigration Association was addressed to the "Colored Citizens of the South," promising them a veritable paradise, where land and peoples were free. Colored citizens only had to join the wagon trains westward.

"That flyer has been sent to thousands of churches and newspapers in the South, and the response, praise God, has been tremendous. A stream of black humanity has begun to flow toward Oklahoma. Some are walking, some have horses or mules, some even have wagons. I'm sure they'll all get here, even if they have to crawl."

"Well, mister," Gypsy said, "that's all well and good, but the District's gonna be opened by a run. The one who gets there first gets the homestead. How's any folks on foot going to beat horses?"

"That's where you guides come in. You all know this country. Most of the people who make the run on horseback, they're likely to be strangers here. Many'll get lost or won't know where to go or won't be able to locate the section markers. You men will lead our people into those areas where they'll have the best chance of finding a claim. Well then? What d'you say? Are you with us?"

"But why," Gypsy wanted to know, "would you be wanting to send us all the way back south? Why not let 'em get out here on their own, and then we'll lead 'em in when the run starts?"

"Think, men! Those people are babes in the woods. I would be surprised if any of them have ever been more than a hundred miles away from home. They don't know how to deal with frontier situations. They need leaders. They need you."

"Yeah?" Chickasaw Charlie said. "What's the pay?"

"A dollar a day."

Charlie hooted. "Hell, I can make more'n that punching cows."

"I realize it's not much, but remember it's the immigrants themselves who'll be paying your wages. These are your people, and they need your help. Will you help them?"

Three of them nodded grudgingly and said yes, they would take the job. Gypsy was the only holdout. He told Mossburger that he saw a disaster in the making. Of all those dirt-poor immigrants coming in, damned few would actually get a homestead. What would happen to those who didn't? And even if a few did manage to get a homestead, how would they build cabins and buy seeds? It would be a year before they could make a crop; what would they live on till then?

"I tell you, mister, this time next year you might have thousands of those poor babes in the woods wandering around out here without any land or shelter or anything to eat."

Mossburger asked, "Have you ever been to the South?"

"Can't say I have," Gypsy admitted.

"They couldn't be any worse off," Mossburger asserted.

"They're alive, ain't they? Out here, they may not be very long."

As Mossburger was trying to figure out how to answer that, Gypsy turned his attention to two men who entered the saloon. On second glance he saw that one of them was dressed as a man and carried a gun like a man, but the hip on which the .44 rested was unmistakably feminine. It was a woman, all right, and not just any woman either, but Rose Maddox herself, the Rose of Cimarron, possibly the most famous woman outlaw in the Territory. Gypsy had first met her about eighteen years ago, when she'd had a price on her head. As far as he knew, she had gone straight for a number of years now, but here she was, packing a .44, accompanied by a man who might have passed for a pig farmer except for the two revolvers he carried. Gypsy guessed from pictures he had seen on WANTED posters that the man was Ole Yantis, a back-shooting killer known to be a member of the Boss Beeson gang. Gypsy wondered which one of the two had been riding the piebald and what they were doing here at Guthrie Station. And where were the five or six others they had been riding with earlier in the day?

Rose pretended not to know Gypsy. As she came into the saloon, her eyes swept across every face in the room, and Gypsy was sure there was a flicker of recognition in her eyes when she saw him. She and Ole Yantis stepped up to the bar and ordered whiskey.

"So what do you say, Mr. Smith?" Mossburger asked, trying to draw him back into the discussion. "Will you do it?"

Still glancing at the Rose of Cimarron from the corners of his eyes, Gypsy said, "Naw, I reckon not. You best count me out." He reached for his saddlebags and bedroll on the floor beside his chair and said loudly enough for Rose to hear, "Now, if you'll excuse me, gentlemen, I'll go on out and take care my horse."

HE WAS in the stables behind the hotel, currycombing his horse, when Rose emerged from the back door of the saloon. She gave him a follow-me look and headed for the two-hole privy behind the hotel. When she disappeared behind the door of the first privy, he followed and went into the second. The plank partition between the holes was thin enough to allow for conversation in normal tones.

"Well, if it ain't the Rose of Cimarron herself," he said through the partition.

"That you, Gypsy Smith?"

"What's left of me, Rose, after all these years. How you?"

"Not so good, tell the truth. Ain't like the old days, is it? You see that skunk I'm riding with?"

"Ole Yantis, ain't it? Last I heard, he was with the Beeson gang. You riding with the likes of that bunch these days, Rose?"

"Just for this job," she said. "And looks like I'm gonna have to mess it up. You done me a favor once. I reckon I can return it."

"Well, I do recollect the last thing you said to me." Gypsy peeked through the quarter-moon aperture in the door and caught sight of three riders coming in from the south. They were about a quarter mile away. "You said you always paid your debts."

Rose took a deep breath and said, "Beeson and his bunch is coming here to kill them you're with."

"That so? Now, why'd anybody want to do a thing like that?"

"They been hired to do it: to kill that—What's-his-name? Mossburger? Some land company up in Kansas hired 'em, I hear. Idea is to keep colored homesteaders from coming in here. They gonna string Mossburger and the others up, take pictures for the newspapers in the South. I'm telling you so's you can save y'self."

"Tell me, though, how'd you get mixed up in something like this? I heard you'd gone straight."

177

"Well," she said sheepishly, "times're hard, and . . . well, I sort of teamed up with Kid Bannister. You heard of him?"

Gypsy recalled the name and face of a kid on a WANTED poster.

"Me and him's sort of a team now, see," Rose said. "He wants to get in good with Beeson. Personally I think Beeson and his boys are a bunch of no-good egg suckers, but the kid . . . well, I sort of tagged along to look out for him."

"Three men riding in from the south," Gypsy said. "Who're they?"

"That'd be the kid, with Bill Ballenger and crazy Nez. Beeson and Bill Harney'll be coming in from the north in a little while. Coming in scattered so's not to alarm nobody."

"Dynamite Bill Ballenger? He must have a pretty good reward on his head. And Boss Beeson must be worth at least a thousand."

"Well, in case you're thinking about trying to collect it, just remember, there's been lots of bounty hunters tried it and most of 'em are dead. It wouldn't break my heart to see them get what's coming to 'em. But leave me and Kid Bannister out of it."

"You don't have to worry none, Rose," he said.

"Good luck," she said. Gypsy watched through the quarter moon in the door as Rose walked on back to the saloon.

Gypsy carried his saddlebags and bedroll with him when he went back into the saloon. But rather than rejoin Mossburger and the others at the table, he took a place at the front end of the bar, so that he had a clear view of the whole room. He placed the saddlebags and bedroll on the bar in front of him.

The three men had entered the saloon just before Gypsy. Dynamite Bill Ballenger, having ordered a drink, was cursing and saying to Lipscomb, "Call this swill whiskey? Be all right for niggers and women, maybe"—giving Rose and the blacks at the table a contemptuous glance—"but white men don't drink this swill. Where's your good stuff?"

"Yeah," said the one Gypsy guessed to be Nez. "Give us the good stuff or we'll—" He looked at Bill Ballenger. "What'll we do, Bill, if he don't? How 'bout I blow his head off?" He put his double-barreled shotgun on the bar.

Kid Bannister stood a little apart from them. He had a delicate, slightly feminine face, with the expression of someone trying to keep his courage up.

Lipscomb tried to placate them with another kind of whiskey. Ballenger drank it and poured himself another, but he complained that it, too, wasn't good enough for white men. He took the bottle to Mossburger's table and slammed it down.

"This the kind of panther piss you niggers drink, ain't it?"

Trying not to be goaded, Mossburger said, "If you'll excuse us, we're trying to conduct some business."

Ballenger snatched up one of the flyers. "Yeah, I know what kind of 'business' you're trying to conduct."

Nez followed Ballenger to the table and aimed the shotgun at Mossburger's face. Ballenger pulled his .44, and the others in the gang followed suit, all except Rose. She turned to face the tables, leaning back against the bar, resting her elbows on it.

"Now you all get your hands up," Ballenger said, "and stand up real slow. Unbuckle your gun belts and let 'em drop."

"What's the meaning of this outrage?" Mossburger demanded.

"Shut up," Ballenger said.

"The knives, too," Ballenger said to Nat Sayers and Chickasaw Charlie, both of whom carried bowie knives on their belts. They dropped them into the pile of gun belts on the floor. "Now step back. Against the wall, all of you. You, Rose!" he barked. "Take these guns out and put 'em on the packhorse."

Rose said, "You're supposed to wait till Boss gets here."

"Just do what you're told."

"To hell with you." She turned around to face the bar. "I take orders from Beeson, not from you."

Perhaps to avert a clash between Rose and Ballenger, Kid Bannister tried to divert their attention by pointing his gun at Gypsy and saying, "What about him?"

Gypsy was primed to go into action on the merest fraction of a second. He had not thought to act until Boss Beeson and the other gang member showed up, but now that Chickasaw Charlie and the others had been disarmed, he had to be ready for the next best moment for action.

"You," Ballenger said to Gypsy. "What're you, anyway?"

"Me Cherokee," Gypsy said.

Ballenger seemed skeptical, and Gypsy's fingers moved imperceptibly a little farther up into the bedroll; but the sound of men's boots clumping across the station platform outside made him hesitate.

Boss Beeson and another member of the gang—Bill Harney—came into the saloon, pushing the station agent in front of them. Beeson had a .44 revolver in his hand, and Harney carried a Winchester rifle. Beeson was a tall, lean man in his mid-fifties, clean-shaven, wearing a black beaver hat and a long, dirty duster. He had the baleful eyes and beaked nose of a bird of prey. Harney was a small squint-eyed man with a gray beard streaked by snuff stains.

"Get over there," Beeson said, using the muzzle of his .44 to nudge the station agent toward the bar.

"We got 'em, Boss," Ballenger said proudly. "Look."

Beeson glanced at the flyer, then looked at Mossburger. "Yeah, you're the one."

"You know who we are?" Ballenger asked Mossburger. "This here's Boss Beeson, and I'm Bill Ballenger. You never heard of us? Back in the war, we used to ride with Quantrill's Raiders, and when we made raids into Kansas, you know what we'd do when we'd catch us an uppity nigger like you? We'd string him up to the nearest tree. And that's what we gonna do with you and your friends here."

"You can't be serious," Mossburger protested. "My God, man, this is not the South."

"Yantis," Beeson said as he holstered his gun, "you and the kid go get things ready."

Ole Yantis and Kid Bannister hurried out of the saloon.

Bill Harney had begun to stare at Gypsy. Finally recognition broke through. "Hey! You're that bounty hunter, ain't you? Gypsy Smith? Yeah, I know you." Having leveled his rifle at Gypsy, he said over his shoulder to Beeson, "Hey, Boss! You know who this is? This's that bounty hunter that got Bob Abernathy."

"That right, boy?" Beeson asked.

Gypsy remained silent. Nez had turned around and leveled the shotgun at his head.

"Bob Abernathy was a good old friend of mine," Beeson said. "How much reward you get for taking him in?"

"More'n he was worth," Gypsy said.

"And you know what happened to him?"

"Sure. Hung him."

"That's right," Beeson said. "And I'm going to hang you just like they hung Bob. Now unbuckle that gun belt."

With a pistol, a rifle, and a shotgun pointed straight at him, Gypsy figured he didn't have much choice, but he obeyed with an almost provocative slowness and let the gun belt drop to the floor.

"Now get over there with the rest of them," Ballenger said.

Reaching for his saddlebags and bedroll on the counter as if to take them with him, his hand went inside the bedroll, gripped the sawed-off shotgun, and pointed the bedroll at Nez. He pulled the trigger, and Nez's body hurtled backward. Within a split second—before anybody could realize what had happened—Gypsy had fired the second barrel, this time at Harney, who caught the load of buckshot in the chest. Harney's rifle discharged when he was hit, but by then Gypsy had dropped to the floor behind the corner of the bar, where he snatched his pistol from its holster and—all in one continuous dancelike movement—rolled from behind the counter, already firing at Ballenger and Beeson.

Ballenger fired two hurried shots from his .44, one of which nicked Gypsy's cheek, before Gypsy's first pistol shot hit him, spinning him around, sending him crashing over a table. Beeson's .44 had barely cleared its holster before the second bullet from Gypsy's pistol hit him in the stomach, slamming him back into the fire in the fireplace.

Then Gypsy was on his feet, ready to fire again but finding himself momentarily without a target. Rose had thrown up her hands; Nez and Harney and Ballenger were dead.

Chickasaw Charlie, Nat Sayers, and Joe Peek scrambled for their guns. Alerted by the sound of running footsteps, Gypsy swung his .44 around to bear on Ole Yantis as he appeared in the saloon's doorway. Kid Bannister was about three steps behind him.

Rose yelled, "Stay out of it, Kid! Don't—"

But her voice was cut off by a shot. Gypsy's instinct didn't allow

181

him to hesitate for the merest fraction of a second. The bullet struck Yantis between the eyes, and his body was propelled backward and off the platform into the mud near the railroad tracks. This left Gypsy aiming at Kid Bannister, who, though he had pulled his gun from its holster, was so startled that he hesitated to shoot.

Gypsy saw that hesitation and shouted, "Drop it, Kid!"

But he neither dropped it nor aimed it. Instead he began backing up, confused, panicked, his eyes darting everywhere.

"I don't wanna have to kill you," Gypsy warned.

Rose cried from inside the saloon, "Jimmy, for God's sake, do what he tells you. Drop it!"

For some reason—defiance, spite, contrariness—Rose's plea caused the kid to raise the pistol. Before he could pull the trigger, however, three almost simultaneous shots fired from the pistols of Chickasaw Charlie, Nat Sayers, and Joe Peek hit the kid in the chest.

Rose cried out, but her cry was lost amid the cries and screams from Beeson, who, having thrashed his way out of the fireplace, now dashed headlong for the front door, his clothes and his hair on fire. He raced out the front door and across the station platform toward the horse trough beneath the water tank, on whose lowest crossbeam hung three noosed ropes that Yantis and the kid had placed there. Beeson threw himself into the horse trough.

Gypsy stepped outside the saloon. He was brought up short by the sight of Beeson's body floating facedown in the trough; then he went to the spigot on the pipe leading down from the overhead tank, turned it on, and put his head beneath the flow of water.

The station agent came to the trough and said to Gypsy, "I'd like to be able to tell my grandchildren I shook the hand of the man who wiped out the Beeson gang. This is a historic occasion!"

After shaking the water from his hair, Gypsy had taken a bandanna from his hip pocket and was drying his hands when the agent extended his own, which Gypsy shook without pride or enthusiasm. It was always like this after a gunfight: the slight nervousness, the hollow feeling in the pit of the stomach. When the fight was over and the danger past, he began to feel a sort of queasy nervousness and embarrassment, as if he couldn't quite believe what had happened.

Rose had stopped at the body of Kid Bannister and pulled his head onto her lap. She was weeping.

Gypsy left the water tank and approached her. "I'm sorry. I tried to get him to . . ." He faltered, shrugged. "I'm sorry."

Rose said, "With me for a mother and Curly Bill Bannister for a father, being an outlaw was in his blood, I reckon. But he was . . . just no good at it. I tried to tell him. He wouldn't listen."

Mossburger stumbled about the platform, gesturing wildly toward the hanging ropes draped over the crossbeam of the water tank. "This! This!" he said to Gypsy. "*This* is why."

"Why what?"

"Why you should go. Think, man. Think what'd happen if those poor ignorant colored immigrants met up with a gang like this. Don't you see? *This* is why you should go!"

Gypsy shifted his weight to one leg, looked up and down the railroad tracks, and said, "Maybe so."

Surprised, Mossburger asked, "You'll do it then? You'll go?"

"I reckon so," Gypsy said.

Chapter Four

WHEN Gypsy first set eyes on the immigrants in a campground on the banks of the Mississippi River just below Memphis, there were about a thousand of them. It was his task to get them organized by cutting out all those who were too sick to make the trip or too poor to provision themselves along the way. He gave them their choice: "If any of you are gonna make it, get rid of those who can't."

This reduced the band to about five hundred, though even most of those didn't look as if they could arrive at the Oklahoma District in time for the run. To do so, they would have to travel at least twenty miles a day, every day, for twenty-two days. How could they possibly do it? Especially the ones who had no means of transportation other than their feet, some of whom didn't even have shoes?

Gypsy didn't have much confidence in some of the conveyances either. One man had a kiddie cart pulled by a big billy goat; another had a sled dog harnessed to a child's red wagon. An old woman rode a saddled milk cow. There were bicycles, burros, and pushcarts.

But all was not hopeless. Of those that followed Gypsy out of Memphis, about a hundred seemed well equipped for the trip. Some had well-matched teams of sleek Missouri mules and horses to pull good wagons that were loaded down with farm tools and household belongings. Some rode Indian ponies; some rode plow horses; a few rode Thoroughbreds.

From among those who had good riding horses, Gypsy chose ten section leaders to ride herd on the immigrants, to keep them moving. There were two things for which he would allow the caravan to stop: a burial or a birth. It was a harsh rule, but what choice did Gypsy have if they intended to get to the Oklahoma District in time for the run?

One mule-drawn wagon became very special to him. It belonged to a handsome young woman named Drusilla Pointer. She had glossy black hair that bobbled on her head in long pigtail ringlets. She had a tall muscular body with smooth skin the color of roasted coffee beans. And you could tell from the way she handled her pair of spavined mules that she was a strong and independent young woman, a woman who cooked a good supper every night for herself and six children, and who was—to top it all off—a schoolteacher.

The children had come to her as pupils. Over the years, however, these four girls and two boys, ages six to twelve—all orphaned or abandoned—had more or less adopted her as a foster mother or big sister, and she had more or less adopted them as her own.

She had taught in a one-room Tennessee schoolhouse that had been burned down one night by the Ku Klux Klan. Shortly afterward she had bought herself a span of mules and an old wagon, heaped the wagon with household goods and books and the six children who had nowhere else to go, and joined the caravan headed for the Promised Land. And though it was a brutal and demanding trip, she didn't neglect the children's education. Every night after supper they gathered around the campfire and took turns reading from their textbooks.

It was these nightly reading lessons that first brought Gypsy Smith into her camp. Could he come and sit with the other students when

185

they had their lessons? She suspected he was more interested in her than in reading, but she was soon surprised and puzzled to see that he really was trying to learn how to read—puzzled because it seemed such a humble thing for a proud man to do.

And he was proud. That had been the first thing she noticed about him on that day he rode into the Memphis campground on his black mare. The aura of authority that he carried about him was so self-assured that he had no need to be arrogant or abusive. She had never heard him raise his voice. She admired that in a man. And yet he wasn't at all aloof. He could still plunk himself down among the children around the campfire and take his turn reading. What was she to make of him, this man who could be a man among men and a child among children?

One morning he rode up beside her wagon, touched his hat brim, and said, "Morning, Miss Drusilla. Fine morning, ain't it?"

"*Isn't* it," she said, and gave him a quick look to see if he resented the correction. "Looky here, you want me to correct you anytime you make a mistake or only when we're in a study class?"

"Why, Miss Drusilla, you just correct me any old time. My mama, she used to say there wasn't no shame in being ignorant, the only shame was staying ignorant."

To hear him mention his mother prompted her to try to draw him out by saying, "Smart woman, your mama. Was she a slave?"

"Most of her life, yeah." With a little more prying, Drusilla learned that his mother had been owned by one of the chiefs of the Cherokees, a big cotton plantation owner, who had adopted the white name Smith. Gypsy was his son.

"He acknowledged you?" Drusilla asked. "Gave you his name?"

"Yeah. I was a sort of half son, half slave. The Cherokees, see, didn't treat their slaves the same way white folks did. They was slaves, sure, but they was still human beings, and when they was set free in '65, they was adopted into the tribe as Cherokees."

As the wagon bumped over the rutted road, Drusilla leaned forward, elbows on her knees, the reins held slackly in her hands. "Looky here, Gypsy Smith—" She hesitated a moment, summoning up her determination, then blurted out, "Are you a married man?"

"Was once. Comanche, she was. That was a long time ago, when I was no older than you are right now. What's that? Twenty-one?"

"Twenty-two. So where's she now?"

"Dead." He absently brushed a horsefly off the mare. "Typhoid. I was in Kansas. Came back and half the camp was dead. The boy, too."

"The boy? You had a son?"

"Two years old when he died."

"I'm sorry," Drusilla said.

He shrugged. "Oh, well, that was . . . a long time ago."

"You never wanted to get married again?"

"Lordy, no, Miss Drusilla. Wouldn't be fair to a woman being married to me. Ain't likely I'll ever stay in one place too long."

A rider suddenly appeared, coming along the caravan from the front at full gallop, calling, "Gypsy! Up front!"

Gypsy had already touched his spurs to his mare's flanks and sent her leaping forward into a run. At the head of the column the caravan had stopped in front of a burning cross that had been planted in the middle of the road. The cross was about eight feet high, wrapped thickly in kerosene-soaked rags.

Gypsy rode close enough to feel the heat and smell the kerosene. He put the sole of his boot against the flaming end of the cross member and shoved it over.

"Keep 'em moving," he called to the caravan leaders.

A little farther down the road they found a crudely lettered sign nailed to a roadside tree: WE HANG STRANGE NIGGERS IN THIS COUNTY.

That night Gypsy posted twenty guards around the perimeter of the campsite and admonished them not to shoot unless their lives were in danger. "If you see any suspicious movement, just fire a warning shot in the air, and we'll all come running."

Later, after he had fed his mare and staked her out to graze by a creek bank, he made his way through the many cooking fires in the campground and arrived at Drusilla's camp.

"Will you join us for supper?" Drusilla asked. "We've got plenty. Fried squirrel, beans, and hot biscuits."

Having very little capacity for polite lies, he said, "Well, if you're sure you got plenty. I'm sick of my own cooking."

187

"Mingo," she said to the oldest girl, "get another plate."

Gypsy was served the first plate of food, and though ravenous, he waited politely until all the others had their plates of food in front of them before he picked up a piece of squirrel. But he suddenly stopped when he noticed that the others were looking at him in a puzzled and perhaps even mildly reproachful way.

"Maybe Mr. Smith will say grace," Drusilla said.

Gypsy dropped the squirrel leg back onto the plate. "Oh. Oh, well, you see, I'm afraid I don't know any."

"Well then, Clarence," Drusilla said, "I think it's your turn."

Gypsy sheepishly followed their lead as they bowed their heads over their plates and Clarence gave thanks to the Lord, after which they all ate heartily enough, though the children didn't seem to be in their usual high spirits.

"It's because of the Klan," Drusilla said. "We all have some pretty bad memories."

After the dishes were cleaned and put away, they all gathered around the dying campfire, and Drusilla, by the light of a coal-oil lantern hanging from a tree, read to them from the Bible.

Watching her, Gypsy saw in her face and heard in her voice a goodness and a gentleness that touched him in a way he'd seldom been touched before. At the same time, however, he felt as if he were a stranger standing in darkness and peering through a window at a firelit scene that he could never share.

He pushed himself to his feet. "I best be making my rounds, see the section leaders and all."

"You kids go ahead—say your prayers and go to sleep," she said. "I'm going to walk a ways with Mr. Smith."

Drusilla accompanied him across the crowded campground only far enough to be out of the hearing of the children, then stopped and said, "You're not a Christian man, are you, Gypsy Smith?"

"No, Miss Drusilla, can't say as I am."

"Were you ever?" she asked, as if there might be hope in history.

"Oh, when I was a kid, I reckon."

"You think it's just for children, then?" she asked in a tone that held no trace of challenge or argument.

"Oh, I don't know," he said, slightly abashed. "I reckon it's for anybody that it helps. Whatever gets you through the night."

She nodded. "Well, good night, then." She gave his arm a light, brief touch before she turned and walked back toward her camp.

AFTER they had crossed the border into the Cherokee Nation, immigrant trails from other parts of the country began to converge. Most of the immigrants were white, and they went their own way. But occasionally a band of Negroes would come out of a side road, and many of them, having been harassed along the way by the Ku Klux Klan, joined the caravan for protection, so that by the time it reached Tahlequah, it numbered nearly a thousand persons—all Negroes except for one, a woman named Eula Rasmussen, whose white skin was not her only notable difference. She also had a harelip.

She was from Minnesota and had walked all the way, leading an old mule loaded with everything she owned in the world. She was dressed in a threadbare coat, a patched ankle-length dress, and one of those field-hand sunbonnets designed to protect the wearer's face from the sun. It also gave protection from curious and pitying eyes.

As a baby, born to some unknown mother who didn't want a harelipped child, she had been abandoned on the steps of an orphanage in Minnesota. Her deformity left her little or no chance of being adopted, so she lived in the orphanage for fourteen years and then was sent out to live and work on a farm.

But Eula didn't waste time feeling sorry for herself. She was a sensible girl. She recognized that she would never have a normal life, with a husband and a family. The best she could hope for would be to have a farm of her own someday, a home in which she would not have to hide her deformity by eating in dark corners. So that became her prayer, her hope, her obsession. From her meager wages as servant and field hand she saved every nickel and dime she could. Her best guess was that she would have enough money to buy herself a farm by the time she was forty or fifty years old.

Then she heard about free land that could be had in Indian Territory by any settler who could win out in a land rush, so she used her savings to buy herself a mule and headed down the road.

She first came into contact with the all-Negro caravan when she found herself sharing a campground with them. It had rained a little that day, causing her matches to get wet. She went to Drusilla Pointer's camp to ask for some live coals from her fire.

Drusilla was very suspicious of the white woman at first, because of the way she kept her face hidden. But when she caught a glimpse of the ugly split in her upper lip that exposed her teeth and gums, Drusilla's suspicions melted to sympathy and pity and shame.

The next morning Eula Rasmussen, leading her mule, walked along the road with the caravan, not as part of it but as if she and the caravan were merely traveling in the same direction at the same speed. But she usually stayed within talking distance of Drusilla Pointer's wagon so that the two of them could exchange idle snatches of conversation to help pass the time of day.

That night in the campground, when Eula once again came to Drusilla's campfire to ask for some hot coals, Drusilla asked her to stay and share their supper of hush puppies and turnip greens, and so grateful was Eula for the invitation that she ran back to her own fireless camp and took from her pack a jar of cherries that she had brought all the way from Minnesota. She used Drusilla's Dutch oven to make a cherry cobbler for their dessert.

Thereafter Eula joined Drusilla and her small band every night for supper. She never came empty-handed or went away without doing some chores around the camp. But the surest bond of their partnership was forged when they were halfway across the Creek Nation, only three days away from the Oklahoma District. It was then that Drusilla woke up to find that one of her two mules was dying. The mule's death left Drusilla in a predicament. Now she would have to either drop out of the caravan or abandon her wagon and most of their belongings, including the books with which she had planned to start a new school in the new land.

Eula brought her own mule to Drusilla's wagon, harnessed it with Drusilla's remaining mule, tossed her belongings onto the wagon, and said behind her hand, "Let's go to Oklahoma."

They reached Fort Reno on April 18, four days before the run. Even the complainers were now glad that Gypsy Smith had driven the caravan so relentlessly. Without the four days to rest their exhausted animals, they wouldn't have had a chance in the run.

The rest did wonders for their spirits, too. They began to share the yeasty feeling of excitement that was growing more intense every day among the thousands of land seekers who were gathering along the borders of the Oklahoma District, a feeling that they were part of something bigger and more important than themselves.

Gypsy felt it—a rare feeling. For most of his life he had been a loner. But that last night before the run, as he sat with Drusilla and the children around their campfire and listened to the sounds of celebrations coming from the other campfires along the starting line, he actually enjoyed the giddy feeling of belonging to something bigger than himself: a place, a people, a tribe, a family.

Drusilla must have sensed what was going through his mind, for when he got up to leave, she walked a little way with him. A three-quarter moon and millions of stars lit the landscape. They stopped beneath a big cottonwood tree.

"And what about you?" she asked. "What'll you be doing tomorrow night? Your job'll be finished."

"Yeah, but I 'spect I'll stick around for a little while. Oughta be real entertaining, seeing people start a town from scratch."

"We all wish you'd be part of it."

"Well, I tell you something, Miss Drusilla—"

"Oh, I do wish you'd stop that 'Miss Drusilla' stuff! It sounds so—so patronizing. You sometimes treat me as if I were a child. I'm not a child, Gypsy Smith, and you're not an old man."

"No, no, you sure ain't no child, Miss Drusilla, honey, but, well, the fact is, I'm nearly old enough to be your—"

"Never mind." She turned to face him in the shadows. "That's not important. Not to me. Is it to you?"

He reached out and adjusted the shawl on her shoulder. Then he let his fingers stray up her long smooth neck to her cheek.

"Right now, Miss Drusilla, honey, it don't seem important at all."

He pulled her to him and kissed her mouth. She put her arms around his neck with the eagerness of someone greeting a long-lost lover. He picked her up around her slim waist and held her so that

191

their mouths were on the same level. She was breathing fast now, but when he made a motion to lay her down on the green grass beneath the cottonwood tree, she, as if suddenly waking up, said no, and pushed away from him. She hesitated for a moment, then said, "Well, I'd better be getting on back. Good night."

He watched her walk away through the moonlight and shadows. He heard crickets singing in the woods behind him, and from the myriad campfires strung out along the starting line, the sounds of celebrations continued. He waited, listening, trying to sort out his feelings, but that seemed impossible, so he walked on toward the grove of mesquite trees where he had left his bedroll.

THE morning of April 22, 1889, the day of the first run into Indian Territory by homesteaders, broke clear and fair. Troops of cavalry from Fort Sill had been sent to patrol the line and prevent the runners from stampeding into the District before the starting gun sounded.

Leading his black mare, Gypsy wandered for most of the morning among the black immigrants, advising, exhorting, encouraging; but as the noon hour began to draw near, he was putting his own mount through warm-up gallops. Amos Fulton, the representative of the Oklahoma Immigration Association, had persuaded him to make the run himself in order to try to secure one of the three claims on which were located the springs that formed the headwaters of Cottonwood Creek. These would be the three most valuable claims in the vicinity of the new townsite, and it was imperative that they not fall into unfriendly hands, for the new town would need the water from the springs to survive until wells could be dug.

Gypsy thought he had as good a chance as any. Among the horses making the run were Kentucky Thoroughbreds that could outrun his black mare, Girl, over a distance of three or four miles, but couldn't outlast her over the ten-mile distance to the headwaters of Cottonwood Creek. Besides, Gypsy figured he probably knew the country better than any of the other riders, and that would be his edge.

He had ridden by Drusilla's camp that morning to see how things were going. They had stripped the wagon of everything except a canteen, and all the children except Clarence were being left behind with the belongings.

"Clarence'll be back to get you as soon as we stake a claim," Drusilla promised as she and Eula climbed up on the wagon seat.

Gypsy escorted Drusilla's wagon up to the starting line. In some places the line was already two or three deep with horses and wagons and buggies and buckboards and bicycles and foot runners, but Gypsy helped Drusilla to jockey the wagon into a good place.

He touched the brim of his hat to Drusilla. "Well then, here we go. Best of luck to you, Miss Drusilla."

"You, too, Gypsy Smith."

He touched his hat to Eula, too. "And good luck to you, Miss Eula."

She had her hand over her mouth, so he couldn't see if she was smiling, but there was excitement in her voice when she said, "Thankee kindly. You, too."

A dead silence settled over the line as the troopers waited for the last few seconds to tick away. At high noon they fired their weapons, and at that moment a great roar was heard up and down the line as the runners echoed the signal shots with shots of their own—with accompanying whoops and screams—and the mighty horde plunged forward in a convulsive movement. The race was under way.

The riders on the fastest horses leaped into the forefront of the stampede. Buckboards and buggies and wagons knocked into one another; some locked wheels; some overturned. Others, pulled by runaway horses, plunged into ravines at full speed and smashed.

Gypsy saw only a little of this. He had left the starting line with the lead horses, though he himself didn't try for the lead, not at first. He put Girl into a steady lope, and after a mile the frontrunners had begun to winnow out. Gypsy counted only eight riders in front of him, all mounted on good horses, most of them probably headed for the valuable allotments at the Cottonwood springs. At about two miles, three of them had begun to falter badly, allowing the black mare to gain ground rapidly enough to overtake them within another mile or two. And while the Thoroughbreds in the lead were no longer gaining ground, they were still holding their half-mile lead, and Gypsy began to realize that the black mare was going to have to be tested as she had never been tested before.

He saw one of the front-runners go down in a ravine. That left only four: Leroy King, one of the black caravan leaders, on his Kentucky Thoroughbred, and three white men, one riding a buckskin, another riding a sorrel, and the other one—the one in the lead—riding a big, beautiful chestnut stallion. All were racehorses, and all had obviously been trained for a long-distance run.

The next to go down was the sorrel. Its legs went wobbly, and the rider slipped off; then he looked on in despair as the horse collapsed.

That left three in front, and it wasn't long before Leroy King's Thoroughbred began to falter. Leroy had to slow the horse's pace, with the result that Gypsy had almost overtaken him by the time they were approaching the low, rolling, tree-covered sandhills that lay between the racers and the Cottonwood springs allotments.

Gypsy knew a detour through the sandhills that cut at least a mile off the distance. He veered off across the prairie, found the narrow old trail, and pulled the mare down to a fast trot. The slower pace through the difficult ground gave Girl a breather.

When Gypsy came out of the sandhills, he was at least a quarter mile ahead of the chestnut and the buckskin. Now *he* was the front-runner. The other riders, astonished when they saw him, laid their quirts to their horses, but the buckskin simply had no more to give. The chestnut stallion, on the other hand, did have more, and he gave it all in a burst of speed that finally brought him up even with Gypsy. Now it was between the two of them.

As the chestnut pulled alongside Girl, the two horses running neck and neck, Gypsy glanced at the rider—a well-dressed young white man in a black Stetson hat and a Prince Albert coat—and nodded in respectful recognition. The white rider returned the salute by touching the tip of his quirt to the brim of his hat.

They were within three quarters of a mile of the Cottonwood springs when Gypsy made his move. He leaned forward and shouted, "All right, Girl, you ready? Here we go!" He took off his hat, slapped it against Girl's haunch, and touched his spurs to her belly, and within three strides she was in a full, flat-out run, thundering across the land. "Lay it on, Girl. Lay it on!"

The big chestnut, lashed by the rider's quirt, made one last desperate, lunging burst of speed, but the horse began to fade, and soon, realizing he had lost the race for that allotment, the chestnut's rider broke off, gave Gypsy another salute, then turned toward another, less valuable parcel.

"You did it, Girl!" Gypsy shouted. "Bless your heart, you beautiful thing, you did it."

He pulled her down to an easy lope as he neared the one-hundred-and-sixty-acre allotment that was now his. It was a pretty piece of land, with plenty of oaks and maples, and with meadows of bluestem grass sloping down toward the cottonwood trees that marked the spring and outlined the gently winding course of Cottonwood Creek.

WITHIN two hours after the run started, every lot in the townsite had been claimed. Some lots even had as many as three and four claimants. By two o'clock tents were going up everywhere. By nightfall perhaps as many as a thousand people had converged on the townsite, all of them Negro, most of them losers in the race, hungry and dejected, not knowing where to go or what to do now.

Those who had been successful in getting town lots gathered before dark on the lot reserved for the town hall to celebrate and congratulate and listen to a speech by Amos Fulton of the Oklahoma Immigration Association, who suggested that the town be named Freedom. Other all-Negro towns—six in all—were planned by the Oklahoma Immigration Association, but Freedom was the first to have a name and a town council, and on that basis laid claim to being the first all-Negro town in Oklahoma Territory—or, for that matter, in the United States.

Since some of the disputes over town lots were becoming gun-fights, the immediate need for a law officer was obvious. Fulton suggested Gypsy for the job. The crowd concurred by acclamation.

Fulton sent a boy called Fast Talking Charlie out to Gypsy's claim to tell him the news, but Gypsy wasn't on his claim. He had hired an old man, one of the many losers in the run, to stay and guard against claim-jumpers while he went looking for Drusilla.

She and Eula had jolted in the wagon across the broken land

195

southeast of town for hours and finally stumbled across two un-staked quarter sections side by side, about three miles from town.

"They're ours!" Drusilla cried as she and Eula leaped from the wagon and ran to drive their stakes into the rocky soil.

Gypsy found Drusilla's camp just as she and the children were unpacking the wagon. They were all excited by the novelty of having land that they could call their own, but Drusilla was worried, too, because by now somebody else had also staked the claim. Drusilla was sure she had seen the man moving through the area *after* she had already driven her own stake.

"What can I do?" she asked Gypsy.

Dismayed and disgusted by the chaos the run had created, Gypsy said, "The only thing I know for you to do is, you get over to the land office at Guthrie Station soon's you can and file your claim."

He wondered who in hell—or in Washington, as the case might be—could think up such a crazy way to give away land.

"Look, I best get on back to my own claim while I still got one," Gypsy told her, "but I'll drop by later, see how you're doing."

On his way back he saw Fast Talking Charlie, mounted bareback on a big Clydesdale. He had a message for Gypsy that he delivered in such a rush of words that it was incoherent.

"Wait a minute. Slow down," Gypsy said. But even after Charlie had slowed down, Gypsy still couldn't believe what he was hearing. "I been what?" he asked.

"Yeah, that's right, Mr. Fulton and the folks all 'gree the new town be named Freedom and you be the town marshal."

"Oh, hell," Gypsy groaned.

Chapter Five

*O*N THE first day of the new city of Guthrie its citizens formed an assembly for the purpose of nominating candidates for a five-member city council. The next day the city council, having been duly elected by acclamation from a crowd of thousands gathered in Government Square, held its first meeting and began to pass laws.

One of these councilmen was Shelby Marcellus Hornbeck. He was barely twenty-eight years old, but he was already a leader. As a boy growing up in South Carolina, Shelby Hornbeck somehow always seemed to end up ruling whatever roost he found himself on. And that was exactly what he intended to do in Oklahoma: get rich and rule the roost. He almost got himself elected mayor. It was only his youth and lack of experience that lost him that election. The mayoral candidate who got the loudest chorus of yea votes from the settlers gathered on Government Square was a middle-aged man who had once been the mayor of Springfield, Ohio.

This loss in no way daunted Shelby Hornbeck. For the time being, he would be satisfied to be the leader of the city council and establish for himself the reputation of a reasonable and just man. In this, too, he was successful, though it soon became apparent to the other councilmen that Shelby Hornbeck had one blind spot: He had a quiet but profound contempt for the dark-skinned races.

Shelby's preoccupation with racial matters soon got in the way of the council's more important business. For instance, the other councilmen thought Shelby was just wasting their time by proposing a law that would make interracial marriage a criminal offense, as well as a law that would make it illegal for coloreds and whites to attend the same school, eat in the same restaurants, or even be buried in the same cemetery. What was the point? There weren't more than two or three hundred Negroes in all of Guthrie. There were more important things to do at the moment, such as establishing a fire department and creating judgeships.

So Shelby Hornbeck's proposals for racial laws were put aside. Even so, it was his attempt to introduce the laws in the first place that brought him to the attention of the one man in the Oklahoma District who had the power to help him realize his greatest political ambition of becoming the first elected governor of the future state of Oklahoma. That man was Milton Ford.

When Milton Ford, ensconced in the opulent elegance of his private railroad car, heard of Shelby Hornbeck's good works on the city council, he sent his private secretary, Leonard Gerke, to fetch the young councilman. Shelby followed him out onto the wagon road that led past the land office, where thousands of homesteaders waited to register claims.

Two guards armed with sawed-off shotguns patrolled the area around Mr. Ford's private railroad car, and a U.S. deputy marshal acted as doorman when Shelby followed Gerke up the steps and inside. Paneled with polished walnut, hung with tapestries, lit by crystal chandeliers, the car's parlor had the look of a Faustian fantasy. A partition of elaborately carved and polished walnut separated the parlor from a room in the rear section of the car. The connecting door was kept closed.

"Excuse me. I'll tell Mr. Ford you're here," Gerke said, and disappeared through the door to the inner sanctum.

There were five other men in the parlor. The only one Shelby knew was Silas Renfro, the U.S. marshal for the Oklahoma District. He was standing in front of a map that showed the Guthrie townsite, with many of the lots marked with a red X. Shelby quickly surmised that the red X's identified lots that had been claimed by the Oklahoma Land Company, of which Milton Ford was president.

The door to the inner sanctum opened, and Gerke beckoned Shelby. Shelby entered the gloomy interior. Tapestries covered the windows, shutting out all sunlight. The only light came from a crystal chandelier. In one corner, propped up on pillows on a huge scrolled bed, was Mr. Ford himself, the man who owned railroads, gold mines, newspapers, and factories.

Mr. Ford waved Gerke away and said to Shelby, "Sit down, young man. Brandy? Cigar?"

Shelby sat down as Mr. Ford was saying, "So you're the young man I've been hearing about, trying to get some laws passed to keep the niggers in their place."

From an ornate side table, Shelby took a glass of brandy and a cigar, even though he didn't drink or smoke.

Mr. Ford dipped the unlit end of his cigar into a glass of brandy, then sucked the smoke through the brandy-soaked end. He fixed his eyes on Shelby and said, "Young man, you know who I am?"

Shelby hesitated before answering. "Yes, sir."

"I," Mr. Ford went on, "am, as of today, the biggest landowner in the Oklahoma District. And when Oklahoma's made a state, I'll be the biggest landowner in the state. I'm sure you'll agree that that makes the political future of the Territory of vital interest to me."

"I can see how it would, yes, sir," Shelby said.

Mr. Ford prided himself on being a very quick and shrewd judge of character, and thus far he had been favorably impressed with Shelby Hornbeck. Shelby had shown himself to be polite, cagey, and self-composed. And he was a strikingly handsome young man—not in a pretty-boy way, but in a rugged, square-jawed, blond-haired way that would win the approbation of both sexes.

"Young man, it's men like me and you who made this country what it is, but when it comes to voting, why, my vote has no more power than that of some penniless baboon who can't even sign his own name. And they're flooding into Oklahoma by the thousands. What are we going to do about it? Eh? What?"

"Well, sir, as you know, I've been trying to get the city council to pass some laws regulating—"

Mr. Ford waved him to silence. "Laws aren't going to be enough now, I'm afraid. Now that they're here, you can't make a law against 'em staying, can you? No. We're going to have to have something stronger than laws. So what's the answer? What?"

Shelby knew Mr. Ford had the answer, and all Shelby was expected to do was to listen.

Mr. Ford cleared his throat and said, "I was just thinking, just thinking about that organization you folks in the South got, the Ku Klux Klan. Now, wouldn't it be something if Oklahoma had its own Klan, to keep 'em running, keep 'em on the move? Eh?"

So that was it. Up until now Shelby had been puzzled about the nature of this interview. Now everything came into focus.

"Well, sir," Shelby said, "I wouldn't be at all surprised if that actually happened. Most of the homesteaders here are from the South, you see, and it's reasonable to assume that there'll be Klansmen among them. It would be natural for them to get together and form a realm here in Oklahoma, with dens in all the major towns."

"Well, I'm glad to hear that. Glad to." Mr. Ford nodded. "Incidentally," he went on, "I'm looking for someone from Guthrie

199

who'd make a good candidate for territorial representative when we get territorial status. Somebody I could back. And believe me, when I back a man, I can damn sure get him elected. Know anybody who might make a good candidate, do you? Eh?"

"Yes, sir, as a matter of fact, I do."

"Who? Yourself, eh?" Mr. Ford said, as if he could divine Shelby's clever-devil thoughts.

"Yes, sir."

Mr. Ford appeared to give the idea some thought and then, with a slight frown, said, "Tell me, young man, are you married?"

"No, sir."

"Ah. Too bad, too bad. Voters like their candidates to be married. However"—he waved that consideration away with his cigar—"there's plenty of time for that. Eh? Eh? Well then, let me ask you this. If you were elected as representative to the territorial legislature, I suppose you'd push to get those jim crow laws enacted?"

"Absolutely. As soon as possible," Shelby answered with quiet but emphatic confidence.

Mr. Ford gulped the dregs of his brandy and set the glass on the bedside table. He extended his right hand to the younger man.

Shelby rose from the chair and took the outstretched hand. The hand was old and bony, with slack white skin, clammy and cold, and the fingernails were so long they curved like claws.

"You're my man," Mr. Ford said. "My man." And coughed.

OVER two thousand Cheyennes and Arapahos were encamped around the agency on the night of July 23, 1890. They had been told to gather there to vote on accepting the provisions of the General Allotment Act. The Bureau of Indian Affairs went through the motions of having them discuss the matter and vote on it, even though the conclusion was foregone: No matter what the vote, the Cheyennes and Arapahos were going to have to give up tribal ownership of the reservation's five million acres and accept individual land allotments of one hundred and sixty acres each. The four million acres left over would be opened to homesteaders, and that was that, and there was no use arguing about it.

But argue about it they did, and though the Indians called the white men everything from betrayers and thieves to forked-tongued devils, the white officials remained unmoved.

Their only moment of real concern came when Ghost Dancer appeared as if out of nowhere. Most of them had heard of this man, the most feared war chief of the Cheyennes, who had taken on the trappings of a legend. In the last year he had been riding a big, beautiful white stallion that had been presented to him by a group of Apache Ghost Dancers. The horse, with its silken white mane and tail, acquired the name Ghost.

Ghost Dancer lived in the wilderness with a few devoted followers and was seen only rarely, when he attended a Ghost Dance in some remote place, far from the prying eyes of white men.

Though the Ghost Dance had been outlawed, it was still spreading through all the reservations of the Plains Indians. It was claimed that if the Indians faithfully practiced the Ghost Dance, an Indian messiah would soon appear and bring an end to the white man's reign on earth. The Indian police and the white soldiers sometimes hunted for Ghost Dancer, hoping to catch him in the act so that he could be sent back to prison, but they could never find him.

No wonder, then, that a hush fell on the crowd that evening in dusty July when Ghost Dancer, carrying a war lance with seven scalps attached—seven white scalps, it was said—and mounted on the sleek white stallion, rode out of the twilight shadows and stopped on the outer edge of the grumbling throng.

All eyes turned on him, but he remained impassively silent until Chief Hehyo stood up and said in a voice loud enough for all to hear, "We will now hear what Ghost Dancer has to say."

Gaunt and solemn, Ghost Dancer said, "It is useless to exchange words with the white man. His words have no truth or honor. So I say this only to the Human Beings who are gathered here to listen once more to the white man's lies. The day the white settlers come to take our land, that will be a good day to die."

Then he rode his white stallion out of the agency and disappeared into the gathering twilight, leaving the Indians with feelings of both dread and wonder. They realized, as the white men did not,

201

that Ghost Dancer had just made the Plains Indian pledge to sacrifice his life—to throw himself away, as the Indians termed suicide.

The white men from Washington dismissed Ghost Dancer's words and saw no reason to continue the meeting. It was getting dark, and they wanted to get some supper before going out to see the lunar eclipse that was due to take place just before midnight.

The Indians had heard the white man's prophecies that the moon would disappear for a while that night, but who could take such prophecies seriously? It was just another effort by the crazy white men, by boasting of their magical powers, to frighten the Indians into voting to relinquish their tribal lands. So they remained unconvinced even when, just before the eclipse was supposed to take place, all the white people at the agency began to gather in the square and gaze expectantly up at the full moon.

Maxwell stepped out of his house a few minutes before the eclipse was due to begin. Rachel and Dexter were already in the front yard, and Nora soon joined them. It was a measure of her curiosity that she would come out of the house when there were so many Indians about. Seeing some horseplay developing among a few of the older boys gathered in front of the school, Maxwell left the yard and walked toward the school. Rachel dashed after him.

"You should've stayed with your mother," he said.

"I wanted to be with you," Rachel said.

The students stopped their horseplay when they saw Maxwell approaching. He took his place in front of them with Rachel beside him and pulled a gold watch from his waistcoat and sprang the lid. The hands on its moonlit face stood at eight minutes after eleven.

"All right," he announced to the students, "any second now."

They turned their faces toward the moon. As they waited, Corby emerged from among them and edged forward, like a metal filing being pulled by a magnet, to stand beside Rachel.

Then a dark shadow began moving—so slowly at first that it was almost imperceptible—across the face of the moon.

The Indians reacted to the beginning of the eclipse with a great collective intake of breath, and then for a few seconds were gripped by a profound silence. But soon moans of terror began to be heard.

The first shouts were from the medicine men, who began issuing frantic orders, telling the Indians what to do to frighten the Great Bad Spirit and make it turn loose the moon. So the Indians began yelling and screaming, banging on drums and pots and pans, firing their rifles and pistols at the shadow on the moon. As the black shadow continued to creep across the face of the moon, the pandemonium became more desperate and frenzied. Some Indians began to gash their faces and arms and breasts. Others hurriedly cut off their hair.

But the dark shadow continued to devour the moon, and the pandemonium continued: the shrieking, the banging of pots and pans, the ceaseless barrage of gunfire, the howling of dogs, the crying of children. And the panic proved contagious. Nearly all of those at the agency felt themselves being sucked into it.

The students felt it, and many succumbed. As soon as he realized what was happening, Maxwell ran to the teachers and shouted, "Get the children back inside!"

But before all the children could be herded back into the building, another great hush slowly descended upon the throng when they saw the edge of the moon gradually emerging from the dark shadow. Then, as they began to realize that their tactics had worked, the Indians' shrieks turned to yells of triumph.

Maxwell remained at the school until most of his charges were rounded up and sent to their dormitories. Then he and Rachel went back across the square, threading their way through the singing, dancing, celebrating Indians. When they arrived at the house, they found that Nora and Dexter were no longer in the front yard and that the front door was standing open. Maxwell hurried into the house and was met by Dexter rushing out of the front bedroom.

"It's Mother!" he cried. "Something's wrong with Mother."

Maxwell found Nora cringing in a corner of the bedroom closet. She, too, had succumbed to the panic. Her body shuddered, and her eyes were like those of a small animal caught in a trap.

"Nora?" He knelt and reached for her hand. "Nora, what is it?"

Dexter and Rachel stood behind Maxwell, staring over his shoulders at their mother's stricken face. Maxwell told Dexter to run and fetch the agency doctor, Dr. Gresham; then he coaxed Nora out of the closet and held her trembling body in a comforting embrace.

"What is it, Nora? What's wrong?"

"I'm afraid I'm—" She faltered, then said in a small, weeping voice, "I'm afraid I'm losing my mind."

With soothing words and gentle handling he got her to lie down in bed and then gave her a spoonful of laudanum to quiet her nerves.

"Nervous exhaustion" was what Dr. Gresham called it. "A condition with many causes and few cures."

"Will she get better?" Maxwell asked as they conferred on the front porch that night.

Dr. Gresham said, "I don't know, John. Her problems are more than just physical, but I think, with a few days in bed, she'll be her old self again."

But Nora was never her old self again. She recovered enough to function around the house, it was true, but she seemed forever befuddled about something. And she seldom combed her hair anymore or bathed or changed her clothes.

The only thing that held her interest was her garden. In a fenced-in area behind the house she had cultivated a plot in which she tried to grow vegetables and herbs. In spite of her labors, however, the garden did not thrive, for she often planted things in the wrong place at the wrong time. Still, she could be found on just about any day weeding, watering, digging, with a sort of dumb distraction. Once Maxwell even found her working in the garden at night, on her knees in the moonlight, a trowel in her hands, gouging at the rocky soil.

"What're you doing here?" he asked gently, kneeling beside her.

"These turnips. I have to work them. They're not growing. Because this soil is so ungiving. This country doesn't like me. Nobody likes me. My own daughter doesn't like me. You don't like me."

"Oh, Nora, dear heart, that's not true." He reached out and gently stroked her graying hair. "We all love you."

She looked at him with surprise. "Do you? Do you, John?" She began to weep. "Do you love me a little?"

"Oh, Nora, of course I do. I love you. I'm sorry if I don't tell you often enough. Please come back in now."

The next day she was in the garden again, on her knees, troweling the soil with a sort of meek desperation, glancing over her shoulder as if she expected to see someone or something creeping up on her.

Then one day in September it finally happened: She glanced over her shoulder, and this time she saw it, something that struck terror in her heart. It had the appearance of a cloud, but a peculiar cloud, a sort of huge gray-green mass moving toward the agency.

Then she noticed that others at the agency were becoming alarmed by it, whatever *it* was. She could see people dashing about, shouting to one another, and the mounting terror she felt caused her to run whimpering into the house.

From the side window in the front room she could see the mysterious cloud coming. She could also see Maxwell and Rachel leave the school building and race across the square toward the house.

"Grasshoppers!" Maxwell said as he burst into the room; then, to Rachel, "Go get Dexter. Hurry! Now look, Nora, we don't have much time. We've got to cover as many of your plants as we can before they get here. Grab quilts, blankets, winter coats, gunnysacks—anything." He pulled the oilcloth cover from the table as he hurried through the kitchen and headed for the garden.

Nora still couldn't quite comprehend what was going on, but being told that her plants were in some sort of danger stirred within her a fierce protectiveness. She hurriedly stripped the beds in Dexter's and Rachel's rooms, then dashed into the garden.

As Nora bent to spread the covers, a few grasshoppers landed on her shoulders and head and began to tug at her dress and sunbonnet with their jaws, eating the cotton cloth. Then the main body of the cloud descended. Within a few seconds the earth was covered with them to a depth of two or three inches, a squirming mass of bodies covering every inch of ground, every plant and shrub and blade of grass. Cornstalks bent to the ground under their weight, bean vines were mashed flat, branches snapped.

With grasshoppers completely covering her body—eating at her clothes and sunbonnet, crawling up her legs under her skirt, crawling on her face, in her eyes, in her hair—Nora shrieked and stumbled around, trying frantically to brush the insects off.

Maxwell tried to restrain her, but she tore away from him, trying to rip her clothes off, clawing at the grasshoppers on her face so frantically that her fingernails raked bloody scratches in her skin. She stumbled and fell to the ground, squashing so many grasshoppers beneath her that her dress became covered with a brown slime.

Maxwell picked her up and carried her through the unrelenting blizzard of grasshoppers to the house. He carried her into the front bedroom and dropped her onto the bed. To his horror he saw that some of the insects had managed to get inside. Nora's panic seemed to have gone into the realm of madness. In trying to claw the insects out of her hair, she had crushed many of them, matting her hair with the brown slime. Now, rather than trying to get them out of her hair, she was trying to pull her hair out.

Maxwell pulled Nora's hands together behind her back and then, holding both her hands in one of his, jerked one of the flimsy curtains off the window. He used it to tie her hands and then used another curtain to tie her feet. By now her body was exhausted enough to become still, but the sounds themselves were unceasing, the wails, moans, and sobs of a mindless horror.

"SOMETHING needs to be done, John," Dr. Gresham said one day in December. They were in Maxwell's office. "I know of a pretty good asylum up in Ohio. I could write and see if they'd take her."

"Would she like that, do you think?"

"I doubt she'd know the difference, to tell the truth." He scratched at his bushy beard. "The fact is, John, she's not getting the attention she needs. She needs someone with her all the time."

But where was Maxwell to find a woman who would take care of Nora? He could have hired one of the older Indian girls from the school, but given Nora's hatred and fear of Indians, there was no telling what she would do if one tried to feed and bathe her.

That evening at supper he told Dexter and Rachel what Dr. Gresham had suggested. Dexter was aghast.

"A crazy house? He wants to put Mother in a crazy house? No! Never. Never, by God, as long as I have a breath left in my body."

These days Dexter seemed to look for pretexts to show that he was equal to any man and the superior of most, and his job at the agency gave him ample opportunity to prove it. As one of the agency's census-and-allotment clerks, he never let the Indians forget how much power he had over their lives. Maxwell was sorry now that he had used his influence to get Dexter the job; but Dexter, having graduated from school, had let it be known that he would soon be going off to Oklahoma City to look for work, and Nora, before her breakdown, was desperate to keep him at home.

"Dexter, nobody *wants* to put your mother in an asylum. I'm just telling you what Dr. Gresham says. He says—"

"I don't care what he says. One of them crazy houses'd kill her."

"She's not getting the kind of care around here she needs. The doctor came in here today and found her lying on the floor near a dead stove, half frozen. And why? Because you neglected to come home this morning, as you were supposed to, and put wood on the fire. Do you call that taking care of her?"

Dexter stared at his plate for a moment, chastised, but he was bristling again when he looked up. "I couldn't help it. I was swamped with work. We're supposed to process a hundred Indians a day, and we can't do half that many with the help we've got, and them red niggers arguing with us all the time about their allotments. I don't see why Rachel can't do more. Her going to school's not half as important as what I'm doing."

"Red niggers? You know I don't like racial slurs in this house."

Dexter pushed his plate away and stood up. "Then I'll go eat at the hotel. At least nobody there tells me what words I can and can't use. And the food don't taste like pig slop." He slammed the door as he left the house.

Dexter had at least been right about the food, Maxwell thought. It did taste a little like pig slop. He and Rachel had thrown together a meal from tin cans—corned beef hash, spinach, hominy.

"You're not hungry?" Rachel asked.

He shook his head.

Rachel pushed her plate away. "I'm not either."

"Maybe we should go to the hotel, too," Maxwell said jokingly.

Rachel started to speak, but she was silenced by something she saw behind Maxwell's back. He turned to see Nora in the bedroom doorway. Leaning against the doorjamb, dressed in a rumpled nightgown, her gray hair uncombed, gaunt and frail, she stood in the lamplit shadows staring at them with meek, mad eyes.

FOR a week or so after the run of '89, Freedom had a population of about two thousand people—Negroes, all of them. Most were settlers who had lost out in the run, and they were glad to take jobs as carpenters, laborers, masons, well diggers, waiters, and washerwomen. This labor force, combined with substantial investment capital coming in from Negro businessmen in the North, resulted in the rapid construction of a town hall, a schoolhouse, and a cluster of false-fronted buildings on Main Street.

Boomtown fever was acute in Freedom, where the builders not only experienced the excitement of seeing a town taking shape before their eyes but enjoyed the additional novelty of being able to vote for and elect men of their own race as their leaders.

Gypsy Smith had nothing but goodwill and admiration for the people who were building Freedom, but he didn't want to be the town marshal. He didn't want the responsibility. And the salary was too small to be an inducement. But he had made the mistake of allowing Mayor Amos Fulton to talk him into it. "At least for a little while," Mayor Fulton had pleaded, "until we can find somebody else who can handle the job. We need you, Gypsy."

Gypsy was flattered to be considered so valuable, but the only person whose opinion could affect his decision to go or to stay was Drusilla Pointer. If he stayed in Freedom, it would be because of her.

Drusilla had been hired as Freedom's new schoolteacher. The officials had decided to build a school on a site at the north end of town. The plans also called for a three-room cabin to be built behind the schoolhouse as a rent-free residence for the teacher.

Drusilla couldn't have been more delighted. Now she would be saved the time and expense of building her own cabin. So she and the children broke camp, loaded the wagon with their belongings, and moved to Schoolhouse Hill, where they pitched their camp until the teacher's cabin could be built.

Gypsy knew that Drusilla hoped he would stay around. She had said so. He reminded himself, however, that she might not mean anything special by it; that was just the way she was. She had a particular caring spirit that made her different from all the other women he had ever known, and it was that capacity to care, that generosity of spirit, that Gypsy found so appealing.

And yet it was this difference that made him reluctant to push his advantage with her. Also, he had never before been involved with a black woman. His wife had been a Comanche, and after she died, there had been a Kiowa girl who took his fancy for a while. As for Negro women, there had never been any in his adult life, and he didn't know quite how to deal with them, what was expected of him.

So he was having a hard time trying to figure out what he really felt about her. He didn't have a name for it, except that it was an entirely new kind of feeling, a kind of protectiveness.

Then something happened that profoundly affected his growing intimacy with Drusilla: Lieutenant Beauregard Pierce came to town. Lieutenant Pierce was a troop commander of the buffalo soldiers, the all-Negro 10th Cavalry Regiment stationed at Fort Sill, on the Comanche-Kiowa reservation. Lieutenant Pierce was the regiment's only Negro officer.

Lieutenant Pierce was the best known of all the buffalo soldiers. His fame began when he was graduated from the U.S. Military Academy at West Point with high honors. In addition, he had received the Congressional Medal of Honor for saving the life of his white commanding officer in a battle with a Comanche raiding party.

Gypsy had met Lieutenant Pierce a few times in the field and considered him a passing acquaintance. But when the lieutenant greeted Gypsy that day in Freedom in the town-hall tent, Pierce almost made it seem that they were long-lost friends. With an outstretched hand and a practiced smile he said to Gypsy, "Well, here he is, the man who got the Beeson gang. Glad to see you again, Gypsy. It's been a while."

"Yeah," Gypsy said.

"And congratulations on being named Freedom's marshal."

"Thanks."

Lieutenant Pierce was a tall man with wide shoulders. He habitually rested his left hand on the hilt of his saber. Every button on his tailored tunic was buttoned; his pants were creased, his boots highly polished. His clean-shaven face, cinnamon brown, seemed as smooth and flawless as silk. His hair was combed like a white man's: parted on the left side and plastered to his head with pomade.

He said to the mayor and other men present, "I'm going to be here for a couple of days, gentlemen, to give my troops and horses a chance to rest. Where can I find a good bivouac area for my outfit?"

Gypsy volunteered his own claim. "There's water there and forage and wood. Half mile northeast of town. I'll show you."

Lieutenant Pierce put his hat carefully on his head. The right side of its broad brim was turned up and fastened to the crown with a cavalry rosette, giving him the look of a dashing cavalier.

"Until tonight, then, gentlemen," he said, confirming his acceptance of an invitation to join the city fathers for a small celebration in honor of Freedom's beginning.

He and Gypsy crossed the busy and noisy street. The first sergeant ordered the soldiers—thirty-seven in all—to mount up, and the column was soon ready to move out in double file, but Lieutenant Pierce's attention was distracted. He had seen Drusilla Pointer, who had brought her brood of waifs to see the buffalo soldiers. Leading his horse, Lieutenant Pierce approached Drusilla, touched the brim of his hat to her, and said to Gypsy, "May I have the honor of an introduction?"

Noting the admiration in her eyes, Gypsy introduced Drusilla.

"Mrs. Pointer," the lieutenant called her.

"Miss," she corrected.

"Ah," he said with obvious delight at the news. "I should've known. You're not nearly old enough to be the mother of this robust ménage. Your brothers and sisters, then?"

"We orphans," Sassy, one of the children, said.

Mayor Fulton stepped forward to say, "Miss Pointer is going to be our schoolteacher.' To her he said, "You'll be coming to the celebration tonight?"

"I don't know. We've got lots of work to get done."

"Oh, please, 'Silla, can't we go?" Ruby begged, and the others began with their own pleas.

"I join the children in urging you to come, Miss Pointer," Lieutenant Pierce said. "And I hope I can look forward to a waltz."

"Well," she answered, doubtful but flattered, "we'll see."

Lieutenant Pierce bowed slightly, swung astride his blaze-faced chestnut gelding, and dashed smartly to the head of the column.

Gypsy was the first to know that Lieutenant Pierce had developed more than a casual interest in Drusilla Pointer. Drusilla was perhaps the next to know, though just about anybody at the town celebration that evening could see that the lieutenant had more than a passing interest in her.

The celebration began shortly after sundown. On a makeshift platform, with nail kegs being used for stools, sat many of the town's dignitaries: Mayor Fulton, of course, and Preacher Pangborn, and the town's special guest, Lieutenant Beauregard Pierce. Gypsy was not among them.

Preacher Pangborn led the settlers in an opening prayer, and then Mayor Fulton gave a rousing speech about the new "land of the Negro," where colored folks would at last have power over their own destinies. The crowd responded with "Hallelujah!" and "Amen!"

Then Lieutenant Pierce, the main attraction, was asked by Mayor Fulton if he would please say a few words to the audience.

To a burst of applause and encouraging calls, Lieutenant Pierce stepped to the front of the platform. "I want to welcome all of you brave and hardy people here to your new homeland. You've shown that colored folks can be pioneers, too, and I'm proud of you. You're a credit to your race. As my friend Professor Booker T. Washington said, 'Brains, property, and character for the Negro will settle, once and for all, the question of civil rights: Excellence is the best antidote for racial bigotry.' In plain English, we'll show 'em!"

He waited for the cheers and applause to die down and then ended by saying, "But enough of this speechmaking. I was told there'd be some music and dancing around here tonight."

He made his way from the platform through the parting crowd to where Drusilla Pointer stood, surrounded by her foster children.

211

The stage was turned over to the musicians, and the dancing commenced with a waltz called "Love's Old Sweet Song." Lieutenant Pierce asked Drusilla if she would do him the honor.

She was wearing her Sunday dress, a plain but pretty thing. Her hat was a little boater with wax daisies on the crown. Compared with the gold-braided splendor of Lieutenant Pierce's uniform, her attire was almost dowdy, but they did make a handsome couple.

At first Drusilla was uncertain of her ability to do a grand ballroom waltz, but Lieutenant Pierce led with such ease and grace that she soon caught on and let him whirl her around.

When the dance ended, Drusilla was out of breath. She said to Lieutenant Pierce, "You're a very good dancer," and he answered in his courtly way, "A dancer's only as good as his partner," then added, "You certainly have a lovely smile."

Gypsy didn't want to make a speech, and he didn't know how to dance, so he had stayed away from the area lest he be expected to do either. He passed by the dancing area once. His eyes swept the dancers; he located Drusilla standing beside Lieutenant Pierce, like a little brown hen standing beside a champion cock. The lieutenant smiled down at her and said something, and she smiled up at him. They seemed to be getting on very well. Gypsy went on his way.

By September the town of Freedom had assumed the essential shape and size that it would have for all its days. Main Street was hardly more than a wide path churned and rutted by horses' hooves and wagon wheels. The false-fronted frame buildings that housed most of the town's businesses were clustered along Main Street, while the residents' houses and shacks were scattered helter-skelter across the town's back streets. The town had a small brick bank, two churches, and a two-story town hall with a jail in the basement.

Gypsy lived in the jail. Two cells had been built for prisoners, but the town treasury found that it couldn't afford steel bars, so Gypsy moved a cot, a cast-iron stove, and a few pieces of makeshift furniture into one of the cells. He took most of his meals at the hotel.

He had kept his homestead quarter section. He had thought to sell it after the wells had been dug in Freedom and the spring on his claim was no longer essential to the town's water supply. But there was no urgency to get rid of it. So mostly he lived in his barless jail cell. Prisoners, when there were any, were kept in the cell next door, chained to the wall.

Gypsy didn't like most of the duties of a town marshal and finally threatened to quit unless they agreed to hire a deputy marshal to take over some of the unpleasant chores, such as emptying the prisoners' chamber pots. Thus it was that Buck Tyson, a toothless old black cowboy from Texas, was hired as his deputy.

The real reason Gypsy stayed on in Freedom was his unresolved feelings for Drusilla Pointer. It was true that he hadn't seen much of her during the summer, because he hadn't wanted to get in the way of Lieutenant Pierce's courtship. But whenever he did see her—even when she was with the lieutenant—he never failed to feel a confused mingling of emotions that included joy and sadness, goodwill, and an almost aching envy of the man who would make her his wife.

Lieutenant Pierce and his troops had gone back to Fort Sill, but during the summer he had made periodic visits to Freedom to court Drusilla. Naturally everyone believed that the dashing young officer and the pretty young schoolteacher were headed for the altar.

Gypsy had decided that on the day Drusilla announced her engagement to Lieutenant Pierce, he would turn in his badge and ride out of town. One Saturday in late September he came out of his office and there was Miss Drusilla Pointer emerging from Frank's General Store and Post Office down the street. In one hand she held a basket filled with groceries; in the other she held a letter to which she was giving her total attention, and she was smiling.

But when she glanced up and saw Gypsy, her smile vanished. She shoved the letter down into the groceries in the handbasket, saying, "Looky here, Gypsy Smith, why don't you ever come around and see us anymore? The kids miss you."

"The *kids* miss me?" he teased.

"Oh, all right, then, I miss you, too," she grudgingly confessed.

"Well, Miss Drusilla," he said, "I got that lieutenant of yours figured to be a mighty jealous man."

"Damn you, Gypsy Smith!"

"Such language! A nice churchgoing schoolmarm like yourself."

"Well, you're enough to make a preacher cuss. And don't call me a school*marm*. I'm a school*mistress*. A *marm* is married. I'm not."

"But from what I hear, you soon will be."

"I have hopes. I wasn't cut out to be an old maid."

"No, Miss Drusilla, you sure wasn't. You're too good a cook for that. Why, someday somebody'll want to marry you just for the way you fry chicken." He nodded toward the two plucked chickens in her shopping basket. "That what you having tonight?"

"And giblet gravy, yes. Supper's at six, if you care to come."

"I'll be there, thank you kindly."

The fried chicken that night was fine, and the children enjoyed having Gypsy around again, but Drusilla seemed distracted. Gypsy asked her what was wrong, but it wasn't until the next day that she told him. Returning from the barbershop, he found her waiting for him, sitting on a bench in his office.

When Gypsy said, "Good morning, Miss Drusilla," she managed a small smile but seemed to avoid his eyes.

"What's the matter?" He hung his floppy-brimmed planter's hat on a peg, but she still seemed reluctant to talk. "Look, you can tell me, can't you? You can tell your old uncle Gypsy."

She stared at her hands, folded in her lap, and took a deep breath. "I got a letter from Beau yesterday. He asked me to marry him."

Gypsy tilted his head. "You gonna do it?"

"I'm not sure yet. I wanted to ask you what you thought."

"Why should it make any difference what *I* think?"

She gave him a quick look. "You know damned well it does, Gypsy Smith. Don't play the dunce with me."

Gypsy walked to his desk and sat down in his chair, facing her. "Well, Lieutenant Pierce is young. He's educated. A distinguished young officer. What more could a young woman want?"

She had resumed looking at her hands.

"You love him?"

"Sometimes I think I do," she murmured, "and sometimes . . ." But then she threw her shoulders back. "Yes, I do."

"Well then . . . It'd mean giving up your job as a school-teacher. You'd probably have to follow him around from one army post to another for the rest of your life. You willing to do that?"

She got up, grabbed her shopping basket, and stepped to the door. "Well, I'll tell you one thing I'm not willing to do"—she turned to face him—"and that's end up an old maid. Good-bye, Gypsy Smith." She went out the door, leaving Gypsy to watch her as she walked across the dusty street and out of sight.

Taking the building's central stairs two at a time, Gypsy went upstairs and walked into Mayor Fulton's office unannounced.

He took off his badge and tossed it onto the desk. "I quit."

Mayor Fulton needed a moment to appraise this development. "What's the matter? Can we talk about this?"

"Nothing to talk about, Amos."

"But what'll I tell the council? They'll want to know the reasons."

Gypsy said, "Tell 'em 'personal reasons,' " and turned to go.

The mayor stood up and pleaded, "Can't I persuade you to put personal reasons aside for now? We just got a report this morning that the Klan has formed a den in Guthrie. It's only a matter of time till we get floggings and lynchings, and God help us, it may come down to a race war. We need you with us, Gypsy. If it comes to a fight . . ."

Gypsy said simply, "It ain't my fight, Amos."

"You! With your black face? Where d'you think you can go to get away from it?"

"Back to the reservations, to live with the savages. What y'all call civilization's too complicated for this old cowboy," Gypsy said, and walked out the door.

Chapter Six

THE race into the Oklahoma District became known as the run of '89, to distinguish it from subsequent runs, such as the run of '92, when the Cheyenne-Arapaho reservation was opened for settlement. And the government, by announcing that April 19, 1892, was the date that the reservation would be opened, effectively announced the date of Ghost Dancer's death. He had publicly proclaimed that the day the settlers took over the last homeland of the Human Beings would be a good day to die.

Three of his followers volunteered to join him in what was seen as a suicide pact. They sent out the word that they, just the four of them, would meet the onslaught of settlers on the day of the run of '92 in a place called Lame Cow Valley and kill as many of them as they could before they themselves were killed. Ghost Dancer even sent a challenge to Colonel Caldwell, the commanding officer at Fort Reno, telling him that if the army wished to stop them, the colonel should bring all of his troops to the valley by midmorning on the day of the run and be prepared for a fight to the death.

Colonel Caldwell could hardly believe it. Four Indian warriors challenging three hundred U.S. cavalrymen? Was the man crazy?

Colonel Caldwell had no choice but to oblige. It could prove inconvenient, of course, since his troops would be expected to be on the starting line of the run, policing the settlers; but if Ghost Dancer and his cohorts showed up by midmorning, there would be time to kill them and get back to the starting line before the run began. In any event, he couldn't take the chance that some white settlers might be killed by four suicidal Indians. So, early on the morning of the nineteenth he marched three troops of cavalrymen— nearly three hundred soldiers—out to Lame Cow Valley and waited.

Indians converged on the valley from all parts of the reservation, gathering on the ridges on both sides.

Maxwell, Rachel, and Corby arrived in a surrey at Lame Cow Valley more than two hours before the run was to take place at high noon. They left the surrey in a draw and climbed the ridge to where Chief Hehyo and his band had gathered, where they could easily see the settlers jockeying for positions along the starting line. They were also directly above Colonel Caldwell's cavalrymen.

"What is my old friend Maxwell doing in this place?" Chief Hehyo asked after greetings had been exchanged. "Why are you not down there with the white people who have come to take our lands?"

Maxwell filled a pipe. Lighting it, he took three puffs, then passed the pipe to Chief Hehyo as he said in Cheyenne, "I have no wish to take any land from the Human Beings, Grandfather."

Chief Hehyo had no teeth at all now, and his mouth was like a slit in his prune-puckered face as he puffed on the pipe. "Then you are the only white man who does not. Look at them. The white man must breed like grasshoppers. They come with the greed of grasshoppers and destroy everything in their path. That is what I think."

"I think you may be correct," Maxwell said. "But my worry now is not about the loss of lands; it is about the loss of lives. I have been told that the Human Beings have come here only to watch Ghost Dancer and the others throw themselves away. But perhaps the soldier chief is not entirely certain that the Human Beings have not come here to fight alongside Ghost Dancer."

"We told the pony soldier scouts that we come in peace."

"*Pava*—good."

THE nearly three hundred troopers—some kneeling, some standing, some mounted—had formed a three-tiered firing line that stretched almost across the valley floor. Sitting astride a big sorrel in the center of the formation, Colonel Caldwell surveyed the Indians scattered along the ridges.

"But where is Ghost Dancer?" he asked, pulling out his watch to check the time. "If he's coming here to get himself killed, I wish he'd come on and get it over with."

At ten forty, one of the colonel's uniformed scouts rode up on a lathered horse to report that he had spotted Ghost Dancer and three other warriors in a ravine at the other end of the valley.

"All right," Colonel Caldwell told the scout, "pass the word. Make sure the troopers are ready. Won't be long now."

Major Phillips, Fort Reno's executive officer, looked at the bristling arsenal of carbines. "Why do they do it?" he asked.

Colonel Caldwell swept his eyes toward the spectators on the ridges. "They're doing it for them."

"For them?" Major Phillips asked.

"They want the other Indians to see them make a stand and die, showing them how to die proudly."

The major snorted scornfully. "Sounds crazy to me."

217

"Well, in that case maybe I'm crazy, too," the colonel said, "because if I were Ghost Dancer, I think this is the day and this is the way *I'd* choose to die."

Quite suddenly four Indian warriors in full battle regalia rode up out of a ravine at the far end of the valley, about four hundred yards in front of the troop formation. They stopped abreast on the rim of the ravine, and a great cheer went up from the multitude of Indians on the ridges. Ghost Dancer, astride his milk-white stallion—flanked by Hawk's Head, Howling Wolf, and Little Pipe—raised his lance high into the air in response to the cheers.

"Well, by God, there they are," Major Phillips said as murmurs of awe and admiration swept through the ranks of the waiting troopers. "Hold your fire!"

All four of the warriors were dressed in Ghost Dancer shirts decorated with bright red sacred designs of suns and horses and lightning flashes. Their faces were painted in black and red and yellow designs. Little Pipe and Howling Wolf each wore two eagle feathers attached to their scalp locks, while Ghost Dancer and Hawk's Head, both chiefs, wore magnificent warbonnets made of eagle feathers tipped with downy red plumes. Ghost Dancer's rifle was slung across his back.

On their ornately decorated and nervously prancing horses, the four warriors began to sing their death songs. The Indian spectators along the ridges fell silent. The death songs continued for perhaps a minute, and when the last notes had echoed down the valley and died in the still air, Ghost Dancer aimed his lance at the waiting soldiers and shouted at the top of his voice the traditional Plains Indian battle cry *"Hoka hey! Hoka hey!* It's a good day to die!"

The other warriors raised their rifles over their heads, and each in turn yelled the war cry *"Hoka hey! Hoka hey!"*

Ghost Dancer plunged his lance deep into the earth and left it there, like a planted flag. He then jerked the Winchester off his back. The horses started down the valley in a prancing walk. The sound of drums began to be heard from the ridges, their rhythms matching the rhythm of the horses' hoofbeats: slow at first, and then faster as the horses hit a cantering stride. And now an unnerving new sound came from the ridges, the sound of hundreds of women ululating in rhythm to the drums.

"Hold your fire," Colonel Caldwell ordered. He wanted to give the warriors every chance to change their minds, but they showed no indecisiveness. When they had covered about half the distance to the waiting troops, they kicked their horses into a full gallop, then dropped their reins onto the necks of their horses and began firing.

"All right, if that's the way they want it," Colonel Caldwell grimly said to Major Phillips, "cut 'em down."

"Fire!"

The first volley from the nearly three hundred Springfield carbines brought down the two outside riders, Little Pipe and Howling Wolf. To the amazement of the cavalrymen, both Ghost Dancer and Hawk's Head were hit and badly wounded, but both managed to stay on their mounts, and both kept firing. The troopers, in their awe and excitement, had apparently aimed most of their fire at the outriders, leaving it to others to bring down the magnificent warrior on the beautiful white stallion. But when two troopers were felled by the incoming fire, the others were quick to follow the major's orders: "Reload! Fire at will."

Hawk's Head's pony turned a forward somersault, but Hawk's Head, though bleeding, leaped from the falling horse and hit the ground running. Raising the rifle in his right hand, he fired wildly one more time before a barrage of bullets tore his body apart.

Ghost Dancer, also bleeding from a number of wounds, got within about forty yards of the formation before the wounded white stallion screamed and reared up. Ghost Dancer fell from the horse and collapsed facedown in the grass. The cavalrymen, apparently assuming Ghost Dancer was done for, slacked off in their firing, and that was when he leaped to his feet, pulled a scalping knife from his belt, and started running in a zigzag course toward them. Many were so rattled by the man's ferocity that they could hardly get the cartridges into the carbines and take aim at him. But enough were still firing to knock his legs out from under him. By then he was within less than twenty yards of the formation. One of his legs had been broken by a bullet, but he put the knife between

219

his teeth and began crawling toward the formation on his belly.

Within ten yards of the line, Ghost Dancer collapsed. His body quivered violently for a moment in its death agony. Before he died, however, he raised his head one last time. Then his eyes began to close and his face slowly sank back to rest on the earth.

Checking his pocket watch once again, the colonel glanced over his shoulder toward the settlers on the starting line and then nudged his horse forward. He rode to Ghost Dancer's body and looked down at it. He heard the women on the ridges begin to keen for their dead. To Major Phillips he said, "Bring the bugler up."

"Bugler, front and center!" Major Phillips shouted, and then rode out to face Colonel Caldwell. "What call, Colonel?"

"Taps," Colonel Caldwell said, and in response to the major's look of confusion, he added, "These were brave men, Major. I think we can honor them without dishonoring ourselves. We have time yet. Bring the troops to attention."

The major called the troops to attention, ordered them to present arms, and told the bugler to blow taps. The officers drew their sabers and held them in salute position as the first bell-toned notes from the bugle silenced all other sounds in the valley. Even the keening and crying Indian women fell into an astonished silence and then, like all living things in the valley, listened.

The only movement that could be seen was a young Indian on foot, dashing toward the place where Ghost Dancer had fallen.

It was Corby. In his schoolboy's uniform and unarmed, he was allowed to approach, but he waited until the last sad, sweet sound of taps had faded before he came up to the body. Maxwell and Rachel watched as Corby dropped to his knees in the grass and reached out to touch Ghost Dancer's blood-covered back.

"Good-bye, my father," he said, and added the customary Cheyenne farewell to one who is leaving this life to travel to the Spirit Land: "*Nimeaseoxzheme*—may your journey be a good one."

A FEW months later Chief Hehyo, wearing a top hat, rode into the agency, sitting in a dusty and ragged overstuffed parlor chair in the back of his creaky old wagon. A boy held a parasol over his head.

The chief's youngest son, Long Shadow, was on the wagon seat, driving the team of pinto ponies. The wagon was accompanied by two riders leading a fine-looking young bay stallion between them.

Maxwell and Corby were behind the house, repairing the corral fence, when the Indians arrived. Maxwell reached up, shook hands with the old chief, and asked, "To what do we owe the honor of the chief's visit?"

"My eyes grow weary and weak," the old chief said, squinting in his effort to see Corby. "Is this boy the son of Ghost Dancer?"

"Yes, Grandfather," Maxwell said.

"I bring a gift for him. A gift that will make a man of him," said the chief. "It is good that he learns the white man's medicine, but when will he learn the ways of the Human Beings? He has no father now. Who is to teach him how to be a man?"

The chief paused, then said, "I have brought this pony as a gift for Ghost Dancer's son. On the day Ghost Dancer threw himself away, I also was ready to die, but I vowed I would live long enough to see that his son became a man of the Human Beings. To tame this horse will make him such a man, and then I will be free to die."

With beseeching eyes Corby asked Maxwell, "Please?"

"Now, dangit, Corby," Maxwell said, "you know I can't allow you to keep a horse at school. If I made an exception in your case, every boy in the school would want one."

Rachel came out of the house with six glasses of iced tea on a tray. The sweet tea, with chunks of ice in it, was greatly prized by the Indians, each of whom swallowed it in mighty gulps.

"But Daddy," she said, "why couldn't he keep the horse in our barn? No one has to know it's his."

"I'd work for free, cleaning the barn, taking care of him," Corby pleaded. "He wouldn't be any bother to you, I promise."

"But this is a *wild* horse," Maxwell said. "Look at him." The bay was a very handsome piece of horseflesh, but it would take an experienced wrangler to handle him. "Why don't you just wait till you graduate and then get yourself a horse that's already broken?"

"Thank you, sir, but it's this one I want."

Maxwell sighed. The fact that the stallion was a gift from Chief

Hehyo made it almost impossible to refuse. Finally he sighed again. "Well, I don't know. . . . Maybe you can keep him here till you finish school. But you have to take full responsibility for him, mind you. You'll have to feed him and take care of him."

Chief Hehyo concluded that permission had been granted. "*Pava*—good. It is done. I have done my duty to the boy. Now I can go to sleep and rest my weary eyes."

Corby could hardly wait to begin the process of taming the stallion. "This's something I have to do by myself," he told Maxwell. "That's what Chief Hehyo said."

"All right. But you don't know anything about breaking horses. You're going to get yourself killed."

"I'll be all right."

But Maxwell worried. He watched daily as Corby crawled into the corral with the stallion, ready to offer the stallion a lump of sugar or an apple. But no matter what kind of present Corby offered him, the stallion would make a dash at him with teeth bared and hooves slashing and kicking.

Finally Corby decided he had to take stronger measures, so he cut off the horse's water supply. "Either you drink water that I give you, or you don't drink at all."

By the next morning the stallion was thirsty enough to approach the bucket with his neck outstretched, his nostrils flaring. Yet even after gulping the water with gurgles and snorts and groans, he showed his ingratitude by trying to bite Corby's hand.

But every approach became easier, and by the end of the first week of drinking from the bucket, the stallion allowed Corby to reach out and pet his head and scratch his ears. And by summer Big Red—as Corby called the stallion—even allowed Corby to enter the corral and currycomb his red coat and black mane.

One day Corby brought Bess, Maxwell's gentle old mare, into the corral and tied the two horses together. Bess's gentleness had a calming effect on the stallion.

Maxwell knew of no other wrangler who would have gone about breaking a wild horse the way Corby did. An ordinary wrangler, armed with spurs and lariat and saddle, would have entered the corral to break the horse, and it would have been a desperate fight from beginning to end. But Corby wasn't trying to break the bay stallion; he was trying to win the animal's cooperation.

Maxwell found himself taking as much pride in the boy as he would have taken in his own son. It was good to have Corby around as a balm for the disgrace that Dexter had recently caused by getting himself fired from his job. It seemed that Dexter had been supplying land speculators with confidential information from the agency's files. He had denied it, of course. It was the Indian Bureau's policy not to publicize wrongdoing on the part of employees. Unless the crimes were of such a magnitude that they couldn't be hushed up, they were usually handled by quiet dismissal. Dexter said he didn't want the job anyway, that they were doing him a favor by firing him. He was meant for better things than being a pencil pusher in a dirty, backward Indian agency.

Dexter had left for Guthrie, and Rachel soon got a postcard from him, telling her that he had gone to work for none other than Shelby Hornbeck. He said he would soon be sending money to help pay for a nurse for his mother so that Maxwell wouldn't have an excuse to send her to an asylum. The money never came.

So the pride Maxwell felt in Corby was a sort of antidote for Dexter, and Maxwell never failed to take an interest in the progress Corby was making with his stallion.

"Why're you doing that?" he asked one day as he stood with Rachel at the corral. Corby stood near Big Red, doing nothing more than holding his hand firmly against the animal's chest.

Corby mumbled, "Just letting him get used to me."

"Well," said Rachel, "he sure ought to be getting used to you by now, much time as you spend with him."

She was jealous. Since the day he had come into possession of the stallion, Corby hardly had a moment for anyone else. He had always been Rachel's best friend, and now a horse had come between them. But changes were taking place within her body that summer that made her feel secretive and set apart. As her breasts budded and her gangly limbs began to show the first signs of womanhood, she sometimes found Corby glancing at her in a peculiar way.

Maxwell bought Rachel a pony for her fourteenth birthday. It was a pinto pony, as she had wanted, but it was a rather lazy animal. What's more, she had to use her mother's shabby old sidesaddle. She said she would rather ride bareback, but Maxwell said, "No, the time's come when you must learn to ride like a lady. You can't be a tomboy *all* your life."

She sighed, reconciling herself to the inevitable.

Even so, she sometimes disobeyed him, such as the day she climbed up behind Corby on the bare back of the old mare Bess, sitting astride, her dusty bare feet dangling down, her skirt bunched up around her thighs. That was the day Corby took Big Red out of the corral for the first time. He had the snorting stallion tied halter to halter with the old mare. Corby and Rachel rode the mare bareback as she ambled toward the river with Big Red in tow.

It was late August and the day was hot. On the river was a pool that the Indians used as a swimming hole. A few Indian children were swimming when Corby and Rachel arrived, but they quickly vacated the hole when they saw what Corby was going to do.

First he stopped the horses on the riverbank, where he took off his boots and trousers; then, dressed only in his shorts, he got back up on the mare and rode her out into the pool, pulling the snorting and plunging stallion along with her, leaving Rachel to sit in the shade of a cottonwood tree on the bank and watch.

When the horses were chest-deep in the water, Corby gave the stallion a few soothing pats and words, then slipped off the mare's back and onto the stallion's. The stallion was startled into a momentary immobility, which gave Corby time to grab a handful of the stallion's mane; then—with explosions of water and tossing head, thrusting body and whinnies of indignation—the battle was joined.

There were whoops and yells from Indian children on the riverbank, and now and then he could hear Rachel's voice among them, calling, "Whooo-eee! Ride 'im, Corby. Ride 'im!"

By their third visit to the swimming hole, the old mare got tired of having her head jerked and snapped by the lunging young stallion, so she decided to leave the water. Corby leaped off Big Red and grabbed her reins to keep her from gaining the riverbank, but it was Rachel who solved the problem by dashing fully clothed into the water and taking the mare's reins from Corby.

"I'll handle her." She pulled herself onto the mare's back and swung astride. Her flimsy dress, streaming water, clung to her skin.

"No." Corby was standing waist-deep in the muddy, hoof-churned water. "You might get hurt."

"Oh, come on, I'm not a kid. Stop treating me like one."

Corby let his eyes linger a moment on her body beneath the clinging dress. She blushed and pulled the dress away from her skin.

"All right," he said. "Get her into deeper water."

On their fourth visit to the spot, Rachel brought a picnic basket and Corby brought his flute. They let the horses graze peacefully on the riverbank while they sat under the cottonwood tree and ate. Afterward Corby played his flute. It was made from the hollow wing bone of an eagle. While he played, Rachel borrowed his pocketknife to carve a heart into the soft bark of the huge old cottonwood. Within the heart she carved "RM+CW."

Corby didn't know what it meant. He reached up and placed his hand on the sign, as if attempting to divine its meaning by touch.

"Means we're . . ." She fell silent, then blushed. "Well, that we're sort of sweethearts, I guess." She giggled. "Means we're betrothed."

IT WAS over a year before Corby finally climbed into the saddle one day and found the stallion willing to do his bidding without any show of contrariness or mistrust. That day they celebrated their partnership with a wild ride across the prairie. Corby had never before experienced such speed, and the joy of it caused him to let out a long Indian howl of triumph.

After they had gone about half a mile, they met a band of Cheyennes on their way to the agency—the Hehyo band, with old Chief Hehyo's wagon in front. The Indians were in full ceremonial regalia, some with warbonnets and feathered headdresses that hadn't been worn for years. Their faces were painted like warriors of old.

Corby guided Big Red directly to Chief Hehyo's wagon. Inside, sunken into the shabby and dusty overstuffed parlor chair, was Chief Hehyo. His shrunken body was dressed in the relics of a scalp-hunting warrior: a moth-eaten warbonnet, a bear-claw neck-lace, a porcupine-quill breastplate.

"*Vahe, namsem,*" Corby said, gentling Big Red to a prancing walk alongside the wagon.

Without opening his eyes, the old chief turned his dust-covered face toward Corby and asked, "Who speaks?"

"It is I, Little Raven, son of Ghost Dancer."

Chief Hehyo's toothless mouth stretched into a grin. "Little Raven, yes. I gave you a stallion to break. What happened to him?"

"I am riding him, Grandfather."

The old chief crowed like a rooster. Then he opened eyes clouded over with cataracts and able to see only vague shapes.

"How many winters have you, boy?"

"Sixteen, Grandfather."

"A boy whose medicine is strong enough to break the wild stal-lion is ready to take his place among the men of the Human Beings. I think you should now drop your boyhood name and choose your manhood name. Has Little Raven considered this?"

"No, Grandfather. At the school we were not allowed to have Indian names or to change our white names. The same will be true at the school called the Carlisle Institute in the place called Penn-sylvania. They asked if I want to go to this school, now that I have completed my studies at the agency school. If I do go to this school, I must keep the white man's name I was given."

"So what will Little Raven do?"

"I am not sure, Grandfather. I have considered returning to the Human Beings rather than go to the faraway white man's school. What does Chief Hehyo think?"

The old chief worked his toothless mouth for a moment. "I want to say, 'Return to our lodge fires so that you will know what it is to be a Human Being before it is too late.' But I know it is already too late. Go to the white man's school. His medicine is stronger than ours. To live, you must learn it. The time of the white man has come. The time of the Human Beings has gone." Then, spent, he closed his eyes, withdrawing into darkness and silence.

Seeing that the powwow between Corby and the chief was over,

227

a few of the young men challenged Corby to race to the agency.

Gypsy Smith and Maxwell were standing in front of the telegraph office when they heard the pounding hooves of the racing ponies coming in under the log-arch entrance to the agency, the race's finish line, with the red stallion in the lead.

"That's Corby?" Gypsy asked. He hadn't seen the boy in four years. "Well, I'll be." He watched Corby trying to bring the stallion under control. "And that horse! Where'd he get him?"

"Old Chief Hehyo gave it to him as a coming-to-manhood present. I'm sure he really didn't expect Corby to be able to break it, but by God, he's done it . . . maybe."

Big Red plunged through the pedestrians and riders along the street before Corby finally managed to bring him to a stop.

"Corby broke him? All by himself? Well, I'll be."

Corby was now bringing Big Red back toward the finish line in a prancing, side-stepping gait.

Gypsy snorted. "Where'd he learn to ride like that?"

Maxwell shrugged. "Beats me."

"Rides like a Comanche. Now there's a boy after my own heart."

Chapter Seven

Gypsy Smith had brought a herd of mustangs down from the Cherokee Outlet to sell to the settlers. He had stopped at Agency— the name of the town that was growing up around the Cheyenne-Arapaho agency—for some supplies and a quick visit with Maxwell. He was also looking around to see if he could find some other way to make a living. The Cherokee Outlet was soon to be thrown open to settlers, after which there would be no more wild land or wild horses.

Gypsy was forty-three now, and sometimes felt fifty; and his aching bones and stiffening joints had begun to prefer the comfort of a rocking chair to that of a rocking saddle. He had even begun to reflect fondly on the days when he had been a town marshal and could sometimes sit around all day in a nice warm office, with his feet on his desk. So he considered it almost providential when he checked at the Fort Sill post office one day in August and found a letter waiting for him from Amos Fulton. Amos wanted to know if Gypsy would consider returning to Freedom and once again become its town marshal. Very dangerous troubles were developing. The Klan, in cahoots with local white ranchers, had begun a campaign to rid the country of Negro communities and to discourage new Negro settlers from coming in.

"I feel it only fair to warn you," Fulton wrote, "the Klan has threatened to kill any colored man found wearing a lawman's badge."

Gypsy left for Freedom the next morning. He was riding an Appaloosa now. His clothes were a mixture of Mexican and Comanche, the results of a recent trip to Mexico, where he had bought a peon's straw sombrero and a vest made of rattlesnake skins.

He followed the stage road to El Reno. Riding at a leisurely pace, he kept his eyes on the countryside, bemused by the grim marvels of encroaching civilization. In spite of the barbed-wire fences, however, and in spite of the windmills and wheat-thrashing machines, in spite of the churches and schools, in spite of all these nature-taming implements and institutions, the land was not prospering. For the second time in as many years drought had withered the crops. For eight weeks now no rain had fallen.

The drought was causing some farmers to desert their homesteads. Thousands more were still pouring into the area, however, to make the upcoming run into the Cherokee Outlet. With more than ten million acres of virgin prairie up for grabs, and more than a hundred thousand settlers expected to grab for them, the run of '93 promised to become the biggest and most famous land rush.

Gypsy could have reached Freedom by late afternoon on the second day, but he was covered with dust and hadn't shaved in a week. So he decided to make camp for the night, get himself spruced up a little, and then ride on into town in the morning.

He found a good camping place on Dead Indian Creek, where he could bathe, wash his clothes, shave, and scrub his teeth with sand. He refused to admit to himself that all this sprucing up was for Miss Drusilla Pointer. He hadn't seen her in nearly four years. He had assumed that she would be married by now. He knew that she hadn't married Lieutenant, now Captain, Beauregard Pierce, had known it ever since the day—only a month or so after he had left Freedom and gone back to live with the Comanches—when he visited Fort Sill and happened to meet Lieutenant Pierce. "How's the missus?" he had asked the lieutenant, and the lieutenant had replied in a voice as hard and cold and sharp as an icicle, "There is no missus."

Gypsy learned later that Drusilla had called off her engagement to Lieutenant Pierce shortly before their wedding. Nobody seemed to know why. Whenever Gypsy happened to meet someone from Freedom, he always brought the talk around to her and learned that she was still unmarried. Everybody, including Gypsy, agreed that was a crying shame, she being such a pretty young thing and all, and it wasn't because she didn't have plenty of suitors. But it had been over a year now since Gypsy last had word of her, and he figured she was bound to be married by now.

Camped under trees on the bank of the creek, he was awakened that night by the sound of hoofbeats. There were maybe ten horses coming in a steady gallop, headed northeast toward Freedom.

He tumbled out of his bedroll, snatched up his sawed-off shotgun, and hurried to his horse. Then, obscured by the shadow of the trees, he trained his eyes on the road. The light from a dust-reddened quarter moon wasn't enough to let him see for more than a few hundred feet, but as the horses came into sight, he could hardly believe his eyes. Rather than a posse or a formation of cavalry troopers, as he expected, he saw a sort of white cloud, a white blur, undulating along the road. Then he began to distinguish riders and horses within the mass, and realized what he was seeing: Klansmen, about ten of them, dressed in their hooded white spook costumes. Even their horses were fitted out in flowing white costumes.

Gypsy automatically swept his eyes over each of the horses and men, searching for some distinguishing mark, but the costumes covered all such identifiable markings. Only on the last horse did he see something helpful: The horse had white stockings on one front leg and both rear legs.

As soon as they had galloped past his hiding place, Gypsy dressed, saddled his horse, and spurred the Appaloosa into a run. He figured the Klansmen were headed for Freedom, but when he had ridden to within five miles of the town, he sensed by the diminished amount of dust in the air that they had probably turned off onto a side road.

He glanced eastward and saw something he assumed was a lantern flickering on some faraway homestead. But the light began to change to a pale glow that emanated upward and then began spreading. A grass fire? He headed toward it. From the brightening glow on the horizon he guessed that the fire was spreading rapidly. Soon he topped the crest of a rise and saw the roaring flames.

Somebody's house and fields were burning. As he rode toward the farm, he began to see, in the vast flickering light of the flames, the silhouettes of people fighting the fire. One of them, a woman, was running toward the house, screaming, "Not my house!" Flames swirled furnacelike from the windows and doors, roaring skyward.

As Gypsy rode into the yard and dismounted, he recognized Eula Rasmussen. Running at full speed, she collided with the heat from the burning house as though the heat were a soft wall. She was sent reeling backward, her arms raised to protect her face.

Gypsy grabbed her shoulders from behind. She struggled to get free, to once again dash toward the flames, but Gypsy pulled her away, saying, "Take it easy, Miss Eula, there's nothing you can do." She wilted to the ground. Her sunbonnet had fallen off, and she made no attempt to cover her harelip as she sat staring at the house while it collapsed into a huge pile of sparks and glowing embers. "Not my house," she moaned. "Oh, please, not my house."

DRUSILLA was coming down the dusty farm road in a buckboard, bringing wicker baskets filled with sandwiches and jugs of hot coffee to the firefighters. Gypsy recognized her even from a distance. She wore a man's floppy felt hat and the high-buttoned dress of a country schoolteacher. And she was just as attractive now, at twenty-seven, as she had been at twenty-three.

Pulling the team of mules to a dusty stop as Gypsy approached on the Appaloosa, she said, "Morning," as if to a stranger. "Is the fire out?" Perhaps because she was riding directly into the glaring red light of the rising sun, she didn't recognize him.

231

"All 'cept the mopping up. And a good-morning to you, Miss Drusilla." He removed his hat with a flourish.

Drusilla brought her hand up to shield her eyes. "Gypsy?" she cried. "Gypsy Smith! Lordy mercy, is that *you*?"

Excited at seeing him, Drusilla began a series of questions that almost left her stammering. Where had he been? What was he doing here? Would he be staying in Freedom for a while? How did it happen that he was out here fighting a fire? And when he told her that he had followed a gang of Klansmen to the fire, she said, "So it was the Klan. Poor Eula. Lord, how hard she worked on that house, and how she loved it! For years she scrimped and saved every nickel and dime to buy a board, a windowpane, a doorknob. I've never in my life seen anybody work harder, taking in washing, scrubbing people's floors—anything to make a few pennies she could put into that house. And now . . . her own people." She shook her head at the wonder of it. "Why?"

"She says they throwed a rock through her window, had a note tied to it accusing her of being a nigger lover."

"I'll take her back with me. She can stay with us."

"Us? Does that 'us' include a husband, Miss Drusilla?"

Her smile was uncertain. "Not yet, but I still have hopes. And how about you, Gypsy Smith? Where'll you be staying?"

"Me, I'm looking forward to clean sheets on a soft hotel bed."

"Getting soft at last?" She smiled, flashing her white teeth. "Well, I better be getting this stuff on down to the folks at the fire."

Gypsy touched the brim of his hat and turned in the saddle to watch the buckboard go jolting down the road.

He rode on to town and found that it hadn't changed much since he left. While it had never become the bustling farm town that the founders had hoped for, it had at least held its own against the withering forces of drought and the lack of a railroad; and now, with caravans of new Negro settlers using it as a staging area for the upcoming run into the Cherokee Outlet, it had even temporarily regained the look of a frontier boomtown.

Gypsy left the Appaloosa in the livery stable; then he rented a room at the hotel and went to the barbershop, where he got a haircut, a shave, and a hot bath. It was in the tub that Deputy Buck Tyson found him.

"Damn my hide, Gypsy Smith," he said, clicking his teeth. "I'd done give up on ever seeing you again."

"So how you doing, Buck? Got some new teeth, I see."

"Damn things don't fit too good," Buck complained, and went on, with a click every few words. "Listen. Amos Fulton wants to get the town council together right away. When can you come?"

"Evening'll be soon enough. I been fighting that fire all night, and I ain't doing nothing till I get me some shut-eye."

Buck hurried away, and before the water had even turned cold in Gypsy's bath, a delegation of city officials burst into the room. Besides Fulton, there was Freedom's current mayor, Philo P. Sawyer, and a new member of the city council, Dr. Homer Upchurch.

"Sorry to barge in on you like this, Gypsy," Amos said, "but with all this Klan activity, we figure we haven't got any time to lose. They may be back tonight to burn somebody else out. Who knows?"

"What d'you want me to do?" Gypsy asked.

"It's my job to coordinate public policies between the all-Negro towns. We've decided to fight the Klan," Amos said. "That's why we need you. I'm prepared to offer you a job not only as marshal of Freedom but as boss over every marshal in every one of the fourteen all-Negro towns in the Territory. The marshal we got here in Freedom now, Rufus Margrave, he's a good man, but . . . Well, we got to put a stop to these Klan raids. Pretty soon the Klan'll be as strong here as it is in the South, and by then it'll be too late."

"Who are the Klansmen? Got any names?"

"Nobody knows who they are," Fulton said. "Only the members know who the other members are, and it's worth their life to betray that knowledge to an outsider."

"Might be best to start with the Olanco Ranch," Mayor Sawyer said. "They're in this up to their necks, burning people out so they can take over their claims. It's owned by the Oklahoma Land Company. Shelby Hornbeck's the chairman of the board. You heard of him? He's Guthrie's representative in the territorial legislature, and he's being groomed for governor when we become a state."

233

"A Klansman?"

Amos tilted his head doubtfully. "Nobody knows for sure."

"I'll need a posse. Thirty or forty men. No hotheads."

"What do you intend to do?" asked Dr. Upchurch. He was a young physician, light-skinned, with black horn-rimmed eyeglasses and a small goatee that gave him a scholarly appearance.

"Nothing much we can do right now," Gypsy said. "I'll ride out to the Rasmussen place, try to pick up their trail. But without names to go on, we'll just have to wait for their next move. Then we'll be ready."

MAXWELL had been reluctant to pressure Corby into continuing his studies at the Carlisle Institute after he graduated, with honors, from the agency school in June of '93. It wasn't that Corby objected to going to Carlisle; he just sort of dillydallied the days away, unable to make a commitment to live in the white man's world, and he decided to stay around the agency at least for the summer and make some money racing Big Red.

Rachel encouraged his procrastinations. She couldn't bear the thought of his going away and leaving her to spend a friendless and funless summer at the agency by herself. So she made it easier for him to stay by suggesting that he move into the barn after graduation. Maxwell went along with the idea because the alternative was for Corby to go back to living with the Indians, and the influence of Indian life, Maxwell feared, might prove irresistible. So they all fixed up the tack-and-feed room in the barn as a place for Corby to stay until autumn, by which time, it was assumed, he would have become reconciled to going to Carlisle.

It proved to be a nice little room. Maxwell put in two windows, Rachel hung flour-sack curtains, a cot and a table were borrowed from the school, and a lantern provided a reading light. Corby was especially pleased with the room, since it was next to Big Red's stall.

So the summer passed pleasantly enough until one day in late August, when a delegation of agency ladies led by Mrs. Poggemeyer came to Maxwell's house—ostensibly to visit Nora but actually to have a talk with Maxwell about his daughter.

"Rachel needs to be sent away from here to a school where she can learn to be a proper young lady," Mrs. Poggemeyer told him. "Otherwise we're afraid she's going to . . . Well, you must realize that her and that Indian boy should be separated."

Maxwell didn't know whether to reproach the ladies for their suspicions or thank them for their concern. But while he told himself that the affection between Rachel and Corby was nothing more than childhood friendship, he began to watch them more closely and saw certain signs—touches, glances—that were more appropriate to childhood sweethearts than to mere friends.

One night when Rachel was in the kitchen cooking beans and ham hocks, Maxwell said, "Rachel, I think it's high time you went away to school. And I know just the place: Miss Finwick's Young Female Academy in St. Louis. Miss Finwick's an old colleague of mine from St. Louis, and I've no doubt she'd find a place for you for the fall term if I ask. It's a nice school. You'd like it, I'm sure."

Rachel wiped her hands on her apron. "School? St. Louis?" Her expression became one of excitement. It would be a delightful adventure, a chance to see new places, wear pretty clothes, meet new people, live in a great teeming city. But suddenly that look collapsed into a frown. "Oh, but Mother. Who would . . . ?"

"I'll find somebody. Don't you worry. In the meantime let's get Miss Clarksdale started on a new wardrobe for you. We can't have the girls at Miss Finwick's thinking you're a little backwoods waif."

Rachel was once again flushed with excitement. "Tell me about the school in St. Louis. Does it have lots of students? But what if they're all silly and I can't stand them?"

Maxwell answered her questions until supper was ready to be dished up, at which time he took a plate out to Corby.

He seemed surprised at the news. "She *wants* to go?"

"Oh, yes. Very excited about it. I'm going to take her to St. Louis on the train. If you decide to go to Carlisle, we could all make the trip together. Make it sort of a holiday. After we dropped Rachel off in St. Louis, you and I could go on to Pennsylvania together. It's about time I paid a visit to the institute, seeing as how I've sent them nearly three hundred students during the last sixteen years."

"And how many *vehos* have they sent back?" Corby asked.

Maxwell was disturbed to hear the inflection Corby gave to the Cheyenne word for white man, an inflection that made it a venomous racial epithet.

DRUSILLA and Eula stood near the opened door of the stagecoach. Eula wore a new dress and a new sunbonnet. Drusilla wore a bright yellow silk scarf over her head, which she drew around her face whenever a gust of hot September wind swirled a cloud of dust around her.

Gypsy approached just as the stagecoach driver and the shotgun guard came out of the depot carrying a strongbox between them.

"Aw right, let's get loaded," the driver called out.

Drusilla and Eula hesitated for a moment, and then suddenly threw their arms around each other, Eula saying from beneath her sunbonnet, "God bless you, Drusilla, and thankee for everything."

With her hands on Eula's shoulders, Drusilla said, "You be sure to write us once in a while, y'hear?"

Speaking from behind her hand, Eula said, "I'll do that, I surely will. Bless you. And bless you, too, Marshal," she said to Gypsy. "And thankee for your help."

Gypsy touched the brim of his hat. "Bye, Miss Eula. And don't you worry. You'll be all right. John Maxwell's a good man."

The driver waited as Eula climbed into the coach, then slammed the door closed. He climbed up into the driver's box and slapped the reins across the horses' backs. The coach jerked into motion.

Drusilla waved. "Bye, bye," she called. "Be sure to write now."

Eula waved from the window until the dust hid her from view.

"I left my grocery basket at the store," Drusilla said to Gypsy. "Walk with me? I'd like to talk to you about Clarence." She continued as they went along, "He's beginning to worry me. He's only sixteen now, but he's beginning to think of himself as a man. You understand? With girls, I mean. Doesn't even try to do his schoolwork. He'd like me to expel him. Then he could hang around with that Fast Talking Charlie and the other hooligans in town."

"Want me to horsewhip him?"

Ignoring his bantering, Drusilla said, "I thought maybe you

could give him a good talking-to, a man-to-man sort of talk. He needs to be told by a man how a boy can get into trouble with girls."

"Well, I'm just the man who can tell him about *that*."

"It's not funny, Gypsy. The other night he got caught, he and Charlie, peeking into—into a neighbor's window, watching a woman get undressed. Her husband caught 'em. He said if it ever happened again, he'd have Clarence arrested."

"All right. Sure. I'll have a talk with the boy, but I wouldn't take it so serious. Never knew a boy his age who didn't try, one time or other, to get a peek at a naked woman."

Gypsy followed her into the store. Her shopping basket was ready to go, but it was heavy, so Gypsy carried it home for her.

She invited him to stay for supper, and he accepted, not only for the pleasure of her company and a home-cooked meal but because he thought he might find an opportunity to speak with Clarence. When he didn't, he was just as glad to put it off for another day.

"Plenty of time for that," he said to Drusilla when, after supper, they were sitting alone on the porch swing in the dark.

"You mean you've decided to stay on in Freedom this time?"

"Well, I'll tell you, that might partly depend on you."

"Me? What's it got to do with me?"

Sitting in a porch swing, Gypsy learned that evening, was not the best place for courting a girl. Whenever he tried to turn sideways and maneuver for a kiss, Drusilla gave her end of the swing a shove, causing it to wobble, making a kiss difficult. She also had a fan—which was perfectly natural on a hot, airless autumn evening—but it wasn't easy to kiss a girl while she was fanning herself, especially if she fanned herself faster and faster as the mood grew more intimate.

"Fact is," he said in a sort of warning tone, "I been thinking about settling down, maybe getting married and all that."

The fan went a little faster. "And you—you're telling me—" She faltered but finally blurted out, "You want to marry me?"

"Well," he drawled, "I 'spect I could be talked into it."

She sprang to her feet. "You 'could be talked into it'! You've got your nerve, Gypsy Smith. Why, a girl'd have to be crazy to marry you. You think you can just run off for four years, without so much as a postcard in all that time. . . ." She abruptly crossed to the porch railing and stood with her back to him, the fan going at full speed. "And you talk about being talked into it. Why, I wouldn't marry you if you got down on your knees and begged me."

He slowly got to his feet and moved to stand behind her. "Now that's real disheartening, Drusilla darling." He put his hands softly on her shoulders, careful not to make any quick moves, as if approaching a skittish animal.

"Don't you 'darling' me." But her body wasn't as rejecting as her words. She allowed his hands to remain on her shoulders.

"Real disheartening, indeed." He leaned down to kiss her neck.

The fan stopped. Contending forces within her held her immobile for a moment as Gypsy nuzzled her neck, but then she spun around so forcefully that his hands were jerked from her shoulders. "Looky here, Gypsy—"

He cut her words off with a kiss.

Gypsy and Drusilla stood kissing in the darker shadows on the porch, so the man approaching the house didn't see or hear them. They were taken by surprise the moment his foot touched the porch. Drusilla tore herself from Gypsy's embrace and whirled to face the man. "Homer! Dr. Upchurch, I didn't—we didn't—"

"Oh," he murmured. "Scuse me. I didn't—I didn't see you there. I was just out for an evening stroll, you see, and thought I'd—I didn't know you had company."

"You know Marshal Smith, of course. We were just going to have a glass of cool tea. Would you join us?"

"Tea? Uh, no, thank you. I just thought I'd drop by for a minute, see how you were." And now his voice took on a barely discernible edge of jealous resentment. "I'd better go."

Gypsy noticed her face as she watched Dr. Upchurch disappear into the darkness. She was obviously fond of the young man. Gypsy touched her shoulder and said, "Drusilla darling—"

"No." She jerked away from his touch. And now the fan was going again. "You'd better go, too. I can't trust myself with you anymore tonight. Lordy mercy, you do bring out the devil in me."

He said good night without trying to kiss her again, but he had stepped off the porch and gone only a few feet when she called his name. "Gypsy Smith," she said. "Do you love me?"

"Ain't it obvious?" he answered matter-of-factly.

After a pause she said, "We'll see. G'night," and went inside.

Gypsy pondered the implication of that "We'll see" as he walked down the long, dark, gentle incline into the lamplit town, and came to the suspicion that his capacity for being a husband to a spirited young wife and a foster father was going to be tested. He knew that the children would come first with her—as Lieutenant Beauregard Pierce had found out, to his sorrow. Drusilla had told Gypsy that she had broken off her engagement to Lieutenant Pierce because, only a few days before their marriage, he informed her that there would be no place for the children on the army post. She vowed that any man in the future who might want her as a wife would have to prove he had room in his heart for a half-dozen waifs.

Well, Gypsy didn't mind being tested. He thought it was a good idea, in fact. He rather enjoyed sitting around at night after supper, telling the children of his adventures as a frontiersman, buffalo hunter, wild-horse wrangler, and Indian scout.

But Drusilla's request that he have a man-to-man talk with Clarence left him feeling a little inadequate. So he procrastinated—a day passed, two days, a week—and then something happened that made Gypsy sorry indeed that he had put off the talk even for a day.

MAXWELL met Eula when she came in on the afternoon stage from El Reno. Scanning the passengers as they stepped off, he said to one, "Miss Rasmussen, is it?"

"Yes, sir," she said, and dropped her hand for a second to let him see her harelip. Then she lowered her head again to hide her face beneath the sunbonnet.

"Well," Maxwell said, slightly rattled, "welcome to Agency, Miss Rasmussen. Which bag is yours?"

"This here bundle's all I got. Fire burned up everything else."

"Oh, yes, the fire. I read about it in the newspaper. Terrible business. I'm sorry. Here, let me carry that for you."

"No, thankee, it ain't heavy."

"Well then," he said, starting for the house. Eula walked at his side but a little behind. "I'm sorry the house's in something of a mess at the moment. My daughter's leaving to go to school in St. Louis in a few days, so we've been doing lots of packing but very little housework, I'm afraid. That's why we were so glad to get Gypsy's telegram about you. My daughter—Rachel's her name— she's been doing most of the work around the house and helping to take care of her mother, who's an invalid. Did Gypsy tell you?"

He stopped. She stopped.

"Yes, sir, he told me," she said, feeling awkward. She had expected to be treated like a servant, not like a guest.

"Well, there'll be time to talk about all that. I expect you'll want to wash up a bit first, after such a dusty trip."

"A pan of water'd be a blessing, thankee kindly."

He opened the front gate and stepped back. "After you."

"Thankee." Flustered again, she passed through the gate but fell behind again as they went up the walk.

Rachel was watching at the window as Maxwell and Eula came up the walk. She opened the door for them and gave Eula a thorough scrutinizing as she was introduced. The few housekeeper-nursemaids who had come and gone over the years of Nora's illness had been middle-aged women, used-up women who didn't have anything better to do. But Eula was different. She didn't seem old and used up. True, there was the puzzling way she hid her mouth when Maxwell introduced her as Miss Rasmussen and she said, "First name's Eula, if you want to call me that."

Rachel's eyes went to Maxwell for an explanation of why Eula was so shy about showing her face. And to divert her attention, he said, "I thought you were over with Miss Clarksdale getting your new dresses fitted."

"I was, but I couldn't stand still, worrying about Corby. He left a little while ago, said he didn't know when he'd be back."

"Well, we won't concern Miss Eula with that," Maxwell said. "Come, the washstand's out on the back porch."

"What's this about Corby?" he asked Rachel when he returned.

"I don't know. He said he was going on a vision quest. Whoever heard of an educated Indian going on a vision quest? I thought only ignorant blanket Indians did that. Oh, Daddy, does this mean he's going back to the blanket? Can't you make him go to Carlisle?"

"It'll be all right. I expect I'll have him in Carlisle before the year's out. But you go on back over to Miss Clarksdale's and get those dresses properly fitted. I have to talk to Miss Rasmussen."

"Say," Rachel whispered, "why's she keep her face hidden?"

"Harelip," he whispered.

"Oh," Rachel said. "Oh, the poor woman."

Chapter Eight

*F*ast Talking Charlie was bent over an operating table, sweating, clenching his teeth to keep from crying out, while Dr. Upchurch picked buckshot from his buttocks with a pair of needle-nosed tweezers. Sixteen-year-old Clarence sat on a chair nearby, his head in his hands.

"How bad?" Gypsy asked as he and Buck Tyson entered the room.

Dr. Upchurch dropped another extracted pellet into a metal dish. "The pellets are just under the skin. Nothing to worry about medically. The worry is, who shot 'em? A white man, they say."

Gypsy turned to Clarence. "All right, Clarence, let's hear it. I want to know who shot you and why, and I want to know *now*."

"Yes, sir," Clarence murmured, raising his head, his face blanched with fear. He stumbled evasively into the story, and within a few minutes Gypsy knew the worst of it.

The two had been shot by a white farmer named Tully, who had caught Charlie fornicating with his fourteen-year-old daughter as Clarence stood by. It seemed that Charlie had been seeing the girl, whom he had met one day at the swimming hole on Cottonwood Creek. She confessed that she often came there to hide in the bushes and watch colored boys swim.

The white man came crashing through the bushes, carrying a shotgun. The boys started running before he fired. The man was too far away for the buckshot to do any serious damage.

241

"All right," Gypsy said. "Buck, as soon as the doc gets 'em patched up, bring 'em down to the jail."

"Jail?" Charlie whined. "What's we done to get locked up?"

"For your own protection, you young scamp," Buck said.

Gypsy hurried back to his office, where he found Deputy Rufus Margrave at Gypsy's desk doing some paperwork. On taking over the job of marshal from Rufus, Gypsy had kept him on as deputy.

"You know anything about a white farmer name Tully?" Gypsy asked. "Got a farm about five miles northeast of here?"

"I knows they's a white farmer living out there. Why?"

"Find Mayor Sawyer and Judge Cale. Ask 'em to come here. You know where Amos Fulton is?"

"Last time I heard, he was up in Langston."

"Send him a telegram. Tell him he better get on down here soon's he can. We got trouble."

Late that afternoon Sheriff Alva Harriman and six deputies rode into town, accompanied by Lester Tully and his daughter in a dilapidated buckboard.

Gypsy stepped casually out of his office and leaned against a gallery post. In his left hand he held a double-barreled shotgun. His right thumb was hooked beneath his cartridge belt, near his Colt.

Sheriff Harriman was not corpulent, but seemed so because he had a turkey wattle under his chin that wobbled when he spoke. "Gypsy Smith, is it?"

"Marshal Gypsy Smith," Gypsy corrected.

"*The* Gypsy Smith?" the sheriff said. "Well, I hear you're one of the few darkies 'round these parts that can read. So I assume you read the telegram I sent, and you know why we're here. As you can see"—he jerked his head toward the Tully wagon—"we brought the victim along to make identification. If the boys you're holding are the ones who so brutally violated this young girl, we'll be taking them back to Guthrie to stand trial. Now bring 'em out."

"Well, Sheriff, I 'spect you can read, too," Gypsy said, "so you know the telegram I sent you said we was going to keep the boys here. We'll give 'em a fair trial, and if they be proved guilty, why, we'll just take 'em out and hang 'em. You got my word on it."

"Your word? Nigrah, your word don't mean a damned thing to me. Now I hope I don't have to educate you on matters of legal jurisdiction, boy, but I'm the sheriff of this county, and the territorial courts are in Guthrie, and that's where those boys'll be tried and hung—if proved guilty," he added, as if amused to think there could be any doubt about it. He leaned sideways in the saddle, preparing to dismount.

Gypsy snapped the order: "Don't get down."

The sheriff glared at Gypsy. Then his body slowly settled back into the leather-creaking saddle. "Now you listen to me, boy—"

"No, you listen to me." Gypsy raked his eyes across the other riders, who, following the sheriff's lead, were making tentative motions toward their guns. "Each one of you's in the sights of a gun right now. Better take time to think about that."

Their eyes darted here and there, searching out the hiding places of the alleged guns; none was anywhere to be seen.

"You're bluffing," Sheriff Harriman said.

"Am I?" Gypsy raised his voice. "All right, men, show y'selves."

From behind the false-front parapets atop the two-story buildings on both sides of the street, and around the corners of nearby buildings, men stepped into the open with weapons leveled at the sheriff and his party. There were probably thirty men in all.

"That look like a bluff to you, Sheriff?"

The sheriff trembled with stifled fury. "Nigrah, do you have any idea what you're doing? This'll get you hung."

"Maybe so. But at least you'll have to hang me before you hang them two boys for something they didn't do."

"Didn't do! Why, look at her. You can see what they done. They brutally raped and beat that girl."

Gypsy approached the girl huddled on the seat, a shawl draped over her downcast face. She didn't lift her head, but he could see the bruises on her face, the black eye, the swollen mouth.

"Missy, did them boys beat you? Or was it your pa?"

"Get away from her, you black bastard," Tully said. "My daughter ain't talking to you. Get away!" He made a move toward the shotgun lying at his feet on the floor of the buckboard.

"Tully," the sheriff barked, and the man pulled back.

Gypsy stepped away from the buckboard and chanced to see the legs of one of the horses in the rear of the group. It had three white stockings—one in front, two in back. The horse's rider was a young man with long blond hair and a sly, mischief-loving demeanor.

Going back to the gallery, Gypsy announced, "If that girl wants to file charges against the two prisoners, I'll be happy to oblige her, and I guarantee they'll be brought to trial." He paused briefly. "But they'll be tried right here in Freedom by a jury of their peers. Till then I reckon there ain't nothing else to say. So if you gentlemen'll just be on your way now, we'll all get on back to our chores."

"Well, they told me you was crazy, but I declare, I had no idea you was *this* crazy. You think we won't be back?" He snorted with contempt. "Well, you just start counting the hours, boy. You don't have many of 'em left. By this time tomorrow you'll be dead."

"Maybe so, Sheriff, but I'll take a lot of men with me when I go."

The sheriff swung his horse around with a jerk of the reins and kicked it into a gallop. The other riders fell in behind him. Lester Tully stood up in his buckboard to whip his plow horses into a run, as if terrified of being left behind.

Once the hoofbeats faded in the distance, Rufus Margrave emerged from the marshal's office still clutching a shotgun.

"That deputy with the long blond hair," Gypsy asked, "know anything about him?"

"A little. Name's Sonny Boy Reeves. Big Mama could tell you 'bout him. He sneaks into town to see one of her girls. Why?"

"He's a Klansman."

"What?"

"I'm going to Big Mama's for a minute. I want you to put three guards out here in front and three in the back."

Gypsy went down a side street to Big Mama's hoodoo parlor and sporting house, a two-story building sitting off by itself in a weedy lot behind Cooley's livery stable. A tumbleweed blew past as he mounted the squeaky steps to the porch. Big Mama had been watching through the window and opened the door before he knocked.

"Is they gone?"

"For now."

She quickly shut the door against the wind and dust.

"Rufus tells me you got a white boy comes here sometimes, a deputy from Guthrie?"

"Yeah. Sometimes he sneak in the back way to see Lulu Belle."

"Which one's she?"

"She in her room. You want to talk with her?"

Big Mama led the way in her flapping house slippers down the hallway to the last door, the room closest to the back entrance.

A homely coffee-colored girl with uncombed hair, Lulu Belle was maybe twenty years old but looked forty, and one side of her face was disfigured by a razor scar.

"What's y'all want?"

"I want you to tell me about a white deputy—name's Sonny Boy. He ever mention the Ku Klux Klan?"

"He ax me was I ever whupped by the Klan. Ain't no Klan gonna whup me. I cut 'em wid a knife. That's what I tell 'im. He just laugh. He say maybe he whup me someday. I tell 'im, he do, I cut 'im good."

Gypsy said to them both, "Look, if this boy ever comes back here, I want to know about it immediately. Send somebody to tell me."

Back at his office, Gypsy told Rufus Margrave to find out everything he could about Sonny Boy Reeves. Rufus started to go. "Miss Drusilla's here," he said. "She brought the boys some supper."

Wearing an apron and a dusting cap, Drusilla came up the stairs from the basement jail carrying an empty wicker basket.

"You shouldn't be here," Gypsy said sternly, but relented, adding, "But the boys do have to eat. How are you?"

She came to him and lightly, awkwardly touched his forearm. "Not very well, to tell the truth. I'm tired. And so afraid."

"Here. Sit." He guided her to the chair behind the desk.

"Those men . . . Rufus said one was a Klansman." She stared into the lamplight, her eyes glistening with tears. "They came here to lynch the boys, didn't they?"

"I 'spect so." He sat on the edge of the desk, reached out to touch her shoulder. "But don't worry. We ain't gonna let that happen."

She placed her hand on his, pressed it. "Thank you, Gypsy," she said. "I'm so tired. How long are we going to have to run, Gypsy? Where can we go to get away from them? Why do they *hate* us so much? What'd we ever do to them? Why won't they ever leave us alone?" The tears were streaming down her face now. "Why do they want to kill our children?"

"I don't know. I got no answers."

"Well, if you got no answers, how about a comforting hug?"

"Got plenty of them." He opened his arms and enfolded her. "It's gonna be all right. Everything's gonna be all right."

Arms around each other, they stood, slightly swaying, and not another word was said until she, in a small voice muffled against the folds of his shirt, said, "Thank you, Gypsy. I feel safe here. In your arms, I mean." She lifted her head and gave him a searching look, then took a deep breath. "Gypsy Smith, would you marry me?"

He chuckled. "Why, Miss Drusilla, I thought you'd never ask."

With a small cry of joy she threw her arms around his neck, and in a jumble of words, as they covered each other's faces with kisses, she said, "You will?" and he said, "Sure," and she said, "When?" and he said, "Why, tomorrow'd be just fine with me," and she cried, "Tomorrow!" and he in a more sensible tone said, "Well, as soon's this business is over with anyway," and she said, "I love you," and he said, "I love you, too, Drusilla darling," and for a moment it seemed they were already hearing wedding bells.

It was the fire bell. Somebody had begun to ring the bell in a series of three rapid clangs, rest, three rapid clangs, rest.

"The signal for the men to assemble," Gypsy said. "Something's up. Come on, we got to get you home."

He snatched the shotgun off the desk and ushered her out. They saw men dashing toward the town-hall building. One of them was Rufus Margrave, panting and sweating.

"They're coming!" he said.

"How d'you know?" Gypsy asked calmly.

"The telegraph wires've been cut. They must be on their way."

"I 'spect so. Here, you, Abe," he called to a man driving up in a buggy, "take Miss Drusilla home." He helped her into the buggy. "Go home and stay inside. I'll send a couple men up to guard the school."

"Isn't there anything I can do?"

"Well, you might get started making y'self a wedding gown."

She touched his face. "God bless and keep you, Gypsy Smith."

The buggy pulled away. He stood and watched as it was swallowed up by the darkness and dust.

He stepped up on the gallery and faced the crowd of men gathering in the street. Some were on foot, others on horseback, some with lanterns, all with weapons. He told Buck Tyson to put about twenty mounted sentries around the town. "And don't start shooting till you know what you're shooting at, y'hear? I want to move the boys out of here to a good hiding place. Anybody know of one?"

Ike Jones said, "Well, how about my storm cellar? They'd be safe there even if a cyclone blew up and the whole town burned down."

"Sounds good." To Rufus he said, "Fetch the boys up."

Carrying lanterns and shotguns, Gypsy and Rufus, accompanied by Ike Jones and a guard called Geezer, escorted the frightened boys from the jail to the storm cellar in a weedy lot behind Ike Jones's home. Gypsy left the boys in the moldy-smelling cellar with instructions to stay inside until someone came for them. He left Geezer, a teamster with a reputation for toughness, to stand guard.

About an hour later Buck Tyson hurried into the marshal's office with the news that the Klan had been spotted. With his false teeth clicking, he announced, "Man on the north water tower saw 'em riding this way. Says there was a bunch. Thought I'd take a ride out that way, see what they're up to."

Gypsy told him to go ahead.

The men in the office moved out onto the gallery, where they waited to see what would happen next. With his sawed-off shotgun dangling from his left hand, Gypsy leaned against a gallery post and calmly smoked a cigarette. Rufus paced back and forth on the gallery, a rifle cradled in the crook of his arm.

After a half hour they heard a shout from the man on the water tower at the south end of town. "Fire to the west! Prairie fire." And soon Gypsy could see, low on the horizon, the first yellowish glow.

"Lord Almighty," Mayor Sawyer groaned, "with a wind like this, we'll be lucky if we can hold it at the firebreaks."

The fire bell began a continuous clamoring peal, and people rushed out the lamplit doorways of the buildings and houses along Main Street to see what was happening.

Staring wide-eyed at the rapidly swelling dome of fiery brightness on the horizon, Rufus said, "Gypsy, we got to let somebody know what's going on here. I could ride to Andersonville, use the telegraph there. Let the federal marshals know, anyway. Not that we'll get any help, but they ought to know."

"All right," Gypsy said. "Go ahead."

Rufus bounded to his horse and swung into the saddle. "I'll be back soon's I can." He galloped off down the street, heading south.

The bell on the fire wagon clanged as the wagon came around the corner onto Main Street, with two horses straining in harness. Alongside the wagon, with its red water tank and coils of hose, trotted a number of volunteer firemen. They began darting here and there, shouting, "Turn out! Turn out! Prairie fire. Turn out!"

Mayor Sawyer and Ike Jones looked questioningly at Gypsy.

"Go ahead," he said. "I'll hold down the fort here."

"What if the Klan comes in while we're out fighting the fire?" Ike Jones asked.

"Long's they don't know where the boys are, they won't get what they came for."

"And what," Mayor Sawyer asked, "if it's you they come for?"

"Well, they won't have no trouble finding me."

Left alone on the gallery, Gypsy watched the streets come alive like a disturbed anthill, watched, too, the fire on the horizon. It was coming fast; within an hour it had reached the outskirts of town. Though perhaps five hundred people were fighting it, they couldn't stop it. Soon structures on the edges of town were ablaze.

Gypsy, wearing a red bandanna over his nose and mouth to filter the smoke and ashes, had remained at his post in front of his office. By now Main Street was thronged with many who had fled their campgrounds outside town, bringing with them their livestock and wagons and hastily loaded belongings.

Buck rode up on his lathered mount. Reining to a stop, he said, "Oldfield says he saw sixteen Klansmen in a bunch about two mile

south of town, whupping some colored man they'd caught and tied to a tree. Says he couldn't get close enough to see who it was."

Acting on a vague apprehension, Gypsy said, "Hold down the fort here while I check on the boys. Heard some shots over that way a few minutes ago. I best go see. Geezer's house's on fire. I doubt he'd stay at his post and watch his house burn down."

Gypsy crossed the street and strode along the sidewalk. Suddenly a woman burst forth, screaming, "Marshal, Marshal." It was Lucille Jones, Ike's plump wife, running as fast as her heavy legs could carry her. "It's you! Thank God! The Klan. They just left. They shot out the light in my kitchen."

Gypsy grabbed Lucille's shoulder. "What about the boys?"

"I don't know. I didn't see. Lord have mercy. When they shot through my window, I fell down on the floor, didn't get up till—"

But Gypsy was already running. Darting into the weedy lot, he called, "Geezer!" before he saw the cellar door smashed open and Geezer nowhere about—and the boys gone.

"Get the posse together," Gypsy shouted to Buck as he ran back to his tethered Appaloosa. "They got the boys." He jerked the reins loose and vaulted into the saddle.

Buck stammered, "What? How—how'd they find—"

"Had to be Rufus. They caught him and whipped it out of him. I'll try to pick up their trail south of town. I figure they'll swing around east to get back on the main road to Guthrie. Get some men, head north fast, try to get between them and Guthrie."

He slammed his heels into the Appaloosa's sides, causing the horse to leap into a full gallop within a few strides. Gypsy rode south at breakneck speed, while the stinging sparks from the blazing tumbleweeds whirled around like swarms of angry insects.

At each intersecting farm road he stopped and dismounted. He finally found what he was looking for: the hoofprints of many horses turning east onto a little-used section road. In the light of the burning fence posts along the road, he saw that the hoofprints were sprinkled with ashes, indicating that the riders had passed this way before the fire. They were probably thirty minutes ahead of him.

It was at Five Mile Ford that he found the boys. It was about four o'clock in the morning, and the moon was going down. He had slowed the Appaloosa as he headed into the creek bottom, when he realized that he had glimpsed something strange in the moon-soft shadows beneath a tree.

Silhouetted against the red blaze of the setting moon, the two bodies swung by ropes from one of the tree's lower limbs. He had to ride to within a few feet of the bodies to recognize the boys, with their faces twisted grotesquely above the hangman's nooses. The initials KKK had been carved into their chests.

The first indication that he had ridden into an ambush was from his horse—a snort, ears pricked up. Then he heard from some-where behind him the faint metallic click-click sound of a gun being cocked. Instantly he drew his own revolver and jerked around in the saddle to fire at a glimmer of white in a thicket of trees.

And just as instantly his shot was answered by a fusillade of bullets. Three of them struck Gypsy. One grazed his head, one struck him in the right chest, another went through his upper right thigh. He was knocked from the saddle and crashed facedown in the dust. He was unconscious for an unknown time, though it couldn't have been very long, for when he regained the hazy glimmerings of consciousness, he could hear the hoofbeats of the riders coming toward him. He tried to move, to find his gun, but he couldn't.

When he blinked away the blood that matted his eyelashes to-gether, he could see the hooded Klansmen on their horses as they moiled around his body. He could hear fragments of voices, words. "I knew he'd come. Didn't I tell you he'd come?"

With the right side of his face pressed against the ground, he could see the legs and hooves of the horses as they churned around him, and he could see among them a horse with three white stock-ings. The man on that horse was slumped forward. On his white robe was a huge stain of blood. Voices were saying, "He's bleeding pretty bad. . . . Take him on to Guthrie. We'll catch up."

Two men dismounted and bent over Gypsy.

"Is he finished?"

"Shot in the head."

"What d'you want us to do with him?"

"Cut him. I want the rest of those Nigrahs to see what happens to any black bastard who wears a lawman's badge."

Gypsy heard his clothes being cut. He tried to reach out, but he couldn't move. Then he could feel the knives cutting into his flesh, cutting into his groin. He could see the men bending over his body, cutting, and he could hear the knives, cutting, and these were the last things he saw and heard before he dissolved into darkness.

Chapter Nine

AFTER Maxwell strapped the trunk to the luggage rack of the surrey, he helped Rachel into the back seat. Eula handed Maxwell a big basket of food for their journey, and he climbed in beside Rachel.

They had gone about five miles when Maxwell, from the corner of his eye, caught sight of something in the dust-blurred distance: a rider traveling along the crest of a ridge about a half mile away. Rachel leaned over to see out from under the surrey's tassel-fringed top and immediately cried, "It's Corby!" She threw herself across Maxwell's lap so she could lean out and wave and yell, "Corby!"

The rider didn't respond.

"There's more than one Indian with a bay horse," Maxwell said.

"Oh, of course it's Corby." Rachel pushed the driver's shoulder. "Stop the horses. Let me out!" She jumped down before the wheels had come to a full stop and ran around to the other side so the rider could see her. She waved both hands. "Corby, come here!"

The rider stopped when the surrey stopped but still failed to respond to Rachel's frantic waves and yells.

"Come on, Rachel, get back in. We'll be late for the train."

She waved once more, this time in a sad, resigned way, and said in a small voice, "Bye, Corby. Bye. . . ."

Then the rider raised his hand and made the sweep-the-sky signal of the Plains Indians, which meant "go in peace."

Delighted to have a response at last, Rachel waved again, and finally, at Maxwell's insistence, she got back into the surrey, and they resumed the dusty, jolting journey to El Reno.

DEXTER HAD RECEIVED A LETTER from Rachel asking him please to meet her train at the station in Hennessey so they could say good-bye. He was living and working in Guthrie these days but had to be in Hennessey that day on Oklahoma Land Company business.

When Dexter left Agency, he had gone straightaway to the Hornbeck Building in Guthrie, where he found the clerks who had bribed him to give them information about Indian allotments. They had promised him a job if he got fired for helping them. Granted, it wasn't much of a job. In fact, it amounted to little more than being an errand boy. Dexter believed that he was meant for better things than being a courier or passing out handbills entitled "The White Man Rules the World." He read the handbill many times, memorizing it as if it were the gospel of a new religion, and Shelby Hornbeck its minister. Hornbeck was everything Dexter had ever wanted to be: rich, powerful, handsome, aristocratic, a born leader.

As a born leader, Shelby Hornbeck knew a born follower when he saw one. So as soon as Dexter proved to be both reliable and obedient, Shelby saw to it that he was moved up the ladder from flunky to tax collector, a job in which Dexter proved particularly adept, especially when it came to collecting taxes from Negroes and Indians. He was good at kicking down doors.

The two-ten train from El Reno pulled into Hennessey Station right on time. As it came to a stop, Rachel leaned across Maxwell's lap and waved through the opened window to Dexter.

Dexter was twenty-one years old now. Though he dressed well and carried a .44 Colt high on his hip, he was a rather average-looking young man, with a flabbiness about the waist.

Rachel and Maxwell emerged with the last of the passengers. Rachel pushed her way through the crowd to embrace her brother.

"Well, look at you!" Rachel said, stepping back. "You look like a bigwig. Doesn't he, Daddy?"

The greeting between Maxwell and Dexter had been in the nature of grunts and nods, and now Maxwell said, "Sure."

"Well, I'm doing all right," Dexter boasted. "And you? Off to school, huh?"

"Yes, isn't it wonderful! Oh, I'm so glad you came," Rachel said.

253

"The conductor told us we'd be here for an hour. Let's find a place and have a picnic, shall we? Eula packed some fried chicken and yams and mincemeat pie. She's the new woman looking after Mother."

They left the station and strolled toward Turkey Creek. As they walked, Rachel chattered on about Miss Finwick's Academy.

Dexter shrugged. "I reckon that's what Mother would've wanted—for you to be among others of your own race. But what about Mother—"

"Don't start that," Maxwell interrupted. "Nora's in good hands."

"Here now, how's this?" Rachel said, diverting their attention to a shady willow tree where there were logs to sit on.

They sat, and Rachel brought from the wicker basket a piece of fried chicken for each of them. Once they began eating, she asked Dexter, "So how is it? Eula's chicken, I mean."

Dexter tossed a gnawed chicken bone away, wiped the grease from his mouth and asked, "Who is this woman you hired to stay with Mother? What makes you think you can trust her?"

"Eula is a good woman. Good with your mother," Maxwell said.

Rachel added, "Eula Rasmussen. You might've heard of her— the woman whose house was burned down by the Klan over near Freedom a couple of weeks ago."

"*That* woman?" Dexter glowered at Maxwell. "Is *that* who you hired to take care of my mother? A notorious nigger lover."

Maxwell cleared his throat and said, "Well now, Dexter, I'm not sure I know what you're implying by that melodramatic epithet. But if you're implying that Eula's some sort of degenerate, you can set your mind at ease. Eula's the last person in the world I'd ever suspect of doing anything improper."

Dexter stood. "Yeah? That's why the Klan burned her out!"

Maxwell hooted with derision. "Oh, yes. The Klan! Those noble knights who burn the houses of helpless women and lynch kids. As rotten a bunch of bastards as ever walked the face of the earth."

Dexter's body shivered with anger. "You think you know so much, but you're stupid!" He flung the words at Maxwell with the force of long-suppressed hatred.

"Dexter!" Rachel cried.

Dexter had started to leave but stopped and whirled around. "You know something, old man? You better watch out. You're just the kind of nigger lover the Klan likes to take care of." He strode away.

Maxwell was stunned by the virulence of Dexter's reaction. Why should he take ridicule of the Klan so personally? It was as if, by cursing the Klan, Maxwell had cursed Dexter himself.

And the answer struck him with the shock of revealed truth: "My God, he's one of them."

IT SEEMED to Dr. Upchurch that he had slept for only seconds, but the room was suddenly flooded with morning light, and someone was knocking urgently on his door.

"Doctor? It's Marshal Smith," said Nurse Deever through the door. "You said to let you know if there was any change. He's coming to, looks like."

Dr. Upchurch bounded out of bed. Scrambling into his scattered clothes, he left the room and rushed downstairs to the operating room, where he found Gypsy Smith alive—barely alive, but at least alive. And that was a miracle. Gypsy Smith had been at death's door, and now he had come back.

But the Gypsy Smith who had been to death's door was not the Gypsy Smith who came back. This became uncomfortably apparent during the weeks following the operation, as Gypsy slowly recovered his senses. His first coherent sentence to Dr. Upchurch was an order concerning people who came to see him: "Keep them the hell away," a prohibition that included even Drusilla.

With his head, chest, thigh, and groin swathed in bandages, Gypsy Smith lay on a bed in the infirmary, as grim as a corpse.

It was Dr. Upchurch who had to tell Drusilla that Gypsy refused to see her, and she, hurt and baffled, made him promise that he would convey her plea to Gypsy that she be allowed to see him. He kept the promise, only to be told, "Mind your own business." After that, the doctor tried to assuage Drusilla's baffled pain by telling her that Gypsy was still in a state of shock.

The only person Gypsy finally consented to see was Amos Fulton. One day near the end of Gypsy's third week of recovery Fulton sent a note saying he had some news about the KKK. He was soon ushered into Gypsy's presence. Fulton sat in a chair beside the bed. Gypsy stared fixedly at the ceiling throughout the visit.

"Well," Fulton said, "our informants tell us that Sonny Boy Reeves was admitted to the hospital in Guthrie on the morning after the lynching. Gunshot wound in his side."

Gypsy's flat metallic voice had an edge of grim satisfaction as he said, "Sonny Boy Reeves."

"Did you shoot him?" Fulton prompted, but when Gypsy finally responded in a croaking whisper, it concerned somebody else.

"Rufus?" Fulton said. "He's dead. They killed him." He paused, then said, "Is there anything I can do for you, Gypsy?"

"Yes."

"What?"

"Go away."

Two weeks later, after Gypsy had learned to walk on crutches, he left the infirmary under cover of darkness. Still dressed in his pajamas and bandages, with his .44 Colt strapped around his waist, attended only by Big Mama, who carried his few belongings in a paper bag, he made his way, grimacing with pain, to Big Mama's house. There he took refuge in one of the upstairs rooms to do his convalescing. Other than the doctor and Big Mama herself, no one was allowed to enter the room.

Drusilla tried, only to be told by Big Mama, who met her at the door, that Gypsy still wouldn't see anyone.

Big Mama's heart went out to the girl, a feeling that increased with each succeeding visit until, on the fifth, she put her arm around Drusilla's shoulder and said, "Honey, when Gypsy say he want to see you, why, I run give you the message myself."

Drusilla's lip trembled like a child's. "Please, let me go to him. I want to help him, to love him."

Big Mama knew it was hopeless, but she gave it a moment's thought. "I tell you what. I go speak to him. You stay here."

Drusilla stepped to the porch railing and waited. From where she stood, she could see the small graveyard north of town, with five new mounds of earth—five new graves, one of them Clarence's.

Then she heard Gypsy's voice from inside the house, talking to Big Mama. It triggered an irresistible impulse. She opened the screen door, went into the house, and climbed the stairs.

Big Mama turned with a startled and reproachful look when Drusilla entered the room, but Gypsy didn't turn to look at her directly. Dressed in rumpled pajamas, he sat in a cushioned chair near the window, his Colt revolver and cartridge belt hanging from the back of the chair. The head wound was covered by a patch of gauze now, and his head and his chin were covered with a month's growth of glossy hair.

Big Mama snapped, "Lordy, girl, didn't I tell you—"

"Hello, Gypsy."

"What d'you want?" he said in that inflectionless voice.

Big Mama made a tactful and unobtrusive exit from the room.

"What do I want!" Drusilla said. "I want to help you. I want you to let me love you. Gypsy, please. . . ." Her voice faded when she saw that her words were having no effect at all.

He had become gaunt and drawn. His cheeks were hollow, his eye sockets cavernous, and the fire of life had gone out of his eyes. "I'm a dead man," he said, and then turned back to the window. "Say you buried me along with Clarence. Forget me."

"Please, Gypsy. Please don't do this. Don't send me away."

But his answer was one of unfeeling finality: "Good-bye."

With a deep sigh of regret she turned to leave, then turned back again and, holding her hand outstretched, approached him as cautiously as she would a wounded animal. She put her hand on his shoulder, half expecting him to flinch, but he didn't respond at all.

"Go with God, my friend," she said, and turned and left the room. The tears didn't begin until the door was closed behind her.

Big Mama appeared and put her arm around Drusilla's shoulder as they descended the stairs. "You do like he say. You forget Gypsy Smith, get on with your life. You young yet. They'll be other men. That young doctor, now. Everybody knows he sweet on you, girl, and I couldn't think of a man who'd make a better husband. Tell you the truth, I 'spect that's what Gypsy himself'd want, too. Might help him to know you was happy and not grieving fo' him."

"Grieving?" They faced each other on the porch. "No. I'm all out of grief. I only want to help him."

"Help him?" Big Mama seemed amused by Drusilla's innocence. "Honey, how you gonna help him do what he got to do?"

"Do? What is it he's got to do?"

"You think he gonna let them Klansmen get away with what they done?" She shook her head. "Lawd, when that man gets well, look out. Them Ku Kluxers better give they souls to God, honey, 'cause they behinds gonna belong to Gypsy Smith."

ON HIS vision quest Corby went out and sat on a mountain for three days and nights without food or water or sleep, but no vision came to him. His thoughts were mostly about food and water and sleep.

So he came back without a new name or a sacred medicine bundle. But he would try again, and to learn what he must do next time, he began visiting Indian villages, seeking out medicine men.

"You think you can have a vision while your hair is cut like a white man's and you wear white man clothes?" said Bear Smelling Sweet Grass. "Also, you are too young. Come back in two winters, and I will teach you things you must know."

He let his hair grow. He sometimes wore nothing more than a breechclout and moccasins while he was staying with the Indians, but whenever he returned to the agency, he always dressed in his agency-issue clothes so that he wouldn't be an embarrassment to Maxwell. He slept in his old room and performed his old chores. But he had changed. Now he went about his chores in a joyless way. Without Rachel he was very much alone and very lonely.

Rachel's letters helped. She wrote both Maxwell and Corby each a letter at least once a week during the first few months she was gone. Whenever Maxwell or Eula took one of her letters to Corby out to him in the barn, he would stop whatever he was doing and devour it as a starving man would devour food.

At first the letters were filled with laments of how lonely and homesick she was and how much she missed him, the most wonderful friend any girl ever had. "It is as if I left a part of myself there," she wrote.

All this was balm for Corby's own painful feelings. But within a couple months the tone of her letters began to change. Rather than homesickness, she talked about her new friends and new adventures in the big city. These letters left Corby apprehensive and bitter. He feared he would eventually lose her to the outside world.

Her letters began to be shorter and less frequent, and by the spring of the following year her communications with Corby had dwindled to random picture postcards on which she sometimes scribbled nothing more than "Wish you were here!"

Without Rachel's letters to lure him back to the agency, Corby began to wander farther and farther afield and stay away longer. The Comanches gave him a new name: Nakoni—Wanderer.

Lamp in hand, Big Mama tiptoed up the stairs and tapped lightly on Gypsy's door. "He's here," she said. "That white deputy. He down in Lulu Belle's room, slobbering drunk."

Jerking his pants on over his winter underwear, Gypsy said, "Send somebody to the stable. Tell 'em to saddle my horse and bring him around back, quick."

When she left, Gypsy quickly dressed, strapped on his gun, and packed his saddlebags. During his convalescence he had kept from going crazy by looking forward to this moment.

Wearing his heavy winter coat and a scarf and gloves, carrying a .30-06 rifle, he stepped out of his room and into the dark hallway. Big Mama, lamp in hand, was puffing up the stairs again.

"Thank you, Big Mama, for everything," Gypsy said. "I left money on the table, but I still owe you plenty. If you ever need anything—"

"Oh, hush now. Owe me? No. You's family. Just take care a y'self."

Descending the stairs quickly and quietly, he went to the front door. A gust of cold wind carrying a few flakes of grainy snow swirled around him as he stepped out onto the front porch. The dark streets were deserted. Only a few lights could be seen here and there. A half-moon glowed dimly through a layer of clouds.

Gypsy strode quietly to the rear of the house, where he found the sorrel with three white stockings tethered. He gave the shivering horse a pat on the neck, then took the rifle from the saddle scabbard and flung it away. He checked to make sure the saddlebags contained no weapons, then stealthily mounted the stairs to the back door and stepped into the dark hallway.

Lulu Belle's door was the first on the right. A dim light shone beneath the door. Gypsy could hear sounds from inside. He tried the door, found it unlocked, and nudged it open. There, facedown in bed, was Sonny Boy Reeves.

When Lulu Belle caught sight of Gypsy creeping up, her eyes widened. Gypsy put a forefinger over his lips and put the cold muzzle of the rifle against the nape of Sonny Boy's neck.

"Get up," Gypsy said.

Sonny Boy, terrified, cowered away from the rifle. "What—"

"You know who I am?" Gypsy asked.

Sonny Boy nodded vigorously.

"Then you know you better do what you're told. Get up."

Sonny Boy thrashed out of bed. Gypsy picked from among a pile of clothes on the floor Sonny Boy's Colt revolver and shoved it into the pocket of his own coat. He then tossed the clothes to Sonny Boy, who scrambled to get dressed. Drunkenly slurring his words, he said, "You'll never get away with this, boy."

"Get your coat on."

But Sonny Boy balked. "Now you listen, boy—"

Gypsy slammed the butt of his rifle into Sonny Boy's stomach. With a cry of pain he fell to his knees and clutched his chest. Gypsy grabbed Sonny Boy's long hair and jerked his head upward. "Have I got your attention? From now on you gonna be living from minute to minute, and the minute you give me any trouble, I'll kill you." He shook Sonny Boy's head. "Got that in your head, buckra?"

Sonny Boy made a few affirmative noises. Gypsy let his hair go. "Get your coat on."

Sonny Boy obeyed. Gypsy took a pair of handcuffs from his coat pocket and cuffed Sonny Boy's hands behind his back.

Outside, Gypsy helped him into the saddle on the three-stockinged sorrel, then mounted the Appaloosa and led the sorrel in a gallop out of Freedom toward the Cimarron River.

Riding head-on into the blue-cold northern wind, the two men hunched forward in their saddles so that the brims of their hats protected their faces against the occasional swirls of ice-crystal snow. Gypsy kept the horses going at a pace that brought them to the frozen Cimarron before daybreak. They then turned northwest to follow the river's floodplain. At noon, with a sickly pale sun filtering through dark snow clouds, Gypsy stopped in a cottonwood copse.

After unlocking one of the cuffs, Gypsy half dragged Sonny Boy to a nearby lodgepole-pine sapling, then snapped the opened cuff onto the tree. Sonny Boy jerked angrily against the sapling, cursing under his breath. Gypsy tossed one of the blankets from his bedroll to Sonny Boy; the other, along with the sawed-off shotgun, he dropped at the base of a big cottonwood tree.

"Build a fire," Sonny Boy begged. "I'm freezing to death."

"No fires."

He took the bridles off the horses and tethered them to the trees, then took some jerky from one of his saddlebags. He offered some to Sonny Boy, who turned his nose up. "Suit y'self."

Wrapped in his blanket, Gypsy sat huddled against the trunk of the cottonwood and gnawed on the strips of cold, hard beef.

Sonny Boy crouched down at the base of the sapling, whining his misery. "Say, looky here, what d'you want with me?"

"You gonna tell me the names of the other fifteen Klansmen."

Sonny Boy sputtered, "What? Klansmen? What Klansmen?"

"Them that rode with you on that lynching raid."

"Raid? What lynching raid?"

"Freedom."

Sonny Boy was flabbergasted. "What? *Me?* You got the wrong man. I don't know nothing about no Klansmen's raid on Freedom."

Gypsy tugged his blanket tighter around his shoulders and said, "You better sleep. We got a long night ahead of us."

Sonny Boy lapsed into a silence of misery and frustration.

A steady snow began falling later that afternoon. Gypsy roused Sonny Boy, who had fallen into a shallow sleep, and again clamped the handcuffs on Sonny Boy's wrists before putting him on his horse.

They rode all night. The snow stopped after midnight, and at dawn a pale red sun rose. Gypsy headed southwest and entered the

Glass Mountains by midafternoon, the weakening horses staggering through the snowdrifts.

Just before sundown they reached an old cabin built years before by trappers and used since by wild-horse hunters and outlaws.

Gypsy half helped, half dragged Sonny Boy into the cabin and then locked his hands around the oak center pole that held up the cabin's smoke-blackened log rafters. He unsaddled the horses and tethered them near a pond, where they could feed on the bark of trees and could get water.

Within an hour he had a lantern lit, a fire burning in the old iron stove, and a pot of stew simmering. The stew had come from a can in a cache of supplies he kept there.

When the stew was ready, Gypsy took chipped enamel plates from a shelf and dished it up for both of them. He placed Sonny Boy's plate on the floor. "I would let you eat at the table, but I 'spect no buckra Klansman would want to eat with no nigger."

"Look, Marshal, you got me all wrong," Sonny Boy insisted between slurps of stew. "I mean, I ain't got nothing against niggers. Nothing at all. And I ain't one of them Klansmen neither."

Gypsy ignored him until they both had finished their stew. Then it was time to get down to business. He unlocked one of the handcuffs and pulled Sonny Boy to his feet and once again handcuffed his wrists together behind him. He then got his lariat from his saddle and dropped the slipknot over Sonny Boy's head.

"What? What're you—" Sonny Boy's voice was cut off when Gypsy tossed the coil of rope over one of the rafters and pulled it taut until Sonny Boy had to stand on the tips of his toes to keep from being choked. He tied the loose end of the rope around the center pole, leaving Sonny Boy half hanging, half standing.

"Now you're gonna stand there till you tell me the names of all the Klansmen with you when you lynched those boys, or until you can't stand on your toes anymore and hang yourself."

"I can't, dammit. I swore an oath. I'd die first."

"Suit y'self." Gypsy ambled back to the table and sat down on the bench. "Agonizing way to die, slow suffocation is."

"Oh," Sonny Boy moaned, doing a little dance on the tips of his toes to keep his balance. Anytime he let himself down as much as an inch, the noose cut into his windpipe, cutting off his words as he pleaded, "I can't—I took a sacred oath. They'd kill me if I told."

As Gypsy casually rolled a cigarette, he said, "And if you don't, you'll die right where you are. You tell me what I wanna know, I'll put you on your horse and give you a head start. Till dawn, say. You might get to Mexico or California and live a while longer before I catch up with you again."

"But I don't know this country, and it's snowing. What kind of chance is that?"

"A better one than you gave those boys."

Tears began to trickle down Sonny Boy's horrified face, which was turning a bluish white color. His breath was coming in gasps. "Not me. I didn't do it!"

"Who did?"

"It was"—he moaned—"it was Tully and Pinkerton."

"Well, that's two of 'em. You might as well tell me the rest."

"I'll tell. Lemme down!"

Gypsy got up from the bench, stepped to the center pole, and jerked the rope loose. Sonny Boy collapsed on the floor, sobbing.

"The handcuffs," he pleaded. "Take off the handcuffs."

"Better leave 'em for a while, case I have to string you up again."

Gypsy crossed to a shelf above the bunks and found a child's school tablet. He took a pencil and touched it to the tip of his tongue. "All right, let's have the names."

For more than an hour he sat scribbling in the tablet. He put down not only the names of the other fifteen men who had made the raid on Freedom but also where they lived, where they worked, and their physical descriptions. He kept pumping Sonny Boy for information long after Sonny Boy protested that he knew no more.

"I've told you everything I can. Now let me go."

Gypsy took the lariat off his neck and unlocked the handcuffs.

"Now you listen to me, buckra, and you listen good. You better light out for parts unknown, 'cause I'm gonna let the Klan know who squealed on 'em, so if I don't get you, they will. Your only hope is to ride as fast and far as you can, and to keep looking over your shoulder. Someday you might see me there, just before I kill you."

Sonny Boy staggered to his feet. "You gonna send me into strange country with no food, without a gun? What kind of a chance is that?"

"Like I said, a lot better chance than you gave those boys."

Gypsy picked up the lantern and followed him outside, where snow had begun falling again. Sonny Boy, fumbling in his frantic haste, finally got his horse saddled.

"You might at least tell me which way to get out of here," Sonny Boy said plaintively as he struggled into the saddle. "How'm I supposed to find my way in this damn snow?"

"That's a problem, all right," Gypsy conceded. "But I wouldn't curse the snow if I was you. By morning your tracks'll be covered, so you might actually get away—for a while anyway."

He slapped the sorrel on the rump, sending Sonny Boy plunging into the snow-swirling darkness.

After adding wood to the dwindling fire in the cabin, Gypsy carried a long roll of rawhide to the table and unrolled it, revealing his "Big Fifty" Sharps buffalo rifle wrapped in oily rags.

Gypsy began cleaning the rifle in the light from the rusty lantern, working slowly, admiring the rifle's bigness and beauty, its awesome power. As a buffalo hunter, Gypsy had once dropped a buffalo bull with it at a distance of over a mile and a half, and killed two hundred forty-two buffalo in one day. It was on that day that the jubilant skinners, following the frontier tradition of giving special names to special rifles, named Gypsy's buffalo rifle the Grim Reaper.

The next morning when Gypsy rode out, he found Sonny Boy where he had fallen in the snow. He was frozen stiff.

Chapter Ten

NORA died of pneumonia in late May, 1894. Dexter, wearing a shiny new deputy sheriff's badge, was among the mourners, but Rachel wasn't. Maxwell had purposely delayed sending her a telegram until it was too late for her to get back home in time for the burial. What was the sense in her coming all the way from St. Louis on the train just to attend the funeral and then turning around and going back?

In his funeral eulogy Reverend Poggemeyer didn't go so far as to call it a blessing, but he did say that Nora's suffering had earned her a place at the right hand of God, and one should not mourn for a woman who had been released from suffering and attained heaven.

Dr. Gresham fell in beside Maxwell as they left the graveyard. "Listen, John," he said. "I'd like to have a word with you sometime about your housekeeper."

"What about her?"

"Nothing urgent."

They had reached the edge of the town square. Here their paths would diverge toward their respective residences, but Maxwell, reluctant to part from the doctor without an explanation of his enigmatic reference to Eula, turned to face him.

"She'd make a good nurse," Dr. Gresham said somewhat evasively. "The way she worked with Nora . . ."

"Yes, I don't know what I'd've done without her."

"There's something you might want to mention to her."

"Yes?"

"There's a surgeon in Philadelphia who's perfected an operation to correct harelips. He has an article in the latest *Journal of Modern Medicine*. It's in my office if you want to look at it sometime."

"An operation?"

"Sort of expensive, but it would mean a whole new life for her."

"My God," Maxwell said, trying to imagine it. He hardly knew what Eula looked like beneath that bonnet. He knew she had grayish green eyes and a small button nose, but he'd caught only glimpses of her face.

"Come by the office sometime. I'll give you all the information I have." He angled across the square toward his house.

Preoccupied, like a man contemplating a moral conundrum, Maxwell strolled toward his house. That medical science had progressed to the point of being able to correct a congenital deformity such as harelip wasn't surprising to him; what was surprising was the enormous impact such an operation would have for someone

265

like Eula. A young woman in her prime, hardworking, a woman with an enormous store of grit and goodness—why, without the harelip she would be snapped up as a wife by some young cowboy before you knew it. And he didn't want to lose her. So maybe he shouldn't even tell her about it—a thought that caused him to flush with shame to realize how monstrously selfish he was being.

He stepped into the house. Dexter was there, in Nora's room, going through Nora's things.

"What're you doing?"

"I'm taking some of Mother's things," Dexter said, ready to take offense. He had placed an opened carpetbag on a chair and was stuffing it with mementos: a Bible, a jewelry box, a matching silver hairbrush and hand-mirror set. "If Rachel wants any of these things," Dexter said, "we'll settle it between us." He strapped the bag closed. "At least they'll be safe with me."

"And why wouldn't they be safe here?"

"Well, with the housekeepers you bring in here, who can tell?" Dexter spoke loudly enough for Eula to hear.

"I resent your insinuation that Eula might steal. I think you owe her an apology."

"You just go ahead and resent all you want to."

Stepping back into the kitchen, Maxwell watched as Dexter stepped out of Nora's room and headed for the front door, where he stopped and turned to face Maxwell again. As if loath to leave the house without at least one more gibe, he said, "Oh, yeah. Speaking of lawbreakers, that teacher's pet of yours? Corby White? I got reports he's in the peyote cult now."

"I don't believe it," Maxwell said.

"Yeah? Well, I guess you'll believe it when I come to arrest him one of these days. Don't say I didn't warn you."

Dexter left the house. For a moment Maxwell pondered the vicissitudes of fate that had given him for a stepson Dexter Bingham, an abrasive white-supremacist bullyboy deputy sheriff.

As for Corby, had he really joined the peyote eaters? Maxwell wouldn't be at all surprised. In place of the Ghost Dance, a religious cult called the Native American Church had been spreading rapidly throughout the Plains tribes, in which the eating of peyote was a sacrament. Naturally, the white authorities saw the cult as something that had to be stamped out.

DEXTER returned for Corby a month later. Maxwell was in his office. Dexter entered, and nodding curtly, he said, "Where's that teacher's pet of yours? I got a warrant for him."

Maxwell leaned back in his swivel chair. "On what charge?"

Dexter said, "Peyote eater. Got an informer willing to testify in court. Where is he?"

"I don't think I'll tell you. As a county deputy, you have no jurisdiction here on federal land."

Dexter pointed toward the agency's headquarters building. "Maybe you'd like to talk to Agent Tanner. He knows what I'm here for, and he's given me the authority to do it. Now, where is Corby? If you don't tell me, you could be charged with harboring a fugitive."

Maxwell slowly rose and leaned across the desk. "I'm the man who put a roof over your head and food in your mouth for how many years, Dexter? And you come around here threatening to arrest me? Listen, boy, you may think that badge and gun make you a big man, but you're just another bullyboy jackass to me."

"Yeah? Yeah?" Dexter sputtered. "Jackass, am I?"

Maxwell said, disgusted, "Let's go see Tanner."

Maxwell saw the wagon cage as soon as he stepped outside. At first he couldn't quite believe his eyes. It was a circus wagon; enclosed with iron bars and a gingerbread roof, it had once served as a cage for circus animals. Now, parked in front of the agent's office, it was hitched to two teams of mules and filled with Indians.

"What the devil is this?" Maxwell asked.

"An arrest wagon," Dexter said condescendingly.

A cluster of people had formed around Orville Snipes, the agency's chief clerk, who appeared to be writing down the names of the prisoners. Beside him was Dexter's cohort, a young deputy named Roscoe Brown, who was identifying the prisoners. Some of the prisoners were sprawled on the floor of the cage, passed out, while others sat and stared through the bars.

Maxwell whirled on Chief Clerk Snipes. "Does Mr. Tanner know about this? The way they're being transported in a circus cage?"

"A-yep. Shows lawbreakers what'll happen when caught."

"I'd like to know why these county deputies are being allowed to arrest people on federal land."

"I understand," Snipes told him. "The Indian boy. Works for you. You're upset. I understand. But have to cooperate with local authorities, don't we? Bureau's orders. Too bad about the boy, but can't play favorites, can we? Not going to be trouble, I hope."

Maxwell knew then that he wasn't going to be able to prevent Corby's arrest. "There'll be trouble, all right," Maxwell said, "if you send these deputies after him. Corby won't surrender to this one"—indicating Dexter—"without a fight. I better get him. Tell these deputies to stay here. I'll be back within an hour."

Hurrying to his barn, Maxwell saddled his strawberry roan and took the wagon road to Arapaho, a small new town about two miles from the agency, with a few stores and a racetrack, the town's main attraction. Indians came from miles around to see the horse races.

Maxwell rode to the windmill that marked the racetrack's finish line, where he found Corby accepting the admiration of the spectators and stuffing his winnings into the pocket of his jeans.

"Won again, did you?" Maxwell said.

Corby gave Big Red's neck a pat. "Never lost yet," he said. "Not often we see you here at the track. Something wrong?"

"Dexter's at the agency. He's got a warrant for your arrest."

"What for?"

"Says he's got somebody who'll swear you're a peyote eater."

Saying softly, "Ho, Big Red, easy, boy," Corby took the saddle blanket and tossed it over the nervous stallion's back. To Maxwell he said, "Thanks for warning me."

"I didn't come here to warn you. I came here to get you. Now Corby," he added hastily, "if you're thinking about running, don't. That's what he'd like you to do. That'd be a much more serious offense than the one you're charged with."

Corby said, "I'm not going to let him put me in jail."

Maxwell swung down from the saddle. "Listen to me, *naha*. I'll do everything I can to get the charges against you dropped. I'll hire a lawyer. I promise. But," he added emphatically, "even if you do have to go to jail, it'll only be for thirty days. If you run, they'll put you in prison for a long, long time, and if you give Dexter any justification, he'll kill you."

Corby turned. He seemed to be thinking the matter over.

"Listen," Maxwell continued, "trust me on this. I know what I'm talking about. Just come on back to the agency, give yourself up, and I'll ride with you to El Reno and do everything I can to help."

Without meeting Maxwell's eyes, Corby made a nod of assent.

They rode back together. The spectators around the wagon cage had thinned out. Dexter and the other deputy, Roscoe Brown, appeared when they saw Maxwell and Corby ride up.

Dexter ordered Corby into the cage. Deputy Brown brought a huge key from his pocket and opened the cage door. Corby slowly swung down from the saddle and handed the reins to Maxwell. He caught one of the iron bars and swung up into the cage. Deputy Brown locked the door, then climbed up into the driver's box.

Dexter unhitched his horse. "He'll appear before Judge Slater in the morning," he told Maxwell as he mounted.

"I'm coming with you," Maxwell said.

Dexter shrugged. "It's a free country."

"Is it?" Maxwell asked, glancing at the cage. "Is it, indeed?"

Dexter rode to the front of the wagon cage. "Move out," he told Deputy Brown, and took the lead on the muddy road to El Reno. Leading Big Red, Maxwell rode alongside. He had no illusions about why the Indians in the wagon cage had been arrested. It wasn't because they had broken the law; it was because each Indian in the cage represented a twenty-five-dollar fee to the arresting lawmen. This load alone would bring Dexter and Roscoe Brown a tidy six hundred dollars.

As they were passing through a stretch of barren land called Gypsum Flats, Deputy Brown suddenly jerked backward in the driver's box and gave a strangled cry, a cry punctuated by the puffy, faraway crack-boom of a rifle. Then he pitched slowly forward and fell crashing into the mud beneath the wagon's wheels.

Both Maxwell and Dexter wheeled their horses and sprinted behind the wagon cage, frantically scanning the countryside in the direction from which the shot had come. Maxwell leaped to the ground and dropped to one knee beside the wagon. Dexter jerked his rifle from its scabbard as he swung out of the saddle and knelt beside Maxwell. "Where are they? You see 'em?"

"Haven't seen anybody," Maxwell answered.

"Where'd it come from?"

"Those creosote bushes yonder is my guess."

"That's a mile away," Dexter said. "No rifle can shoot that far."

"Buffalo rifle. I've heard they can shoot that far."

They kept watching the bushes, waiting for another shot. When it became apparent that the sniper wasn't going to fire again, Maxwell said, "If it's somebody trying to set these Indians free, when's he gonna make his next move? My guess is, he got who he wanted, then took off."

Dexter considered that possibility, then said, "I got to go get some help. You stay here." He snatched up his horse's reins and shoved his rifle back into the scabbard. "I'll make a fast run to El Reno, bring back a posse." He crouched behind the horse's neck, using its body as a shield, and kept trotting alongside until he was out of range of the buffalo rifle.

"Key," an Indian in the cage said after Dexter had left.

Maxwell reached into Deputy Brown's pocket and brought out the key, unlocked the cage door, and swung it open. The livelier ones jumped to the ground running. Most headed back down the road toward the agency, but a few of them took off cross-country.

Corby jumped down from the cage and took Big Red's reins.

"I'm going to drive this rig to El Reno," Maxwell said to him. "I don't suppose it'd do any good to ask you to come along? Be best if you turned yourself in. Make it easier to get that charge dropped."

"No," Corby said, flatly refusing Maxwell for the first time.

"Thought not. Well then, help me get him into the cage, will you? Can't leave him here in the road."

Corby helped Maxwell wrestle the deputy's body into the cage.

"Listen," Maxwell said, "might be best if you go out and stay with the Hehyo band. Just long enough for me to get this mess straightened out. Then you can come on back. We've got to do something about your life before you throw it away."

Without touching the stirrup, Corby vaulted into the saddle. "If I throw it away, it'll be as my father threw his away." He spun Big Red around and galloped back down the road.

SHERIFF Alva Harriman had a revelation about the killing of Deputy Brown. It was only one in a series of mysterious deaths that had occurred during the last few months in Logan County, but Deputy Brown was the second man known to him personally who had been shot with a buffalo rifle. Sheriff Harriman obtained from the coroner a list of all the people within the county who had met violent deaths within the last year, and from this list he compiled the names of seven men whom he had known personally.

First there was Brod Clemmens, the owner of a Guthrie grocery store. He was shot with a .44 at close range.

Twenty-five days later Potter Gibbs, a cowhand on the Olanco Ranch, was found with four Comanche arrows in him, but no Comanches had been reported in the area.

On February 10, 1894, Justin Williams, another cowhand at the Olanco Ranch, was blown out of his saddle by a monstrously big .50-caliber slug that could only have come from a buffalo rifle.

A few weeks later a tax collector named Pat Buchanan, a good horseman, was dragged to death by his own horse.

Next came Clifford Arnette, a clerk for the land commission. His wife found him in the privy, his throat cut ear to ear. A butcher knife lay at his feet, so suicide had to be considered.

But there was never any doubt that Lester Tully, the next man to be killed, was murdered. On the night of April 7 he was shot in the chest with a slug from a .30-06. The killer left no clues or tracks, and nobody could say who did it or why.

Then came the killing of Deputy Roscoe Brown, the second man to be killed with a buffalo rifle, and Sheriff Harriman had his revelation: All the men on the list had been murdered by one man, and he knew who that man was.

271

Harriman hurried down the street to the new Hornbeck Building, where he found Shelby Hornbeck in his walnut-paneled office. Harriman showed him the list.

"Know what all these men have in common besides being dead?"

"They were members of the brotherhood."

"What else?"

Hornbeck's face registered the answer immediately. "Freedom."

"That's right. Sixteen men made that raid on Freedom last year. Since then, seven of them's been killed. Somebody's got a list."

"Gypsy Smith," Hornbeck said. "We should've finished him."

"He was shot in the head. All of us thought he was dead."

"Find him," Hornbeck ordered. "Kill him. But keep it in the Klan. If he should be arrested and brought to trial, we'd all be exposed, and my chance for the governorship would be jeopardized. And call a meeting of the den for tonight. The others'll have to know about this before somebody else gets killed." But at that very moment Roy Pinkerton came into the sights of Gypsy's rifle.

MAXWELL drove the wagon cage on to El Reno, where he found a judge who, for a bribe of fifty dollars and a few drinks of whiskey, was willing to see that the peyote charge against Corby was dismissed. Even so, Maxwell expected that Dexter and the other lawmen would want to question the wagon-cage prisoners to see if they had any connection with the sniper. To his surprise the lawmen acted as if they already knew who the sniper was.

The newspaper stories said that the killer's identity remained a mystery, but rumor named Gypsy Smith. Lynch mobs, sometimes led by lawmen, combed the country, looking for him. One posse, led by U.S. Marshal Silas Renfro, with Deputy Dexter Bingham at his side, rode through Agency, asking about Gypsy Smith.

"Why're you looking for Gypsy Smith?" Maxwell asked Marshal Renfro, but got no answer. The posse rode away.

"Oh, the poor man," Eula murmured that night. "To be run down by lynch mobs. He was right kind to me over in Freedom." Eula had recently received a letter from Freedom. Drusilla wrote with news of her marriage to Dr. Homer Upchurch.

Maxwell had always valued Eula highly as a housekeeper, but it wasn't until he saw how deeply she sympathized with Gypsy's outcast state that he realized how fond he had become of her as a person. And this brought a new rush of guilt. So reluctant had he been to lose her as a housekeeper that he had delayed telling her about the operation that could repair her mouth. Now he told her.

She seemed struck dumb by the idea, as if the consequences were too profound for her to comprehend.

"If it's just the money," he said, "I'll give it to you as an advance against your salary. You can work it off over the next year or two."

"But who'd take care of the house while I was gone?"

"Don't worry about that. Rachel's coming home for the summer. She can take care of things around here till you get back."

Eula went to the stove. "I don't think so. I'd be too scared."

"Why? What's there to be scared of?"

"I reckon I done got used to being the way I am, and if I was some other way, I wouldn't know how to be."

"Well, if you change your mind, the money's always available."

"Thankee kindly. You're a right good man."

A week later he went to St. Louis to bring Rachel home for her summer vacation. Although still a gangling girl of fifteen, Rachel had acquired at Miss Finwick's Academy a certain grace, a softer way of speaking, and a snobbish attitude toward backwoodsy ways.

When it began to appear that Corby wasn't coming back to the agency anytime soon—he had gone with Chief Hehyo and a small band of Cheyennes on a visit to Wyoming—Rachel seemed to resign herself to enduring the hot, dusty, fly-buzzed monotony of the place.

But after a month had gone by, she told Maxwell one afternoon, when she found him sitting in his rocking chair on the back porch drinking iced tea, "I want to leave here and go back to St. Louis. I can't stand this place any longer. May I go back, Daddy?"

To him she seemed very much like her mother at that moment. "Why, Rachel, I never heard you complain about it before."

"Sure—before I knew anything else existed. And anyway, that was when Corby was here. But who knows when he might come back or even *if* he's coming back. Anyway, I'm tired of waiting."

"Well, what am I supposed to do? Just jump up and take you back to St. Louis anytime you get bored and want to leave?"

"I can go on the train alone. For goodness' sakes, Daddy, I'm old enough to travel without a chaperon."

"No, you're not, young lady, so let's hear no more about that."

Rachel flounced inside.

Eula came out onto the porch, drying her hands on her apron, and said, "I reckon I could ride with her to St. Louis. I'd be going through there, anyway, wouldn't I, on my way to Philadelphia?" After a brief pause she continued. "I been thinking, maybe I ought to try that operation. I mean, if you still don't mind loaning me the money, and all."

"Mind? Why, I'd be delighted." But at the same time Maxwell felt a quiver of apprehension.

Two weeks later he took them to the train depot in El Reno. It was almost time to board the train when he gave Eula the envelope containing the money, saying, "There's a little something extra in there. I thought you might like to buy yourself a new dress."

He thought for a moment that she was going to embrace him, but she restrained herself, saying only, "I don't know how to thankee, Mr. Maxwell. You're a right kind man." Then she rushed aboard the train.

As the conductor was calling, "All aboard," Maxwell and Rachel embraced. Her eyes puddled with tears as she said, "Oh, Daddy, I'm sorry I've been such miserable company. Eula's right, you're a good man. You deserve a better daughter than me."

"Now, now, you're the best daughter a man could have. Go on, get aboard. Be good now, and mind Eula, you hear?"

With a hissing release of steam and a chattering of spinning wheels, the train began to pull away from the station. He walked along the platform and called, "Good luck!" feeling in some strange way that he was saying good-bye forever to both of them.

THE small band that accompanied Chief Hehyo to Wyoming hoped to reach the reservation of the Northern Cheyennes before the chief died. He had been getting weaker and weaker during the trip, until finally he wasn't even able to get out of the tattered over-stuffed chair in which he rode, without help from Corby and the other young men. He made the journey with his eyes closed, saving what little sight he had left for the ancestral hunting grounds.

The condition of the chief continued to deteriorate as they drew closer to the Wind River country and to the place on top of the Bighorn Mountains where the old chief planned to open his eyes. He had described to the driver of the wagon exactly where to stop, a place where he would be able to see the valley of the Wind River and the trees and the mountains and the fat-grass prairies where millions of buffalo used to feed.

When they finally reached the place—at dawn about three weeks after they had left the reservation in Oklahoma Territory—it was Corby and the medicine man, Iron Shirt, who helped the old chief out of the wagon. With the Wind River valley stretched out before him in all its springtime splendor, he took a deep breath and opened his eyes. His old skin-and-bones body shook with excitement as he threw up his hands and cried, "Look! They have come back!" He jerked out of Corby's and Iron Shirt's hands and tottered a few steps toward the valley. It was obvious from the way he stumbled over rocks and into bushes that he could see nothing, yet he held his arms out toward the valley and cried, "They have come back! The buffalo. Look, buffalo beyond counting!"

When he tottered and fell, Water Bird Woman, his grand-daughter, rushed to pull him to his feet. "Come along, Grand-father. There are no buffalo there. You have lost your mind. Come back to the wagon."

"Leave him alone," Corby said, helping to steady the tottering old man in an upright position.

"You see the buffalo, don't you, boy?" Chief Hehyo cried.

"Yes, Grandfather, I see them," Corby said.

"Buffalo beyond number! Never again will our children cry with empty bellies." He sighed with weariness and contentment. "I have lived to see the buffalo return. Now I can die a happy man."

To everyone's surprise he lived for another two months, bed-ridden and blind, senile and shrinking, until one day in August he curled up into a fetal position and stopped breathing. Corby was with him when he breathed his last.

"Good-bye, Grandfather," he said. *"Nimeaseoxzheme*—may your journey be a good one."

THREE months after Maxwell saw Eula off at the El Reno railroad station, he once again stood on the platform. He watched the passengers disembark from the train, but she wasn't among them. Had she missed the train?

Among the passengers remaining on the platform was a young woman who seemed to be waiting to be recognized, waiting for him to recognize her, apparently, since she was looking directly at him. But his glance glided past her completely before being jerked back by a shock of recognition. "Eula?"

She was a woman of about Eula's age, all right, plainly but prettily dressed, with ash-blond hair brushed upward and bundled on the crown of her head, topped by a small hat that bobbled wax cherries. She had hazel eyes, a small button nose, and a smiling mouth. But it wasn't until she brought her hand up to cover her mouth in that old gesture of self-consciousness that he said, "My goodness, it *is* you!"

"Yes, sir, it's me."

He stepped closer to get a better look at her mouth. She hung her head. He put a finger under her chin and lifted her face. Other than a pink thread of a scar running from the base of her nose to her lip, one would never have known that she had once had a harelip.

"Well," he said, at a loss for words, "wonders will never cease! Welcome back."

"Thankee."

"Well then, shall we be on our way? Allow me," he said, and picked up her carpetbag and started for the buggy. And when he noticed that she had, from old habit, fallen in behind him, he took her arm and escorted her to the buggy and helped her in, shaking his head with wonderment at the change in her.

On their way to Agency he tried to make conversation by asking about Philadelphia, but all she said was, "It's a right big place."

"Think you'd like to live there?"

"Oh, no, sir, not me. I best stay right here. I've et so much Oklahoma dust already, I done become part of the place."

Slapping the reins against the horses' rumps, he said, "Well, I wouldn't be truthful if I didn't tell you I'm really glad you're back." He had started to say "back home" but caught himself.

"Thankee. I'm right glad to be back."

He chuckled with delight, and when she glanced at him for an explanation, he said, "I was just wondering what their faces are going to look like when the folks in Agency get a look at you."

He naturally assumed that they would be as astonished and pleased as he had been, though he was to realize over the course of the next few days and weeks that his astonishment wasn't entirely due to Eula's transformation, but to his own.

He found himself tingling with a new enthusiasm for life. His walk took on a new and sprightly bounce. He surprised people with his cheerfulness. He was happy. He was excited.

He was in love, but he didn't know it until about three weeks after Eula's return, when from his office window he saw her in front of Simon's store conversing with a young cowhand. Eula had come out of the store carrying a number of parcels, and the cowhand had offered to help her. Eula shook her head, but the offer alone had suffused her face with delight.

That look stabbed Maxwell with dread. Sooner or later he was going to lose her to some young cowhand or homesteader. And it was then he had to admit to himself that he was in love with Eula.

It was true that Eula seemed perfectly content to remain as his housekeeper. She felt profound gratitude to Maxwell and couldn't do enough for him in repayment. She made his favorite foods, listened raptly whenever he read to her at night from a book or a newspaper, and always spoke to him in the tenderest of tones.

Still, Maxwell knew that gratitude alone wouldn't always hold her. What could he do?

It was Mrs. Poggemeyer who suggested the solution. Busybody that she was, she came to see Maxwell in his office one day and hinted to him that it wasn't fitting for him—a respectable man and the superintendent of the school—to be living alone in a house with a pretty young woman who wasn't his lawful wedded wife. It was different, she said, before Eula got her mouth fixed. But now people were beginning to talk.

"And what am I supposed to do?" Maxwell protested. "Fire her?"

"Fire her? Heavens, no," Mrs. Poggemeyer said. "Marry her."

Maxwell could think of about a dozen reasons why not to marry her, not the least of which was the great difference in their ages. It wasn't until he stopped thinking that he resolved the situation.

It happened one evening when he came home and found Eula kneeling beside a wooden box on the floor near the kitchen stove. Within the box were a half-dozen fluffy yellow peeping chicks.

"A coon got their mother last night," she explained. "I thought I'd bring 'em in here for a night or two, keep 'em from being cold and afraid out there in the barn without a mother to protect 'em." She held one of the chicks cupped in her hand. She put some bits of crushed corn on her palm, and the chick pecked at it. She smiled. "Feels funny. Wanna see?"

He knelt on one knee beside the box. Eula dropped some crushed corn on his outstretched palm, then took one of the chicks and put it in his hand. The chick began pecking at the corn. The little beak made pricking sensations against his skin.

"Eula, would you marry me?"

He hadn't meant to ask that question. He hadn't planned it at all. It just popped out in a casual way, as if asking for the time of day.

The question gave her such a start that she flushed a deep red and stammered, "What—what did you—"

"Oh, I know, I know," he added hastily, putting the chick back in the box. "I know that, well, I'm fifty-one years old now, and you're what? Twenty-eight? So I can understand if you don't want to. It's just that . . ." That what? he wondered, afraid now that he had made a fool of himself.

Recovering her composure at last, Eula replaced her chick in the box, brushed the corn from her hand, and sat back on her heels.

"I'd be right honored," she said.

At first Maxwell was incredulous. "You mean it?"

"Yes, sir," she said, and fell silent, unable to meet his eyes.

And Maxwell, who hadn't been a lover for more years than he cared to remember, was at a loss. But then with a nervous chuckle he said, "Well then, I suppose you could stop calling me sir, couldn't you? And Mr. Maxwell? My name's John."

"Yes, sir," she said, but smiled. "I mean, yes, John."

He stood up. "Well, we'll need to make some plans, won't we? I mean, like when? And where?" He reached down and took her hands and helped her to her feet. "And a honeymoon! Where'd you like to go? New Orleans? San Francisco?" He stopped his nervous chattering when he saw that something was wrong. "What is it?"

In an agony of embarrassment she said, "There's something . . . afore we get into all that, I'd like to . . ." She couldn't finish.

"What is it? Don't be afraid. You can tell me."

She methodically smoothed her apron down for a moment, then abruptly looked up at him. "Well, y'see, I ain't never been kissed."

He looked at her blankly. Had he not been in an agitated state himself, he would have understood immediately.

"And I—I've always wondered, you know, what it'd be like. Since we're going to be married, I was wondering if . . ."

Smiling with a sudden rush of relief, he took her in his arms and kissed her lips.

"So that's what it's like!" she said, delighted. "Why, it's right nice, ain't it?"

Chapter Eleven

AFTER that first summer vacation Rachel decided that she would stay in school through the summers, thereby enabling her to graduate in three years rather than the usual four. This decision was made easy for her when Maxwell wrote that Corby, after his summer with old Chief Hehyo in Wyoming, had gone back to the blanket—had, in fact, gone to live on the Comanche reservation.

It grieved her to know he was throwing his life away, but what could she do? She had her own life to live. So she stayed in school and was graduated from the academy in June 1896. When she returned to Oklahoma Territory at last, she was eighteen years old, and she had changed. No longer a gawky girl, she had filled out to pleasing proportions, with fashionably coiffed auburn hair, a complexion that had lost its freckles but none of its healthy glow, and bright hazel eyes.

Maxwell traveled to St. Louis to attend her graduation and to bring her back home. Eula, now his wife, had been feeling poorly and therefore didn't accompany him on the trip.

The train stopped for two hours in Guthrie. Rachel had wired Dexter to meet them at the station there, and he was on the platform when the train pulled in.

Their greeting was confused and awkward, especially on Dexter's part. But Rachel handled the situation adroitly by giving him a quick sisterly peck on the cheek and saying, "My, how handsome you've become. I'm surprised you're not married yet. You must have to beat the girls off with a stick."

Dexter managed a smile as he grunted, "Not really. But look at you. You're all growed up. Pretty dress," he added.

"You like it?" She stepped back to give him a better look at her bustled gray cheviot dress. She wore a Robin Hood hat of dark gray velvet with a plume of white egret feathers.

"Two hours, huh?" Dexter said. "What'd you like to do?"

"I don't know about Daddy," Rachel said, glancing at Maxwell, "but I'd like to stretch my legs a bit. Maybe you'd show us around your little town?"

"Little!" Dexter snorted. "Well, I guess it's not so much compared to St. Louis, but we got an opera house now."

"Really! Daddy, would you like to go see?"

"You two go ahead," Maxwell said. "I'm going to get myself a cold beer. But don't forget, the train leaves at three twenty."

Without Maxwell present, Dexter seemed a little more congenial as they strolled along the brick sidewalks of Harrison Street. When he saw the admiring attention that Rachel was getting from the men along the street, he felt himself swelling with pride.

"So you're a deputy sheriff now," she said admiringly.

"A special deputy," he boasted. "I'm one of the bodyguards assigned to Shelby Hornbeck."

"Shelby Hornbeck? And why would he need bodyguards?"

He glanced at her to see if she was being a tease. "Are you kidding? Men don't get as powerful as him without making enemies along the way. And a lot of Radical Republicans'd like to kill him, I reckon, 'cause they know there ain't no other way of stopping him from becoming governor once we get to be a state. There"—he nodded toward a three-story brick building across the street—"that's his. The Hornbeck Building. Biggest office building in Guthrie. Would you like to see it? I could show you through."

"Oh, would you?" she begged.

They crossed the street, but before they reached the building, Dexter's attention was diverted by a buggy approaching.

"That's Mr. Hornbeck's buggy," he informed her.

A fancy yellow-wheeled leather-hooded buggy, pulled by a matching team of blue-roans and escorted by two bodyguards, came to a stop near Dexter and Rachel. The bodyguards exchanged greetings with Dexter.

But all talk ceased when Shelby Hornbeck himself emerged from the building and hastily descended the marble steps to the sidewalk, pulling on yellow kid gloves. Ordinarily Shelby would have passed Dexter without even a nod, but this time he stopped and said, "Howdy," speaking to Dexter but glancing at Rachel. "Is *this* the young lady you referred to as your kid sister?"

Flattered by such unusual familiarity, Dexter stammered, "This's her, all right. My sister, Rachel. Growed up some since I last saw her. Rachel, this here's Mr. Hornbeck."

Shelby touched the brim of his Stetson. "Miss Bingham."

"Maxwell," she corrected. "We're half sister and brother."

"Miss Maxwell," he said. "When Dexter asked to be relieved from duty this afternoon so he could meet his kid sister at the depot, I had a vision of a twelve-year-old with pigtails and freckles."

"Sorry if I've disappointed you," Rachel said, smiling.

"Disappointed?" he said. "Why, how could you possibly be a disappointment to anyone?"

"Thank you, sir. You pay a pretty compliment." She had once read that phrase and had been waiting for a chance to use it.

"I'm showing her around town," said Dexter.

"That so? Well, I'm just on my way out to Kingstree." To Rachel he said, "Kingstree's the house I'm building just southeast of town. If you're sight-seeing, you might be interested in it."

"That's kind of you, Mr. Hornbeck," Rachel said, "but I'm afraid I have to get back to the depot before three twenty. My train—"

Shelby pulled a gold watch from the watch pocket of his pants and sprang the lid. "Why, that gives you plenty of time. It's only ten minutes from here. That is, of course, if you'd like to. . . ."

"Oh, sure," Dexter said. "Sure we'd like to, wouldn't we?"

And it wasn't entirely to please Dexter that she nodded her assent. She was dazzled by the man. At thirty-five not only was Shelby Hornbeck strikingly handsome, rich, powerful, and—as far as she knew—unattached, but he had the courtly manners of a southern aristocrat.

Rachel sat between Dexter and Shelby, and as the buggy made its way toward Kingstree, Dexter babbled on. "Kingstree was the name of Mr. Hornbeck's family plantation back in South Carolina before the War Between the States," he informed Rachel. "Before the Yankees burned it down."

"I'm sorry," Rachel said, "about your house."

"It's kind of you to say so. It was a beautiful house. But the new Kingstree will be, too. At least *I* think it will be. I hope you agree."

She did. When she first saw the mansion standing on a hill overlooking the Cimarron River, she said, "Oh, my. It *is* beautiful."

Two-storied, with a veranda running all the way around it, made of beige brick with four huge white columns in front, Kingstree stood on the hill, stark and imposing, like some ancient Roman temple.

They were met on the steps by a middle-aged woman dressed in black. Shelby introduced her as his widowed aunt, Mrs. Bertha Dolph, who had kindly agreed to serve as Kingstree's hostess "till the house has a mistress of its own," he said, and by this remark Rachel gathered that Shelby wasn't yet a confirmed bachelor.

"Like it, do you?" Shelby asked, pleased by Rachel's exuberance.

"Oh, I love it. You're so right to be proud of it. My goodness, it just goes on and on, doesn't it? How many rooms did you say?"

"Twenty-two."

"Well, we haven't got time to see them all, but I'm certain this'd be my room, if it were my house." They were in one of the second-story rooms in the east wing. Pointing with her parasol, she said, "A vanity there. A mirror there."

"You're very decisive for someone your age," Shelby observed approvingly. "You seem to know exactly what you want."

"Oh, I do," she boasted. "I certainly do."

French doors led from the room out onto the second-story veranda, from which Rachel could see Guthrie.

"Which one is the Hornbeck Building?" she asked.

Pointing, Shelby said in his mellifluous accent, "That one there. Look down my arm, sight on my thumb."

She put her face against his shoulder, squinted one eye, and sighted along his arm. Their heads were only a few inches apart when she abruptly lifted her face from his shoulder and caught him staring at her. His golden hair shimmered in the sunlight, and his blue eyes met her gaze for a moment, and it struck her that Shelby Hornbeck was the most handsome man she had ever seen.

"Mr. Hornbeck!" A messenger on horseback came galloping up the graveled lane toward the house. Stopping beneath the veranda, he shouted, "O'Keefe's called a quorum on bill three twenty. The speaker wants you back quick as you can."

As the messenger galloped away, Shelby said to Rachel, "Politics. I'm afraid we'll have to go back in a hurry."

"Suits me," Rachel said. "I love a fast ride."

When they were settled in the buggy, Shelby took the buggy whip from its socket. "Ready?"

Rachel nodded. Dexter nodded, too, though Shelby hadn't been speaking to him. Shelby barely flicked the whip at the pair of blue-roans to set them into a gallop, a rather slow gallop at first.

Rachel asked, "This is as fast as they'll go?"

Shelby smiled. When they turned onto the main road, he flicked the team into a fast gallop. As the buggy jolted along the rutted road, Shelby glanced to see how Rachel was reacting. Most of the women he had known would now be babbling with fear and holding on for dear life, but the only thing Rachel was holding on to was her egret-plumed hat, and the look on her face was one of exhilaration.

"Faster!" she cried, like a child on a carnival ride. Dexter was frightened and on the brink of jumping out.

Entering town, Shelby slowed the team down to a brisk trot.

"Thank you," Rachel said. "That was fun."

"I'm glad you enjoyed it. Perhaps we can do it again sometime."

"I'll look forward to it."

RACHEL introduced Maxwell to Shelby when Shelby returned her to the train depot in Guthrie. Maxwell shook hands with him, but it was obvious that he had to exercise great self-control to keep from making some disparaging remark to Shelby about his politics.

When they were on the train, unable to contain himself any longer, he told Rachel, "That's the man who's responsible for all the Territory's jim crow laws, who's made it against the law for me to sit on a public conveyance with my own students, against the law for teachers of one race to teach the children of another."

Her seeming lack of outrage only incensed him further. "No doubt he built his house with money he bilked out of the Indians."

Rachel stared at her father, wondering if they could be talking about the same Shelby Hornbeck. She knew nothing about business and politics, and didn't want to know anything about them. "Now Daddy, let's not get into a tiff before I even get home, all right? Let's talk about something else. Tell me more about Corby. Oh, I do wish I could see him again."

"Don't you realize that if Corby were on the train with us now, he'd have to ride in the car reserved for coloreds?"

"Then I'd go ride with him," she declared, which mollified him somewhat, for he knew it was true.

Still, she didn't dismiss Maxwell's opinion of Shelby Hornbeck lightly. She had seldom known her father to be wrong about anyone. But now that she was eighteen and had been away to school, she felt she was permitted to have her own point of view, and in her opinion Shelby Hornbeck was a prince. Who but a prince would have said, "Why, how could you possibly be a disappointment to anyone?" And just like a prince in a fairy tale, he even invited her to a ball, the Commemoration Ball to celebrate the grand opening of Guthrie's new opera house.

She received the gold-trimmed invitation on the fourth day after her return to Agency, and it was Dexter who carried the invitation. He rode horseback all the way from Guthrie to Agency during the night to deliver it to her. "Do you have any idea how lucky you are?" he asked Rachel. "This'll be the biggest social event ever in Guthrie, and you'll be in Mr. Hornbeck's private box!"

"But where would she stay?" Maxwell wanted to know.

"I'll get her a room near mine at the boardinghouse," Dexter said. "It's perfectly respectable—run by a preacher's widow."

They were in the front room of the house. This was the first time Dexter had set foot in the house since the day of Nora's funeral. Eula had tactfully gone to the barn while the three of them talked.

"Well?" Dexter said to Rachel. "Will you come?"

To placate Maxwell, she would have probably declined had she not become so bored with life at Agency. When she first got home, she had sent a letter to the Comanche village to let Corby know that she had returned from school and would like to see him. There had been no response. So, fingering the gold-trimmed beribboned invitation, she said, "Yes, I will. It'd be fun. Tell him I accept."

Dexter sighed with relief. "That's settled, then. Let me know which train you're coming in on. Well, I better go get a room over at Bixby's Hotel. Gotta get some sleep before I start back tonight."

"Sleep?" She was puzzled by Dexter's hurry to be gone. "Well, if you need sleep, there's an extra bed here—"

"No, no," Dexter interrupted with a contemptuous look toward Maxwell, "don't worry 'bout it."

After he was gone, Rachel said, "What's the matter with him?"

"It's Eula. Oh, it's me, too, I suppose. Mainly, though, it's Eula. Being under the same roof with her makes him nervous."

"Why? What'd she ever do to him?"

"I think the question might be, What's he done to her?"

"Well," she demanded, *"has* he ever done anything to her?"

Maxwell mused for a moment. "There are . . . well, rumors." He paused to puff on his pipe. "Did you ever wonder why Shelby Hornbeck has bodyguards, like Dexter? And did you ever wonder why Dexter travels cross-country only at night?"

"Yes. Why?"

Maxwell knocked his pipe against the potbellied stove. "To keep from getting ambushed. Somebody's out to kill them. People say it's Gypsy Smith. They say he's got a list of all the Klansmen who did that to him and those two boys three years ago, over in Freedom. They say quite a few of the men who made the raid are dead already, and Gypsy's hunting the others down one by one."

"Dexter? Oh, Daddy, you can't mean it."

"I don't know. I have my suspicions, but I don't know. If he was, though, it's likely the same bunch that burned Eula out."

Rachel's eyes snapped with anger. "I'll ask him."

She left the house and marched down to Bixby's Hotel, where she found Dexter sitting at a table by himself in the dining room.

"Dexter, I want to talk to you." Taking a chair, she lowered her voice as if asking for a confidence. "I want to know if you and Shelby Hornbeck were in that bunch that burned Eula's house."

"That's ridiculous," Dexter sneered without blinking an eye.

Stymied by the force of his denial, she hesitated a moment. "Dexter, tell me the truth. Do you and Shelby Hornbeck belong to the Ku Klux Klan? I want the truth now."

The waitress, an Indian girl dressed in a soiled apron and gingham dress, came to stand beside their table. Dexter gave her his order, and as soon as she was gone, he glowered at Rachel.

"No, I do not belong to no Ku Klux Klan. Neither does Shelby Hornbeck. Now are you satisfied?"

Rachel studied his face, then dropped her gaze. "Yes. Well, all right." She got up. "I'm sorry, but I had to know."

As she was leaving the building, a voice from behind said, "Rachel?" It was the Indian waitress from the dining room.

"I'm Molly Iron Shirt," she said in a whisper. "I got a message to you from Corby."

At the mention of his name Rachel felt a surge of love and longing. "Corby! Where is he? Why hasn't he come to welcome me back?"

Molly Iron Shirt's eyes glanced about furtively as she said, "The Native American Church is having a peyote ceremony a few miles from here, in a hidden place. Corby asks if you can come."

Intrigued, Rachel said, "But how would I find him?"

"I can take you there. Soon as my shift's over. Two o'clock. If you want to go, meet me behind the building."

Rachel went home and spent the next few hours modeling dresses, wondering which one she could fancy up for the ball. As two o'clock drew near, she snatched up her wide-brimmed straw hat and left the house. She put the sidesaddle on Maxwell's strawberry roan and rode to the windmill behind Bixby's Hotel. Molly Iron Shirt was on foot, carrying a small bundle in her hand. She swung up behind Rachel and sat sideways on the horse's haunches. "Take the trail upriver about five miles," she said.

The ceremony was taking place in a vale through which ran a small creek. In each of five canvas tepees, priests were beating drums, rattling gourds, blowing whistles and flutes, and chanting.

"You stay here," Molly Iron Shirt told Rachel in the place where the worshippers had picketed their ponies. "I'll get him."

Rachel tied the strawberry roan to the picket rope. A few women were carrying pails of water from the creek to the tepees, and a few children splashed about in the nearby creek.

When Corby emerged from the center tepee, a flute in his hands, she couldn't be sure it was really he, so tall had he grown. And he had grown into a handsome young man. His glossy black hair hung in two braids down his bare chest. He wore only moccasins, buckskin pants, a beaded Indian necklace, and a headband.

Rachel restrained an impulse to run to him; she waited, instead, until he reached her and said, "*Vahe,* Rachel. Welcome home."

Unable to control herself any longer, she threw her arms around him and pressed her face into the hollow of his shoulder.

"Oh, Corby, Corby, how I missed you! But *you,*" she said in a suddenly reproachful voice, pulling away from him. "I've been home four days now, and you haven't even come to say hello. I was beginning to think you'd forgotten me. My goodness," she said then, as if she had just noticed, "how *Indian* you've become."

"And how white you've become." He touched her cheek.

"Is that what you've done? Chosen the Indian's road?"

"Well, I could say I've chosen, I suppose, but I can't be sure that I've *been* chosen. For that, I'd have to have a vision quest."

"You've not had a vision quest yet? Why not?"

"You wouldn't understand."

"You might try me. We used to understand each other."

"When we were children, yes, but we've changed."

"Sure, but we are still best friends, aren't we?"

"Friends? Is that all?"

Searching his face for meaning, she felt a slight panic when she saw the kiss coming, but she didn't stop it. She even returned the kiss for a moment, so sweet and gentle and loving was it.

Drawing away, he said, "What we always felt was the love of mates, not the love of friends."

He kissed her again, and this time the kiss quickly became passionate. Rachel joined in the passion for a moment but then came to her senses and said, "No, we mustn't. Please. Let me go."

He released her with a readiness that surprised her, but disappointed her a little, too.

"I mean," she said, "what if . . . something happened?"

"Whatever happened, it'd be all right, long as we were together."

It was only then that she comprehended the full dimension of what he was suggesting. "You mean . . . go off and *live* together?"

"Yes."

"In some tepee somewhere? Sleeping on a dirt floor? Cooking rabbit stew over a campfire? Corby, I'm not a squaw."

Happiness vanished from his face, replaced by sullenness.

"Be sensible," she said. "We'd be outcasts. We'd be beggars."

"How little you know me if you think I'd ever beg. And as for being an outcast, what's it like *not* to be?"

"Oh, I'm sorry. I didn't mean— I have to go."

"Then go." He raised the flute to his mouth and played a song.

"That's beautiful. Does it have words?"

"No, but it has a meaning. A Cheyenne warrior was trying to get a captive Cherokee woman to be his mate, but she thought Cheyennes were savages. So he began courting her in the Cheyenne way, with a flute. When she heard his song, she was finally convinced he wasn't a savage after all. Anybody who could play a flute like that, how could he be a savage? So she became his woman."

"And they lived happily ever after?" But she repented her sarcasm and added sincerely, "Well, she was right. Anyone who played that song as beautifully as you do couldn't be a savage." He put the flute away and hoisted her onto her horse.

"So it's not because I'm a savage that you're afraid of me?"

Settling into the saddle and arranging her skirt, she smiled at him, then reached down to touch his cheek with her fingertips.

"My darling Corby, don't you understand yet? It's not the savage in *you* that I'm afraid of. . . ."

A BOUQUET of red roses waited for her in her room at the Simpson Boardinghouse in Guthrie, the first flowers she had ever received from a man—and not just any man, either, but Shelby Hornbeck.

Dressed in her prettiest dress, she greeted Shelby promptly at six, thanked him for the roses, told him he looked dashing in his dark evening suit with its high stiff collar, white silk vest, and swallowtail coat, and marveled when he blushed.

He'd brought along a chaperon, Aunt Bertha, who sat in the back seat of the surrey in her widow's weeds, like a totem, as they whisked through traffic toward the opera house, escorted by three bodyguards on horseback, one of whom was Dexter.

The lobby of the opera house was festively decorated, and Rachel was ogled by the women of Guthrie society. For Shelby Hornbeck to have brought this chit of a girl to the opera house to meet the most important people in the Territory clearly indicated that his intentions toward her were serious and honorable.

Shelby introduced her to Territorial Governor William C. Renfrow. She also met a United States Senator, a justice of the territorial supreme court, and a number of millionaires. She charmed the lot. It was obvious that Shelby was very pleased with her performance.

Dexter stood guard outside Shelby's private box. Aunt Bertha sat behind Shelby and Rachel. She was soon snoring, and Rachel welcomed her lack of vigilance. It gave her a chance to watch Shelby from the corner of her eye without being watched herself. And not only was she once again dazzled by his handsomeness but she was also fascinated by his strangeness. He wasn't at all what she would have expected a man of such wealth and political power to be. He acted more like, say, a successful minister. He had that look of rectitude about him, a look of unassertive but self-confident moral superiority. And that carried over to the ball later that evening, where Rachel learned to her surprise that Shelby didn't dance.

"You'll excuse me, I hope. I just never liked doing it well enough to learn how"—implying that he'd had better things to do. "But if you like to dance, please do. I'm sure you won't lack for partners." It was as if he were encouraging a child to run along and play.

So Rachel accepted the request for a dance from Governor Renfrow and thereafter many of the young bachelors. She often glanced at Shelby and found him talking to men, most of whom were older, with big cigars and big paunches.

Their conversations always seemed to falter when Rachel returned. Once she asked Shelby what they had been talking about.

"Politics. Nothing to bother your pretty head about," he said. "Are you enjoying yourself?"

"Oh," she said breathlessly, fanning herself, "I've never danced so much in my life. Could I have a sip of your punch?"

She pointedly turned the cut-glass cup around so that she drank from the same place on the rim where his lips had been, all the while looking up at him to make sure he noticed.

The intimacy of the act seemed to stir something in Shelby. He finally said, "Would you like to get some fresh air?"

"Oh, yes! What shall we do? Go for a midnight ride?"

He smiled apologetically. "I'm sorry. I'm afraid I promised Aunt Bertha I'd have her home by twelve o'clock. But what about tomorrow? Would you take a ride with me? There's something I want to ask you," he hinted, then added, "We could have a picnic."

"Without Aunt Bertha?"

"Without Aunt Bertha," he replied.

The next day they had their picnic under an old lightning-scarred oak tree high on the escarpment overlooking the Cimarron River. The bodyguards carried the wicker hamper from the buggy and put down the picnic blanket. Never before had she seen Dexter so eager to be of service to anyone. And like good servants, as soon as the picnic was prepared, Dexter and the other two bodyguards took up protective positions at a discreet distance from the picnic site.

Rachel anticipated their spending an hour or so laughing and talking, but she soon realized that Shelby never laughed and apparently had very little sense of humor. Politics and power were the only subjects that seemed to interest him, yet those were subjects he thought women shouldn't bother their pretty heads about. He talked about his politics of white supremacy, but only grudgingly and because Rachel required some explanation of her father's charges against him. "It's something I'm proud of," he said. "Every white man is a white supremacist at heart—even your father."

Rachel hooted. "I doubt he'd agree."

"He may not admit it, but how could it be otherwise? He's trying to teach the Indians the white man's ways. Why would he be doing that if he didn't believe that the white man's ways are superior?"

That sounded reasonable. And though he became a little testy when she asked him if he was a member of the Ku Klux Klan, he denied it. As for his personal background, he seemed willing enough to talk about his father—a Confederate major killed at the Battle of Shiloh—but of his mother he would say only that she, too, had died in the war. When Rachel tried to find out how, she noticed a look of alarm in his eyes, as if he were afraid of something.

He seldom turned the questions back upon her. He seemed to know all he wanted or needed to know about her and was satisfied just to sit in silence and look at her. There was something in his eyes, something that made her feel very special, and she decided to busy herself throwing pebbles over the escarpment into the river below and let him look as long as he liked. In a few minutes he approached her, saying, as if to a child, "Don't go too near the edge. You might fall, and I wouldn't want to lose you."

"But I'm not yours to lose."

"I'd like you to be," he confessed.

Her quizzical gaze caused him to avert his eyes.

"In what way?" she prompted coyly.

"Well, now that you mention it," he said in a businesslike way, "there is something I want to say to you. I haven't had much experience with women. But that's only because I never found one that I liked and admired enough to—to want her to be the mother of my children." He looked straight at her. "Until now."

"Why, Shelby Hornbeck, is this a proposal?"

"Yes. If you'd consent to be my wife, I could give you everything you ever wanted. I could take care of you and keep you safe."

"You make it sound a little like a business proposition. What would I be expected to give you in return?"

"A son," he said without hesitation. "I want a son."

She looked up at him for a moment in silence. Actually she was waiting for him to take her into his arms, but he just stood there, waiting. And she couldn't answer, because she couldn't imagine agreeing to marry a man whom she had never kissed.

So she put her arms around his neck and kissed him. Like an eager and awkward boy, he pressed his mouth against hers, his lips stiff and unyielding to the point of causing pain.

It had never occurred to her that a thirty-five-year-old man wouldn't know how to kiss. But she could teach him that—and how to dance and how to laugh. But love? She felt none of that in his touch. She wondered if she would have to teach him that, too.

"Do you know what you're doing?" Maxwell asked.

"Oh, Daddy, I do hope you're not going to start that stuff about politics again." She glared at him across his desk.

"It's not just politics," he protested. "How can you marry someone who thinks Indians are an inferior race?"

"And he asks why you're teaching the Indians the white man's ways if you don't think our ways are superior. To me this is all just politics—men talk. You men get to run the world and decide such things. You don't even let us vote. What business is it of mine?"

"Well, maybe it should be your business when they burn down people's houses and lynch kids."

"Oh, he's not in the Klan. He didn't burn down Eula's house."

"You're sure?"

"Of course I am. I asked him. He said he wasn't in the Klan, and I believe him." She leaped up from the chair and took an aimless turn about the office. "Why—why, for heaven's sakes, he's a church deacon!" she cried in triumph. "What's more, he doesn't drink, smoke, gamble, or chew tobacco."

"None of which precludes him from being a Klansman. I'm sure most Klansmen are churchgoing men who don't kick their dogs. But that doesn't mean they don't lynch a Negro now and then."

"Oh, for goodness' sakes," she said, "we're obviously never going to agree on this. I might as well go."

"All right, all right." He threw up his hands in surrender. "I'll try to give him the benefit of the doubt. But I still don't see why you're going to marry him in a *month*. What's the hurry?"

"*He* wanted to wait. It was *I* who didn't. D'you know why? Because I'm sick to death of this place, and I'd give anything to be mistress of my own house—in Guthrie."

Rachel had chosen not to share with Maxwell her most urgent reason for wanting to be married: her feelings for Corby. Since the day she had responded to his kisses with a passion equal to his own, she knew she couldn't trust herself to resist him for long.

Maxwell said, "What about love? I haven't yet heard you say you love the man. Do you?"

"Of course I do. Yes, I do. I love him." She crossed to Maxwell, stood beside his chair, and put her arm across his shoulders. "You'll like him, too. I know you will, when you get to know him."

DURING the month preceding her wedding date, Rachel made her own wedding gown. She had help from Miss Clarksdale and Eula, but she did most of the work. It gave her something to do.

Against her better judgment she had hoped each day to see Corby again. Molly Iron Shirt told her that he had gone off somewhere. The news left Rachel both angry and sad. She and Maxwell lamented his going back to the blanket, though Maxwell usually ended up sighing and saying, "Well, maybe it's for the best." One evening after supper he said, "Being colored in a white society is a losing game. Who can blame him if he doesn't want to play?"

Rachel, suddenly defensive, snapped, "Well, it's not *my* fault."

Momentarily surprised by the tortured logic of that response, Maxwell said, "Why, Rachel, nobody said it was." Then he looked at her more closely. "What's the matter?"

"I'm just . . . well, sort of nervous, that's all." Turning to Eula at the other end of the table, she said, "That's natural, isn't it, Eula? You were nervous, weren't you? About getting married?"

Eula blushed. "Considerable. But I never doubted I wanted to."

That touched the source of Rachel's nervousness. She was having second thoughts that left her irritable and short-tempered.

Such was her disposition on the day before she was supposed to go to Guthrie, the day that she put the last touches on her wedding gown and modeled it in front of the swing mirrors on the dresser in the main bedroom. Maxwell and Eula had gone to El Reno to buy wedding presents, so Rachel had the house to herself.

She wasn't pleased with what she saw in the mirror. The gown and veil made her look like a bland, sweet doll.

But all thoughts of the wedding went out of her head when she heard what she thought were galloping hoofbeats that came to a stop in the backyard. She tossed the bridal veil onto the dresser and darted through the kitchen to the back screen door.

Corby had tied the sweat-lathered red stallion at the corral water trough and was coming up the footpath to the back porch. He was dressed in faded blue jeans and a flimsy, dirty, buttonless blue work shirt. He was hatless and wore his hair in braids.

She cried his name and stepped out to meet him on the back porch. She had an impulse to throw her arms around him but held back when she saw the anger in his face.

"What is it?" she said. "What's the matter?"

"So it's true." He raked his eyes up and down the wedding gown. "Molly said you were getting married. I didn't believe her."

"Yes. Sunday. Why, Corby, you're not jealous, are you?"

Taking offense at the ridicule, he raised his voice to match his hostility. "And why should I be jealous? This"—scornfully gesturing toward her wedding gown—"is not the Rachel I loved. You know what you are now? A *vehoa.*"

She didn't spare the venom when she struck. "A white woman? Yes, and I'm proud of it. And who're you to look down your nose at me? Just take a look at yourself. You've become a dirty Indian. Look at your hands, how disgustingly dirty they are."

Moving with a sullen slowness, Corby lifted his hands and looked at them. They were black with charcoal from his last campfire. He put his hands on Rachel's shoulders and wiped them on the pristine whiteness of the gown. Then he spun around and left the porch.

Glancing down at the two smudges of charcoal and dirt on the shoulders of her wedding gown, Rachel cried out with shock and charged after him. She caught up with him, and began hitting him with the butt of her hand, as furious as she had ever been in her life. "Damn you, Corby. Damn you!" she cried.

He let the blows rain down on him without defending himself. He strode toward the barn, and she ran after him, pummeling him.

"How dare you ruin my wedding dress." Rachel's fury foundered, and by the time they reached the barn, she had ceased striking him, and her voice took on a plaintive edge. "How could you do such a thing. Look what you did."

Grimly silent, Corby strode on into the barn, scattering chickens before him, and into his room, with Rachel following. He went to the window at the foot of his bed and stared out, keeping his back to her. "I'm sorry. You were right. I'm jealous."

"What right have you to be jealous?"

He jerked his head around to fix her with his suddenly accusing eyes. "I love you. What rights does that give me?"

"None. None at all unless I said I'd be yours."

"And you did, dammit, you did. You carved a sign in the tree by the river that said we were betrothed."

"For goodness' sakes, Corby, we were *kids*. We're not kids any longer. And there can never be anything like man-woman love between us."

"Why not?" he asked, and in the face of her exasperated disbelief, he added, "Don't marry that man. Marry me."

She searched his face for signs of insanity, but he seemed quite reasonable. "What you're saying is plumb crazy," she said.

"Maybe so, but that never stopped us before, did it? We always had fun doing crazy things, didn't we? Well, let's do the craziest thing in our lives. Let's go to Mexico and get married."

She couldn't help being caught up for a moment in the romantic vision, and though she resisted being thrilled by it, her hesitation in refusing him outright gave him the courage to kiss her.

She allowed the kiss for a moment and even enjoyed the sensual pleasure of it, but soon she pulled away. He, rather than desist, grasped her by the shoulders and pulled her to him and kissed her again. She tried to turn her face away, but his lips followed.

"We mustn't do this." She was admonishing herself as well as him. "We mustn't." But she didn't try to stop his kisses. "No!"

"Yes. Listen to your heart. What does it say?"

It was then Rachel realized that she was no longer in control of her body. Oh, but we mustn't, we mustn't—she spoke the words in her mind, but her tongue refused to form them. What it was murmuring instead was, "Oh, Corby . . . my darling Corby."

Afterward they lay in bed for a long while in a silence broken only by the sounds of animals in the barn and barnyard. Then Rachel sniffled, and Corby used his thumb to wipe away her tears.

"Tears?" he asked. "Why?"

"Oh, Corby, what've we done now?"

"Something we've always wanted . . . were meant to do."

She shook her head as if shaking off a spell. "No." She sat up in the bed. "Just look at it!" She was noticing the dark smudges on the gown. "I'll have to hurry and wash it before Daddy gets back."

Corby scooted off the bed, saying, "Wait. Wait a minute now. You mean you're still going to marry him? After *this*?"

"Of course," she said without hesitation.

With a glance toward where they had lain, he stammered, "But you—you said just now . . . you said you loved *me*. And yet you're going to go ahead and marry *him*?"

"Yes."

"Why? You don't love him."

"Yes, I do," she insisted. "It's different, that's all. But listen to me, Corby. Even if I didn't love him, I'd still marry him, *because* I love you. We can't be together anymore, not after this. We can't allow this to happen again. Because no matter how much I love you, I'm not going to run off with you and live as an outcast squaw."

They stared at each other in silence for a moment, as if neither had anything left to say, and then Rachel moved to the door.

"I have to go." At the door she turned and said in a sadly resigned tone, "Good-bye, then, Corby. I don't think we should see each other again until—until afterward."

He turned his back on her. "Go to hell," he said.

Chapter Twelve

THE Southern Methodist Tabernacle in Guthrie sat on the edge of town, across from wooded acres set aside for a future city park. From the edge of these woods Corby watched the wedding procession. Concealed by bushes, he sat on Big Red and saw the bride and groom emerge from the church amid a rain of rice and cheers.

So it was done. Corby had needed to see it with his own eyes. Now, faced with the finality, he rode back to the Comanche reservation, where he resumed preparations for a vision quest.

His mentor and teacher was the venerable medicine man Three Rains, who had prepared Corby for all eventualities, but couldn't tell him where and when the vision quest should take place. Three Rains spoke to the Great Spirit about it, but all the Great Spirit told him was "From the place of the dead, follow the wolf."

Corby found this very cryptic. "Look for the signs," Three Rains said. "From the place of the dead, follow the wolf."

Corby kept his eyes open, but months went by, and still he saw nothing that he could interpret as a sign. He never missed an opportunity to visit burial grounds, but he never saw a wolf that he could follow from any place that might be called a place of the dead.

Indeed, he never saw a wolf at all until late in February, 1897.

He had gone rabbit hunting. A recent blizzard had covered the ground with snow, and Corby was riding Big Red across a snow-whitened meadow when he happened on a squatter's cabin. It was a plain board shanty of the kind being built by thousands of home-steaders who had begun entering the reservation illegally. No smoke came from the chimney. Snow was piled about ten feet high, completely covering the front door. So nobody had gone in or out of the shanty since the blizzard ended two days ago.

He dug the snow and ice away from the front door on the unlikely chance that someone inside might still be alive. After half an hour he finally forced his way inside. There was not a stick of furniture in the place. The small tin stove, the floor, and the walls were covered with hoarfrost. In the farthest corner of the room lay a pile of bedding. Stepping closer, he saw the three bodies: a woman and two small children, stiff in death, with frost in their hair and on their faces. Their eyes were closed as if in sleep.

Turning away, Corby glanced around the room, automatically reconstructing the bitter struggle that the woman had waged to stay alive. She had demolished every piece of furniture, every box, every picture frame that would burn, and in the end had even burned the axe with which she had demolished the furniture.

On a nail near the door a page from a child's school tablet had words scrawled on it in pencil:

> My dear husband we et the last of the food yesterday and burned ever thing there is to burn even the Bible. We have prayed for you ever day but we are afraid the storm is so terable you have become lost or will not come back in time. If that be true I pray that we will all meet again in Heaven. We are going to sleep now.

There was nothing to do but leave them there like that. If the husband was coming back, he should find them as they were. Corby put the note back on the nail and went outside, closing the door behind him. He mounted and rode toward the south no more than a half mile before he topped a small rise and, struck by what he saw, brought Big Red to a halt.

About a hundred yards away was a white wolf feeding on something. As soon as Corby topped the ridge, the wolf raised its head, saw Corby, and ran. Corby kicked Big Red into a plunging run through the snow, giving chase. But when he passed the place where the wolf had been feeding, he reined Big Red to a sudden stop.

It was a man's body—no doubt the husband who had gone for help. Again Corby thought it was best to do nothing. The ground was frozen, so he couldn't bury the body. Besides, those who would come looking for him would want to know what happened.

So he left the body there and went riding after the white wolf with the excitement of one whose destiny was about to be revealed.

In the first few months of marriage Rachel had busied herself with furnishing and decorating the house, but after that she found she had nothing to do. Aunt Bertha kept the accounts, hired and supervised the staff, and decided what would be served for dinner. She kept the keys to all the locked drawers and rooms and closets and cupboards on a ring that she carried on her belt.

When Shelby came home late from a meeting one night, Rachel accompanied him to his study, demanding to know why it was that Aunt Bertha was responsible for running the house, and not she.

"Seems to me most women would consider themselves lucky not to have to do such things," he said.

"Well, I'm not most women. Sometimes I feel like an empty-headed doll that's been dressed up and put on a shelf and told to stay there until you get ready to notice me—which isn't often."

"Well, there's just so much work that I have to do. You know that. And as the next election gets closer, there's going to be even more. I'm sorry, but"—he gestured toward his desk—"what would you have me do? I have responsibilities."

"*I* don't have *any*. Yet *I'm* the mistress here, not Aunt Bertha."

A small indulgent smile played in the corners of his mouth. "All right. I'm sorry. I hadn't realized you were so dissatisfied. Tell you what, I'll ask Aunt Bertha to let you help her with some of the household accounts. In the meantime, I have to get on with my work." He nodded toward his desk.

"Tonight?"

"There's a board meeting in the morning." He stroked her shoulders. "Be a good girl. Go on to bed. I'll be up in a little while."

Upstairs, Rachel slipped into a nightgown, touched her neck and arms with perfume, and crawled into the huge canopied bed, where she waited for Shelby in case he decided to try once again to beget the son he wanted. She wasn't really optimistic, however. She hadn't the least idea how to help him, how to arouse him, how to make him want her. It had been a shock to her on her wedding night when Shelby had been unable to consummate their marriage, and she came to believe that he had at some time in his life been deeply hurt.

One December night when Rachel and Aunt Bertha were decorating the Christmas tree, Rachel asked, "What's wrong with him?"

"With Shelby? Why, is there something wrong with him?"

"There's no—no *joy* in him. You know something? I've never seen him laugh. I mean, really laugh. Have you? Ever?"

"Well, I don't know. I guess he's always been pretty serious. He's had to be a man, and do a man's work, ever since he was eight. All of us were ruined by the war, and Shelby lost everything. He didn't have much to laugh about, let me tell you. But I've said all I'm going to. You want to know more, you best ask him."

Rachel found an opportune moment one night shortly after Christmas. She and Shelby were sitting before the fire, and Rachel looked up at the portrait of his mother above the mantel.

"She must have been very young when she died," she mused. "What did she die of?" And she saw a sudden tension grip his body.

"Why do you want to know?"

"Because I want to know about *you*. Please?"

Staring into the fire, he slowly, bit by bit, revealed to Rachel the very first memory of his life, an unspeakable secret that began with swirling flames and screams and cries of horror.

"Near the end of the war Yankees swept through South Carolina on a raid, gave the slaves firearms, told them to revolt against their masters, to burn the crops and plantations. They did. They went wild, drunk on whiskey and vengeance, became marauding bands. They burned Kingstree. My father was away in the war—dead,

301

though we didn't know it at the time. Mother got us out, just the two of us, out of the house with our lives, but that was all. For days we stayed in the woods, dodging marauding bands of drunks. We ate roots, frogs, berries, slept on the cold ground, running like hunted animals. And then . . . there were two of them. They found us, ran us down. 'Run, Shelby, run!' my mother—"

He broke off, too distraught to go on for a moment, then cleared his throat. "They caught her, tore off her clothes. I tried to protect her. I ran at them, crying, hitting, trying to make them stop, but they knocked me away. She told me to turn my head. She didn't want me to see . . . but I saw. And I swore I'd get back at them someday."

When his words finally trailed off and died in a brooding, malignant silence, Rachel, her eyes filmed over with tears of sympathy, said, "Oh, Shelby, how awful for you. Your poor mother. . . ."

"She died a few months later. She lived only long enough to see that I was safe and had a good home with Aunt Bertha, and then she turned her face to the wall and willed herself to die."

"The poor woman. And the men who— Did they get away?"

"The Klan caught them," Shelby said.

NEAR sundown Corby found himself on the north bank of the frozen Red River, about twelve miles from where he had first seen the wolf. The sky was threatening more snow, so he decided to give up the chase for the present. Surveying the area for a likely place to spend the night, he spotted a cave about halfway up a bluff.

He unsaddled Big Red, left him tethered to a leafless cottonwood tree, and made his way up the scree to the cave. In the last light of the sinking sun he saw the remains of recent campfires near the entrance, and there was even a cache of firewood.

"Anybody here?" he called back into the dark shadows of the interior. No answer came except the echo of his own voice. He built a fire near the cave entrance and used a cedar fagot as a torch to explore the rest of the cave. He found a small sump hole that someone had dug to collect the water seeping from a fissure. On one wall of the cave he was surprised to find a number of pictures and symbols carved in the alabaster, pictures of animals and humans and mysterious markings reminiscent of those on tepees. Huge horned buffalo—with small, sticklike men attacking them with sticklike lances—ran across the wall; and a wolf was sitting on its haunches, its head tipped backward, howling at a full moon.

"The Cave of the Ancient Ones," Three Rains said gleefully when Corby told him where he had spent the night. "*Haiya!* Medicine Bluff. And a white wolf led you there! The cave will be the place of your vision quest. It should begin on the night of the next full moon." This meant a wait of nearly a month, but Corby had plenty to do in the meantime to purify himself and make himself worthy of a vision.

When the full moon of March drew near, Corby was escorted to Medicine Bluff by Three Rains and two lesser medicine men. They gave him his last food and water, then took Big Red and left.

As Corby stood motionless on the bluff, looking to the east while the sky grew light and the sun came up, his ordeal began. He looked into the sun as it climbed into the brightening sky, and by midmorning he felt as if his eyeballs were going to explode. His legs became so weak that he could hardly stand. Yet he went on staring and standing and chanting until the sun went down.

Though blind and scarcely able to move on his cramping legs, he crawled down the steep rocky face of the bluff to the entrance of the Cave of the Ancient Ones. Following Three Rains's instructions exactly, he stopped in the entrance of the cave and turned around and around in a dizzying dance as he chanted a prayer, asking the Great Spirit to give him the strength to endure four days and nights without water, food, or sleep.

Next he built a small fire and took the ritual items he needed for his quest from his rawhide pouch. With sacred paints he decorated his face and body in swirls of yellow and white and black. Shaking a buffalo-skin rattle and blowing a shrill whistle, he began a slow shuffling dance. He danced until the fire died out and then, on the verge of collapsing, groped his way to the entrance of the cave. In the light of the full moon he sat down cross-legged, shivering with cold, light-headed with hunger and lack of sleep.

When he had been without food or water or sleep for three days and two nights, his light-headedness began to grow into hallucinations. Standing before the sacred rock drawings, he felt the world swirl into dream shapes and dream sounds. Falling, he thrust out a hand against the alabaster wall, and his hand fell exactly into the outline of a hand carved by the Ancient Ones; his eyes fell on the scene of the giant buffalo being hunted by sticklike men with lances. Then the wall gave way, and he felt the carved hand fold itself around the shaft of a lance, and he was running, panting, shouting. He had become one of the carved stickmen, and the giant buffalo had become hundreds of buffalo, thousands of buffalo, stampeding, driven by the hunters.

He was standing in the river. He didn't know how he had got there. He didn't remember leaving the cave, but he found himself standing knee-deep in the rolling red waters of the Red River, and he heard the river say, "I am the blood of the earth. Drink of me and be strong."

He dipped his cupped hands into the waters and drank, and then he reached down into the water and brought up the first pebble he touched. This would be the first relic in his medicine bundle.

As he was climbing back to the cave, he saw a raven perched on a limb. Preening, the raven dropped a feather to the ground and said, "Take that for your medicine bundle," and Corby was pleased to have a gift from the bird that was a messenger between the earth and Great Spirit in the sky.

"There is a spider's web just inside the cave," the raven said. "You will need his power, too."

Yes, the power of the spider, the most intelligent of all creatures, would be his, too. He found the web and rolled it into a tiny ball.

These relics he placed inside his pouch; then he picked up a stone and went to the sacred rock drawings. He wanted a chip of alabaster from inside the carved outline of the howling wolf. He drew back the stone and struck. The wolf howled. Corby believed at first that the howl had come from the alabaster wolf, but then he realized that it came from outside the cave.

In the next moment, Corby found himself hunting the wolf. He made his way through some woolly buckthorn bushes on the riverbank and drew near a tamarisk thicket, whence came the snarling howls of the wolf. Before entering the thicket, he drew his knife.

Caught in a trap was the huge white wolf that had led Corby to the cave. The wolf growled and lunged at Corby, only to be brought up short by the chain on the trap on its broken rear leg.

"You are finished, my brother," Corby said. "With such an injury, even if you escaped, you would soon die."

"I know," said the wolf. "I am to be a sacrifice."

Suddenly elated, as if everything had become clear to him in a flash, Corby said, "The white wolf is to be my animal helper?"

"Yes, if you can release me from this worthless body. But I warn you, it will not be easy. I will fight you to the last breath."

Corby hesitated. The wolf was huge—probably six feet from the tip of its nose to the tip of its tail—and weighed as much as Corby himself. So Corby found six sticks and used his belt to lash the sticks to his left hand and forearm like splints. Then, with the knife in his right hand, he advanced on the wolf.

The wolf backed up; then, snarling ferociously, it lunged. Corby used his stick-encased forearm as a shield, and the wolf sank its fangs into the sticks, cracking them like bones as Corby's right hand went under the wolf's head. In one quick slashing movement he cut the wolf's throat. The light of life slowly faded from its eyes. Corby chanted a prayer that would let the wolf's released spirit enter his own body. "Give me your strength, O wolf. Give me your cunning, O wolf. Give me your fierceness."

And when he felt a shudder run through him, a sort of convulsion of ecstatic strength, he knew that the wolf's spirit had entered him, and he knew—for the first time in his life—who he was.

"I am White Wolf."

DEXTER and Sheriff Harriman strode to Shelby's study at Kingstree, entered without knocking, and closed the door behind them. The sheriff slapped his hat against his leg in fury and frustration.

"We got to do something," he said. "Shelby, we *got* to."

"Calm down now, Alva. Getting all riled up won't help anything." Shelby moved to the liquor cabinet. He gave them each a glass and filled their glasses with whiskey. "All right now. Sit down. Tell me what happened."

With his lower lip trembling, Sheriff Harriman related to Shelby what he himself had recently been told over the telephone: Two more of the men who had made the raid on Freedom four years ago had been killed—both shot from ambush the night before.

"The fools. How many times have they been warned?"

"Yeah, they got careless," Harriman admitted, "but it just ain't possible for us to go on like this, year after year, and not get careless sometime or other. We got our lives to live."

"Well, it fairly amazes me," Shelby said, "that the combined forces of more than five thousand men of the brotherhood scattered across the Territory can't find one pitiful nigger and kill him."

"Well, it amazes me, too, but the fact is, he's got us at a terrible disadvantage, because we've got our lives to live and jobs to do, and he just lives for one thing only: to kill us."

He gulped the whiskey and wiped his lips with his hand.

"And here we are," he continued, "the last three men left alive. Which one of us is gonna be next? I get up in the morning and ask myself, Is it me today? I tell you, he ain't gonna stop till he's killed every one of us. Now, it seems to me we got to put his face on WANTED posters and tack 'em up in every post office in the whole damned Territory. With a five-thousand-dollar reward on his head, dead or alive, we'll have every bounty hunter in the Territory on his trail, like the hounds of hell."

"And what if he gets taken alive?"

"He won't be. Nobody's gonna take him alive—he'll see to that himself. And if he don't, I will."

Shelby considered the proposition for a moment, then dropped his hands in a gesture of resignation. "All right. Go ahead. But make sure that black bastard never comes to trial."

THE first time Rachel saw Shelby leaving the house with a valise, she called down to him from the second-story veranda and asked if he would be gone all night. When he said he'd be back by midnight, she asked him why he was carrying an overnight bag.

"Taking a change of clothing, just in case," he had said, and rode away with his bodyguards before she could ask, "In case of what?"

Another night, after he had returned home late with the valise, she observed him taking it to the basement. The next day she went to find it, tingling with curiosity to know what was in it. But the valise was nowhere to be found among the basement's stored provisions. That left only an antique wardrobe, which was locked.

Then one day in March, when Aunt Bertha was down with a bad cold and had been ordered by her doctor to stay in bed for a few days, Rachel was entrusted with the ring of household keys. So she went down into the basement to the wardrobe and fumbled through the keys until she found the one that fitted.

Unlocking the wardrobe, she paused, then steeled herself and jerked the door open. A Ku Klux Klan robe hung from a hanger. A conical hood was folded neatly on the shelf above. On the floor of the wardrobe was the empty leather valise.

Acting on impulse, she took the costume to her room. When Shelby came home that evening, she met him at the bedroom door dressed in the costume. She stood in silence, facing him, allowing the costume to charge him with deception and dishonor.

For a moment Shelby seemed too stunned to react, but then an expression came over his face that Rachel had never seen before. Shoving the door closed, Shelby jerked the hood off Rachel's head as he muttered, "How dare you? How *dare* you? Get out of that robe this instant."

Hurriedly pulling the robe over her head, she said, "I dared because you lied to me. You told me you didn't belong to the Klan."

"If you ever again do anything so disrespectful and foolish, I'll take my belt off and give you a good licking—something your father obviously neglected to do in the past. And if you don't think I will, you just try me."

"Oh, I don't doubt you're capable of it, considering all the people you and your Klansmen have bullwhipped. You must be pretty good at it by now."

"You keep on, you're going to find out."

"Well, I *am* going to keep on. I'm going to keep on till I find out

307

the truth. It was you and Dexter and your other bullyboys who burned Eula's house that night, wasn't it?"

"I'm warning you for the last time."

But she couldn't stop now. "I'm not afraid of you. I know what you and your Klansmen did to those colored boys from Freedom. Oh, you must be proud of yourselves, mutilating *children*."

He stared at her, his nostrils flaring, his eyes narrowing.

"But you made a bad mistake when you did it to Gypsy Smith, didn't you?"

He slapped her.

"You bastard!" she cried, and tried to strike him.

He caught her wrist and squeezed until she cried out with pain. "What do you know about Gypsy Smith?"

She thrashed against him. "No more than anyone else who's heard the rumors of what you did to him. But even if you did take his manhood, he's still probably a better man than *you*."

She didn't even see the hand that struck her, that spun her around and sent her sprawling across a chaise longue. Hearing a loud ringing inside her skull and seeing only a multitude of small exploding lights, she was unaware that Shelby stood over her and had slipped the black leather belt from his pants. But she looked up in time to see him swing the belt. She tried to scramble away, but the stinging slash across her shoulders slammed her back down.

Then he caught her dress at the collar and ripped downward. She cried out, struggling against him, but her kicking and cries only increased his frenzy. He began lashing her naked flesh, but after a dozen hard lashes, the blows tapered off, until he stood above her, breathing heavily. Then she became aware that he had dropped the belt and was unbuttoning his fly in a frenzy, tearing at the buttons. She tried once more to bolt, when he fell upon her.

After the assault Shelby, with anger so profound it could only be called insane, told her, "We made a bargain. I made you my wife and gave you everything a wife could want, and you were to give me a son. When you fulfill that bargain, you'll have my permission to leave."

"You can't keep me here against my will."

"I can do anything I damn well please."

After he was gone, she threw all his things out of the east wing apartment into the hallway. She locked the doors and wedged straight-backed chairs underneath the door handles, and she took a pistol from a bureau drawer and kept it under her pillow. It was a pearl-handled little snub-nosed .32 revolver, a gift from Shelby.

In the days following the assault, Shelby spent little time at home and, as far as Rachel knew, never once ventured upstairs. But remaining a prisoner at Kingstree was never one of her options. She was going to leave Shelby, of that there was no doubt; the only consideration was how to leave without incurring more violence, more trouble. Her Negro maid—who, with Aunt Bertha's permission, kept the barricaded apartment supplied with food and water—agreed to sneak a letter out of the house and mail it to Maxwell for her.

WHEN Rachel first heard the music, she thought it was the sad sweet song of a night bird but soon realized that it was a flute.

With a wave of excitement sweeping over her, she tiptoed along the veranda to the outside stairway leading down to the gardens, and went down the stairs as silently as possible. Once on the ground, she raced across the backyard toward the shrubbery whence had come the sound of the flute, and then as she passed an oak tree, a hand suddenly reached out and grabbed her arm and swung her around, and she found herself looking into the barbaric face of an Indian warrior. She almost cried out with fright.

"Is it really you?" she said at last. The white wolf–pelt cloak he wore reeked of smoke and sweat and death. "What're you doing here? You could get yourself shot."

Aunt Bertha's voice came from the house. "Rachel? Is that you out there? What're you doing? Who're you with?" Her darkly dressed form could be seen in the shadows on the back veranda.

Rachel shoved Corby behind the tree. "Nobody. There's only me. I'm just out for a little walk."

She watched in silence as Aunt Bertha's silhouette passed in front of a lighted window and disappeared into a briefly lighted doorway; then she whispered, "Come on, we've got to get out of sight."

She took his hand and led him hurriedly into the lighted barn—

310

the only barn in Guthrie with electric lights. She hastily closed the door and turned to him, smiling now.

Corby touched with his fingertips the discoloration around her right eye. "What happened? Did he hit you?"

"No. I bumped into something. Oh, Corby!" Putting her arms around him, she pressed tightly against him. "I'm so glad to see you. But what're you doing here?"

"I went to Agency to tell your father about my vision quest, and he let me read the letter you wrote."

"But I told him I didn't want any help. I got myself into this mess; I'll get myself out. I don't want you or Daddy getting mixed up in this. Shelby can be dangerous." She touched the discolored eye.

"So he did beat you."

"Once, but never again." She fell silent, suddenly on guard.

They could hear the buggy approaching the barn.

"It's Shelby. Come on," she whispered urgently, and clambered up the ladder to the hayloft, Corby following close behind. Once in the loft, they dropped down onto a pile of hay and listened to Shelby's bodyguards enter the barn.

It was Dexter's voice they heard first. He and two other men unhitched the blue-roans and put them in their stalls. Then the lights went out and the door closed, leaving the barn in darkness.

Rachel whispered, "We have to get you out of here. Soon as Aunt Bertha tells Shelby she saw me out here, he'll come looking."

They had to crawl on hands and knees in darkness, feeling their way toward the edge of the loft until they reached the ladder. Corby descended first, then waited for her at the foot of the ladder and took her in his arms.

"Come with me, Rachel."

"What? Now? Don't be crazy. When I leave here, I'm going to St. Louis. I have friends—"

But her words were cut off when the lights in the barn suddenly came on. Just inside the barn door stood Shelby and Dexter and the other two bodyguards. Shelby was carrying a double-barreled shotgun. Dexter and the other two had their pistols drawn.

Approaching, Shelby said, "What's this redskin doing here?"

Rachel stepped protectively in front of Corby. "He's an old friend of mine come to visit. He was just leaving. Go on, Corby."

"Stay right where you are." Shelby gripped the shotgun as if preparing to fire. "Put your hands over your head."

Corby hesitated.

Dexter jabbed him forcefully over the kidney with the muzzle of his .44 Colt. "You heard him. Get your hands up."

Corby raised his hands slowly and contemptuously enough to show them that he wasn't afraid.

"Leave him alone," Rachel said.

Dexter jerked the horn-handled hunting knife from its sheath on Corby's belt and flung it away onto the floor.

"What're you doing?" Rachel demanded of Shelby. "I told you, he's a friend of mine from the agency."

"Get in the house," he said to her. "I'll deal with you later."

"Let Corby go, and I'll—"

"Do as you're told." He grabbed her arm and flung her toward the door with such violence that she fell sprawling across the floor.

Corby's reaction was purely automatic: He lunged at Shelby and struck him with his fist across the face, a blow that knocked Shelby backward against the buggy. And then one of the deputies—Billy Blankenship—cracked Corby on the back of the head with the barrel of his revolver, knocking him to his hands and knees. Then the men grabbed his arms and jerked him to his feet.

Frightened and furious at the same time, Rachel had scrambled to her feet, but didn't know what to do.

A small drop of blood trickled from Shelby's nose. Slowly raising his fingers, he looked at the blood on his fingertips.

"You *struck* me?" It was as if Corby had committed some sacrilege beyond comprehension. Then he said, "Tie him up."

"What're you gonna do?" Rachel demanded. "Leave him—"

Her words were cut off with a stinging slap across the face.

"I told you to get in the house," Shelby said through clenched teeth. "Now *go!*"

Rachel turned and dashed out of the barn.

"Tie him to the ladder."

While Deputy Blankenship held the muzzle of his Colt to the back of Corby's head, Dexter and Harry Dahl tied his hands above his head to one of the rungs of the ladder.

Shelby leaned his shotgun against a nearby horse stall, then crossed to the tack room and brought out a coiled bullwhip. "We're going to teach this redskin manners," he announced. "Strip him."

Harry Dahl jerked the wolfskin cape off over Corby's head. Dexter took out his pocketknife and slit the buckskin shirt from collar to tail, and drew aside the flaps to leave Corby's back naked.

With the solemnity of an executioner, Shelby said, "For the crime of striking a white man, twenty-five lashes, and as many thereafter as it takes to teach you to stay in your place."

Corby muttered, "If you whip me, you better kill me, 'cause I'll—"

The first lash of the whip silenced him, leaving a long red welt. Blood trickled down his back. His body contracted convulsively at each lash, but he didn't once cry out. By the tenth lash, Corby's back was a swollen mass of welts and cuts. By the thirteenth lash, the shock and pain had made him almost insensible.

That was when Rachel burst into the barn, brandishing the pearl-handled .32 revolver that Shelby had given her. She held it in both hands and pointed it directly at him. He raised the whip to strike again but now held it as if paralyzed by disbelief at what he saw.

"Stop it!" she cried, approaching Shelby. "Turn him loose."

Not one of the three bodyguards moved except to look back and forth between Rachel and Shelby, not knowing what to do.

"Cut him down, damn you!" she cried.

Her words released Shelby from his paralysis. He brought the whip flashing overhead to strike Rachel on the shoulder. The pain of the lash caused every nerve and muscle in her body to contract in a cringe. So close were the sound of the whip striking and the sound of the pistol that she didn't realize she had fired until she saw Shelby clutching his chest, blood pouring through his fingers.

With his face turning the color of cold ashes, Shelby looked at Rachel in a peculiarly pleading way as he collapsed onto the floor.

Dexter rushed to Shelby's side and dropped to his knees, saying, "What the hell've you done?"

The other two bodyguards made a move toward Rachel.

"Stay where you are," she warned. "I'll shoot you. I will."

They stopped in mid-stride, exchanging questioning glances.

"He's dead," Dexter said. "You killed him."

"Rachel," Corby called, "my knife. Give me the knife."

Keeping the bodyguards always in front of the pistol, she picked up the knife and placed it in Corby's hand. Panting and cursing, he cut the rope that bound his wrists and lunged for the shotgun that Shelby had left leaning against the horse stall.

Harry Dahl was the first by a fraction of a second to draw his Colt, but it had not cleared the holster when a blast from the shotgun hit him in the chest. Billy Blankenship managed to get his gun clear of the holster, but before he could bring it to bear, the second blast of buckshot hit him, sending him sprawling across the floor.

Corby flung the empty shotgun away, snatched the .32 revolver from Rachel's hands, and aimed directly at Dexter.

"Don't shoot," Dexter begged in a small voice, cringing, holding up his hands as if to ward off the bullet. "Don't kill me!"

"No," Rachel cried. "Corby, you can't! He's my *brother*."

The sight of Dexter cringing there on the floor, pleading, caused Corby's fury to subside into disgust. "He may be your brother, but right now he's the worst enemy you got. He's the only witness to all this. If we let him live, he'll put our necks in a noose."

"No, no," Dexter said. "I wouldn't do that. Honest I wouldn't."

"Shut up," Corby snapped; then to Rachel he said, "You'd better think about it."

Rachel actually seemed to be giving it some thought, much to Dexter's consternation, but she finally gave the only answer it was possible for her to give: "Let him go."

"You got off lucky this time, *veho*," he said to Dexter, "but if you ever cross my path again, I'll kill you." Then he told Dexter to stand up and take off his gun belt. Corby took the gun belt and snatched up his wolfskin cape, saying to Rachel, "Come on, we've got to go."

"Go?" she said. "Go?"

"We haven't got much time."

"Corby . . . what've we done?"

"What we had to do."

"And what—what're we going to do now?"

"What we have to do."

Rachel allowed him to lead her, running, out of the barn and past the paddocks and down the sloping pasture toward where Big Red was tied in a distant darkness of trees.

Chapter Thirteen

THEY followed the Cimarron westward. Around midnight a drizzling spring rain began to fall. The moon disappeared behind the clouds, and Corby had to let Big Red pick his own way slowly in the darkness. Dawn brought a short respite from the rain, but it began again before they angled southwest toward the Glass Mountains.

At midday they reached the old trapper's cabin Corby had discovered during one of his wandering sojourns into the wilderness. Within a few minutes they had a fire going in the rusty iron stove, fueled by a cache of dry firewood left by some former occupant. While Corby went out to tend to Big Red, Rachel hung the wet blankets and the wolfskin on the smoke-blackened rafters to dry.

Corby brought the saddlebags in and tossed them on the plank table. "Some dried apricots and jerky in there, and a little coffee."

While he undressed, she stole a glance at him when he turned his back, and couldn't turn away.

"Oh, your poor back," she murmured.

Corby took the saddle blanket, wrapped it around his waist, and tied it on with a frayed piece of rope. "I saw some Indian turnips out by the pond," he said, and began to make coffee. "I'll see if I can catch us a rabbit tomorrow, make some rabbit stew."

Rachel had been fighting back tears ever since leaving Kingstree, but at the mention of rabbit stew, the tears overflowed. "Oh, Corby," she said, "what's going to happen to us?"

"It'll be all right. Rain's washed out our tracks. Not much chance they'll find us here. Not many people know about this place."

"Maybe not now, but they'll keep hunting till they find us."

"With any luck we'll get to Mexico."

"And if they catch us?"

"They won't." He put another stick into the stove. "But if they do . . . Well, there's something you better know so you'll . . . well, just so you'll know. I'm not gonna be taken alive."

For the next three days the rain continued in gusty showers, and the cabin was dark and dank. They made a bed from the cabin's old mice-gnawed mattresses and two blankets. The festering wounds on Corby's back forced him to lie on his stomach when he slept.

The dried apricots and jerky were gone by the end of the second day, leaving them nothing to eat. The next day Corby went out in the rain to see if he could catch something. When he returned, he said, "Better put out the fire. I heard some shots. Might be signal shots."

"But you said they wouldn't be able to track us in the rain."

"They're not tracking us. If it is a posse, they're just poking around, hoping to stumble across us." He strapped the gun belt around his waist.

"Is there going to be shooting?"

"If it's a posse and they find us, yes, there'll be shooting."

She couldn't sleep that night. Afraid, hungry, guilt-ridden, and confused, she lay there, hearing the rain dribbling off the roof, trying to reconcile herself to dying.

But the sun came out the next morning, and the world was reborn. Rubbing sleepy eyes, Rachel and Corby emerged from the dark cabin like two animals awakening from a winter's hibernation to behold a transformed earth. The dogwoods around the pond were in bloom, birds sang as they built their nests, and geese in V formations were flying northward in a cloudless sky.

"I'll saddle up and take a look around," Corby said. "Soon's I get back, I'll dig some worms. We'll have fish for breakfast."

After he rode down the trail, she turned and went back into the cabin to get the fishing pole. If Corby could catch fish, so could she.

While she was looking around outside for some worms, she jumped a rabbit and gave chase. Dashing barefoot through the grass, she chased the rabbit until it went to ground in a hole.

Rachel dropped to her knees and thrust her arm into the hole, trying to reach the rabbit, but found instead a bulging rawhide bag and an Indian bow and quiver of arrows. With her heart racing, she hurriedly untied the rawhide flap, and what she saw made her gasp with wonder: a can of coffee, cans of tomatoes and peaches, as well as watertight canisters filled with cornmeal, dried beans, and a mixture of dried fruits and nuts. There was also a tin of salted bacon, a box of matches, some salt, some ground pepper, three boxes of shells for guns, and a bar of soap.

"Come see what I've found," she said when Corby returned.

He dismounted and squatted beside the rawhide bag. "Somebody's cache." He picked up the bow and arrows. "Comanche. But what's a Comanche doing here? Anyway," he continued as he examined the bow, "with this, I'll have us a deer before sundown."

"What about the posse?"

"Maybe forty or fifty men camped on the river last night. Probably a posse. I saw them ride on up the river with Arapaho outriders, looking for signs." He strung the bow and notched one of the arrows on the bowstring to test its strength.

"Are we safe here, then?"

"Probably safer here than anywhere else—for the time being, at least. In a week or two they'll get tired looking and call it off. Then we can head out for Mexico."

Corby went hunting with the bow and arrows and brought back a buck. They kept only enough fresh meat to last for a few days and cut the rest into thin strips and hung them above the stove to dry.

When he brought another deer, Rachel helped him skin and clean it and even helped tan the hide. "When it dries, I'll make you a pair of moccasins," he said. "We'll make a squaw out of you yet."

One day while Corby was out hunting, she took the bar of soap to the pond, stripped naked, and waded into the chilly waters to wash herself and her hair and then her clothes. Shivering, she emerged from the pond and spread her clothes out on bushes and combed her hair as it dried in the sun. She was lying naked in the grass, soaking up the sun, feeling the wonder of being alive, when he returned.

He didn't say that he had always loved her and only her, but she

317

knew that was what he meant when he said, "You're the only one," and she confessed that she had never loved anyone else. Doomed now, what did they have to lose?

For Rachel it was as if she had been lost for years and finally found herself in a place where she had always wanted to be: in Corby's arms. Nothing else mattered. Let them be outcasts, let them be hunted fugitives; she no longer cared, as long as they were together. And if and when the hunters ran them down— "We'll die together," she said.

During the three weeks that they stayed at the cabin, they slept outside at night, making their bed in different places. This was partially a precaution against being taken by surprise, but it was also a matter of choice. Corby preferred sleeping outside, and Rachel delighted in making love under the stars.

Back at the cabin one day, she tried on the moccasins he had made for her. "Not very fancy," he said, "but they're double-soled, so they'll last till we get to Mexico, anyway."

"Now, if I only had a deerskin dress, I'd be a squaw."

"You think that's all it takes? Just clothes?"

"What does it take? I'm serious, Corby, I would like to become an Indian. Can't you adopt me into the tribe or something?"

"Maybe. But the first thing you'd have to learn is that Indians attach a lot of meaning to a name."

"I know that."

"Then why do you keep calling me Corby? I've told you my name's White Wolf. I'm no longer Corby. A vision quest is a serious thing. The name given by the Spirits should be respected."

"You're right," she said. "From now on—cross my heart—White Wolf, White Wolf."

Neither of them wanted the idyll to end, but there came a day when their supplies were running low, and Corby—White Wolf— said they had better start for Mexico. "Somebody's bound to stumble on to us here sooner or later."

Then he came across a fresh set of a shod mule's hoofprints about a quarter mile south of the cabin. He put Big Red into a lope, tracing the rider's trail. He was within sight of the cabin when he found the place where the rider had stopped. He read the signs: hoofprints about twenty-four hours old, leading away from the area. He sent Big Red plunging down the slope toward the cabin.

When Rachel saw him, she hurried out to meet him.

"We've been spotted." He swung down from the saddle. "One man, on a mule. I figure he probably lit out for Guthrie. Posse could be here anytime now. Let's grab a few things and go."

Inside the cabin, he stuffed his saddlebags with jerky and boxes of ammunition while Rachel folded the blankets and the wolfskin. Then they heard the voice.

"Hello, the cabin!" It was a man's voice, calling from a distance.

White Wolf grabbed the rifle, then opened the door far enough to see the trail approaching the cabin.

"Hello, the cabin. I'm coming in. Hold your fire. I'm a friend."

White Wolf aimed the rifle through the opening of the door. "That's far enough," he shouted. "Who are you? What d'you want?"

The rider pulled up and raised his right hand in the Indian gesture of peace. "Gypsy Smith!" he called. "I bring news."

Rachel dashed to the door to get a look at the approaching figure. "Look, it *is* him. It's Gypsy Smith."

White Wolf and Rachel stepped out to greet him. And though they did recognize him, it wasn't the Gypsy Smith they had last seen over four years ago. He was gaunt now, almost skeletal, with a beard in which there were streaks of gray. He wore a plain dark worsted suit and a farmer's dark Sunday hat. He could easily have passed for a farmer, except for the many weapons he carried: a Winchester rifle, a Sharps buffalo rifle, and two .44 Colts in hip holsters.

"Howdy. Long time no see." He shook hands with White Wolf, touched the brim of his hat to Rachel. "Miss Rachel."

"News?" White Wolf said anxiously. "What news?"

Dismounting, Gypsy said, "There's a posse on its way here, 'bout four hours behind me. Marshal Renfro and maybe sixty men."

"Four hours?" White Wolf asked. "You sure?"

"Seems you was spotted yesterday by somebody looking to collect that thousand-dollar reward."

"A thousand dollars?"

"You didn't know? You're worth a thousand, dead or alive."

"Let's talk inside," White Wolf said, "so we can be getting our things together."

Looping his sorrel's reins over the hitching post beside Big Red, Gypsy followed White Wolf and Rachel into the cabin.

Noticing the rawhide bag and canisters they were packing, he said, "I see you found my cache."

"Yours?" Rachel said, and stopped packing.

"We didn't know," White Wolf said. "If I'd known . . ."

"Forget it. In your place I'd've done the same thing." Gypsy took a tin-can cup from the shelf behind the stove and half filled it with lukewarm coffee. "But I come to help you get away if you want me to. And I was gonna try to talk you into letting Miss Rachel go. Though," he said to Rachel, "I gather you wasn't kidnapped."

"Kidnapped?" she said.

"The newspapers say Corby came to your house, killed your husband and two deputies, then dragged you away, kicking and screaming."

Rachel and White Wolf exchanged puzzled glances, and then she said, "That's not true. I killed Shelby, not Corby—White Wolf—and I'm here with him because it's where I want to be."

"White Wolf?" Gypsy said, and White Wolf told him that he had been on a vision quest and now had a new name. Gypsy nodded; then he said to Rachel, "It was your brother who gave out the story."

She said, "Dexter. Why would he lie?"

Gypsy shrugged. "Beats me, but he was the only eyewitness, and that's his story." After another sip of coffee he said, "Anyway, we'd better get going. We'll head south for the Red River, where I have another cache. Maybe we'll steal another horse along the way if we can do it without calling attention to ourselves. If not, I know some Comanches down on the Red who'll sell us a couple. From there we'll head out to Mexico."

"That's where we planned to go," White Wolf said.

"We'll go together then—if you want to. Have to travel mostly at night till we get to the Red. With you riding double, it'll take four, five nights of hard traveling. Maybe six."

320

"But why're you doing this for us?" White Wolf asked.

"I figured I owed you a favor for killing Shelby Hornbeck. But you might've saved y'self the trouble. He didn't have long to live anyhow."

"I've heard you have a list," Rachel said. "Was Shelby on it?"

"At the top."

"And Dexter? He's on it, too?"

Leading them out of the cabin, Gypsy said, "He's probably with the posse chasing us. I 'spect he'll have a little surprise in store for him if they catch up with us." Gypsy swung up into the saddle.

White Wolf put the saddlebags on Big Red. Then he secured the blankets behind the saddle as a riding pad for Rachel. Mounting, he reached down to catch her arm and swing her up behind him.

Gypsy said, "You up to this, Miss Rachel?"

She put her arms around White Wolf's waist and said, "I'm up to anything."

Gypsy tipped his head with admiration. "Let's go, then."

BECAUSE of the blowing sand, a person could walk through the Little Sahara without leaving tracks. Headed northwest, they crossed the Cimarron and entered the desert about midnight. To save the horses, they dismounted and walked, struggling and plunging through the deep sand. At White Wolf's instructions, Rachel held on to Big Red's tail and was half pulled through the dunes.

While still in the desert, they turned due south and came out on the Cimarron near Slocum's Crossing, where a wooden bridge spanned the river. They recrossed the river, mingling the hoofprints of their horses with those already in the dust, and then angled eastward across an open range.

"That ought to buy us a couple of days," Gypsy said.

About an hour after dawn they went into a dry gully to make a cold camp. They ate jerky and a few dried fruits, with Gypsy and White Wolf taking turns at lookout duty. The horses were allowed to forage, and Gypsy poured water from his canteen into his hat and let each horse have a swallow. They left at dark.

On the second day, Gypsy took his binoculars and climbed to the peak of a small ridge to have a look at the terrain behind them.

White Wolf and Rachel spread their bedroll under a mesquite tree.

"I been thinking," White Wolf said. "You're not a fugitive. You could wait for the posse, say you escaped, and go back to your old life."

Rachel crawled across the blanket and took both his hands in hers. "Listen to me, my love. I have no life to go back to. It's you and me now. All we've got is each other now—now and forever."

"But if they catch us . . . like I said, I won't be taken alive."

"And I wouldn't want to live," she said without hesitation.

On the third night of traveling they crossed the South Canadian River; on the fourth night, the Washita. On and on, until the horses began to show signs of exhaustion.

"We'll let 'em rest up after we get to the Red," Gypsy said, gnawing on a piece of jerky. He and White Wolf were hunkered down on a creek bank, filling their canteens. "And we'll treat ourselves to a hot meal. I got a pretty good cache in a cave down there."

"What cave?" White Wolf asked with more than idle curiosity.

"Indians call it the Cave of the Ancient Ones. You know it?"

"Know it! That's where I had my vision quest."

"That so?" he said. "Well, it's always been a sacred place for Indians. With any luck we'll be there by day after tomorrow."

When Gypsy went to make camp, White Wolf and Rachel bathed in the creek. They swam, splashed each other, and embraced.

AN OLD wrangler from Fort Sill called Coot was searching for some runaway army horses when he came across the fresh hoofprints left by White Wolf's and Gypsy's horses. He followed the tracks to Beaver Creek, where he saw Rachel and White Wolf cavorting in the water. He made a fast ride back to Fort Sill.

A reporter from the Oklahoma City *Daily Democrat* was at Fort Sill at the time. After hearing Coot's story, he immediately wired a dispatch to his newspaper, saying that the renegade Cheyenne killer and Mrs. Shelby Hornbeck—"reportedly a kidnap victim"— had been spotted about twenty miles from Fort Sill.

The word that Corby and Rachel had been spotted reached U.S. Marshal Silas Renfro in the town of Woodward, where he and his posse, having lost the fugitives' trail in the Little Sahara, had been waiting for just such a break. The marshal loaded his posse onto a train—the horses in livestock cars, the men on flatcars—and headed for Fort Sill. Among the posse were Sheriff Alva Harriman and Deputy Dexter Bingham, both of whom were in the small group of posse leaders who met in the Fort Sill office of Deputy U.S. Marshal Clovis Pinkard. Coot, the old wrangler who had spotted Corby and Rachel, showed the posse leaders on a map where he had seen them. "But," Coot said, "I'm considerable suspicious that the woman ain't being held agin her will."

Dexter snapped, "Whatever my sister's doing, she's being forced."

Coot tipped his head to Dexter. "If you say so."

"There's two more posses on the way," Deputy Pinkard said to fill the strained silence. Tapping his finger on the map, he continued. "They're gonna move up here, where Beaver Creek empties into the Red. They'll make sure the fugitives don't cross the river into Texas. We got 'em boxed."

"Looks like," said Marshal Renfro, idly fingering his long, drooping frontiersman's mustache. "Well then, let's go get 'em."

ON THE morning of the fifth day, Gypsy, from his vantage point on a rocky ridge, saw through his binoculars a small thin cloud of dust rising in the distance. When White Wolf came to relieve him, Gypsy handed him the binoculars and pointed toward the dust.

"Posse?" White Wolf asked, looking through the binoculars.

"Whoever it is, they're coming at a pretty good clip. Fresh horses, likely."

"Wouldn't be Renfro's posse, then," White Wolf said. "By now their horses'd be as jaded as ours."

"Maybe," Gypsy said, taking the binoculars back. "But if we was spotted along the way, it might be a new posse. If that's the case, there'll be other posses showing up pretty soon."

"There." White Wolf pointed to the east, where another cloud of dust had begun to rise from the land, maybe ten miles distant.

Gypsy trained the binoculars on the dust. This time he could see the men and horses of the second posse as they rode. They didn't seem to be soldiers or Indians.

"Looks like another posse, all right. Big one. I reckon we gonna have to make a run for it."

No longer concerned about being seen, they now kept to the open roads and trails as they rode toward the Red River's Horseshoe Bend.

When they crossed over Kiowa ridge, they stopped behind some boulders to give the horses a rest. Gypsy scanned the country behind them with his binoculars. He watched the two posses come together. Combined, they numbered sixty or sixty-five men. He glanced back at their two lathered and fatigued horses. Neither of them seemed to have enough strength left to outrun the posse's fresh horses for another ten miles, which was about how far it was to the Cave of the Ancient Ones, where they could at least make a stand.

"Well, we better get going," Gypsy said. "To beat 'em, we'll have to ride flat out all the way. Think your horse can do it?"

"He'll give it everything he's got," White Wolf said.

They began the long run off the ridge down into the Red River basin, following an old Indian trail, with Gypsy in the lead on the sorrel and Big Red close behind. Rachel, with her arms around White Wolf's waist, hung on tightly as they plunged through gullies and ravines, the horses' hooves clattering on rocks.

Once, they came around a corner and almost collided with a Mexican on a burro coming from the opposite direction. Had the Mexican been riding a horse, Gypsy would have stopped and taken it, but a burro would do them no good, so they rode on.

The Mexican had hardly recovered from the near collision when he began to hear the thundering hoofbeats of many, many horses galloping toward him. This time he rode the burro off the trail.

Marshal Renfro raised his hand and brought the posse to a halt. He had one of the Arapaho trackers fetch the Mexican. He asked the Mexican if he had seen two riders pass this way.

"*Sí, sí, señor. Dos caballos. Tres jinetes.*"

At first Marshal Renfro thought the Mexican was merely confused. "*Three* riders? Two horses and *three* riders?" He held up his fingers so the Mexican would be sure of the numbers.

"*Sí, sí.*" The Mexican held up his fingers to show that he, too, could count. "Two horses, three riders."

When Marshal Renfro asked for a description of the riders, the Mexican said the one riding single on a sorrel was *un negro*.

Marshal Renfro's eyes narrowed menacingly. "And the other two? An Indian and a white woman? Riding double on a bay?"

The Mexican wasn't so sure. Possibly a white woman, *sí*.

Renfro murmured, "I wonder . . ."

WHEN the posse was within two miles of catching up with them and coming on fast, Gypsy reined the sorrel to a stop. They were about a mile from Red River now.

"You two go on. I'm going to slow 'em down some." He dismounted and reached for his buffalo rifle.

White Wolf was reluctant. "If there's going to be fighting . . ."

"Ain't gonna be no fighting. You go on. Head for the cave. I'll be along directly."

They rode on.

From a saddlebag Gypsy took a buckskin bag filled with cartridges and jerked the binoculars from their case. He hurried to an overlook. The posse was about a mile and a half away when it first came into view around a heavily wooded spur of Kiowa ridge.

He pushed the aiming stick into the ground, rested the long barrel of the buffalo rifle in the fork of the stick, and lying prone on the green grass, waited, watching through the binoculars.

Which would it be, Sheriff Harriman or Dexter? He would only get one good shot.

He set the sights on the buffalo rifle for four thousand yards, took aim at Sheriff Harriman, and waited—waited for that optimal moment. He took a deep breath and gently squeezed the trigger.

Sheriff Harriman, riding abreast of Marshal Renfro in the front of the posse, toppled backward before they even heard the shot.

As panic and confusion gripped the front ranks of the posse, Marshal Renfro shouted, "Cover! Take cover!"

The men scattered, looking for a rock or a bush to hide behind.

Dexter was almost babbling. "That was a"—trying to get Renfro's attention, trying to make him understand—"a buffalo rifle."

"Why, that must be nearly a mile away," Deputy Pinkard said.

"Gypsy Smith," Dexter cried. He had been riding directly alongside Sheriff Harriman, so Gypsy could just as easily have killed him as the sheriff. "Don't you see, Marshal? It has to be Gypsy Smith."

WHITE Wolf and Rachel were riding west along the Red River's northern escarpment when he saw the riders coming fast, about thirty or forty of them, widely scattered.

"Another posse," he said. "And they've spotted us."

White Wolf pulled Big Red to a stop near the foot of the scree leading up to the mouth of the cave. He slid to the ground and helped Rachel off the horse and jerked the saddlebags off.

"Up there! Take these and run for the cave." He flung the saddlebags to her. She caught them and scampered up the scree.

He took the .30-06 rifle from its scabbard, then reached under the horse, unfastened the cinch, pulled the saddle off, and said, "Go on, Big Red, you're free!" He slapped him on the shoulder.

But the sound of the slap was almost simultaneous with the splat-thunk sound made by a bullet hitting Big Red. Big Red screamed and staggered sideways toward White Wolf, then tottered and fell.

"Damn you," White Wolf said to the oncoming riders. With bullets ricocheting all around, he began scrambling up to the cave.

He got within a few feet of the cave entrance when his right leg was knocked from under him. He fell sprawling amid the rocks, and when he tried to get up and go on, he couldn't move his leg. Blood streamed down beneath his buckskin pants.

When she saw him fall, Rachel, who had reached the mouth of the cave, started down the incline toward him, but he shouted, "Go back! Go back!" and she stopped.

He leaned against the rocks, brought his rifle to his shoulder, and fired at the advancing possemen, knocking a man out of the saddle. But then another one toppled from his horse without White Wolf's firing another shot.

The shot came from somewhere above him. Gypsy, lying prone on the top of Medicine Bluff, was firing down on the posse with the big buffalo rifle. The possemen were thrown into panic and pinned down by the deadly accuracy and range of the terrible-sounding gun.

White Wolf dragged himself the rest of the way up the scree to the mouth of the cave, which was protected by boulders that made a perfect parapet. Safely inside, he sat with his back resting against the boulders. Rachel fell on her knees beside him.

"Cut the pant leg," White Wolf said, handing her his knife.

Rachel slit the blood-soaked leg of his buckskin pants to above his knee, exposing the wound in the calf of his leg. She used his belt as a tourniquet just above the knee.

Gypsy, carrying the buffalo rifle, leaped into the cave and hunkered down behind the parapet of boulders. "If that's the best those buggers can shoot, we got nothing to worry about." Then, seeing White Wolf's leg, he said, "Ah. I see you wasn't so lucky. How bad is it? Let's have a look."

Kneeling beside him and inspecting the wound, Gypsy said, "I'll get some medicine and some sticks for a splint, case it's broke."

Leaning his rifle against a boulder, Gypsy went to the pile of rocks where he had left his cache, which had a few medical supplies. He and Rachel washed the wound and bandaged it with strips torn from her blouse. Using sticks and rawhide, they made a splint.

Then they began to hear the rumble of hoofbeats and the faraway sounds of men's voices. Gypsy glanced over the parapet to see the possemen. "Well, that must make about a hundred of 'em altogether. What d'you think about them odds, *navestax?*"

"What can we do?" White Wolf asked.

"Do? Well, first we make us a cooking fire and have us a hot meal. What d'you fancy? Pork 'n' beans? Canned stew? We got a week maybe. As long as the food lasts anyway. We ain't in much danger of getting shot by them. Hell, two of us could hold off an army from up here." He paused for a thoughtful moment and then added, "Unless, of course, the army had a cannon. . . ."

RENFRO turned to Deputy Pinkard. "Put a cordon of men around that cave so they can't slip out." He turned to another of his nearby deputies. "Harry, I want you to ride to the telegraph office over at Waurika Station and send some telegrams.

327

"The first telegram goes to School Superintendent John Maxwell at Agency. Tell him we got his daughter and her kidnapper trapped down here. Tell him he might want to come on down here.

"Then send one to the commanding officer at Fort Sill. Tell him we got Gypsy Smith and that renegade redskin Corby White trapped in Medicine Bluff Cave. Tell him I'd be obliged if he'd send me down a cannon quick as he can."

Chapter Fourteen

*I*T WAS a little before five the following afternoon when Maxwell reached the river. He had hitched a ride in a buckboard bringing supplies to the possemen. By then a throng of excited and even festive people had gathered behind a long sandy ridge that protected them against rifle fire from the cave.

As Maxwell's buckboard was approaching, another group of riders could be seen coming in from the west, a column of men in dark blue uniforms, riding two abreast. Following them came a horse-drawn cannon and a canvas-covered supply wagon. A cheer went up from a few of the lawmen and spectators when they first saw the troopers approaching, but the cheers died quickly when one of them with binoculars said, "Hey, they sent them nigger troops."

Dexter went out to meet Maxwell and said by way of a greeting, "We's beginning to wonder if you'd get here in time."

"How's Rachel?" Maxwell said.

"Far's we know, she's all right. That teacher's pet of yours got shot in the leg, but they're still up in the cave, all three of 'em."

"Mr. Maxwell," Renfro said, "glad you could make it."

He led Maxwell to a lookout point at a nearby crevice in the sandhill, from where they could see the opening of the cave. "That's where they're holed up, and there's no way out. Think you can talk that renegade redskin into surrendering? Or at least letting your daughter go?"

"I can try."

"Well, I'll give you till we get the cannon set up, and if they choose not to surrender, they can just kiss tomorrow good-bye."

Nettled by Renfro's cold-bloodedness, Maxwell said, "Even if my daughter's still there?"

Renfro gave him a stern look. "Mr. Maxwell, we got evidence that your daughter's not being held against her will. Maybe she began as a kidnap victim—*maybe*—but now she's acting more like an accomplice. Still, we're willing to hold our fire till you've had a chance to talk to her, see if you can get her to come out."

The approaching column of buffalo soldiers was drawing near. At its head rode Captain Beauregard Pierce—who sat easy on a big dun gelding—dressed in his gold-braided uniform. When he signaled with a raised hand, his first sergeant called, "Column, halt!"

"Marshal Renfro," Captain Pierce said as a greeting.

Renfro nodded. "Captain."

Speaking from the lofty height of his horse, Captain Pierce said, "We brought the howitzer." He peered over the top of the sandhill toward Medicine Bluff. "That's the cave?"

"That's it."

He turned to his first sergeant. "Bring up the gun."

Maxwell was puzzled when Dexter took him aside and said in an undertone, "Listen, tell Rachel that everything's going to be all right as long as she keeps her mouth shut about what really happened at Kingstree that night. Understand? She don't have to worry none about going to prison if she does what I tell her."

"What d'you mean? What did happen?"

"Never mind. You just tell her—"

He was interrupted by Renfro, who identified Maxwell to Captain Pierce. "He's gonna see if he can talk 'em into surrendering. How long'll it take you to get the cannon set up?"

Captain Pierce glanced at the howitzer. "Fifteen minutes."

Turning back to Maxwell, Renfro said, "All right. I'll give you thirty minutes to see what you can do."

"Thirty minutes?" Maxwell asked scornfully. "Hell, I can hardly walk up there and back in that time. I want at least an hour."

Renfro pulled a watch from his serge trousers and tapped it with a forefinger. "Five fifteen. You got an hour."

"LOOKS LIKE YOUR FATHER'S coming," Gypsy said over his shoulder.

Rachel dashed from the campsite to the parapet. "It is!" she cried. "It's Daddy."

White Wolf sat against the wall, his splinted leg stretched out in front of him. He motioned to Gypsy.

Gypsy went over to where White Wolf sat.

"Listen," White Wolf grunted, "Mr. Maxwell's gonna try to get us to surrender. Help him convince Rachel to go, will you? No need for her to die here with us."

"You're sure that's what's gonna happen, are you? That we're not gonna get out of here alive? You don't believe in miracles?"

"Like what?" White Wolf leaned on the damp rock wall.

"Who knows?" Gypsy gazed at the ancient picture carvings on the cave wall and said, "You might pray to those Indian gods of yours for a little miracle. Barring that, though, *navestax*, I 'spect this's where me and you come to the end of the trail."

"HELLO, the cave," Maxwell called when he was near the opening. "I'm coming in." He dropped down behind the parapet of boulders and found himself facing Rachel. With her ash-soiled face and uncombed hair, she looked like the ragamuffin she had been as a child.

He opened his arms to her, and she flung herself into his embrace. "Daddy!" She clung to him like a child. "Oh, Daddy, I'm so glad you came."

He held her close in silence, brushing his hand over her tangled hair, patting her shoulders.

"Come," she said then, pulling back and trying to smile. "Come see Corby. Only he's not Corby anymore. He's White Wolf now."

As Maxwell and White Wolf shook hands, White Wolf said, "Good to see you again, *nihoe*"—Cheyenne for "my father."

"I, too, *naha*," Maxwell said, using the Cheyenne word for "my son." Then he shook hands with Gypsy. "It's been a long time."

"Ain't it, though? Over four years. I hear you married Miss Eula, and that she's pretty as a picture these days."

"How is Eula?" Rachel asked.

"Just fine. She's saying special prayers for you. But I don't know if prayers are going to be enough to . . . Listen to me, all of you. They just brought a cannon in from Fort Sill. They've told me to tell you that you're going to have to surrender or you're going to die. And you've only got a few minutes to make your choice."

"Choice!" Gypsy snorted. "The only choice for me is to die here today or by a hangman's noose tomorrow. And I'm sure not gonna give them Klansmen the satisfaction of seeing me swing. Now I'll get back to lookout duty—let you talk to these two alone."

"And you?" Maxwell asked White Wolf. "Can I convince you to give yourself up? You don't have a chance if you stay here."

"They'll hang me. You know it. And you know, too, that a Cheyenne who dies by hanging can never enter the Spirit Land."

"Maybe in court . . . maybe we could make a case."

"No. I killed those two deputies, and they think I killed Hornbeck, too. I don't stand a chance, and you know it."

With a flicker of desperate hope in her eyes, Rachel said, "I could tell them the truth, that I killed Shelby, that it was an accident."

"You?" Maxwell said. "*You* killed—"

"I didn't mean to," she said.

"It wouldn't matter," White Wolf said. "They'd just send you to prison and hang me anyway." As if that matter were settled, he took Rachel's hand. "But you—you must go."

"No!" She shook her head. "I'm staying with you."

Maxwell took a deep breath. "Now listen to me, Rachel. Corby's right. There's no reason for you to die. As far as the officials know, Corby killed Shelby, and as long as Dexter sticks to his story that you were kidnapped, they'll never know any different. Rachel, you're young. You've got a long life ahead of you."

She lowered her head. "If he dies, I wouldn't want to live."

After a moment of silence White Wolf picked up the coffeepot and slowly poured the water over the splinted and bandaged wound on his leg. "Helps keep it cool," he explained, and handed the pot to Rachel. "Get me some more water, would you?"

Rachel took the pot and darted toward the sump hole in the back of the cave. White Wolf turned to Maxwell and said in a voice barely above a whisper, "Give me a minute or two with her, and then when I tell you, take her away. By force if you have to."

Maxwell placed a hand on White Wolf's forearm, pressed it gratefully. "Bless you for that, Corby. Can't I also convince you?"

"No. And stop calling me Corby. My name's White Wolf, and it's what you must call me in the time we have left. White Wolf is the name the Spirits will know me by. I spent just about all my life being confused about who I was. I wouldn't want it to be that way throughout eternity."

As Rachel was returning with the water, Gypsy announced from the parapet that a band of Comanches was approaching. Maxwell hurried to the parapet to get a look. They were riding at a canter, headed directly toward the cannon.

White Wolf took the pot of water from Rachel and set it aside and took her hands in his. "Come here. Sit. I want to talk to you."

She took a seat beside him. "I know what you're going to say, and I don't want to hear it." She looked down at their clasped hands.

"But you have to, Rachel, for my sake as well as your own. "Listen to me. Do you *want* to die?"

"No," she blurted. "Of course not. But I don't want you to die either."

"But I have no choice. You do. And as long as you live, as long as you love me, the part of me that's within you will go on living. Don't you see?"

She was crying. "But I *can't*. I can't just leave you here to die."

"Yes, you can. Do it for me. Go on now. Say good-bye and go."

She threw her arms around his neck. "I can't! I can't!"

"Please, Rachel. Do it for me. Live for me."

He signaled to Maxwell, who left the parapet and came to put his hands on Rachel's shoulders. He was prepared to pull her away by whatever force was necessary, but to his surprise he found that she didn't resist. There was something like resignation in the way she released White Wolf, in the way she took his hand and kissed the back of it as she said, "I love you," and then pressed the back of his hand to her cheek. "I've always loved you. I always will."

"And I've loved you all the days of my life," he said.

Maxwell pulled her gently to her feet. "Come on now, Rachel."

She allowed herself to be turned away. Limply she followed Maxwell's guidance.

Maxwell turned back to White Wolf, who was struggling to stand. "Good-bye, *naha*."

"Good-bye, *nihoe*. You've been a good friend to me all my life. For that, *haho naheto*."

Maxwell spoke the traditional Cheyenne good-bye to one who is about to die and travel the Hanging Road to the Spirit Land: "*Nimeaseoxzheme*—may your journey be a good one." And then he turned and strode back to the parapet. There he briskly shook hands with Gypsy. "Good-bye, Gypsy, and—*nimeaseoxzheme*."

"Thank you, and you, too, when your time comes. And good-bye to you, Miss Rachel," Gypsy said, touching the brim of his hat. "You take good care of yourself now, y'hear?"

"Good-bye, Gypsy," she said. "I'll never forget you."

Maxwell took her arm and gently nudged her forward. "Come on now. We're out of time."

"HERE they are," called one of the men on the ridge of the sandhill, announcing the arrival of Maxwell and Rachel.

They came through the crevice in the sandhill, Maxwell with his arm around Rachel's shoulders. As soon as they were safely behind the sandhill, a swarm of reporters surrounded them. They said, "Were you a captive, Mrs. Hornbeck? How have you been treated?"

It was Dexter who took the situation in hand. "Get away from her. Step aside." He took Rachel's arm and guided her toward Marshal Renfro, who gave her an icy look and asked, "You all right, Mrs. Hornbeck?"

Rachel said nothing. She seemed to be in a state of shock.

"She's all right," Dexter said. "She just needs to rest for a little while. Ain't that right, Rachel?"

She didn't appear to have heard, but Renfro got on with the business at hand by saying to Maxwell, "Well? What's the report from the cave? They're not going to surrender?"

While Maxwell gave his report, Dexter hurried Rachel to the army supply wagon that stood a few paces behind the cannon.

In the distance a drum had started. The Comanches had begun their medicine dance for White Wolf and Gypsy.

Dexter helped Rachel into the wagon. Beneath its canvas cover they sat on crates, facing each other. "You all right?" he asked.

She looked at him for a moment with vacant eyes and said, "Why're you doing this? Why're you being so nice to me?"

In a whispery voice he said, "I'm gonna be nice to you from now on, Rachel. We're gonna be nice to each other from now on."

But she wasn't gulled. "Why'd you lie about who killed Shelby?"

"Lie? Lie? Listen, I'm gonna tell you exactly what happened that night in the barn, and it's exactly what you have to tell anybody else who asks about it. You hear?"

"Why? What do you care?"

"Why, can't you figure it out? You're a very rich widow."

She gave him a look of smoldering hatred. "Damn you. I should've let him kill you."

INSIDE the cave Gypsy was crouched down behind the parapet of boulders. White Wolf had resumed his seat on the ledge a few yards in from the cave entrance. From his saddlebags he had taken the small containers of paints and proceeded—slowly, ritualistically— to paint designs on his face.

"Going out in style, are you, *navestax?*" Gypsy asked, though he knew the tradition. It called for a warrior's face to be painted before burial, so the Spirits would know that he had died a warrior.

When he had finished with the paints, White Wolf secured the wolfskin to his back, like a cape, and pulled the wolf's head over his own, like a hood. Now he was ready to sing his death song. But first he said, "Gypsy, I'm sorry that you're here on account of me. If you hadn't come to warn us, you could've got away."

Gypsy shrugged. "If they didn't get me today, they'd get me tomorrow." Then he grunted with a sort of bitter amusement. "You know the only thing I regret? I won't be taking Dexter with me. Complete the list. Yes, sir, if I could just get a shot at Dexter, I'd die a happy man." He raised his head up above the boulders to see what was happening below. "Guess you can't win 'em all."

The buffalo soldiers had the cannon ready to fire. It was apparent that Gypsy wasn't going to get his chance at Dexter.

"And the worst thing about it all," Gypsy said, "it's gonna be colored men who kill me, and their commander is my old pal Captain Beauregard Pierce himself." He snorted. "He's gonna kill a black man on orders from a white man so he'll be a credit to his race."

"WELL, Captain? You ready to fire?" Marshal Renfro said.

"Anytime," Captain Pierce said. "Get your men off the bluff."

To a nearby deputy, Renfro said, "Send word over to the men in the cordon. We're going to fire the cannon."

Within the supply wagon, Rachel clamped her hands over her ears, trying to shut out the multitudinous sounds of a bizarre celebration: the crackling rifle fire, the shouts and laughter and curses of drunken men, the distant sounds of the Comanches chanting and dancing to throbbing drums. But then came the voice of the gunnery sergeant, "Fire!" And suddenly the air was rent with a sound like that of a thunderclap.

GYPSY saw the puff of smoke. A second later he heard the explosion, then the long screeching sound of the oncoming projectile. "Here it comes!" He dropped behind the boulders.

The projectile hit the face of the bluff about twenty yards to the east of the mouth of the cave. The earth shook; a geyser of rocks and dirt spurted from the bluff and cascaded down.

Inside the cave, the walls shook and rumbled. Rocks fell crashing from the ceiling; dust spewed through cracks in the wall.

"Getting zeroed in," Gypsy said. "Next one'll probably be a bracketing shot on the other side. It'll be the third or fourth one that gets us."

He got up, picked up his hat, slapped it against his leg, then put it on and adjusted it squarely on his head as he walked back to White Wolf. "Well, *navestax,* if you don't mind me leaving you here, I think I'll go out fighting."

White Wolf nodded. "I'd join you if I could."

Gypsy held out his hand. "It's been good knowing you."

"You, too, Gypsy." They shook hands. "Who knows? Maybe we'll make the journey to the Spirit Land together."

"Maybe so. If you Indians are right, maybe we will. If the Christians are right, though, I 'spect I'll see you in hell."

Then they heard the second boom of the cannon. They froze for the few seconds that it took the projectile to hurtle toward them. This time it struck on the west side of the cave, about ten yards from the opening. Again the earth shook and a great cascade of rocks and boulders rumbled down from the bluff.

The concussion from the blast knocked Gypsy down, but neither he nor White Wolf was hurt. Gypsy got up and brushed himself off.

"Well, they're almost on target now, looks like. The third one'll likely be it. I better get out there while I can." As he made his way through the fallen rocks toward the opening, he pulled the .44 Colt from the right holster. At the parapet he turned to White Wolf. "What's that the Cheyenne warriors used to say when they were going into battle? '*Hoka hey!* It's a good day to die'?"

And without waiting for an answer, he touched the muzzle of the .44 to the brim of his hat as a parting salute; then, pulling the other .44 from his left holster so that he had a gun in each hand, he leaped up onto the parapet.

He stood on the boulders for a moment, in full view, his arms raised high into the air, and then he yelled at the top of his voice, "*Hoka hey,* you sonsabitches! It's a good day to die!"

DEXTER pulled Rachel's hands away from her ears, saying, "Listen to me now. We've got to get our stories straight—you were protecting Shelby, and Corby took the gun away from you and shot—"

When the cannon fired the second time, something snapped in Rachel. She jumped down from the wagon and dashed toward the cannon, pummeling the four black soldiers who were operating the gun, crying, "Stop it!"

Maxwell rushed to Rachel, but it was Dexter who grabbed her. "Let her go," Maxwell said to Dexter.

Dexter ignored him. Angrily he pulled Rachel back toward the supply wagon, holding her arms pinned behind her back while he pulled a pair of handcuffs from his belt.

Maxwell grabbed his arm. "Leave her alone. I'll take care of her."

Dexter shoved Maxwell away, manhandling Rachel again. So disdainful was he of Maxwell that he was taken completely by surprise when Maxwell, recovering from the shove, jerked Dexter around and brought a fist up into his solar plexus with all his strength. Dexter clutched his abdomen, gasping for air.

"Leave her alone, I said."

Dexter stepped back out of Maxwell's reach, staring at him with eyes widened by fear and respect as well as surprise.

Maxwell put his arms around her. "Rachel, there's nothing you can do."

Then his attention was diverted as someone shouted, "It's Gypsy Smith. He's come out."

Gypsy stood on the lip of the cave in full view of everyone, his arms raised, as an expectant hush fell over the gathered throng. All rifles were trained on him. Then they heard him cry, *"Hoka hey!"*

Gypsy fired two shots from his .44 Colts before the hundred or more rifles opened up on him. He pitched forward and fell, tumbling and sliding down the scree, and came to a stop about one third of the way down the bluff.

"Hold your fire!" Renfro shouted, and the rapidity of the firing quickly diminished, leaving only an occasional shot from some drunk who wanted to be able to say that he had shot Gypsy Smith.

"Well," Renfro said in a coldly gloating voice, "that's that. Maybe we should have a moment of silence for the passing of the great Gypsy Smith." But there was real admiration in his voice when he added, "No matter what the color of his skin, gunfighters don't come any better than he was." He began rolling a cigarette, and to Dexter, who had joined the group to witness Gypsy's death, he said slyly, "Well, Deputy Bingham, I reckon you'll be able to sleep lots better now."

Dexter didn't answer, but he did look very relieved.

After Renfro put the pucker string between his teeth and pulled the tobacco sack closed, he said, "Well, Captain? What d'you say we get the rest of this over with and go home?"

Captain Pierce was on the point of ordering his gun crew to fire the third round from the cannon when they began to hear a sound, a very peculiar sound, coming from the cave—someone singing. The cave acted as a sort of gigantic megaphone, amplifying the sounds with its echoes. It seemed as if the singing were coming from the earth itself.

"What the devil is that?" someone asked.

"Singing!" someone exclaimed incredulously.

"His death song," Captain Pierce explained.

A hush began slowly to settle upon all the men at the scene.

"Well?" Renfro said.to Captain Pierce.

"We'll give him time to sing his death song."

When the death song ended, Captain Pierce turned and nodded sharply to his gunnery sergeant, who whirled on the gun crew, raised his right hand, and then brought it down. "Fire!"

For the third time the roar of the cannon momentarily deafened the bystanders. Everyone stood motionless for the three seconds it took for the screaming projectile to reach the bluff and hurtle directly into the mouth of the cave. The sound of the explosion was an earth-shattering roar as the mountain collapsed in upon itself.

The Cave of the Ancient Ones had ceased to exist.

POSSEMEN, Klansmen, spectators, and Indians began streaming closer to look at the damage done by the cannon. Marshal Renfro dispatched a group of deputies to recover Gypsy Smith's body. He stayed behind to question Rachel, though his questions seemed more in the nature of a formality. "Just a few confusing points to clear up" was how he put it.

"What d'you want to know?" Dexter asked, hovering at Rachel's side, protective, with a lawyerlike alertness.

Ignoring Dexter, Renfro said to Rachel, "I want to know about Mr. Hornbeck—how he was shot and under what circumstances."

"I told you," Dexter said. "The Indian took the pistol away from Rachel and killed Mr. Hornbeck with it."

338

"After he'd killed the bodyguards with Hornbeck's shotgun," Renfro prompted.

"That's right," Dexter said. "She had gone into the house to get the pistol, because the Indian was holding us at gunpoint."

"Deputy, haven't you got something to do?"

"I didn't mean to interfere, but she's obviously in no condition yet to answer questions, and as long as I know the answers . . ."

It was true that Rachel, still in a stupor of shock and despair, seemed incapable of responding. Renfro sighed and said, "Well, how about a simple yes or no?" After a slight pause he added, "Is it true what Deputy Bingham says?"

To Dexter's surprise and great relief, Rachel finally broke the surface of her stupor by saying in a very small voice, "Yes."

Renfro pursed his lips beneath his drooping mustache for a moment, pondering some grave decision, and then in a conciliatory voice said, "Well, I reckon that about clears it up." He made it sound as if he had never entertained a suspicion about her. After all, if Renfro couldn't prove that she was at least an accomplice in her husband's murder, then she was, as of that moment, the inheritor of the bulk of the Hornbeck estate, which made her one of the wealthiest women in Oklahoma. It would be very injudicious to make an enemy of her.

Then he said to Maxwell, "I'll get you and Mrs. Hornbeck a buckboard to the nearest train station."

"Thank you," Maxwell said with more politeness than sincerity, "but we've accepted an offer from Captain Pierce to ride in the supply wagon to Comanche Station. By the way, what's going to happen to Gypsy Smith's body?"

"Oh, we'll take it back to Guthrie, turn it over to the coroner."

"If nobody claims it, I'd like to know, so I can. I wouldn't want him to be buried in a pauper's grave somewhere."

"Oh, I'm sure them niggers over in Freedom'll claim it. I'm sure they'll give him a real hero's burial."

Dexter and Marshal Renfro had a picture taken together, standing on opposite sides of Gypsy's body, their rifles cradled in their arms, like big-game hunters displaying a prize trophy.

It was almost dark by the time the mules were hitched to the supply wagon, and Rachel and Maxwell climbed inside for the bumpy ride over rutted wagon trails to Comanche Station. Maxwell used his coat to make a padded seat on one of the supply crates and sat close enough to put his arm around Rachel's shoulders if she should need comfort or support. But for a long while they rode without touching and in a strained silence. Finally Rachel, wiping her tears with the handkerchief Maxwell had given her, asked him, "Do you blame me?"

"Blame you? For what?"

"For lying. For agreeing with Dexter's lies, anyway. For playing the innocent victim."

"Nobody could blame you, my dear, for saving yourself."

"But I didn't do it for myself," she protested.

Maxwell puzzled over that remark for a moment, but before he could ask for an explanation, she said, "Do you think White Wolf would?"

"Blame you?" After a moment's silence he said, "You did exactly what he wanted you to do."

"I didn't do it for myself, though," she said again.

"What do you mean? If not for yourself . . . ?"

"For the child," she said. "I did it for the child."

"The child?" he asked, but it was not really a question, because he knew the answer.

ABOUT THE AUTHOR

"You ever heard that Waylon Jennings song 'Ramblin' Man'?" Clancy Carlile asked a visitor recently. "Well, I guess that's me. My father was one, and his father was, too."

Carlile's paternal grandfather, of Scotch-Irish descent, participated in an Oklahoma land rush, riding on an old mule with no saddle. He got a parcel of land but lost it in a poker game. Later he married a Cherokee woman—Carlile's grandmother-to-be—who inherited a one-hundred-sixty-acre spread, but that, too, was eventually lost in a poker game. Carlile's father, a sharecropper in Oklahoma, moved out to California with the Okies—"*Grapes of Wrath* stuff," Carlile calls it.

After serving in the army in Korea, Carlile went to college on the GI Bill. Before graduating, he published his first book, *As I Was Young and Easy.* A later novel, *Honkytonk Man,* was made into a movie, directed by and starring Clint Eastwood. Carlile wrote *Children of the Dust* over five years, while living in the Cascade Mountains of Oregon and in Tucson, Phoenix, St. Augustine, Captiva, Mendocino, and, finally, Las Vegas, which, for the time being anyway, is about the closest thing to home for this ramblin' man.

Clancy Carlile

MRS. POLLIFAX
and the
LION KILLER

Dorothy Gilman

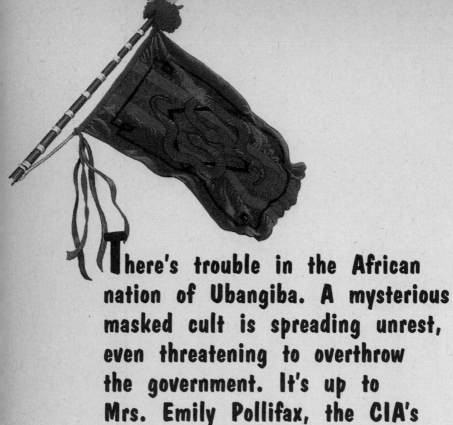

There's trouble in the African nation of Ubangiba. A mysterious masked cult is spreading unrest, even threatening to overthrow the government. It's up to Mrs. Emily Pollifax, the CIA's agent extraordinaire, to uncover the all-too-human face behind the dangerous mask.

1

"SHE mustn't go alone," Cyrus was saying. "Absolutely not. It could be dangerous for Kadi. We both know that."

Mrs. Pollifax looked at her husband, seated on the couch with his left leg heavily encased in plaster and propped on a stool, and she didn't know whether to laugh or to cry. "Cyrus, I can't possibly leave you and go with her," she told him. "Your cast won't be removed for eight more days, you need help with your crutches, you can't drive, you can't manage cooking or shopping."

"She mustn't go alone," he repeated firmly. "No matter what appeals have come from Ubangiba and young Sammat, she mustn't go alone."

Mrs. Pollifax acknowledged this with a sigh. "What's to be done, then? We've practically adopted Kadi. Or did she adopt us?" she asked with a smile. "She's spent every weekend with us when not at art school, and of course I feel responsible. She's like family."

"Like quicksilver," Cyrus said. "Eager. Curious. Can't have any harm come to her. Those three men . . ."

He didn't finish his sentence, but he didn't need to. Mrs. Pollifax had met Kadi Hopkirk eight months ago, spending an extraordinary week together that ended with the CIA whisking them off to Africa, to the country of Ubangiba. It was a relationship that Mrs. Pollifax had assumed would end when she and Kadi parted, but much to her delight it had only begun.

They had known Kadi was an orphan, but they'd been unprepared for the nightmares that had awakened them on a number of the weekends she spent with them. Kadi had never cared to speak of what she'd seen that day when her parents were executed at their mission station during one of Ubangiba's coups, but over the months of knowing her, Mrs. Pollifax and Cyrus had managed to extract from her several small details. Kadi had been returning on foot to her father's clinic with a bag of salt when she heard gunfire and her father's nurse, Radia, screaming. She'd stood behind a screen of bushes at the edge of the compound to see what was happening. "There were three men," Kadi had said, tight-lipped.

Cyrus had said, "Did Radia know who they were?"

Kadi had shaken her head. "They caught and blindfolded her before—before—"

"Then did the three men see *you?*" Cyrus had asked.

Kadi had shrugged, saying, "I hid, and by night the arrangements had all been made to smuggle me out of Ubangiba."

Now Kadi had announced that she had to go back in response to Sammat's call for help. But both Mrs. Pollifax and Cyrus had wondered if those three men had survived the brutal reign of President Simoko, which followed the coup, and—if they were still alive—what might happen when Kadi returned.

Cyrus interrupted his wife's troubled thoughts to say, "Mrs. Lupacik! Here last month when you had the flu. She could move in, take over. Strong as an ox. Professional nurse, too. Good cook, and frankly, m'dear, a vacation would do you a world of good."

A vacation, thought Mrs. Pollifax with amusement, when Sammat is in trouble and has sent for Kadi for support and help?

A troubled African country, Ubangiba, she reflected, small and impoverished. Kadi had grown up there with Sammat, who happened to be the grandson of King Zammat VIII; he had been sent as a boy to her father's mission school to study and be trained for college abroad. In those days it had not been an impoverished country. It was after the king's death that Ubangiba had been looted and despoiled by coups and atrocities. Sammat's father was the first leader to be assassinated; he had been succeeded by President-for-Life Chinyata, until he in turn was assassinated in the coup by President-for-Life Simoko. It was during this period that Sammat had been sent off to Yale University, apparently placed on hold by Simoko's government for some future use.

When President-for-Life Simoko had been assassinated, the chiefs of the Shambi and the Soto tribes had pleaded with Sammat to become *mfumo,* or chieftain, and restore heart to the devastated country. He might be young—only twenty-three—but he was, after all, the grandson of their beloved King Zammat.

It appeared that Sammat had indeed been producing a few miracles: Inflation had fallen, and he had persuaded the Shambi and the Soto tribes to select representatives to write a constitution.

"Except they don't all understand what a constitution means," Kadi had said. "The Soto are mostly nomads, and only a few have had any real education. They've really been quite neglected, so they're very suspicious, and Dickson Zimba, a Soto, *has* had schooling and is a real troublemaker."

"Ambitious," Cyrus had said. "There's always one."

"Many of the Shambi are city people, some of them educated abroad. Sammat is Shambi, too." In the end, Kadi had told them, "They agreed to take all their disagreements and problems to Sharma, the eldest wise man." It had been decreed by Sharma that what the country needed for untangling all the knots and settling the arguments was not a chieftain, a *mfumo,* but a king.

"A king!" Mrs. Pollifax had exclaimed. "Sammat a king? He doesn't want to be a king, does he?"

"No, but he's the only one left of the royal line, and a king is believed to have magical powers, you see, and is always respected."

Mrs. Pollifax had said doubtfully, "Of course, he's young, and I suppose a king has more panache than a mere chieftain."

Cyrus had said with a twinkle, "Being a retired judge, I'd certainly be interested in this Sharma's technique in handing down his judicial decisions."

347

"And you'll be *meeting* him," Kadi had cried triumphantly. "We're all invited to the coronation." She had beamed at them. "You'll be really impressed by Sharma. He's a diviner, and he must be at least a hundred years old. Sharma sees things. He is wise."

Mrs. Pollifax had said quickly, "We'll go, won't we, Cyrus? Your cast will be off by then. You may not even need a cane."

"Blessed thought," Cyrus had said. "Of course we'll go, m'dear."

That had been ten days ago—a peaceful ten days that had ended last night with Kadi's midnight telephone call from Manhattan, where she lived. At the other end of the line Kadi was blurting out, "I've just heard from Sammy, Mrs. Pollifax, and he's in *trouble*."

"What do you mean, trouble?" asked Mrs. Pollifax.

"Rumors, terrible rumors," Kadi continued in a rush of words. "He says there may be no coronation. He may not even be able to remain a *mfumo*, because someone's been circulating terrible rumors about him. And the people are growing uneasy, too. Joseph—he's Sammy's assistant—has not been able to learn anything."

"But learn what?"

"Learn who is behind the rumors," Kadi said impatiently, and then with suspicion, "Have you been asleep? Have I waked you up? I'm sorry. It's just that—"

"Kadi," said Mrs. Pollifax firmly, "just tell us what's the matter. Clearly."

In a sobered voice Kadi said, "He sounded desperate. It all began nine days ago. He says he's stuck in the capital, where no one tells him anything. He suddenly can't trust anyone."

"But what rumors?" asked Mrs. Pollifax reasonably.

"I don't know," Kadi cried. "He said, 'But there is more, Kadi, much more,' and then we were cut off. I have to go back and help. I must. You understand, don't you?"

"Kadi," Mrs. Pollifax said, "I hear you, and I suggest two things: Go to bed and get what sleep you can, and then call Sammat in the morning to learn exactly what he meant by rumors and by his saying 'there's more, much more' before you were cut off."

Kadi said anxiously, "Maybe we weren't cut off. Maybe someone was listening."

348

"All the more reason to wait," Mrs. Pollifax told her calmly. "At eight o'clock in the morning it will be four o'clock in the afternoon in Ubangiba." Realizing that it was already Friday, she added, "I'll meet the six-o'clock train today, as usual, and we'll talk."

It was after she put down the phone that Cyrus said for the first time, "She can't—mustn't—go alone."

MRS. Pollifax, glancing at her watch, said, "Kadi's train is due in ten minutes, Cyrus. I've got to go."

He nodded. "And I'll put in a call to Mrs. Lupacik while you're fetching Kadi. See if she's free to move in for a week."

"Oh, Cyrus. . . ."

"Yes, m'dear, but we've become surrogate parents, and I think her true parents would want this and be glad for it."

Driving to the railroad station, Mrs. Pollifax admitted to herself that accompanying Kadi to Africa would normally be delightful, but she realized how tiring the trip would be after the recent flu. On the other hand, she knew that she could never forgive herself if harm came to Kadi. And after a dark and difficult January and Cyrus's fall on the ice, a week in the sunshine could be therapeutic.

Kadi was waiting at the railroad station when Mrs. Pollifax arrived. She looked trim in black stockings, black shoes and a beige trench coat. Kadi was small, with a rather plain, fine-boned face, brown hair and huge eyes, green and thickly lashed. It was her eyes and an aura of eagerness that drew people's glances. She was different, with an endearing oddness.

Definitely, thought Mrs. Pollifax, this child has experienced enough horror in her nineteen years, and of course I must go.

AT DINNER Kadi said, "It took hours, but I got through to Sammy this afternoon. He wouldn't say much, but he said—he said the rumors about him have something to do with witchcraft."

Cyrus gave Mrs. Pollifax an amused glance, but she was not amused; she did not underestimate for a moment what Kadi was saying. Africa's culture was ancient, and ancient beliefs might be hidden, but they were not easily exorcised. Witchcraft was serious.

"You have your art classes," Cyrus reminded Kadi gently.

"Yes, but you have to remember, I was born in Ubangiba," she said earnestly. "Fourteen years of my life I lived there, and it's more home to me, still, than New York. Sammy and I are like brother and sister. He trusts me. I can find out things for him. I grew up in a village. I know the people and they know me, and it's in the villages that rumors start."

The telephone rang, and Mrs. Pollifax rose and said, "Hello?" and then carried the phone to Cyrus. "Mrs. Lupacik."

Cyrus answered and listened, nodded and said, "Thank you. Bless you for that. I'll call you back in half an hour."

Hanging up, he said to Kadi, "But you're not to go alone, Kadi." And to Mrs. Pollifax, smiling, he said, "Mrs. Lupacik is free, and happy to take over while you're gone."

"You mean—" Kadi gave a deep sigh of relief. "Oh, I'm so glad." Turning to Mrs. Pollifax, she said, "Sammy's last words on the phone today— I nearly cried. He said, 'Please, *kam kwik, kwik, bo.*'" To Cyrus she explained, "We used to talk pidgin English a lot. I think someone may have been listening in on the phone or in the same room with him."

"What does it mean?" Cyrus asked.

She said soberly, "It means 'come quickly, quickly, friend.'"

2

IT WAS high noon on Monday, three days later, when the plane began its descent over Ubangiba, the smallest and possibly the poorest sub-Saharan country on the continent. The shadow of the plane moved across the desert, darkening it like a great flying vulture. The monotony of sand and goats was presently replaced by greening fields, clusters of thatched conical huts, a network of red-clay roads, a suburb of square cement bungalows, and then they were flying over the capital of Languka, with its two incongruous white palaces, one now a hospital, rising above the crowded alleys and dung-colored buildings—a city that had endured riots, massacres, hunger and decay.

As they landed, a cargo plane near the terminal building was being unloaded by men in overalls. Three huge crates sat in the sun, and what looked to be a backhoe was being driven down a ramp.

"Machinery," breathed Kadi, looking over Mrs. Pollifax's shoulder. "Sammy had such hopes they could afford a backhoe. It must be for opening up the coal mine in the south that the geologists found. I just hope they've enough gas to run it."

A worry about gasoline seemed a strange comment, until Mrs. Pollifax remembered that President-for-Life Simoko had bankrupted the country by designing a second palace, to outshine the palace that former President-for-Life Chinyata had built.

"And look! There's Sammy," cried Kadi.

Sammat was striding across the tarmac toward them. He wore a crisp white shirt, which heightened the rich dark color of his skin. His was a strong face, the features well cut, with intelligent eyes under a slash of black brows, and young as he was, there was a natural grace and dignity about him that made one aware of his being the descendant of African kings. He was not in any regal costume. Today he was wearing knee-length khaki shorts, high socks and sneakers. The only sign of his being special was the uniformed guard, Joseph, who walked at his side with a gun at his belt.

"Kadi," shouted Sammat, and as they descended from the plane, he gave her a very American hug and then turned to Mrs. Pollifax, beaming. "Friend Pollifax," he said.

Joseph reached for Mrs. Pollifax's hand, and remembering the traditional handshake, she shook it, clapped her own hands three times, shook his hand a second time and clapped again. He repeated the greeting to Kadi.

"You see what has come for us as well as you?" said Sammat, pointing to the cargo plane. "On Thursday, digging begins in the south. We've had more tests made, and it's anthracite—good coal!"

Kadi said teasingly, "But Sammy, future kings aren't supposed to

351

wear shorts and be at the airport watching a backhoe come in and meeting a pair of *mzungu*."

Sammat straightened his broad shoulders. "If I still become king," he said firmly—and Mrs. Pollifax noted the if—"I will be a different sort of king. I will be accessible."

Joseph nodded. "*Yanga mfumo* go everywhere. He spare none of us."

"Come, let's go," said Sammat, and led them through the shadowed terminal and customs, and out into the bright sun again. Pointing to a dusty four-door sedan, he had just opened the rear door for them when a Land Rover came speeding up the road from the city, blowing its horn with something like hysteria. Close to Sammat and his party, the Land Rover swerved, came to a stop, and two policemen jumped out, shouting, "*Yanga mfumo, ngoozi!*"

Sammat gasped, "Another? *Again?*"

Kadi stiffened.

"What's he saying?" asked Mrs. Pollifax.

"He says something terrible's happened."

"*Inde, inde,*" the man said, and resorting to English, "Behind the Bang-Bang Snack Bar."

Jumping into the front seat of the car, Sammat started up the engine. Mrs. Pollifax slid into the rear seat, then Kadi, and following the police in the Land Rover, they sped down the boulevard that led straight as an arrow to the Simoko palace.

The road was not empty. A barefoot woman in a turban and multicolored wrapped skirt herded a line of goats along its edge; bicycles swerved to give the cars the right-of-way. The native market lay ahead, with its bright ragged awnings and stalls, but strangely deserted, until Mrs. Pollifax saw why: There had been an exodus across the boulevard, and the crowd from the marketplace had gathered under the neon sign of the Bang-Bang Snack Bar.

Sammat stopped at the edge of the crowd, his brakes squealing. To one of the police in the Land Rover he called, "Show me." To Kadi and Mrs. Pollifax he said, "Please, stay in the car."

Sammat and the policeman disappeared down a shadowed alley. Through the crowd Mrs. Pollifax could see the Bang-Bang Snack

Bar, very modern but adjoining a shabby storefront. On the other side, separated by the alley, rose a high, crumbling mud wall with a wooden padlocked gate. Over this gate hung a sign that read BIKES SOLD CHEEP. RING BELL.

Mrs. Pollifax leaned out the open window of the car and tried to discern words. In the mumble of voices one word seemed to be repeated over and over: "*Mkambo?*" and "*Inde! Mkambo!*" accompanied by a wail, obviously of mourning. Then Mrs. Pollifax saw Sammat emerge from the alley between the buildings, and he looked shaken and suddenly very tired.

Sammat took his place behind the wheel and headed down the boulevard toward the white hospital/palace glittering in the sun. The entrance, lined with brilliant bougainvilleas, fairly bristled with small, upright wooden signs, each one in English, with line drawings for those who could not read. The largest read HOSPITAL, followed by EMERGENCY ROOM TO LEFT; MATERNITY CLINIC; TEACHING HOSPITAL; and a more modest sign with arrows: EXPERIMENTAL FARM, AGRICULTURE CENTER.

Sammat stopped the car and turned to them with eyes looking as if he'd glimpsed hell.

Mrs. Pollifax said gently, "What happened back there, Sammat?"

Tight-lipped, he said, "A murder, but—" He stopped. "Later," he said flatly, and opened the car door and slid out. "I'll show you to your room. We've prepared one at the top of the palace. Then I must leave you and speak to Dr. Merrick, and also meet with Police Inspector Banda."

About the murder, of course, thought Mrs. Pollifax. She remembered Sammat's "Again? *Another?*" and she wondered.

As Sammat walked around the car, Kadi said sadly, "I don't feel very welcomed."

Mrs. Pollifax squeezed Kadi's hand. "I think we've arrived at a difficult time, Kadi. Sammat is a very worried young man."

Sammat gave Kadi a warm smile. "I'm glad you're here, really glad, Kadi, and if you want to see Radia, she's head nurse now here in our emergency room."

"Then I can see her this afternoon. How wonderful!"

To Mrs. Pollifax, Sammat said politely, "And you must visit our greenhouses later and see the experimental farm."

Mrs. Pollifax brightened at this. Her geraniums at home blossomed nearly all year in her greenhouse, well nourished by her conversations with them. "I'd like that," she told him.

Inside the palace, the marble-floored hall was filled with people waiting for treatment. Sammat pointed to the balcony at the top of the main staircase, from which ropes were suspended, knotted and secured to stretchers waiting on the floor. "We have no elevator, and while the clinic and the emergency room are down here, the operating room is on the second floor."

"Very ingenious," murmured Mrs. Pollifax as they began climbing the broad staircase. The room on the third floor that she and Kadi were to share was small and plain.

"You'll both want to rest. We'll have dinner together early, at five. In the meantime," he said with a rueful smile, "welcome to Ubangiba."

When he had gone, Kadi said, "Well, I'm not going to rest, not if Radia's downstairs. I'll just say hello. You don't mind?" she asked.

It occurred to Mrs. Pollifax that the last thing she wanted was to become Kadi's shadow or an obligation. Nor did she want to rest, either. What she wanted after the long plane flight was to connect with her surroundings. She said vaguely, "Oh, I might take a short walk. Just to see a little of the town."

"Then wear a hat. The sun can be ferocious," Kadi reminded her. "Don't go far. I really won't be long."

When Kadi had gone, Mrs. Pollifax opened her carry-on bag and changed into lighter clothes. She left the room, descended the staircase and walked out into the heat of the afternoon.

At once, there were people, shops and stalls to capture her interest, and Mrs. Pollifax enjoyed people. She passed shops selling jewelry, secondhand furniture and leather shoes in rainbow colors. At the corner she was intrigued by a man seated on a strip of canvas and surrounded by jars of what looked to be dried snakes and baskets full of strange-looking herbs. Reaching a sign announcing THE BANK OF UBANGIBA, Mrs. Pollifax entered and exchanged her currency for a wad of Ubangiban *gwar,* which she stuffed into her purse. Continuing up the boulevard, she thought that she might walk as far as the Bang-Bang Snack Bar and the gate next to it, with its sign BIKES SOLD CHEEP. She was pleased at being out in the world again, but what interested her most of all was the fact that in the absence of cars, so many citizens of Languka rode past her on bicycles. Mrs. Pollifax decided that she would like to have a bicycle, too. When in Rome, do as the Romans do, she reminded herself.

She reached the gate of the bicycle shop and stood back to read again its stern instruction: RING BELL. Through a crack in the wooden boards of the gate she could see a square earthen compound, its opposite wall formed by a small house with a door. To her left a few bicycles leaned against the wall in the sun; to her right a long and ragged awning shaded a forest of old bikes. She grasped the rope and pulled. A giant of a man emerged from among the bicycles, big-shouldered and broad-faced, with a shaved black head that gleamed like polished mahogany. He was not young. He wore shabby jeans and looked disgruntled, even hostile, as he opened the gate a few inches and stared at her. "Yayezz?"

There was a terrible scar running from his cheekbone to his jaw. This and the shaved head, the hostile gaze, the absence of any other people beyond the gate gave her pause, until, refusing to be afraid, she told him, "I have come for a bicycle."

"*You?*"

"Me."

He grudgingly opened the gate, saying crossly, "Come in."

The gate closed behind them. He loomed above her, taller even than Cyrus and massively built. "My bikes be old and used. No pretty bikes here for a *mzungu.*"

She said tartly, "Did I ask for a pretty new bike?"

"But you come to me—Moses. Why? *Ku zonda?*"

She looked at him with exasperation. "What I want is a bike, and I must say, you're a very strange salesman."

"Bikes along the wall be for selling." He pointed, not moving.

Feeling quite cross at his lack of hospitality, she approached the dozen bicycles leaning against the wall but found only four of them

355

designed for a woman wearing a skirt. She mounted a large and very ancient one, put her feet to the pedals and rode in a circle around the man, swaying wildly. He watched without expression as she returned the bicycle to the wall, but when she mounted a second one, he retreated to a bench to watch, possibly to avoid being hit. There he sat as she tried out the remaining bicycles. At last she made her decision. "This green one—how much?"

He shrugged. "Two hundred *gwar.*"

She said accusingly, "That sounds like forty U.S. dollars!"

"Yayezz," he drawled.

A dozen retorts came to her mind, but the sun was hot, and she felt suddenly weak. Worse, a feeling of abrupt and violent alienation swept over her. Suddenly she had no idea what she was doing here or why she wanted a bicycle. She grasped the pole of the awning and clung to it, willing herself not to faint. Then the earth tilted sideways, and she had time only to gasp before she slumped to the ground.

When she opened her eyes, she was lying on a bench in the shade, and this strange giant of a man was fanning her with a newspaper. "Breathe," he told her sternly.

"I *am* breathing."

"Breathe deep."

As she struggled to sit up, he helped her, nodding. She managed a feeble smile. "Thank you. I'm sorry. I've never fainted before. *Never.*"

He said gruffly, "But there is no need to apologize. I know what it is like to faint. I know what it is like to be sick."

Startled, she said, "Suddenly you just spoke perfect English!"

He shrugged. "I saw you at the airport with *Mfumo* Sammat. You came with Dr. Hopkirk's daughter."

She nodded. "Yes. Did you know Kadi's father?"

"Long ago, yes. Everyone knew Dr. Hopkirk."

"He was murdered when? Five years ago? Six?"

"So I heard. I was in prison until last year, when *Mfumo* Sammat came back and freed us." His hand moved to touch the thick rope of scar on his face. "The lucky ones . . . died early."

"Torture," she murmured, nodding.

He looked at her. "Why did you come to Ubangiba?" he said.

"I had some sort of irrational fear that Kadi might be in danger here and shouldn't come alone."

He thought about this. "You were kind, then, and very wise. Are you some kind of police?"

"Oh, no," she told him. "That is, not exactly. And who are you?"

"Me? Nobody."

"You've not always mended and sold old bicycles, surely."

He said meditatively, without expression, "Long ago I was a *mwamuaa,* a man. There was a house, a wife, two sons—all dead now. When Zammat the Eighth was king, I was with the police. After he died, after his son was assassinated, President Chinyata took power, and many went to prison, most especially the police. He killed and killed. Now I am nobody, mending old bicycles. I hide myself away, as a nobody must." He sighed. "I am sorry that you come to this country when there is so much trouble."

"What trouble?" she asked quickly.

Ignoring this, he said, "I would give the bicycle to you, but it won't put food on my table. I will sell it to you for one hundred *gwar.*"

She nodded. "Twenty U.S. dollars is fair," she told him, "and you've been very kind, and I do apologize for suddenly—"

He said in a harsh voice, "You are tired. You are not young. Rest, sleep and then you will fly home, yes?"

Startled, she said, "Home? Oh, no." She added with a faint smile, "And how can I go home when I have just bought a bicycle?" She counted one hundred *gwar* into his huge palm. "I'm Emily Pollifax," she told him, "but you haven't told me your last name."

"Just Moses."

So he trusted no one, even with his full name. Accepting this, she was about to climb onto the bicycle when he said, "Do not be too free where you ride. Be watchful."

"Watchful?"

He regarded her thoughtfully. "It would be wise. Where there is *imfa—zitatu imfa* now—there will be no pity." He strode to the gate, opened it and waited for her to go. She wanted to ask him what he meant by "no pity" and what the words *imfa* and *zitatu* meant, but his face was tight, and she pushed the bike past him to the street. "I hope I see you again, Moses."

The gate was half closed, when he said flatly, "There are no lions in Ubangiba."

Now that was a non sequitur, she thought, since everyone knew there were no lions in Ubangiba. With a wave of her hand she mounted the bike and pedaled rapidly down the boulevard. With much ringing of the bicycle's bell she succeeded in threading her way among her fellow cyclists, narrowly missing several of them, and overlooking their gasps of alarm, she returned successfully to the palace.

3

FIVE of them sat down to dinner that evening in a tent set up in the garden behind the hospital's kitchen. Joseph had joined them, followed by a Dr. Merrick. "White medicine man," he said with a smile as he shook hands with them.

Their dinner was a modest one of yams, hard-boiled eggs and stewed chicken with a bread sauce that resembled a dumpling. When they had begun eating, the sky had been ravished with color, but now they were surrounded by night, with an evening chill stealing into the tent. Two candles sputtered on the table, alternately shadowing and illuminating their faces, and Mrs. Pollifax, observing each in turn, gained the impression that Joseph did not like Dr. Merrick. Jealous perhaps, she thought. Joseph, no doubt, had a proprietary feeling toward this *mfumo,* who had promoted him from palace servant to assistant and guard. "My right hand," Sammat had said of Joseph. He was of medium height and broad-shouldered, with a small head, the flesh drawn taut across high, sharp cheekbones; his eyes were small, alert and intelligent. A serious man, Joseph. Sammat said he claimed to be in his forties. He was born in the shantytown outside Languka, and there was a wariness about him, a watchfulness, Mrs. Pollifax thought.

Dr. Merrick, on the other hand, bore the ease of a privileged life. He was British, probably forty, with gray-flecked black hair, thin patrician features, a quick and friendly smile. Eventually his talk was of the backhoe that had arrived that morning.

Sammat turned to Kadi and Mrs. Pollifax. "Thursday we leave in a cavalcade to see the backhoe make its first major excavation of the mine. I think you will find it'll be a real celebration. Joseph, the buses—has the paint dried yet?"

Joseph nodded. "I go see now." He rose and left.

Dr. Merrick, glancing at his watch, said, "Time for me to get back to work, too, but delighted to meet you both. Thanks, Sammat."

In the silence that followed, Mrs. Pollifax heard the rhythmic beat of drums in the distance. "Talking drums?" she asked.

Sammat smiled faintly. "Not tonight. What you're hearing is the Picadilly Popcorn Rock Band. Very talented. The second palace has an auditorium, and they're rehearsing there tonight."

"Cool," said Kadi politely, giving Sammat a puzzled glance. "And a cavalcade on Thursday, with a bus?"

"Three buses, very old," he said ruefully. "The chiefs and the subchiefs of the Shambi and Soto will go with us. And all the rites are being taken care of tomorrow. The medicine men will be making sacrifices to the spirits in the hills so they won't be angry."

"Will we meet the Mr. Zimba," inquired Mrs. Pollifax, "whom you described to Kadi as a troublemaker?"

"Dickson Zimba? Oh, yes. He'll go with us, but 'troublemaker' is really too strong a word." He grinned. "How about 'gadfly'? He's certainly made himself an opposition party. He does have ideas— some of them very good—and he intends to be a leader of the Soto. But unfortunately, he argues *interminably.*"

"What sort of man is he?" asked Mrs. Pollifax.

Sammat shrugged. "Not old. About twenty-eight or thirty, and son of one of the subchiefs. Ambitious. He's an accountant in one of our offices. Quite a firebrand when he makes a speech. He wants change, but we disagree on what's possible just now. He doesn't appreciate the World Aid people being here, for instance. I suspect he wants all white people sent home, but he forgets that our best and most talented people have been killed or in prison for years and we have to start all over again."

This reminded Mrs. Pollifax of earlier events in her day. From her pocket she brought out the words that she'd written down phonetically on a slip of paper. "Tell me," she said, glancing at it, "what does *ku zonda* mean?"

"*Ku zonda?* It means 'to spy,' " said Kadi.

So that was who Moses had thought at first she was. "There are three more words. The next two are *imfa* and *zitatu.*"

"*Imfa* means 'death,' and *zitatu* means 'three,' " Kadi told her.

Sammat's eyes probed Mrs. Pollifax's face, but he said nothing.

"Which brings us to the word *mkambo,*" she concluded.

"Oh, that's the word for 'lion,' " said Kadi, "except, of course, there are no lions in Ubangiba."

It was becoming monotonous being told this. Mrs. Pollifax lifted her gaze to Sammat and said, "We've come a long way to help, Sammat, and you've avoided explaining what made you desperate enough to ask for it. *Have* there been three deaths—three murders?"

He rose from the table. "Let's talk in your room."

They walked together back into the palace and up the broad staircase, then the second long staircase, not speaking. They reached the door to the guest room, and Mrs. Pollifax unlocked it.

Once inside, she said, "All right, Sammat, what so shocked you at the Bang-Bang Snack Bar? You spoke of a murder?"

"The rumors began the day after it was announced that I would become king," he said in a hard voice. "Dr. Merrick brought me news of the rumor."

"What rumor?" asked Kadi.

"That I—I, their *mfumo,* their chief—am a sorcerer."

Kadi looked at him with horror. "A *sorcerer?*"

Sammat nodded. "It seemed harmless, ridiculous, at first." To

361

Mrs. Pollifax he said, "In Africa there have always been secret societies, most of them for good, but some of them very very evil." His glance moved to Kadi, and he said gently, "You remember Nomsa, Kadi? The woman who once looked after you."

"Nomsa?" Kadi said. "Sammy, she terrified me!"

"Yes, until your parents learned why you were having nightmares and sent her home. What did she threaten you with, Kadi?"

Kadi said shakily, "With the lion men of Singida. She said if I didn't behave and obey her, the lion men would steal me and hide me in a deep pit, and keep me there until I was old enough to—to go out and kill for them."

"Who on earth are the lion men of Singida?" commented Mrs. Pollifax. "Are they real or a myth?"

"Real enough, unfortunately. A cult of assassins in what is now Tanzania," Sammat said. "Whether they still exist, I don't know, but they *did* steal or buy children. When someone wanted an enemy killed, they went to the cult of sorcerers called the Lion Men and paid to have that enemy killed, and the sorcerers produced a child who was sent out in lion skins and mask, with long sharp fingernails, to kill. The cult terrorized everyone, and always they left their victims clawed to death, as if by a lion."

"But it never happened *here*," Kadi said.

"That's understood, but the man found behind the snack bar this morning had been clawed to death."

Kadi gasped.

"Then it's begun here?" said Mrs. Pollifax. "A secret society?"

He said grimly, "Very neatly timed, with rumors that I am a sorcerer."

Appalled, Mrs. Pollifax said, "Then someone is trying, diabolically, to connect you with those terrible murders."

"Oh, Sammy," Kadi said in a shocked voice. "But why?"

He placed his hand on the knob of the door and opened it, but before leaving, he said, "To destroy me, of course."

The door closed behind him, and there was a long silence, until Mrs. Pollifax said gently, "Kadi, does it frighten you? Are you sorry you came?"

"Of course not. You know he asked me to go into the villages—"

"But not alone—*never* alone," Mrs. Pollifax said sternly. "Ever. Promise?"

Kadi grinned. "You're saying I'm not much good yet at the karate you've been teaching me?"

"You know what I mean," Mrs. Pollifax said.

Kadi nodded. "I know."

Mrs. Pollifax, studying her face, wondered if now might be the time to chance the question she had been waiting to ask. It was risky, yet . . . She drew a deep breath. "Forgive me if I ask something that I need to know. Did you recognize any of the faces of the three men who came to your father's clinic that day?"

"No," Kadi said sharply. *"No."* She hesitated. "All right, I saw one of them as they left. He turned his head, and I saw him."

"And he saw you?"

"Yes," admitted Kadi, "but he didn't say anything. He didn't stop. He just followed the other two men down the path."

"Yet one of them knew you were hiding there?"

"Yes, but I was out of the country by night, you know."

Mrs. Pollifax nodded, not at all reassured by what Kadi had told her. It didn't seem to occur to Kadi that the man who had seen her might have told the others and they'd wonder how much she had seen. For that matter, Mrs. Pollifax was not at all certain that Kadi would remember her promise not to wander off alone—the young could be impulsive. A gun, she thought. Kadi was a novice at karate, but she was an expert markswoman. Kadi must have a gun, she decided, wondering how to find a gun in a country where two dictators had long ago banned them out of fear of revolution.

"TRY the black market," Dr. Merrick told her in the morning, looking amused.

"Oh, dear. Must I?"

"Yes, and you'll pay a pretty price for one. You know the public market on the boulevard? Stroll around behind it, and you'll find an ex-mercenary they call Jim-Jim. But you mustn't go alone, of course. Ask Joseph to go with you."

Mrs. Pollifax thanked him. Once he left, she placed her wide-brimmed hat on her head and, with no intention of enlisting Joseph, mounted her bicycle and set out to find Jim-Jim.

The boulevard was alive with people, but it slanted just a little uphill, so that Mrs. Pollifax was puffing when she reached the public market. Dismounting and wheeling her bicycle, she walked around, looking over the infinite variety of wares on display: sacks of charcoal and millet, a stand selling rolled tobacco leaves, an entire aisle given over to cages of live chickens, a cubicle selling dishes, bowls, mirrors and brooms. She winced a little at the sight of dead mice for sale, admired the fresh pumpkin leaves, yams and peanuts, and particularly the woven baskets of all shapes and sizes.

While reconnoitering, she identified two booths with a narrow space separating them. Negotiating through with her bicycle, she arrived in a compound bearing a single acacia tree, around which a number of rascally-looking young men loitered. There was also a thatched hut and a ragged army tent of considerable size, its flaps open to the sun. The young men stopped talking at the sight of her. She bowed politely and headed for the tent.

"Mr. Jim-Jim?" she called, peering inside.

He appeared behind her, startling her, a tall and unsavory-looking European with a patch over one eye and a band of red cloth tied around his head. "The market," he said, pointing, "is that way."

She said pleasantly, "I hear that you sell guns," and walked into the tent.

"Hey!" he shouted, but it was too late.

She had already seen the trestle table fashioned out of rough boarding, with its samples laid out on display. She saw cartons of English cigarettes and of whiskey, cases of food, and several guns half hidden behind a case of Jamaican rum. She leaned her bicycle against a tent pole and glanced over the selection. "Well, well," she said, "an M-1 carbine, a Beretta submachine gun, a Sten. . . . But what I want is a pistol. Do you have a pistol?"

His one eye was gray and expressionless, but both of his eyebrows were scowling. "They cost plenty."

"I'll judge that when I see them," she said tartly.

He walked to the rear of the tent and brought a handful of pistols to dump on the table. Only one or two of them looked new.

"Have you ammunition for this?" she asked, pointing to a Makarov 9-mm. When he nodded, she said, "Then load it for me, please. I'd like to make sure it works."

He reached under the table, slipped in the clip and handed the pistol to her. She decided it would be excellent for Kadi—only a little over six inches in length and light in weight. Pointing it at the farther wall of canvas, she pulled the trigger, which brought a curse from Jim-Jim. "You make holes in my tent!"

"Ah, but how fortunate that I didn't shoot *you*," she pointed out. "How much does this cost?"

"Five hundred U.S.," he told her.

"I'll pay three hundred fifty."

The traditional battle of wills called bargaining began. They settled at last on four hundred U.S. dollars. She unloaded the pistol and placed it and the ammunition in her purse, and counted out the money. Assuring him that it had been a pleasure to meet him, she walked out of the tent with her pistol and her bicycle.

She had drawn more attention than anticipated, however. The group of young men still lounged under the tree, but one of them lazily rose to follow her across the barren compound, toward the public market. Nearing the exit, she laid her bike on the ground and turned to face him.

"I like purse," he said, extending his hand.

"I like it, too," she said, and adjusted her weight to an on-guard stance. When he made his lunge forward, she was ready for him and, with the edge of her hand, karate-slashed him across the jaw. He reeled backward, stunned. She picked up her bicycle, and as she resumed her exit from the compound, she discovered a blond-haired young man staring at her in astonishment.

"I say, I saw what was going to happen," he said, making way for her. "I was going to rescue you."

"That's very kind of you," she said, "and I'm sorry I denied you the pleasure."

He grinned. "Black belt?"

She shook her head. "Brown belt."

"You must be the Mrs. Pollifax who flew in yesterday. News travels fast here. I'm World Aid—the experimental farm. Tony Dahl." They shook hands. "But what were you doing back there?" he asked.

"I made the wrong turn and got lost," she told him.

"Well, now you know," he said. "Going back to the palace?" When she nodded, he said, "Yes, you'd better, or you might still be followed. . . . Come see the experimental farm."

"I will," she promised. Mounting her bicycle, she pedaled furiously back to the palace.

THERE was no time to see Kadi alone on her return. When they finally met again, it was to tour the second palace, which was now called Government House. Mrs. Pollifax could understand Sammat's need to show them what he had accomplished before vicious rumors began to tarnish his accomplishments. So they set off on foot for the nearby palace, built by former President-for-Life Chinyata during the years he had spent looting the treasury.

"It was the first one built. It's not nearly so grand as the palace we've just left," explained Sammat. "Simoko spent twice the money on *his* palace."

This was obvious: The older building was built of sun-dried clay, painted white. Its rooms were smaller, less pretentious, and there was no glittering marble entrance hall. It did, however, have a splendid auditorium and housed the radio station, the offices of the *Ubangiba Free Press* and of World Aid.

The tour was only moderately interesting to Mrs. Pollifax, until they reached the basement, where the newspaper office and the pressroom had been installed. Sammat strolled into the pressroom, followed by Kadi, but Mrs. Pollifax chose to wander down the hall and peer into the empty newsroom. A copy of the *Ubangiba Free Press* lay on the editor's desk, dated a week ago. She glanced at it with interest. Under a banner headline—MR. MWANGO & WORLD AID PREDICT GOOD HARVEST—there was a smaller one: INTERVIEW WITH MR. DICKSON ZIMBA, SOTO REPRESENTATIVE TO COMMITTEE

FOR A CONSTITUTION. Running her eyes down the column, Mrs. Pollifax was caught by a particularly provocative question asked by the interviewer, one Johnson Sovi.

SOVI: We have a new and young head of state, Mr. Zimba, soon to be our king. In the months that he had been at Government House, how would you summarize his performance?

MR. ZIMBA: I'm impressed by his energy, but frankly not by his goals for Ubangiba. He has spent four years in America, and see how he brings in white men and women to organize us. It's back to colonialist days; he speaks of going forward and takes us backward.

Hearing Kadi's and Sammy's footsteps, she quickly replaced the newspaper on the desk.

Sammat looked amused. "Oh, there's no need to hide it. That's last week's issue, and I've read it."

"I don't think he likes you, Sammat," Mrs. Pollifax said.

"Oh, that scarcely matters," Sammat said dismissingly.

But Mrs. Pollifax wondered if it might not matter. She decided that she would like very much to meet this Mr. Zimba and judge for herself if he was a danger to which Sammat was blind.

Strolling back to Simoko's palace, past a block of offices that had sprung up to serve the palaces, they heard the sound of a siren in the distance. It grew louder and closer.

As they reached the palace entrance, a renovated Land Rover, painted white and bearing a huge red cross, raced down the drive and stopped near the hospital entrance. Two men jumped out, unfolded a stretcher and began fumbling in the rear.

"What is it?" asked Sammat, calling to them.

One of the men turned a panicky face to him. "*Yanga mfumo,* another lion attack." Together the two men lifted a bloody body from the car and placed it on the stretcher. A sheet thrown over the man fell to one side, and Mrs. Pollifax caught her breath at what she saw: a torn throat, a dozen claw marks across face and shoulders. She turned away, shocked. "Poor man, poor man," she whispered over and over.

Death number four, she realized bleakly.

367

4

LATER that afternoon Mrs. Pollifax left her room and began the process of descending the two long staircases for dinner in the hospital's staff cafeteria. Reaching the balcony, she glanced down to the huge entrance hall, usually filled with patients waiting to be called. The benches were empty now except for one, on which Dr. Merrick sat wearily. Finishing her descent, she walked across the marble floor and joined him. "Are you resting or waiting for someone?" she asked.

"The police inspector's due any minute. You saw the latest casualty, then?"

"I saw." Frowning, she said, "Tell me, is there any pattern to these killings? Do the victims have something in common?"

Dr. Merrick sighed. "So far, they appear to be random killings." "But the motive?"

He said dryly, "I think you know that as well as I do: to terrify."

"Does it terrify *you?*" she asked.

"Let's just say that I don't plan to go out alone after dark, and I strongly suggest that you and young Kadi do your walking on the palace grounds, in the garden. . . . Ah, here's my policeman— Chief Inspector Banda," he said, rising to greet a brisk, slender man in his thirties, wearing an immaculate dark green uniform. He was clean-shaven, with a thick knot of frown lines between his eyes. Wasting no time in pleasantries, he nodded to Mrs. Pollifax, and the two men walked away in the direction of the garden. Mrs. Pollifax rose and continued on her way to the cafeteria to meet Kadi.

After dinner Mrs. Pollifax said to Kadi, "Let's go into the garden. I've something important to give you."

"A *present?*"

"Not your typical gift," Mrs. Pollifax told her, "but a useful one."

They walked down the hall and out into the garden. The sun had set, and darkness had fallen with the abruptness of a curtain. Lights from the kitchen spilled out across the ground, turning the wall of bougainvilleas a garish pink and illuminating one side of the canvas tent in which they'd had dinner the previous evening. Beyond it rose the dark shapes of new tents being erected for the coronation.

Kadi and Mrs. Pollifax pulled canvas chairs up to a table and sat down. The air was fragrant with the scent of flowers. The sound of crickets made a companionable backdrop, and muffled voices could be heard from the kitchen. Mrs. Pollifax began fumbling in her purse for the Makarov 9-mm to present to Kadi, when abruptly the peacefulness of the night was violated by the sound of a loud hammering in the garden.

"Tent pegs?" said Kadi, frowning. "Who could be working so late? They'll wake the patients in surgery. Don't they realize that?"

"Kadi—" began Mrs. Pollifax, but Kadi had already slipped out of her chair and had vanished into the darkness.

Mrs. Pollifax had half risen from her chair to follow her, when she heard a sound of scuffling and then a scream. At once she was on her feet and running. She called Kadi's name over and over.

"H-here," said a faint voice. Kadi burst into tears. "He—he—"

Dr. Merrick came rushing out with a flashlight. "Who's there?" he shouted. "Who screamed?"

"Over here," said Mrs. Pollifax. "Kadi's been hurt."

His light found them. Kadi was curled up on the ground, one hand gripping her left arm. "It hurts," she sobbed.

The two of them knelt beside her. With the arm exposed to the light, Mrs. Pollifax shuddered at the scarlet gash running the length of her arm. "Who was it, Kadi?" she asked.

"I don't know, I don't know," cried Kadi. "He came out of the dark—just a shape—and he had a knife. And I fought him, I fought him, but he was so—so *strong*," she said on a sob.

Dr. Merrick said, "Kadi, I'm going to carry you into the infirmary now. We've got to treat this at once, you hear?"

But Kadi had fainted. Dr. Merrick carried her out of the garden and through the marbled lobby into the emergency room.

Mrs. Pollifax turned and looked back into the garden before she followed. It was dark and silent now, and she wondered, Had it been a thief bent on robbing the palace whom Kadi had disturbed by accident? Had the hammering been started to deliberately entice *someone* into the garden, or had it been Kadi specifically whom the person in the garden wanted to harm?

As HAD been said, news traveled swiftly in Languka. Sammat, meeting with tribal elders in the old palace, left them to rush to the emergency room only half an hour after Kadi's attack. At seven the next morning Joseph brought a bag of sunflower seeds for Kadi; at half past seven Radia arrived with lovingness and a smile. She was a plain, cheerful woman with a figured red head scarf framing her round-cheeked, pockmarked black face with its full lips and bright eyes. At noon Dr. Merrick brought in the freshly printed *Ubangiba Free Press.*

"Front page, Kadi," he said. And it was true: Near the top of the page there had been inserted a small headline—HOPKIRK DAUGHTER ATTACKED.

Sammat, joining them, said, "And now I must increase the palace guards and station several in the garden. Too late, of course. Mrs. Pollifax, I'm about to visit the old royal compound, and with Kadi out of circulation today, I wonder if you'd care to see it."

"Yes, do go," Kadi told her. "When you get back, I shall be up, I promise you. I don't want to miss tomorrow's ride south to see the backhoe celebration."

As Sammat led Mrs. Pollifax outside to a dusty Land Rover, he said, "The compound's not far. There's only a path to it now, which makes for a bumpy ride."

Just beyond the shantytown, Sammat swerved off to the right and followed an ill-defined path. They lurched and bounced over untilled earth until up ahead Mrs. Pollifax saw the ruins of a wall surrounded by acacia trees.

Sammat, stopping the Land Rover, said simply, "Here in this place lives the soul of our people. This is where the first shrine was made to our ancestors and where generations of kings lived and ruled." As he helped her down from the Land Rover, he added without expression, "The later royal compound—my home—I can't show you. President Chinyata ordered it destroyed when he took over the country."

He led her through the ruins of a huge entrance gate, and they emerged into a great open space, much of it overgrown with grass. Sammat, pointing, said, "Over there, see? That was once the ceremonial hall." She turned and saw the skeletal bones of a long arched hall, open at either end, its sheathing worn away by wind and sun and time.

"And here is the shrine," Sammat said, pausing next to a well-kept line of attached conical huts. "I won't be long," he told her. "Feel free to walk around, but watch out for scorpions."

A private matter, then: She was not to see the shrine.

As he vanished into the shadowed entrance, a faint breeze stirred the grass and made silky, whispering sounds. A place of many ghosts, she thought. The local myth was that centuries before, a quarrel had arisen between Chief Mobolu of the Soto tribe and Zammat, chief of the Shambi, and to avoid war, the two chiefs were bound together in the throne room and a pair of poisonous snakes released, so that the gods might speak and choose which man was to survive and to rule. The unfortunate Mobolu had died, and it was Zammat whom the gods had favored, and from this had come the pair of serpents portrayed on the Ubangiban flag.

The sun was hot, and Sammat's warning about scorpions inhibited exploration. Wandering outside the gate, Mrs. Pollifax found a rock on which to sit and to consider feelings that she could neither define nor name. Perhaps she was experiencing what Sammat had called the soul of his country and also of Africa itself. Here in the ruins no sounds intruded; the leaves in the grove of trees hung limp and still. There was only the earth. Sammat trusted the earth; he wanted Ubangiban farms to prosper, grow fertile and feed all the people. If Sammat was driven out by these terrible rumors of sorcery, what would happen to this sunbaked country?

The appearance of a guinea fowl interrupted her thoughts, and she watched it rush indignantly out of the grove to vanish behind the walls of the compound. Suddenly Mrs. Pollifax felt uneasy.

I am being watched, she thought in dismay. I can feel it. There is someone hiding in among those trees. It's why the guinea fowl rushed out of the grove.

She stood up, uncertain what to do. Then Sammat walked out of the shrine and through the gate, and said, "Shall we go now?"

She did not mention the sensation of having been watched. Instead, as they drove away, she said politely, "Is it true that in Africa you worship your ancestors?"

"We revere our ancestors. We pray to them, hold festivals for them and offer sacrifices—like gifts—and hope for guidance and help. We like to believe our ancestors still watch over us."

"And did you make a sacrifice at the shrine?"

He said soberly, "Of course. And prayed with all my heart for help just now."

She nodded. There was no need for him to explain why.

THE next morning a knock at the door woke Mrs. Pollifax, and she stumbled out of bed, half asleep, to find Joseph in the hall with a tray of food. *"Moni,"* he said. "It be five o'clock."

For a moment she found his knock unforgivable, because she wanted more sleep and Joseph looked incredibly awake and even cheerful. Noticing the gun in his holster, she remembered that she still carried the Makarov in her purse. While she ate, she wondered what to do with it for this day. Having been warned of pickpockets, she finally stuffed it deep inside Kadi's knapsack.

Downstairs, she learned that Dr. Merrick had given in to Kadi's pleas to see the backhoe celebration in the south, but only if she remained in the bus and watched from the window. Dr. Merrick would be going, too; it was his day off, and he'd volunteered to drive one of the buses. Walking outside and seeing the three buses waiting for them, Mrs. Pollifax exclaimed, "Well!" and smiled.

Kadi, emerging from the infirmary with her left arm heavily swathed in bandages, joined her and said, "Wow!"

The first bus was a riot of yellow sunflowers painted on a background of bright red; the second bus was a hot pink, with dizzyingly blue polka dots; and the third was black, with colorful drawings of children playing, men at work and women with baskets on their heads. A loudspeaker was blaring music for the crowd surrounding the buses, and the men were equally as colorful in printed cotton robes. The chiefs and subchiefs had arrived.

Dr. Merrick, looking much younger in jeans and a denim shirt, winked at Kadi. "Hop in," he said, and as each passenger filed into the bus, their names were hurled at Mrs. Pollifax and Kadi. "Chief Kampemba," said Dr. Merrick. "Judge Mutale of the Ubangiban court. . . . Mr. Earnest Malima of the Agricultural School. . . ." Each courteously leaned down to smile at Kadi in her seat and to speak of their *chisoni*—sorrow—at her being hurt.

"And Mr. Dickson Zimba."

On hearing his name, Mrs. Pollifax looked up sharply. No one had mentioned his being so prim-looking a man with such a disapproving glare. He was thin and wiry—like a coiled spring, thought Mrs. Pollifax—and wore gold-rimmed spectacles that magnified intense black eyes. He was the only man not in native garb; he wore a thin black suit and a white shirt. Mrs. Pollifax nodded politely. He took the seat behind them and leaned forward to say importantly, "I am Dickson Zimba, and you—Mrs. Poltiflack?—you are shocked by the poverty of our poor country?"

Turning to look at him, she felt attacked by those piercing black eyes. She said sturdily, "Not so poor that good leadership can't bring great change. And it's Pollifax, not Poltiflack."

"Ha!" he said, and leaned back, saying no more.

She, too, sat back, interested in seeing the country outside Languka, and since it was a drive of over two hours, she was to see a great deal of it: groves of acacia trees, followed by long, dull, flat stretches of bush and scrub, a school, a field of men tying up great bundles of wooden sticks. "Not wood," said Kadi. "Those are millet spikes drying in the sun."

Dr. Merrick drove on toward the long line of hills that loomed now on the horizon, but Mrs. Pollifax could stay awake no longer. She closed her eyes and slept. When the bus came to a stop, she woke up and saw that they had arrived and that the hills had turned into mountains now that they were under them and in their long shadow.

A base camp had been set up here for the miners, furnished with half a dozen tents. The backhoe gleamed bright and yellow in the sun and was surrounded by people. As Mrs. Pollifax looked at the scene more closely, there appeared to be rather a lot of arm waving. She heard shouting and a woman screaming. A swarm of boys raced toward the buses, shouting, *"Imfa! Imfa!"*

Dr. Merrick leaped out of the bus. Mrs. Pollifax bolted after him. When they reached the site, the problem was seen at once. In order to entertain the huge audience that had been waiting since dawn, the foreman, Callahan, had started up his machine and had made a preliminary opening at the base of the hill to demonstrate what a backhoe could do. What had been uncovered was a skull, still half embedded in the earth, its eyeless sockets staring back at a shocked foreman and a frightened crowd.

Dr. Merrick knelt beside the skull and examined it. A minute later he stood and called out, "Steady, everyone. *Not* a new death. What's the word? . . . *Manda! Kalamba! Kale kale."*

"What does all that mean?" asked Mrs. Pollifax.

He grinned. "I *hope* I'm telling them that it's an old grave, very old. I know *kale kale* means 'long ago.' "

They had heard him: The hysteria was fading. Dr. Merrick said to Sammat, who had joined them after disembarking from the third bus, "This skull is old, really old, and friable. You've got to cover this skull right away, or it'll turn to dust. You just may have stumbled on an ancient tomb here, Sammat."

Dickson Zimba said impatiently, "But we want *coal.*"

Sammat turned to the foreman. "Is this precisely where the geologists recommended you start? They found no skull."

Callahan, the foreman, pointed west. "Further along, guv," he said in a cockney accent. "By the red flags. But you can see we're nearer the road and the wells 'ere. What I thought was, if there's coal *there,* there's coal 'ere."

"You must at once move the backhoe farther west now," Sammat told him. "You see what's here."

Callahan returned to the backhoe, climbed aboard it and prepared to move.

"Someone with a shovel. You," Sammat said, pointing to a boy. "Help Dr. Merrick bury the skull, will you?"

"Let me help," said Mrs. Pollifax. The backhoe had roared to life and, like a pied piper, was leading everyone to the new site.

The boy waited, interested, shovel in hand, as the three of them looked over the situation. He said his name was Reuben, and where was he to dig?

"It mustn't be touched," Dr. Merrick said. "I think we just cover it lightly with the earth removed by the backhoe."

Reuben was about to lift his first shovelful of earth when Mrs. Pollifax said, "Wait." She had noticed something in the far corner of the hole, quite separate from the skull. Kneeling, she peered inside, reached out and gently pried loose a small object foreign to the earth. Brushing the soil from it, she said ruefully, "I shouldn't have done this, but *kale kale*, Dr. Merrick?"

The three of them, Reuben as well, bent over her discovery. In the palm of her hand was a circle of metal—iron or bronze—a little over two inches in diameter, with an openwork center laced with curious, raised designs. There were two metal loops at one edge, suggesting that once it might have been linked to a chain.

"Snakes," said Reuben, leaning close to look, pointing with one long dark finger.

Dr. Merrick nodded. "You're right. Definitely they're snakes. I think we show this to Tony Dahl, the World Aid chap at the farm. He spent his college summers with an archaeological team in Egypt. We'll take this to him after lunch. You'll like him."

"I've met him," said Mrs. Pollifax, and with a twinkle in her eye added, "Just what *are* you thinking?"

"I'm thinking that our friend, the future king Sammat, may have an archaeological find on his hands here that could be of far more value—historically, at least—than his coal mine. The only problem," added Dr. Merrick with a frown, "is how superstitious the natives are going to be about this, coupled with rumors of sorcery and four lion murders."

By the middle of the morning they were on their way back to the capital, leaving the backhoe to its excavating. Once at the palace, the guests poured out of their buses, and Kadi, holding Mrs. Pollifax's arm, made her way to Sammat to congratulate him.

He turned at once to her. "Did the trip tire you?"

"I'm okay. I missed most of the fun, but I was glad to be up and out again."

His eyes moved beyond her, and he frowned. "Now what on earth is wrong with Joseph?"

They turned to see the usually calm Joseph pushing his way ruthlessly through the crowd, his eyes blazing with anger. "*Mfumo,* a terrible thing," he shouted. "While you gone, thievery! The secret files kept by President Simoko. In the Strong Room."

Sammat said sharply, "Show me." And to Mrs. Pollifax and Kadi, "This is a serious business. You must excuse me."

"We'll come with you," said Mrs. Pollifax. She and Kadi followed in their wake as Sammat and Joseph made their way through the entrance hall. They continued past a long row of doors and stopped at the last one. It was ajar. They descended into what appeared to be a cement bunker lighted by two feeble bulbs. In the middle of the room stood a young man in a palace guard's uniform. Behind him rose a ceiling-high latticework gate of iron, with a padlock that guarded a smaller room—a vault—fitted with metal drawers. Several of the drawers had been strewn across the floor.

"*Mfumo,*" said the guard, saluting, "I see this and run to tell."

"Good." Sammat walked up to the gate. "Why is it locked?"

"I no touch," said the guard, backing away.

Joseph said in horror, "You mean the lock wasn't broken?"

"Picked," said Mrs. Pollifax knowledgeably, looking at it. "A lock like this would need a little time and a special tool, but a professional could probably do it in ten minutes. What was kept here?"

Eyes narrowed, Sammat said softly, "We've not had the time to go through Simoko's files. There's been so much to do." For a moment he looked very tired, almost defeated.

Kadi, seeing this, rallied to say crisply, "Whatever's stolen would have to be important, Sammy?"

"I suppose in the wrong hands, yes," he said. "But what is most alarming is that whoever did this knew of the Strong Room and how to find it."

"How many know?" asked Mrs. Pollifax.

"Myself. . . . Joseph."

"Police? The palace guards?"

He shook his head. "No one in *my* police. President Simoko's police or aides perhaps. Joseph, who among Simoko's people would have had access?"

Joseph shook his head. "Nobody, I swear. Only President Simoko come here all the time I work in palace. It was known by us, but nobody know which door—only President Simoko."

Straightening his shoulders, Sammat said to Joseph, "At least not much was taken. Someone was very selective, but until we examine what's here and learn more—"

Joseph looked horrified. "You be chief! The *mbala* be found *now*. Punished! Given *mwabvi*."

"The ordeal poison?" Sammat gave him a sharp glance. "There will be no ordeal poison." And to the guard sternly, "No one is to hear of this, you understand?"

The guard nodded.

Sammat said quietly to the others, "Shall we go?"

"As you see, I make many mistakes," Sammat said later, as they stopped in the garden before parting. "I was careless."

"You can't think of everything," Mrs. Pollifax reminded him. "It's been only ten months since you returned, and you've thought of people, not documents and old records."

"Yes, Simoko is the past;" added Kadi, "and you've been thinking of the future. How can you call that a mistake?"

Sammat's hand moved to his forehead to shelter his face. "Nevertheless, something very important has to have been taken from those files to dare such recklessness. A guard checks all the doors, and always the door to the Strong Room, on every round that he makes. Yet someone moved through that padlocked gate inside like a *mzukwa*—a ghost."

"No ghosts," said Kadi firmly.

He smiled faintly. "It's more comfortable to think it a ghost than a fellow human being who can so easily pick locks." He sighed. "I must call Inspector Banda and have the room checked for fingerprints." He looked at Kadi and then at Mrs. Pollifax and suddenly gave them a quick and radiant smile. "I find myself at this moment infinitely grateful you are both here with me."

Mrs. Pollifax said nothing. She was thinking that any enemy of Sammat's could certainly make good use of a dictator's secret files, especially if included among them was a list of informants and spies. It was chilling to realize that President Simoko might be dead but that the people he had corrupted and depended upon were still very much alive.

5

 THE experimental farm, explained Dr. Merrick, occupied fifteen acres of once barren land behind the palace. To Mrs. Pollifax it looked like a giant patchwork quilt of bright varying shades of green. A tall cistern fed a modest irrigation ditch that trickled past small earthen dams against a background in the distance of what looked to be fruit trees. Next to the crudely built warehouse stood the greenhouse.

They found Tony Dahl in the warehouse, inventorying sacks of seed. When he looked up and saw them, his gaze lingered on Kadi with special curiosity. "Oh," he said, flushing, "you have to be Dr. Hopkirk's daughter. Is your arm better?"

Dr. Merrick said dryly, "She's threatening a visit to Sharma if she's not healed inside of twenty-four hours."

"But we're here now to show what we found this morning," said Mrs. Pollifax. Holding out the circle of metal to Tony, she dropped it into his palm.

Tony examined the object, turning it over and over in his hand. "Where did you find this, anyway?"

Dr. Merrick explained, and Tony murmured, "Hmmm. Bronze, very delicate. I'd say it's a medallion of some sort." He looked up at them. "It really does make one think—"

"Of what?" asked Mrs. Pollifax.

"Of doing a bit of careful probing where the skull was found. I mean, to see whether it's a real find. But I'll need permission," Tony said. "Quickly, too, because tomorrow's my day off. Where can I find our busy *mfumo?*"

"He was last seen with Inspector Banda heading down to the storerooms," Merrick said.

"I'll go and look for him. Think there'll be enough gas for my motorcycle?"

"We'll steal enough from *somewhere.*"

Tony said shyly to Kadi, "Perhaps when your arm is okay, you'd care to ride with me on my motorcycle?"

Kadi, glowing, said, "Oh, I'd *love* to."

"That should be better medicine than either Sharma or I can give you," Dr. Merrick told her. "Well, my day off ends all too soon. Have a good evening." Following Tony, he turned to say, "Incidentally, Tony is a *very* nice young man."

It was Kadi who blushed now.

Mrs. Pollifax realized that if she was to reach Cyrus by phone in Connecticut, she had better start the process at once. After escorting Kadi to the infirmary, she began to look for a telephone. What she found instead was Sammat and Inspector Banda talking in low voices in the garden. Pausing, she said, "Excuse me for interrupting, but have you made any headway in finding out who attacked Kadi on Tuesday night?"

"There was a full footprint," Inspector Banda said in a clipped English accent, "but unfortunately, before we could photograph and measure it, a workman blurred it, leaving only a heel mark."

"In any case, that was Tuesday," Sammat said with a sigh. "We now have this entry into the Strong Room, discovered this noon. Inspector Banda has just completed dusting for fingerprints."

"And found none," Mrs. Pollifax said, nodding.

Inspector Banda gave her a sharp glance. "You say this. Why?"

"Because it was done by a professional." She hesitated. "Through a certain government department in the U.S., I've come to know such men who picked locks with ease. They would have worn gloves."

Inspector Banda, startled, gave her a closer look. "We have no experts like that in Languka. In my entire lifetime I've heard of only one person with such a gift. You recall Philimon Tembo?" he said with an inquiring glance at Sammat. "But he's been dead for years."

Sammat frowned. "He could have trained someone."

Banda looked doubtful. "I'll make inquiries." He shook his head. "But so long ago."

Mrs. Pollifax asked, "Sammat, where can I find a telephone?"

"My office. . . . Joseph's there," he said. "Second floor."

"Thank you," she said, and with a nod to the inspector went off.

JOSEPH, it seemed, did not know the word for privacy. He sat unmoving at his desk while Mrs. Pollifax struggled to get her call through to Connecticut. He was shuffling papers, but she knew he was listening, and she found this oppressive. When at last she heard Cyrus's voice, she joyfully shouted, "Cyrus!"

"Well, m'dear," he said, "great relief to hear."

"How are you?" she said lightly. "Still bored and dipping into soap operas?"

He chuckled. "Seems Mrs. Lupacik likes soap operas, too. Very interesting conversations we have." He paused and then said, "You're not alone, I take it."

"Perceptive, as always. Definitely not."

"Then how's Kadi?"

"Well," she said cautiously, "she's been in the infirmary."

Cyrus's voice changed. "Kadi? What's happened?"

"A knife wound, a few stitches. She's up and around now."

"But not an accident, I take it. Who did it?"

"No clues," she said. "It was in the palace garden and at night."

"Next time find an empty room to call me, damn it," he said

impatiently. "I can only imagine what you're *not* saying. Nobody after *you*, I hope?"

"I've met some very interesting people and am quite well, Cyrus. Only five more days until your cast is removed?"

"So the doctor says," he growled. "I'll join you as soon as I can."

"Then Cyrus—" She stopped, aware of Joseph's eyes on her.

"Yes?"

Very softly, quoting Kadi, she said, *"Kam kwik, kwik, bo,"* and hung up.

HEADING for the infirmary to see if Kadi would be there overnight, Mrs. Pollifax found Kadi in bed, with Radia hovering over her.

"She do too much," Radia said chidingly.

"Okay, okay, I admit bed feels awfully good," Kadi confessed with a smile.

Dr. Kasonde, the native physician who worked with Dr. Merrick, made his way down the aisle between beds. "You are Mrs. Pollifax?"

Looking at him, she realized that he was the first plump Ubangiban she had met; her scrutiny met with a round black face radiating cheerfulness. "I am, yes," she said, shaking hands with him. "How is she really, Dr. Kasonde?"

"Basically tip-top," he told her. "But she needs rest to heal. We do not wish an infection."

"But how long?" wailed Kadi from her bed.

He smiled. "We will see in the morning."

Mrs. Pollifax followed him down the aisle to the nurses station. "Dr. Kasonde, tomorrow morning I'd like very much to find and visit the diviner named Sharma. Is he in Languka?"

He nodded gravely. "You wish to consult about this attack on Miss Hopkirk, am I right? He is not far. You bicycle down the road to Government House—the second palace—and across the road from it, there is a path. It runs past an orchard, and then you reach a field and beyond this, there is Sharma . . . a house of wood and roof of thatch."

"Thank you, Dr. Kasonde," she said with equal gravity, and with a wave to Kadi she left.

IN THE MORNING, AFTER A QUICK breakfast of porridge and tea, Mrs. Pollifax walked around the building to the front entrance and extracted her bicycle from the rack. Pedaling down the road toward Government House, she found the path to Sharma's.

It proved a level, well-traveled path at first, skirting a tall hedge of thick brush. Eventually she negotiated a field of scrub and clay and saw a screen of trees ahead and two huts in among them.

She braked, slowly wheeling her bicycle closer. At that moment, from one of the huts, there emerged a diminutive man, wearing several layers of dusty robes that ended at his bony knees, with a circle of pure white goatee at his chin. Mrs. Pollifax and the strange little man observed each other with interest.

She cleared her throat and said, "You— Are you Sharma?"

"*Heya*, the American!" he exclaimed. His voice was light, lyrical, faintly mocking. "Come closer." He indicated the bench next to the door of his hut. "I am Kamuzo Sharma, yes."

"Emily Pollifax," she said, sitting beside him in the sun.

He turned his head to look at her with soft brown eyes. "You are troubled. I see that." Studying her face, he added, "You have come a long way to visit our country."

"Yes," she said, "and to meet *you*."

It was peaceful sitting there. The bright sun filtered through the leaves of the trees, leaving dapples of gold on the earth. A scent of herbs sweetened the air. Off to her right the trees thickened, shading a growth of scrub that rustled a little now in the breeze.

Except, she realized with a start, there was no breeze.

She said abruptly, "I feel watched, Sharma. I *feel* this," and stared into the underbrush, from which she sensed watching eyes.

Sharma said gently, "There are watchers . . . and there are watchers. Shall we go inside now?"

He led her through one dark, cool room into a smaller one. Its reed walls were hung with marvelous woven designs on cloth; carved masks; gourds; totemlike figures; stalks of drying herbs.

"You must take off your shoes and sit," he told her. With a flap of his robes he sat down, and removing her shoes, Mrs. Pollifax joined him on the rough wool rug.

Delving into a leather bag at his side, Sharma drew out an assortment of objects and tossed them across the rug. Holding out the emptied bag, he said, "This is *ku-uzira*—to blow with your breath into it, please."

Intrigued, she did as he said, whereupon he picked up a colorful stick, twirled it and put it to one side to begin studying the objects that lay between them. These were cowrie shells of varying sizes and tints, a few smooth stones, a curiously shaped piece of wood, and several feathers. For a long time Sharma observed them, until he closed his eyes, and she wondered—it was quite possible—if he had gone into a trance.

Opening his eyes, he did not look at her. "You are not here by accident. Since coming here, already you have been very close to evil but not knowing it. It has brushed past you. You have met it, but it is not given to you to recognize it. Not yet. You and Dr. Hopkirk's daughter have souls tied together like *chingwe*—rope— or what you would in the West call fate, and in turn Kadi Hopkirk is tied by fate to *Mfumo* Sammat, like *mbale* and *mlongo*—brother and sister."

There was silence, and then, "There will be more deaths. It is a sickness in the country. Only when the fever breaks will there be a healing and no more sickness."

She said bluntly, "Who attacked Kadi?"

He gave a last glance at the cowries and for the first time looked directly at her. "That is all," he said. Rising nimbly and walking to a wooden bowl, he looked over its contents and brought to her a thin leather necklace laced with feathers and shells. "Wear this," he said. "These have been given much power. To protect."

She hesitated. "Have you one for Kadi?"

He shook his head. "No."

"But . . . why not?" she faltered.

He said gently, "Because it is you who will need protection. Now I must rest."

She nodded and quietly left, wearing the necklace around her neck but troubled and frustrated by what he had told her—so much and yet so little.

Mrs. Pollifax found Kadi in the infirmary, dressed but sitting quietly on her bed, reading. She looked up and said, "Sammy was looking for you."

"For me?"

"Yes. He wondered if you'd help. He's in the Strong Room, and Dr. Merrick wouldn't let me go." She suddenly smiled. "I'm being let out of captivity later this afternoon, at four o'clock."

"I congratulate you. And now I'll see what Sammat wants."

The Strong Room was identifiable by a soldier standing guard beside its door, rifle in hand and a properly stern look on his face. A moment later Sammat was escorting Mrs. Pollifax through the iron gate into the cool, dim concrete vault. He said, "So many papers on the floor! I tried Joseph—him I trust—but he didn't understand what might be of importance."

She saw two chairs and two small tables, on which documents—most of them in English—were piled high. Sammat said, "Take that table on the left. I really appreciate any help you can give me."

"What are we looking for?" asked Mrs. Pollifax.

He said ruefully, "I have no idea, frankly. Something important enough for someone to want. Half of a report, with the other half missing, a page gone. . . ." He shrugged.

Mrs. Pollifax made herself comfortable and began the process of sifting through the papers. A list of names she put aside for Sammat to see, but most of President Simoko's old papers were receipts and copies in triplicate of orders for guns, uniforms, caviar, a hundred cases of champagne. The man had lived well.

She had nearly completed sorting them when Sammat murmured, *"Heya."*

"What is it?" she asked.

"The name of Hopkirk—a report on them." He placed it in front of her and leaned over it. "This is not in English. It reads, 'Hopkirks—known friends of rebel leader Willie Chiume, head of the Freedom Party. May sixth, Dr. Hopkirk set broken leg of rebel-traitor Reuben Matoka. May tenth, removed bullets from two members rebel group: M. Chona, E. Mutale.' "

"But that was his job as a doctor," protested Mrs. Pollifax.

"And here," Sammat said grimly, "here at the end, in Simoko's clumsy writing, is the word *chherra*—set a trap."

"For the Hopkirks?"

Sammat nodded. "Where is that list of names you found?" She handed it to him. He glanced at it. "These men were executed by"—he frowned—"by M, S, S2 and B." He looked thoughtful. "Somewhere, *somewhere* here, there has to be a list of names identifying them. Simoko's secret police were called the Seketera, meaning the 'Witch Finders.' But the people called them simply the Death Squad."

"A codebook, then?" said Mrs. Pollifax, riffling through the remaining papers. "I'll look for a code list."

"I will, too," Sammat said, and returned to his table, to say a moment later, "Here's more on the Hopkirks. On this list Simoko has scribbled 'Hopkirk, spy.' " He shuffled through more papers and groaned. "And here is the order of execution for Dr. and Mrs. Hopkirk, by X12, X2 and X8. On the last day of July."

X12, X2 and X8—Kadi's three men, thought Mrs. Pollifax.

Sammat handed her the slip of paper, and she stared in dismay at the words that so coldly and ruthlessly ordered the murder of Kadi's parents. But something about the paper struck her as odd— it didn't have the weight of the others that she'd held. "This is a copy, Sammat. The original order of execution's not here."

Sammat looked over her shoulder. "You're right."

"The thief could have taken it, then?"

"There is no doubt he stole many things."

"And the letters X12, X2 and X8 each represent a name. But their names have to be somewhere," she said angrily. "What about the other file drawers?"

Sammat walked over to the wall of closed drawers. "Here, at the far end, are President Chinyata's files. His drawers are labeled 'Police,' 'Army,' 'Receipts' . . . The British had taught President Chinyata order. He was much more efficient than Simoko— Chinyata's soldiers and police were fingerprinted and photographed. No hiding behind initials there.

"Now we come to President Simoko's files, which take up most of the vault. Here are the empty slots for the three drawers found on the floor, their papers scattered. These are the drawers that interested our burglar. I've skimmed through the rest, and they hold exactly what they say."

Mrs. Pollifax said thoughtfully, "There would have *had* to be a codebook, a list of every member of Simoko's Death Squad, with the assigned initial and number. And it's gone."

"There's something else missing as well," Sammat said grimly. "The names of the so-called rebels who called themselves the Freedom Party. We found only a report of six of them executed, but there would surely have been a complete list of every suspect."

"So you think the burglar found both the names of the Freedom Party members—"

"And those who survived his executions."

"—as well as the codebook identifying the men of his Death Squad."

He looked helplessly at the files and then at Mrs. Pollifax. Neither of them dared to put into words the infinite possibilities behind what was missing.

6

Once the Strong Room was securely locked, Sammat said, "We must tell Kadi what was discovered."

"And not discovered," said Mrs. Pollifax.

They walked across the entrance hall and into the infirmary, where a surprising scene met them. Kadi stood beside her bed in blue jeans, T-shirt and sandals. Next to her stood Tony Dahl, and at the head of the bed stood both Dr. Kasonde and Dr. Merrick.

Kadi, seeing them approach, called out eagerly, "Tony's found things. It's exciting. He came back early to show us. Look!"

A blanket had been spread across the bed, on which a number of strange and interesting fragments had been placed. Mrs. Pollifax found it an adjustment to shift her attention from the files in the Strong Room back to the discovery of the skull.

Smiling, Tony said to Sammat, "I was very careful, sir. We built a small shaft at an angle to the skull, sifted every inch of earth, and see what was found! Look, here's the broken lip of what was a good-sized pot of coarse clay. Here's a stone bead, carved by hand. And look at this two-inch fragment of a beaded copper chain. It could be part of a necklace belonging to the skull. And of course, there's this medallion Mrs. Pollifax found. I'd like your permission, sir, to call my archaeologist friend Dr. Gibbons. He's in London just now. I can take photographs in detail of what's here and send them along to him. I think he might want to come see for himself."

"Well, by all means call, then, and take your photographs," Sammat said politely, and with a twist of a smile he left them to their newfound treasures.

Tony began picking up the items from the blanket. "I'd better get back to the field office and call Dr. Gibbons." He smiled at Kadi. "Want to come along? I can offer you a soda to celebrate your discharge from the infirmary."

Kadi said, beaming, "That sounds great."

"You're not to overdo things this first day," Dr. Kasonde told her firmly.

Tony grinned. "I promise I'll return her in forty-five minutes."

"And once returned, Kadi," said Mrs. Pollifax, "I've something important to give you. A sort of present."

"More celebration!" exclaimed Kadi, and with a wave of her hand she made her exit.

Once outside and walking alone with Tony, she found herself suddenly lighthearted and absurdly happy. Tony said, "You're not staying until Sammat's coronation next month?"

She said quickly, "I'll be back for it. I came this time— Well, Sammat asked for help."

"But you *will* be back," he said.

She looked up at him and smiled. "I certainly will."

"What help did he need of you?" he asked curiously.

"A little detective work. Because he's in trouble." But she didn't want to talk about Sammat or about leaving Ubangiba, not now, and she changed the subject. "Isn't it exciting, what you found today in the south? If it's important, will they let you take charge?"

"Whoa," he said, looking down at her and smiling. "Archaeology doesn't work that way, and besides, I've a real commitment now to World Aid." Reaching for her hand, he held it companionably as they walked to the field office.

He unlocked the door of the office, and they entered a room whose rough-board walls were papered with thumbtacked schedules, memos, maps, charts and lists; the only furniture, a small gas-run refrigerator, a desk and three chairs. But the desk held that rare object—a telephone—and the refrigerator held several tins of cola, one of which Tony presented to her with a flourish.

"Have a seat," he said. "There could be a miracle, and I'll get through at once to London."

Today, it seemed, there was a miracle, because presently she was hearing words like rim section, transverse grooves and biarcuate bosses. It sounded very professional indeed, and as she watched Tony's eager face and how he ran his hand through his tousled blond hair, she was thinking, I like him, I like him. If I'm not careful, I'm going to fall in love with him.

When he put down the phone, he looked satisfied. "He was impressed. He'll let me know how impressed later."

As they strolled back to the palace, again hand in hand, they were both oddly silent. His motorcycle was just inside the entrance, and she followed him as he wheeled it outside.

Mounting it, he said to her, "I really hate to think of you leaving even for a few weeks. I never thought I'd meet someone like you."

She said gravely, "I feel that way, too. I'm surprised."

He flicked on the ignition. "And if I'm not careful," he said sternly, echoing her own earlier thought, "I'm going to fall in love with you."

With a roar the motorcycle sped away down the driveway, leaving Kadi to whisper, "But don't be *too* careful, Tony, please?"

"AND NOW," SAID MRS. POLLIFAX when Kadi was once again in the room they shared, "now at last for the gift, so to speak, that I was about to give you in the garden the other night." She brought the pistol out of Kadi's knapsack.

"B-but," Kadi stammered, "where on earth did you get this? Guns are banned here."

"I bought it on the black market. Dr. Merrick told me where."

Kadi said, "I do wish I'd had it that night. I was such a fool. . . . And I've shoved deep every memory of those three men. You think the person who attacked me in the garden was really after *me* and connected to that nightmare day?"

"Not necessarily that particular man," said Mrs. Pollifax. "You also glimpsed two other men."

Kadi shook her head. "But I didn't *see* the other two men—only their backs as they walked away."

"Would those two men know that?" she asked. "Kadi, the man who saw you need only have said later, 'The girl was watching. She may have seen *everything*.' You can't overlook the fact that you could still be in some danger if any of those men—X12, X2 and X8—are alive."

"All those initials! What are you talking about?"

"Sammat and I found the orders to execute your parents in the Strong Room this afternoon, Kadi. The killers were referred to as X12, X2 and X8. We couldn't find their names."

"Oh, no," Kadi said.

"So here is the pistol. I'll help make some kind of holster."

There was a glitter of tears in Kadi's eyes. She leaned over and kissed Mrs. Pollifax on the cheek. "I truly thank you for this."

"Now, shall we go down for dinner? Dr. Merrick recommended a quiet evening so that by tomorrow you can do anything you choose. Within reason," she added quickly.

WHAT Kadi chose to do the next morning was to buy presents. "Something to celebrate my release from the infirmary," she said. "A present for Cyrus, and for you, and for my woodcarving teacher at school. I used to visit Esau Matoka and watch him carve little wood sculptures. You'll come, won't you? Esau's not far—just off the boulevard."

"Think you should walk that far?"

"I feel fine, and I'd love to walk."

They began their walk up the boulevard, and Mrs. Pollifax was touched by how many people stopped Kadi to point to her bandaged arm and ask how she was feeling. Strolling past Moses's bicycle shop, Mrs. Pollifax paused at the Bang-Bang Snack Bar. "Let's go in," she said. "It looks very American, and I'm thirsty."

The interior was indeed very American, with Formica tables lining the wall; plastic-covered red seats; and a long counter, with two men in white jackets dispensing food and drink. She and Kadi ordered colas.

Sipping them and facing the window, they were talking, when Mrs. Pollifax glanced up to see a man standing outside and staring intently at the two of them. She recognized him: It was Moses. But before she could lift a hand to wave at him, he had vanished. She said, "The man who sold me my bicycle—I just saw him outside looking at us through the window. I somehow had the idea he was a recluse and never left his compound."

Kadi laughed. "How could anyone never leave? They'd have to buy food, wouldn't they?"

But there had been something disturbing about his gaze and the intensity of it. He was watching us, Mrs. Pollifax thought. Oh, well, she decided with a shrug, and finishing her soda, she smiled. "Esau Matoka next?"

"Oh, yes," Kadi said eagerly, and they walked out into the sun again and crossed the boulevard to the street where Kadi's friend lived. It proved to be a narrow, unpaved lane, shaded by trees and lined with fences. The houses themselves were substantial, being of concrete, with tin roofs. "A luxury," Kadi said, pointing to the roofs. "Expensive."

Mrs. Pollifax felt that even she could have located the Matoka house, because its door had wonderfully carved posts on either side of it. The house had been painted a pale blue, and there were beds of bright flowers. Definitely an artist lived here.

Kadi opened the low gate. "He works in the back, but I'll ring the bell anyway."

The bell hung on a rope beside the door. As Kadi grasped the rope, the first chime was accompanied by a thin scream. Abruptly Kadi silenced the bell, listening. A second scream rent the silence, and without a word Kadi was running around the house to the rear, and Mrs. Pollifax was racing after her, her heart pounding.

He was lying in the dust of the path behind the house, one hand clutching a small carved figure. A slender man, the back of his gray shirt torn into shreds, his neck oozing blood.

It was Kadi who screamed now, and Mrs. Pollifax grasped her and turned her away, saying, "Don't look, don't look!"

"But it's Esau," she sobbed. "It's Esau."

"Go and get help," Mrs. Pollifax told her. "Hurry, Kadi."

Sobbing, Kadi obeyed, calling out as she went, "Help! Somebody help!"

Mrs. Pollifax knelt beside the man and studied what she could see: the mark of claws on his right cheek, the terrible marks on the back and the neck. She doubted he was still alive.

The dust had scarcely settled from his fall to the earth. He must have been attacked at the very moment that she and Kadi walked up the path to his house, and this meant the killer couldn't have gone far. Glancing around, she observed her surroundings. Some nine feet away stood Esau's workshop. Behind this rose a thicket of vines and brush, at one point broken and flattened. The killer came through to him from the rear, she thought.

With a shiver she returned her attention to Esau and sat quietly, keeping watch over him, brushing flies away from the still and bloody body. And once again there came over her the feeling that she was being watched, just as *she* kept watch over Esau.

Out on the street she heard voices at last, but at the same moment, off to the right behind the workshop, she heard the snapping of dried twigs. Someone was retreating in haste, and she thought furiously, I really *was* being watched; there was someone standing there all this time.

The yard was suddenly full of people: two young men in police uniform and three little boys and several women, awed and curious. There was the sound of a car, and Inspector Banda came hurrying in, followed by Kadi. It was Inspector Banda who turned over the body, and after one quick glance Kadi looked away.

"Come, Kadi," Mrs. Pollifax said gently. "Leave it to the police now." She guided Kadi out to the street and then to the boulevard. As they reached the snack bar, a movement next door to it caught her eye. The gate to Moses's bicycle compound was just closing and then was abruptly slammed shut.

7

THERE had now been five lion deaths. In Ubangiban the word for "five" was *zisanu*, explained Tony Dahl the next morning. Mrs. Pollifax said crossly she wanted no more deaths to count off in either English or Ubangiban.

"Fair enough," said Tony, "and anyway, what I came to you with is an invitation. Dr. Gibbons is flying in this morning from London. He'll only be here overnight. Considering what a dreadful day Kadi had yesterday—and you, too," he added quickly, "I've been given the day off to drive him down to look over the site near that coal mine. It would be good for Kadi, don't you think?"

"I agree," said Mrs. Pollifax. "Ah, here she comes now."

Kadi looked her rosy self again—she had the resilience of youth—but Mrs. Pollifax noticed that her eyes held a sadness, a wariness that were new. Tony was right, though—a trip south would be a happy distraction, and his company even more so.

"He's coming so quickly?" Kadi said in surprise. "You haven't even sent the photographs, have you?"

Tony said modestly, "Well, he knows me, you see." He glanced at his watch. "His plane's due in twenty minutes. Let's see if Mr. Zimba's brought the World Aid jeep yet."

"Dickson Zimba?" said Mrs. Pollifax.

Tony nodded. "This week he's been doing some accounting work for us at World Aid." He added ruefully, "For some reason we all take great care to call him *Mister* Zimba. Wouldn't dare otherwise! There's something about him."

Mrs. Pollifax smiled. "Yes. I've met him."

Dickson Zimba was seated stiffly behind the wheel of a Land Rover, on which the insignia of World Aid was barely visible under coats of dust. With equal stiffness he climbed out, gave Kadi a curious glance and Mrs. Pollifax a curt nod, and walked away, very erect and elegant in a black silk suit. He must, thought Mrs. Pollifax, have *hated* delivering the jeep to Tony.

THE plane arrived on time, and Dr. Gibbons surprised Mrs. Pollifax. If Tony hadn't identified him, she would never have guessed this boyish, elfinlike man to be Dr. Gibbons. He was thin, his face was thin, his white hair was thin, but there was a mischievous quality about him. He was wearing polished loafers, chinos and a shirt without a tie; he carried a tweed jacket over one arm and an attaché case in the other hand. She guessed him to be in his late fifties.

Tony said dryly, "I have to warn you—he'll keep forgetting your names. But I think you'll like him."

Seeing Tony, he rushed toward him, saying, "Oh, my, oh, my, here you are, and with this exciting news! And you've found two lovely women as well. Both of you are Red Cross?"

"It's World Aid here," Tony told him politely.

"Oh, yes, of course. We can visit the site now?"

"Have you a suitcase?" asked Mrs. Pollifax.

He looked at her in astonishment. "I have, yes. So good of you to remind me," he said, and once this had been retrieved, they set out for the south.

It was a pleasant drive, and they arrived at noon. Nearly a mile to the west Mrs. Pollifax could see the tents and huts of the mining crew, the backhoe standing idle. Mounds of earth stood pyramid-like behind it, wrested out of the hills.

The trench that Tony had made on his first visit had been roughly filled in for concealment. From his suitcase Dr. Gibbons removed a trowel, a square of screening framed in wood, innumerable plastic bags and sacks, two cameras and what looked like a miniature Geiger counter. By the time Tony joined him, carrying a shovel, Mrs. Pollifax and Kadi had retired to one of the few bushes growing out of the hillside that was large enough to provide shade. There they sat companionably.

Something worried Tony. "Footprints," he pointed out. "People have been here. Look." He walked several paces from the trench. "Someone's dug a hole here."

Kadi joined him to look. "Deep?"

Mrs. Pollifax called out, "There's another hole off to your right."

Dr. Gibbons walked over to examine it. "Anybody else know about what you found here?" he asked.

"The entire infirmary," Kadi said, looking chagrined.

"Nothing to be done about it now except praise the gods they didn't know where to dig. Let's get to work. You, Mrs. . . ."

"Pollifax," she told him kindly.

"Yes. Keep an eye out for people."

The afternoon wore on. The sun moved across the sky, and fingers of shadow slipped down the hill, but there began to be no doubt that what they had found by accident was proving to be a real find. The trench was deepened and extended, and when Dr. Gibbons rose at last, leaving Tony to fill in and rake over the trench, even Mrs. Pollifax was excited. They had found a broken half of a curved and hollow bronze object, intricately decorated, that Dr. Gibbons thought belonged to a *siwa*, a ceremonial horn. There were also fragments of bone, three more stone beads that matched the one found earlier by Tony, and a small flat bronze rectangle with an intricate, raised design.

"What now?" asked Mrs. Pollifax.

"I take these back to be tested, cleaned, examined, photographed and dated, and start begging funds to really get something major started here." Dr. Gibbons looked wistfully at the trench site. "Hate to leave, hate to."

The four of them carefully inspected the site, agreed that all signs of digging had been erased and began the long drive back to the capital.

In midmorning of the next day Mrs. Pollifax and Kadi strolled slowly up the boulevard, and Mrs. Pollifax learned that a visit to the market was very different in Kadi's company. A stall with mysterious powders displayed on its counter was a magic shop, Kadi explained. A goatskin that Mrs. Pollifax thought might be of interest as a small rug had not been properly dressed, Kadi said.

As they wandered, Kadi said, "Look! Violet Kamangu's here today. She makes glorious necklaces. Violet, how are you?"

"Kadi! And the bicycle lady." She rose and hugged Kadi, while Mrs. Pollifax stared at her, staggered by her beauty: The woman had the profile of Nefertiti.

She had a tray full of necklaces, fashioned of bone, shells, beads and grasses. "But nothing of Esau's," she told them sadly.

"These necklaces are certainly unusual," Mrs. Pollifax said.

Violet picked up a necklace of carved bone and hung it around Mrs. Pollifax's neck. Purchases were made, gossip exchanged, and when they turned to leave, it was to find Dickson Zimba standing behind them.

"Mr. Zimba," murmured Mrs. Pollifax.

He bowed stiffly. "I feel I was most rude to you on the bus, Mrs. Pollifax. Just now, passing, I hear you speak of Esau Matoka's art? Please, to make amends, across the street in Mbuzu's shop I know there is one of his carvings. I do invite you to see."

The shop was near the bank, in a row of five narrow cement-block cubicles. There was a door, and one very dirty window with bars, and a sign—MBUZU'S. GIFTS. FURNITURE.

Dickson Zimba opened the door, ushered them inside and firmly closed the door behind him. They entered a long and narrow room, made even darker by a door at the rear of the shop that had been left open to an almost blinding sunshine. As her eyes adjusted to the darkness in the store, Mrs. Pollifax realized it was empty of Mr. Mbuzu. A counter held trays of gaudy imported jewelry.

"But nothing of Esau's here," protested Kadi.

Only junk, thought Mrs. Pollifax, glancing around, and she looked at Dickson Zimba. "Nothing of Esau's," she repeated.

Zimba's eyes blinked rapidly behind his spectacles; the glasses magnified his eyes and he looked— How *did* he look? Embarrassed? Pleased? Abruptly Mrs. Pollifax realized that she and Kadi were exactly where they must never be: isolated in a room, in the company of a stranger who had artfully persuaded them here . . . into a potential trap? She took a step back, staring at him. Kadi sensed her distress and said to Mr. Zimba, "Go. . . . We have to go. *Must.*"

"Please, no," said Mr. Zimba in a choked voice. Then his gaze shifted beyond them, to the open back door, and he looked startled. Turning, Mrs. Pollifax was just in time to see the silhouette of a huge man outlined against the sun. The figure of Moses filled the doorway, moved and was gone. Then the front door opened, and a black man in a brightly colored robe walked in. When he said, "Mr. Zimba! You be customer?" Mrs. Pollifax breathed a sigh of relief.

Dickson Zimba spoke to the man in Ubangiban. Mr. Mbuzu opened a rusty safe and drew out a tall cup that had been marvelously carved out of a satiny brown wood, a full ten inches in height.

"Esau's work," breathed Kadi. "He's carved a ceremonial cup."

The purchase was made, Kadi thanked both the shopkeeper and Dickson Zimba, and they walked out into the hot noon sunshine. "But please," Kadi said, "what were you thinking back there? You looked, you looked . . ." She fumbled for words.

Mrs. Pollifax could only repeat what had occurred to her at that earlier moment. "I realized we were exactly where we shouldn't be, cut off from the street and in the company of a man—"

"Don't finish," Kadi said quietly. "It suddenly came to me, too. You really think that maybe Dickson Zimba . . ."

Mrs. Pollifax sighed. "I have a lively imagination, Kadi."

"But he did have an awfully strange look on his face," Kadi said, frowning. "And then came that spooky figure at the back door—a giant! I wish I could have seen his face. But then he just disappeared. Did you see him?"

"I saw him," said Mrs. Pollifax, and thought, Yes, and saw him two days ago staring at us through the window of the Bang-Bang Snack Bar, and an hour later his gate was closing after we had found Esau murdered, and all the time that I waited beside Esau's body, I was being watched.

Had it been Moses?

Who *was* Moses? She had asked him, and he'd said, "Nobody."

She remembered that when she first saw his hostile glare, she had been tempted to flee. Yet after meeting him, she had ended up liking Moses very much indeed.

She thought unhappily, Perhaps it's time now to ask how sane a man may be after being imprisoned and tortured for seven years. I don't want to think it, but I must.

She felt a sudden, urgent need to call Cyrus and to talk of familiar things with him, such as Mrs. Lupacik, soap operas and whether it had snowed since the morning she left.

"Has it snowed?" she asked Cyrus when her call was put through to Connecticut.

"Emily," he said, "why are you calling me from Africa to ask if it's snowed? Don't like the sound of your voice, either. You're in trouble. You alone now? Can you talk?"

"Guardedly," she told him, "but for a few minutes *you* talk."

Mercifully, he understood. He said there had been an inch of snowfall during the night; that Mrs. Lupacik was sure that in the soap opera *Time and Tide,* Winsome Aubrey couldn't possibly be a thief; that Mrs. Lupacik had sternly removed eggs from his diet.

"Is that mundane enough for you?" he said. "Your turn now. Speak."

Mrs. Pollifax carefully edited what she had been going to say, aware that Cyrus felt helpless enough without adding worry to his circumstances. She explained what it meant in Ubangiba to be rumored a sorcerer, that in rapid succession there had been several odd deaths and that Kadi was fine now.

"I can read between the lines, m'dear," he said. "Odd deaths indeed! Be careful, Em, you hear?"

LATE THAT AFTERNOON, WHILE KADI was picking beans with Tony at the farm, Mrs. Pollifax walked into the office of the *mfumo* and asked Joseph when she might see Sammat.

Joseph looked at her and frowned. "He be busy. Up at four a.m. today. Many conferences. He be on *telephone* now."

"I see." She frowned. "Joseph, you work with Sammat."

"*Mfumo* Sammat," he put in quickly, correcting her.

"Yes, but how is he really? Is he eating and sleeping well?"

"Pretty good," Joseph said stiffly, "but he work too hard."

"Joseph, do you think Mr. Dickson Zimba likes your *mfumo*? He is known to be difficult. He is not—not an *enemy*, is he?"

Joseph's face tightened. "Enemy?" He considered this. "He have *mapundi*." He reached for the English word. "Insolence? Recklessness? *Mapundi*."

The door to the inner office opened, and Sammat appeared, tall, serious and frowning. When he saw her, his face brightened. "Ah, friend Pollifax," he said. "You come at just the right moment. Let's buy two sodas from the cafeteria and sip them in the garden."

As they walked down the hall to the staircase, Mrs. Pollifax said lightly, "Does Joseph disapprove of me?"

Sammat grinned. "I think this week he disapproves of *me*."

"Joseph? Why?"

"One of the big problems in Africa is nepotism," Sammat said as they descended the staircase, "and I'm determined to prevent it. Joseph is testing me, once again approaching me about a cousin of his needing a job, when the young man hasn't even completed school. No, he doesn't disapprove of you." Reaching the cafeteria, he insisted on paying for two sodas and led her out to the table and chairs beside the low wall of bougainvilleas.

"I wanted to ask you," said Mrs. Pollifax, "has Inspector Banda any suspect or suspects yet in the murders?"

Sammat's lips tightened. "In the murder of Esau Matoka a few shreds from the lion mask were caught on the branches of the underbrush behind the workshop. They are synthetic, fake."

"The mask has been made with local material that could be traced?"

"He hopes so."

Frowning, Mrs. Pollifax said, "But it's the motive behind the murders that interests me, as it must you," she added carefully. "It began after the decision was made that you be crowned?"

"Yes. Everything was going very well until then," said Sammat.

"Someone objects, then, to your increased power? You *must* know of someone you've affronted."

He sighed. "I cannot name an enemy, and now there have been five lion deaths. Inspector Banda is as baffled as I."

Mrs. Pollifax nodded. "You hoped that Kadi might circulate among the villagers and help, Sammat. But since she's been incapacitated, I've been trying to substitute for her."

He said gently, "If Inspector Banda can make no headway—and he is very good—what can a *mzungu* do?"

"A *mzungu*," she said quickly, "can see what you may not, simply because she is a *mzungu* and foreign here."

"You do not even speak the language," he reminded her.

She smiled faintly. "People are the same all over the world, Sammat. Black, brown or white, we have the same longings, hopes, triumphs, failures, fears, anxieties, worries. Even a *mzungu*—an experienced one—can notice, watch, regardless of language."

Sammat said ruefully, "Then I apologize."

She said, "What about Dickson Zimba?"

Sammat laughed. "But I've told you—he's quite harmless, you know. He heads the Soto delegation. He will rise quickly."

She looked at him with exasperation. Surely, he was not unacquainted with evil, not when his father had been assassinated. Sammat, she decided, was determined to think well of everyone. She wanted to shake him and say, "Sammat, someone wants to destroy you!" Then it occurred to her that perhaps he had known so much tragedy in his young life that he had survived only by suppressing memories. Or perhaps what he was really suppressing was fear.

She rose, saying quietly, "Do sit here and relax, Sammat. And thank you for the treat."

She would have gone directly to her room, but as she passed into the marbled entrance hall, she glanced through the glass doors and saw Kadi outside, talking to Tony, seated in a dusty pickup truck. She changed direction to join them.

Seeing her, Kadi said, "Tony's been worried about what he calls the dig. Would you believe it? Yesterday he borrowed this World Aid truck, drove south and camped out there for the night."

Tony said, "Yes, and heard voices. I turned on my flashlight and scared them. They'd been poking around our trench. I saw three shadowy figures run away."

"But that's dangerous for him," pointed out Kadi, "and now he's leaving again to guard the site. Do you think I could lend—"

She was going to mention her pistol, and to forestall this, Mrs. Pollifax said firmly, "No, Kadi. . . . Tony, why don't you speak to the mine foreman down there, explain the situation and ask if some of the tents the workers live in could be moved closer to the site? There's no reason why a few of them couldn't keep an eye out for prowlers."

"Good thinking," said Tony, switching on the engine. "I'll reach the site before dark." He revved up the motor and roared away, leaving a cloud of dust behind him.

KADI had enjoyed picking beans at the farm on Monday, but she had torn her blue jeans, and the next morning Mrs. Pollifax watched with amusement as she sewed up the long tear with bright red wool borrowed from Radia in the infirmary.

"You'll begin a new style," commented Mrs. Pollifax.

"Ha," sniffed Kadi. "I just wish I'd brought more clothes." She sat back and said thoughtfully, "You know, I do hope no one steals anything from the dig. It's exciting to think what it could mean, especially for Ubangiba, if it turns out they find something really important. It would be horrid if anybody should steal what's there."

"Agreed," said Mrs. Pollifax.

Kadi brightened. "If the mine foreman moves some of his men nearer the road to guard Tony's dig, it would be fun to borrow another truck and go down and camp out in that truck for the night. And on the way back the next morning, we could stop at my village—where I grew up—and I could show it to you."

"But first joining Tony at the site for a camp-out?"

Kadi blushed. "I don't know why not. We could sleep in the back of the truck, and it would be quite safe, wouldn't it? I'd have my pistol and you have your karate, and in the morning, visiting my village, I'd be doing what Sammat hoped I would do: talk to people and learn things."

This was a new Kadi, impaled by first love or infatuation, thought Mrs. Pollifax, and she briefly lamented the exigencies of being chaperon as well as guardian for a teenaged girl. Kadi was a darling but vulnerable. Tony was older—well into his twenties—capable and very nice indeed. The problem was how to guard Kadi without imprisoning her.

Choosing a neutral subject while she thought about this, she said, "It is high time you find out what friends in your village are feeling and saying about Sammat."

Kadi nodded. "Radia was there on Saturday. Her relatives are still back in the village, and she visits them once a month."

"Has she said how they're reacting to rumors that Sammat's behind these murders? Are they turning against him?"

"The rumors trouble them," Kadi acknowledged. "Sorcery is a terrible thing, but Sammy's the grandson of King Zammat, and superstitious they may be, but King Zammat was really loved. Oh, he was regal but so kind. Wise, too. And a king, you know, has always been the heart and the soul of the country. It's why the people—in my village, at least—are very disturbed." She added sadly, "I don't know how long it will be before the rumors win and they turn on him or riot. I can't believe they'd *kill* Sammy," she said, "not when he's the last of the royal line."

Mrs. Pollifax thought, It takes only one person to assassinate a chief or a king, and it will surely be the man who hides behind a lion mask.

Kadi gave her a pleading glance. "But what about the overnight camping trip?"

Mrs. Pollifax said carefully, "I have nothing against such an expedition, Kadi, but I have to add one stipulation. It would be foolhardy to go without added protection. If Sammat will assign a soldier or two, or a pair of armed and trustworthy men, only then."

"For just a simple camping trip?" protested Kadi.

Mrs. Pollifax said tartly, "Nothing is simple just now in Ubangiba."

SAMMAT agreed to at once assign two armed security guards, Bristol Tanko and Roy Siwale, to accompany them on their trip.

After joyfully telling Mrs. Pollifax this news, Kadi raced off to the experimental farm. While she was gone, Mrs. Pollifax put in a call to Cyrus, borrowing Joseph's office again.

Her call went through quickly, but the connection was poor and Cyrus's voice muffled. "Cast's off!" he announced in triumph.

"Cyrus, I'm so glad. When can you travel?"

"Not for a few more days," he growled. "Muscles flaccid, doctor tells me. Three days of intense physical therapy ahead."

"Can you walk?"

"Gingerly. Not coming home yet, I take it?"

She winced. "Not quite yet."

"Right." She could picture him nodding his head. "This is Tuesday. I'll make reservations today and hope to be on the Monday flight into Languka."

She wondered what to say, until brightening, she confided that an overnight camping trip was being planned. This sounded carefree and innocent—she only wished it felt so—and on that note their conversation ended. She hung up, relieved that Cyrus hadn't noticed anything in her voice that suggested worry.

While she had been closeted in Joseph's office calling Cyrus, she found that plans had been quickly made. Tony was going to steal half a day from his weekly day off, and they were to leave for the south tomorrow, on Wednesday, after lunch. They would go in two pickup trucks, loaded with bedrolls and sleeping bags and picnic dinners for themselves and the two guards, returning Thursday to Languka by nine o'clock in the morning.

Tony would also, at the last minute, add a volleyball.

Mrs. Pollifax would remember that volleyball for a very long time.

8

THE two guards, Roy and Bristol, were cheerful young men drawn from Sammat's palace guard. They knew Tony and had an easy, bantering relationship with him.

Blankets and bedrolls were piled in the back of the two pickup trucks. Mrs. Pollifax was given a seat next to Roy, who would drive the first truck, while Kadi rode next to Tony in the second truck, with Bristol in the rear among the bedrolls, rifle in hand.

It was late afternoon when they reached their destination and parked in the shadow of the hills. Across the treeless, barren strip of land they could see the backhoe shining in the sun and figures moving around it. Whatever villages existed in the neighborhood were hidden behind the woods that rimmed the broad field lying at the base of Tony's dig.

They inspected the site, and Mrs. Pollifax noted how regretfully Tony left it. "You want to dig more," she said, smiling.

"Gets in your blood," he admitted. "At least nobody's visited it today. Apparently, they come only at night, when it's dark."

They reached into the hamper for sandwiches—*sangwis* in pidgin, laughed Kadi—and sat on the bedrolls in the truck. Tony dug among the blankets and brought out the volleyball. "We can kick this around," he said, gesturing toward the expanse of field around them.

This was received with enthusiasm. They climbed down from the truck, and Tony produced a campstool for Mrs. Pollifax to sit on. After inspecting the ground for scorpions and snakes, he set it up for her.

"Soccer?" asked Roy.

Tony pointed to Kadi's bandaged arm. "We kick the ball, okay?" They agreed and formed a circle that gradually expanded, the

405

four of them making a great deal of youthful noise. Mrs. Pollifax watched from the sidelines. Their shouts brought attention, and presently half a dozen of the mining crew, all Ubangibans, wandered down to watch.

Seeing them, Kadi called out, "Want to play, too?"

Tony shouted, "Yes, spread out! Come play kick-the-ball!"

With enthusiasm they formed a great circle, and the ball shot back and forth from one to another, with much laughter.

Callahan, the foreman, strolling down to see what was happening, said, "They're a good lot of men, I can tell you. I've 'ad worse. The girl yours?"

Mrs. Pollifax glanced toward Kadi, who had established herself near the woods. The ball came toward Kadi, and she kicked it away. Mrs. Pollifax heard Kadi's neighbor shout, "Good show."

"Kadi's a good friend," she told Callahan, glancing at the sun. "But it will soon be dark. I think they should stop." Already she could see a pale crescent moon in the darkening sky. She glanced again toward Kadi and was startled to see no sign of her. Her eyes moved quickly around the field, and she felt a first clutch of fear.

"Where's Kadi?" she called to Tony.

He turned toward her. But already Mrs. Pollifax was running across the field. To the young man who had called "Good show" she cried, "Where is she? Where's Kadi?"

Tony, catching up, said to the young man, "What's your name?"

"Jacob Bwanausi."

"Jacob, the girl—Kadi—where has she gone?"

"I see her turn. She go thus." He pointed toward the woods and to the edge of the field among the trees. "I hear her call out in very happy voice, 'Philimon, it's really *you*?' Then ball is kicked to me, and when I look back, she be gone. This be all I know."

"A *happy* voice?" echoed Mrs. Pollifax.

Jacob nodded. "This I hear. She sing it like a song."

"She can't be far," gasped Tony. "Callahan, can we borrow your men?"

"You already 'ave 'em," he said dryly, and shouted orders.

But it was Mrs. Pollifax who led the way, preceding even Tony and repeating over and over to herself that Kadi's voice had been happy at whomever she'd seen. But where was she now, and who on earth was Philimon? And if Kadi hadn't wanted to go, why hadn't she used the gun she wore in the ankle holster they'd so carefully made?

In spite of her frightened thoughts, her experienced eye was noting how the tall grass had flattened to form a path: Someone had walked here to the field and watched them play, and had made himself known to Kadi. But Kadi would never *never* go with a stranger. Why had she trusted the man who had called to her?

Something was terribly wrong.

Eventually, after pushing their way through the underbrush, they met with a rutted thread of a road. Jacob, pointing to the left, said, "That go to village. Other way to main road, Languka."

Bristol said, "I'll go to the village. I know it."

Tony nodded. "Good, and Jacob and I will try the main road."

They rushed away in opposite directions. Mrs. Pollifax turned to Callahan and said, "What I want is a telephone. Fast."

Callahan led the way back, with Mrs. Pollifax and the remaining men behind him. Once through the woods, it was a mile to Callahan's trailer, and Mrs. Pollifax was ushered in.

Callahan reached for the telephone and waited. "I hear nothing," he said. "Phone's dead."

"There should be an operator?"

"Goes through the army barracks' switchboard in Languka. They do the connecting. Damn fools," he growled. "They set it up two weeks ago for me, and already it's not working."

She said quietly, "Or the line's been cut."

He stared at her. "That would mean the girl disappearing was *planned?* What the 'ell's going on?"

Mrs. Pollifax told him. Then, "I've got to get back to the capital."

"I'll drive you down to the pickup truck. Come along now."

They found Tony standing beside the truck. "Any news?" he called.

"Mr. Callahan's phone is dead," she told him. "We've got to get to the police, Tony, to Languka."

Grimly he said, "Let's go."

407

IT WAS A SLEEPLESS NIGHT. MRS. Pollifax and Tony waited with a stunned Sammat in Inspector Banda's office, while in another part of the police station Jacob Bwanausi was questioned. Hours later the three of them drove back to the palace, made tea and coffee in the deserted cafeteria and carried their cups to Sammat's office, where they sat, each of them trying not to think what might be happening to Kadi and whether they would see her alive again. Certainly, Inspector Banda had refused Mrs. Pollifax even the small comfort that Kadi could have gone willingly with her abductor or have even known him.

"To put it bluntly," he'd said, "why would she consider leaving you and Mr. Dahl when she was having a very good time on a picnic she herself had planned?"

This, of course, was unanswerable.

Around three in the morning their silence was interrupted by Joseph. He had just heard of this terrible news, he said. "Who could have done this? Inspector Banda be good man, he must—*must*— know who do this."

"He doesn't," Sammat said wearily.

"But what he be doing? He *must* be finding who did this!"

He seemed genuinely upset, and Mrs. Pollifax appreciated his concern, but she also wished Joseph would calm down or go away. His excited questions were quite unlike him, until she recalled his emotional outburst over the Strong Room's having been entered.

At dawn Inspector Banda came in his Land Rover with Jacob Bwanausi to pick up Mrs. Pollifax; they were both to be taken south to show him precisely where Kadi had vanished. Tony had work to do at the farm, while Sammat had appointments.

It was a long, hot drive. Once at the site, the next hours seemed unending. Each of the kick-the-ball players was questioned. Inspector Banda combed the woods, looking for footprints or signs of violence. He found nothing. After this, while Mrs. Pollifax waited, he drove out to the main thoroughfare and turned up the road leading to the nearby village. When he returned from questioning the elders, however, he had learned one small thing at last.

"They tell me a very old truck was parked at the side of this narrow road leading into the village for a couple of hours late yesterday afternoon. It was parked pretty much in line with the path out of the field, the route Kadi would have been forced along."

Forced, thought Mrs. Pollifax, trying not to think of Kadi's being forced anywhere. "Do you have a description of it?"

He sighed. "Only that it was used and shabby. Possibly an old army truck. But at least we can assume for the moment she's no longer in this immediate area—that is, if the truck belonged to her abductor. I'll ask for soldiers to begin searching down here in the south. My police will start with Languka, a house-to-house search for Miss Hopkirk and someone named Philimon and for a truck of that description." He added politely, "We will find her, madam."

Mrs. Pollifax thought it generous of him not to add "dead or alive."

That evening Dr. Merrick knocked on Mrs. Pollifax's door and walked in. He said, "I caught a glimpse of you this afternoon, and you looked awful. I'll bring you a sleeping pill to help you sleep tonight. You're imagining the worst?"

"Of course," she admitted.

"So let me point out one heartening detail, my dear Mrs. P. Twenty-five hours have now passed since Kadi was abducted, and each poor soul murdered by the lion killer was discovered inside of twelve hours. Whoever this devil may be, he wants his victims found quickly, for the terror of it, and kills accordingly."

"I suppose that helps, but I was thinking of the attack in the garden on Kadi," she told him. "The day of her parents' murders by Simoko's men she was returning to the clinic when she heard the gunshots, and hid and watched from the bush. She saw the face of one of the killers, and at the same time, he turned and saw her, which makes her a witness and dangerous to them if they're still alive."

Dr. Merrick said quietly, "You feel the attack in the garden could have been one of those three men?"

"It's been a worry to me from the beginning," she admitted.

"Hmmm," he murmured thoughtfully. "That *could* be important, Ubangiba being such a different place now—law and order established, courts and judges, et cetera. But following through on that possibility, wouldn't this have to mean that one of those chaps has become so well known and so respectable now that to be recognized as one of Simoko's hit men would ruin him?"

She gave him a quick glance. "That's very shrewd of you. It would certainly explain motivation this many years after the murders, wouldn't it?" She nodded.

"If a man has a reputation to protect and sustain."

"A man of reputation," she repeated, and smiled. "Dr. Merrick, you've give me something graspable at last, and I thank you." She nodded, satisfied. "I'll take the sleeping pill, because I see that I've a busy day ahead tomorrow."

BEING unaccustomed to a sleeping pill, the effect of it carried Mrs. Pollifax beyond her usual eight o'clock. She woke at half past nine. After a good night's sleep she still pulsed with determination, but now she wondered how on earth she could use it to find Kadi when no one else could. Well, she thought, lying here in bed and thinking doesn't help. It was time to visit Sharma, talk with Inspector Banda and with Sammat, ask questions.

Quickly dressing, she began her trip downstairs, but on reaching the second-floor balcony, she was surprised to hear a buzz of angry voices below. Looking down into the huge lobby, she was even more startled to see small groups of workingmen with worn and dusty faces talking among themselves with angry gestures.

Behind her a door slammed, and Sammat hurried toward her, followed by Joseph. "They've found the lion man," he said curtly. "The killer." To Joseph he said, "Take over, Joseph. Mrs. Pollifax will come with me. They may have news of Kadi."

"But who did they find?" she asked as they rushed down the staircase.

"I don't know. Inspector Banda left an urgent message to come at once. A car's waiting."

They hurried outside, where a palace guard was waiting with the Land Rover. In the car, Sammat explained, "It was a busy night here in Languka. They questioned every Philimon they could find, and now something has happened."

It was not far. They drove through the gates into the police station's compound, and here, too, were clusters of men waiting. As they climbed out of the Land Rover, the inspector came out to meet them. "They've found him. And here they come now," he said as a closed sedan inched its way into the compound.

The curious onlookers began to follow, until Inspector Banda called out sharply, "Keep them out! Close the gate!"

The car came to a stop, the rear door opened, and an armed policeman stepped out, reluctantly followed by a handcuffed man in a pale gray robe and sandals.

It was Dickson Zimba.

"Oh, no," groaned Sammat. "Not Dickson!"

Zimba looked frantic. He shouted to Sammat, "I am not guilty of this. No! *Bozaa*—a lie!" He burst into tears, and his glasses fell off. The guard scornfully plucked them from the ground and pocketed them, and led him into the police station.

Sammat, stunned, said, "I don't understand. Zimba?" and to Inspector Banda, "Any sign of Kadi Hopkirk?"

Inspector Banda's stern face softened. "Nothing. No sign. It was Officer Chibabila who shone his flashlight through a window last night and saw a lion mask lying on a bed. It seems that Mr. Zimba rents a room behind the Bang-Bang Snack Bar, and this was his room. We were told that frequently he returns to the desert to see his father, and that's where he was found. No, there was no sign of Miss Hopkirk ever being in either place." He gave a brisk nod and turned. "Now I must question him, please."

For Mrs. Pollifax it was unbearable to look into Sammat's face, because she, too, was shocked. Who could have believed it would actually be Dickson Zimba? In that one moment of his defeat, leaving the car in handcuffs, he had been not a monster but as vulnerable as any human being, whose glasses fell off and who wept.

She grieved for Sammat, and yet in spite of the shock and horror of its being Zimba, she recognized in herself a sense of relief. She'd been growing very afraid the killer might be Moses, with whom she'd shared those brief moments of warmth.

411

She sighed. The killings would end now, but Kadi was still missing. If Kadi had not been found with Dickson Zimba, in either his rented city room or in the desert with his father, then it was possible that Zimba had nothing at all to do with her disappearance.

Which brought her to Philimon again.

Sadly Sammat glanced at his watch. "I must go back and prepare a message to transmit to the people, telling them the killer's been found. Tomorrow is Joseph's day off, and suddenly there is too much to do." He added in an anguished voice, "But why Dickson Zimba? *And where is Kadi?*"

She could only shake her head, finding no comfort for him.

They drove back to the palace. The lobby had emptied. Sammat hurried to the staircase to return to his office. Mrs. Pollifax hesitated; then she crossed the entrance hall and headed to the infirmary.

She found Radia in the doctor's office. "Kadi—have you news, please?" Radia asked.

Mrs. Pollifax shook her head. "You're my last hope, Radia. I need information. I don't know whether you've heard that it's possible Kadi left willingly with her captor?"

"Willingly?" Radia looked shocked. "I hear nothing of this!"

Mrs. Pollifax said dryly, "Possibly because Inspector Banda doesn't *believe* she went willingly. They were all playing kick-the-ball that afternoon, and Kadi was over near the woods. The young man nearest saw her walk to the edge of the woods, as if called there by someone. He heard her say in a happy voice, 'Philimon, it's really you?' and when he looked again, she was gone."

"A trick," gasped Radia. "A trap."

"It sounds that way now," admitted Mrs. Pollifax.

"But this Philimon—who could that be?"

Mrs. Pollifax sighed. "Someone she'd not seen in a long time. Perhaps someone she knew back in the old days."

"In the old days," repeated Radia. "Yes, that could be."

"So, Radia, I ask you, did she know anyone named Philimon back then? Did she perhaps go to school with someone by that name?"

Radia said slowly, "There was a boy named Pharaoh, I remember. I knew many names of children but not all, no."

"Perhaps a friend to Dr. or Mrs. Hopkirk? Oh, Radia, think *hard*."

"I am thinking." She frowned. "Police Inspector Tembo was good friend to Dr. Hopkirk. His name was Pharaoh, I think, but it could have been Philimon. It's a long time ago now."

Mrs. Pollifax said quickly, "Where can we find him?"

"Inspector Tembo? Oh, he is dead long since."

Tembo. . . . Radia was echoing something Mrs. Pollifax had heard before. "When did this inspector die?" she asked.

"Die?" Radia's voice was harsh. "He be shot. So many killed! After the hunger riots President Chinyata kill, kill, kill."

It was coming back to her now: They had been talking about the Strong Room, and Inspector Banda had said, "In my entire life I've heard of only one person with such a gift"—at picking locks, wasn't it? But he, too, was dead.

"Yes," said Mrs. Pollifax, suddenly thoughtful. "Thank you, Radia."

She walked out into the marbled hall and up the staircase to the second floor and to Sammat's office. "Is he here?" she asked Joseph. "It's important. I must see him."

"He be very sad," he told her reproachfully. "At Mr. Zimba."

"So am I," she said tartly, "but I must see him."

Joseph rose and knocked at the door of the inner office. When Sammat called "Come in," she entered and found Sammat sitting in his chair, staring out the window.

He turned in his chair to look at her. "I have been wrong about Dickson Zimba. It is like a wound in me. But worst of all is no news of Kadi. I feel helpless," he said. Tears glistened in his eyes. "It is I who begged her to return here to Ubangiba and now . . ."

"I came to ask for the keys to the Strong Room," she told him. "The records there—I want to see them again."

He rose and without a question went to a wall safe, opened it and withdrew the keys. "Return only to me," he said in a dull voice.

There was no guard at the door to the Strong Room on this trip. Unlocking the hall door and slipping inside, Mrs. Pollifax turned on the overhead light, went to the gate of the vault, unlocked the enormous padlock and entered.

She went directly to a line of drawers marked with the name of ex–President Chinyata. A methodical man, Chinyata, in both his killing of dissenters and his files. Turning to the police file, she saw that it was arranged alphabetically, and she riffled through until she reached T, her eyes moving quickly down the sheet of small photos. And there was Police Inspector Philimon Tembo.

Her reaction was so violent that she quickly covered the page with one hand and looked over her shoulder, frightened lest someone be in the room with her and see what she was discovering. Because Police Inspector Tembo was *not* dead, as everyone believed. He was very much alive. "So that's it," she whispered.

She stared a long time at the photograph, reappraising every event that she'd witnessed and every preconceived idea that she'd nurtured. This new dimension that she'd unearthed solved nothing, and yet it changed everything.

Sharma had said, "You have been very close to evil, but not knowing it." He had also said, "There are watchers . . . and there are watchers."

After returning the keys, she would go to see Sharma. She must.

Mrs. Pollifax unlocked her bicycle from the palace rack and set off down Government Road. The well-worn path to Sharma's hut had been preempted by a family of guinea fowl, looking like plump and indignant matrons in pinstriped suits, and it was necessary to sound the bell until they made an exodus into the brush. At first glance Sharma's compound was empty. She leaned her bicycle against a tree and called out, "Hello? Hello!" and walked up to the door and peered inside.

A girl came around the corner of the house. "Oh," she said, and smiled. "The *mzungu*."

Mrs. Pollifax smiled back. "Yes. Is Sharma here?"

The girl shook her head. "He take a flat tire to bicycle repair. There is place next to Bang-Bang Snack Bar."

"Moses?"

The girl brightened. "That be—that *is*—where he will be."

It was by now midafternoon, and the sun was searing. Mrs. Pollifax anchored her straw hat more securely on her head, thanked the girl and rode away. She reached Moses's gate and found it ajar. Dismounting, she pushed the gate open and wheeled her bike inside. Moses was leaning over a bicycle in the center of his compound. She called out, "Moses, is Sharma here? I'm looking for him."

Moses straightened and looked at her as if he had never seen her before. "Sharma come, Sharma go," he said gruffly.

"I see," murmured Mrs. Pollifax. "Know where or when I can find him?" Her glance drifted past him to a clothesline, from which hung two pairs of blue jeans of different sizes.

"No. Sharma come, Sharma go," he repeated testily, seeing her eyes fixed with interest on his clothesline. "He be back early morning for new tire is all I know."

She nodded. She was beginning to understand why she was not welcome, and turning away, she wheeled her bicycle out of his compound. But as she rode down the boulevard, she knew that her visit had not been wasted. She had learned why Moses did not want her there, and this interested her very much.

It was five o'clock when she entered the cafeteria. She was hailed by Dr. Merrick, who looked at her and said, "You strike me as being hellishly tired. Kadi, of course."

"Kadi, yes," she said.

"Tony Dahl has been rushing into the infirmary every hour to ask if there's news of her," Merrick said. Glancing around, he said, "Ah, Joseph, about to leave for your day off tomorrow?"

"Yes." Removing a slip of paper from his pocket, he said very formally, "I have message for Mrs. Pollifax. It be from your husband. On his way, he say, and see you Monday morning airplane."

Mrs. Pollifax thought, He's coming too soon, but she managed a smile and a thank-you to Joseph.

In his friendly voice Merrick said, "And what do you do with your days off, Joseph? Sleep?"

"Oh, no," Joseph said. He looked affronted. "I have many books to study that *Mfumo* Sammat lend me. Accounting and *Robert's Rules*, taxes and World Bank."

"Impressive," commented Dr. Merrick. "Enjoy it if you can."

"Yes, thank you," Joseph said, and left them.

At that moment the talking drums began, and the few diners in the cafeteria were silenced, listening to that distant pulsating beat, so stirring to the senses. Mrs. Pollifax pictured its reverberations flowing with the winds to the south, where another drummer would send its message west, until finally all of Ubangiba knew the lion killer had been found and that rumors of sorcery had been false.

Excusing herself, she went up to her room and lay down on her bed, listening to the distant drums. In the morning she would forgo bicycling and walk to Moses's bicycle shop, hoping to find Sharma, there to pick up his repaired tire, or, even better, encounter him on the way, which would save her a great deal of time.

IN THE morning Mrs. Pollifax set out on foot at half past eight. The great wooden gate to the bicycle shop was closed; Mrs. Pollifax rang the bell and waited. When there was no response, she began pounding hard on the gate, calling out Moses's name.

It was by now nine o'clock, and the shop was obviously closed— to herself and to Sharma and to anyone else. Moses had said he expected Sharma in the morning. Why, then, was he not here?

Baffled and frustrated, she turned away and reluctantly walked back down the boulevard to see if Sharma was now at home. She made her way to the path leading to his home and walked across the field toward the wood. Reaching his compound, she called out to him, but there was no reply. Finally, exasperated, she sat down on the bench outside Sharma's house to wait.

A gray pigeon alighted on a nearby branch and then fluttered away. It was very quiet, but she did not feel at all quiet; she felt abandoned. Where, she wondered, had everyone gone?

She decided to give up waiting and return to the palace. She set off down the narrow path, grateful to the trees overhead that provided a welcome shade. Soon the trees thinned, replaced by a virtual hedge of thick, high, leafless brush.

She had not walked far when she became aware of cautious footsteps behind her. She stopped; the soft pad of feet stopped, too. She told herself there was no reason to feel uneasy; the lion man was safely imprisoned. But why did the footsteps pause when she did? Her heart began pounding, and she could feel beads of sweat forming on her forehead. Impatiently she wiped them away with her sleeve. She thought, I could go back and confront whoever it is, or I could start running very fast. If instead she stepped out of the path and hid herself in the tall brush, she could learn who was seemingly stalking her. Stalking. . . . She shivered at the word.

She pried open a space for herself in the wall of wild scrub and vines and inserted herself among the thick branches. A heavy and oppressive silence followed. No one came down the path.

Until abruptly there came the sound of steps crashing through the forest behind her. Not by the path, but behind her.

She turned and screamed in terror.

He stood only four feet away from her, both hands lifted to kill, the fingers clothed in long, terrifyingly sharp claws, the face concealed behind a huge mask of tawny fur with two slits for eyes, a ruff of pale wool crowning the lion's head.

Her thoughts raced: No screaming. Fight, fight!

She waited, eyes concentrated only on those terrible claws. The man took a step closer—so close that she could hear the heavy breathing behind the mask. Trembling, she steadied herself. Nerves taut, she made her first move, lashing out defensively at one of those two claw hands, blocking the one as his other fell to her shoulder, ripping the flesh of her shoulder and neck. The pain was excruciating, but steeling herself—it was her life now or his—she aimed a forward kick to his knee, and her hand whipped out with a quick, hard karate slash to his solar plexus.

He fell back with a groan and sank to the ground, clutching his abdomen with his left claws. She watched, fascinated, as he lifted the right hand to his mouth and with his teeth savagely tore away the glove of claws, freeing the hand to begin fumbling among the folds of the dark cloak that he wore.

She marveled that he could still move after such a savage blow to his abdomen. She saw that it was a gun he was bringing out from under the cloak. Move, she told herself. Move! But she stood frozen. The noise of the gun firing shocked her out of her unholy trance; the sound of it reverberated through the woods. She felt nothing. Instead it was the lion man's gun that spun out of his hand.

Bewildered, exhausted and in shock, she became aware of someone behind her and turned. "Moses?" she faltered.

Moses broke through the underbrush and strode to her side, glanced briefly at her bloody shirt and continued past her to the man on the ground, who was struggling feebly to crawl away.

"Take my pistol and keep him covered," Moses said.

When Moses leaned over the masked figure, she closed her eyes out of dread. Only when he straightened did she open them to see the face of the man who had tried to kill her.

It was Joseph.

"Oh, dear God," she whispered.

His face twisted in a grimace of pain, Joseph turned his head away from her.

Moses was bringing out a length of rope from his pocket. "Help me," he said. She nodded, and when he lifted Joseph, she was at least able to slide the rope under him. Once Joseph was firmly trussed, Moses rose to his feet, looking down at her from his great height. "You're hurt. Can you make it to my truck?"

With a wry smile she glanced at the pistol he'd given her to hold. "Would you like Kadi's pistol back now?"

His smile lit up his scarred dark face, but he didn't reply. Joseph had slipped into unconsciousness. Moses plucked him from the ground, slung him over his shoulder, and together they limped out of the woods.

IT was palace guard Roy Siwale, driving from Government House to the palace, who first noticed them. He saw Moses carrying a man on his shoulder, followed by Mrs. Pollifax, dragging behind her what looked to be the head of a furry animal. Stopping the car, he jumped out and raced toward them.

As Roy Siwale reached them, Mrs. Pollifax said, "We're taking this man to the infirmary in Moses's truck. Tell Inspector Banda to come with guards. Here is the lion man."

"But this is Mr. Joseph Kamwi, *Mfumo* Sammat's assistant!"

"Yes, and he tried to *kill* me," she told him indignantly.

Moses spoke. "Mrs. Pollifax be hurt. Quick, quick! Help us. My truck by Government House. Drive it here."

Roy acquitted himself efficiently, then went to get Inspector Banda. Joseph was placed in the back of the truck, and Mrs. Pollifax sat over him with the gun while Moses drove the short distance to the palace. At its entrance, Mrs. Pollifax handed the gun back to Moses and walked through the glass doors to find help.

Crossing the marble floor, she reached the door to the infirmary and stood there. Radia gave a cry of horror.

"Mrs. Pollifax," gasped Dr. Merrick, running down the aisle between the cots.

She leaned for strength against the doorframe and said quickly, "In the truck outside. Please hurry. He tried to kill me. . . . Moses has him. . . . It's Joseph."

"Put her to bed," Dr. Merrick said to Dr. Kasonde, and promptly hurried off.

Mrs. Pollifax, rallying, said to Dr. Kasonde, "I can't stay. Please just give me a bandage and stop the bleeding. There's more to do."

"But you need rest," Dr. Kasonde told her. As he cut away her shirt to examine the wounds, he said in a shocked voice, "*Claw marks?* How is this? Who—"

"Sammat has to be told. It's Joseph."

"Joseph tried to *kill* you?"

"He's the lion man, not Dickson Zimba."

"Good heavens!" Dr. Kasonde said, and to Radia, "Tetanus, antibiotic, antiseptic, bandages and— What's this?" He gently pried loose from the neck wound a necklace of bloody shells and feathers. Giving her a surprised glance, he said, "You had protection, Mrs. Pollifax. Where did you get this?"

419

She had almost forgotten the necklace. "Sharma," she told him, adding softly as he worked, "When I told him I'd rather Kadi have it, he said it would be I who would need it more."

"A very wise man," Dr. Kasonde said, nodding.

"Are you through now?" she asked as he knotted the last bandage, and seeing Moses approach, she told the doctor, "Inspector Banda will be coming. Please tell the inspector—Sammat, too—that I'll be found at Moses's bicycle shop."

Dr. Kasonde gave big, shabby Moses a startled glance and said only, "But of course."

LEAVING his truck outside on the street, Moses grasped Mrs. Pollifax's undamaged arm, and they entered the bare compound, noon-hot in the blazing sun. "Lean on me," he told her. "Lean hard." They walked past the awning-shaded area to the door of the little house, where he unlocked the door.

The door opened, and Mrs. Pollifax walked into a room whose dimness blinded her after the bright tropical sun outside. She could make out a chair, a table, a shabby couch. A figure seated on the couch leaped up and cried, "Oh, thank God! We were so afraid for you." Racing toward her, Kadi stopped, seeing the bloodied shirt, and looked at Moses questioningly.

He nodded. "I follow Joseph. Joseph followed *her*. But she is great fighter, Kadi. And she knew you were here."

Kadi burst into tears and flung herself at Mrs. Pollifax. Moses tactfully removed her. "Gently, gently. She's hurt," he said. He brought Mrs. Pollifax a chair, and she was relieved to sit down.

Kadi's face was tearstained. "But to leave you, to know how you'd worry—it was awful."

"And we *did* worry, terribly," Mrs. Pollifax told her, her voice unsteady. "It never occurred to us, or to me, until yesterday that a mysterious man named Philimon could have kidnapped you—removed you—to save your life."

Kadi smiled. "But how did you know I was here?" she asked.

"Because certain references to a Police Inspector Tembo, long since dead, began to interest me," said Mrs. Pollifax. "I made another trip to the Strong Room, and found his photograph in the old files, and discovered that he was very much alive." There was a twinkle in her eye as she added, "And when I paid a call on Moses yesterday, I noted a line of bright red on one of the pairs of blue jeans drying in the sun."

Kadi laughed. "Oh, I *wish* I could hug you. When I heard that Dickson Zimba was arrested and Joseph still free, we were both afraid for you. I don't think you realized how vulnerable you were. Tell her, Philimon. *You* knew."

Moses said gravely, "It was my fear that he'd plan to use you as bait to bring Kadi out of hiding. He was desperate to find her. It must have been a great shock to him when Kadi returned to Ubangiba. Who knows what he feared? That she'd already recognized him, or that at any minute a word, a gesture would give him away and she'd remember him? From what Kadi has told me, those three murderers never knew how much she saw that day."

Kadi said sadly, "Yet I would never have recognized him. I saw the face of only the one man, and it wasn't Joseph."

"But he didn't know this. And to become the lion man," said Mrs. Pollifax with a shudder, "stalking people with those terrible claws—he must have gone mad. Utterly."

Moses, glancing out the window, said, "Here is Inspector Banda now, with *Mfumo* Sammat, who is looking most upset. We must go to meet them."

"But not Kadi, not immediately," urged Mrs. Pollifax. "One thing at a time. Poor Sammat has had so many shocks, and I suspect Inspector Banda is furious at having to come here, to a bicycle shop, to find me."

Her prediction proved to be right. As she advanced into the yard, an angry Inspector Banda said curtly, "My car is outside. We've come to drive you to my office, where you should have gone in the first place to make your statement."

Mrs. Pollifax smiled at him. "In a few minutes, Inspector Banda, in a few minutes." Pointing, she said, "It's shaded over there under the awning, and there are benches."

She at once sat down, in effect forcing them to seat themselves on the opposite bench, while Moses stood protectively behind her.

Inspector Banda gave Moses an annoyed glance and said dismissingly, "You can leave us now."

"Oh, no," she said, "because the story you have to hear is Moses's story and has been all along. His name is Philimon, you see."

"Philimon!" exclaimed the inspector. "This—*this* is the thief who stole Miss Hopkirk?"

"Scarcely," she said calmly. "He removed her from danger. As soon as he read in the newspaper about the attack on Kadi, he knew there would be another." Leaving the bench, Mrs. Pollifax walked around it to stand beside Moses. "He goes by another name now. I'd like you to meet former Police Inspector Philimon Tembo."

Inspector Banda sighed. "Enough. This is ridiculous, impossible! Tembo is dead."

Sammat, frowning, said, "My father knew Inspector Tembo, but for myself, I know only that he was very tall. This I remember, but I don't recognize this man."

Mrs. Pollifax smiled. "Then perhaps the best witness to that is Kadi." Lifting her voice, she called, "Kadi? Come join us now."

"She's here?" gasped Sammat.

"She's been here all the time, quite safe, thanks to Moses, or to Police Inspector Tembo."

The door to Moses's house opened, and a subdued Kadi walked out into the sunshine. "Hello, Sammat. I'm awfully sorry, but, you see, it was important." She went to Moses, reaching for his hand and holding it. "None of you may have remembered Philimon, but I did. He came often to see us, and he was a *friend*."

Moses looked down at her with affection.

"All right," said Inspector Banda, as if conceding the point, and to Moses, "Just how did you know she was in danger?"

Moses pointed to Mrs. Pollifax. "It's she who reminded me. I had to think back. . . . Three men, I heard, three of Simoko's Witch Finders executed the Hopkirks, but the daughter had been smuggled out of the country. Suddenly last week the *Free Press* published news of an attack on Kadi in the palace garden, and then I knew. I knew Mrs. Pollifax was right to worry. One of the men was still alive, and Kadi had to be killed. I knew I had to learn the names of those three men in the Death Squad who murdered the Hopkirks. Learn if they were alive and who they were."

Banda said sharply, "You mean you found their names?"

Moses drew a sheet of paper from his pocket and handed it to Inspector Banda. "The names," he said, "as you can see, are Mbuza Msonthi, Johnston Milingo . . . and Joseph Kamwi."

Inspector Banda was staring at the sheet in disbelief. "This is government paper. You could have only found it if— Is it possible?" Turning to Sammat, he said, "You remember my saying that I'd heard of only one man skilled in locks—Philimon Tembo?" And to Moses, "It was you who robbed the Strong Room!"

Mrs. Pollifax, remembering, gasped. "So *that's* why Joseph was so upset. Not the faithful, outraged assistant protecting his chief, but a man terrified at being identified as one of the Death Squad."

"He was as upset as I have ever seen him," Sammat said grimly.

"But how did you know about the Strong Room?" Mrs. Pollifax asked Moses. "You told me you were in prison when the Hopkirks were killed."

Moses said dryly, "In prison there is talk. That is how I knew Chinyata's files had been moved to the new Simoko palace. For a little while, before they hanged him, there was in my cell a young man who helped build the Strong Room for President Simoko— where it was, the thickness of the walls, the iron gate, the locks. I remembered."

"And you survived. But how?" asked Inspector Banda. "Tembo was killed, yet here you are alive when everyone believed you dead."

Moses's smile was rueful. "And so I was. Philimon Tembo's number was Prisoner 186432, and Philimon Tembo was executed the second day he was in prison. A man named Moses Chona was 186452. . . . Poor devil. But suddenly I was Moses Chona. Just one number different, and I lived. And nobody noticed."

Mrs. Pollifax said with a frown, "But none of this explains why Joseph suddenly pinned the lion deaths on Dickson Zimba. Had he grown worried, even frightened?"

Moses said in a harsh voice, "Don't you see? Planting the mask and claws in Dickson's room was a calculated risk, a trick. It gave him time." Moses lifted three fingers. "In perhaps three days Zimba would have been proven innocent, but what better way to bring Kadi out of hiding than to place a copy of his mask in Zimba's room? Everyone relaxes. Dickson is the lion man. Mrs. Pollifax perhaps grows careless. If not . . ." He hesitated.

Inspector Banda said, "And if not?"

Moses sighed. "Once Kadi was safe, I followed Joseph. Two nights ago I watched him as he dug a grave out in the woods."

Startled, Mrs. Pollifax said, "Whose grave? Kadi's?"

"Yours, I think. If you didn't lead him to Kadi, his only hope of bringing her out of hiding was to have you mysteriously disappear and never reappear. And by the time Kadi had been dealt with and Sammat blamed for it, Sammat would have been lucky to flee the country. And his accuser, Joseph, would have become the savior of Ubangiba."

There was silence, and then Inspector Banda turned to Moses accusingly. "Why didn't you bring the information to me?"

"What evidence could I bring you? I had no idea he was the lion man. And would you have listened to Moses the bicycle man?"

"You could have told me who you are."

"*Were.*" Moses smiled faintly. "Philimon Tembo died in prison, Inspector Banda. I prefer to remain Moses. But to save the daughter of my dear friend Dr. Hopkirk—yes, I could still manage a little detective work."

Banda smiled at Moses, his tense face relaxing for the moment. "And what did you so magically tell Miss Hopkirk to persuade her to go with you?"

He said simply, "That I knew who attacked her—it was Joseph. That he would try again to kill her, but no one would believe me. I could only say to her 'Trust me,' to hide her for a little time. To be safe. While Kadi was safe in the infirmary, I kept an eye on Mrs. Pollifax when I could. I felt that she could be in danger. Once Kadi disappeared, it was Mrs. Pollifax whom Joseph followed."

Mrs. Pollifax remembered Sharma's saying, "There are watchers

. . . and there are watchers," and she asked, "Was it you I felt watching me the first time I visited Sharma?" When he nodded, she said, "And you followed me even after hiding Kadi in your house?"

He shook his head. "Oh, no. Once she was safe, it was Joseph I followed, Joseph I watched."

Frowning, Kadi said, "What about the other two men who killed my parents?"

"I have made inquiries," Moses told her. "Dead, both of them, under very strange circumstances, frankly. I would suspect that Joseph silenced them."

Sammat stirred with a sigh and stood up. "It has been a terrible four weeks, but now that it's finished, I am thinking of Dickson Zimba, who has suffered enough. Inspector Banda, we must see that he's released."

The inspector nodded. "Yes, of course."

"Perhaps he'll have been sufficiently humbled now to be of more help to you," suggested Mrs. Pollifax to Sammat.

Inspector Banda walked over to Moses and said gravely, "I will see you again, Inspector. I think I, too, have been a little humbled. I see that I can learn much from you, please."

"I will be here," Moses assured him with a smile.

EPILOGUE

ALL during the night the city of Languka celebrated. There was music, and the constant beat of drums, and dancing along the boulevard. Watching from the balcony of the palace, Kadi and Mrs. Pollifax were joined by Tony Dahl, who shouted, "I've been looking all over for you." He waved a cablegram. "It's just come from Dr. Gibbons, and it's good news."

It seemed that Dr. Gibbons was to arrive on the same plane as Cyrus. Two of the artifacts from the dig had been found to date back to the fourteenth century; there was no doubt that Ubangiba had a promising archaeological site to be excavated.

Sammat, looking his old self again, responded at once to Kadi's mischievous suggestion that Cyrus and Dr. Gibbons be met with a band. "Piccadilly Popcorn Rock Band?" he said with a grin. "Sure, why not."

And so it was that a larger than usual welcoming committee lined up on the tarmac to meet the eleven-o'clock plane. There was Dr. Kasonde—"To look after my two patients," he said. There was Mrs. Pollifax and Kadi, Tony Dahl and Sammat, and lurking in the background was Moses, who would soon vanish, guessed Mrs. Pollifax. And of course, there was the Piccadilly Popcorn Rock Band— six young men in matching crimson blazers, white shirts and black trousers.

The plane began its descent, touched ground and came to a stop. The door was opened, and a stewardess appeared, followed by Dr. Gibbons and then Cyrus, carrying a cane over one arm.

"There's Cyrus!" cried Kadi joyfully, pointing.

Reaching the middle step, Cyrus paused to look into the faces of the people waiting below him, and it was now that he saw Kadi with her left arm still swathed in white gauze, and then he saw his wife with a bandaged throat and her arm in a bright red sling.

His comment was as pithy as only Cyrus could make it, and loud enough to be overheard. He said simply, "Good God!"

Whatever else he said was drowned out as the Piccadilly Popcorn Rock Band struck up a lively rendition of "When the Saints Come Marching In," and at this, Mrs. Pollifax felt a rush of emotion. There would be no more evil rumors of sorcery and no more lion killings. Sammat was still *mfumo,* Kadi was safe, and for the moment Ubangiba had returned to its usual precarious state of normalcy.

And Cyrus had arrived.

ABOUT
THE AUTHOR

Dorothy Gilman

During her research for *Mrs. Pollifax and the Lion Killer*, Dorothy Gilman was able to draw inspiration from a source close to home: her own collection of African masks and carved wooden figures, which she acquired during various trips to Africa. These objects helped her to evoke the spirit of the people who created them, just as her extensive reading provided information that she needed for the book. Still, she believes, there is nothing that can capture the true nature of a region better than seeing it firsthand.

Dorothy Gilman currently lives in Connecticut. But like her peripatetic heroine, her wanderlust has led her to dozens of countries worldwide. Indeed, knowing where Mrs. Pollifax's next adventure will be set is usually only a matter of knowing where the author has traveled lately. (Here's a hint: Her most recent trip was to Jordan and Syria.) "Some authors choose a title first," she says. "I choose a country." Of course, there are still a few places in the world Dorothy Gilman hasn't visited. But when she does, can Mrs. Pollifax be far behind?

THE **MA**
BULLET

GIC

HARRY STEIN

The goal is a magic bullet: a drug to destroy cancer cells, leaving healthy cells untouched. Idealistic doctors Dan Logan and Sabrina Como are sure they're on the right track with a chemical called Compound J. But there are some who would like to see Dan and Sabrina fail. Because in the high-stakes world of advanced medical research, sometimes it's not patients but careers that come first.

*T*HE *first change was infinitesimal—a mutation in a single nucleo-*
tide of a single cell deep within her right breast. It is impossible
to say what caused it or even if it was necessarily destined to have
any impact. Still, from that moment on, that cell was unique among
the several trillion in her body.

She was seventeen years old.

Over the next decade the cell mutated several times, behaving
autonomously. Its nucleus changed. Its metabolism increased.

Her career was going exceedingly well.

Eight years later the cell undergoes a sudden, dramatic change.
The DNA within its unstable nucleus begins mutating hourly. Nor-
mal signals directing it to stop reproducing are ignored. Within a
month it has spawned close to a hundred daughter cells.

Between her two young children, her work, and her husband, she
jokes that she doesn't have time for problems.

It takes four years for the next great mutation. The malignant
cells now number in the hundreds of thousands, but, even if taken
all together, are no larger than the head of a pin. Some, however,
have already learned how to live outside the breast.

One afternoon, doing laps in the White House pool, she feels a
dull pain in her lower back. She ignores it. The backache lasts
twenty-four hours and disappears as suddenly as it arrived.

DANIEL Logan lay on a gurney in a dim cubicle off the emergency room in New York's Claremont Hospital. He'd been this way for an hour, seemingly forgotten by the nurses moving in the corridor just a few feet away. Heaven knows he needed the rest. He hadn't made it home from that damn party until nearly dawn, and as senior resident in charge, he'd had to report to the ER at noon.

Logan sat up and swung his feet off the gurney. He left the cubicle and walked into the doctors station. Through a glass partition staff could survey newcomers and assess which cases required immediate attention, while charting the heartbeats of those already under their care, on a large EKG monitor suspended from the ceiling. Logan glanced up at the monitor. Nothing going on.

He turned to Janice Richman, the young intern on duty. "Janice, will you keep an eye on things? I'm gonna grab a bite to eat."

"I'll join you," said an attendant named Ruben Perez. "I had a break due two hours ago." They headed for the cafeteria.

The only food available at this early evening hour was from vending machines. As Perez ate something passing as chicken soup, Logan poked at a container of Jell-O.

"By the way, how's that old guy Friedman doing?" Perez asked.

"Which one is he?"

"You doctors." He shook his head. "Fever? Abdominal pain? Low hematocrit? I brought him in around three o'clock."

It was not unusual for orderlies to take an interest in their charges, but the depth of Ruben's concern was exceptional, as was his understanding of medicine. Born in the Dominican Republic and raised in the South Bronx, Perez was only a few years older than Logan; and the young doctor knew—and knew that Perez did too—that if he'd had the education, he'd have made a hell of a doctor himself. Over the course of dozens of conversations like this one, their mutual regard had blossomed into firm friendship.

"I sent him to intensive care," Logan replied.

"He's a nice guy. Think he'll make it?"

"No." Logan paused. "You're right. After a while you almost do stop thinking of them as people. Nice guy, huh?"

Perez nodded. "He was in the first wave that landed on Normandy. Great stories to tell."

"I'll look in on him before I go. Promise."

Perez stirred his soup. "So . . . tell me about the party."

"Not much to tell."

" 'Not much to tell,' " echoed Perez sarcastically. "The man attends one of the social events of the season and makes me read about it in the *Daily News*."

"Hey, for me it was work." Logan smiled.

In fact, the event honoring Dr. Sidney Karpe, one of medicine's most celebrated names, had gone well for Logan. A one-man industry, Karpe wrote books, provided medical commentary for TV news shows, and had a long roster of celebrity clients. That he was a mediocre doctor hardly seemed to matter, for his greatest skill lay in choosing associates to handle the nuts and bolts.

Which is where Dan Logan came in. The most gifted young doctor emerging that year from the city's top medical facility, he'd been wooed by the great man, with a starting salary of $170,000. And last night, at Karpe's elbow, he'd been introduced to movie stars, politicians, and financiers as Karpe's soon-to-be partner.

But there was no way Logan was about to report any of that to Perez, stuck at Claremont with little hope of escape.

"Fine," said Perez. "Did you enjoy the *work?*"

"Some of the women were quite attractive. But you know how shy I am."

"Yeah, right. Logan, you're the kind of guy the women's magazines are always talking about."

" 'How to Meet Terrific Eligible Bachelors'?"

Perez grinned. " 'Guys Who'll *Never* Commit.' "

"Anyway," said Logan, "I felt awkward in a tuxedo. It's not me."

"You go to that place I told you? Did it fit right?"

"Yeah, it fit right. I wasn't about to look like a *total* jerk."

Indeed, Logan knew he'd seldom looked better. Still boyish at twenty-nine, he was aware that his loping gait, longish hair, and quick smile could lend him the air of a spirited undergraduate. Last night, he knew, he'd looked like a comer.

"So did you commit to Karpe?"

"Not yet."

"Why not?"

Why not? The truth was, Logan wanted it several irreconcilable ways at once. Ambitious for success and status, he also clung to a brand of idealism his colleagues would take as naïve, and he ached for reasons to respect himself. Too, there was the matter of . . . *sport,* the skill and gamesmanship involved. It could be nothing short of thrilling when a mix of intuition and hard work cracked a case that baffled other doctors. He knew full well that within Karpe's practice such opportunities would be rare and the opportunities for creativity even rarer.

"We both know," he began haltingly, "how clinical work can beat you up emotionally. I've been thinking about how nice it'd be to do pure research. I want to show you something." He reached into the pocket of his white jacket, pulled out a crumpled envelope, and handed it across the table.

Perez withdrew the single page and put on his glasses to read.

Dear Dr. Logan:

Thank you for your application to the American Cancer Foundation. I am pleased to inform you that you are among those selected for final consideration. As such, you are invited to visit the ACF to be interviewed by members of our staff. Please contact Dr. Shein, the supervisor of the fellowship program, at the number listed below, to arrange a mutually convenient date.

The signature belonged to the ACF's director, Dr. Kenneth Markell, one of the world's greatest names in cancer research.

Perez let out a low whistle. "I'm impressed."

"That isn't why I showed it to you."

"What, you want my advice? How the hell should I know what to tell you? Just that you should be flattered."

"Hey, it's a form letter. They probably send out hundreds." Logan rose. "Aren't we supposed to do some work around here?"

BACK IN THE ER THINGS HAD picked up. Four patients waited to be seen, among them a chest pain and a chronic asthmatic.

"Where's Richman?" Logan asked Nurse Clancy behind the desk.

She nodded toward the line of examining rooms. "With a dirtball"—hospitalese for malingerer.

Logan peered beyond the cubicle curtain. Janice Richman was examining a woman of perhaps thirty, blond, and very attractive. "Excuse me, Dr. Richman . . . ?"

Richman excused herself and joined him in the hallway.

"What's the story?"

"I don't know. Cough and fever. Vital signs are okay."

"Well, don't take too long. They're stacking up out there."

Logan had the chest pain and the asthmatic placed in examining rooms, when Janice Richman appeared abruptly.

"Could you have a look at this?" She couldn't hide the panic, and was already hustling back down the hall to the examining room. "That woman. I left her alone for a few minutes and . . ." The woman he'd seen earlier was totally transformed. Wild-eyed, her blond hair damp with sweat, she was trying to climb over the railings of the bed.

"What's her name?"

"Betsy Morse."

Logan rushed over to the bed. "Betsy, calm down. We're here to help you." He tried to ease her down by the shoulders; her skin was burning. "Richman, I need your help."

But the harder they tried to hold her down, the harder she fought. Her face contorted, she was kicking violently.

"Clancy," yelled Logan, "get in here!" Nurse Clancy appeared almost instantly. "Tie her down. Get security to sit on her. Get a rectal temperature. She's hot as a pistol. One milligram of Haldol IM stat! Let's get her someplace we can hook her up to the EKG."

Security took over. The young woman's EKG tracing showed ventricular tachycardia—the chaotic fluttering of a severely injured heart. She was out cold. No blood pressure. No carotid pulse. Furiously Logan began cardiopulmonary resuscitation.

"Call a cardiac team and get a respirator up here!"

The message thundered over the loudspeakers: "Cardiac team, emergency room. Cardiac team, emergency room."

Logan ordered saline pads applied to the woman's chest. "Run up the paddles to three hundred watt-seconds!"

The energy of the shock literally raised her from the bed.

Logan looked at the monitor. Flat line.

"Keep pumping!" he screamed. "Where's the respirator?"

Bleary-eyed, the cardiac team rushed in. While continuing to work at the young woman's chest, they began administering drugs, desperately trying to flog the heart into action. One by one the drugs failed.

"Anyone have any other ideas?" said Logan with pretend calm.

Silence.

Logan snapped off the EKG. "Thank you, everybody."

"Another one in a box," said one of the cardiac guys softly, trying to maintain his sanity.

Glancing across the room, Logan caught Ruben Perez's eye. He reached into his pocket and felt the envelope.

T HE moment he entered the grounds of the American Cancer Foundation, steering the rented Taurus onto a long sloping drive lined with spruce and maple, Dan Logan understood why this place was referred to as a campus. With its vast manicured lawns and elegant Federal-style buildings it conveyed as strong a sense of dignity and purpose as any ivy-covered institution of higher learning.

There was simply no research institute in the world like the ACF. Born of postwar can-doism in 1946, the ACF now comprised some fifteen buildings. Here a small army of Ph.D.'s and M.D.'s worked toward curing cancer. The ACF also contained its own hospital, the Eisenhower Medical Center, staffed by some of the finest oncologists in the world.

If Logan became a part of this place, he could *accomplish* something. How many times, growing up, had he heard a TV reporter soberly intone "Authoritative sources at the renowned American Cancer Foundation announced today . . ."?

Parking his car outside the administration building, he made his first appointment with five minutes to spare. It was with Raymond Larsen, chief of the department of medicine. Dan had seen his name often in the prestigious *Annals of Internal Medicine.*

Tall and ramrod straight, Larsen bore a distinct resemblance to Lee Marvin and carried himself like a marine drill sergeant, all brusque impatience and snarly command. He even wore a brush crew cut straight out of a '50s movie. How, Logan wondered fleetingly, does this guy manage to deal with patients? Larsen motioned for the younger man to be seated. Logan studied the room as Larsen leafed through his file. The walls were bare except for diplomas from Princeton and Harvard. The broad mahogany desk bore only a telephone and a neat stack of papers. No knickknacks. No photos of loved ones—if there were loved ones.

"I see you have a recommendation from L. D. Greiner," spoke up Larsen suddenly.

"Yessir." Logan had studied with the Nobel prizewinning chemist as a postdoc in molecular biology at Stanford, before opting for medicine. Greiner's glowing report on him was one of the things that made his résumé leap out from the pack.

"Opting out of molecular biology just six months after you got your doctorate doesn't say much for your stick-to-itiveness."

"I loved the work," Logan said. "It's just that there was a . . . coldness to it. A lack of connection between what I was doing and any practical application. Whereas with medical research—"

"You get to *help people,*" Larsen finished the thought, and with horror Logan realized that he was mocking him.

"Something like that," he agreed.

"You realize, of course, that we have many promising applicants for the fellowship program. And only a few slots to fill."

"Yes, I do."

"Good. I don't like people to have any illusions." He shut the file. "Well, thank you for coming by. You'll be hearing from us."

437

THE INTERVIEW, SCHEDULED FOR half an hour, had taken less than ten minutes. It was forty minutes until the next one. Shell-shocked, Logan was not even sure he wanted to go to it.

Taking a seat on a bench outside the administration building, he felt the beginning of a dull ache behind his eyes. Without noting the irony, he wondered if he could get an aspirin in this place.

"Hi."

Logan looked up, startled. Before him stood a short, balding man in his early forties, his bright eyes and droopy little mustache lending him an almost comic appearance.

"Hello," Logan returned laconically.

"I work here," offered the other. He indicated his white lab coat, in case there was any doubt. "I saw you just came outta Larsen's office. What an ass, right? Mind if I sit down?" He immediately did so. "You're at Claremont? Lotta rich patients, I bet."

Logan's face reflected his surprise.

His companion pointed to the Claremont Hospital security pass dangling from the lapel of Dan's coat. "You like New York? You're not from there originally."

"No. But I like it. Actually, I'm from Illinois."

"I am. From New York. You wouldn't've guessed, right? Tell me how you ended up at Claremont."

Dan found himself running through the story of his life in medicine. The excruciating first couple of years of medical school. The joy that came in the third year with the start of hospital rounds. Internship and residency and his interest in oncology.

"Why oncology?" asked the other.

Logan glanced at his watch. "Oh!" He leaped to his feet. "I've got to go. I'm late for my interview. Nice meeting you."

"Just hold on a sec, Logan. You ain't late for your interview. You're in the middle of it."

Logan was speechless. "Dr. Shein?" he said at last.

"Call me Seth. Time on my hands—figured I'd come to you."

Despite himself, Dan smiled. As head of the ACF's clinical oncology program, Shein probably had less free time than the guy across the river in the Oval Office. "So what now?" asked Logan.

Shein nodded toward the administration building. "There."

His office turned out to be immense, but Shein's personality seemed to instantly fill it.

"So," he said, sitting in his antique swivel chair and throwing his feet up on his desk, "tell me about your work with Greiner."

Logan sat in an old dilapidated upholstered chair at the foot of the desk. "Well," he began, "we were trying to see if there were unique genes that expressed themselves in glioblastoma. We took the DNA, sliced it up with a restriction enzyme, and packaged it with a virus—"

"Then," cut in Shein, "you let the virus infect the bacteria and so forth. Read about it. Just wanted to hear it in your own words."

Logan looked at him curiously.

"You'd be surprised how many people try to bluff me." He snorted. "Can you believe it? *Me?*"

It didn't surprise Logan that Shein, among the most gifted researchers in his field, should flash a huge ego. A certain arrogance was in the makeup of every successful scientist he'd ever known.

Shein paused. "You must have some pretty good offers, no?"

Logan played it straight. "A few."

Shein nodded. "Karpe's got a great practice, all right. You'll be in the society columns in no time."

The younger man stared. Was there anything Shein didn't know?

"But you know what? You're not going there. You're coming here. You're gonna help us cure cancer."

"*What?* I'm . . . accepted? But are you authorized . . ." He hesitated. "I mean, Dr. Larsen—"

"Look, Larsen knows you're my kinda boy, and he's out to protect his turf. That's the way it works around here. Now, you'll start at fifty-one thousand."

Logan swallowed. "Karpe is offering three times that."

"No negotiation. This is a nonprofit foundation, remember?"

Crestfallen, Logan remained silent.

"What, you think this is a bad career move? This is the big time, Logan. Me, I got security clearance and everything. You know what even a couple of years at the ACF does for your résumé? The big drug companies start top researchers from this place at three hundred grand, plus a piece of whatever patents they develop."

Logan weighed this a moment. "Why would you need security clearance?"

"Are you kidding? Where do you think the big shots"—he nodded in the direction of Washington—"come for treatment? Especially if they want to keep it under wraps." Abruptly Shein was on his feet. "C'mon, I want to show you the labs. And the medical center." He smiled. "I mean, that's where you're gonna be spending most of your time, right?"

LATE that night in his modest apartment in New York, Logan was unable to sleep. He went into the living room and found what he was looking for on the top bookshelf: *Microbe Hunters*—about the pioneers of microbiology. It was a vintage edition, published in 1938, that he'd had since childhood. He flipped through to the glossy section: old-fashioned engravings and photographs of the geniuses honored on its pages. Stiff, serious men, wearing black suits and grim expressions. All, that is, except Paul Ehrlich, the conqueror of syphilis. Slim, bearded, and bespectacled—appearing to be in his mid-sixties—he stared out from the page with a quizzical, almost childlike expression.

Studying the photograph, Logan smiled. As a kid, he'd lionized Ehrlich the way other kids did John F. Kennedy or Reggie Jackson. Even now he found the story profoundly moving: this impish little man, for more than a decade working against incredible odds to find "the magic bullet" that would cure the ancient scourge.

THE buffet luncheon at Seth Shein's Arlington home was billed as a social occasion—casual dress, significant others invited—but Dan Logan knew that career would be at the top of the agenda. In just two days the incoming fellows would begin working at the ACF, and this hazy June afternoon was the first time they would be meeting some of the key members of the hierarchy. Logan decided that khaki pants and a blue blazer were right for the occasion.

Seth Shein greeted him at the front door of his impressive Tudor home, a plastic cup of Scotch in his hand, wearing shorts and an extravagant Hawaiian shirt. "Kinda overdressed, wouldn't you say, Logan? It's a damn pool party."

Logan looked stricken. "I guess I am."

In fact, though the temperature hovered in the mid-eighties, most of the junior fellows had also dressed for success. All but a couple of the senior fellows, who'd been at ACF for a year, wore shorts.

Shein led Dan onto the patio, making introductions. "Allen Atlas," he said, moving him in the direction of a tall, hollow-cheeked young man in a tailored blue suit, "Dan Logan."

Dan and Atlas shook hands, eyeing one another with interest.

"Allen went to school at Vanderbilt," noted Shein evenly—then suddenly assumed an exaggerated southern accent. "In *Tennes-seeeeee*. But we won't hold that against him. Now, Dan here," he added, in apparent comparison, "went to Princeton as an undergraduate and Stanford for his Ph.D.

"Nice to meet you," mumbled Atlas, eyeing him coolly.

"Same here," replied Dan.

"Oh, Seth . . ."

They wheeled to face a dowdily dressed, middle-aged woman bearing a pitcher of iced tea. Her face was incongruously pretty.

"I'm sorry to interrupt," she said, "but there's a telephone call."

Shein gave her a quick peck on the cheek—"Dan Logan, Allen Atlas . . . my wife, the endlessly patient and still beauteous Alice Shein"—and headed into the house.

There was an awkward pause. "Well," she said, "I do hope you young men will be happy here at the ACF."

They offered their thanks, and she walked away.

The newcomers seemed to be keeping almost entirely to themselves, clustered in groups. Logan headed toward one of these at the far end of the pool. He already knew John Reston, the other junior associate recruited from Claremont. "Well," exclaimed Reston, "look who's here!" He made introductions: Amy, not an associate but Reston's petite, blond girlfriend; Barbara Lukas, tiny, with a staccato delivery and a degree from Duke; Paul Bernstein, quick with a smile, by the look of it a little too smooth; Sabrina Como, a striking young Italian with a mane of black hair, large green eyes, and an incredible accent.

Abruptly Seth Shein joined them. "You all making friends?"

They agreed they were.

"Good. We like to leave the backstabbing to the senior staff."

This brought an uncomfortable laugh. Dan began to suspect that the Scotch was getting to Shein.

A moment later the thought was confirmed. Smiling at Sabrina Como, Shein announced, "Appearances to the contrary, we recruit our foreign associates only for their *scientific* potential."

Sabrina looked at him evenly, showing nothing.

"And I'm sure women are treated very well at the ACF," offered Reston's friend Amy breezily. "Appearances to the contrary."

The junior associates turned to her, horrified. "Why don't I leave you people alone to get acquainted?" Amy said, and she moved off in the direction of the buffet table. Reston offered a helpless shrug. "Sorry."

"Don't apologize," interjected Shein, laughing heartily. "Believe me, hang around here long enough, you forget what someone with guts sounds like." And chuckling to himself, he left them.

"You should know," offered Sabrina, "I really am not bothered by such things."

"Well, you should be," snapped Barbara Lukas. "He has no business commenting on your looks one way or the other."

"Ah," she said. "I must study to learn to recognize such insults."

Logan, suppressing a smile, looked at her with interest. Lukas turned to Reston. "She your wife?" she said, nodding after Amy.

"Girlfriend," replied Reston. "She's a lawyer with the FCC."

"He's right—she's got guts. I should've said something."

"I hate to be a realist," said Paul Bernstein, "but saying what you think isn't exactly the best policy around here. I had a long talk last night with one of the senior associates. There are a few people to watch out for." With a tilt of the head he indicated a balding young man in horn-rimmed glasses near the buffet table. "See him? Peter Kratsas. Larsen's number two."

"Who else?" asked Dan.

"Greg Stillman."

There was a surprised silence. The name needed no explanation. Dr. Gregory Stillman, world-renowned specialist in breast cancer, was one of those chiefly responsible for the ACF's reputation.

"C'mon," said Logan finally, "someone's exaggerating."

Bernstein snorted. "Talk to the senior associates—this is a guy who describes *himself* as a vicious s.o.b. He thinks other people respect him for it." He paused for effect. "And they do."

A few minutes later Logan moved alongside Reston at the buffet table. "You buy any of that?"

Reston shrugged. "Hard to tell. Maybe we were just watching a guy working real hard to impress a woman."

"Well," said Logan, "we survived Claremont."

The remark called for no elaboration. Claremont was a political minefield, famous for the willingness of young doctors to cut one another up.

"Right," agreed Reston. "No way this could be as bad as that."

Logan smiled. "You don't go looking for trouble. You find out early who the key players are, and make a point of staying on their good side. You make yourself helpful to attending physicians."

"Now we're getting into my territory. It's called being obsequious."

"Being *careful*. There's a difference."

Reston grinned. "All right, *strategically* obsequious. Honorably obsequious."

Logan laughed; this guy seemed to be a soul mate.

They were cut off by the roar of a motorcycle zooming up the driveway. Skidding to a stop, the driver, in black leather—his face obscured by the black-tinted Plexiglas of his helmet—dismounted and strode into the midst of the gathering.

"Who the hell is *that?*" whispered Reston.

"Stillman!" called out Seth Shein from across the patio, as if in response. "Get that damn thing off my lawn!"

Stillman removed the helmet, revealing a beet-red face, topped

by thick black hair matted with perspiration. He looked to be in his late thirties. His surprisingly unimpressive features—a doughy face and droopy eyelids—lent him a sense of sleepy disengagement.

From then on, it was Stillman's show. Purposefully, he began making the rounds of the newcomers and exchanging a few words. Given Bernstein's earlier warning, Logan found himself surprised that the man seemed quite the opposite of an ogre.

"I read your recommendations," he told the young doctor. "We're looking for good things from you."

"Thank you, sir," said Logan, immensely pleased.

"Chicken, Greg?" offered Seth Shein, suddenly at their side, thrusting a plate of barbecued chicken Stillman's way. He smiled, but there was utterly no warmth in it.

Stillman speared a leg. "Why not?" Suddenly he was a different man, his eyes alive, looking younger, energized.

"Why not a breast, Greg? Isn't that your specialty?"

"Not after you've been handling it, Seth. At that point, the patient is usually beyond hope."

"At least I don't run experiments that risk lives."

"That's true. Your experiments don't do anything at all."

Logan was aghast. It wasn't merely that Shein had had too much to drink or even that these two so clearly loathed each other. What was remarkable was how little effort either made to hide the fact.

Abruptly Stillman turned back his way with an ingratiating smile. "Aren't you hot in those clothes, Doctor?"

Not knowing what to do, Logan nodded tentatively.

"I know I am," said Stillman, unzipping his leather jacket and tossing it at Shein's feet, quickly followed by his boots and leather pants. Underneath he wore a pair of swim trunks.

"First rule of medical research," he announced. "Never shy away from the unorthodox because of what people will say." He shot Shein a look and dived into the pool. With strong, even strokes he made his way to the other end.

"You," hissed Shein in Logan's direction, "are going to have to choose sides." And, though still dressed, dived into the pool after the other man, racing frantically to overtake him.

Two days later, his first day of work, Logan reached the ACF grounds before seven, though the initiation session for incoming associates was not scheduled to begin till eight thirty.

The encounter between the two senior scientists had thrown him badly. Sure, Logan had often seen gifted men under stress act like spoiled five-year-olds, and knew he would many times again. Still, as he replayed the scene in his mind, the question grew ever more insistent: What the hell had he gotten himself into?

Just as he drew his newly purchased used Ford into the parking lot, the heavens opened. Using the Washington *Post* for an umbrella, he made a dash for the administration building, arriving soaked. He headed for the cafeteria, got a cup of tea, and took a spot at a corner table to dry out.

John Reston stopped by with a full tray. "Hope you don't mind me making a pig of myself," he said, indicating his plate. He sat down and crammed a forkful of eggs into his mouth. "You feeling all right? You seem down."

"Aren't you? After the other day?"

"Naaah. Look, guys like this, we're hardly even in their field of vision."

"So who's running the orientation meeting?"

"Larsen."

"Really?" Logan shuddered. "The guy hates me."

"Welcome to the club." Reston ran a napkin across his mouth.

LARSEN was precisely as Logan remembered him. Sitting at the head of a large conference table, flanked by his lieutenant—Peter Kratsas—and a grim-faced secretary, he opened the meeting by indicating the two thick spiral-bound notebooks that had been set before each new associate. "Your first assignment is to master the material in these books. All of it. No excuses or exceptions."

That was it. No word of welcome. No banter.

"Each of you will be responsible for charting the progress of between one hundred twenty-five and one hundred fifty patients," Larsen continued. "As you know, our job here is to develop and test new cancer therapies. Every patient has agreed to take part in a carefully controlled course of treatment. You must see to it your patients do not deviate from the instructions they have been issued, that they understand that if they fail to follow through in any way, they will be dropped from the program." He nodded in the direction of his lieutenant. "Dr. Kratsas will give you a brief overview of the trials currently in progress."

Kratsas's sudden smile was ingratiating, a conscious effect to dispel the chill that had settled over the room.

"First," he began, "I want to extend a personal welcome. I'm sure I speak for the entire senior staff in saying that we are always available as colleagues and friends."

Logan glanced at Larsen, who stared straight ahead, showing nothing. Sure, Logan thought, that guy'll be my friend, all right— the day jelly beans cure cancer.

"Now then, as I'm sure you know, our experimental treatments fall into three categories. A phase-one trial is by definition a new form of treatment. Subjects' malignancies are highly advanced, and we recognize, going in, that chances of meaningful success are remote. Usually, what most interests us is gauging the maximum dose of a new drug the human body will tolerate. Its impact on the malignancy is often of only secondary concern. We are currently conducting only two phase-one protocols."

He cleared his throat and took a sip of water. "Perhaps only ten percent of the drugs that go through a phase-one test move on to a phase-two trial, aimed at determining a compound's effectiveness against malignancy in a specific organ. In turn, no more than about ten percent of those drugs—*one* percent of the total—are sufficiently promising to warrant phase-three trials, which test the new treatment against the best existing therapy."

He picked up one of the notebooks and let it fall to the table with a bang. Several of the young associates started. "Heavy, huh? It contains, among other things, a rundown of all thirty-six current protocols. Familiarize yourself with them all by Wednesday, when

447

you assume charge of your full complement of patients." He turned back to Larsen. "I think that about covers it."

Larsen nodded crisply. "After your patient-care year you will, in turn, pass on your patient roster to next year's incoming fellows. And assuming we are pleased with you"—here he stopped for a millisecond—"you will then be attached to a lab in which to pursue your specific interest."

A bell sounded outside the conference room, followed by the loudspeaker. "Code blue. Twelfth floor. Room thirty-eight."

"Never mind that," snapped Larsen. "Let's continue."

"Dr. Larsen." His secretary had spoken barely above a whisper, but Logan picked it up. "That's Mrs. Conrad."

He hesitated, frowning, then rose. "Take over, will you, Dr. Kratsas?" he said, moving briskly toward the door.

"WHO's Mrs. Conrad?" ventured Logan several hours later. Rich Levitt, the senior associate whose patients Dan was about to inherit, stared at him across his tidy desk. "An ovarian patient. The wife of *Senator* Conrad."

"Is Mrs. Conrad the top VIP here now?"

"Absolutely." He paused. "As far as I know. Sometimes— rarely—there are people who get seen only by the top guys. They might even check in under phony names."

"You're kidding me."

Levitt sighed. "Look," he said, rising to his feet, "I think it's time you met some of my—soon to be your—patients."

"At least this part will be familiar," Logan said, following suit.

"The patients here may not be what you're used to. You were treating yours individually, improvising as circumstances changed. Right?"

"Of course."

"Well—I can't emphasize this too strongly, Logan—here you have zero treatment options. Your job is to enforce the protocol. Period. Sometimes you'll be going *against* your better judgment."

"What happens if a patient starts questioning the protocol?"

"Happens all the time. Just make sure the patient doesn't *leave* the protocol. Because then you're messing with an entire study." He paused. "Trust me, if a patient drops out on your watch, the senior guy running that study will have your tail. Some of those guys are killers."

"I get that impression."

Levitt nodded. "You have any idea how fierce the competition is for funding? Every time someone wins, someone else loses."

Levitt explained that in the case of Shein and Stillman the animosity dated to Shein's long-ago support of a young ACF researcher who had come up with a novel approach to breast cancer. Stillman vigorously resisted—and won—on the ground that the data on which the conclusions were based were incomplete, though soon afterward he wrote a protocol himself based on the same idea. Quite simply, Stillman regarded breast cancer as his turf, and Shein had earned an enemy for life.

"That's par for the course. The top guys hate each other." He shrugged. "They all have their own little fiefdoms and their own loyalists. The ultimate aim of each is to defeat all the others. But sometimes, for strategic reasons, they forge alliances against a common enemy. Get it?"

"So what you're saying is, I'd better stay on *everyone's* good side."

"You'd better also be ready for some of what you'll run into from patients."

"I've dealt with some pretty bad attitudes."

"Our patients are a different breed. Many have moved heaven and earth and traveled thousands of miles to undergo a treatment that might end up doing nothing. The ACF is a roll of the dice, and not many shrinking violets take it."

"They're fighters. Nothing wrong with that."

Levitt nodded. "The truth is, if you've got cancer, there's no better place to be treated. But basically we and the patients have different agendas. We're interested in finding ways to cure cancer. They want *their* cancer cured." Rounding a corner, they came to a bank of gleaming elevators. "Let's go see Rochelle Boudin. She's one of Larsen's."

"Oh, right," said Logan. He had already gone over the patient files Levitt had prepared. "She's in the control group for the drug combination they're testing against Hodgkin's. On ACE chemo."

The protocol in question was a phase three. ACE, an acronym for the three compounds involved in the treatment, had been pioneered almost twenty-five years before by Dr. Kenneth Markell, current head of the ACF. If it was less than completely effective, it significantly reduced tumor mass eighty percent of the time.

"What's the problem? The report says she's doing well."

"This woman is the *mother* of all pains." Levitt paused. "And there's also the father—her husband, Roger."

After a couple of minutes in their presence Logan had a hard time deciding which of them he liked less: the endlessly self-pitying Rochelle or the arrogant Roger. The problem today was that Rochelle was due to start a new round of chemotherapy. "It will have to be postponed," her husband put it to Levitt. "She's not ready."

"I'm afraid that's not possible. You know very well that, according to the terms of the protocol—"

"Damn the protocol! Look at her—she's looking great. She's feeling fine! Why put her through this now?"

"I feel like I'm losing control," said Rochelle, bottom lip trembling. "It's not fair that you make me feel that way."

Levitt exhaled deeply, trying to maintain his composure. "I understand. The treatment is extremely unpleasant. But we do this for a reason. We've been charting the lab values very closely and—"

"So have we," cut in Roger, "and we've taken the numbers elsewhere for independent evaluation."

"You've *what?*" For a moment Logan thought his colleague might lose it. But almost instantly he recovered. "Mrs. Boudin," he said blandly, "it is your right to take that information to anyone you see fit. It is also your right to remove yourself from the protocol." He stared at the floor a moment, then cleared his throat. "If you choose to do so, kindly inform me as soon as possible so I can prepare the appropriate paperwork."

He turned and began walking from the room. Logan followed. "Doctor?"

They turned. It was Rochelle, her eyes moist. "Could you come back tomorrow? Just to answer a few questions?"

He nodded crisply. "Certainly."

As soon as they reached the hall, Levitt clapped his hands together. "Meaning," he added, grinning, "that *you'll* be back."

THAT night Logan was so immersed in the notebooks it was nearly dawn before he was aware of the time.

Each of the thirty-six protocol proposals ran at least twenty-five pages, but to Dan every one was like a chapter of an epic detective story, suggesting a new approach to the age-old mystery of cancer.

Logan was not surprised by the number of compounds that had demonstrated activity against malignancy—at least in a test tube or a rat. What did take him aback was how many of the most promising drugs had in some form been known to scientists for decades. It was just that their potential uses had never before been fathomed, let alone tested—no one, until now, having made the essential leaps of logic and imagination.

The next morning Reston caught the bounce in Logan's step as soon as he saw him approaching the administration building lobby.

"Who'd *you* sleep with?"

Logan laughed. "I have the feeling I'm not going to be sleeping with anyone for a long time—unless I find someone who gets turned on by randomized trials in Hodgkin's disease."

"Ah, you've been going through the protocols."

Logan nodded. "Boy, some of the work that's being done here. I mean, I'm reading this stuff and thinking, What the hell do these people need me for?"

"Don't give me that false-modesty crap." He snickered. "You're thinking the same thing I am: How soon before I get to run a protocol of my own?"

Logan smiled. "Me? I'm just a humble junior associate."

"Like hell. Logan, they know we're ambitious. Ambition is part of what they were after when they brought us here."

451

"*Controlled* ambition. In the service of the greater good."

Reston nodded. "You're right. The first order of business is figuring out which of the senior guys to try and get as a godfather."

"Good morning, gentlemen."

They wheeled. There, to their intense discomfort, stood Gregory Stillman. How much had he heard? His small, hard smile gave away nothing.

"Logan and Reston, isn't it? The Claremont twins." His eyes narrowed slightly. "I try to get to know the junior associates personally. Tell me, do you have some time right now?"

The two young doctors exchanged a quick glance. Logan knew full well that Shein would take it as a betrayal; he also suspected that this might be precisely what Stillman had in mind.

Reston quickly made the decision for him. "Sure. We were just going to grab a bite in the cafeteria."

Ten minutes later they were in Stillman's office, listening to the story of his own rapid rise within the ACF hierarchy. His brilliant career, as the younger men well knew, was built on his pioneering work in the molecular origins of breast cancer. In his studies he investigated which agents within cancer cells enabled them to replicate with such deadly efficiency.

"Would you like to hear what I'll be working on next?" he asked. "This is going to be the next great breakthrough."

His visitors' faces lit up. Opening a drawer, Stillman withdrew a manila folder.

"This began over a year ago," he said. "A patient came in with an inflammatory carcinoma. I had given up hope on her, and then, to my surprise, some of her tumors spontaneously disappeared. It turned out this woman was taking a course of drugs and enhanced vitamins for a completely unrelated condition."

"May I ask what condition?" interjected Reston.

Stillman shot him an annoyed glance. "Sure. After I've had our work patented." He resumed his professorial tone—and changed the subject. "There are a number of interesting things we've been working on in this lab."

From the folder he withdrew two black-and-white photographs.

"This is a photomicrograph of malignant breast cells growing in a culture dish. And this," he said, displaying the second photograph, "is the same cell growth after a six-week exposure to one of the chemotherapeutic agents we've been developing. It involves a new mycotoxin—one of the ones brought back last year from the Amazon."

The change was uncanny. More than half the cells were clearly dead or dying.

"That's unbelievable!" exclaimed Reston.

Stillman nodded crisply. "Yes, it is." He turned to Dan. "Bear in mind I've got more protocols going at the ACF than anyone. Almost twice as many as Shein."

LOGAN spent the rest of the day in the computer room, trying to learn the system. Every procedure at the ACF—from ordering antibiotics to tracking patients' progress—went through this machine.

When he was finally done, it was after eight p.m. Yet Logan dragged himself up to the twelfth floor to Rochelle Boudin's room.

"Sorry I took so long," he said apologetically.

"Where's Dr. Levitt?" replied Roger, clearly not a man big on pleasantries.

"He's off service." Logan paused. "You'll be dealing primarily with me now."

"What do you know about my wife's case?" demanded Roger.

"I'll be working under the senior physicians, of course. But, please, I want you to feel comfortable discussing anything at all with me."

Rochelle looked him over for the first time. "I'm not sure any doctor can ever understand how we feel."

"Try me." With his gentle prodding she told the story of her illness. When she finished, Logan started asking questions: What at the ACF gave them the most trouble? Was it the course of treatment or a communications problem?

"Both," said Roger. "This is Rochelle's life we're talking about. Almost no one in this place seems to get that."

Logan nodded. "I heard what you said before about your sense of having no control. I understand that, and I promise you I will make a real effort to be more sensitive to it." However, he explained, he expected that they would make an equal effort to observe the protocol. "I've got to run now," he said. "I'll come by tomorrow."

Rochelle looked at him gratefully. "Thank you, Dr. Logan."

So, he thought, allowing himself a smile as he moved from the room, maybe *that's* how to handle these two.

IT WAS not until the third Sunday after his arrival that Logan finally had more than a couple of hours for himself. He grabbed the Washington *Post* and headed for a small park he'd passed every morning en route to work.

It was exactly what he needed on this lazy summer afternoon: high grass, lots of shade trees. He kicked off his loafers, lay down in the grass, and closed his eyes. From a ball field a hundred yards away came the sounds of a softball game: dim exhortations, the crack of ball against aluminum, an occasional cheer.

"Hey. Excuse me?"

Dan opened one eye and squinted at the silhouette looming over him. A guy with a baseball glove. "Yes?"

"You want to play some ball?" He nodded vaguely in the direction of the field. "A couple of our guys've left."

Logan was a softball player from way back. "Can I borrow a mitt?"

"You can use mine."

For two innings Logan was exiled to the fourth outfielder spot. But when he finally came to bat and lined a triple over third to drive in two runs, he was instantly transformed into a hero. As soon as he'd come around to score, Kevin—the catcher, the man in charge—sat down beside him on the rickety bench. "You from around here?"

"I just moved here. I'm a doctor with the ACF."

The other, impressed, gave a low whistle. "Not bad."

"How about you?"

"Me? I'm with the IRS." He pointed at a fellow in glasses coaching third base. "Bruce Ryan's a doctor too. I'll introduce you."

The next inning Kevin was as good as his word. "So," said Ryan, "you're at the ACF."

Logan could not help but note this seemed less in the spirit of fellowship than sullen challenge. "Right. How about you?"

"Just a radiologist, with Prince William County Hospital."

"Ah. That's supposed to be a good facility."

"Don't worry, I make good money."

What kind of answer did *that* call for? "Glad to hear it."

"I knew another guy at the ACF. I met him at a party a few years ago. A first-year fellow. Cooper-something."

"It doesn't ring a bell. He must be gone by now."

"Coopersmith, I think. Real sharp guy. He was working on a protocol he'd set up."

Logan smiled indulgently. "No. That's not possible. First-year fellows don't run protocols. We get the scutwork."

The other shook his head. "No, I'm sure of it. That's why it made such a big impression on me, 'cause he was so young. Anyway, that's some hot-stuff place. That's the trade-off, isn't it? Guys like you get the glory. Guys like me get the dough."

Just then the batter lined to center for the third out of the inning, and Ryan headed back out to the field.

Logan walked up to Kevin behind home plate. "Look, I've really got to get going."

"Oh, really?" The guy looked genuinely disappointed. "Well, look, we're out here every Sunday. You know where to find us."

As he walked from the field, Logan made a mental note to check out a recent junior associate named Coopersmith.

BEFORE the end of summer Logan was entirely at home at the ACF. What was asked of him was no more than he'd always asked of himself: lots of hard work and willingness to take on more.

The work routine was standard for junior associates: three days a week working the hospital, the other two dealing with protocol patients in the clinic on an outpatient basis and evaluating new candidates in the screening clinic. Somehow, remarkably, thus far he had managed to remain on good terms with everyone who mattered. Half a dozen senior men—even Larsen—had indicated that in time he would be welcome as a member of their team.

Indeed, he'd already begun viewing the day when he'd have to actually make such a choice with apprehension. The consequences on his career were incalculable: the implacable enemies it would create, the doors it would forever slam shut.

Allen Atlas, the junior associate from Vanderbilt, seemed to have made himself all but indispensable to Peter Kratsas, spending virtually every evening in the senior man's lab.

"I really can't stand that guy Atlas," said Reston to Logan one evening in Reston's Dupont Circle apartment. "You notice how he's started to parrot Kratsas on every damn subject?"

"Look at it this way. He's picking up as many enemies as friends."

"You know that from experience, right?"

"Hey, I don't need that from you."

"I don't mean it as an insult. I'd change places with you in a second."

Logan laughed uncomfortably. Reston was right: Talented as Reston was, no one who counted at the ACF seemed to have noticed, and the fact was becoming a matter of some awkwardness between them. "You're just biding your time, that's all," Logan said. "And at least you've got a terrific woman. Anyway," he added, "don't exaggerate. It's not as if I run the place."

"Not yet. Thank goodness."

Reston's girlfriend, Amy, emerged from the kitchen, holding a knife and a couple of tomatoes. "Hey, John, aren't *you* supposed to be doing dinner?"

"Yeah, yeah."

Reston and Logan rose to follow her back toward the kitchen.

"Amy," said Reston, "we gotta set Logan up with someone. He's trying to use our relationship to get me to feel sorry for him."

She stopped and smiled at Dan. "Are you kidding? There must

be a thousand women on Capitol Hill who'd love a guy like you."

"I think Danny's already got someone in mind," added Reston.

"Who?" asked Amy.

"Sabrina Como," Reston said.

"Oh, the Italian bombshell." She nodded at Logan. "You've got good taste."

Logan smiled uneasily. "I really don't know where he comes up with this crap." Actually, he knew perfectly well: Reston had been around more than once when Sabrina's very presence turned Logan into an awkward parody of his normal self. "Look," he added lamely, "I don't know a thing about the woman, except that she's a terrific doctor. For all I know, she's involved with someone."

"No, she's not. I checked it out with Sylvia"—the hospital pharmacist, also the hospital's foremost gossipmonger.

Logan shook his head. "I tell you, Amy, if this guy put half the energy into science he does into being a wiseass, he would be *running* the ACF."

Two hours later they were sitting in the living room, sipping Amaretto, still savoring Reston's splendid northern Italian dinner.

"You ever hear of Ray Coopersmith?" Logan asked his friend. "He was a first-year associate at the ACF four years ago—and he got a protocol through."

"Like hell. That's impossible."

"I've seen the paperwork."

The documents were in the antique wooden filing cabinet outside Larsen's office, with hundreds of other earlier protocols.

"I found the record of the proposal, but not the results," Logan went on. This was not unusual: Protocol data could run hundreds of pages and were generally filed away on computer disks. "It was something about shooting radiolabeled antibodies directly into the bloodstream to go after prostate tumors directly instead of relying on standard chemo. Interesting idea."

"Prostate? Who'd he get to sponsor this? Larsen?"

Logan shook his head. "A genitourinary guy—someone named Locke. I think he's now in private practice."

"So now you want to do something on your own? *You?*"

"*Us.* Maybe. Why not?"

"Why not? Because, frankly, I don't even register on their radar around here. But I'm perfectly willing to talk—when you've got something serious on the drawing board."

IN FACT, Logan had been toying with an idea for weeks, ever since Larry Tilley had stepped into his examining room.

A Kansas City lawyer, thirty-four and gay, Tilley was on a phase-two AIDS protocol for a drug called Compound J, designed to interfere with viral reproduction. The protocol seemed to be totally ineffective in yielding practical results. No real news there. The AIDS virus had long been a particular source of frustation to ACF researchers, on a par with the most baffling cancers in its complexity.

Tilley had come back in for tests. He'd been feeling dizzy lately, but not from overactivity. "It usually happens when I've been resting. I get up from a chair and feel like I'm going to faint."

"Have you been thirsty a lot lately?"—worth asking, but barely. Simultaneous changes in blood pressure and heart rate can be symptomatic of extreme dehydration.

To his surprise Tilley nodded. "But that comes from taking the drug, doesn't it?"

"Well, let's see. I'm going to want to run some tests."

"How long am I gonna have to stay around?"

"Probably no more than a few days. Meantime, I'm going to give you a couple of liters of intravenous fluids and see if that helps."

Briefly it looked like a miracle cure. By the following day Tilley reported he was feeling better than he had in months.

But the day after that, the dizziness was as bad as ever. As test after test came up dry, the patient's few days in Washington became almost two weeks. Logan's curiosity mounted, until finally the tests yielded the reason: Tilley's adrenal cortex had ceased to produce the hormones that enable the kidneys to retain salt and water. Apparently, Compound J was blocking the normal function of the organ.

458

And yet, going over the proposal, Logan found nothing to indicate that the drug might have so alarming a side effect. Nor, as far as he knew, had it so affected any other patient. What could produce such a result? And could such a discovery have some meaningful practical application?

LOGAN did some of his best thinking at the ballpark, and Shein had told him that the ACF had a box at the Orioles' new Camden Yards stadium. He picked up a ticket for that evening's game.

Arriving early for batting practice, he bought himself a hot dog and beer and settled in. It wasn't until the fourth inning, with the Angels enjoying a three-run lead, that he reached into his briefcase and withdrew Larry Tilley's case history. His plan was to review it, looking for some clue in Tilley's past.

"Dan?"

He looked up, and there to his astonishment, a cardboard food tray in her hands, stood Sabrina Como.

"I hope you do not mind to be bothered."

He replaced the papers in his briefcase. "No, of course not."

"Most times no one else is here." She took a seat beside him.

"Aha. . . ." He stared at her wonderingly. "You like baseball?"

She nodded. "It is a game of numbers. I like numbers." She pointed at the scoreboard in right field. "The Orioles, they are not doing so well. Only three hits, and two errors already."

Logan strained to think of something to say. "So . . . what are you eating?" Why was it that every time this woman spoke to him, forty points seemed to drop from his IQ?

She picked up the hamburger from her tray. "Not the best."

"Well, at least it beats the food at the ACF." He hesitated. "Is hospital food any better in Italy?"

"No, maybe even not so good. What could be worse than days-old pasta?" She turned away to stare out at the field.

"So, are you enjoying your work at the ACF?"

"Enjoying? It is like a medieval Italian city-state. It makes me go back and read Machiavelli."

Gratefully Logan burst out laughing. "That's true."

459

"Some of the people there—just *horrible!* Like this Larsen and Stillman. Experts in ovarian cancer and breast cancer—no?—and they do not like women. How could such a thing happen?"

On the field, the Orioles were rallying. There was a roar as a ball shot between a pair of infielders into left field.

"Back in Florence, where I did my training, I had a specialization in endocrinology. But here"—she shrugged to indicate her frustration—"what is the use of such a specialization?"

"I didn't know you were an endocrinologist."

"Yes, and very good too." She laughed. "No good hiding it under a bush."

Her laugh was lovely. He leaned forward. "Listen, I've got something you might be interested in. . . ."

He withdrew the pages from his briefcase and outlined Tilley's case, stressing his apparently bizarre reaction to the protocol drug. Eyes fixed on the field, Sabrina listened intently.

"You know," she said, "I have several patients also on the Compound J protocol. One of them, she has similar symptoms, only not so severe." She paused. "You have been to the library at the foundation? You have checked for information on Compound J?"

"I've made a start. Unfortunately," Logan confessed, "I'm not strong in languages. Only English and some German."

Sabrina shook her head. "This is truly a disgraceful thing about you Americans." Then, worried that she might be offending him, "I don't mean this in a bad way."

He couldn't keep from laughing. "I can see that."

"Anyway, my English is not so perfect also."

"Just drop it, Sabrina. You're in too deep."

"Anyway," she added, her green eyes luminous, "this is why I went into medicine—the fun of the hunt."

"That's a nice way of putting it."

"And you?"

He thought a moment. "The same." He glanced at his watch and reluctantly rose to his feet. "I'm afraid I have an early flight to New York tomorrow."

"New York? Ah, you maybe have a friend there?"

Incredibly—or was it his imagination?—Logan thought he detected a note of jealousy. "Well, yeah. He's getting divorced."

"You are a good friend," she said, her tone betraying nothing. She extended her hand. "I am pleased to know you at last. You seem to me like not such a bad guy after all."

Her smile was so disarming Logan missed the faintness of the praise. "Thank you, Sabrina. That's nice of you to say."

CATCHING a morning shuttle out of National Airport, Logan made it into midtown Manhattan at half past twelve.

Ruben Perez was waiting in front of The Plaza Hotel. As Logan approached, Ruben held up a deli bag. "I figured we'd eat in the park."

"Some things never change." Logan grinned as they shook hands. "Why do I keep imagining you have class?"

"Hey, not all of us make doctors' dough."

"*I* don't make doctors' dough. I'm at the ACF, remember?"

"That's why I didn't suggest a restaurant. Didn't want to embarrass you."

Having established nothing had changed between them, they began comparing notes on their respective work environments.

"You're not gonna believe this," said Logan, "but a lot of people'd say the ACF's as bad as Claremont. Maybe worse."

His friend shook his head vigorously. "Oh, c'mon, man. You *forget* what Claremont was like."

"I'm telling you, some of these guys at the ACF are unbelievable bullies. Cross 'em, and you can kiss your career good-bye."

"So how you handling it?" They sat on a bench.

The simple question seemed to hit a raw nerve. "You just work hard and try like hell to stay out of harm's way."

His friend was taken aback by Logan's intensity. "Hey, man, sounds like they're working you too hard down there."

"Sorry."

"Anyway, how'd we even get started on *your* problems?"

461

Logan couldn't help but smile. "Fine. Your turn." He extended his hand. "Give me my sandwich, and talk to me."

Ruben's impending divorce was far messier than Logan had realized. His estranged wife was drinking heavily. Increasingly bitter, she'd been denying him access to their young daughter. He'd begun to feel he had no alternative but a custody fight. "It's so damn hard," he said, brushing a sleeve over suddenly damp eyes.

Awkwardly Logan threw an arm over his friend's shoulder. "You know I'll do everything I can." He'd almost forgotten—perhaps only now fully grasped—the depth of his feelings for this man.

Later, as Perez hurried back to Claremont, Logan headed for the movies, where he spent the rest of the afternoon. Afterward he decided to stay for dinner at his favorite Thai restaurant. After ordering coffee, he called Washington to check his messages.

The first two were routine: a hospital secretary with word of a protocol patient who'd checked back in; a college friend planning to be in town. The third caught him by surprise: Sabrina Como wanted to talk with him.

Logan checked his watch—it was eight sixteen. Dialing Sabrina's number, he got her machine and left a message: He was hoping to make the nine-o'clock shuttle. He'd try her from home.

Sabrina was waiting for him at the gate. Her long dark hair was pulled back in a ponytail; instead of one of the stylish suits to which he'd grown accustomed, she wore jeans and a sweatshirt.

He stood there, stunned, his heart racing.

"I hope there is no one else to meet you," she said simply.

"No. I was going to take a cab."

"I have brought my car." She hesitated, seemingly embarrassed. "Perhaps I should not have come. But I have some news."

"What kind of news?"

"Today was my day of not working."

"Your day off?"

She nodded. "I went to the library. I want to show you some references I found. They are on my computer at home. If it is not too late?"

As they headed toward the garage, she began telling of her discovery: Poring over documents well into the afternoon, she'd come upon an editorial in a vintage German chemicals periodical on what appeared to be a fairly close relative of Compound J.

"They do not give the name. But they talk about the structure. And of polynaphthalene sulfonic acids, as in Compound J. And what this paper says is *tremendous* interesting."

GLANCING around her small apartment, Logan noted how clearly it mirrored Sabrina's personality—no-nonsense yet quietly tasteful.

She inserted a disk into her computer. "This paper was published in 1924."

"Nineteen twenty-four?" He tried to keep his skepticism in check. "What exactly does it say?"

The screen filled with text. "You speak German, no?"

Logan pulled up a chair and set about trying to decipher it. It took formidable powers of concentration not to be distracted by Sabrina sitting a few feet away, eyes alive with anticipation.

What instantly struck him about the brief article was its tone. Written in the aftermath of the German defeat in World War I, its point was that Germany's scientists, for all their lack of financial resources, remained vastly superior to their detested counterparts in England and France. The compound—"the work of a former researcher with the great Paul Ehrlich"—was merely mentioned; its alleged cancer-fighting properties cited, without substantiation, as another example of German brilliance.

"Sabrina, there are claims made here, but there's no evidence."

"Don't you see, Dan? They talk of cancer! This is important."

He shook his head slowly. "It's so little to go on. I've got to tell you, it's hard to imagine they would even have recognized an anticancer agent."

She flashed unexpected irritation. "You are very arrogant, Logan, for an American living in the 1990s."

"Sorry." He shrugged. "I'd like to believe, but I just don't. Anyway, Compound J has already been eliminated as an anticancer agent by cell-line tests." Such tests, in which drugs are tried against

463

malignant cell growths in petri dishes, are a shorthand method of determining which compounds merit further trials.

"A cell line is not human," she said heatedly. "How cancer cells interact with healthy cells, these things cannot be seen in a test tube." She was right, and he knew it. "It is a pity you do not know French," she added sharply. She had another, longer document on-screen. "This is from the Pasteur Institute in Paris. You maybe have respect for them?"

He peered at the screen though he spoke scarcely a word of French. The date was 1937. "What does it say?"

"It is observations of one of their researchers who worked in a clinic in Guinea. Two women with infections from spirochetes—they had breast malignancies also. And after three injections for the infections, the *tumors* began to shrink."

"What are you saying? Some relative of Compound J was active against breast cancer?" It was so far-fetched as to defy belief.

She nodded. "Perhaps. From what it says."

"Does it give any details of the compound's structure?"

She scrolled down. "Consisting of fused polycyclic sulfonates." She smiled at him. "Sounds a little familiar, no?"

Despite himself, he was starting to share her excitement. "Anything else? Any names attached?"

She indicated a name in a footnote: M. Nakano. "It talks of an unpublished paper this person wrote about the compound," she noted. "The name is Japanese, no?"

"Nakano. Didn't Paul Ehrlich like to use Japanese chemists in his lab? From what I've read, he had enormous respect for their work ethic."

Sabrina shrugged. "That is history, not science." Then, abruptly realizing what he was getting at, "Ah . . . the other article?"

He nodded. "Ehrlich died around the beginning of World War One. Who's to say this Nakano character wasn't the one from his lab who continued work on this compound after the war?"

Logan could no longer hide his mounting enthusiasm. Hadn't the Tilley case already impressed on him that the compound could be enormously active? If in certain circumstances it inhibited the growth of healthy cells, who was to say it couldn't also block the growth of malignant ones?

They talked for the next two hours, discussing the many ways such a theory could go awry. Sabrina yawned, and Logan suddenly thought of the time. "It's late. I guess I should be heading home."

She looked at him directly. "Is this what you want to do?"

Logan was taken aback. Could this be a proposition? More likely Sabrina's English had fallen short. "Do I want to?" he repeated.

Sabrina rose from her chair and walked over beside him. "Do you want me to drive you home, or perhaps stay tonight with me here?" She gently stroked his cheek. "I would like you to stay," she added. "It will disappoint me if you do not."

In reaction to his startled silence, she kissed him lightly on the cheek—then began undoing his shirt buttons.

"I guess I don't want to disappoint you," he said, smiling.

UNCHECKED, *the malignancy has begun to work at her lumbar vertebrae. With every sharp twist or turn, the tension comes to bear on the weakened bone.*

Though she denies it, even to herself, the condition is starting to impact her daily routine. She is often exhausted. Usually alert and remarkably perceptive, now she more and more lacks focus.

In his office, her physician won't let it rest. His training and instincts tell him, even in the absence of hard evidence, that something is terribly wrong. He informs her that he has scheduled a series of tests at Bethesda naval hospital.

She has fourteen months to live.

LOGAN and Sabrina decided to keep what had happened between them to themselves, dealing with one another at the ACF with strict professional detachment.

"You must see the sickness at this place, Logan," Sabrina cautioned the following evening at her apartment. "Your passion for this work, it's the same as mine. But if we go ahead—"

"If?"

"We must understand how dangerous these people can be."

"Of course," he said blithely. "But let's just not get paranoid about it."

"This is wrong. We *must* become paranoid. And you especially."

"Oh? Why's that?"

"Because you like to trust people. And please them. Science you know well—but people, I think, hardly at all."

Their first sharp disagreement involved John Reston. Sabrina strongly resisted letting him in on their secret.

"Look, Sabrina, we can't do this alone. If we're to have a shot at getting a protocol accepted, we'll have to come at them with a team in place. Reston's a terrific doc. And I trust him."

"I do not. There's something about him I have never liked."

The argument exasperated Logan. Of course, he too would prefer to lock others out—for personal as well as professional reasons. Already, between them, there existed the kind of respect and trust lovers can take years trying to achieve. Why tamper with that? Never had Logan dreamed he could find a woman like this: someone to whom he was not just wildly attracted, but whose passion for this specialized work equaled his own. Yet he had far less faith than she did in her intuition about human beings. Her suspicion of others could sink them before they even got started.

It came to a head when Logan reported on the unsettling conversation he'd had with Steven Locke, the former ACF genitourinary researcher he'd finally tracked down in Dallas.

"Coopersmith was bad news, that's all," Locke had said.

"Why? I don't understand."

The other sighed. "He faked his data, and he brought other people down with him. End of story. Look, I've got patient rounds to make." And he was off.

Now, hours later, Logan felt he had the exchange in perspective. "It was a scandal," he told Sabrina. "It left some casualties. But that has zero to do with us."

"Maybe you are right," she replied with unexpected mildness. "But this Coopersmith was also a first-year associate, no? This will give them another reason not to let us try a protocol." And before long she was using this as further reason not to include Reston.

"This Reston, you must stop looking at him as a friend."

"I'm sorry. He *is* a friend. But I knew him as a scientist first, and *that's* why I want him. He has skills we need."

"What skills? To be a wise guy? That is mainly what I see."

"That's not fair, Sabrina."

"What, then? What are these special skills?"

"Look, Sabrina, this whole thing could fall apart for lack of enough competent hands and heads. It's happened before. Who knows? *That* might've been Coopersmith's problem."

He thought he could sense Sabrina's starting to waver. She indicated a stack of research to review on the table. "Let's get to work. In three hours I must go back to the hospital."

"Well, I guess I should start the introduction to the proposal."

"Good." She gave him a chaste kiss on the cheek.

"Though writing has never exactly been my strong suit."

"At least it's your own language. I'm sorry I cannot be much of a help in this."

"You know"—he grinned—"Reston's a *helluva* writer."

"COMPOUND J?" repeated Reston three evenings later in the trendy Georgetown restaurant to which Logan had invited him. "For *breast* cancer?" He snorted. "It's a bust. Everyone knows that."

"Maybe they've just been using it against the wrong disease."

"I think we should order." Reston flipped open the menu.

"Look, I understand your reaction. It's a lot to digest."

"I'd say it's indigestible."

The truth was, Logan saw his friend as a kind of test; the objections he raised were those they would face within the ACF.

Given how the discussion had started, neither man pressed it. Only with the arrival of their food did it resume. "All right," Reston picked up suddenly, "let's hear some evidence."

"Where is it written that cell lines are reliable models for what goes on in a living patient? I mean, making a judgment based on cell line is like looking at an elephant's toenail and thinking you see the whole elephant."

Reston looked up from his cassoulet. "Okay. So what?"

Logan raised the Larry Tilley case. "If a drug seems to be that active against a healthy gland, you've got to at least wonder if it won't be active against a diseased gland."

"That's reasonable speculation. But why does it lead to cancer?"

"Sabrina Como and I have been doing some research." He told him about Sabrina's initial finds in the archives.

Reston was dismissive. "You're giving me stuff from the '20s and '30s?" He shook his head.

Logan glared at him and pulled a folded sheaf of photocopied pages from his inside pocket. He handed them across the table. "Try telling me *this* is ancient history. It's a paper presented when we were third-year residents."

The paper's author, a Professor Engel of the University of Minnesota, was an expert on the proteins called growth factors, produced by all cells. He had shown that some tumors, especially those of the female breast, develop the ability to secrete growth factors into surrounding tissue, where they bind with receptors on neighboring cancer cells, signaling those cells to reproduce. This creates an endless circle of secretion and growth.

Yet Engel had noted a curious phenomenon: Sometimes, inexplicably, drugs containing polynaphthalene sulfonic acids—like Compound J—appeared to block the binding process.

"How's that for evidence?" asked Logan. "If we can show this stuff screws up a cancer cell just a little bit more than it does normal surrounding cells, we have ourselves an anticancer drug."

Reston burst out laughing. "Logan, you're crazy. Finding a drug that works among the millions of compounds out there is like hitting the lottery on your first try."

"Come on, John, you know as well as I do that this is enough evidence for a protocol."

Reston fell silent. "Who else knows about this?"

"Only you, me, and Sabrina."

Reston leaned forward and spoke softly. "You're gonna get massacred on this, Logan. Breast cancer belongs to Stillman. You're going to have to get one of the other top guys behind it."

"I know that."

"And by a process of elimination . . ."

"There's only Shein."

The implications were clear to both. Shein wielded far less power at the ACF than most of the others.

Logan leaned forward. "So you with us, or what?"

Reston shook his head with resignation. "Ah, what the hell. I guess we've gotta give it a try, right?" He paused. "You'd better start thinking of how you're gonna suck up to Shein."

As IT happened, Shein made things easy for him. Two days later the senior man called Logan into his office and closed the door.

"You speak German, don't you, Logan?"

"Enough to get by."

"Getting by doesn't impress me. I can do that with my Yiddish."

"Actually, I've been working on it a lot lately."

"I know. I see you've taken a lot of material out of the archives."

Logan just stared. Was there *anything* this guy didn't know?

"I'm going to the International Chemotherapy Conference next month in Frankfurt, and I'm gonna need another set of eyes and ears. Yours."

"Seriously?"

"Write it down: December fifteenth through the eighteenth. It'll give us a chance to get to know each other a little better."

"SAY, Logan," hissed Shein, eyeing a tall blonde in an elegantly tailored suit, "get a load of that." They were standing by the baggage carousel at the Frankfurt airport. "Trust me, Logan, we're going to enjoy ourselves here."

Logan was already starting to have second thoughts about this venture. On the plane, while most of the other passengers dozed in the darkened cabin, Shein had downed a steady supply of Bloody

Marys and recounted his exploits on other trips, such as with the research assistant at the conference in Rome and the English physician in Tokyo.

Logan couldn't miss the desperation behind the braggadocio—the sense that this man, so widely admired, had a void in his life that could not be filled. Suddenly Logan felt himself to be less a colleague than a chaperon. A few hours before, his primary concern had been choosing the right moment for trying to enlist Shein's support for their trial of Compound J. Now he had to worry about the esteemed scientist's embarrassing the ACF . . . and possibly taking him down with him.

Half an hour later at the Hotel International, Shein underwent another metamorphosis. Relaxed and bright-eyed, he stood in the large, tastefully appointed lobby, greeting colleagues from around the world, seeming to effortlessly recall not just their names but minute details of their research.

Dead on his feet, Logan quietly excused himself and went to his room. In less than five minutes he was out.

When his eyes opened again, it was afternoon. He picked up the phone and asked for Shein's room. No answer. But Shein *had* left a message for him: "Papa's gone a-hunting. Don't wait up."

The conference would not officially open until the morning. Shein was not due to speak until the following evening. Surely by morning . . .

But Shein was not at breakfast the next day, nor, Logan discovered, had he even picked up his credentials at the front desk.

In the end Logan decided the best choice was to pay attention to the conference. In Shein's absence, wasn't it more vital than ever that he serve as the senior man's eyes and ears?

The work being discussed and evaluated here was of immense importance. Never before, not even at the ACF, had Logan seen so much talent in one place.

By the time the last afternoon lecture ended, it was nearly five o'clock. Shein was scheduled to speak at eight, immediately after dinner. Where could the guy be? What was wrong with him?

Logan made his way to the large room off the lobby given over to poster sessions. It was reminiscent of a high school science fair. Lining the aisles, edge to edge, were easels, each about six feet high and four feet long. Anyone with information to display had merely to scrawl a shorthand description on a poster, paste on a bit of supporting data, and wait for interested customers. Logan slowly began to make his way past the exhibits.

"Where the hell *you* been?"

He would know that voice anywhere—and *never* had he been so glad to hear it. Though red-eyed, unshaven, and still wearing the same clothes in which he'd arrived, Shein appeared just fine.

"Dr. Shein, I was worried about you."

"About *me?* Didn't you get my note?" Suddenly he leaned in close. "I gotta change for my damn speech. Come up with me."

Shein was fairly bursting with news.

"Remember the woman at the airport?" he asked in the elevator.

"The blonde? You were with *her?* How'd you find her?"

Shein smiled with pride. "I read her luggage tag."

As they headed down the corridor, Logan glanced at his watch. The speech was in less than twenty-five minutes. And his colleague evidently hadn't given his talk a moment's thought.

He needn't have worried. Shein was brilliant. Speaking without notes on the granulocyte colony–stimulating factor—a genetically engineered protein that enables bone marrow to quickly regenerate, thus allowing extremely high doses of chemotherapy—he kept the overflow audience in the main auditorium mesmerized, along the way getting laughs from this gathering of senior scientists that would have delighted a veteran borscht belt comic.

IT HAD *been eighteen years since she had written on local politics for the Sacramento* Bee. *Sometimes she could see herself, hair still shoulder length, wearing one of those ridiculous pantsuits, working away at her old Underwood, struggling to meet a deadline.*

The choice to set aside a promising career had been hers. Fourteen years ago, when Charlie was born, she had wanted to stay home to watch her children grow up. Seven years later, by the time her second child, Allison, was old enough for school, her old life no longer seemed feasible. Now, unavoidably, John's political career came first. It wasn't easy living in his shadow, but theirs was a good marriage. She respected him. She saw herself as a partner in far more than name only. He trusted her absolutely.

Perhaps even more, she realized now, than she trusted him. For almost a week after the gnawing ache in her lower back returned, she failed to mention it to him. After all, the doctor said the biopsy was only a precaution. It was set for day after tomorrow.

Still, she decided she'd let John know afterward, when the results came in, when she was free and clear.

THE following morning Shein was gone again, but Logan had other things on his mind. This was the day he was to visit the building in which Paul Ehrlich had conquered syphilis—now a cancer research center. Its directors had taken advantage of their proximity to the conference to arrange a tour. For Logan this was a pilgrimage. He was coming to this place imagining that he might pick up some small sense of what made the great man tick.

The chartered bus deposited Logan and two dozen others before the institute shortly before eleven. Instantly he was disappointed. From the outside it was curiously unimpressive: a massive, ivy-covered cube of gray stone. The only sign of its remarkable history was a tiny metal marker in the corner.

Entering, Logan was further disheartened to note that the reception area was filled with the kind of ultramodern furniture Logan had come to associate with eager-to-impress Park Avenue physicians like Sidney Karpe. The few remaining traditional touches now seemed out of place: a pair of large, ornate Oriental vases filled with peacock feathers, a stately turn-of-the-century portrait of the wife of the building's original owner and Ehrlich's benefactress, an alabaster bust of the scientist himself. Inwardly, Logan shuddered. This had nothing to do with the magical place that had stirred his boyhood imagination.

Midway through the conducted tour, Logan slipped down the stairs and asked the receptionist where the bathroom was. She nodded in the general direction of the front hallway. "Go through there and down the stairs, then straight on to the next room. Turn left, and left again. You will see it on the right."

He was certain he'd done precisely as told—which is why he was confused to suddenly find himself in a narrow corridor that dead-ended against a wooden door. Was this it?

Tentatively he pushed the door open—and instantly knew he should close it again. Wooden stairs led downward into the basement. But after a moment's hesitation he flicked on the light.

What he saw convinced him to go the rest of the way down: vintage lab equipment, neatly arranged within old glass-fronted oak cabinets. There were oversized bronze microscopes, a polished steel balance, handblown glass condensers with beautiful spiral cooling coils. Over all lay a thick cover of dust.

Had these once been used by Paul Ehrlich himself?

In the corner he noticed a stack of wooden crates. Gingerly he lifted off the top one and set it on the floor. Within were exquisite old bottles with raised lettering that had once contained chemicals. Each was protectively wrapped in yellowed newspaper.

Logan's eye was drawn to a crumpled sheet of lined notebook paper wedged in a corner of the crate. He picked up the page and smoothed it out. In pencil—difficult to read in the dim light—was the date 25 November 1916, followed by a line of tight script. But what seized his interest was the sketch beneath: twin hexagons sharing a common side and, protruding from the end of each hexagon, additional sulfonate molecules. He took a deep breath, sucking in the musty air. What he held in his hands defied all logic: a primitive version of Compound J!

Carefully he folded the page and stuck it in his pocket. His heart racing, he rejoined the group.

SABRINA gave John Reston no reason to suspect she'd opposed his involvement with the project. In fact, in the couple of days since Logan's departure her ill will had dissipated. Given the handicaps under which the team would be operating, the proposal had to be flawless. And it was only now, with Reston at the computer keyboard, that Sabrina knew that Logan had been right: Reston was a gifted editor, and his involvement could be crucial to the outcome.

"You are excellent with words, Reston," she said, reading over a rough draft of the introduction to the proposal. "Who would not wish to support such a protocol?"

"It's called piling on the bull." He paused. "Say, got any liquor around here? I figure it's time for a break."

"Why? The sooner we start, the faster we will end, no?"

She turned her back on him. Suddenly, incomprehensibly, she felt his arms around her waist, his breath against her neck.

"John, what are you doing? Stop. Right now!" She twisted her upper body, trying to pull away.

"But you look so good." He kissed her neck, pressing against her. "C'mon, Sabrina. What's Logan got that I don't?"

"Bastardo!" With a violent lurch she wrenched herself free.

He held up his hands like a basketball player unjustly charged with a foul. "You're not interested—fine. It was worth a try."

"You get out, Reston. Right now!"

"C'mon. Don't be stupid. Let's get back to work."

"You get out now."

"Look, it won't happen again." Already he was reaching for his jacket. "I'm sorry, Sabrina." He stepped toward the door. "Please, let's just keep this in perspective, all right? And to ourselves."

Two hours into the return flight Logan was still trying to find an opening for the subject of Compound J.

"Dr. Shein, I had a particularly interesting experience when I went to the place where Paul Ehrlich once worked."

Shein appeared to be dozing. "I know about that lab. They're not doing anything worth wasting your breath on."

"It has nothing to do with that. I ran across some equipment in the basement. I have an idea it's from Paul Ehrlich's own lab."

Shein sat up and looked at Logan in genuine surprise. "What were you doing in the basement?"

"Well, see . . ." Flustered, Logan reached into his inside jacket pocket for the sheet of paper. "I found this."

Putting on his reading glasses, Shein looked it over, then shot him a hard look. "Logan, when the hell you gonna come clean? You and I both know this is an early version of the chemical structure you and the Italian babe have been looking at."

"That's right," Logan acknowledged.

"What do the words say? Translate."

"Well . . ." Logan hesitated. "It basically describes the compound in the picture. But the language is stilted. I was thinking it might've been written by one of Ehrlich's Japanese researchers."

"Deal in facts, Logan. What does this little find of yours *mean?*"

"Well"—he paused—"we'd read that this compound may have originated in Germany, way back when. It's fun to find what seems like direct confirmation."

"Logan, you're a scientist. You want fun, go body surfing. Now, I want the whole story of what you've been up to."

So over the next couple of hours Logan told it, starting with Larry Tilley's appearance in the examining room. Shein sometimes seemed impatient—cutting into the narrative with a sharp comment or a challenging question—but his interest never wavered.

"Compound J for breast cancer?" he said at the end. "Well, it's a novel notion—I gotta give you that. Where do you stand now?"

"I'm hoping Sabrina and Reston will have something on paper when we get back. We've put a lot of time in this project. We think it has real potential."

"It's just you three?" His tone was ominously noncommittal.

"So far."

Shein settled back in his seat. "It's a good idea. I'm impressed. Of course, I'll wanna see your data."

"So you're interested? You'll help us?"

"Why do you think I took you along on this damn trip?"

S TARING at a page of the proposal, bone-tired, Reston suddenly began to laugh. Across the room Logan and Sabrina looked up from the pages they'd been reading.

"I don't know about you guys," explained Reston, "but I've read this damn proposal so many times, it doesn't even register anymore. It might as well be in ancient Greek."

"We are all tired, Reston," snapped Sabrina. "That's no reason to stop working."

"Look," Logan said now, "we're all nervous about Shein's reaction to the draft. Why don't we try and relax?"

"Bet I'm not as nervous as you," offered Reston. "Shein expects nothing of *me.*"

"Thanks a lot for the reassuring word," said Logan.

In fact, since he was the one who'd recruited Shein as their advisor, Logan had infinitely more at risk than his colleagues. So far, Shein had kept his distance, choosing to let the three junior associates work out the draft of the protocol proposal on their own. It was a courtesy and also a challenge: Only now, having studied it, would he let them know whether he'd give them his full backing.

"Well," said Logan, sighing, "we'll know in"—he glanced at his watch—"anytime. How do you like that? The s.o.b. is late!"

"Me, I am not worried," reassured Sabrina. "It is good work."

Titled "A Phase-Two Clinical Trial of Compound J in Metastatic Breast Cancer," the proposal had, at fifty-five pages, plus reprints of six articles and other supporting data, the solid feel of a corporate annual report. That was part of the point, of course.

They'd paid unusual attention to the informed-consent document that made up the proposal's concluding section, listing all the possible toxicities that other researchers might have discounted. One of their toughest decisions—since Compound J could not be absorbed orally—involved the choice of which intravenous delivery system would prove more effective: a continuous drip, in hopes of wearing down cancer cells, or concentrated doses via a large slug known as a bolus, aimed at overwhelming the cancer cells with toxins, which could also place healthy cells at greater risk. They'd finally opted for the drip as the more responsible, sounder choice.

"Sorry," offered Shein, when he finally turned up at Logan's apartment, forty minutes late. "A guy from Health and Human Services came by my office, and I couldn't get rid of him."

"That's okay. May I take your coat?" asked Logan.

"No. What I have to say won't take long."

It felt like a blow to the solar plexus, but Logan showed nothing.

"Not a bad place," observed Shein, glancing around the room. "You furnish it totally through the Salvation Army, or did you step up to Goodwill?"

"Actually, Dr. Shein, I went to Ikea."

"What's wrong with you, Logan? Losing your sense of humor?" From the inside pocket of his rumpled tweed jacket Shein removed a folded copy of the protocol proposal. It appeared to have been well read. "You got something to drink in this place?"

"Please, Dr. Shein. The proposal."

Shein cast Logan a baleful glance. "Okay. It's good. Very good." He looked from Reston to Sabrina, the relief apparent on both faces. "Not that I don't got some criticism. I don't like the drip. You gotta go with the bolus."

"We were trying to minimize damage," offered Logan.

"Screw that. You do a trial like this, you face that there might be fatalities. Because basically what you're doing is poisoning people within an inch of their lives. You can't make omelettes without breaking eggs."

There was a long silence in the room.

It was Sabrina who broke it. "Dr. Shein, you are talking about the therapeutic window, no? The dose that will be toxic to cancer cells, but not toxic for healthy cells."

He nodded. "You got it."

"And this is a tiny, tiny margin . . . even for the best drugs."

"The trick is finding it. That's what separates great cancer docs from the chaff—the willingness to go right to the edge and not flinch." Shein smiled. "Fortunately, you'll have me to help devise solutions. By the way, when you rewrite the proposal, I want you to tone down that damn informed-consent provision. You don't have to go out of your way to imagine every possible side effect."

"We just wanted to be candid. And responsible."

"Listen, what you had there scared the hell outta *me*. The committee knows all that anyway."

THAT NIGHT, WITH RESTON gone, Logan produced a bottle of champagne. Yet, though he'd planned this moment for weeks, it was astonishing how soon it began to feel like an anticlimax.

"Is there something wrong?" he asked Sabrina as they sipped their second glass.

"I am just a little tired."

He slipped his arm around her. "Get used to it. The *real* work hasn't even started yet."

"This Shein," she said, with a forced smile, "he has the morals of a cabbage. But he is not dull."

"No. Anything but that. Get him an organ grinder and a little suit, and he'll do handstands in the street." He paused. "I only wish he'd stop making nasty cracks all the time."

She looked at him closely. At the beginning his face had struck her merely as conventionally handsome; now she was equally taken by the deepening worry lines—evidence of what she knew to be character. "He doesn't mean it. It is a sign he likes you."

"Much more of his friendship and I'll put a gun to my head." He smiled. "Look at it this way—Shein's my cross to bear. You've got Reston."

Reston. She simply could not trust him. She reached for the champagne. "If I show you something," she spoke up suddenly, "can we keep it just for ourselves? Nothing so important, but I do not want Reston involved."

"I guess so. If you want."

She rose, crossed the room, and retrieved a sheet of paper from her briefcase. "Here," she said, handing it to him. "Not much, but it has some new details."

It was a copy of a German newspaper announcement dated August 18, 1924: Dr. Mikio Nakano, associate director of the medicinal chemistry division of the I. G. Farben Company, was to speak the following day at the Frankfurt League of War Wives. His subject was advances made by Farben scientists against disease. The item identified the speaker as a native Japanese, age thirty-four, formerly an assistant to the great Paul Ehrlich.

"Where did you get this?" asked Logan, looking up.

"I contacted all the important German chemical firms. I asked if they had any information on this man."

"But I. G. Farben no longer exists."

"It was in the files of Hoechst, one of the successor companies."

"So we were right about this guy—he was with Ehrlich." He looked at her. "You're unbelievable, you know that?"

"No, just curious. Same as you."

But he could see she was her old self: her intense preoccupation replaced, at least for the moment, by an openness appealing beyond description. "You're also very beautiful," he added spontaneously. "You've definitely earned some more champagne."

"No, thank you." She took his hand and kissed it gently. "I think now is the time to do the rest of our celebrating."

↔

18 August 1924
Leverkusen

Why did I accept work at Farben? They use me like a trained monkey! Have to waste whole afternoon giving a speech.

More proof Farben has little interest in project. Herr Direktor says too much lab time spent on compound—questions its commercial potential. Harder to get laboratory time for the work.

Compound #157 useless. Unstable at room temperature and poorly soluble in aqueous media.

Begin tomorrow on #158.

↔

Logan was a bit shaky when he arrived at the hospital the next morning for rounds. Splashing water on his face to wash the bleariness from his eyes, he was suddenly aware of a nurse waiting off to the side. He turned and stared at her.

"I hate to bother you with this, Doctor."

"Boudin?"

She nodded. Over the months Rochelle had grown ever more difficult. Almost daily—even when he was not on hospital duty—Logan received word she needed to see him. If it wasn't about her dosing schedule, it might be the quality of the hospital food or perhaps even a TV program on cancer research she'd seen.

The truth, of course, was that what she mainly wanted was a friend. In recent weeks Rochelle's husband, Roger, had all but disappeared. There was less and less conviction in her claim that he was just away on business. Obviously, such a scenario is always poignant, and had it been someone less manipulative, Logan might have found her circumstance more touching.

"She started asking for you as soon as she woke up this morning," the nurse said. "Her latest white cell count is in."

"Oh, God." In general, he had no problem with the ethical guideline giving patients full access to their medical records, but Boudin made a habit of abusing it. "What is it?"

"Forty-two hundred." She handed Logan the sheet.

"So she wants to cut down on her dosage again?"

She nodded. "That's what she wants, all right."

Resignedly he started moving toward her room.

"Dr. Logan?"

Logan wheeled, and was startled to see . . . Stillman!

The senior man approached him, hand extended, smiling. "I was just wondering if you might have a couple of minutes to talk."

"Well, I'm on my way to see a patient."

"Who?"

"Rochelle Boudin."

"Lucky you." Another smile, this one full of comradely understanding. "Come see me in my office afterward."

A moment later, stepping into Rochelle Boudin's room, it was all he could do to mask his reaction—curiosity, tinged with anxiety—to what had just occurred.

"Good morning, Rochelle," he said with brisk efficiency.

She was watching TV. "Have you seen my white cell count?"

"I have. I know it seems low. But I assure you, we're not close to the danger zone."

"I want to cut the dose. I *insist* on it."

"Rochelle, you know the terms of the protocol—"

"I'm so sick," she interrupted. "Can't you give me a break?"

"Please, Rochelle, you know that I—all of us—have only your best interest at heart."

480

"Do you?" she asked, suddenly girlish. "Sometimes I can't tell."

Logan glanced at his watch. "Listen, Rochelle, I've got a very busy morning. I have to go." And he headed for the door.

"Will you be back to see me later?"

But he pretended not to hear.

When he reached Stillman's office, the senior man indicated the chair facing his desk. "What have you been up to lately?"

Logan offered a stiff shrug. "Nothing much. This and that."

"This and that. Sounds like you could put your time to better use." He paused, leaning forward. "I'd like you to join my team."

"Your clinical research team?" Logan was stunned. "Really?"

"That drug I talked about to you and what's-his-name?"

"John Reston."

He nodded. "I'm almost ready to bring it to trial, and I have to beef up support staff. I've seen your work. You're good." When Logan didn't respond, he pressed on. "Assuming things work out satisfactorily, you'll get your name on the paper." He laughed. "Somewhere."

Logan knew how unusual such an offer was. He appreciated what it could mean to his career. He also knew that, because of Compound J, he had to find a reason not to accept.

"Sir, could you possibly tell me a bit more about the drug?"

Such a question from a junior researcher might have seemed presumptuous, but Stillman, utterly confident, took it in good grace. "Well, it's an antigrowth-factor strategy. I'm not ready to go into more detail."

Still not ready, Logan wondered, with it almost set to go before the review board? Suddenly he was hit by a gut feeling: Stillman had zero faith in this drug. It was just another variation of the same old stuff. *That's* why he wouldn't come clean. Stillman was thinking only short term—the hype, and the funding it would bring in.

"Can I think about it?" Logan waffled. "It's a huge decision."

Stillman's eyes flickered with annoyance, but he held it in check. "Certainly," he said. He got to his feet and extended his hand. "Like I tell people, that's one of the things I like about you, Logan. Not an impetuous bone in your body."

BEFORE their protocol could go before the review board, Logan and his associates had to get the man who'd be most unhappy about such a project to sign off on it: Raymond Larsen. As chief of the department of medicine, he ran the system into which any new protocol had to fit.

In Logan's view there was no chance Larsen would hold up the project: He couldn't afford to put himself in the public position of trying to block a reasonable idea. Too, vitally, Compound J had the backing of Seth Shein; and Shein enjoyed the support of Kenneth Markell, the powerful head of the ACF. If nothing else, Larsen understood the realities of institutional politics.

For Larsen, however, the Compound J protocol would represent a double humiliation: proof positive that this first-year associate, this *nothing,* had not only rejected his overtures but gone with his nemesis Shein instead.

Clearly, Logan would have to make at least some attempt at damage control. Now he walked toward Larsen's office, clutching the final draft of the protocol.

The senior man was not in.

"May I leave this?" he asked Larsen's secretary.

Looking at him dismissively, she pointedly laid the envelope to the side and went back to work.

When Logan returned toward the end of the day, Larsen was back—and when he saw his face, he knew he'd read the proposal.

"Sir, I was hoping you might have a few minutes to talk."

Larsen glanced at his watch. "I'm afraid that's quite impossible, I'm due at the lab in five minutes. If you'll excuse me."

Logan followed him out into the corridor. "Dr. Larsen . . ."

Abruptly Larsen stopped and faced him. "*What?*"

The unmistakable note of anger made Logan flinch. But there was no turning back now. "I was wondering if you've had a chance to read what I left you."

"I looked through it."

Logan tried not to sound unctuous. "Sir, I'd appreciate any comments as to how it might be improved."

"My *comments?*" Larsen stared at him coolly. "I'm late, Logan." And turning on his heel, he strode away.

ACTUALLY, the reaction Logan was most worried about was Stillman's. It was not long in coming. As he was about to call it a day, he saw the senior man heading his way.

"So," said Stillman sharply, before Logan could say a word, "I guess I've got your answer to my invitation."

"Dr. Stillman—"

"I have no interest in your explanation, Logan! Just know that I can make your life hell. You stuck a pickax in my back, and now you'd damn well better watch yours."

"LOGAN"—Sabrina's tone was less consoling than practical—"we knew Stillman would not be so happy, right? Larsen also. And maybe others. But what can they do to us?"

Logan shrugged. "Not much—once we get the proposal through. But they've got six weeks to try and sabotage us."

In fact, the petty annoyances began almost immediately. Suddenly various functionaries around the hospital and labs were slower to cooperate with routine requests. Reston one day found that for no apparent reason his dial-out number had been changed, and a new one was not readily available.

A week later Peter Kratsas ordered Sabrina to desist from giving her patients occasional pieces of chocolate.

"And while he tells me this," she reported late that evening, "he is smiling, like it is a big joke!"

"That's exactly what it is," concurred Logan. "Patients' families bring them stuff to eat all the time. Ignore him. It's only temporary. Just a couple more weeks."

Of course, neither lost sight of the key fact: Things were right on track. If their adversaries had real power to get at them, they'd never have had to resort to such pettiness.

"That's very easy for you to say, Logan," she said with a sudden smile. "Me, I have four pounds of Perugina chocolates in the closet. Soon I will have the mice and roaches."

Logan managed to smile back. "I haven't told you the latest. Guess who just discovered he now needs clearance to get a Tylenol from the hospital pharmacy?"

T HE Compound J team waited outside the administration building's third-floor conference room. Logan would represent the team before the board members. He was already on a first-name basis with four of the seven: Dr. Lauren Rostoker of surgical oncology, Dr. Brendan Herlihy of the department of medicine, Dr. Myra Manello of radiation oncology, and Marilyn Lennox of nursing services. The remaining three included a bioethicist based at Georgetown University; an Episcopal minister from Annandale, Virginia; and Marion Winston, a pleasant-looking woman from patient services.

The board stayed behind closed doors for fifteen minutes. Then the three junior associates were invited to join them.

"Well," began Herlihy, chairing the meeting, "I must say a lot of solid thinking went into this idea. However, as you know, we are able to approve only a very small number of protocols—those that meet the strictest criteria for scientific merit and ethical accountability. Dr. Logan, you are speaking for the team?"

"Yessir." Logan smiled and began to lead them through the case for Compound J, emphasizing the significance of the various reports of the drug's activity, spanning decades. "What we have already observed is clear evidence that it is capable of blocking growth factors from binding with cell-surface receptors. The thing is that as long as this drug has been around, it has *never* undergone a rigorous clinical trial for activity against metastatic breast cancer. That is a situation that we now hope to rectify. Thank you."

"What about your informed-consent document?" It was Winston, the patient-care rep. "As you've acknowledged, this is a very toxic drug. I have it on the very best authority that you have not covered all likely eventualities. For example, cerebral hemorrhage. Or heart attack."

Of all the possible calamitous effects of Compound J, the chances that these were among them were infinitesimal. Still, Logan worried she might be scoring points with the others; following Shein's instructions, they *had* passed lightly over the unsettling matter of side effects. The room suddenly seemed overheated.

"Well," Logan said evenly, "listing every *possible* eventuality would have involved pure speculation. That's the point: We need to know more about this drug."

"I see"—Winston again—"and you're planning to use these patients as human guinea pigs."

"I didn't say that." Logan collected himself. "Isn't there a certain degree of uncertainty in a test of any new compound?" He looked hopefully at the medical personnel around the table.

No one gave a word of support.

"Dr. Logan," said Winston, her voice taking on a hard edge, "public confidence in breast cancer trials has been badly shaken in recent years by doctors more concerned with their own reputations than with the well-being of patients. Frankly, certain aspects of your own history have been brought to our attention. Are you aware of a patient named Rochelle Boudin?"

"Yes. I've helped care for Mrs. Boudin."

"I have interviewed Ms. Boudin personally." She held aloft a notebook in grim triumph. "She says you are chronically indifferent to her needs and rarely, if ever, tell her the full truth. I must tell you that Dr. Larsen fully shares her view of the situation."

So that was it? Larsen! "Ms. Winston, I don't know what you expect me to say. I've done my best with Mrs. Boudin, as with all my patients. I—"

"Look." He was interrupted. "This is *absurd*. We're talking about the *wrong* things here."

Logan jerked around to see Shein standing just inside the door.

"You want to talk about the informed-consent document?" he picked up. "Fine, blame me. I'm the one who told 'em to make it short and sweet. But don't throw out the baby with the bathwater!"

Everyone knew Shein's intrusion was highly unorthodox, but no one was about to stop him. He moved to stand beside Logan.

"What are we really here for?" he continued. "We have a problem in this country with metastatic breast cancer. Now, in my considered view, based on twenty years in the business, our friends here have come up with a novel and rational idea that represents hope for women who otherwise have none. If, God forbid, it were my wife, I'd sure as hell want her on this protocol, even if I don't know every one of the damned toxicities."

IT TOOK the review board a half hour to reach its decision. The Compound J team was granted a modified protocol—a smaller and more closely monitored version of the one they'd proposed.

The note on the bottle of champagne that arrived at Seth Shein's door that evening didn't even try to be clever: "All the gratitude we can ever express will never be enough."

According to the guidelines imposed by the board, the Compound J team had to have a hit—a demonstrably positive result—within the first fifteen patients. That placed even greater than normal importance on putting together a patient roster. "It's easy," as Shein pointed out, "to kill a good drug with a bad trial." And the easiest way to screw up a trial is to stock it with patients whose chances of doing well are already compromised going in.

Unfortunately, potential candidates for this protocol would likely fall into that category, since, having proved resistant to one therapy, they would likely be resistant to others. The best the team could reasonably hope to do was locate fifteen women whose exposure to such treatments had been minimal.

As in every other protocol being conducted at the ACF, a summary of the Compound J test was duly recorded in the foundation's community outreach system. The description of the protocol was followed by an appeal for likely candidates. Over the next few weeks calls slowly began to come in, but three weeks into the process only a handful of women were even being considered.

The ice was finally broken late one Friday afternoon. Sabrina got word that Rachel Meigs, a junior associate interested in the protocol, needed to see her immediately in the screening clinic.

"I think I've got a live one for you," said Meigs when Sabrina arrived. "I finished the exam about half an hour ago."

Sabrina looked into the waiting room. Except for a young woman, evidently very pregnant, it was empty. "That one?"

Meigs nodded. "That one. I think you'll like her."

Entering the room, Sabrina extended her hand. "Hello. I am Dr. Como."

The woman struggled to her feet. "Hi. I'm Judy Novick."

Only now was it apparent: Aside from her bloated midsection, the woman was emaciated. She wasn't pregnant; her abdomen was full of tumor.

It took a moment to compute. Of *course;* a week or so earlier Sabrina and her colleagues had studied this woman's X rays and slides. Although tests confirmed that a breast tumor had metastasized to the liver and was laying waste her body at an awful rate, the only treatment she had undergone to date was a single course of adjuvant therapy. She'd been referred to the program after the most active drugs available had proved useless. And she lived in Bedford, Pennsylvania, little more than two hours from the ACF.

"Now," offered Sabrina, "I am sure you have some questions, no? And I have some questions for you also."

"Well, I really don't even know what all this involves."

"The first thing I will tell you," replied Sabrina, "is that this is an outpatient trial. We might need you here in the hospital at the beginning, but afterward you would live at home."

"But what does it do?"

Sabrina's tone was at once straightforward and sympathetic. "I can only tell you of our hopes. This is a very new treatment, but it is something some of us believe in very much."

"How many patients has it been tried on?"

Sabrina hesitated. "You will be the first—number one." She smiled. "This is kind of an honor, no?"

The woman looked away. "I don't know whether to be flattered or horrified."

Sabrina had never imagined this part of it would be so tricky.

Suddenly she found herself having to sell the protocol—and to a patient she wasn't even sure she wanted. "You are possibly a good candidate for this treatment," she offered simply. "And this is not a thing we can say to very many."

For a long moment Novick said nothing. Then, "It's not an easy decision, but this is my only chance, isn't it? I'm not one of those people who lie to themselves."

"Still," Sabrina said evenly, "before we agree, you must think about it a little. I want you to look carefully at the informed-consent document. And talk with your family and with your doctor. And I must talk with my colleagues."

Novick nodded. "Fine. But if we're doing this, I'd like to get started. The sooner the better."

↔

3 October 1927
Frankfurt

Cannot believe my good fortune—Emma's family does not disapprove! I am proud, but must also be realistic. A Japanese son-in-law cannot be easy for any German family to accept.

Versions #284, 285, and (especially) 286 of compound continue to give hope. When it works, nothing is more beautiful than chemistry.

Except Emma.

Must now write my family in Japan. How will *they* take idea of a German Jewish daughter-in-law?

↔

As WORD of the Compound J protocol spread, the patient accrual phase began clicking along surprisingly smoothly.

One day in the screening clinic Logan was alerted by his beeper to an incoming call while talking with a candidate, one Sally Kober. She was missing a kidney as a result of an auto accident in her teens. Since she was sixty-six, this was of little consequence, but under other circumstances, it might have been used to keep her out of the program.

Logan switched off the beeper and smiled at the patient. "I'll get to that in a few minutes. Just a doctor calling about someone

488

who might be interested in this protocol. *You're* already here."

"And immensely good company," she observed, laughing.

Logan couldn't help but be struck by this woman. A veteran of a radical mastectomy twenty years before, she seemed to be taking the ominous appearance of the new node above the clavicle with amazing calm.

"Now," she said, "this thing I've got is pretty desperate, isn't it?"

"I wish the news were better," he replied.

Unconsciously she passed a hand over her steel-gray hair. "Are you a football fan?"

He nodded, confused. "The Dallas Cowboys."

"Oh, please. You struck me as someone with common sense." She smiled. "I love the Giants."

"You're excused—you live in New Jersey."

"I will bet you, right now, on the first game the Giants and Cowboys play next season."

"It wouldn't be right taking your money."

She laughed. "It's called faith. It's a convenient way of betting on myself to still be here."

"I've only known you fifteen minutes, but *that's* a bet I'll take."

She waved her hand. "Enough flattery. Go return that call."

"Hello," answered a male voice.

"This is Dr. Daniel Logan at the American Cancer Foundation. I was given this number but no name."

"Yes, Dr. Logan. You've got the right number."

"Did you call? Are you a doctor?"

"Yes, I'm a doctor. But I'm afraid I don't have a patient to refer to you. My name is Ray Coopersmith."

Logan walked into the Hotel Jefferson in Richmond, Coopersmith's choice for their meeting. Though it was early on a Saturday evening, the lobby was nearly deserted. Logan was about to take a seat in one of the chairs beyond the main staircase when he happened to look up. There, at a table behind a wrought-iron railing on the second floor, a man was nodding at him.

"I thought for a second you wouldn't see me," said Coopersmith when Logan reached the top of the stairs. He extended his hand. "Ray Coopersmith."

Though probably no more than a few years older than Logan, Coopersmith looked middle-aged. Tall and rail thin, with dark hollows beneath penetrating eyes, and thinning hair in need of a trim, he had an edgy, unfocused quality Logan had noted in gamblers and junkies.

As they took their seats, Logan noticed, with a rush of sympathy, that the man's worn suit jacket didn't quite match the pants.

Coopersmith ordered a gin and tonic; Logan, a beer. They stared at one another for a long moment.

"So what are you doing these days?" Logan asked.

"I'm getting by," he said with sudden, unmistakable rancor. "Don't worry about me. I'm practicing medicine."

"Where's that?"

"At a clinic. In Petersburg. Why? You gonna check me out?"

Logan chose to ignore this. "I read your protocol. Impressive."

The waiter brought the drinks.

Incomprehensibly, Coopersmith snickered. "Maybe I'll read yours sometime. Breast cancer. Smart. A glamour disease. Me— genius!—I go after prostate. Try to get funding for *that*."

This was the opening Logan had been looking for. "I heard it wasn't lack of funding that got you in trouble."

Coopersmith's head jerked left, then right. "Who said that?"

"Steven Locke. He said you faked your data."

"That's bull. The data was good data," he insisted. "But they said it was uninterpretable."

"Who's that?"

"Larsen. Stillman. Kratsas. That bunch. They were against me from the start. What I'd give to ream out those bastards!"

Logan stared at him. *That's* why this guy had gotten him down here? "Look, Ray, I appreciate the warning, but it's not news about these guys."

"You don't know what you're talking about. You don't know the half of it."

"Really, I understand what you're saying."

"You're such an arrogant s.o.b. You fit right in at that place!" He shot him a malicious grin. "Bet you don't like hearing that, do you?"

Logan was caught short by the savagery of the attack. "Look, I've gotta be getting back. I don't think this is doing either of us any good."

Unsettling as this was, Logan found it useful. This guy was wildly unstable. Who could doubt that that had been the heart of his problems?

Coopersmith's strangled laugh caught him by surprise. "You're a jerk, Logan!"

LOGAN liked Faith Byrne the instant he met her.

"So, Doctor," she greeted him in the examining room, "who does a girl have to suck up to around here to get well?"

He laughed. "I'm afraid sucking up won't do it."

"Ah. In other words, it's you."

This sixty-two-year-old widow from the Boston suburb of Brookline—with lively blue eyes beneath a halo of white hair—was obviously going to keep him on his toes.

"I want to tell you it was my own decision to come down here and see you people," she told him five minutes into their session. "My doctor wanted to give me the same old stuff. But I told him no." She looked directly at him. "I've read up on my chances."

The manifestation of Byrne's malignancy was unusual: hundreds of tiny pink nodules cutting an angry swath across the chest wall and around to the back. But the young doctor saw this as no impediment to her inclusion in the trial. The key fact was that she had been exposed to only minimal levels of adjuvant therapy, and that had been fifteen years ago, at the time of a mastectomy.

There was something else: Faith was an irresistible chance to stick it to Stillman. He found in her paperwork that she had rejected the chance to go with the senior man's protocol.

"Why's that?" he soon felt comfortable enough to ask. For a

patient seeking innovative treatment to turn down a doctor with Stillman's reputation was almost unheard of.

"*Why?* You kidding? I *met* the guy. Call me weird, but I like to feel I'm gonna get more consideration than a slab of beef."

Despite himself, Logan burst out laughing.

WHEN she was accepted five days later, Faith became the eighth woman on the protocol. A half-dozen other prospects waited to be seen. The time had arrived to begin administering the drug.

By custom, protocol patients receive treatment in the order in which they've signed up. That meant Judith Novick would lead off.

Logan was aware this was not ideal. The progress of the early patients would be watched closely by their senior colleagues; and of all the patients on the roster, Judith was in the worst shape.

It was Reston, at a meeting one Sunday morning around Logan's dinner table, who raised the issue. "Look," he said, "I say we launch with someone else. Judith Novick is too far gone."

Sabrina stared at him murderously. "We made a contract with Judith Novick. This cannot be changed now. Compound J can be as toxic to a person with a small tumor as a large. In fact, if Judith does well, it would look even better for us, no?"

"Sabrina"—Reston smiled indulgently—"I admire your compassion. But when Judith Novick goes, she's gonna take one of our fifteen slots with her. And you know as well as I do that because she's weak, the toxicity is likely to be heightened."

He waited for a response, but there was none. He turned to Logan. "Look, Dan, why can't we just drop her back a few slots?"

Logan looked toward Sabrina, then back to Reston. "So it's up to me? Well then, we go ahead as planned."

Abruptly Reston was on his feet. "Dammit, what kind of power does she have over you anyway?"

"I'm just afraid that to change now," Logan replied calmly, "would be to draw the wrong kind of attention to ourselves. Either we believe in Compound J or we don't."

But already Reston had grabbed his coat and was heading for the door. "To hell with you both! With this whole project!"

Two weeks later, on the morning of Judith Novick's first treatment, Reston was there with the others. An intense seriousness of purpose marked the occasion. This was their debut—a time, if ever there was one, to look beyond petty squabbles.

The patient was pale, her midsection appearing larger than ever beneath the flimsy hospital gown. The tumor measured an astounding ten by ten centimeters.

"Don't you worry, dear," the research nurse, Sadie McCorvey, said. "It'll be over sooner than you know." She inserted the IV line into the patient's arm and taped it in place. "We'll begin the drug in just a few minutes."

But the items that were wheeled into the room a moment later could not have been reassuring: an EKG machine, lights glowing; then the paddles, ready to go if her heart stopped; followed by the mobile crisis center known as the crash cart, each of its drawers bearing a different drug in a hypodermic.

Novick was so focused on these that she failed to notice that McCorvey had removed the clamp on the IV. If she was to have a negative reaction, it would come within the first five minutes.

The Compound J team waited eight.

"Well," spoke up Judith Novick finally, "when are you going to give it to me?"

Sabrina laughed and pointed toward the liquid flowing through the clear tubing. "You see. No problems."

If it hadn't been unprofessional, Logan might've grabbed Sabrina and kissed her. Instead, he turned from one to the other, grinning. "Let's hear it for anticlimaxes!"

Logan made three visits to Novick's room during the next six hours. Sabrina made four. Even Reston stopped by a couple of times. Always she was resting comfortably, watching TV or reading. "Is something wrong?" she asked Logan finally.

"Not at all!" he exclaimed, feeling just slightly foolish. "Just making sure you're okay."

By the third day she was ready to go home. Gingerly Logan felt the tumor. By now he knew it intimately—not only its size but its

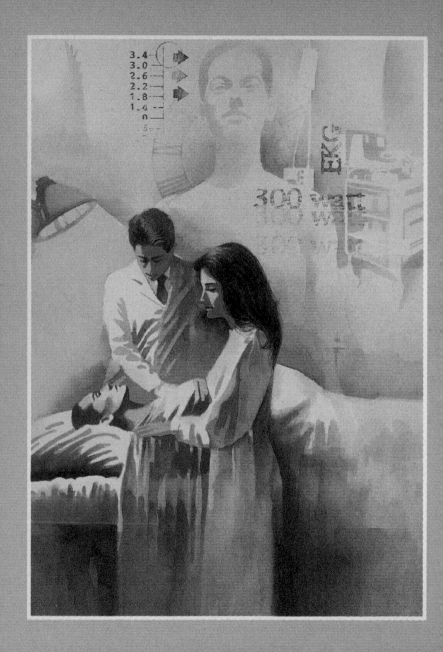

feel, its distinctive contours. Could it be slightly softer than before? No. That had to be his imagination.

Abruptly, there came a knock at the door.

"What is it?"

"I'm sorry, Doctor," said a nurse, opening the door a crack. "Mrs. Byrne is on the phone, and she says it's very important."

"Okay." He smiled at Judy Novick. "Just keep on keeping on. We'll see you on Tuesday for your next treatment."

He picked up the phone at the reception desk. "Faith?" he said, with concern. "This is Dr. Logan. Is something the matter?"

"You told me I have to wait a month and a half for treatment." There was a hardness to the voice.

"Yes."

"So how come someone else has already gotten hers?"

"Who told you that?"

"Never mind who told me. That isn't the point."

"Faith, listen to me. The drug is administered according to when patients joined the protocol."

"I don't give a damn about that. I've got to look out for me."

"Faith," he said, "we'll have to discuss this later."

"When?"

"*Later.*"

It wasn't hard to pinpoint Faith's source: Marion Winston, the patient-care representative, who made it policy to let every patient in the protocol know that, as she put it, she "was available to mediate misunderstandings with medical personnel."

When Logan stopped by her office intending to raise the subject of Faith's call, Winston stopped him short with her opening words. "I heard from Mrs. Byrne. Apparently, you are not being very responsive to her needs."

"Listen, our job is to be fair to everyone on the protocol."

"Good. Well, just so we're clear: I see it as *my* job to empower these women. So that they can also help decide what's"—she made quote marks with her fingers—"fair."

"I see. So you suggested that Faith call?"

"She was troubled. I said it was up to her to let you know."

"I see," he repeated with practiced calm. "Look, Ms. Winston, I hope we can work together to minimize friction."

"Of course." She eyed him coolly. "That's always my intention."

"I'm just saying that Mrs. Byrne was made needlessly upset. It doesn't *matter* to her chances what order she goes in."

"Well, then, why not move her up? We both know there are others on this protocol who truly don't care what order they go in."

Logan's head was starting to spin. He sighed. "I'll give it some thought."

She offered what under other circumstances would pass as a friendly smile. "Faith and I would appreciate that."

WHEN Judith Novick showed up at the hospital the following Tuesday for her second treatment, the change was unmistakable. "I'm feeling great," she said. "Less tired than I can remember."

Standing beside her in the examining room, Logan and Sabrina exchanged a quick glance. Both knew that even if what they were seeing was in reaction to the drug, it could prove fleeting.

Still, there was no question the tumor was more yielding to the touch. And when they measured it, they found that it had shrunk three quarters of a centimeter—not significant but encouraging.

In any case, Novick wasn't waiting for the doctors' authorization to celebrate her new vigor. "This past week has been so wonderful," she announced. "I've been seeing people again. My husband took me to the movies. The other day I even went out shopping."

"That's terrific, Judy," agreed Logan. He hesitated, not wanting to play the ogre. "But go slow. It's still early."

"I know. I don't have any illusions." Suddenly she smiled, her face radiant. "But, I'll tell you, I almost don't care. I never thought I'd ever feel this good again—even for a day."

↔

15 May 1929
Frankfurt

Version #337 showing heightened activity in rats. Some tumors shrinking twenty-five percent! Must guard against overoptimism. Sixteen years on the project, and toxicity as great a problem as ever.

Was the right decision to come to Christian Thomas Company. Herr Thomas follows work closely. Very interested in progress.

Emma keeps me balanced, listens to my frustrations and complaints. If it ever comes, my success will be her success.

↔

As SHE lay in bed waiting for her treatment to begin, Faith Byrne appeared calm. "You're not gonna feel a thing," encouraged Nurse McCorvey, inserting the IV line into her arm.

Since Faith had assumed the fourth slot—it had previously belonged to a certain Hannah Dietz, who welcomed the delay—the procedure was starting to feel so routine that Logan was the lone Compound J team member on hand.

"That's right," echoed Marion Winston. "Easy as pie." She placed her hand lightly on the patient's arm. "I wish I were as comfortable as you look in that bed."

"Hey, feel free to change places," said Faith. She strained to get a look at the IV bottle bearing Compound J.

"You want me to tell you when it starts?" asked McCorvey.

"Of *course*. It's my life."

McCorvey gingerly removed the clamp. "Now."

The patient exhaled deeply, staring up at the ceiling.

Two minutes went by. Then a third.

"Something's not right," spoke up Faith suddenly. "Stop the medicine. Please!"

"What is it? Tell me." Logan looked over at McCorvey. Her face reflected his own intense concern.

"I feel chilled all over! I'm getting nauseous."

Logan discounted anaphylaxis—a severe toxic reaction—almost at once: Faith's breathing was not labored, and her color was good. "What's her pressure?" Logan asked McCorvey.

She checked the monitor. "One twenty-five over eighty."

"Heart rate?"

"Seventy-five." Both normal.

The problem, he could only conclude, was nothing more than acute anxiety. Logan nodded toward the crash cart. "Prepare a milligram intravenous of lorazepam." A Valium analog.

497

He leaned in close to the patient and spoke soothingly. "Faith, we're going to give you something to help you relax."

"No! What I need is epinephrine!"

Lunacy. Epinephrine speeds up the heart rate. "I really don't think that's necessary," he reassured.

"Doctor, the woman is telling you she's in crisis. I would like you to call for backup!" demanded Winston.

Startled, Logan looked across the bed at her. "What Mrs. Byrne is describing is not life-threatening," he replied calmly. "We've been through this procedure several times already."

With a sudden wail Faith Byrne again commanded all eyes. "Oh, God, *please,* don't let them kill me."

Winston took her hand. "I promise you that's *not* going to happen. Dr. Logan, I must insist that—"

By now Logan had to make a physical effort to maintain his surface calm. "If it'll set your mind at ease . . ." He dialed the nurses station. "This is Dr. Logan in room three fourteen. I'd like some backup here. Stat."

As he hung up, he glanced at his watch. "I just want to tell you, we're already past the danger point."

Now that all concern had passed, Logan eyed the patient-care rep with cool disdain. "Ms. Winston, you are not medical personnel. I would *really* appreciate it if you would stand back now."

"I happen to be doing my job, Doctor."

"What is this problem?" There, in the doorway, stood Sabrina.

Logan nodded to her. "I'm afraid we've had a bit of a misunderstanding. But everything's under control now." He looked down at the patient. "Feeling better, Faith?"

"I don't know. I guess so."

"Nonetheless," said the patient-care rep, "I believe Mrs. Byrne would feel a lot more comfortable if Dr. Como took over now."

Logan stared at her. "Is that what you want, Faith?"

Byrne didn't hesitate. "Yes, it is."

"Well, it's all yours, Dr. Como," he said with a brittle smile.

And Logan strode from the room, leaving the woman he loved to supervise what had, in fact, been an entirely routine procedure.

LOGAN hoped against hope that word of what had happened would not get around the ACF. After a week he'd almost begun to believe it was possible.

Then one afternoon Allen Atlas sidled up to him in the junior associates lounge. "I hear you've been rejected by one of your protocol patients." He was grinning broadly. "Isn't it supposed to work the other way around?"

"Don't worry about me. Or our protocol."

"Dr. Stillman sends you his regrets about Mrs. Byrne. He knows her, you know."

"I heard. She turned you guys down flat."

"Is that what she told you? Logan, you're even more gullible than I thought. The woman has a borderline personality disorder. It was in her file. Stillman took one look at it and sent her packing."

Of course. It explained everything. When such an individual's expectations go unmet, good can turn into bad in a nanosecond. No one would ever knowingly include a borderline in a drug trial.

"I didn't see any report on that in her file," Logan said.

"Oh, no?" Atlas smiled, even more broadly. "Maybe that part of it didn't get sent along. These things happen."

FORTUNATELY, there was more than enough work to keep Logan from dwelling on having been pushed into a mistake. Patients already on the protocol—half the eventual total—were now reporting semiweekly for administration of the drug, a thorough examination, and a consultation. On top of which, Logan, Sabrina, and Reston had their obligations at the hospital. Under the circumstances, their workdays often continued past midnight.

Late one Thursday night the phone rang in Logan's place: Sabrina needed to compare notes on a patient. While they were talking, there was a call-waiting beep on her end.

"Who could it be at this hour?" she wondered. "Hold a second."

A moment later she was back. "It is Marion Winston. Something has happened to Judith Novick. I will call you back."

The wait was less than three minutes, but it felt like a decade.

"Logan, it is terrible news. She had a bad fall. A fractured skull. She's in a coma. At the Bedford General Hospital in Pennsylvania, where she lives."

Logan was numb. "What's Winston doing in the middle of it?"

Sabrina knew better than anyone how sensitive the topic was. "Judith's family gave the hospital her name," she said gently.

Logan found himself irked that Winston hadn't seen fit to notify him, the head of the Compound J team. Thirty seconds later he had Winston on the line. He could almost see her stiffen at the sound of his voice. "Dr. Logan, I've passed all the pertinent information to Dr. Como."

"Can you tell me exactly what happened?"

"She fell. That's all we know."

"At home?"

"No. It was at a mall. On some steps by the parking lot."

What the hell was wrong with her, shopping at that hour? Her balance was off. I warned her to take it easy!

"Is that all, Doctor? Obviously, keeping her on the protocol now is out of the question . . . *permanently.*"

Logan was surprised. "Why? She seems to have had some response to the drug already."

"Because it could be that your drug caused her to black out. We don't know what happened to Mrs. Novick. In my view this must be regarded as a possible drug-related toxicity."

THE odds were one in ten thousand that the drug had anything to do with Mrs. Novick. As for the other patients, no one, it seemed, was being made sick by Compound J, and obviously, that was good. Yet none had signed up merely *not* to be made ill by the drug. The truth seemed to be that this stuff was doing nothing at all.

Early one Monday morning, busy with their respective hospital duties, Logan and Sabrina heard themselves paged over the intercom. They were to report immediately to the outpatient clinic.

There they found Reston, as sober as Logan had ever seen him.

"This is it," he said. "We can kiss our careers good-bye. We've got a toxicity problem." He indicated the examining room to his right. "Hannah Dietz." Dietz, a feisty refugee from Hitler's Germany, was the patient who'd switched places with Faith Byrne. "She reports profuse bleeding from the gums," said Reston. "Every time she brushes her teeth."

Sabrina led the way into the examining room. "Hello, Hannah," she said to the heavyset woman with steel-gray hair—and then spotted the man sitting in the corner. Balding, with a seedy, unkempt mustache, he appeared in his early sixties, a few years younger than the patient. "Hello, Phil."

Phil, her "companion," accompanied her on visits to the ACF.

"Well, well, the gang is all here," said Hannah pleasantly.

"Yes," said Logan. "Dr. Reston's told us about your problem."

"Just some bleeding when I brush."

"Have you noticed if you've been bruising more easily than usual?" asked Logan. The obvious thought: The drug was playing havoc with the proteins responsible for coagulation.

She shrugged. "No, I have not noticed."

"Well," said Logan, "I think we'll take a little blood. And maybe keep you here a couple of days for observation."

Late that afternoon the blood test showed what they'd expected: At least one of the proteins in the coagulation cascade was seriously malfunctioning.

It had to be Compound J.

"Damn!" erupted Reston. He kicked a chair violently, sending it crashing to the floor. "What now?"

"You are a child, Reston," said Sabrina disgustedly. "Vitamin K should bring the prothrombin time down, and with little risk."

"That's not the point!" raged Reston. "You realize this is going to have to be reported to the institutional review board."

"Don't overreact," Logan cut him off. "If we can tune up Mrs. Dietz quickly, we're just about back to where we were."

"Hold on." Reston held up both hands. "No *way* she stays on this protocol. The next time the bleeding could be internal—and fatal."

"You know as well as I do, she hasn't a chance otherwise."

"Not my problem. What are you, Logan? Suicidal?"

"You can just forget it. I'm not going to cut her loose. We've already lost Judy Novick. We're down to fourteen as it is."

"I was against keeping Novick too! That was another mistake."

"I will arrange for the vitamin K treatment," said Sabrina, walking briskly from the room.

"WHAT'RE you reading?"

Startled, Logan looked up at Seth Shein. He'd deliberately chosen this spot—a bench in a quiet nook behind the library—to avoid being bothered. "Just a letter."

"Who from?"

"A researcher, retired. An old guy. It's nothing."

Shein sat beside him on the bench. "Lemme see it."

Logan handed it over and watched for a reaction.

> My dear Dr. Logan:
>
> Greetings and best wishes. My name Rudolf Kistner. I live now in the city of Köln, as a pensioner.
>
> Formerly I am an organic chemist. I write you because I learn from my readings of the protocol you conduct at the American Cancer Foundation. Many years ago I worked also with compounds of sulfonate derivatives against cancer. In those times we had many hopes for such drugs.
>
> It would be a great favor if perhaps you could take a moment to tell me of your labors. I am old now, but I have much time to think and wonder. For this, one is never too old.
>
> With very sincere regards,
> Rudolf Kistner

Shein handed back the letter. "The guy's gotta be ninety years old. Straight outta the Dark Ages." He paused. "Listen, Logan, I gotta tell you something. You really got Stillman going. He's scared to death he's gonna be shown up by a bunch of punk kids."

"Us?" asked Logan reasonably. "Why?"

"Why?" Shein's voice dropped. "Because Stillman's finally faced the fact that *his* protocol's gonna be a total disaster, that's why."

"That's great," Logan said uncertainly.

Shein clapped him on the back. "The bigger his failure, the bigger my success." He stood up. "Now what I need from you is not to let up. Wring some activity outta that stuff of yours, and it'll be the stake through his heart."

WHEN Sabrina reached Logan that night from the hospital, he could hear the exhaustion in her voice. A couple of hours earlier, word had come in that Judith Novick had died.

"I have heard something today about Reston from Rachel Meigs. She says Reston makes fun of Compound J right in front of Stillman. Even Atlas. I despise this guy."

"You were right all along, Sabrina."

"I don't tell you this to be right. But we must deal with it."

"Unless the protocol pans out. I know this guy. Believe me, if things start going better, Reston'll be right back with the program."

SHE *was in her private office when she was told her doctor was waiting to see her. As soon as she saw his face, she knew the news was bad.*

"Mrs. Rivers, I hope you'll forgive me. I've taken the liberty of—"

Abruptly John entered the room. He was ashen-faced, not a politician now, but a husband. Wordlessly, he stood by her chair and kissed her. "I love you, Elizabeth," he said.

"That bad?" she said, glaring at the doctor.

"I'm afraid that the biopsy shows a malignancy."

There it was: the death sentence.

As he launched into a jumble of medical jargon, she scarcely even listened.

"So you're saying this is bone cancer?" asked John.

"No, sir. Based on what we see, the disease originated in the breast and metastasized to the bone."

"Then what are we talking about? Breast surgery?"

The doctor shook his head sympathetically. "I'm afraid, sir, that at this point breast surgery would only eliminate a small portion of the disease. I recommend we call in Dr. Markell at the ACF."

"How dare you?" she suddenly erupted. She glared at the doctor

503

again. "This is my life! What gives you the right to supersede my wishes?"

"Mrs. Rivers, I'm sorry. It just seemed to me that your husband had the right—"

"Well, that's not your call to make! You're worried about your own neck!"

"Elizabeth, please. You're upset."

"Damn right I'm upset! I've got cancer. And his only thought is how he's going to look in front of the President."

"Mrs. Rivers, I assure you that's not true. I'm sorry. Perhaps I did use poor judgment."

Her fury was spent, and a moment later she was sobbing. "I don't understand it. I've done everything I'm supposed to. Self-examinations. Mammograms."

Her husband took her in his arms. "It's not your fault, darling. What we've got to think about now is fighting it."

"I just want to say that there is every reason for optimism," the doctor said. He nodded out the window in the direction of the ACF across the river. "They're doing remarkable things there."

THEIR first year at the American Cancer Foundation came to an end the second week in June. With the rookies coming in to take over the hospital scutwork, the second-year associates were now moving up to lab work—which for both Logan and Sabrina meant going to work directly under Seth Shein.

Their role was simply to clone and sequence a certain gene so that more senior people would have material to work with. Logan, with his advanced degree in chemistry, found it mind numbing. Day after day it was like following directions in a cookbook: "Add three lambdas of the restriction enzyme Xba to DNA; spin for fifteen minutes;" and so on. He soon began regarding the routine sessions with the protocol patients as a relief.

Increasingly Logan was aware that the Dietz case had left Compound J ripe for ridicule. True, toxicity had been minimal and treatable. But coming as it did within weeks of Novick's fall, there was also the psychological factor. Before, Compound J's opponents had merely been able to say it was a harebrained idea. Now they could say—with pleasure—it was a harebrained idea *that makes people even sicker.* Like it or not, the Compound J protocol was now regarded at the ACF as being in trouble.

One afternoon when he and Sabrina were perusing accumulated protocol data, Logan started going over the numbers of a patient named Marjorie Rhome, a forty-eight-year-old dental assistant from Dover, Delaware. By the luck of the draw, Logan hadn't seen her in over a month. Reston had handled her last three visits.

Her file, like that of every other patient in the protocol, was now over a hundred pages. As Logan scanned the results of her blood work from three weeks before, something caught his eye: The woman's creatinine level, a measure of kidney function, was at 1.7. Immediately he skipped ahead to the results of last week's visit. The level had jumped to 1.8. Normal is 1.4.

"Sabrina, look at this!"

She grasped its significance instantly. "My God," she said softly.

Elevation of the blood creatinine level meant the kidneys were not clearing it properly. Which could mean that they were not clearing far more dangerous substances, particularly potassium, which can make the human heart come to a dead standstill.

"Reston must've missed it," said Logan bitterly. As far as Logan was concerned, the final straw on Reston had been his erstwhile friend's decision to do his lab work under Larsen's associate, Kratsas.

They spent the next hour going over the files of all of the other patients on the protocol, looking for the same syndrome. They found it in one other: Faith Byrne was also at 1.8.

"This is a real problem," said Sabrina intently. "If the level goes to two point zero or two point one . . ."

"They'll have to leave the protocol. And if the creatinine level continues to rise, we may be talking a worst-case scenario of chronic kidney failure or even permanent hemodialysis."

The fact was, Logan had been turning an idea over in his mind for a while—since Hannah Dietz's toxicity. Only now it began to seem less an intriguing possibility than an imperative.

"I think we should take this drug back to the lab," he told Sabrina. "Try to find some way to cut down on its toxicity."

"But the drug we are using—*that* Compound J—by the terms of the protocol, it's the one we must stay with," she argued.

"You're right," he said. "But I'm trying to think beyond that. We've got to redesign the molecule. This is the Compound J we've got, right?" He sketched an awkward rendering of two spheres, with three spikes protruding from each, connected by a long, thick tube. "Basically, we've got three parts that more or less fit together: two naphthalene rings, each bound to three sulfonate groups—those are the spikes—and connected to one another by an organic polymer. Think of it as a modular couch, with the larger section in the middle."

He looked up and she nodded. "It looks more like a lobster."

He laughed. "Anyway, the bridge between the two outer modules might be too long. If we could shorten it . . ." He went on, explaining how in scientific terms what he proposed was quite elementary, how it could even be achieved in a matter of days.

WITH Shein's permission they got the lab to themselves the following weekend—by happy coincidence, the three-day Independence Day holiday. All was ready, including a dozen lab rabbits bearing tumors induced by a carcinogen.

The procedure Logan had in mind required six chemical reactions in a set sequence. If they were to succeed in concocting the slightly altered compound—Compound J-lite, as they'd begun referring to it—each step had to go flawlessly. It was intense and grueling work, punctuated by long, frustrating breaks as they waited for one or another chemical reaction to reach completion.

That first night, close to one a.m., Logan noted approvingly the brown gelatinous liquid bubbling on the heating mantle. "You want to take a nap?" He indicated a room with a cot off the lab. "I'll do the next part."

He worked through the night, finishing early Saturday morning as Sabrina sauntered back into the lab. "How is the work?"

"Terrific." He held aloft a beaker bearing yellowish liquid. "My turn to nap. I've written down instructions for you for the next step. It's simple as pie, but you know where to find me."

Six hours later she gently jostled him awake. "I have finished," she said softly. "Come see."

The container of liquid she held aloft seemed to be of precisely the right hue.

He beamed. "See that? You're a natural. After we boil off the liquid and recrystallize the residue, we'll be left with a white powder. That's the material that will make up the modules."

"What now?" she asked.

He stretched. "Now we start on the bridge material."

The procedure that followed took most of the next two days. Basically, as Logan told it, the various elements they were fitting together were analogous to pieces in a Tinkertoy set. "Certain pieces fit together, and others never will. You can't make an amide out of a carboxylic acid and a tertiary amine. Yet a carboxylic acid and a primary amine can fit together as neatly as a key in a lock."

Finally they were left with a second batch of white powder. It was seventy-five hours after they'd started. Outside, on this Monday evening—the Fourth of July—the sun was starting to set.

Logan, exhausted, allowed himself a small smile. "Just one more step. Combining them with a condensing agent to make the Compound J-lite molecule."

Less than two hours later Compound J-lite was a reality. On the table before them was fully one hundred grams of it.

Logan picked up the phone and called down to the animal-holding facility in the basement. "Good evening. This is Dr. Daniel Logan in Dr. Shein's lab."

"Yessir. How may I help you?" It was Hassan, the young Bangladeshi guy, one of the crew of four or five that ran the place.

"My colleague Dr. Como and I will be down shortly. I believe we have twelve rabbits with induced tumors. . . ."

"Yessir. Would you like me to prepare them for you?"

"Yes, please. I'd appreciate that."

By the time they made it down to the basement, the animals had been moved from the holding area to an adjacent lab. The rabbits, each in its own cage, were a sad-looking bunch, grotesque versions of the adorable creatures found in pet shops every Easter. The fur of each was pocked with pink tumors—rough to the touch and rock-hard. Untreated, none would live longer than three weeks.

After they'd injected each of the rabbits, Logan summoned Hassan. "You can put these back now."

"Yessir." He nodded. "Are there any special instructions?"

"Only to let us know if there is anything unusual."

"Yes. I will."

As a precaution, the meeting was not at the White House but across the street in the Old Executive Office Building. One of the participants, ACF director Markell, might be recognizable; his picture had been in the newsweeklies. So had that of the man at his side: the renowned breast cancer specialist, Gregory Stillman.

Dr. Paul Burke, the President's personal physician, introduced Charles Malcolm, special assistant to the President for domestic affairs. Stillman maintained a careful reserve. Markell had told him nothing in advance—a sure sign of the meeting's importance.

Dr. Burke turned to Stillman. "It's about the First Lady. She's got breast cancer, with widespread metastases to bone."

Stillman nodded soberly. "I see. I'm terribly sorry." But inside, the contradictory emotions were already stirring. This was a wide-open shot at superstar status. But it could also be a bear of a case.

Burke handed him a large manila envelope. Wordlessly, he opened it and held a CAT scan up to the light. Then he turned to the thick file of lab reports. Almost immediately he spotted two negative prognostic factors: The tumor was estrogen-receptor negative, and the tumor cells were undergoing an extremely high rate of DNA synthesis and mitosis.

"Obviously," said Burke, "we hope you will take the case."

"Of course," responded Stillman.

"Good," Malcolm picked up. "I don't know much about these things, but I assume you'll want to start immediately."

"Yes."

"I'll talk to Mrs. Rivers today," said Burke. "Perhaps you could set aside Friday morning." It was less a question than an order.

"Yes, of course."

"Obviously, this is highly privileged information. You are to discuss it with no one. That includes family members."

AT NOON Faith Byrne underwent her weekly exam at the outpatient clinic. So far, Logan and Sabrina had kept the creatinine problem to themselves. But they could no longer avoid facing its implications.

When Sabrina walked into the physicians lounge, Logan could tell the news was not good.

"Her creatinine is at two point zero."

He closed his eyes and shook his head. "Does she know?"

"No. I wished to talk first with you."

"We've got to be straight with her. Keeping her on the protocol will endanger her health. Shall I go in with you?"

"No," said Sabrina. "There could be trouble. By myself is best."

Fifteen minutes later Sabrina returned. "Logan, come. This situation, it is impossible."

Reluctantly he followed her into the examining room. Byrne was perched on the edge of the examining table in a hospital gown.

"Hello, Faith," he began pleasantly. "Dr. Como tells me you have some questions about your blood test results."

"Is *that* what she tells you? Well, *I'm* telling you your results are wrong. I feel fine. I have been coming here for three months, and no one's said a word about this so-called problem until today. You'll have to come up with something better than this before I let you kick me out of this protocol."

Logan was at a loss. "Perhaps I can give you a clearer idea of what the problem is," he said, "You see—"

"I'm sorry, Faith, I got here as soon as I could."

And there, stepping into the small room, was Marion Winston.

"Ms. Winston," said Logan, "perhaps you can help Mrs. Byrne understand that, for all our past differences, we're on the same side."

"Are we? Would *you* have called me—as Faith did?"

"Well, no. But I'm glad you're here. I know how much respect you have for the integrity of the informed-consent document."

"You see," added Sabrina, "this is set in the terms of the protocol. If a patient's creatinine level rises above two point zero, then she *must* leave the protocol. It is too dangerous to continue."

"No," cut in Byrne, "you've got it backward. It's too dangerous for me *not* to continue. I'm going to *die* if I don't continue."

"Look," Logan said, "we cannot in good conscience continue to administer this drug to a patient who manifests this kind of reaction. Now Faith, this examination is over. You may get dressed."

Winston put a hand on the patient's shoulder. "Go ahead," she said gently. "You and I will talk in my office."

As Byrne walked slowly toward the adjoining changing room, Winston lingered behind. "I just want you both to know that we are not going to let this stand."

ARRIVING on campus next morning, Logan found a note in his ACF mailbox instructing him to report to Dr. Raymond Larsen.

"You've done it now, Logan," Larsen began.

"How do you mean, sir?" The senior man's obvious enjoyment of this scene only reinforced Logan's intention to play it cool.

"Do not insult my intelligence, young man. I'll come straight to the point. In the five months of this protocol all you've established is that this drug is highly toxic."

"I'm aware of that, sir. But it is still relatively early."

"And," Larsen continued, brushing this aside, "you do not seem to know how to get along with patients."

Logan started to respond, then stopped. This guy wasn't interested in a dialogue. "What do you suggest?"

"I don't *suggest* anything. You *will* do the following." He paused. "Inform each of the patients on this protocol, on her next visit, of the extraordinary risks we now know to be associated with this compound. Each shall then be given the option of leaving the protocol." He shook his head, as if in consternation. "I wish I were in a position to offer each of them my personal apologies."

Logan was dumbstruck. In effect, Larsen was killing the program. Was this the way it was going to end? Without his even making a coherent argument on its behalf?

But he also knew that words were not going to mean a thing.

↔

10 August 1936
Frankfurt

The heat unbearable these last days. Still, dare not leave the apartment. Much trouble in this part of city—beatings, broken shopwindows, etc.

By new laws, Emma can give piano lessons only to other Jews. Her father fears he will lose store. Some friends trying to get out.

Reduced to two days a week by Herr Thomas, so have set up alternate facility in basement. Early tests on version #531 of compound, new synthetic modification, show excellent potential. But laboratory supplies getting harder to come by, like everything else.

↔

MORE than an hour later, sitting on a bench in the quad on this brilliant summer morning, Logan could still scarcely believe it. He recognized the reaction: shock.

He would wait to call Sabrina. No need to hit her with it yet. She was stuck all morning in Shein's lab.

Logan glanced at his watch. Marjorie Rhome, the other patient with a creatinine problem, was waiting for him in the outpatient clinic.

To date, Logan had had only a brief introductory meeting with her. Sabrina had conducted the woman's initial interview, and so far, her clinic exams had been covered by Sabrina or Reston.

Both confirmed Logan's own first impression: that this woman was genuinely *nice*. Above all—and this was the quality often hardest to come by in such a situation—possessed of real balance. Logan recalled this by way of reassurance, since he was going to have to conduct her exam this morning.

Even before his conversation with Larsen, that prospect had loomed as gruesome; after all, there was every reason to suppose that her creatinine level, too, had edged up beyond the acceptable range. Even the slim possibility that her level would be encouraging offered no hope. For here he was, under orders to trash his own program.

"Sorry I'm late," he said, extending his hand as he entered the examining room and offered his customary reassuring smile.

"No problem, Doctor, really." A heavyset woman with a pleasantly round face and sharp blue eyes, she seemed just as concerned with reassuring him.

"You've been feeling all right? No new special aches or pains?"

"No. Actually, I've been feeling pretty darn well."

"Good. If you'll just take a seat on the examining table."

Even as he grinned his idiot grin, he knew he'd have to work toward the subject at hand: her future with the protocol. But he'd wait for the results of her blood work. They should be in anytime.

Logan scanned her chart. Yes, he was reminded, her problem was intraparenchymal lung nodules—a dozen or so BB-size growths in each lung field. Her prognosis could hardly be worse.

He flipped to the page on her personal history.

"So," he said, "how are your kids?"

Her face lit up. "Oh, fine, thank you." She laughed. "But keeping me busy. You know teens."

"Actually, only by reputation."

"Of course, you're hardly older than that yourself."

He smiled, imagining the incredible degree of will this woman must possess to maintain even a semblance of a normal life.

He placed his fingertips on either side of her neck and began working down, feeling for supraclavicular nodes.

"That's good," he concluded. "Still clear. Mrs. Rhome, would you mind getting to your feet now?"

She slipped off the examining table.

Gently he felt her abdomen for the liver edge. He couldn't feel it. Also good—the organ wasn't yet distended.

He was interrupted by a knock on the door. "Doctor?"

The dreaded test results. He opened the door and took them. "Excuse me, Mrs. Rhome, just a moment."

"Take your time, Doctor." To his surprise she began *humming*.

There were three pages, but his eye went right for the line that mattered: Creatinine, 1.9.

He didn't know whether to be pleased or despondent. On the one hand, she could remain with the protocol. On the other hand, he'd just been robbed of his easy out. Now he would have to discuss the dangers of this trial.

She stopped humming. "What's the word, Doctor? Good news?"

He laid aside the blood results. "Status quo."

"Well, where I come from, no news *is* good news."

Distractedly he slid the X ray from its envelope. "Mrs. Rhome, there's something we've got to discuss."

"Shoot." He detected a trace of concern through the breeziness. "Do you know what creatinine is?"

"Not exactly."

He stuck the X ray onto the view box and snapped on the light. "Well, it's a measure of kidney function." He turned and faced her. "We track it through blood tests."

"Is there a problem with mine? Because, frankly, I feel great."

"Well, yes and no. I'm sorry to say that we've had to take one woman off the drug because her creatinine rose to dangerous levels. Yours is not quite that high yet."

He paused. That was strange. He had turned back to look at her chest X ray. The lungs appeared clean.

"But you're saying there's a danger of that?"

"It's something we have to watch. . . ." His voice trailed off as he examined the film more closely. "Excuse me, Mrs. Rhome, you did have a chest X ray taken this morning, right?"

"Of course. Just a little while ago."

"And how long ago was the last one taken?"

She shrugged. "Oh, two weeks ago."

Taking the X ray from the view box, he held it sideways and read the name: Rhome. Putting it back in place, he looked at it again.

No way. Someone must've mislabeled this thing!

He picked up her previous X rays—all four of them, in chronological order. He stuck the most recent one up alongside the other.

No question. Both lacked a right breast shadow where she'd had the mastectomy. But one showed nodules. This new one . . .

Logan's heart began to pound. He turned to her with shining eyes, trying desperately to maintain a professional bearing. "Mrs. Rhome, I'd like to take another X ray." He dialed the nurses station. "This is Dr. Logan," he said evenly. "I'm going to need another chest X ray on Mrs. Rhome. Stat."

Hanging up, he said, "Excuse me just a minute."

As soon as he was out of the room, Logan dashed down the corridor to the in-house phone in the doctors lounge.

"Logan?" asked Sabrina, concerned. "Why are you calling? Is it about your meeting with Larsen?"

In fact, the brief session with the head of the department of medicine—which only minutes before had been the central fact of his world—now seemed completely beside the point. "No, no. I'm at the outpatient clinic. Can you get right over here?"

She was there in ten minutes. He handed her two X rays and watched as she held them up to the window.

"These are of Mrs. Rhome."

"Yes. And so?" But now, as she looked from one to the other, he saw her expression change. She sat down on the window ledge and held the latest X ray to the light. "I think we must take another picture, no? To be sure."

"Sabrina, this *is* the second X ray."

She nodded soberly. "Still, we must not give false hope."

"No. Of course not."

Such conservatism came with the territory. Still, even as they went for dispassion, neither could deny what they were feeling: complete and utter elation.

"So," pressed Sabrina, "what should we tell her?"

Logan erupted in a smile. "That's the problem, isn't it? Words don't do the job."

Ultimately, they elected to let the patient make the discovery. When they returned to the room, Sabrina put the X rays side by side on the light box. "Would you like to see?" she offered.

Rhome shrugged. "I doubt it'll mean heads or tails to me."

But as Sabrina indicated the nodules in the first picture, then indicated the same area in the second, entirely clear of tumor, Rhome turned to her with a sense of wonder that was almost childlike. "Does that mean what I think it does?"

"It's a very hopeful sign," agreed Logan. "*Extremely* hopeful."

All at once there were tears in Marjorie Rhome's eyes. "Oh, dear God!" And opening her arms, she drew them both into an embrace.

As soon as Logan and Sabrina were alone again, back in the doctors lounge, he smiled sheepishly. "It got a little sentimental in there, didn't it?"

Sabrina's eyes were moist. "Oh, Logan," she said, throwing her arms wide, "I can hardly believe this."

He took her in his arms and held her tight. Now she began crying in earnest. "Shhh," he comforted her. But as she continued, he fell silent, his face buried in her hair. He didn't want her to see that he was crying too.

WHEN Sabrina answered her door that evening, Logan was standing there with an armful of sunflowers. "Just so you won't forget who's the sunshine in your life," he announced. "To Marjorie Rhome, I sent roses."

She laughed. "So did I." From behind her back she withdrew two giant packs of Chunkys. "So you will remember who is the sweetness in yours."

He took her in his arms. "As usual, I got the better deal."

She kicked the door closed behind her as they kissed.

"I tell you, Sabrina," he said, pulling back, "I've been flying all day. I can hardly stop myself from telling people."

"I know. When are you seeing Reston?"

"Nine. At his place." Something suddenly hit him. "Oh, I got something to show you." From his breast pocket he withdrew a folded letter. "It was in my box this afternoon."

She recognized the envelope as identical to the earlier communication from the elderly German chemist. This letter was longer.

My dear Dr. Logan:

Greetings and best wishes. I am pleased to hear from you in your letter of 31 May. Your protocol sounds interesting indeed.

You ask me about the work we did long ago. It was under a Japanese named Mikio Nakano, who worked for the great Dr. Paul Ehrlich on this problem of cancer of the human breast.

I came to know Nakano in 1927, when he arrived to work in the Christian Thomas Company in Frankfurt. He was the chief chemist, and I was only a young assistant. But we got on well.

Our main work at Thomas was with petrochemicals, but Herr Nakano was most interested in cancer experiments with sulfonate derivatives. He was certain he could find a cure. Herr Thomas at first believed also. But the compounds were highly toxic. So after a time Nakano left Thomas.

But I know he did not stop working on this problem. He was determined. After all, Paul Ehrlich spent twenty years on the toxicity problem in his treatment for syphilis.

Please, sir, write me more details of your work.

With very sincere regards,
Rudolf Kistner

"You see," Sabrina said softly, "it does not all begin with us. This man, he had the same ideas."

"I wish he could have seen what we saw today."

She looked at him quizzically. "How do we know he did not?"

AN HOUR later Logan entered Reston's apartment with mixed feelings. Obviously, as a member of the team, Reston had a right to the extraordinary news; in fact, he should have been told of it hours earlier. On the other hand, he had distanced himself from the project. The thought of Reston now sharing in the glory, if, in fact, there was to be any, was almost too much to swallow.

"So, Danny boy, what's so important it couldn't wait till tomorrow?" Reston asked. "Another damn toxicity?"

"Actually, no. It's about Marjorie Rhome." Logan held up the X rays. "She's clean."

Reston sat up. "*Clean?* Really?" He got to his feet. "Lemme see those."

He studied them only momentarily. "Amy!" he shouted. "Get in here. Hurry."

She came rushing in, wearing a terry-cloth robe, a towel around her hair. "What?" Then, spotting Logan, "Oh, Dan. I didn't know you were—"

But already Reston had her in his arms, dancing her around the room. "We've had a hit, Amy! The drug actually works."

"What?" She turned to Logan, what she was hearing apparently striking her as flatly impossible after months of negative talk about the drug. "Is it really true?"

He shrugged. "Looks good so far. Of course, it's early . . ."

Reston walked over and extended his hand. "I guess all the rough times were worth it, right?"

"Hey, we all did our part."

"Right." Reston laughed. "And don't you forget it."

THE next morning Logan was both pleased and surprised to discover that Seth Shein had not already gotten his hands on the information. "Take a look at these," Logan said, sliding Marjorie Rhome's X rays across the desk.

Shein did so—but his face remained disappointingly impassive. "This is your second creatinine patient?" he asked finally.

Logan nodded. "That was my concern when she came in."

"And what was her creatinine level? Or were you so swept away by this triumph that you forgot to check?"

"One point nine. Not good, but still eligible."

"We don't know if this result is going to stick, do we? Nor have you come close to licking your toxicity problem."

"No." What was going on here? Logan wondered. Could it be that Shein resented this success?

Shein suddenly grinned and threw out his hands. "That said, I am bowled over. Congratulations, Logan. This is gonna kill that bastard Stillman. *Kill* him." He actually cackled. "And I have a pretty good idea you're going to be seeing other results."

"Really?" Logan sat up in his seat. "Why?"

"Paid much attention to your rabbits lately?"

"The rabbits? Not since yesterday morning when I gave 'em their second dose."

"Better take a look, then, don't you think?"

A moment later in the animal-holding facility with Shein, Logan spotted the change even from across the room. At least half the animals looked healthier, their movements brisker. He went closer. On almost every one the tumors were markedly smaller.

"My God!" exclaimed Logan. "But it's only been four days."

Shein nodded. "I think you playing around with this molecule achieved something interesting: You didn't alter the effects of Compound J, but you accelerated the process. You'll see more responses. It's just taking longer than you thought."

"Why? What makes you so sure?"

"What seems to be happening is that this new stuff of yours isn't cleared by the body as rapidly as Compound J, which means its effects are enhanced."

"So you think we can expect a *major* response rate?"

Shein gave him that familiar look of contempt. "How the hell do I know? We're dealing with human beings, not rabbits." He paused. "But it's a pretty good bet you're gonna get a response in more than just one."

Logan stared at the rabbits. "That's good enough," he said.

IT WAS little more than a week before they had their second response. Reston noted it first. Back on board with a vengeance, he'd been seeing virtually every protocol patient in for her regular exam, hoping to come up with a hit of his own. It was ironic that the patient turned out to be Hannah Dietz, whom Reston had tried to remove from the protocol.

Reston smiled. "I see you've licked that bleeding-gums problem, Mrs. Dietz."

"Yes, yes. No more of that, thank goodness." She nodded. "My Phil is such a good fellow. You know what he tells me all the time now? 'We beat one, we'll beat the other.'"

Dietz had a palpable rocklike tumor of five by four centimeters, easily monitored by touch. When Reston began manipulating it, he was struck by the change. Not only had there been a significant reduction in size, but what remained was now rubbery, blending seamlessly into the surrounding tissue. He made little effort to hide his excitement.

"Mrs. Dietz, I swear, this tumor of yours seems almost *gone*."

Mrs. Dietz took a moment to react. "Really?"

"What we'll need to do is a biopsy."

The cytologist charged with performing the biopsy—a good friend of Reston's—finished the job in less than two minutes. At Reston's request the results were back before noon the next day. Not a single malignant cell had been found. Reston let out a whoop and dashed across campus. He reached Shein's lab, breathless, his face bright pink.

"What the hell happened to you?" asked Logan.

"I got some news," he panted. "Come outside." He turned to Sabrina. "You too, signorina."

In the hallway he thrust the page their way.

"Hannah Dietz . . ." began Logan.

"Is *clean*. You're holding her bill of health."

Logan smiled broadly. "I can hardly believe it." He stopped. "Wait a minute, when did you examine her?"

"Yesterday," said Sabrina, eyeing the page.

"Why didn't you say something before this?"

"He wants the credit," said Sabrina in a low voice, turning to Reston with disdain. "This Reston, he does not change."

"I wanted to be *sure*," Reston countered.

"I presume," said Logan, betraying his irritation, "that you told her before you came running over here."

He hesitated. "Not yet. I'd like to tell Shein first."

"We can handle that."

"I'm sure you could." He snorted. "I'm sure you'd love to cut me out of this thing entirely, the way you have from the beginning."

Logan shook his head and sighed. "Go ahead," he said, gesturing extravagantly toward the door to Shein's lab. "He's all yours."

TRUE TO FORM, SHEIN WAS publicly uncommunicative about the surprisingly positive results. But to Logan he said, "I've been thinkin' about settin' you up at grand rounds."

Logan was incredulous. Grand rounds presentations, held every Tuesday in the main ACF auditorium, were the most prestigious forum afforded by the foundation; speakers were generally top scientists, both American and foreign, hoping to draw attention to major research developments. "You think I'm ready for grand rounds?"

"Nothin' to it," said Shein. He paused. "Go into detail about some of the responses you've had."

"*Both* responses," corrected Logan. "There've been only two."

"Two outta fourteen ain't bad. And I bet there'll be more."

In fact, they had a third response only a couple of days later: sweet old Mrs. Kober, whose supraclavicular node had seemingly vanished.

Sabrina, who conducted the exam, brought Logan the news, along with a note from the patient.

Dr. Logan,
  Don't forget . . . we have a bet on the Giants versus the Cowboys next season.

  Sally Kober

  P.S. Suddenly I am feeling *much* better about my chances of collecting. Thank you.

It was the day after that, that Logan was summoned back to Larsen's office.

The head of the department of medicine fixed him with a cool stare. "I thought it was understood that I would be kept informed of the status of your protocol."

"I'm sorry, sir," Logan stammered. "There must have been a misunderstanding."

"I'm sure. How convenient for you."

"But we've done exactly as instructed. Every patient we see is made aware of the toxicities associated with this drug."

"And how many patients have chosen to discontinue treatment?"

"None, sir."

"*None?* And you expect me to believe that you've told them the whole truth? You're a *liar,* young man!" he suddenly shouted. "You should never have been accepted into this program."

But sitting there across from him, Logan felt a remarkable sense of well-being. Larsen was aware of the growing regard for Compound J at the ACF, and there wasn't a damn thing he could do about it.

"I'm sorry you feel that way, sir," replied Logan.

"You'd just better pray," Larsen spat back, "that when all is said and done, everything you've told me holds up."

"Yessir," said Logan.

Abruptly Larsen stood up. "I really don't think," he said scornfully, "that you and I have anything more to say to one another."

As GRAND rounds approached, Logan's excitement and apprehension grew. Shein was naturally keyed into his mind-set. "What're you worried about, Logan? You got it made."

"I guess I'm concerned because Markell is going to be there."

"That's right. He is." Shein nodded thoughtfully. "I see what you're sayin'—you'd better be absolutely *brilliant.*"

"Thanks. I needed that."

Logan was well aware of the extraordinary complexity of Shein's relationship with the imperious head of the ACF. They were intellectual soul mates. Formerly Shein's mentor, Markell had turned into his protector—the reason, for all Shein's calculated outrageousness, his enemies couldn't touch him.

LOGAN stood on the stage in the vast amphitheater, looking out over the crowd, heart pounding. Only perhaps a third of the hall was occupied, but that meant at least four hundred people. He was most conscious of the three in second row, center: Raymond Larsen, Allen Atlas, and Gregory Stillman.

Shein stood in the back. Sabrina, in the first row over on the left, smiled at him, then quickly averted her eyes. She's almost as nervous as I am, he thought. At least Markell didn't show.

For the first several minutes of his speech Logan scarcely dared look at his audience. But gradually the terror began to lift, and by the time he showed his first slide—a vintage photo of Paul Ehrlich, sitting amid mounds of journals—he'd found his rhythm and he noticed that his audience was gratifyingly attentive.

Markell entered the hall midway through the presentation. A short man, with a fringe of white surrounding a bald pate, he had the bearing of Caesar. He didn't bother to take a seat, merely stood in back, arms folded, listening. Shein took his place beside him, unconsciously assuming the same posture.

By the time Logan reached his climax, even the occasional bout of coughing in the hall had ceased. "I want to tell you about one of the patients on the protocol," he said.

He nodded toward the projectionist, and the slide showing Marjorie Rhome's initial X ray appeared on the screen. He briefly discussed her case before nodding to the projectionist again. "This is the same patient's chest X ray after eight cycles of treatment with Compound J." There was a murmur in the hall. He paused a moment. "That was only our first response. It has been followed by two others."

For presentation purposes these cases were less dramatic, but moments later when he concluded the speech, it was to highly respectful applause.

Logan acknowledged this with a broad, unaffected smile. But when he glanced down at the second row, his apprehension returned with a rush. The three of them were still there. And when Logan caught his eye, Stillman was clearly mouthing the words "Toxicity. What about toxicity?"

"WELL, well, hail the conquering Logan," greeted Shein, half an hour after the speech, when Logan reported to work at the lab. The several other junior associates within earshot grinned. Logan noted that Sabrina was not among them. "Thank you," he said.

Shein led him to a quiet corner. "I think you mighta done yourself some real good out there, boychick."

"Really?" asked Logan. Still shaken by Stillman's taunts, he was starting to think his failure to suggest a plausible approach to the toxicity problem might outweigh all the rest.

"Listen, usually Markell walks out on these things." Shein pointed to the door. "I told Dr. Como to take the rest of the day off. You too. You've earned it."

"Thank you, Dr. Shein."

"Seth."

"Right." Smiling, Logan began heading for the door.

"Oh, Logan . . . that kid down in animal land wants you there."

Logan's pretense of good humor vanished as soon as he was out of the room. *No way* this guy would call unless it was serious. What he found when he reached the animal-holding facility exceeded his worst expectations. Every rabbit that had been dosed with Compound J-lite lay dead in its cage.

Every one.

A moment later Sabrina walked in, also summoned by Hassan. She gasped in horror. The word "toxicity" hovered in the air.

Logan moved slowly down the line of cages. "When did this happen?" he asked Hassan.

"I cannot say for certain. This is how I found them this morning."

Logan turned to Sabrina. "What now?"

On the one hand, to drop Compound J-lite after it had achieved such spectacular results would be to essentially write it off as a failure. But continuing to experiment with the new compound might only kill more rabbits. And if word of *that* started getting around, it could be a disaster.

Sabrina walked to Hassan's desk and picked up the phone. A few minutes later Dr. Carrie Schneider, a friend of theirs in pathology, sauntered into the room and peered in at the cages, surveying the carnage. "How many you want done?"

"I don't know. At least three or four, I guess. We need to know what killed them. As soon as possible."

THEY were at Sabrina's late that afternoon when Logan called in for the report.

"I can't be too precise here," Carrie Schneider told him, "but you've definitely got liver failure. That's your cause of death. I don't have any toxicology reports yet. But the three livers I've looked at so far are congested and grossly inflamed."

He thanked her and a moment later was off. "Well," he said to Sabrina, "at least we've come up with a foolproof way of killing rabbits. That stuff is potent."

She made no reply.

"But I keep thinking about those first results on Compound J-lite. Every one of those little rabbits hopping around with a smile on its face. *Something* in that molecule works." He paused. "Ah, well, I guess it was too much to hope for."

The next week, as reaction to the grand rounds talk continued to filter in, it became clear that the young doctor's star had never shone more brightly. "You just never know the talent they've got buried away in this place," remarked one senior staff member. "Who'd have guessed we had one of Paul Ehrlich's heirs right here at the ACF?"

THERE'D been so much good news lately that when the phone call came in, it took a while for its gravity to register.

"Dr. Logan?" said the male voice.

"Yes."

"This is Phil Lester." He waited for some sign of recognition. "I met you with Hannah Dietz."

"Oh, yes, of course." Abruptly his antennae were up. Why wasn't Hannah on the phone?

"I think something's not right with Hannah. Last night, in the middle of the night, she started vomiting."

"Has the vomiting been continual?" The guy's tone was so moderate, it was hard to believe anything could be seriously wrong.

"Continual? Yes, I would say so. She's just exhausted. And she's also sweating a lot. She's like a dishrag."

This woman should be in a hospital. "You were right to call. She should be looked at."

The words were all it took to crack Phil's veneer of calm. "I knew it. It's bad, isn't it? Should I take her to the hospital here?"

Where the hell were they? Somewhere in the New Jersey burbs! Chances are no one there would even know what to look for.

"Look, if at all possible, I'd like to get her in here." Logan's mind was racing. "I have a thought. Can I call you right back?"

A helicopter! That way she could be on-site in little more than an hour. The ACF used them occasionally, but only for dire emergencies, and that required clearance by the director's office.

In seconds he had Shein on the line. Less than a minute after that, Shein called him back with formal authorization.

"Thank you, Dr. Shein."

"Thank me if it pans out. Otherwise, keep me the hell away from it. We're both spending a lot of capital here, Logan."

AN HOUR and a half later when the copter put down on the quad, Mrs. Dietz was hustled into the hospital on a stretcher. Logan and Sabrina were waiting for her. Reston had declined an invitation to participate in the treatment.

One sight was all it took to assess the gravity of the patient's condition. She was extremely pale and completely disoriented. Most worrisome, the whites of her eyes had a distinctly yellow cast, evidence that her liver was no longer functioning properly.

Phil, alone in the waiting room, was doubled over, head in hands. Logan touched him gently on the shoulder. "Phil," he said softly, "we're going to be running a few tests, but you haven't been forgotten. If you feel you need to speak to me, tell a nurse."

He nodded. "I understand. Thank you, Doctor."

Mrs. Dietz was already hooked up to an IV line to counter her dehydration. The monitor over her head revealed that her heart was racing and she was hypotensive. But the greatest concern, based on her obvious sense of confusion, was the possibility that she was encephalopathic—another sign of liver failure.

Still, she appeared more alert now. Sabrina was leaning over her, talking soothingly. "Hello, Hannah. Do you recognize me?"

The old woman smiled. "How are you, Dr. Como?"

"Good. Will you do something for me?" Sabrina asked.

"Yes?"

"Hold your arm out straight." She demonstrated with her own.

It is the simplest test for hepatic encephalopathy. When a patient is suffering the condition, the hand will jerk back and forth spasmodically. Which is precisely what Mrs. Dietz's now began to do.

Sabrina looked to Logan. There was no need for words.

"You can put your arm down." Sabrina managed a smile as she stroked Hannah's forehead.

"You're a very kind girl, do you know that? Very loving."

"Thank you. From you, I consider this a great compliment."

Hannah opened her gray eyes wider. "I'm going to die now."

It was a declaration. Nor did the doctors doubt it was true. As she drifted off to sleep, Sabrina remained watching the beautiful old face. She touched Logan's hand. "You should get Phil."

He was there when she fell into a hepatic coma a few minutes later, and still there early that evening when she peacefully died.

The initial autopsy report came in two days later. As he read through it, Logan shuddered: A congested and grossly distended liver. Fulminant hepatic necrosis. Almost identical to the rabbits.

THE speed of the improvement startled her. Three days after she started radiation therapy, the pain in her back began to subside; within a week she no longer felt it at all.

"I feel like the Tin Man in *The Wizard of Oz*," she delightedly told her husband that night. "Like someone took an oilcan to me and made all the stiffness disappear."

Her husband, the President, took her in his arms. "That's so wonderful, darling. Maybe the worst is over."

"I hope so. They say so much of it is attitude. Well, I'm going to test that theory, because no one's going to top my attitude."

Gregory Stillman knew not to be fooled, of course. They'd killed only a single localized tumor—just a symptom, not the disease itself. Still, for the time being, there was no reason to disabuse the patient of her optimism, especially this patient.

"Things are looking pretty good right now," Stillman told her after the ten days of radiation. "I'm going to want to keep a close eye on you, of course. There's still disease there."

"Isn't that what we should be doing now, rooting out what remains of the disease?"

"It's not that simple." He opened his briefcase and withdrew a book—a copy of his own *Basic Principles of Breast Malignancy.* "Read this. I'd be pleased to discuss any questions you have then."

She looked at him, incredulous. If he hadn't just pulled off what she regarded as a minor miracle, she'd have been tempted to fire him on the spot. After their first meeting she'd been prepared to assume that his manner was a matter of shyness or discomfort due to her position. But no, it was the real thing. Stillman might be a gifted cancer specialist, but he was hardly someone she'd choose as a friend.

"I would suggest an examination every two weeks," he continued. "But call me if you experience any unusual physical symptoms of any kind."

The first three exams were uneventful. But she arrived for the fourth with a dry, rasping cough. This was not necessarily cause for concern. And in fact, when he took a chest X ray, it was clean.

Five days later he reached her at the White House. "Just checking on that cough."

Before she could respond, he heard it. "It's no big deal," she insisted. "Aside from that, I'm feeling strong as a horse."

"How you're feeling otherwise doesn't interest me. I'd like you to come in tomorrow."

"No!" Tomorrow truly was impossible. She resented his peremptory manner. "It will just have to wait until next week. And frankly, Doctor, if we're going to continue, I'd appreciate a bit more courtesy."

Like most bullies, he instantly backed off. "I didn't mean it as it sounded, Mrs. Rivers. My only concern is your health."

"It concerns me also, Doctor. But this can wait till next week."

"Of course."

The following week the new X ray showed it clearly: a streaky density, like a cirrus cloud, in the left lung. The tumor was growing within the walls of the lymph vessels inside the lung. Radiation had taken them as far as it could. He'd have to begin chemotherapy—

and soon. This was a very sick woman. He knew it, and now she knew it too.

For the time being, at least, he suspected she wouldn't be giving him much trouble.

AFTER Hannah Dietz's death Logan called Shein's office.

"Sorry," Shein told Logan. But his voice was so flat, he might have been a stranger. "Nothing to do now but tough it out."

Three days later Sabrina had some more bad news as she let Logan into her apartment.

"There was a call a while ago. From Pennsylvania. Mrs. Rhome died today."

He hardly reacted at all. Whether by training or instinct, they pressed on. If Compound J was killing the very women whose cancer it destroyed, there still remained one such woman unaccounted for.

When there was no answer at Mrs. Kober's home, Logan suspected the worst.

"Relax, Logan," said Sabrina, though she was thinking the same thing. "Probably she's just not at home."

"Where would she be at ten o'clock at night?"

"You left a message. When she gets it, she will call."

They spent a fitful night. When Sabrina awoke early to call again, she spoke with diminished conviction. "If she's in trouble, someone would call us," she said to Logan. "This is what happened with Mrs. Dietz and Mrs. Rhome."

"Both of them had family. Mrs. Kober is alone."

↔

1 November 1937
Frankfurt

Today I learn Eisenstadt has been arrested in Berlin. One of our greatest chemists. For what? No reasons are needed anymore.

Best results yet on version #612. Toxicity marginal—diminished energy and slight loss of appetite. Reason for hope?

Emma nearly ill with fear. Cannot blame her. Who will be next?

↔

LOGAN FOUND A NOTE FROM Larsen in his box. He would learn it was identical to ones Sabrina and Reston found in theirs. Written on the stationery of the department of medicine, it was vintage Larsen.

> In light of recent developments surrounding the clinical trial of Compound J, you are requested to meet with representatives of the department of medicine tomorrow, October 14, at 3:00 p.m. in the department conference room.

Larsen clearly intended to rake them over the coals and probably, if he could find a way to circumvent normal procedures, try to shut down the Compound J trial by executive fiat.

Beyond that, realistically, what could he do? Eight months remained on their two-year contracts. The likeliest scenario was a stern reprimand, a PR move designed to ward off potential embarrassment. Patients on this trial were dying. If the press got wind of it, the ACF had to be seen as having taken some action.

Even Sabrina, the ultimate pragmatist, chose to see the positive aspects of what was obviously to be a painful encounter. They would take their shots, but at least there was to be a dialogue, a chance, after all the simmering hostility and silent undercutting, for them to make their case. Who could doubt, even now, that it would be a mistake to abandon this drug?

"This night will be hard, I think," she told Logan as they pulled up before her apartment. "Waiting is the hardest."

"Tell me about it."

She led him inside, then punched a button on her answering machine to check her messages. There came a familiar voice. "What's all this fuss about?" demanded a perplexed Mrs. Kober. "I get back from my sister's, and there are three messages on my machine. Anyhow, if you still need me, I'll be in tonight. If not, I'll be in next week for my treatment." She laughed. "Hooray! The last one."

"That's some good news, no?" said Sabrina. "Maybe an omen." Snatching up her book, she dialed the number.

It turned out that Mrs. Kober had indeed felt ill briefly several days before. "A little fluish, you know? A few chills, a little vomiting, and it went away. Why, what's going on?"

Sabrina shrugged. "Some people on the protocol have gotten quite sick, so we are checking. But it sounds like you are fine."

"I *am* fine, you sweet girl."

When Sabrina got off, she grinned at Logan. "For her, I really think this drug has worked."

"Forget the omens. That's called *ammo.*"

As SOON as they walked into the room, it was clear the process was rigged. Larsen sat at the head of the conference table. Around him were a who's who of the protocol's enemies: Gregory Stillman, Marion Winston, Peter Kratsas, and, representing their peers, Allen Atlas.

Also present, of course, looking utterly miserable in his seat at the opposite end of the table, was John Reston. As Logan and Sabrina moved to their own places nearby, he nodded but edged his chair a couple of inches in the other direction.

Larsen looked solemnly around the table. "You are all by now aware of the deaths of several patients on the Compound J trial. I am sure you share my sense of the extreme gravity of this situation." He paused, leaning forward, his blue-gray eyes boring in on the Compound J team. "It is my intention to rectify it."

Only now did Logan see with absolute clarity how bad it was going to be. There would not even be the pretense of allowing them a say. The verdict was already in. It was just a matter of going through the formality of reaching it.

Larsen turned to the patient-care rep. "Ms. Winston, I believe you have some preliminary observations."

"Yes, I do," said Winston evenly. "There is considerable evidence that at least one member of this team, Dr. Logan, has been extremely negligent in regard to patients. I would like to bring before this group two women who have had what can only be called emotionally devastating experiences under this doctor's care."

The women, of course, were Rochelle Boudin and Faith Byrne.

Called in first, Boudin went through the litany of Logan's supposed abuses. How he'd systematically neglected her needs and failed to deliver the treatment her condition demanded. "He just always made me feel," she summed up softly, "that the fact I had cancer was an inconvenience to *him.*"

Byrne, who followed, was even worse. In self-dramatizing detail she told the story of her initial treatment with Compound J, emphasizing her concern—and his complete absence of same—over what turned out to be the drug's very real dangers. Never mind that she showed no danger signs; never mind that she was sitting here, right now, *alive.* Around the room Byrne's fable was met with sympathetic nods.

"The worst of it," chimed in Winston, "was that, against her will, Dr. Logan subsequently removed Mrs. Byrne from the protocol. I personally regard this as an act of petty vindictiveness."

At this, Logan actually came close to smiling. Which was he? A monster for knowingly subjecting patients to a dangerous drug, or a monster for not allowing them to take it?

But by now, logic seemed the furthest thing from anyone's mind.

"I'd like to say something," said Allen Atlas when Byrne left the room. He glanced meaningfully toward Stillman and Kratsas. "I don't know if this is the appropriate time to raise this, but Drs. Logan and Como developed a second, related drug. They call it Compound J-lite, I believe."

Logan was stunned. How did Atlas even know about the variant?

"When tested in lab rabbits," continued Atlas, "this compound showed a good deal of activity—followed by extreme toxicity."

"I think what Dr. Atlas is driving at," picked up Stillman, "is that this is the same pattern observed in the deceased patients. It seems the possibility must be considered that these doctors substituted the second drug for the one that had been approved for protocol use."

Instantly Logan was on his feet. "That's a lie! We did *not* violate the protocol."

"Logan is right," said Sabrina loudly, pointing a finger Stillman's way. "You know we did not do this thing! Why would you say so?"

It was as close to losing control as anyone had ever seen her, and momentarily Larsen seemed at a loss. "Dr. Como . . . *please.*"

"No. To say such things, *that* is wrong—not what we did!"

"All right," said Larsen, decisive again, "we are going to take a break now. And when we come back, I expect both of you"—he stared at Logan and Sabrina—"to control yourselves."

Leaving the room quickly, they retreated to a quiet corner, seething. "I'm going to bring up Mrs. Kober," said Logan quietly. "We've gotta say something on the drug's behalf."

"They will not let you."

"Oh, here you are."

And there, to their astonishment, stood Gregory Stillman.

·"Sorry to interrupt," said Stillman ingratiatingly. "I know it's tough in there." He nodded back toward the meeting room.

Sabrina eyed him with undisguised loathing.

"It's not personal. We're competitors, sure, but we share the same goals. Your friend Reston understands that." He actually managed a smile. "I've been talking with him."

Logan and Sabrina exchanged a glance, but made no reply.

"Look," added Stillman, a model of sweet reason, "no one denies you've had some interesting results. But when there are questions about methodology, we've got an obligation to raise them."

Logan knew what this was about. "You want to take over this drug, don't you?"

"That's a hell of an accusation. Let's just say that given the history of this protocol, it's obvious it could use an experienced guiding hand." He looked from one to the other. "I'd even say Compound J's finished without it."

The bastard's intention couldn't have been clearer: Compound J was to become a Stillman project. Their dogged work would earn them nothing. For who could doubt that once Stillman had his hands on their research, he'd cut them out entirely?

"I take it Reston's already agreed to this?" asked Logan.

"Happily. He wants only to see this drug succeed."

Logan paused thoughtfully. "Well then, I hope you enjoy working with John Reston as much as we have."

Stillman's face darkened. "That's it?"

"Yes," said Sabrina, taking Logan's hand, "that is it."

"Fine," snapped the other, turning on his heel. "See you inside."

WHATEVER SATISFACTION THE exchange with Stillman gave them vanished the moment they reentered the room. At the table, where Boudin and Byrne had been, sat Ray Coopersmith.

He wore the same anxious expression Logan remembered from their meeting at the Hotel Jefferson. Only now his suit, gray with muted pinstripes, appeared to be brand-new.

"Dr. Coopersmith," began Larsen, "we understand you met some time ago with Dr. Logan. This was at your instigation?"

"His." He looked around the room and smiled broadly.

"That's a lie," said Logan.

"Dr. Logan, I am ready to conduct this hearing without you." Larsen turned to Coopersmith. "Now perhaps you might fill us in on your background with this institution."

Coopersmith exhaled dramatically. "I was a junior associate here five years ago. And I was good too."

Larsen nodded. "That strikes me as a fair assessment."

"But I screwed up. I was working on a phase-two prostate cancer trial." He stared down at the table. "I altered some data."

There was a silence in the room—a sympathetic silence.

"It was stupid. I'm trying to live it down."

"Why do you think Dr. Logan wanted to see you?"

"He wanted to know how to pull the same thing. How to get away with underreporting toxicity."

To Logan it was too preposterous. What could they have offered him? Reinstatement?

Coopersmith gave a sudden maniacal grin. "Of course, he also wanted to talk about you, Dr. Larsen. And you, Dr. Stillman."

"About Dr. Stillman and me?"

The grin grew even wider. "He told me he hated your guts. He said you were scum." Coopersmith, clearly improvising wildly, couldn't have been enjoying himself more. "He said he wanted to show you up and I was the man to show him how."

Logan felt a presence looming behind him. Instinctively he turned—Seth Shein.

"Did he make any other remarks about senior personnel?" Larsen soberly asked.

"Yeah," cut in Shein. "He said everyone was scum!" He began pointing around the table. "You, you, you, you, and me—scum! That's just the way we've all heard Dan Logan talk, isn't it?" He eyed Larsen with contempt. "What the hell do you think you're doing?"

But Larsen only smiled. "Dr. Shein, I'm so pleased you could join us. Won't you take a seat?"

"I'm comfortable here."

"Dr. Coopersmith, we thank you. You've been very helpful."

Rising from the table, Coopersmith walked from the room, glancing blankly at Logan as he did so.

"So you found Dr. Coopersmith's presentation enlightening?"

"Come off it, Larsen, you really think anyone's gonna believe this?"

"The point is," said Larsen, "that these people conspired with a known fraud. Dr. Logan's clear intention was to fabricate data. We have just heard that—"

"We've heard lies. That's all you've got—lies!"

"Forget that," interrupted Stillman. "None of that matters. Are you ready to go on record to defend these people and their protocol? The real point, as Dr. Shein knows, is that this protocol has become an embarrassment." He cast Shein a malevolent glance. "He gave a group of incompetent young doctors the power of life and death over a group of women, and the result has been tragic."

"This protocol has merit, Stillman," Shein said, but with considerably less fire.

"You are willing, then, to assume public responsibility for any further patient deaths that result?"

Shein stood there, his face at once showing anger and intense anxiety.

"Well, we're waiting," piled on Larsen.

For a moment longer Shein stood silent. "All right," he announced finally. "Logan got in way over his head. He's got talent, but he's arrogant, and he doesn't know when to listen. He takes stupid risks."

535

"Then we all agree," said Stillman evenly. He nodded at the chair. "I'd appreciate your joining us. *Please.*"

Shein assumed his place at the table.

"You may leave now," said Larsen, indicating the Compound J team.

THE letters Logan and Sabrina received that evening were identical: You are hereby advised that your contract with the American Cancer Foundation has been terminated, effective immediately.

T HE worst of it—which neither Logan nor Sabrina wanted to discuss—was that they'd no longer have each other. The ACF had always been, literally, their common ground. Stripped of her standing at the foundation, Sabrina had no possibility of work at a comparable level outside Italy. They would be an ocean apart.

"At least at Regina Elena they make me feel welcome," she said. "They do very good work also. Serious oncology."

He could see that already she was pulling away in self-protection. Probably he should do the same. "When do they want you?"

"They say at the end of October. But I must go sooner, I think." She momentarily averted her eyes. "The faster to leave, the better."

"You're right."

"And you, Logan?"

He shrugged. "Don't know yet. I'll mull things over for a while, get organized, sort out my options." He looked at her tenderly. "It would definitely be better if I were doing this with you."

Instantly her reserve melted away. She gave his hand a tender squeeze. "One day, Logan. I promise."

"I'VE been looking over the latest data on Elizabeth Rivers," said Kenneth Markell, indicating the pile of folders on his desk. "Frankly, Greg, the bottom line is, standard chemo isn't working."

"How aware of her progress are they at the White House?" Stillman asked.

"They're not idiots, Greg. Burke *can* read X rays."

The latest X rays were what had them both so concerned. Not only was the tumor in her lung growing, it now appeared as a nodular density.

"Well then, he also shouldn't expect magic."

"Ah, but that's the thing of it—they do." Markell rose. "It's time to give it to them. I want to go experimental. Let's talk about the results of your protocol."

"Well," Stillman said, smiling, "I haven't killed anybody."

"That's not exactly the kind of endorsement I had in mind."

"Maybe not. But in experimental breast treatments around here lately, that makes it unique."

Markell shook his head. "That's all the White House would have needed right now—a public stink about some kid doctor at the ACF hyping his results. Where's Logan going, anyway?"

"I have no idea. One of them's still around, though—Reston, the one who came clean. He's got promise. Why not give him a break?"

Markell looked at him with sudden impatience. Who was Stillman kidding with this ersatz magnanimity? "We've already had this conversation, Greg. What I want to hear about is your results with dyronium nitrate."

"We've had some encouraging responses. No appreciable tumor shrinkage, but seventeen of the thirty-eight women have shown considerable periods of stabilization. In several cases we're at six months and counting."

Markell sat back down behind his desk. "Let's put her on this stuff of yours. Maybe she won't get better, but your job right now is to see to it she doesn't get worse."

LOGAN settled himself onto the sofa next to the phone. Glancing down at the yellow legal pad in his lap, he picked up the receiver.

His plan was simple enough. There were more than twenty comprehensive cancer centers in the United States. Before this week was over, he intended to hit every one of them.

He knew not to be overly optimistic. Still, hadn't he been among the prize recruits in the nation? And despite the recent unpleasantness, it was reasonable to assume that his time at the ACF could only have increased his market value.

His first call, to the Washington Memorial Cancer Center in St. Louis, quickly confirmed that feeling. Here, as at a dozen other institutions around the country, Logan already knew a higher-up— in this case a crackerjack oncologist named Bradley Merritt, formerly associated with Claremont Hospital.

"Dan Logan," Merritt said. "What a terrific surprise!"

"Well, Brad, just thought I'd say hello."

There was some small talk about Claremont and assorted souls they'd both known there, before Merritt said, "I assume you're not calling just to reminisce."

Logan chuckled. "No—much as I enjoy it. Frankly, I want to find out how things are over there."

"You asking if there are any openings?" Logan had the impression he was trying to restrain his enthusiasm. "Look, Dan, do me a favor. Don't call anyone else today. Let me speak to the director here and see what kind of package we can put together. Will you do that for me?"

"I guess so." Logan couldn't believe it: The guy was *desperate* for him.

"Thanks, Dan, really. Just sit tight. I'll get back to you."

THE call came that evening. As soon as he heard Merritt's voice, he knew something had gone terribly wrong.

"Uh, listen, Dan," he began. "I've spoken to our top guys. It seems we're in a holding pattern right now. No new hires."

"Oh. I see."

"Look, I'm terribly sorry. I'm sure you'll land something terrific."

"Oh, yeah." But the knot in Logan's stomach meant he already suspected otherwise.

Over the next two days he called the remaining twelve institutions in which he knew a senior staffer by first name. At no fewer than four, the St. Louis experience was repeated: strong initial enthusiasm unaccountably dissipating within twenty-four hours.

Logan knew that at every one of those institutions, someone had checked in with the ACF. There was only one office to which such calls would have been directed: that of Raymond Larsen.

Thursday morning he set about cold-calling the second group of institutions on his list—those in which he would be known, if at all, only by reputation. The five calls he made produced not even a flicker of interest. In a couple of instances, judging from the tone on the other end, he even had the impression that his call had been *expected.*

Could it be that Larsen was even seeking out potential employers and blacklisting him?

He dialed the Instituto Regina Elena.

It took several minutes for the receptionist to track Sabrina down. As he waited, Logan could hear the sounds of a busy hospital, at once familiar and exotic: footfalls on a hard corridor, the chime of nearby elevators, a *Dottore Ferlito* being paged, scraps of conversation—the language so melodic it might have been poetry.

"Logan, it is you!"

"Who else?" He was determined not to show her the depth of his distress. "I've been missing you, Sabrina. A lot."

"I also, dear one." She laughed, a marvelous sound. "You see, it is so easy for me to say from far away."

"You sound great. You doing okay?"

"Yes, I think so." She paused, and her voice fell. "I must tell you something. Larsen, he called the director of this hospital, saying bad things about me. Untrue things."

"How'd your director respond?"

"She told him she doesn't want to hear this. She knows me for years, far better than him."

He laughed, imagining Larsen's reaction. "That's great! One small victory for humankind." Then, despite himself, "I envy you."

There was an awkward silence. "And you, Logan? You are okay?"

"Of course. I'm still looking. I'm working on it."

There was another pause.

"Listen, Logan, I must go. I am on duty."

"I'll call you soon. As soon as I know something."

"*Ciao,* my love." He heard a kissing sound. "*Ti amo.*"

A moment later Logan was staring down at his yellow pad. There remained seven institutions on the list. But by now he wasn't even sure it was worth the trouble trying them.

JOHN Reston was frustrated. He hadn't expected it to be like this. Hadn't he done his penance? Yet still they didn't trust him. What did he have to do to put his past behind him? Others at his level, a lot less sharp than he, were right at the center of the work on Stillman's protocol, a sure road to glory. And here was he, still in Kratsas's lab, still doing scutwork.

So when he got the call to report to Stillman's office, he made it over in less than five minutes.

"Close the door," said Stillman. "Take a seat."

Reston perched on the edge of it. "I was hoping you'd call. I was going to come over and see you."

"I like that attitude. Because I've got important plans for you."

Reston smiled. He was about to hear about Stillman's wonder drug. At long last he was being ushered into the charmed circle.

Stillman hesitated, seeming to study Reston's face. "Tell me about Compound J."

"Compound J?" Wouldn't they ever let him forget Compound J?

"And the other one. What'd you call it—Compound J-lite?"

Reston sat there blankly. "The whole thing was a disaster," he said. "All I want to do now is forget about it."

"Doctor," Stillman said, with sudden impatience, "I want you to level with me. Why was the decision made to go back to the lab? What structural problems were identified with the molecule?"

Reston hesitated, and Stillman moved quickly to reassure him. "I promise you, should we resume research on these compounds, you shall continue to play a prominent role."

"You're thinking of doing more work on Compound J? *Why?*"

"I'm a scientist. The drug did show some activity. And as for its toxicity problem, clearly you discussed ways of mitigating it. I'd like to know what they were."

"But aren't you focused on your own protocol?"

In the second it took Stillman to answer—"I can do both"—

Reston began to suspect the truth. Stillman's drug doesn't work!

But simultaneously, Stillman was reaching a disturbing conclusion of his own. "Tell me, Doctor. Do you even know the chemical structure of Compound J-lite?"

There was an undercurrent of menace to the question, and Reston caught it. But there was no way he could bluff this one. "Lab isn't my strong suit, but I took notes. I think I still have them somewhere."

Stillman didn't believe him for a second. "I'll want to see those." He smiled congenially. "As I say, it's only a vague possibility, but if we do pursue this, you'll be key."

The meeting was clearly over. Reston rose to his feet. "Till then, maybe you can find me something else worth doing around here."

"Absolutely. I'll see to it." Stillman nodded. "In the meantime of course, we never had this conversation."

AMONG the first people Logan had called after the axe fell was his friend Ruben. Perez was now working part-time at a small start-up company in lower Manhattan, a research lab involved in AIDS drug-delivery systems. He was pretty sure the guy in charge could use someone with Logan's credentials. The job held minimal interest or prestige, and the pay would not be high.

Logan reached his decision. Working was better than not working. He called Perez; the spot was still open.

Logan's new boss, Alex Severson, had absolute faith in his method of targeting HIV-infected cells while bypassing healthy ones. Having patented it, the young biochemist had devoted the past year to raising money for his own biotech company, HIV-EX.

The problem, Logan saw, was that the guy was a far better promoter than he was a scientist. Appealing as his idea might be in theory, Logan knew that in practice it was close to an impossibility, and given his reservations about the project, Logan just wasn't sure he could bring to the job the commitment Severson had every right to expect. On the other hand, Severson was ready to give Logan unlimited use of the lab during off-hours.

"I'm not really sure there's enough work here for the two of us,"

Logan told him. He glanced around the converted loft that was HIV-EX world headquarters, trying to conceal his distress; the equipment, what little there was, looked to be reconditioned surplus.

Severson dismissed this. "You'll be my director of basic research. My job is to get out there and round up money. I'm finding I'm pretty good at it. Look, I know how this place must look to a guy like you. But lean and mean has its advantages, starting with the fact that you'll pretty much be your own boss. You do the work, and I'm happy, period, end of story."

No question, the pitch had its points—not the least of which was the chance to work closely with his old friend Perez, the company's only other on-site employee, a sort of all-purpose lab assistant.

As soon as they were alone, Logan threw an arm over Ruben's shoulder. "So that's the big bonus of being here—your company?"

Perez laughed. "Just remember, I got seniority. If it's a conflict between the Mets and the Yankees on the radio, we go with the Yanks."

"Fine," said Logan. "If you're gonna play hardball, I'm gonna make *you* listen to classical music."

"And I thought things around here couldn't get any worse."

SABRINA had to make the trip, if only to satisfy her intense curiosity. True enough, she had nothing more than an address: Philusstrasse 29. A call to the local directory had failed to locate even a telephone number. And her letters to Herr Kistner had gone unanswered.

The first Friday in December she flew to Cologne, arriving early in the afternoon. The address turned out to be a brick building of four stories. The name was the first of eight listed on the directory: R. Kistner, on the ground floor.

She pushed the buzzer. No response. She rang again. Nothing.

Dispirited, she stood there a long moment. What now? She composed a note.

Having wedged it into Kistner's mailbox, she went out into the cold again and was searching for a cab when she became aware of an old man coming toward her. Though he used a cane, he moved remarkably well. She watched him enter the lobby, then proceed to the mailbox and begin reading her note.

"Herr Kistner?" she said, pushing through the front door.

He looked at her a moment, then back down at the note.

"I am from the American Cancer Foundation."

"In America?"

"I have written you letters."

Slowly he unwrapped his muffler. The face that emerged was ancient, a thousand furrows beneath a shock of snow-white hair. If she'd had to guess, she'd have put his age at past ninety.

"I've been working on the study you inquired about. With Dr. Logan. You inquired about our progress. Since I happened to be in Cologne, I thought I might tell you."

Unused to telling lies, Sabrina found that even this modest lie came with great difficulty. But she'd come too far to risk being turned away now.

Wordlessly he led her through the lobby and into his tidy apartment. She was reminded of her grandmother's place in Livorno: the same heavy turn-of-the-century furniture, Oriental rugs, and leather-bound books; the same musty odor.

"May I get you some tea?" he asked.

"No, thank you."

He took a seat in a stiff-backed chair. "Now, please, tell me about your protocol. Your Dr. Logan did not give many details."

"We have had," she replied, choosing her words carefully, "very encouraging results. The drug is active. Of this there is no doubt."

He leaned forward, alert as a fan at a sporting event. "Yes."

"Unfortunately, toxicity remains a problem."

"Of course. As always. Can you give me the details?"

So she began at the beginning, in broad strokes recounting the history of the protocol, except for the final, humbling chapter.

"There's something I wish to ask you," she said. "About Mikio Nakano. What happened to him? And to his work?"

She thought she saw him start. He shook his head. "*Nein, nein.* I do not know. After he left our laboratory, I did not see him."

"But," she said, "you wrote to Dr. Logan that you knew he did not stop working on this problem. How did you know?"

Again he shook his head. "It was very long ago, I am sorry." Grasping the arms of his chair, he lifted himself to his feet.

Sabrina understood she was being dismissed. "I'm sorry to keep asking, Herr Kistner, but you have no idea what became of him?"

"No. I am very sorry, miss." Taking up his cane, he started leading the way toward the door.

As they walked, Sabrina handed him a business card. "Please," she said, "if you recall anything, will you let me know?"

He squinted at the card, then turned to her in surprise. "The Instituto Regina Elena?"

She nodded. "Our study had problems. You see, I am no longer welcome at the ACF. Neither is Dr. Logan."

LOGAN'S spirits picked up somewhat once he got started. The work would never be challenging, but after normal working hours he was able to spread his creative wings. For at last he was free to get back to work on Compound J.

Yet the primitive conditions held him back. Lab animals had to be ordered from a breeding lab in Massachusetts, untreated. Logan decided on immunosuppressed rats, which, at fifteen bucks, were roughly one third the cost of rabbits. The human-tumor cell line necessary to induce cancer had to be obtained separately.

"Damn!" exclaimed Logan, filling out the order form. "I won't even know how to grow the tumors in the rats when everything gets here. I've never done that kind of dirty work."

"I have," said Perez dryly.

"Well, there you are," said Logan, trying to make the best of it. "You've got to help me out."

From the outset Perez had resisted the notion that he serve as Logan's assistant. He had quickly grasped the obvious: Even if, theoretically, such a miracle drug could be concocted, the chances that it could happen here—in this miserable excuse for a lab, with him, Perez, as the entire support staff—were close to nonexistent.

"The truth is," Ruben challenged, "you don't even know what

you're looking for, do you? There are how many changes you could make in that molecule. Ten thousand? A hundred thousand? That could take years."

"Except we've got a head start—Compound J-lite."

"Dan, that's a death drug. It rots livers."

"I'm not convinced of that." He paused meaningfully. "Allen Atlas was in with those animals, Ruben. I'd bet my life on it."

"You're saying he *murdered* your bunnies?"

Absolutely right, buddy! "Well," he said with a stab at moderation, "it's what I hope to find out."

"Look, Dan, why don't you drop it," Perez asked, "at least for now?" He had begun to fear for his friend's equilibrium.

"I know what you're saying," said Logan. "Really. Don't you think I know where I stand?"

"I don't. Tell me."

Logan exhaled deeply. He thought about this all the time—sadly, bitterly—but he'd never once said it aloud. "I have no standing in the scientific community. *None.* Even if we make progress with the drug, right now I'm not even in a position to get it tested. It's possible I never will be." He managed a smile.

"I feel bad for you, man," said Perez softly, his heart going out to his friend.

"Think of this as therapy for me, Ruben. Creative play. It'll keep me off the streets."

Ruben never formally agreed. But when the six rats arrived a few days later, in cardboard boxes with vents, it was he who immediately took charge. "What's wrong with you? They can't live in these. Go to a pet shop and get me some decent cages."

Logan grinned. "Will do."

"And some Purina Rat Chow."

Logan paused. "*Rat Chow?*"

"It costs a little more, but it's worth it."

The breast-tumor cell line came the next day, packed in dry ice, and went immediately into a culture flask. A week later Logan harvested the cells, mixed them in a saline solution, then watched his friend shoot half a milliliter into a tail vein of each of the six rats.

Within a week the first tumors were visible—small bumps on the skin surface. Logan clapped his friend on the back. "C'mon, let's us mix up a new batch of Compound J-lite."

The procedure was identical to the one Logan had followed earlier—only without the time pressure. Soon, despite himself, Perez began to find himself engaged by the process—what became a crash course in advanced chemistry.

As they waited for the newly formulated compound to cool down on the last night, Perez asked, "What about Mrs. Kober? Why did she live?"

Logan had been wondering the same thing for nearly five months now. "I don't know. I've gone over and over the charts. I've even kept in touch with her to make sure she's *still* okay." He shrugged. "Not even an earache."

"It has to be something, right? These things don't happen for no reason at all."

T HEY hadn't made love now in nearly three months. She didn't feel like it—and obviously, under the circumstances, John didn't press.

Although her fears about losing her hair had passed—the two cycles of standard chemo had left it only slightly thinner—she'd never imagined anyone could appear so perpetually fatigued. No matter how much sleep she got, it was never enough to dispel the rings beneath her eyes or lend color to her pale features.

"Does it hurt a lot?" her husband asked softly.

"Only when I look in the mirror." She took his hand. "Please, John, let me know if I ever start reminding you of Camille."

He smiled. "I don't think there's much chance of that." He reached over and flicked off the bedside lamp.

"John?" she said tentatively. "You don't have to spend the night in here."

"I know that." He paused. "Are you worried about the calls waking you up?" He had a standing order that he was to be awakened with any news deemed by aides to be even marginally important.

"No." She laughed softly. "I just wanted to make sure you really wanted to. You know how I hate pity."

"Don't worry. You don't inspire it."

"I worry about embarrassing you, about letting you down."

He rolled over to face her. "Elizabeth, I'm the one who should be embarrassed, putting you through all this pretense. I hate it."

"I'm managing all right. Just keep me away from long flights of stairs. I'm running out of excuses for why I get winded."

"You mean more to me than anything—you know that."

She laughed, but the laugh quickly turned into a cough. "No, I don't. And in the position you're in, I *shouldn't*."

"You can't help it, can you? Always with a wisecrack." He kissed her lightly on the cheek and took her in his arms. "What does your doctor say about the stairs?"

"Stillman?" He couldn't see her face, but the distaste was clear in the way she spoke the name. "Something about the tumor preventing fluid from draining from the lungs. I wish I didn't have to always drag things like that out of him."

"Elizabeth, he's the number one specialist at the leading cancer institute in the world."

"Maybe. But when it comes down to it, they have no idea how to beat this. It's just trial and error. That's their big secret."

They lay in silence for a long while, just holding hands. Suddenly he was aware that she was crying. He took her in his arms again, her face damp against his.

"It's so trite. I so much want to be there when the children get married. I want to see my grandchildren." Burying her face against his shoulder, she began to sob in earnest.

"It's going to be all right," he comforted, stroking her hair.

Safe in his arms, she let the lie pass.

IT WAS Perez who discovered the mess: cabinets ransacked, drawers overturned, smashed beakers and test tubes everywhere.

As soon as Logan entered ten minutes later, he went ashen. "What about the rats?"

"No problem. Better than ever."

Logan hurried back to the storeroom. The rat cages appeared not to have been touched. Already, three days after their first dose, the animals were showing marked improvement. The tumors had begun to soften and shrink, just like the first time.

Returning to the lab, he sat down heavily in a chair. "I can't believe this."

Perez, sweeping up, paused to face him. "Hey, it was junkies, man. It happens, especially in a neighborhood like this."

"Why isn't anything missing?"

"We were lucky."

"Junkies wouldn't take *anything*?"

"I'm not even gonna have this conversation with you, Logan. You're paranoid!"

"We'll see."

"You know why I was most afraid of this?" demanded Perez, three mornings later, holding one of the six dead rats in his hands.

Logan stared at it. "Because I'd say I was right."

"Because you'd take this and misinterpret it. Face it. The drug killed the animals, just like it did before. It doesn't work!"

"Then why was Stillman so interested in it?"

"Oh, man, can't you see what a stretch that is? He's a cancer researcher. He's gonna be interested in any active drug."

"I want to run the experiment again," Logan suddenly decided.

Perez threw up his hands. "Forget it. I want no part of this."

"Please, Ruben, I need you. We can't keep them here, and I don't think my place is much safer."

"In *my* apartment? Logan, you're way over the top, man. You're just *gone*."

But already Perez was thinking about where to put the cages.

The letter arrived ten weeks after Sabrina's return from Cologne. Even if the envelope hadn't borne a German stamp, she'd have recognized the handwriting—slightly shaky, yet still evocative of turn-of-the-century elegance. Rudolf Kistner!

549

My dear Dr. Como:

Greetings and best wishes. Before all else, I must offer appreciation for your kindnesses on your recent visit. Thank you so much for the many details of your protocol with Dr. Logan.

Since your visit I have thought much about the question you ask me. Even now I do not know if I can give the answers you seek.

Herr Doktor Nakano was a very great chemist, I only a young admirer. The work he did was important, but he was not treated as he should have been. I did not learn until after he was made to leave Christian Thomas that Frau Nakano was of the Jewish faith. This was in 1936. After this I did not see him again.

You must understand that I did not support the views of the National Socialists. Few in our laboratory did. We held Professor Nakano in only the highest esteem. Some even continued to correspond with him after he left for Frankfurt. It is in this way that I learned of his continued work on the compound.

Personally, I was not one who wrote to him. This is why I was so surprised to receive from him a letter in November of 1938. I still have this letter. At the time, he was living at Bornheimerstrasse 138. It was quite short—only that he wished for help in leaving Germany. Perhaps he recalled I had a friend at the Swedish legation.

Of course, I could do nothing. At the time, it was not possible. Even now this troubles me. For Professor Nakano's work was truly of the highest order. This is why I write you. Perhaps it is not too late to see his work recognized at last.

Sabrina caught a three-forty flight for Frankfurt. By six thirty she was standing before the building once occupied by Mikio Nakano.

Like the surrounding neighborhood, the nineteenth-century house had seen far better days. Several large windows were cracked; the knocker on the front door and the rail leading up the front steps needed a coat of paint.

The quiet, narrow street was so little traveled that Sabrina's taxi, pulling up before the house, had interrupted a raucous game of soccer. Briefly she watched the game. A dozen or so children were involved, German and Turk, boys and—she was pleased to note—spiritedly defending one of the goals, a girl.

Smiling, she walked up the steps of the house and rang the bell. A middle-aged woman with bright yellow dyed hair answered it. *"Ja, bitte?"*

"I was wondering, please, do you know where I might find the owner of this house?" Sabrina smiled, to establish she was not bringing trouble. "I am trying to discover what's become of an old friend who lived here many years ago."

The woman called over her shoulder, *"Mutter, komm bitte."*

A moment later an elderly woman, frail but with an exceptionally kind face, came shuffling into view, wearing a tattered bathrobe.

Slowly Sabrina explained why she was here.

The old woman shook her head. "My late husband bought this house in 1969. He bought it from a man—Herr Klaus. But he also is gone, many years."

"Well, thank you so much for your time."

Well, thought Sabrina, back on the sidewalk, what now?

She watched the soccer game a few minutes longer before, lacking any alternative, she began randomly approaching passersby on the street, anyone who looked to be over sixty-five. She assumed a general line of inquiry, pretending to be a graduate student researching the recent history of the city. She heard about chronic shortages during the war; about children and grandchildren raised in these houses; and, several times, about how the influx of Turkish workers had made things worse. It was now close to eight p.m.

"Entschuldigung." Pardon me.

Sabrina wheeled around. There stood the girl from the soccer game, her pretty face framed by a tangle of dirty-blond hair.

"You wish to know about the people who have lived here?"

"Yes. This is of great interest to me."

"Come. My grandfather will tell you. He has lived here all his life." She extended a small hand. "My name is Agneta."

She shook it. *"Ich heisse Sabrina."*

The child led her down several residential streets, emerging onto a more traveled thoroughfare with a number of modest commercial

551

establishments. All but one were closed for the day: a small shop, its interior shielded by strings of beads covering the windows. When they entered, Sabrina saw it was a Middle Eastern–style coffee-house, patronized by men of the local immigrant community.

Peering through the acrid smoke, she picked up only one clearly recognizable German in the place—the individual toward whose corner table Agneta was leading her.

He greeted the child with a grin. "Come to visit your old grand-papa or just after another pastry?"

His companion at the table, a middle-aged Turk, smiled broadly, showing several gold teeth.

"Grandpapa, this is Sabrina. She has some questions about the neighborhood."

"Well, then"—he gestured expansively with a workingman's hands—"you have come to the right person. Please, you must have some Turkish coffee. For me, it is an addiction."

He ordered the coffee, and a sweet pastry for his granddaughter. "Now, what is it you wish to know? I am seventy-one years old. Before that, you must find it in a book."

He was so willing, Sabrina impulsively decided to abandon her ruse. "I am told that many years ago, before the war, a Japanese man lived on your street. A scientist, Mikio Nakano."

Instantly, the old man's face softened. "Ah, yes. The professor. I was only a boy, of course. He lived with the family of his wife— Jewish people. He also had a laboratory there. We children liked him very much. He used to give us hard candy."

Sabrina gave a convincing impression of complete calm. "I am trying to find out what happened to him, to his work. I understand that in 1938 he was trying to leave."

He nodded slowly. "Yes, of course. They all were. You have heard of Kristallnacht? The Nazis destroyed his laboratory. Everyone heard of it, even the children. It was very sad to us after all his hard work. This is when he sent away his things."

"Pardon?" Involuntarily Sabrina leaned slightly forward.

"Not only him—many Jews in the quarter. After Kristallnacht they began sending their valuables, what was left, out of the country. I know about it because my brother helped carry some of their trunks to the shipping office. The professor's trunk was one of the first."

"It went to the shipping office? Surely, they would have records there, then."

"*Nein.* The center city was completely destroyed."

"Do you know if Professor Nakano got out?"

"Of course not." He paused. "His family was Jewish. He was not the sort of fellow who would leave them behind. Soon afterward many of the Jews in the quarter—and the professor too—were taken away. It was said to Dachau."

Though none of this was too surprising, Sabrina was unprepared for the force with which it registered. She knew almost nothing about Mikio Nakano, had never so much as seen a picture of him. Yet over the past year, working on the compound, she'd begun to feel an intimate kinship with him. Later that evening, thinking about the thugs destroying his lab, she did not even try to hold back the tears.

"The professor's trunk was sent to America," the old man added now, trying to be helpful. "He had, I believe, a brother-in-law. Many had family there who had gotten out earlier."

She hesitated, almost afraid to ask the obvious question. "Do you happen to recall the family name of the professor's wife?"

"It was so long ago, but yes. I believe it was . . . Falzheim."

"FALZHEIM," mused Logan. "Can you believe it? She got the name from a former neighbor, someone who actually *remembered* Nakano."

Ruben Perez didn't even pretend to be impressed. "So you have the name of his in-laws—maybe. So what?"

"It's a start," shot back Logan. "A *good* start. The guy'd been working on this process for twenty years."

"Right. And he wrote it all down, and it's just waiting for you to find it." He picked up the telephone book. "Manhattan. Isn't this where most of the German Jewish refugees back then settled?"

Annoyed, Logan took it from him and flipped to the appropriate

553

page; not at all to his surprise, there was no such name. For once, his friend's skepticism only reflected his own. Logan knew how far-fetched this possibility was. "I didn't say it was going to be easy."

He started for the door.

"Where you going?"

"Forty-second Street, the main library there. They've got phone books from all over the place there. I'll be back in a few hours."

THE estimate proved way off. There were perhaps seventy directories from large and medium-sized cities throughout America at the library, and it took no more than fifteen seconds to locate in each the page where the name Falzheim might have been—but wasn't. He was back at the office in an hour and a half.

"Let's have the wisecracks now and get it over with," Logan said, marching through the door.

To his surprise Perez just turned from his workbench and nodded soberly toward the far end of the room.

Logan was stunned. There, atop a stool, sat Allen Atlas.

"Hello, Dan."

"What do you want?"

"Nothing much. Just to talk." The guy fairly oozed sincerity.

"I've got nothing to talk to you about, *nothing.*"

"Just ten minutes—that's all it'll take. You won't be sorry."

To himself at least, Logan didn't deny he was intrigued. What was the s.o.b. after? He glanced at his watch. "Ten minutes."

THEY went to the bar two doors down from HIV-EX. "All right," Logan said, as they sat down at a booth, "What do you want?"

"Wait a sec, will you. Won't you at least let me order us something to drink?"

Atlas returned a minute later with two beers and placed one on the table before Logan. "Drink up. It's on the ACF."

"No, thanks."

"C'mon, Logan. This is no easier for me than it is for you."

"Hey, pal, I didn't come looking for you." Logan took a quick swig and glanced at his watch. "You're down to two minutes."

"They've had second thoughts at the ACF about what happened. Dr. Stillman, for one."

Logan leaned forward, his eyes narrow. "Which part are you talking about, Allen? What happened at the hearing, or what happened when I went looking for another job?"

"That's your imagination. We had nothing to do with that."

"Sorry. Time's up."

"Wait!" Atlas grabbed his arm. "Look, Stillman's ready to bury the hatchet. You want a better job, the ACF can help you out."

"Why, Atlas? All of a sudden they're growing consciences down there instead of tumors?"

"We're doing what we've always done—trying to cure cancer. Dr. Stillman's had a chance to go over your data. He thinks your Compound J has promise. He'd like to talk it over with you."

"Tell me something I don't know, Atlas." He shook his arm free. "And tell him I'm happy where I am." He stood up and walked out the door.

Atlas hurried outside after him. "Hey, Logan! Just one more thing—I'm real sorry about your friend Reston."

"What about him?"

"Didn't you hear?" He paused meaningfully. "They found his body in his office the other day. Barbiturates. Apparently, he got tired of living."

Logan just watched as Atlas walked off in the other direction.

A MY answered on the first ring. "Amy? It's Dan Logan."

"Hi. How are you?"

Her flat voice made him realize she was in bad shape. "I'm okay. How are *you*?" He paused. "I heard about what happened."

"I'm doing okay, better. It's been almost a week."

"I'm so, so sorry. You know, even after everything that happened, he was still my friend. It was never personal."

"Well, thanks," she said. "Look, Dan, it was nice of you to call."

Logan was caught short. He didn't want to get off, not yet. There were too many questions demanding answers. Desperately he plunged ahead. "Allen Atlas told me."

"Atlas?"

"He was in New York on business. I just couldn't believe it. It just seems so completely out of character. Do you have any explanation for it? Did he leave a note?"

"Please, Dan. I don't want to talk about it."

"Why not?"

"Good-bye, Dan. Thank you for calling."

Hanging up the phone, Logan turned to Perez, sweeping up the far corner of the lab. "She wouldn't tell me a thing."

"It's not easy being the girlfriend. She probably feels guilty about not picking up the signals."

Logan thought a moment. "This isn't one of those cases. Something's off." He paused. "She doesn't think he killed himself."

Perez stopped his sweeping. "Did she say that?"

"No. But I know her. I also knew him." He stopped. "There's also the way Atlas told me about it. Almost like . . . I don't know . . . a threat."

"Oh, come *on*. Your imagination's working overtime again. Look, the guy did himself in. Period."

Logan smiled. "You might be right. I'm going home. What I need now's some peace and quiet."

HEADING home to his studio apartment, he'd been seized by so powerful a sense of anxiety that, once inside, he ran to the medicine cabinet for a mild sedative. He was perspiring heavily. He took his pulse: 120. What was going on here? Distractedly, aware he was hungry, he was opening a can of baked beans when he was hit with sharp abdominal pains. Within a minute the pains were powerful enough to make him double over. He staggered to the next room and collapsed on the bed.

Now there came a terrific pounding in his head, so intense it all but crowded out thought. Yet he was so weak he could scarcely move. Could this be a flu? But no, it had come on too fast.

Food poisoning? What had he eaten today? His mind raced. For breakfast, only a bowl of Rice Krispies and orange juice. For lunch—what?—some chicken noodle soup, a bagel with jelly, tea.

Wait a second. . . . The beer with Atlas!

The panic suddenly welling up within was even greater than the pain. He felt himself losing consciousness. He had to get to a hospital. He raised himself to his hands and knees.

But it was too much. He actually saw the blackness coming and felt it begin to wash over him.

WHEN he awoke, the room was still dark. The clock read three twenty-three a.m. He was, he realized with a start, still dressed. Tentatively he sat up.

Slowly he got off the bed. So physically traumatic an experience *always* leaves aftereffects—at the least, wooziness and disorientation. But now there was nothing. Except for slight hunger pangs, he felt absolutely wonderful, on a natural high.

This was as frightening as anything yet. The thought was impossible to shake: This had only been a warning.

PICKING up his car at the long-term lot, Logan headed into the Lincoln Tunnel just as dawn was breaking. Doing seventy-five most of the way, he made it to downtown Washington in less than four and a half hours. He headed toward the National Archives.

What he needed was *The Martin Allen Directory of European SS Arrivals, 1890–1940, Port of New York*, which, he'd learned at the New York Library, was available only here.

Since the book had just a record of departures and arrivals—the individual passenger lists being available only on microfilm—Logan was reduced to playing probabilities. In all likelihood, German Jewish refugees exiting Nazi Germany would have left via Hamburg, the country's principal port, between 1933—when Hitler was named chancellor—and 1938. And though there were several companies that sailed between northern Germany and New York, Logan decided to concentrate on the most prominent: the Hamburg-Amerika line.

Hamburg-Amerika had three ships working the route—the

Potsdam, the *Bremen,* and the *Lübeck*—each making some fifteen round-trips annually. Worse, when he requested the first microfilm reel bearing passenger rosters, he found that the lists, numbering as many as fifteen hundred names apiece, were handwritten—and not alphabetical.

It was the very definition of tedium, reading down columns of names by the thousands. He'd chosen to start with the *Bremen.* Working through the morning, he did not find Falzheim. The closest approximation, which he jotted down, was Pfaltzstein, Ernst.

By midafternoon, having moved on to the *Potsdam,* he was up to August 1934, when he made note of a second name that seemed close. Forcheim, Leopold; immediately followed by Forcheim, Hilda and Forcheim, Greta. A whole little Forcheim clan, he realized. He pressed on.

An hour later, dizzy with fatigue, he took a break and dialed the lab.

"You're in Washington?" exclaimed Perez. "What the hell for?"

"Look, do me a favor. Do you have that phone book handy?"

"Oh, c'mon, man. You went down there for *that?*"

"I just want to try a couple of names on you. You got a Pfaltzstein? With a P?" He spelled it.

Logan heard the pages rustling. "No. You know something, I oughta have you locked up."

"How about Forcheim? With an F."

He sighed. "Hey, yeah, I got one. My neighborhood, Washington Heights, 802 West 190th Street."

Logan wrote it down. "Thanks. I'll call you when I get home."

IT WAS past four o'clock when Logan left the building and hailed a cab. He had the driver let him off at the Foggy Bottom Metro station and moved around a nearby corner. The spot allowed him a view of pedestrians approaching the station from the direction of the FCC Building on M Street, where Amy worked.

He waited about ten minutes, and there she suddenly was, moving briskly but, as he had hoped, alone.

"Amy?" he said, feigning delight at a chance encounter.

Startled, she reflexively smiled. "Hi." Then she recognized him, and to his surprise the smile turned genuine. "I had a feeling you were coming."

Taking his elbow, she led him briskly back around the corner.

"Where are we going?"

"I'm trying to figure out where we can talk."

"I got the idea you didn't want to."

"You caught me at a bad time—at home." She glanced over her shoulder.

"What? You think you're being followed?"

"I don't know. Probably we should just keep walking." She laughed uneasily. "You can tell I'm not very good at this."

"Amy, what happened to John?"

She turned to look behind her again. "What'd Atlas say to you?"

"That they found him in his office. That he'd done it with pills."

"That's what they told me too. You knew John. Did he seem the suicidal type to you?"

"No. That's what struck me."

"I don't know what to believe." She said nothing for half a block. "They were after him for information. About Compound J. They were pushing him really hard."

Logan's blood went cold. "Stillman?"

She nodded. "They wanted to know how the stuff worked, things he just couldn't tell them. Because—let's face it—he hadn't been that involved."

"Right." Logan could almost see it: the cocky, insecure Reston, desperate to play the big man, but powerless to do so.

"Obviously, they thought more of Compound J than they pretended. And John got back at them. He *taunted* them about it. At least that's what he told me."

Having walked several blocks, turning corners apparently at random, they now found themselves on busy Connecticut Avenue.

Now that she'd let it all out, Amy was more relaxed. She indicated a nearby bar-restaurant. "I think I need a drink."

But the conversation had had the opposite effect on Logan. "Not me. I'll take a rain check. See you, Amy. Watch yourself."

559

"Funny, I was going to say the same thing to you."

As soon as she'd disappeared into the bar, he jerked around, scanning the busy street. Nothing. But how would he know?

What, he wondered, had Atlas used on Reston? It could have been anything. Toxins from Amazonian plants, so poisonous that millionths of a microgram could kill and yet leave no apparent trace. The ACF had readier access to such compounds than any intelligence branch of any government on earth.

Logan walked quickly to a cab. His car was still in the underground garage by the National Archives. When the cabbie dropped him at the entrance, he ran to it without looking back.

Seated behind the wheel, he tried to collect himself. Suddenly he knew what he had to do.

It took him no more than twenty minutes to reach Seth Shein's home in Arlington. Heading up the walk, he knew he still wasn't thinking clearly. What did he expect? An explanation? Reassurance? He was still considering when Alice Shein opened the door. He saw her shocked dismay. "Seth," she shouted. "Seth, come here!"

A moment later Shein appeared at the door in baggy trousers and work shirt, hammer in hand. Seeing Logan, he recoiled—but recovered immediately. "Logan, you look like hell. Don't think I'm gonna ask you in. No one invited you."

Defiantly Logan elbowed past him into the house, then wheeled on him. "What happened to Reston? What'd they give to him?"

"Reston finally figured out what a nothing he was and did something about it. End of story."

"Why're they killing my lab animals?"

"*Killing your lab animals?*" Shein laughed out loud. "You got it wrong, Logan. *You* killed those animals. What's happening to your mind? You're embarrassing yourself."

The sight of Shein standing there with a smug smile was too much; abruptly Logan snapped. Knocking the hammer from his hand, he slammed Shein against the open front door. "You bastard," said Logan, breathing hard. "You wreck people's lives and don't give it a second thought!"

Pinned tight against the door, Shein was still smiling. "What are you gonna do? Beat me up? Accept it, Logan. You just weren't good enough."

Logan's fingers dug into Shein's arms. "You know that Compound J works! Why else was Stillman after Reston about it?"

"You're outta your head, Logan."

Logan shook him violently. "Tell me, damn you."

"Let go of me," he shouted.

Logan did so.

"Good," said Shein, rubbing his upper arm. "Now get outta here. I got a kitchen cabinet to fix."

"I'm not going anywhere until you tell me the truth."

"Alice," Shein called, "call the cops. Tell 'em we got a psycho threatening a guy with security clearance. And tell 'em to hurry. Also that he's driving a beat-up white Ford—a real piece of crap."

"I swear," Logan said softly, "you won't get away with this." Turning, he walked quickly out the door.

Shein watched him drive off. Then he headed for his office. Did he have the home number of the ACF pharmacist in his address book?

Yes, there it was. Seizing the phone, Shein punched it in.

S OMEONE was following him—he was sure of it. From the start of the New Jersey Turnpike to beyond Trenton, the headlights remained at the same distance behind him, switching lanes as he did, seeming to mirror his every change of speed.

Pulling off at a rest stop, he did not leave the car—just sat staring into his rearview mirror, the exit ramp in full view behind him. Nothing—just a steady flow of cars driving up to the pumps and then off into the night. He eased back onto the turnpike.

Just outside New Brunswick it was back. Or maybe this was a different car. This one stayed with him for ten minutes. But when he slowed down, it zoomed past. A Volvo wagon. A family car.

Had his eyes been playing tricks on him? Or—worse—his mind?

He traveled the rest of the way to the city in the right-hand lane at a steady fifty-five and made it home by one thirty a.m.

Logan collapsed on the bed. What time is it in Italy? he wondered. But before he'd even done the math, he was asleep.

AT THAT moment Seth Shein was wide awake, his every sense on full alert. His eye moved from one to another of the three files open before him on his desk at the ACF, each distinctly labeled in black marker: RHOME, KOBER, DIETZ.

Again he picked up the Dietz autopsy report, almost identical to Rhome's. Both of these women had gone from apparent good health to total physiological decompensation and death in a matter of hours.

But what about Kober? She'd had the same initial positive reaction to the drug as the others. Why in her case had there been no comparable devastation afterward?

Already he'd carefully examined all the women's treatment schedules. They'd been close to identical. Kober had not missed any treatments, nor had her dosage been even marginally reduced.

For the third time, Shein pulled out her CAT scan. There were eight pictures, each representing a slice of the patient's body at a different level. The liver, homogeneous, took up almost one entire picture; in the next he once again noted the upper pole of the left kidney, the kidney hilum, the indentation in it where the blood vessels enter and exit. Then . . . Wait a minute. What was this? Where was the upper pole of the *right* kidney?

Quickly he turned to the notes on her initial examination. Here was confirmation: This woman has only one kidney.

Shein leaned back in his chair. On the face of it, this made no sense at all. In fact, it was *backward*. Like many drugs, Compound J was eliminated via the kidneys. Lacking a kidney, she'd have had *more* drug in her body than the others, not less. Given the drug's established toxicity, she should've gotten sick and died sooner!

He cupped his hands behind his head and closed his eyes. This was always the part where it got to be *fun*.

He didn't quite have it yet, but it was coming.

Logan awoke with a jolt, the telephone jangling in his ear. The room was still semidark. He fumbled for the receiver and answered. But there was only a click as someone hung up.

Instantly the drowsiness was gone. He dialed Perez's number.

"Dan?" Ruben's voice was heavy with sleep.

"Ruben, listen to me. Something's going on." Suddenly he thought, What if his phone was tapped? "Wait. Stay there." He slammed down the phone and, wild-eyed, throwing some clothes into an overnight bag, dashed out the door.

"Ruben?" he said ten minutes later from a pay phone.

"Logan, you're totally messin' up my life."

"Stay there. I'm coming over."

He caught the uptown A train at Canal Street and hid behind an open *New York Times*. It was not yet seven when he pressed the buzzer in Perez's building—and woke him again.

"Look, Ruben, I'm sorry," he said, facing him across his tiny living room. "I know this is tough on you."

In the far corner the rats scurried in their cages; the tumors, induced a week earlier, were visible even from where Logan sat. In a few days they'd begin dosing them with the drug.

Perez, in a bathrobe, leaned forward in his chair and rubbed his eyes with both hands. "What is it now?"

Briefly Logan told him about his experiences in Washington.

His friend took it in soberly, aware of the sharp decline of Logan's emotional state in just two days. "Listen, Dan," he said softly, "I just want you to think about what you're saying to me. I know what the girlfriend told you must've been scary. But think about where she's coming from. Her guy just killed himself."

Logan shook his head. "No. You don't know these people."

"It's the ACF, Dan! They don't *do* this kind of thing." Perez sighed. "Look," he said, rising to his feet, "I gotta get ready for work. You do too."

"I don't think so, Ruben. Not today. Would you mind if I stayed here? Just for a few days?"

Perez disappeared into the bedroom and returned with a key. He tossed it to Logan. "What're you gonna do for clothes?"

Logan nodded at the overnight bag. "But I was kind of rushed. I only brought a couple of things."

"Man, don't you got any other friends?" He shook his head wearily. "Gimme your key. I'll pick up some stuff after work."

PEREZ had been gone a half hour before Logan focused on it: Forcheim G., 802 W. 190th St. Not many blocks away.

Logan showered and put on the jeans and shirt he'd brought.

He walked down Broadway and up a long, curving hill. The building was perhaps twelve stories high. The names on the panel reflected the changing face of the neighborhood, a mix of German-Jewish and Hispanic, with a couple of Russian names as well.

FORCHEIM. APT. 3C. He pushed the buzzer and waited.

"Yes?"

"Ms. Forcheim?"

"Yes?"

What now? "My name is Dr. Daniel Logan. I know this might sound strange, but I'm looking for a man named Nakano—"

He heard the click that signaled she'd snapped off the intercom. "Damn," he muttered, and pressed the buzzer again. No response. He pressed again. And again. He was about to turn away when through the glass he saw the elevator door in the lobby open.

Coming toward him was a woman—probably in her sixties, wearing a baggy housedress, but possessing one of the most beautiful faces he'd ever seen, jet-black hair, lustrous skin, dark eyes slightly crescent-shaped. He knew it even before she opened the door.

"He was my father."

TWENTY minutes later he sat on her faded couch, a cup of tea on the low table before him, as she told her story. She was less than a year old when she came to America with her aunt and uncle, her mother's brother. The plan was that eventually her own parents would join them. "But my mother's parents—my grandparents—were too old to leave. Someone had to stay with them, and I suppose everyone thought because my father was not Jewish . . ."

"It would be safe."

"I was lucky, actually. My aunt and uncle adopted me. I was never alone. My aunt just died last year."

Logan glanced about the room, busy with colorful fabrics, plants, framed photos. His gaze fixed on the small portrait on the window ledge beside him. It showed a youngish Oriental man wearing black-rimmed glasses and a serious expression. "This is him?"

"Yes." She smiled. "But I have others where he doesn't look so stern. When it became clear they weren't getting out, they sent us an album. Would you like to see it?"

"Of course."

"I keep it right here." She reached into a shelf beside her and withdrew an album with a faded fabric cover.

Opening it, Logan was transported to another time, the Frankfurt of pre-Hitler Germany, the backdrop of many of the carefully mounted and labeled black-and-white pictures: elegant little shops, well-tended parks, peaceful streets. But, above all, he picked up a sense of the young family in the foreground. Mikio Nakano, usually in a business suit, but occasionally showing a mischievous or even a silly side; the woman before him, as a chubby infant; her darkly pretty young mother.

"What was your mother's name?" asked Logan.

"Emma. She was a piano teacher. That's how they met. With all his work he decided to take up the piano!" She laughed. "I have all the details. My mother sent over her diary."

"I was wondering, by any chance, did your father also keep a diary?"

She shook her head. "I don't think he had the time."

"I mean about his work."

"Oh." She thought a moment. "Actually, yes, I think there is something, a journal of some sort. . . ."

She went to a closet across the room. "Most of it I can't make heads or tails of, of course. All those numbers and letters." She stood on tiptoes and gingerly pulled down a box from the top shelf. "I think it's in here. Yes, here it is."

She handed him a black-and-white-marble composition book, similar to those Logan himself had used in school.

He opened it. What he saw on the first page sent a shiver down his spine: a rendering of the precise compound with which Logan had been working.

"I hope it's helpful," she was saying.

He flipped to the next page and then to the one after that; then, more rapidly, scanned perhaps ten more. What he was seeing was a series of brief entries, three or four to the page, occasionally accompanied by a sketch of a chemical model. The story being told here was riveting—that of the evolution of a brilliant scientist's thinking as he struggled, over more than two decades, with a problem of almost unimaginable complexity.

Excitedly, apprehensively, Logan skipped to the back of the notebook. The final dozen pages were blank. But on the one that preceded them, there it was: the fully realized compound!

Logan deciphered the German words above it: *"Es funktioniert!"* It works! It was dated two weeks before Kristallnacht.

"Would you mind if I borrow this?" asked Logan, trying to maintain a veneer of calm.

She looked suddenly concerned. "It's very important to me."

"I understand. Of course." How to put this? "I just think you should know your father did some remarkable work here."

"Really?" She lit up. "That's wonderful to hear."

"Only for a day or so. I just want to make a copy of it." He began fumbling for his wallet. "I'll leave you my license, my credit cards—"

With a sudden laugh, she relented. "Never mind. Of course you can. I never imagined anyone would ever be interested."

SOMEONE else might have dreaded this confrontation. Seth Shein relished it.

"Say, Stillman," he said, strolling into his rival's office unannounced, "haven't seen much of you lately."

Gregory Stillman looked up from the paper he'd been working on, his lip curling in a sneer. "Who the hell let you in here?"

"Just wonderin' what you been workin' on." He noticed Stillman had slipped his forearm over the page before him. Shein innocently took a seat.

"I'm in no mood for your idiocy," Stillman snapped. "Get out!"

"Maybe that's the wrong question. What I mean to ask is, who've you been treating with Compound J?"

Stillman rose to his feet, bewildered. "What?"

"Simple question. I looked at the pharmacy records. It seems you've checked out fifteen grams of the stuff. Who for?"

"For research purposes, of course," he said. "I've never denied Compound J seems to have some activity."

Shein snorted. "Don't insult my intelligence," he said, his voice taking on a dangerous edge. "We're talkin' fifteen grams. How many mice you planning to dose? A hundred thousand?"

"That's the most irresponsible kind of speculation!"

Shein hesitated, appearing to consider this. "You know what Logan thinks?" he picked up, his tone almost conspiratorial. "He thinks you poisoned his lab animals. So that you could take over."

"You're throwing Logan at me? A guy who faked his data?"

Shein nodded decisively. "You're right. J-lite's incredibly toxic. No way you killed those lab animals." He smiled; it was impossible to tell he was operating on intuition. "Just the women."

"What? What the hell are you—"

"Simple enough with these new poisons, Greg. Was it chrisan-thetoxin—*that* destroys the liver. All you'd have to do is get a thousandth of a microgram into the IV line."

Stillman came back with a brittle laugh. "Compound J killed those women, Shein. It's an established fact."

"No, Greg. Compound J doesn't have that kind of toxicity. You know that. Why else would you take the chance of feeding it to someone else?"

The other man hesitated, his face suddenly drained of color.

Jackpot!

Shein smiled confidentially. "She must be pretty big stuff for you to go to so much trouble. I figure none of the conventional stuff worked, right? So what were you gonna use—*your* stuff that'd had

567

zero responses? Compound J had some problems, but at least it's active."

"Where do you come up with this crap?"

"Take a look at Kober's file. She only has one kidney."

"What do I care?"

"It means she had more Compound J in her system. The stuff didn't kill her—it probably saved her. Helped her fight off the toxin."

"You're delusional. Do you *know* what you're suggesting?"

"Well, Greg, I know this: Compound J didn't kill those ladies. Just as a matter of professional interest, did you use the same toxin on Reston? He was quite a loose cannon, wasn't he?"

Stillman threw up his hands.

Shein had never imagined there'd come a time when he'd see his rival so utterly vulnerable—and he moved in for the kill. "It's okay if you don't wanna tell me. He's only been buried—what?—a week. No problem exhuming the body and running a few tests."

"Shein, what are you trying to do? Wreck the ACF? I'm not saying there's a word of truth to this. There's not. But if you pursue it, that's what you're going to do. It couldn't come at a worse time."

Shein leaned forward. "Oh, yeah? Why's that?"

Stillman closed his eyes and breathed in deeply.

"C'mon, Greg," he urged gently, almost seductively, "out with it. You know I'm gonna get it anyhow."

Stillman stared at him miserably. Then he picked up the file on his desk and handed it over.

LOGAN had been poring over the notebook in Perez's living room for over four hours, but he was still as light-headed with excitement as at the start. What he held in his hands was close to holy—the lifework of a scientist as remarkable as any he'd ever studied in the classic texts.

It was a complete record of the development of the compound from theory to realization. He could see how Nakano had built on small successes as he went; yet, too, how reluctant he'd been to discard certain key ideas that seemed virtual truisms and how slow to embrace others that appeared at first extraordinarily unlikely.

Logan understood. Nakano had also been convinced that for a dozen frustrating years the toxicity was linked to the length of the polymer's bridge. It was only his belated discovery that the problem lay elsewhere that enabled him to press forward; and even then, ten more years were required to reach completion.

Logan studied the final drawings. The compound Nakano discovered was, in fact, an isomer of Compound J: It had the same number of atoms, but its parts were arranged slightly differently. Logan himself might have gone on working for a hundred years—a thousand—and never gotten it right.

He heard the click of a key in the door and looked up.

"Well," announced Perez, a shopping bag full of Logan's clothes in each hand, "just call me the Bag Man of Washington Heights."

He had just closed the door and was heading toward the couch when there came the sound of heavy footsteps in the hallway, followed by a violent pounding on the door.

"What the hell?" exclaimed Perez, quickly moving for the baseball bat he kept in the corner.

In a panic, Logan slipped the notebook beneath a cushion.

Abruptly the door crashed open, kicked in by one of the four burly men who came rushing in. Three of them had guns drawn. "Which one of you is Logan?"

"Who are you?" demanded Perez.

"Federal marshals. Keep your mouth shut!"

Logan noticed the head man had a small photograph in his hand. It was identical to the one on his ID card at the ACF. Instantly he knew: These guys were ACF security.

"I am." He accepted the inevitable. "I'm Dan Logan."

"Who's he?"

"He's my friend," Logan said. "He didn't do anything."

"He goes too," came the command.

"What about these?" One of the men indicated the rats.

The leader didn't hesitate. "Take 'em."

Both men were jostled out of the apartment and down the stairs, where two cars waited, engines running.

"My fault, man," called Perez before he was pushed into one car. "I was a stupid idiot."

Logan couldn't manage a reply before he disappeared into the second, a Volvo. No way, he reflected miserably. All mine.

He was placed on the back floor, invisible to passersby. "My friend doesn't know about any of this," he insisted. But he had no doubt that if they were ready to eliminate him to steal Compound J, Perez, caught in the cross fire, didn't have a chance.

"Don't worry about it," said the guy in charge.

"How'd you find me?"

"No talking, Doctor. Those are our orders."

Anyway, the answer seemed clear. Having staked out his place, he figured, they'd followed Perez uptown.

For the next thirty-five or forty minutes they drove in silence, across—he surmised, looking up from the floor—the George Washington Bridge, and into New Jersey. When they came to a halt and he was helped from the car, he was surprised to find they were at the edge of a rural airport. Now he found himself hustled aboard a Learjet. A few moments later they were airborne.

"I know where we're going," he said quietly.

Neither of the men flanking him replied.

They came down at a similar airfield—Virginia, he guessed, by the look of the terrain—and he was made to lie down in the back of another car, a Buick sedan.

For another half hour there was silence—until someone tapped him on the shoulder. "Okay, you can sit up now."

With difficulty, he struggled in the cramped space to his knees. Then two pairs of hands helped lift him to the back seat.

"Why?" he said, shaking them off. "You want me to see where—"

He stopped in midsentence, jaw literally going slack. What loomed before him was so staggering, for a moment he was actually unable to process it. They'd just driven through a gate and were heading up a drive toward the imposing structure.

"Is that the—"

"Yessir. The White House."

At the east entrance Logan was helped from the car.

"I'm very sorry for the inconvenience, sir," said the senior man. "There was concern you might try to evade us, and our job was to bring you here as quickly as possible. Right this way, please, Doctor." He escorted him into the building, around a corner, and then up a narrow staircase.

"Excuse me," said Logan, "but isn't this where—"

He nodded. "The private quarters, yessir. Please follow me."

He led the way down a long corridor, knocking at a door close to the end.

"Come in," called the familiar voice.

His escort opened the door and stepped aside to let Logan pass. There, in what appeared to be a sort of sitting room, waited Kenneth Markell, Raymond Larsen, and Seth Shein.

By now Logan was almost beyond surprise. He stared at them.

"Dr. Logan," nodded Markell in greeting, as if the meeting of this group in this place were the most natural thing in the world.

Suddenly conscious he was still dressed in his T-shirt and jeans, Logan folded his arms before him. "What am I doing here?"

"We've got a situation," said Markell. "And it occurred to us that you might help." He paused. "Mrs. Rivers has a chemotherapy-refractory cancer. I'm afraid it's bad."

The First Lady? Logan's mind raced. What Markell was telling him was that she was doomed: They'd tried all the chemo they could, and nothing had worked. "I'm sorry."

"The upshot is she's willing to try any alternative therapy we deem appropriate. The President concurs. The situation is quite desperate."

"We understand," added Shein, "that you've continued to work on Compound J."

He looked from one to the other. "How do you know that?"

"As I expect you know, Doctor, it's our responsibility to keep tabs on such things," replied Markell.

The break-in—it wasn't only Stillman. These monsters! Yet instead of anger, what he felt bubbling up within was something like pure joy. *They* needed *him*. *He* was in control here; *he* had the power. "Where's my friend? They took my friend also."

"He's fine. We had to be certain he was aware of the security implications in this."

Logan nodded. "Shouldn't Dr. Stillman be here? Or did he object to my being called in?"

Shein fielded the question. "Dr. Stillman's leaving the ACF. He's accepted an offer to be the director of the Southwest Regional Cancer Center in Phoenix. That far away enough for you, Logan?"

"Dr. Stillman was the original doctor on this case," added Markell quickly. "Unfortunately, he did not agree with the course we wished to pursue."

Throughout it all, Larsen, having taken a seat in the corner, looked as if he wanted nothing so much as to disappear into thin air. Now Logan confidently turned his way. "How about you, Dr. Larsen? Do you agree with this course of action?"

Larsen cast a worried glance toward Markell. "Actually, I'm new to the case myself. But, yes, it strikes me as fully appropriate."

"It does? You're saying you've changed your mind about this compound? And me? You're offering me an apology?"

Larsen shifted miserably in his chair. Shein spoke up. "Why don't you let me have a few minutes alone with Dr. Logan." He smiled amiably at his colleagues.

Markell nodded. "Absolutely."

Shein steered Logan toward the adjacent bathroom and closed the door behind them.

"Great." He laughed, jerking a thumb toward the room they'd just left. "I enjoyed that as much as you did."

"How'd all this happen?" asked Logan coolly.

Shein shrugged. "Hey, didn't I tell you I'm your guy?" He dropped his voice. "You know the best part? It's a no-lose proposition. If she responds, we get the credit. If not, Stillman takes the blame. He wasted five months on useless treatment."

"Markell's willing to back that?"

"What choice does he have? You got a desperate man in there."

Logan smiled. "Let's go back and talk turkey."

"Well?" asked Markell when they emerged.

"Obviously, we have to do everything we can." Logan paused

thoughtfully, then looked directly at Shein. "I'm going to want to head up my own team, of course."

Shein blanched. For the first time in Logan's experience, he appeared wholly at a loss for words.

"I understand," agreed Markell.

"I'll pick my own people—starting with Dr. Como and Ruben Perez."

"Of course. Whoever you feel you need."

"Good." Logan looked from Markell to Larsen to Shein. "Thank you, gentlemen. Now, where do I get some fresh clothes? I'd like to see my patient."

ON AN evening almost ten months later Logan felt a tap on his shoulder.

"Mrs. Rivers," he said, surprised.

"I believe you promised me a dance, Doctor."

"It must've been one of those lies doctors tell to buck up patients." He grinned sheepishly, aware of the eyes on them. "I don't want to embarrass you in front of all these people."

"That's the same thing he always says to me," noted Sabrina. "This is a guy who just does not know how to have fun."

"Well, I don't embarrass easily. C'mon. Here's a slow song. Don't worry, I'll lead."

She took his hand and led him toward the crowded dance floor, other revelers at the inaugural ball clearing a path as they went.

"So," he said, "I guess congratulations are in order."

"Thank you—but doesn't that go both ways? It looks to me like you guys are quite a success story yourselves."

He smiled. "Right." The reference was to his recent appointment as director of basic research at New York's prestigious Roosevelt Cancer Research Institute—with Sabrina named director of clinical trials. "They're keeping us pretty busy."

"I just hope you'll be available if needed."

"Of course."

Logan was relieved to hear her say it. She looked stupendous and—in this he took even greater pride—her CAT scans had been clean for over five months. But he knew that for some time to come, she would have to be closely monitored.

"Word is you plan to put the drug into a major clinical trial."

"Yes. There's still a lot about this compound we need to know."

"Have you put in for the patent?"

He grinned. "How close are you to the IRS?"

"Don't worry, I can be trusted."

"Anyway, three quarters of the profits are going to Nakano's daughter. Believe me, money was never the point."

Elizabeth Rivers looked at him closely. "I know that."

"*I* DON'T know how to have fun?" demanded Logan, opening the hotel room door. "*Me?* You got me confused with someone else."

Sabrina laughed. "All right, I admit, this kind of fun you know."

He gazed at her with a mix of tenderness and lust. She was wearing a black Versace gown, as drop-dead sexy as it was elegant.

He removed his jacket and shoes and collapsed onto the bed. Idly he picked up the remote and switched it on. "C'mere."

They were so lost in a passionate kiss, the words in the background didn't even register.

"Authoritative sources at the renowned American Cancer Foundation announced today . . ."

ABOUT
THE AUTHOR

Harry Stein

Harry Stein began writing for magazines in 1971, upon graduating from the Columbia University School of Journalism. He achieved his first major fame at *Esquire* in 1980 as the writer of its new Ethics column. His blend of humor and philosophy made the column so popular that fans sported T-shirts saying BUT WHAT WOULD *HARRY STEIN* DO?

Though he has kept up with his magazine writing—he currently writes the Our Times column for *TV Guide*—Stein has also pursued more in-depth projects. In 1983 he published his first novel, *Hoopla*, about the 1919 Chicago White Sox baseball scandal. Then came two nonfiction works: *One of the Guys: The Wising Up of an American Man* in 1988, a painfully honest book that made many near and dear to him furious; and two years later, *Eichmann in My Hands*, with Peter Malkin, about the capture of the Nazi war criminal. Now, having sold the movie rights to *The Magic Bullet*, Stein is on to another medical thriller, about the dark side of antiaging treatments.

Harry Stein lives with his wife, Priscilla Turner—a television writer—and two children in New York's Hudson Valley.

201 239 9603